J. A. Bushman

THE MOUNTAIN OF THE CONDEMNED

Thank you to those who waited all these many years as I labored over my greatest passion, cheering me on along the way. And to those who are no longer here to see it completed, you are dearly missed.

"O mountain…
"I'm begging you…
"O mountain, heed my call…
"We're lost, and this is our only light."

Table of Contents

PROLOGUE   I

CHAPTER ONE

A manor of unrest...4

CHAPTER TWO

Footprints in the old Eldhorium 9

CHAPTER THREE

A snaked path 15

CHAPTER FOUR

The Mousehole...21

CHAPTER FIVE

A gathering of mice and rats...30

CHAPTER SIX

Doubled over...46

CHAPTER SEVEN

Brimstone 54

CHAPTER EIGHT

The ant mill...60

CHAPTER NINE

Unmasked..70

CHAPTER TEN

Embers of a fire..80

CHAPTER ELEVEN

Rekindled..86

CHAPTER TWELVE

The dream of a one-winged mourning dove.................................96

CHAPTER THIRTEEN

Visions 100

CHAPTER FOURTEEN

Bloody drunk 105

CHAPTER FIFTEEN

Blood upon his hand...119

CHAPTER SIXTEEN

Circlet's dread and a horn's howl..134

CHAPTER SEVENTEEN

Her name was Adfirna, and tenderly, Ogormin 153

CHAPTER EIGHTEEN

Cedric's foil...162

CHAPTER NINETEEN

Close to the chest..170

CHAPTER TWENTY

Barking dogs 178

CHAPTER TWENTY-ONE

Catching rain 185

CHAPTER TWENTY-TWO

A clamoring darkness 192

CHAPTER TWENTY-THREE

Deeper cuts 200

CHAPTER TWENTY-FOUR

To tell the truth 210

CHAPTER TWENTY-FIVE

The dark house 218

CHAPTER TWENTY-SIX

Silver to silver 226

CHAPTER TWENTY-SEVEN

To endure 232

CHAPTER TWENTY-EIGHT

From the dark 245

CHAPTER TWENTY-NINE

Wars in the muskeg 263

CHAPTER THIRTY

Six melting candles 284

CHAPTER THIRTY-ONE

A cloud of flies..297

CHAPTER THIRTY-TWO

Sand and vinegar..305

CHAPTER THIRTY-THREE

Dark reflections...316

CHAPTER THIRTY-FOUR

Truthseeker...335

CHAPTER THIRTY-FIVE

Gutter plant..353

CHAPTER THIRTY-SIX

The Eye of the Reaper..371

INTRODUCTION

Eight vassals were appointed when the First King arose—once dukes, now dubbed cardinals. Each ruled their own wynd, beholden to the king, who appointed their own vassals, counts, and barons. Together, they were granted fiefs, and the eight houses grew within this newly established feudal system. Their crests adorned their gifted lands with their allegiance as payment.

The White Raven is one such crest, with Raven Stead as its capital. Known for their tidiness, interpretative wisdom, and righteousness, they represent the North Wynd, while the Copper Hulls of the East Wynd remain bullish and foolhardy.

These were just two of the greater wynds that Young Lord Muna Raihn Parcel knew little about as he spent his days amidst fields of wheat, heaps of barley, fallowed fields, and copper-laden hills. Even less familiar to him were the Blue Pearls, Red Thorns, Free Birds, Felled Leaves, and Black Deer. However, he was well acquainted with the sugarcane, figs, oak trees, and the finest ale of Adjurrah, which his lesser wynd, nestled between the North and the East, had to offer.

Upon the passing of the esteemed Cardinal Ruhi Sohrer Eternis of the Northeast Wynd, his successors ruled the wynd until a lackluster inheritor emerged—one who became more enriched than his predecessors. This wealth was thanks to a graven mountain that drew paying visitors from other wynds to an appended market town, which expanded to accommodate said visitors and guests that sought a glimpse of the mountain and its mysterious, ringing Wall of Thorns. But they were taxed for the privilege.

According to the old charter drawn by Cardinal Ruhi, the first landholder, Sir Amos Ferver Drori the Dreamer, was granted this land in recognition of his astute servitude while taking the hand of the cardinal's second daughter. Upon marrying her, he took his beloved's name, becoming Sir Amos Parcel, and passed his manor down to his heirs. One such heir was Raihn's father, Manor Lord Rahim Partikus Parcel, who harbored a deep grudge against the market town of Cobblestone for mocking their family's heritage of independence and the land that had been gifted to them long ago.

Despite the First King's prohibition on religious practice throughout Eldhona—save for the taxed pilgrims from another land—not all of Parcel Path paid it much heed… The serfs and villeins of Parcel Path repaid their Parcel lords with their blood and sweat, while even the freemen were still insisted upon by the lord of Parcel Path to remain curious, and curious only, about Cobblestone. For, like the mountain to many, it remained a place of great curiosity…even to the heedless Young Lord Muna Raihn Parcel.

PROLOGUE

Above the village, within the valley, a servantless manor trembled on a cold hilltop. Inside, Raihn and his mother gathered around a crackling fireplace in her—the Lady's—chamber. Flickering shadows were puppeted on the oak walls while the unswept floor tickled their masters' jittery feet. Though she was scratching out squawks from her rocker, the clacking of sewing needles competed to be the loudest among the Lady's clamor. And with little else to drown out the sound, it became the focal point of her son's growing frustration, Young Lord Muna Raihn Parcel. He shook his leg anxiously, his gaze fixed on the burning logs. They hiss and pop, but her clacks cope and battle.

Fleeing to the window, his forehead found comfort on the cool glass, his feverish concern somewhat nurtured. His eyes deered into the black of night, howling winds and a pelting shower blowing shivers down his spine.

Still, Mother's busywork contended.

His foot tapped incessantly on the cellar, soft groans purring out from its loose oak.

"Return and be seated, Raihn!" his mother snapped, her voice as sharp as the fire-laden logs. "Please," she added, her tone mellowing from concern.

Reluctantly, Raihn abided, slinking into the rocker.

"He'll be back," she said, though her voice was thin, betraying that assurance.

The needles clicked as anxiously as Raihn's thoughts until the night tide lulled his eyes. The shower murmured on, and Muna Raihn drifted away— the needles abating.

Raihn stirred awake. The last embers of the fire had already crumbled into ash. Unlike its fleeting warmth, a steady glow illuminated the room from afar, sieving through the deeply inset round window. It was their eternal lamp in the sky: Eldhos.

Was it already past daybreak? Had Father come home? Raihn's thoughts churned as he glanced around in a sleepy haze. He'd never have been allowed to sleep this late—certainly not on a petal from his father's coffer. "Mother?" he called, his voice buttering under the shimmer.

She was gone, just like the cackling hearth. In fact, he woke in another chamber. Propping himself up, he realized he was lying in a kingly bed, less lavish than his own three-stack canopy, tucked into the furthest corner of the room. His gaze wandered over his surroundings: the distinctive x-shaped window, a shelf crammed with books, a desk, and an array of canvases.

The old Eldhorium.

He realized this was one of the upper chambers, long ago converted into a private sanctum. But something was off. The room, abandoned for nearly a year, was now pristine, utterly unlike the neglected state he remembered.

Impossible.

Where were the cakes of dust, the rolls of hair, the tangles of cobwebs clinging to every corner?

Raihn swung his legs over the bedside, only to be met with a sharp stab of pain in his heel. A hiss escaped through clenched teeth as he strung curses; his foot struck a familiar box of art supplies lying on the floor. With a frustrated shove, he kicked the box back under the bed. And before he could collect his thoughts, heavy footsteps thudded beyond the door.

"Hello?" Raihn called out, lurching over the bedside with his brows knit together. The moaning oak, sturdy as it was, fell silent then. His eyes became fixed on the copper knob until it rattled.

The door swung open, revealing a familiar figure so large it stooped to enter, shoulder-smashing the frame. Raihn gasped and rushed forward, embracing it. "Is it really you, brother!? Where have you been!?" he asked eagerly. "Did Father find you? He was out all night."

"No, he didn't. You were just dreaming again—are dreaming again."

Their reply was grimmer than Raihn liked. He scoffed. "What do you mean, River? You're right here… I mean, if those boards don't squeal and buckle beneath you, I'd question it."

"Raihn, brother, you must listen well," his younger yet taller brother said, their tone not enthusiastic enough. "Sit."

Raihn slapped his sides. "Sure. Alright," he stuttered. His fingers nervously cross-stitched as he sat upon the wool mattress, pondering the formality. And even after a pinch, he was here. But he had to make sure, pinching once more.

"Stop that," River demanded.

Raihn squinted. "Stop what?"

"All those nervous tics, wipe that pensive look off your face, too."

"I'm just glad to see you, is all," Raihn replied, hesitating as if waiting for River to echo the sentiment. But his brother stayed silent, their expression hardening into something studious and distant.

"Questions plague me," Raihn blurted. "Why do you carry such a peculiar gloom? Are you not as thrilled to see me as I am to see you?" His voice had cracked from frustration; he readjusted from little embarrassment.

River's gaze darkened. "I shan't stall with distracting memories."

Distracting? Raihn frowned. "Okay, but—"

"Enough!" River snapped.

Raihn caught onto his lean, straightening.

River's sharp tone cut through the air and drew a wince. His hand fell atop a black, gleaming trunk beside an aged desk. "Do you remember this?"

2

"…Of course," Raihn murmured.

"And do you remember what I told you about it?"

"If you're suggesting I tried opening it—"

"My mind has changed. Open it."

Raihn unknit a brow. "Right now?"

"Do you have the key?"

"Well, no, but—"

"…Find it."

"You won't give it to me?" Raihn asked.

River lurched forward, their boulder-like shoulders rolling. "I found my escape, and so can you. You must find answers on your own, though sometimes you can read the thoughts from those who are no longer with you… Books tell stories, hidden or forgotten. If you really want the key, then think where my heart lies and look upon it. Hopefully, you won't need a book for that, though."

"Can't you just tell me rather than employ these silly games?"

"Where is the fun in that?" River asked.

They were smirking, their lips all too devious. It had been a while since Raihn had seen any joy, especially from River. His duty to sustain it crept into his want.

CHAPTER ONE
A manor of unrest

RAIHN'S eyes shot open under the muzzle of a bleating black goat. His body, encased in sweat, glistened like a fatty sausage against its salt-licking tongue. He lay through tremors from resurfaced monotonies; the bed was more fitted for him, though still lordly, and the ceiling pushed lower in an already more boxed-in chamber… It was *indeed* a dream.

"Son of a—"

Young Lord Raihn pondered, rolling back his curly black hair. His gaze went to the nearby window where Eldhos still glowed. Its rays ran along his copper-tinted arm, highlighting his faint hairs into rushlights. He felt as though he was suffering from a mind addled by old age, though only eighteen, and began to ponder what was real anymore, still untangling from time made into knots.

"Damn," Raihn groaned, shooing the goat away. He flung off his lavish, silky sheets and threw the bed curtains aside, feeling *unfit* for a three-stack bed and all its silk; not like he'd prefer a serf's hay pallet. Stuffed in his mattresses was: hay at the bottom, wool in the middle, and goose feathers on top, all in his canopy-sandwich-of-a-bed, sprinkled with guilt.

From birdsong and the echoing hammer from the smithy reverberating through the valley of Parcel Village, he cursed again as he ambled toward the window. He swiped his nightcap off and removed his linen nightshirt before dressing himself in "commoner's garb," unlike the finery his parents preferred. Rugged ridges circled his neck instead of a dazzling hem as he donned his *good old tunic.*

A sigh blew from his nostrils as he leaned upon the sill and bathed in light. He gazed at Parcel Path: a secluded village. And on its eastern end is an appended market town—Cobblestone. It bustled with merchants peddling their wares, enriching the coffers of their Rosen King. But to Raihn, it was all just noise. If not for the chance of a flogging, he'd elect to worm back into bed and weave himself into a silky cocoon, but he cracked the window and paced back. His cloth and hair waved in the cool, fig-sweet breeze, but when the breeze faded, a savory, salted scent seemed to slip past his door. Along with it came a feisty warning—his mother demanding he come for breakfast and abandon his bed, which, like his quarters, had been moved to the old servant's wing.

The screen passage outside his door led to various spaces—the buttery, pantry, kitchen, and its adjacent private dining quarter, and finally, the Great Hall. As Raihn slumped through the passage, what pep he had slackened when he came to the family tree framed on the wall. He paused, staring at the blank space inside it where his brother's name had been omitted, until his name echoed again from the dining quarter, pulling him back through the passage.

Nearer the dining room, he endured the rising clamor of his parents' voices—sharp, bitter, and growing more heated. Their words were garbled, but the tension was obvious. Raihn cut through their conversation by stepping in. His father remained hunched over his plate, devouring sausages with barely a glance, while his mother's gaze faltered as she caught sight of him.

"Good morning," Raihn offered curtly, certain their quarrel had been about him.

His mother, Angeline Corty Parcel, an Eirhartic Lady, puckered her lips in a terse nod. Her pale skin, though lighter than Raihn's and certainly his father's Erath tones, shared the same soft features.

Her hands fidgeted, nails digging into her golden hair as she scratched nervously. Elbows braced on the back of her chair, she seemed elsewhere, lost in her ticks. But the sharp cry of Raihn's chair's legs dragging across the floor snapped her out of her reverie. As he joined them, he hoped the tension might fade. Settled into his seat, eyes drifting to the neighboring empty chair despite the food arrayed before him—hummus, pocket bread, tea, and sausage—it all barely registered, his mind mid-wander. But beneath the table, his feet shuffled and crunched over walnut shells and straw that snapped him back.

Seated to his right at the head of the table was a powerful man with gusty lungs, whose long-winded speeches were a staple of the manor. But today, his father, Rahim, barely greeted him, his voice unusually short, breath coming in huffs.

"Today is not a day of fasting," Rahim muttered. "Our people—gifted copper hills from Ruhi, driven to build a new life in this valley—did not do so for my son to loathe it. You are lucky to descend from Mersa and luckier that its lord is no longer alive to smite your disobedience from this stead. A lord should never be late in his hall, but luck finds you again, for we feast humbly."

Raihn considered relaying his dream but thought better of it. His father's intensity snuffed out the idea.

"Are you going to eat?" Rahim barked at Raihn, quickly turning to Angeline next. "And Jelly, crack the window, would you?"

She opened the window, the cool breeze lifting her curls. Her caffeinated motions boomeranged her back, fingers resuming their taps over the back of her chair. Her gaze fell on Raihn again, who wasn't as restive. "Enjoying your food?" she asked sarcastically.

He hadn't touched a morsel, his fists clenched beneath the table. Nodding absentmindedly, his mind drifted again until his father's table-pounding fist snapped him free. A walnut cracked beneath Raihn's heel, his back stiffening as he snatched the fork with a tense grip.

"Your mother cooks, yet you become idle in the abandoned servant's wing. Be grateful I don't throw you before the fire to cook, like a servant, on such a warm day," Rahim scolded, wagging his greasy fork.

His father's beady eyes bore into him from over his clasped knuckles, his full stomach impatient with Raihn's tardiness. Rahim pushed back from the table, offering Angeline a perfunctory kiss before storming off. "Raihn, join me when you've finished," their voice bounded.

Angeline sighed. "He's just tense today."

"He's tense every day," Raihn muttered back, forcing a bite of sausage between his teeth.

Angeline's frustration spilled over as she scraped the remaining food from his plate into a smelly sack, her movements as jerky and rushed as her tone. "Leftovers for the pigs... Go see your father. I meant to ask you to herd Tadda back into the pen...that damned goat got out again. But never mind, I'll do it. Go, see your father. Okay?" She forced a grin that betrayed certainty. It was the same flash of unease that remained an ember, flickering like the hearth in that cold, haunting night.

Raihn paused, his hands tightening where his plate was. *She's hiding something...*

If they had any sheep as black as the escaped goat, there would be two moseying through the manor, now that River is gone. Raihn went into the vestibule, slid on his boots, and pushed himself outside to see Rahim sitting on the oak rocker, gazing eastward over the garden and to the deep valley. Raihn collapsed into the neighboring chair and braced for the awkwardness.

"Late already," said Rahim, his brows draping over his squint. "Eldhos on the rise, I'm going to make this brief. Stomach full—eyes full. Proper start for a working man, and as things will change, you should see the light that shines upon the memory of our ancestors."

"I guess." Raihn shrugged. "Can't really say I feel much grace sitting above a village of our laborers, though."

"They understand why we have this hill, and you know well enough, too," Rahim's tone mounted. "We don't look down at them, we look over them. And without them, I wouldn't be here—we wouldn't be here."

"Is that why you will not grant the serfs freedom? Because we need them?"

Rahim leaned towards Raihn, the creak from his chair narrowing. "If you are so concerned for them, then be a man, Muna Raihn." Rahim fell back, his lip twitching beneath his scruff. "Then you can inherit the land and liberate them yourself."

6

"Why? That's not what you would want."

Rahim's frustration swelled. "I want you to take what is rightfully yours! Because when I am dug into the soil, they will look up from the foot of the hill and wonder who will lead them. Those who toil offer me their grain and their eggs, as Amos intended. For us to prosper, dammit. His dream was to secure his kin a good life."

"To prosper in a tarnished plot?" Raihn remarked, embellishing. "Withering lands under the shadow of a mountain?" he went on, exaggerating more.

"…Do you fear it?" his father asked

Raihn did not answer, his eyes swinging over the valley, hanging onto the mountain's ominous size. Every morning would start with it casting a shadow over them until Eldhos surpassed it. Maybe that was the kind of triumph that Rahim admired at dawn, the kind that he meant for Raihn to witness.

"Our ancestors were not afraid," Rahim continued.

"That was long ago, Dad. I just think we should let those born in bondage—"

"Father," Rahim sternly corrected, his pointer direct. "Now listen, you are next of kin. And while I mean for you to grasp it, do not tear down our independence."

Raihn took a breath, pondering the independence of the villeins and the serfs. "Sure. As you said, Father, they bring us the grain and the eggs."

Rahim took a deep breath, the creaks from their chairs the only sound between them. And when he spoke again, his voice settled into a somber tone. "The peasants seem to gravitate around the market town more and more."

"It's been a year now," Rahim added softly.

"Hard to believe," Raihn replied.

"That it is. He'd be seventeen now, just about a year younger than you. Your mother is distraught, understandably, so perhaps you should keep her company when night falls, just as it did then… I did all I could to find him last year. I hope you know that."

"Of course," Raihn said meekly.

"I took care of him, but he was obsessed."

"I remember…"

"The King's Authority turned me away, said they'd seen no one at the gate." The gate to the mountain, he meant.

"I know, Father. You tried, just like you said. There was nothing else you could have done."

Rahim squirmed, his face flushing with frustration. "River was selfish," he said, his words cutting into Raihn with an unexpected sharpness.

"We all have something we want for ourselves," Raihn replied, rising to his feet.

"Sit," Rahim ordered, his hand clutching Raihn's arm. "I'm not done yet. The world doesn't adapt to you; you adapt to it. You won't inherit respect like you will the manor. The village needs to trust you before they follow."

"I don't want respect from them. And I don't want them to follow like ducks in a row."

"Cute…" Rahim scoffed. "What about from me? You could have so much more than your brother. Shit, you already do, yet you piss it away loafing about! At least he had the guts to leave. But put us at risk he did, like he'd done before, wandering—wandering against my warning. I was so close to working something out," Rahim said, pinching the air, "but then he left. That was his choice!" Rahim was becoming emotional again, anger rising onto his face. "Look, I have little time," his voice wavered through its simmering. "You're to go out today before coming home to your mother. I'll let you go someplace special—by my side, even."

"Where?"

"A place that took some convincing for your mother."

"The Mousehole?" Raihn's brow knotted in confusion.

"I persuaded Angeline to make an exception."

"After the way she scolded me for going before? Like you scolded River for his excursions?"

"You snuck off in the night," his father reminded, his voice softening more. "Anyway…it's time now," Rahim said.

Raihn became anxious, knowing what he'd leave behind for later. There was no patience for it. "Wait!" he cried, jumping straight up. "I have to go back inside. I forgot something."

Rahim looked him up and down queerly. "Very well. Maybe it's best if we don't travel together anyhow. Lord of this village, I am. I can't lurk in a grimy tavern for too long before being noticed. My hood will be over my head once I leave, so keep your eye out and be quick…maybe get your cloak as well."

CHAPTER TWO

Footprints in the old Eldhorium

Up the stairs, there was a corridor with three doors. One on the right being Raihn's old quarters, now made into a study, and two on the left. The first was locked, and the second led to River's abandoned chamber. Raihn passed the first door, then centered himself before the second. Turning the knob, the door swung, offering a jostling truth. His shoulder sank into the doorframe. As told by all the dust, the chamber was back to being pale and dull, unlike how it was in his dream. But something else lay queer—two sets of footprints along the dusty floor. One large set led to the trunk in the corner, while the noticeably smaller pair led to the center of the room where the light of Eldhos struck the floor from the window.

A strange, though disregarded, tingle ran up the back of Raihn's right hand, and through his erratic excitement, he incidentally gulped dust, thus stifled a coughing fit. But upon peering out the window, he saw his mother with the food sack, fighting off the goat she meant to herd back into the pen. He swept his brow, relieved to be alone in the Eldhorium where he could flurry his hacks without rousing suspicion.

The abandoned chamber was in disarray. Dust swirled lazily in the four beams of light that spilled through the X-shaped frame of the circular window. Dead bugs lay in brittle, forgotten heaps on the sill. Nearby, a family portrait hung crooked on the wall, with the word "home" painted across the canvas, licked by thin, milky webs. Other paintings scattered throughout the room suffered the same fate—forgotten relics draped in neglect. An easel stood in the corner, beside a weathered trunk, and a nearby desk was strewn with parchment, smudged by ink from a near-empty pot.

Raihn's eyes moved over the room, tracing threads of memories in each painting. But something caught his attention—pieces he didn't recognize. Grim, unsettling works, likely created during River's more isolated days toward the end of his stay. Raihn stepped cautiously toward the trunk, nudging the lid. *Locked.* His gaze drifted to the bookshelves. *Books tell stories, hidden or forgotten*, he recalled.

His eyes flickered over the spines: a green book, a blue one, then red, gray, and another, a darker blue one.

"Bees and Honey: What Completes Us," Raihn muttered, pulling up a large chair. He felt small in it, just like he did in the kingly bed from his lucid dream, and thumped the curious book on his knee. Most of the books had been in the family long before he was born. Some were gifted, others taken from the dead hands of scribes. Some commissioned… The details were fuzzy to him, not that he cared. Still, this one felt out of place. *Had it come from the study?* He didn't remember ever seeing it.

Kicking up his feet onto the trunk, he skimmed the yellowed, goat-skin pages, growing more eager for each chapter. Raihn flipped through the book, the weight of its pages shifting from right to left like a tipping scale. A chapter caught his eye—*Romance*. He paused. Three inconsistencies marred the page: watermarks. *Tears,* he realized, his thoughts drifting.

Flipping to the final chapter, *Your Escape*, Raihn recalled River's voice: *I found my escape, and so can you.*

He read diligently, but the chapter offered little more than a vague hint toward escapist hobbies. Frustrated, Raihn snapped the book shut, dust spiraling into his contorting face. "Bleh," he muttered, tossing it aside.

Raihn piled more books onto the desk. The next one was a collection of children's tales—stories he knew well. *The Woodsman* and *Cedric's Foil*. The latter was grimmer, telling of a royal favored by his mother but doomed by his carelessness in the garden. Dismissed as irrelevant, Raihn moved on.

The third book was filled with landscapes and cliffs, well-worn, its pages ripped and creased from overuse. *Just pictures.* Flat images. Nothing drew him in, sparking frustration; he slammed it shut. But another book caught his eye—different from the rest. He mothed to its light. *Sacred Flesh.* His brow furrowed curiously over the tome, he thought *perhaps a steamy fire,* an unfamiliar book to him. It storied a fair-haired woman and her clever pig. The pig, said to be as smart as a man, saved the girl from an intruder in Raihn's own wynd, squealing its alert and rousing its owners. The pig was rewarded, fattening as it was fed the invader. Even then, its warmth comforted the girl through winter. Intriguing but a dead-end.

Running out of options, Raihn's gaze wandered. Painted depictions of women and nature hung on the walls, their details softly stroked. *I found my escape, and so can you,* he muttered to himself, recalling River's words.

Then he remembered, like a flash of lightning, the answer. The box he had kicked in his dream. *That's where it must be.* He bolted to the floor at the foot of the bed, sweeping his hand into the dark space beneath. His fingers brushed something coarse, and he froze as something scurried past.

A mouse darted out. Raihn flinched, cracking his head against the bedframe. His breath hitched as dead skin drifted into his tangled hair. Shaking it off, he resumed his search. His hand felt the familiar texture, grain catching on his fingers. He pulled out a small wooden box. "Gotcha," he whispered.

The latch clicked open, revealing only brushes and quills. *That's it?* He frowned. *If not here with art, then where?*

Raihn sighed, sinking back against the bed, frustration burdening him. He thought himself so clever, too, considering escapism. His eyes skimmed the room once more, stopping at the family portrait. *Home. Is that where your heart lies?* Doubt suggested otherwise, considering River left it. Still, Raihn approached the portrait and pulled it off the wall. Behind it, in the shadowed oak, something metallic caught his eye. His fingers probed the gap until they robbered a small copper key. It was heavy, gleaming in his dirty hand.

Raihn's heart raced.

The dream. It was real.

But a sudden pitter-patter broke any inner monologue he had, spine flag-poled, hairs put on end. He listened as a shadow crept over him like a rising tide about to roll. His throat cinched like a tugged slipknot. *Is it Mother?* The key hid in his palm as he turned, only to find a raven at the window, its shadow long, the door still shut. Air found his lungs again, and he relaxed, chuckled, even, but the bird cawed mockingly. *Just my luck,* he thought. *Ravens are bad luck.* Then he knelt before the trunk. *Sorry, Father. I'll have to be a bit longer.* The key was inserted, but the raven's shadow distracted. Glaring over his shoulder, Raihn shooed it with a wave, but the black bird only cocked its head.

"Leave, pestering bird!" Raihn hissed, but the raven persisted. His frustration bubbled, but he dared not raise his voice, fearing Mother might lurk in the vicinity.

The raven cawed three times, rasping closely to something human. Raihn paused, his blood turning cold. *Was it...mimicking a voice?*

"Not yet, not yet," it croaked outside the glass. Its pecks on the glass damned Raihn into a curious submission when a creak staffed his back again. Surely, it was outside the door this time. It set every nerve on edge. He spun around, up on his toes. The door inched open. Angeline peered inside. "What are you doing in here?" she asked.

Raihn stammered, palming the key, "I… I miss him."

Her gaze softened. "That talk with Rahim must have made you senti-mental," she presumed.

"Yeah," Raihn replied clumsily. "Have you been in here lately?" he asked, eyeing the suspicious footprints on the floor.

Angeline shook her head. "Shouldn't you be with your father?"

"Just about to leave." *Is she lying? Whose prints are they?*

Her eyes glossed over, then she closed the door behind her, and whimpers broke on the other side.

Raihn smothered sympathy and returned to the trunk, breath held as he twisted the key. The lid creaked open, revealing only two drawings and a leather-bound book. Confused, Raihn took the first drawing—an image de-picting a well. A reflection stared back at him from the black water. As Raihn studied it closer, a flicker of words shone through the translucence.

He flipped the drawing over and discovered a passage, heart ticking.

I know not the pestering image in my head, never crafted through memory nor made by imagination, seemingly conjured by thin air. I thought perhaps inking it would help purge the constant nag from my mind, but the sight fails me.

Below this image was another. It depicted a wall of woven roots and bramble, adorned with thorns, hewn from the earth to blockade the world from the mountain within them. Normally, this wouldn't be remarkable, as everyone knows of it—its fame spread through renowned artists, despite the King's Authority restricting access. But this image had a unique detail: a bloody hand-shaped indentation.

Raihn plucked up the book and peeled the cracking cover away, discovering that it was not a book but a journal. He thumped through it eagerly and landed upon an entry, reading:

Journal Entry 16
Era of King Stamen, Year 26 under his reign.

I've had an experience. I feel strange. A daze sunk my consciousness into a murky depth. Waves crashed, flooding me with a sense of calling, with faint and old memories I could see from the deep. Despite that, I am uncertain of what they mean. I must know and follow this unexplainable string.

Conflicted, I am at a standstill. I can only twist and turn as my head pulls me in every which way with sharp hooks. In both places, I feel a connection, though I cannot leave. Father won't allow it, bitterer of it the more these days pass over.

Journal Entry 17
Era of King Stamen, Year 26 under his reign.

It happened again. I saw a colossal fang rise over the clouds, sharp and rigid. It was powerful, and my chest felt tangled into knots like the wall of bramble and burls surrounding it. I broke them apart. I became free. Less claustrophobic than in that dream. And yet, I can't stop thinking about it. I see it in my inkpot and my drawings. Even the wood grain on my wall looks like it. The mountain. It is there, everywhere I look.

Strangely, it feels hopeful. But, alas, my anniversary draws near, and I might forget it if the manor is bright again. I recall being younger, smaller, and freer to roam. My guardians seemed happier then, but maybe this year they will laugh again. Seeing them smile might even calm me. I miss their grinning. The manor has become dark. I am haunted.

Journal Entry 18
Era of King Stamen, Year 26 under his reign.

At first, it thrilled me to expect their planning whispers, but they seemed stressed. Yelling. Bickering. And just as I was about to write, Raihn came in, speaking about tomorrow, for he could also hear them. He tried drowning them out with chatter for me, but I still heard them.

At night, I suffer nightmares, perhaps from stress, the second one becoming much worse. I feared the third to be more severe.

I feel as if something is reaching out to me from the dusk.

In some corner of the world outside of my vision, I see the shadow creep even when it is dark. It calls me with a faint whisper. It beckons me, rolling nearer. Though I cannot disobey my father and go against the wind. I can only disobey one: a command or an urge. But I itch for this urge to leave so that I might sleep and cease waking in panicked sweat.

I nestled in early before the night fell. I was shown the light, shining upon a boulder and gleaming over the river. Some aura about it made me feel safe, like a haven, not creeping as the dark did. And there, long, arched nails of polish waved me in. Fingers, gold-tipped, seemed to promise guidance for slumber.

But if so, what is so wrong in the night? The thing that would come for me in my dreams. The thing that came again before I woke, bathing in sweat from a sight of two silver ravens.

And when I wake, I seem jerked at the hand, but nobody is there. It's as though something is trying to take me away.

Journal Entry 19
Era of King Stamen, Year 26 under his reign

It's my anniversary, and it brings me joy. For this one day, I am special. Maybe it's silly to indulge in such wealth, but it is what makes me feel less at home. Strangely, that is a good thing. I forget about these walls in the distraction. Though so far, it's not the greatest anniversary. The subject of my stay has become strenuous. I can hear them when they think I can't, and it doesn't feel all too celebratory, but maybe that'll change.

Right now, nothing has sprung, but I'm sure it'll come. Raihn, unfortunately, wished to see Aggie after all, his own heart's desire, but that shouldn't be long. He promised he would be quick.

The day is passing. Eldhos still hovers, but they neglect my precious time, as Raihn is yet to return. I wondered where he could've gone, but then I heard an axe digging into a tree, meaning Rahim was lashing out. I assume he's still upset over that rumble downstairs. I thought they made up: 'mother and father,' but perhaps more sparks flew from the grindstone after their arguing. However, there was something my father told me today that I was happy to hear…at first. He offered me a new but unfinished stay: a cabin. All of this is the least of my worries at the moment, though, and that says a lot because when I look out my window, I see Angeline and Raihn. Why do they sit there and watch over the village while I'm up here? It's my day.

Maybe the cabin is just to get rid of me. But that is fine. I'll go out the back door and find sleep. If they care to find me, they know where to look, for I'll go with the vision in my dreams, hoping I may not be seen leaving the manor again, as I've feared since Father's last scolding.

What? Raihn wondered. *Seen by whom? Father?* he questioned.

Raihn, frustrated, cursed that it was the last page—the others oddly ripped from the spine—possibly regretful passages. Might it be mentioned within a prior entry, but that would have to wait, for he was in a hurry, and the twist in his stomach brought tears that forbade sight anyway.

"I'm sorry," Raihn panted, stealing time to weep. The passage whirled in his head. "Forgive me."

If River's one goal was to revisit Raihn and to rake him into a deeper sadness, it was working.

Now sounded a good time for ale.

CHAPTER THREE
A snaked path

Raihn shut the front door and exhaled, his shoulders stressed. He fastened the cloak he'd retrieved and clung to his stitched satchel. It was hemmed with many repairs by his mother, still loose-threaded here and there, but trusty no less, carrying his brother's journal.

The valley blew a crisp breath through his black hair, and he could smell the harvest in the air. For him, it was a bitter fragrance, nostalgic of wheat and barley. He thought of harvesting something to peck at, but surely Father was at the tavern by now, waiting, and the thought of moseying through the village balled up his stomach like an orb of yarn. His hankering for a nut dissipated.

Ambling down the hill, the ball grew in his belly. Before him stretched the valley with its thatched-roof huts, the mill, and—he stopped, his attention drawn away. A shadow joined beside his—one that did not belong to a human, but to a creature with wings and talons: a raven. It landed on the path, waddling.

Could it be the same from the sill of the window? Raihn pondered. "Don't you have a gardener to pester?" he asked it. The raven cawed. "That sounds like a no to me. I will not be having any bad luck befall me today. Scram!" he shouted, though the raven tipped its head at him. "…Fine. Have it your way. Though I warn you, if anything happens, I'll have bad luck haunt you next."

Raihn quit yammering with the feathered fiend at the foot of the slope and came to a dirt path. The trail wound past a quaint hut, where an elderly woman knelt beneath her window, plucking weeds. His shoulders stiffened, and his head lowered as he hoped to slip by unnoticed. Breath held, he crept forward until the raven broke the silence with a harsh caw.

"Oh!" the startled peasant exclaimed over her shoulder. "Raihn? Raihn!"

"Damn raven," Raihn muttered through an exhale and with a half-hearted wave. "Good morning," he said, edging away.

"The sky couldn't be any clearer today," she said cheerily.

It was too late—small talk.

"But even I know that's not enough to drag you down here," she continued.

"Yup."

She hobbled toward him, her swollen eyes red from allergies. Stray hairs bristled from a mole on her chin, just below her sunken lips. "What have you got stirring today?"

"I'm just going out, Mrs. Acker," Raihn replied, leaning back instinctively as her face came uncomfortably close.

"I know I'm old, but don't go telling me things I can plainly still see."

Raihn pressed his lips together, unwilling to say more.

She snatched a glance at the raven, her eyes peculiar upon it. She crossed her arms as if to close herself off from a bad omen. "Raihn," she began, her eyes flickering back. "I know what you're doing. You have a hankering for that 'no-good town,' as your father would call it. Well, I can keep a secret," she winked. "Just look the other way if you see me there!"

Raihn laughed, imagining her living it up on the stone streets with a gilded arm of jewelry. "My lips are sealed," he said, loosening up, but then a rotten bellow pierced the air.

"Raihn!"

The Young Lord flinched, then spun, nerves a wreck. "What do you want, Will?" he said to the stocky blond blackguard in a blackened tunic. A coif nested over their ruffled head, and they sported blotchy breeches, where boots met the hem around their dirty ankles.

"To know what dragged you out of the castle," Will snorted back. "But now I see you got Mrs. Acker pullin' your weed!" He cackled. "No girls fancyin' you these days after the way you was."

"You're as warped as the timber of the Mousehole," Raihn said plainly.

Sneering at Raihn, Will curled his lips and stepped closer, his dirt-smudged nose pointing at him like an arrow's tip. "Be careful, Lordling. Word 'round here is that villagers've gone missin'. If I'm lucky, so will you. If it weren't fer yer pop, Aggie's daddy, Bart, would pop you like a zit."

Mrs. Acker, *shockingly,* struck the bitter blonde, leaving behind more sparse specks of dirt on his face.

Will was speechless. They sent off the raven with a feather-fluttering kick, then tramped across the garden.

"I'm not sure which is better, hurting his pride or just plain hurting him," Raihn laughed.

"I was saving you," she corrected.

His brows furrowed. "How so?"

"Your hand," she answered simply.

Raihn's grin died as he looked down his arm, realizing his hands were made into trembling fists.

"Can't have the lord's son laying a crack of ham upon one of his peasants, can we?" she went on.

"Unfortunately not. Thank you," Raihn said earnestly. A smirk crept back while he could hardly remain serious. "But I think a crack of ham would suggest I sit on him triumphantly after kicking his ass."

16

She nodded, nudging his shoulder before returning to her flowers. "Perhaps I should've said pork knuckle."

Raihn grinned even more, considering she wasn't such a bad crone. "Well, then I sound to be made a pig, which I am not, Mrs. Acker. By the way, what did he mean? Who's missing?"

The woman paused mid-pluck, her grip hanging in the air. The joyous air dissipated in a dimming fog. "Bonds break and lovers come and go," she replied over her shoulder, colder than before. "Nothing more to it. His better half had already gone searching for him, and it had left their home empty. Maybe I'll bring their lonely hollow some flowers."

"'His'? Raihn pondered. *Must be some villager's dispute.*

Today was too important to let something so childish get to him. Raihn stepped away, still pondering the shake in his right, dominant hand. He hadn't realized the frustration within him until Mrs. Acker pointed it out. And stranger, it felt a bit fuzzy, as if caterpillars crawled over his skin, his nerves prickly like thorny vines. But Will would likely lasso his gang of misfits and return with a contest to see who the biggest prick was among them. So, Raihn sunk both his concern and hand into his pockets. Soon, he would pour over it with the ale from a hole in the wall.

The last home in the row came into view, with only the smithy remaining beyond the fallow field after it. Metal clanged on beat, ringing louder as Raihn approached a burly man. The smith bent over a glowing blade, hammering it meticulously. Beads of sweat rolled and fell to the wrought metal. They groaned a breath steamier than a cauldron's, a man plowing love in his own garden of sorts. Metal clanged rhythmically, their moans in tandem.

"You really love your work," Raihn cut in.

"Greetings, Parcel son," the smith said, hanging up his hammer and quenching the blade in a barrel of cold water. A wave of steam soared over the sword's purring dunk. "It isn't often I see your face. What brings you to the edge of Parcel Path? Might it be Cobblestone?"

"You know I don't like to be called that, Ballard," said Raihn, though he also did not appreciate the questions about his business or leisure.

Ballard's thumbs hooked the straps of his smock. "Of course, Young Lord."

"Nor do I wish for any title, if you'd please," Raihn added.

"If you wish not to have your surname or title spoken, then so be it, but in return, I ask you to refrain from calling me 'Ballard.' It is much too formal as well. You can call me by my first name," he replied heartily.

"An even trade, Grafton," Raihn grinned.

"And mayhap my question would be answered if not already by another nosey busybody."

Raihn's face twisted with unease.

"Do not overthink my jest," the smith went on, looking at Raihn's expression. "I just wonder if it be business beyond that gate. If so, I would be glad. And whether it be pleasure, I would have my lips speak none of it before another, and neither would I listen to them say it to me, with my hot fingers pressed into my ears."

Raihn's lips pressed, then he said, "Consider it business."

"Good!" Grafton roared, his voice froggy and tight. "Good for a growin' lord in our pasture… Now, with that said, scram while the fire is hot! I have work to do," said the smith, grinning through his scruff.

The gate to Cobblestone stood at the end of the crossroad. Above it was a metal arch, adorned with copper lettering forged by Grafton. And through the open gate was a sea of lapping noise—a feeding frenzy from travelers with pockets deeper than those of Raihn's breeches.

Folk from all over clamored for food and drink or sought guild masters—weavers, butchers, potters, saddlers, chain-mail makers—all kinds of guilds with their apprentices, abiding the weighmasters of the town. And along the street, too, were the merchant houses and cart pushers selling their wares.

Many masons here offered their services, but some knitters lured customers with charm and painted faces. Though they were behind the king's parapet, so to speak, and not at all worried about trouble. They did not shake legs, for they were not common women. They were soft, but their voices could be heard through the crowd, guiding pockets like drapery-waving sirens. With them were seamstresses and jewelers, who were more alluring, pushing copper rings, necklaces, and corsets. Though not all men gleamed in their direction, nor at their pressed-up chests, and not all were kind.

Men from even a distant land arrived from across the sea, docking at the Blue Pearl harbor in the South Wynd. They came over sharp waves and salty winds. Others glided in with an air of freedom, needing no vessels at all, flaunting their status as visitors from the Wynd of Free Birds.

Contrasting the free-spirited arrivals, other men walked with pride as heavy as mountains. Their chests swelled, heads held high, stoney brows glistening with sweat, and dark curls furled over their tunics. These were the men of the Lesser Wynd—the Wynd of Red Thorns. The red hilts at their sides represent their native thorns, red stamps of warn.

Raihn watched as men from the Realm of Red and the Realm of White brushed past each other with disdain, their shoulders colliding, swords rattling from the bump. Thorns scraped against raven feathers like ram horns clipping wings. Red snorted, the white scoffed.

Whatever their purpose—be it trackers, mercenaries, or women—all had gathered here in Cobblestone, beneath the looming shadow of Mt. Miryam. Some stood in awe, their eyes lifted toward the distant peak, where the mountain rose above the Wall of Thorns. The bramble wall was not red, however, but white, "pure," as the Ravens of Raven Stead liked to boast.

But the Ravens made many claims. One such claim was that Lord Robert Redthorn was nothing but a "scoundrel" of a vassal. "A trough-gulper."

Raihn butted into this crowded market feeling slightly overwhelmed, bumping red hilts, blinded by flowing navy capes, and clocking his head into tall men's chest plates. He tried to comfort himself, knowing that nobody here knew who he was and that he would be free from the persistent badgering from those in Parcel Path; however, his relative invisibility meant he could be trampled over without a second thought.

Knocked again.

Moving more cautiously, Raihn's eyes fell on a shabby, crooked booth. The centerpiece of this grim little performance was the very thing he despised most: puppets. A shiver tickled his spine as a jester and a prince struggled to reconcile in the show, their conflict fueled by the meddling of the Prince's father. The scene shadowed over the small audience of children. Their glee turned to confusion, then lament. Raihn felt a similar pang of unease, lips pursed tight. Time to leave.

Dodging the bombardment of males and plates, he made his way with keen eyes and mindful steps. Through the crowd, he saw two pale-skinned fellows of opposite builds on a corner. One was round, the other straight. The hefty one's round belly sported red-striped suspenders that held up dark and baggy trousers over a white, tucked-in tunic adorned with pearly fasteners. Flashier than their garb was the fellow's wide, infectious smile and bushy mutton chops. Their eyes gleamed through clean spectacles, and he looked approachable.

Opposite the sociable man stood a lanky, deathly thin gent with legs tightly pressed together. On his face was a clear-as-glass smile that garnered no attention at all. Under his sharp chin was a burgundy vest with bronze fasteners, which overlaid his white silk upper garment tucked into dark trousers. Both men were remarkably outlandish.

Like witnessing a disaster in slow motion, Raihn couldn't tear his eyes away from the two bumbling idiots. They flailed their arms wildly, pelts held high, their ceaseless whooping and hollering echoing through the air.

Despite their efforts and approachable faces, no pelt exchanged hands during Raihn's spectating. The round one waved his wares at every passerby, while the slender one boasted exaggerated tales of daring encounters with deadly beasts. His voice carried line after line of dubious bravado, and Raihn's keen ear sifted falsehoods.

Eventually, the slender man's energy waned and he sagged into a slouch, breathless from his relentless performance.

Raihn fed his strange fascination with their bumbling failures, then followed the stream of people past the two gingers. His eyes kept on them, and to his dismay, he saw the thin one's attention following back. Their gazes met.

Raihn quickly averted his, feeling oddly discovered. Then, in his periphery, he saw the stranger thrusting his sharp elbow into the other's side as if to say, "Look at that Young Lord."

Do they know who I am? Raihn wondered. He had no clue, bumping a couple of Daints as he fled. The gingers seemed incompetent either way, but then a thought crept into his mind. *What if they're only masquerading as buffoons?* Raihn became cautious at the thought and continued away from them with more urgency than before.

Raihn followed the street until came a dank alley. He'd discern whether he was being tailed by traveling through this convenient passage devoid of strangers. Unfortunately, confirming his suspicions, the pale pair ensued like utter buffoons. They left behind the bustling street and slunk through the piss-reeking alley with their cart's wobbling wheels squawking.

Are those idiots really bringing their cart of pelts?

Raihn fled again and rejoined the lively populace. Glancing over his shoulder, he saw them come from a distance, looking clueless as to where he went. He sighed, turning away.

Before him, at last, the Mousehole.

CHAPTER FOUR
The Mousehole

Once a peaceful hideaway, the meager hole for mice had transformed into a den of rats, filled with scrap and ale. Despite its lackluster appearance, there was no demand for higher quality; that could be found down the street at the ironically named 'Finer Things Inn.' Perhaps the finer things were suitable for Rahim, but Raihn fancied the rugged charm and privacy of the Mousehole, where even the light stayed out.

Scurrying past the battered side of the tavern and dipping his head under the dangling sign that read, 'THE MOUSEHOLE,' he burst inside and faced the howling taverner across the bar.

"Will you shut the damned door!" the taverner bellowed through the gap in his teeth. "Dammit!"

Wafting smog glowed in dim lantern light, and the air reeked of fleck-bacc: a local tobacco commonly smoked in the tavern. Raihn pulled the rattling door closed behind him, shutting out the noise of the bustling streets and cleaner air.

"I forgot you were a troglodyte," he remarked to Benjin Breuer, the taverner.

Benjin blew his long, oily hair out of his face. "Only you forgot, drip, none other than a trog would slither here."

"In an outhouse? Because that's what it looks like," Raihn jested, approaching over straw and dung, passing two drunks sprawled out over tables. One's navy cloak draped over them, unfamiliar to Raihn, but the other was a regular.

Raihn reached the bar and plopped down on a crooked stool.

"Similar, aren't they? Both store shit!" Benjin roared, slamming an oak barrel.

"Y'both sound like children. How do I work for one, and how'd I once have the inclination to screw the other?" said a woman from under her bonnet.

"'Cause you couldn't find work doing anything else," Benjin replied. "But now you're a wench—my wench."

"Well, I did like being on top," she grinned.

"Like you didn't leave most the nailing to Tassy as a prostitute wench."

"Marnie," she corrected, her grin gone. "You pay me to be a wench, and I paid you half for using your shit beds. But I'm not much for the beds anymore, Ben. Nor am I interested in paying half."

"'Cause you like to slack and not make lively this sodden hovel, layin' in the booth these days."

Raihn, barely hearing them, was lost by the sight of the woman's bare legs that dangled from the booth where she lay, her frilled bonnet lazily covering her eyes.

"Still shy?" Benjin asked Raihn, his fat bottom lip peering from under his bushy mustache. "Well, don't be!" he urged, leaning closer.

Raihn shrunk, his cheeks feeling red. "I was just taken aback by the tiny curtains you force upon them. Classy."

"Sorry lad, but them 'curtains' seemed to work on you, creep. An' with an attitude like that, you're gonna find my foot, in your ass, sending you down the street to find yerself at the Finer Things, surrounded by even snootier folk," Benjin bantered. "Just be honest. There's no shame here."

"Clearly," Raihn remarked. "But you can't afford to boot me out of this boring bucket."

"'Boring'!?" Benjin recoiled. "I've got Ma-er-Tassy! A real merrymaker, that one!"

"And that's all you've got," said Marnie. "She's testing the beds most the time, and all the other whores and wenches left. Face it, he's right. You can nearly see my nethers."

"She's right about me being right, Benjin. I can almost see her nethers… But maybe if you advertised my name, things would change," Raihn boasted.

"Your name is already sullied by those familiar with it, and you know it," Benjin grinned. "And I ain't never heard a patron speak of no boy from the hill, 'cause nobody here knows who you are. Only we do. Appreciate that fact. Furthermore, don't blame me or her for your weakness."

Raihn remained quiet as Benjin rested over the bar, inches away.

"Bah," the taverner gurgled, straightening up, awaiting his reply. "Ay," Benjin snapped. "You a'right? You ain't had a drink yet, and you're in a daze."

"I'm fine. Just thinking," Raihn replied, hooked by those men.

"And that's what brings me patrons, thinkin'. 'Ere, have a drink," Benjin said as he topped off a tankard under the barrel's spigot. "On the house," he added, slapping the tankard down, foam rolling.

"Thanks, but you need someone to talk to. Being shut in here all day with drunks kissing tables must be dull. I should be sober."

"Only two're kissing grain. And just so you know," Benjin said, his voice easing to a whisper, "there are two patrolmen seated just over in that corner," he clarified, his voice full of warn.

"You gonna talk to them?"

"I might," Benjin straightened, his voice bright and his eyes glancing at them.

"Uh-huh. Well, I'm surprised to see them here, being served no less."

"A petal is a petal... Besides, they complain just like everyone else, gossiping an' all...politics. 'Enduran trade ending over a new ruler from the east-land' and so on. What do I care?"

"Right, you hate politics."

"Aye, you be right..." Benjin agreed, lowering himself to the bar contemplatively. "Maybe it is time for a wake-up," he said, looking to one of the passed-out drunks. "Can ye speak, Hardy!?"

Hardy, the tavern regular, sat back in a daze with murky eyes, his pint of ale clasped in his hands.

"Hardy!" Benjin burst again.

Delayed acknowledgment crept through until the patron's blank expression reanimated with a lively grin.

Raihn leaned back and crossed his arms victoriously. In no shape to talk, Benjin's patron, Hardy, stood up and teetered off and out the door.

"Damn all, Hardy!" Benjin cursed. "Your stock is long cut, you no-good, drunk bastard of a mule!" the keeper shouted, waving his foil where the notches of their record lay. "You owe me!" Then he turned to Raihn, holding half the tally stick, and explained—or rather—vented, "This is a business, not a place where people come and go for a free drink."

"For the love of god, just say soup circle," Raihn groaned.

Benjin lunged over the bar and pressed his hand over Raihn's mouth. "Mind the company in the corner!" he whispered harshly.

Marnie shot upright, her body tense as she clasped her bonnet tightly. "Lucky they didn't hear you. Watch what you say, Raihn," she hissed.

Her fingers lingered on the bonnet, clutching it as if to steady herself, before she slapped it back onto her head and flopped down with a frustrated huff.

"You know better than to speak of things that do not exist—man above man and all that," Benjin continued. "Nothing is greater than our king—our one king of Eldhona."

Their hand, warty and fat, remained over Raihn's mouth until his warm breath thawed Benjin's hold.

"It seems no harm is done," Benjin sighed, retracting. The patrolmen continued talking amongst themselves. "Like you've said, being cooped up is no good fer ye."

Raihn sat awkwardly, his cheeks flush with guilt over his loose lips.

"It's a shame," Benjin continued in a low hum. "Seems like they're everywhere now. Folks're tight-lipped. Most Authoritarians fancy The Singing Swallow or Finer Things, luckily. Yer father holds a grudge to 'em, even to me. My ol' man was on good terms servin' them Authoritarians sparsely, but...it wasn't too common. These fellas seem to come and hide like mice just as well, cursing their betters. But the lot of 'em have gotten worse these days, it seems."

"Well, speaking of my father and his grudge, brace yourself. He's supposed to meet me here."

"Lovely. He'll stink it up with his judgin' eye more than the tobacco. Why's he comin'?"

"Not sure. To tell me something? He knows this is a bit of a comfort place for me. Might his relay be dire," Raihn guessed.

"That's fine. I ain't bitter. My father contributed to destroying your way of life anyhow," Benjin said intensely, pocketing his tongue under his lip, gazing into the distance. "He built this place. That shit-bag. He left it to me."

It was quiet now. The mood seemed soured, and Raihn struggled to think of something to say. To bring the light mood back—anything. Shifting his weight, he tilted. "Chair's wobbly," he said.

"Yeah? I could use another hand on deck for fixin'."

"My chest doesn't meet your requirements," Raihn scoffed, insinuating that Benjin would only hire busty lasses.

"Raihn, I'm willin' to give you a place to work," Benjin leveled.

"You joking? Father wouldn't allow it," Raihn replied, taking the pewter tankard. "I'm...a Young Lord by end of day and the start of the next."

"Well...we do what we want in the end."

Raihn was feeling bottled up, becoming evasive and changing the subject rather than speaking truthfully, and was uninspired to change. Rather, Raihn glimpsed his satchel and recalled the events from earlier. "I nearly forgot to mention it, but Will said something to me today."

Benjin sighed. "And you didn't give them a smack, I'd wager."

"Almost. But that's not what I mean. He was an erring chicklet, yes, but he was clucking away that people were going missing."

Benjin's brows squeezed together. He parsed his meaning and swept a smirk. "Never repeat that," he said. "Anyway...you worried?"

Raihn evaded the question, waving the tankard. "For curiosity's sake, do you know anything?"

"Two've gone missin'," Benjin replied, leaning in. "Now that you mention it...I overheard them two patrolmen say a man from your village had disappeared. And his beloved raved to the King's Authority, I guess. But the big K.A. took it lightly, shruggin' it off. Her persistence finally chased them into the matter after the village came up with nothing, so I gather."

Raihn leaned too. "So, then what?"

Benjin waved a hand. "Nothin'," he said. "She took matters into her own hands. She went lookin' and not come back."

"So?"

"So, what?" Benjin's brow scrunched again.

"What do you think?"

24

"I dunno—could be some Outcast loose…"

"What Outcast!?" Raihn exploded from excitement.

"Don't get so worked up!" Benjin strained. "Look, I overheard a feared woman was making her way—an anvil. You know, the most fearless of mercenaries and most feared and all that shit. Just seems a bit crowded for a missin' couple. But cold is she, this anvil, so I heard again, abandoning her men to die after their rampage across the line of Bedfort, across the muskeg and into the Frinj up north."

"You hear a lot."

"Part of my societal labors."

"And you know as well as I do that word spreads faster than fire."

"And this is how it happens." Benjin beamed. "'A boring bucket' my right cheek."

Raihn slouched in his stool with his knees pressed against the undercarriage of the bar, relaying his day to Benjin. The raven, the bumbling buffoons—and their wailing cart—all of it. Benjin suggested a ploy for ransom, then a crash racketed in the kitchen behind the bar.

"What was that?" Raihn asked.

"Damned rotted wood and bad nails," Benjin excused, but then came a gnarly meow from the kitchen, summoning truth. "It's an ill-tempered, scarcely haired cat! Thought it might take the mice out of the hole, but it bangs up damn all from its chase!"

As Benjin rolled up his sleeves, ready to get dirty, Raihn saw the cat scratches on his arm as if he were a tally stick. "Good luck," he bid him.

Raihn sat alone, noticing a caged, clucking chicken at the far end of the bar while Benjin battled in the kitchen. Amid its clucks, a tap spurted from behind. Fingernails drummed a looping beat from the back corner. Annoyed, Raihn hunched over his drink.

Tap.

Tap.

It felt like an echo from his past dream, where the clacks of the needles had left him unsettled and agitated. Every clack emboldened him to glare over his shoulder.

And so he did.

His eyes fell on a man with wavy brown hair and a strange brooch that clasped their cloak, shaped like a dog. They're seated at the darkest table, watching Raihn intently. Their observations crossed only briefly before Raihn reverted to his gripped pewter. *Do I have a bounty on my head?* He felt itchy, his throat scratchy from the lingering smoke of fleckbacc that peppered his lungs. He couldn't stand it. *Who are these people?* They seemed to intently spurn a glance as they sat beside the diamond-shaped bars hewn into the wall.

"You awake? Hey, Marnie!" Raihn asked. Nothing. "Damn," he muttered.

Raihn's right hand nervously traced the rim of his tankard as he watched the kitchen door, hoping for Benjin's swift return. Finally, Benjin burst through but was immediately preoccupied with Marnie.

"Come on," begged the taverner, "that stray coughed up a hairball."

An argument broke between them as to who should remove it, Raihn fighting for a breath between them.

"He's no stray. You gave him a home now and named him Cuss! And 'Cuss' is your responsibility," Marnie argued.

"Benjin," Raihn interrupted a third time.

The taverner kicked the booth and spun. "What!?"

"Over in the corner… He's staring at me!"

Benjin stammered, waving out his arm. "So?"

"Benjin!"

"Fine, fine," Benjin folded, taking a look.

"So?" Raihn asked.

"Yeah—eyes like a hawk," Benjin described.

"Then stop gawking! You're making it obvious that we're talking about him," Rayne fretted.

"So? Go stick up for yerself like you almost did with that Will."

"Will is different… He's a serf. I have no idea who this is, what his intentions are…"

"Well, he's comin' this way. Better think quick."

Raihn's shoulders clamped like a vice as he spun around to meet the stranger head-on, but they weren't coming, nor were they even in the tavern. "Benjin, you asshole!" he barked. "How long ago did he leave?"

"Wouldn't know. I haven't seen nobody there all this morn. Was funny seein' you goosenecked, however."

"You lie. He was there, gawking."

"I ain't seen nobody either," Marnie attested. "But I understand."

Raihn was becoming more frustrated.

Benjin rolled his eyes, taking up a rag from the pocket of his filthy apron. "Okay… Give me a description," he said, twisting the rag, keeping his fingers busy.

"His lip was bushy. Soft brown hair. Bags under his eyes. Looked stressed beyond sleep with a brooch of a dog."

"He pearly?"

"I said brown hair. Eirhartic, like Tassy. Well, she's blonde, but…you know."

"Okay, okay, drip. I'll keep a lookout, a'right? That make you feel tender?"

"Thanks, Benjin."

Raihn heard those taps crawling up his spine as if he was being encroached upon. Itching, he looked at the door periodically, gripped by paranoia.

26

"Maybe you should go upstairs," Benjin suggested. "Tassy should be 'bout finished. Get yer mind off things."

Raihn remained quiet.

"Not yer type?" the taverner went on.

"No, it's not that. She looks great."

"I know. She has more curves than my curly hair. Her tits rival the mountain. Her voice…well, that's grating, but that's the least of yer worries—"

"Benjin," Raihn cut abruptly, tired of the womanizing and sexism. "It's not about her looks or anything like that."

"Fine. Yer worry wart is showing. I done all I could to remedy that."

"You just…you wouldn't get it," said Raihn, slumping over his tankard again.

"Sure. I'm just a womanizer. I wouldn't get it," Benjin replied and slapped his thighs with the washrag. "At least I don't feel sorry for myself being a lord."

Raihn sat unaccompanied again as Benjin went to the kitchen. Marnie fastly fell asleep, neglecting the two Authoritarian patrolmen who sat without drinks. Raihn took a final swig, the subdued atmosphere lulling him into a drowsy calm.

Where is he? he thought, regarding his father. Just then, the front door swung open, and light streamed into the hay and up the bar. *Could it be?* Raihn heard footsteps approaching—two patrons, by the sound of it. *No,* his father would come alone. *Just some rat-folk, surely.*

A pale, meaty palm, sparsely freckled, slapped down on the bar top as one of them took a seat. Raihn's heart raced, his breaths quick. The second figure seated itself on his other side, trapping Raihn between them.

The kitchen door banged into the wall, and Raihn jumped from his seat, his heart in his throat. Quivering, he tried to play it off as best he could in front of the newcomers.

"Welcome to the Mousehole," Benjin greeted. "What can I get you?"

"Hodge. My name is Hodge," said the meatier one with a soft hand. "And this is my brother, Herb," he gestured across Raihn, seemingly at the protest of Herb's glaring disapproval.

"Wonderful," the taverner said dryly. "What'll it be?"

"I'll accept your finest wine, thanks," Hodge said with a grin.

"If you want that, fancy-pants, then maybe your suspenders could waddle to Finer Things. I have ale, ale, and oh, yes, more ale."

Hodge huffed. "I'm sure many things are finer than—"

"He loves ale," Herb interrupted with a raised finger.

"Ale it is," said Benjin, finality in his tone.

"What might there be to dine on?" asked Hodge.

"Butter-boiled chicken," said Benjin, to which the chicken in the cage clucked.

"He meant to nibble on," Herb intervened.

"Meats and cheeses."

"So be it."

"And bread!" Hodge added.

"Sure. And what about you? You look like you could go for a bite," the taverner said to the deathly thin Herb. "I have pottage and pig—good stuff."

"I don't doubt it's splendid, but none for me, thank you," Herb said rather snootily.

Benjin barked at Marnie, startling them all. "Fetch this gentleman his nibbles," he demanded before finally giving Raihn a queer eye.

Raihn cleared his throat, suddenly aware he was still standing—a detail that might raise concern. He eased himself back down, maintaining eye contact with Benjin and giving a subtle nod. As he settled, he watched Benjin's gaze shift, taking them all in. Raihn hoped he noticed how he was flanked by the two who perfectly matched the description he'd given earlier.

Hodge's ale came to a head while Herb fiddled with something over his collar that looked to be a newfangled fastener.

"I told you to just yank that shoddy button," Hodge told his brother.

"It's not shoddy, just well-serviced."

"Then find a tailor," Hodge pressed.

"There's no time for such luxuries, brother."

"Always time for comfort," Hodge retorted.

Interrupting their bickering, Marnie barged in, serving scraps.

"Ah, I give you my gratitude," Hodge thanked.

Raihn couldn't take it any longer, his mind spiraling with thoughts of what they might do once Hodge had his fill. It couldn't just be his imagination—they were following him, weren't they? If all they wanted was a drink and a bite, then why were they sandwiching him between them?

Feeling trapped, he pushed back his seat and headed for the door. The bulbous buffoon paused mid-chew, twisting toward him with his mouth still full. Raihn quickened his pace, but just as he reached the door, the remaining drunkard at the table shot out a hand and clamped down on his arm.

"You can't leave," said the thought-to-be-drunk, surprisingly sober. His grip brought out a cry for help from Raihn.

Benjin vaulted from behind the bar to grapple with the attacker. Hodge also clambered off his stool and collided with them, elbowing Benjin.

"How about an intermission before it gets out of hand!" Herb cried.

It was too late for that and it was getting worse. The patrolmen got involved. And the drunk at the table was swinging angrily, landing blows upon Benjin. Even Marnie gasped and darted over.

"Herb!?" Hodge called out in panic, but his brother was already dashing out the door. Amid the fight, Raihn saw him ripping away furs from a pile in the cart just outside as the loose door hung open. He was looking for something.

Tossing away their furs, Herb revealed a dangerous stash: two axes, a club, rope, and a short broadsword.

"Cursed be the eight!" Benjin swore, seemingly catching a glimpse as well.

Herb seemed to ponder the weapons. He chose the club but nearly fell over a bed of loose nails just trying to heave it out with his string bean fingers. And so, he held firm with both hands, slumping it over his shoulder, nearly cracking it, he'd swore aloud. And upon reentering, he was nearly squatting from the club's heft, his hips shaking.

Herb dropped the head of the club upon one patrolman, rendering them unconscious. Hodge aided Herb in lifting it again to club the other.

Benjin and Marnie stepped back, retreating from the chaos. Raihn noticed the cut on Marnie's lip, and the taverner beside her had blood dripping down his knuckles.

"Go upstairs," Benjin told Marnie.

"And leave you two?" Marnie questioned.

"Go," Benjin repeated. "Room number three. Block the door with the cabinet."

Herb appeared to be struggling to hold the club any longer, making Raihn afraid for whoever may suffer its fall.

"Careful," said Hodge to Herb.

Benjin lunged, but Herb struck him down cold. Marnie stood frozen, fear evident in her eyes. She was outnumbered, and Raihn couldn't even help himself—he was pinned down. The navy-cloaked drunk fixed her with what seemed a lascivious stare, and perhaps it was that fiendish gaze that finally drove her to flee. "What are you doing?" the feigning drunk cried. "Get her!"

Herb dropped the club and dashed madly after her up the stairs. His hand hooked her ankle and brought about her fall. She crashed into the upper step, skull first.

Feeling for a pulse, Herb let go of his breath. "She's alive."

"Who gives a damn!" the stranger replied callously, restraining Raihn. "The only one that needs to live is this one! Lest my debt be mountainous. Get the rope."

CHAPTER FIVE

A gathering of mice and rats

Room number three at the end of the second floor was a dismal space containing little more than a wobbly cabinet and a questionably stained bed fit for three. It was a nasty hole where Hodge couldn't bear to sit anywhere.

Raihn was restrained to a chair at the foot of the bed, choking on a salty gag. Xander, the last navy-cloaked 'drunk' from the table who had grabbed Raihn, paced the room before him, cursing bitterly. Sweat stained his cloak as he dragged his hobnailed heels, his face covered in short bristles, with a few frail hairs clinging to his scalp above piggish ears. He continued pacing before coming to an abrupt stop.

"How much longer must we wait?" Xander asked. "Waiting is what got us in this mess to begin with!"

"We've no choice," said Herb.

"Of course we do! I am here solely to repay my debt. If I cannot do that, then I may as well leave this lost cause."

"Leave?" Herb squinted. "You mean stir a panic just before ditching us? Is that all your debt is worth to you?"

"It very well isn't worth waiting here for the King's Authority to come. Not like anyone else will show besides us suckers!"

"Well, if you hadn't assaulted the lad!"

"I had to act!" Xander cried. "Ain't my fault he's squirrelly. And answer me this: did you wheel that stupid heap of pelts when tailing 'im?" Guilt melted the faces of the two gingers. "No wonder!"

"I couldn't just leave it on the corner!" Hodge excused.

"You! I had to push it because you're a cheat!" Herb accused.

Hodge squealed. "I play grass fire water just square! You know I'm bogged by rheumatism."

"Look," Herb said, pinching his nose bridge and focusing back on Xander. "This is your expertise, not ours."

"Kidnapping is not my expertise."

"Would you rather I say killing?" Herb clarified, drawing a muffled groan from Raihn. "We're short numbered either way and must explain why we have the Parcel boy all tied up. We've bound ourselves to demise."

"Then that's it. Let's split," Xander said. "You dipshits left behind our gear anyhow."

Hodge stomped. "I have waited long for this opportunity! And after all, Xander, you are a friend to Magnus."

"And I fell asleep waitin' for him!"

"Wait," Herb waved, "you weren't faking?"

"Well…I was in and out of it!"

Through their bickering, Raihn managed to work out the nasty gag. "Help!"

"Shit! Shut him up!" Xander ordered.

Hodge stuffed Raihn up again and spoke to his compatriots, "We should just tell him."

"I was hired under one guideline, and a professional follows through," the supposed killer said.

"Real professional thus far," Herb scoffed. "Follow through with what? You're ready to abandon ship!"

"Shut it!" Xander barked. He pressed his pinkish ear to the door. "Shit," he whispered.

"Is everything alright?" a voice crept through the door. "I heard some shouting."

"Just some roleplay!" Hodge squeaked out.

"I see! Sounds like a proper way to treat a lady. May I join?" the voice said gleefully, the knob turning.

"Hodge, you dumb son of a bitch, look at what you've done!" Xander squirmed.

"How should I know she'd be so rude as to intrude on something so private!"

"At least she said 'may I,' first," Herb pointed out.

The door cracked, but Xander slammed against it. An audible tumble was heard through the door.

Hodge whimpered, "Oh no. We have to stop hurting these poor people."

The others remained quiet, and Herb nervously picked at his button when suddenly the door burst open and flung Xander to the ground. Raihn muffled a call to warn Tassy as she'd charged in, halting on her toes.

"Raihn? I'm not sure this be your kinda roleplay," she said as she peeped the other guests.

As Xander clambered back up, his cloak hung over his back, and a blade on his hip gleamed. Tassy took a retreating step away before a full sprint, but Xander darted after her. Raihn feared for her life, as this man was said to be some kind of professional killer, and down the corridor, he was seen to be chasing her until they went down the stairs.

A moment passed by, and dead silence staled the air. Raihn huffed and puffed through flared nostrils, yet to know what came of her, but Xander stomped back. He slammed the door and drove a hole through the rotted wall with his foot.

"Calm down," said Herb.

"They're gone," Xander whimpered, sounding like a beaten dog. "They're all gone."

"Who?" Hodge asked. "The girl?"

"All of 'em!" he repeated, "not just the damned girl. I saw nobody downstairs," Xander informed, holding his head between his hands.

"It's all crumbling, like a cake with too much sugar," Hodge said.

As if things couldn't get worse, a voice seeped through the crack of the door when nobody else was expected to be there. "Tassy?" a curious man moused. "Come on back; I'm not done with you," he said flirtatiously.

Xander paused, flustered, and Raihn thought those might be the last words from the man on the other side of the door, whom he presumed to be Tassy's last customer. Xander swung open the door with his other hand, fastening a tight fist. He struck and laid them flat.

"So violent," Herb remarked. "This was a mistake."

"I could have done worse," Xander replied. "He should have kept his nose out of our room."

"At the least, the lady escaped us," Herb moaned.

"'Lady'?" Xander questioned. "Don't mind the strumpet. We have direr concerns."

"And we deserve what is coming," Herb said.

"You mean from the Authority?" Xander's lip rose. "The King's Authority—the ones that grip their leashes over the Eight Wynds? I'd rather drink an old hag's bath water."

"Then we best get along," said Hodge, peeking through the window. "I see them clearing a path, making way to our front door!"

Xander scrambled beside the puffy ginger and stole a glance between the tattered curtains. He spun back, his face a knot of dread. "Too many of them," he said. "Too many to be rallied so quick, right, Herb?"

Taking a gander for himself, Herb agreed. "Indeed, perhaps all the watchmen—many times greater than any patrol. In times such as this, I long for the days when they were the Rose Guard."

"Hah!" Xander hopped away. "Well, it's late for a front door escape now!" He shoved the crooked cabinet in front of the bedroom door, barring any more intruders. "We're already skewered and ready to be cooked! They gathered so fast and not from any word of mouth by any whore or taverner…"

"Who then?" Hodge asked.

"He muses a snitch is among our party," Herb clarified.

"Not a snitch, a rat!" Xander clarified.

"Okay, so who do you propose, then?"

"Who do you think?" Xander scoffed.

"Magnus assured us otherwise," said Herb. "Everyone in our party is trusted. Magnus said he had proof."

"Look around you!" Xander belted, his arm flung out. "Do you see his contact?"

"Excuse me, but we can go without the attitude."

"Well, excuse me," Xander mocked, "but we are in an inescapable pit full of shit. Cardinal Pharloe Hull and the king himself will take turns clipping our fingers!"

"Well, my fingernails are getting quite long," Herb joked, stoking Xander's fire.

"Guys!" Hodge blurted out. "We should focus on one prominent question: what do we do now?"

Taking a beat to think fast, Herb shortly thereafter said, "I might have a proposal, Xander. I suggest leaving him—Raihn," he clarified, glancing at him quickly. "He had no part in this, and he knows naught of our plans."

Raihn, not liking the sound of being left for the buzzards, squirmed.

"Leave him to the Authority?" Hodge questioned.

"They will question him and only learn our names, which are damned already," Herb continued. "The King's Authority will let him go. So, I say, we flee out the window and search for Magnus and make our next move. That is our logical option… What say you, Xander?"

"No!" Hodge interjected again.

The door downstairs bellowed, and stomping ensued.

"Then what do you propose?" Herb asked, his tone frantic.

Hodge froze, fighting for a reliable breath of an answer.

"Exactly," Herb snipped.

As fate would have it, a large stone burst through the back shutter right then and there, hardly missing Raihn. The trio peered outside.

"Magnus!" Hodge shouted.

"Quiet, you daft idiot!" Xander slapped his head and looked at their brother. "Go first, skinny."

Herb crawled through, and Hodge was about to go next, but Xander pulled him away. "Not so fast."

"Why?"

"You know why, tubby," Xander remarked.

Hodge huffed. The cabinet legs screeched as the Authority reached the door, clobbering the other side.

"With haste now! Come on!" Xander yelled from outside.

Hodge went there, then looked back at Raihn, his eyes soft. "I'm sorry you got involved in all this," he said. "Xander's just a bit of a hot egg, and I got a bit scrambled amid the heat. Also, apologies to your friends. I think they may just have some bruises…hopefully."

"Come on, jump, you'll be fine!" Herb encouraged.

"But will we?" Xander asked from below. Another jab.

Hodge continued, "I know you have no reason to trust me, but you should trust the men at the other end of that door even less. Your name, lad. It's important. Consider keeping it secret. Maybe no more fools would drag you into their mess if it were kept quiet."

Not long after Hodge fled, a duo from the town watchmen, responsible for criminal justice and order, rammed through the door, gawking about the nearly vacant room, sniffing for their bone to chew. Today, they might be after a femur, the largest bone in the human body, given the unusual mess that had unfolded around Raihn.

The man who seemed to be the town's bailiff entered with one of his constables, stone-faced and sour of mood. From beneath the long-billed visor of his open-faced helm, his eyes narrowed on the broken shutter. "We're too late," he groaned. "They're gone."

"But what could they have wanted with him?" the constable asked, regarding Raihn.

"That's what questioning is for," replied the bailiff.

"Would you have me inform the anvil? Dame Dawness was reportedly entering the town by contract of the Hulls."

"I am aware. And the lass knows enough, it seems," said the bailiff. "She tried extending her boot in my door."

"She paid you a visit," the constable surmised.

"Her little carrier pigeon, Pate, did…stern little thing, and secretive too," the bailiff said. "And she paid nothing, owing gold petals to the town reeve for the ruckus that dame and those Hulls are stirring. And knowing those Hulls, we best be careful, though I know these alleys better than they do… Damn Hull soldiers skirting around my constabulary, flirting with an anvil. A fine mess they made by chasing their fugitives here," the bailiff grumbled. "Forget her. Gather some lads. I want to know what's going on that is so dire to include an anvil—a woman demanding my submission of authority to her and the Hulls from the East Wynd…"

The constable nodded and left the room, leaving the bailiff to remove the gag from Raihn's mouth, finally, before asking his name. But Raihn stalled, looking empty-headed and clueless. He should have prepared through all that nattering. He thought hard, considering Hodge's suggestion.

"Your name!" the bailiff demanded.

"Lance!" Raihn replied louder than he meant to.

"Lance what?"

"Lance-uh-peddler," he answered, smacking his lips and wincing.

"Why're you doing that?"

"The gag was awful… Try chewing a dirty sock after a long plow, and you might understand the savory taste. Better yet, try this gag yourself."

"…Just recount me the names of the captors, Peddler."

"Herb, Hodge, and Xander."

"That's it?"

"Well…I heard mention of another name. He wasn't here. His name was Magnus."

The bailiff questioned "Lance Peddler" until a figure lurked in the corridor, clad in broad armor.

The bailiff sighed. "Forget something?" He'd asked, then spun around, presumedly realizing the figure was not one of his men. He stammered at their sight, indicating the surprise. Regardless, he'd relayed what he knew to the lurker. "I would surmise that the trees are their shelter," he said. "Scour the perimeter. They won't have anywhere to hide. I want them upon their knees in the court."

"You misunderstand your position, bailiff. This is bigger than a theft in the corner of your house of rocks. These fugitives come from the East Wynd. The Hulls will handle it from here. If you wish to turn over stones, be my guest, but don't get in our way further."

"This is a joint effort at best. The Hulls work within accordance to the Charter of the Rose from First King Eldridge, post War of the Cardinals—"

"I need no lesson nor reminder of political shifts, flatfoot."

"—And I am a representative of his law," the bailiff continued. "Even under the king of my years, King Stamen. The Cardinals of the King's Compass are lieges. They follow the law, and the cardinal of this Intersectional Wynd of Wheat will not sit and abide your stomping!"

"On the contrary, your—Intersectional, mind you—Cardinal obliged per request from Cardinal Pharloe Hull in his Superior Wynd. Pharloe would have had his collection sooner had your blundering street watchers not scared them away."

"…Did you interrogate my men?"

The shadowed man stepped closer, the dark peeling off their copper-rimmed armor. "What was their business here in this tavern of ale and wenches?" the lurking Hull soldier, perhaps knight, questioned. "Anvil Dame Dawness had control of the matter."

"That anvil is but a dark wanderer," said the bailiff, snubbing the question just like his question was snubbed. "And little has she clued in for me and yet have I to collect a letter for said oblige. I'd like to know what the Lord Mayor thinks firsthand."

"This town has made you soft, Bailiff Kelce," the soldier said. "This is not a matter for you to handle, but Pharloe Hull, as permitted by, in fact, your Lord Mayor, who contracted Anvil Dame Dawness," he explained. "Justice will come."

The bailiff appeared disarmed and fatigued and at the end of his wit.

The figure vanished, and then the bailiff cut Raihn's bonds. "Hulls… Damn them. You're free to go," he said bitterly. However, something seemed to have caught his eye. "That satchel. What's in it?"

"Just a journal," Raihn squirmed.

Snatching it, the constable went on. "Got any interesting stories to tell?"

"Not really," Raihn said. "Sometimes you just want to confide in something."

"To 'confide in something'?" Bailiff Kelce echoed, sifting through. "Let's see. Entry four. 'I woke up hungry for a world I could not swallow, and tonight, I'll sleep on the thought of how delicious it could be. For now, I consider myself lucky to sleep contentedly with a family that loves me and shelters me, for just yesterday they gifted me a couple of books so that I could have a taste of the world, and quills and brushes so that I may envision more.'" The bailiff glanced at Raihn with a glint of judgment.

"Yeah—so, that's kind of private. I don't suppose I could have it back?"

Kelce continued skimming, frighteningly close to the final inscriptions as their thumb sprang the pages over. With perhaps only six entries left, Raihn thought to snatch it away. However, his indecision paid off. The bailiff's eyes lingered in almost contempt from under his bill.

Kelce clapped the book shut. "It is not a journal," he said. "It's a diary." Chuckling, he handed it back. "Should get out more often, Lance Peddler."

He must not have read the more interesting parts by some dumb luck, Raihn thought.

By the strap, Raihn slung the satchel over his shoulder before ambling through the corridor where Xander's victim once was—Tassy's horndog customer. But now it was quiet. Lonely. Disheartening. Raihn was just captured by three strange men without understanding why, and his father still had not come. Raihn felt vulnerable and alone, still grasping at what was going on and why he listened to his captor to withhold his true name.

His worry for his father, Rahim, festered, his thoughts jittering him down the stairs. Chairs and tables were on their sides, and the tavern was eerily quiet, but then the front door blasted from its hinges and cracked the wall like a whip. Tassy butted in and embraced him, Benjin and Marnie trailing. She squealed in Raihn's ear, playfully tucking his head under her chin.

"Nice to see you too," he said, his voice muffled against her bosom. His nose felt snug between supple loaves of springy cheese, warm as freshly baked bread. But her low-cut bodice reeked of fleckbacc, while her skin's fragrance fought back with hints of lavender and the savory scent of butter-broiled chicken.

Tassy lightly scratched his scalp, her nails soothing Raihn's overworked brain. He quivered, but after a moment, reined in his desires and pulled away gently. She stood before him, bundled in a ragged bodice, her body curvy yet rigid from its squeeze. She smiled, ignorant to any boundaries, but was harmless.

"Glad you're not dead," Benjin gleamed.

Raihn recovered, plying his eyes away. His heart still pounding, his voice frenetic, "I could say the same. But they got you good. Your head's bleeding."

"Should see my nails. I was bitin' them down, worryin'," Benjin said.

"They were bad before," Marnie teased. "Anyway, what about you, Raihn? You okay? What happened up there?"

"Honestly, I don't know. I'm not sure where I fit in that mess." His gaze lowered; he wondered if maybe he was just excited from the chaos. But even then, Tassy's ever-supportive bodice wasn't calming him, his heart racing.

"You should be with your mother," Benjin said. "And if I see your ol' man, I'll tell him he should be with his family."

"You're not going to shut in?" Tassy asked Benjin, her voice as squeaky as the upper floorboards.

"You go on. I'm gonna down a few and check on Cuss," Benjin said. Tassy gave Benjin a kiss before he slapped her rear like she was a horse to gallop.

Before his giddy-up hand could find the next horse to suffer it, Marnie snagged it. "Not ever in your life," she said. "And I'm staying. Can't have you drinking away all the ale before a patron could be seated at an upright table."

Parting from his friends, Raihn's eyes were blinded when he emerged from the tavern. Eldhos was high in the sky now, and after his eyes adjusted to the light, he saw a flock of folk gathering in the street. They seemed to be drawn in from every which way, piquing his curiosity. He entered the current where these fish swam mindlessly, some muttering and questioning what all the commotion was about down the way. As Raihn went, he spotted posters nailed against stalls flickering through the murky stream. He glimpsed them and parsed from their ink the same man who gagged him up.

Raihn plunged deeper into the quilted mob. Some folks were angry, others scared and murmuring, trading stories about some woman in black.

"She once went feral with her bunk buddies and slayed a dozen Outcast beasts in the north frost. A bloodthirsty lass she is," said one.

"She will summon their rage, that Frinjen Slayer!" another replied.

"Fools!" said a third man, bearded and broad-shouldered. "Quiet yourselves, lest she hear you."

It was a stirring pot here as off-putting spectators marched through town. Raihn budged through them until he saw three broad soldiers standing before a fishmonger and his racks. At the center of attention, among the gazes of onlookers, stood a colossal woman adorned with black armor. She looked nothing like the typical Authoritarian, nor like the copper-lined soldiers beside her.

"Who is she?" Raihn asked aloud, not expecting anyone to answer.

"Notorious mercenary," hummed an old, skinny fellow, slack-jawed and toothless. A string of tip-suckled hay bounced on his fat lip, and he spoke. "A mercenary honored by knighthood, I guesses. But many know her through a bleaker moniker: the Black Anvil. Yeah—a hardened lass that. But it's all hearsay; and it is said that she has a strong will and that power imbues her armor, blackest of all among the anvils: midnight metal and full-grain leather. Ey, hearsay 'bout the killa, yeah. What is true, though, is that she hails from the Lead Belly Foundry. Aye, she does— a harsh 'forge' some call it, near the northern trench that be Crossguard, or more simply, the Line."

Raihn had heard of it from past murmurs in the tavern. Things he wasn't meant to learn about, as his father seemed to maintain a temper for certain understandings. But from more recent events, he recounted what the bailiff had to say about her.

"Upon her back, a brand, I reckon," the stranger droned on. "Like a fine cow, belongin' to a farm, taken in as a calf, milked dry ever since. Wherever she go, all know to who she belongs."

Raihn was increasingly curious. She looked strong, and she had to be, judging by the hunks of black metal that clasped her body. However, her presumably forward leg was cast in iron, as was the rest of her, save for her back leg and, currently, her head.

Jagged, anvil-like pauldrons towered above her unruly hair that was worn shorter than most men's. Studs adorned her knuckles, good for beating, while faulds and chain mail around her hips cascaded to her knees like a skirt. Beyond her imposing appearance, there was something else equally fierce within her that Raihn couldn't put his thumb on. Though he continued to hear meek whispers of her name all around him, 'Dame Renna Dawness…the Black Anvil.' However, Dame Dawness stuck the most.

Beside this anvil was a much shorter and more petite girl with jaw-length blonde hair—someone that Raihn had noticed last. Might it be that 'pigeon Pate' the bailiff had also mentioned. She was watching Dame Dawness's every move, her eyes gleaming with loyalty and admiration. She was frail-looking, bearing armor that was lighter than her mentor's. Her reinforced leather donned meager plates of tidy black armor, resembling that of Dame Dawness's, except over hers was a tattered, brown surcoat embroidered with a white bell.

As was whispered, the bell implied she was once a child of the Salt Rock Corral in Bedfort, a place where the ringing of a white bell meant a child, occasionally two, and less often three, would be legally bound to their new guardian, most often as a servant. This was hardly better than pulling salt from the north mines for their housemaster or sponging the floors of the wayward home, but her eyes rejected that murmur.

Raihn could only surmise that Dame Dawness had once visited this place in Bedfort, south of Crossguard, and had that bell rung. The child would've departed there, overworked and prune-fingered, with salted hair. Abandoning the home between the moor, the Foundry, and the cluster of mines.

She must be thankful to be whisked away from there. Her knees wouldn't be planted into the worm-wiggling soil. However, now she scrubbed Dame Dawness's armor and carried with her a bag of sand and a bottle of vinegar for the removal of rust. And fresh upon her hands was the potent smell of stinging vinegar that wafted through the crowd. The apprentice stood proudly. A blackened great helm that was far too big for her head rested awkwardly on her arms as she clenched a large heater shield that displayed Dame Dawness's coat of arms: the anvil.

Before the slimy fish racks, Dame Dawness retrieved what appeared to be some rolled-up parchment from a man clad in armor. Uncoiling the furled flyer, the Eirhartic woman presented it to the old fishmonger. And around Raihn were bubbling heads, taking glimpses, as if a cauldron clamoring in the heat.

"Have you seen this girl?" Dame Dawness asked. All fell silent at her deep tone. "You are inclined to tell me," she said tersely.

The monger looked the flyer over. "I see lots of faces, but I wouldn't forget this one," he shrugged.

Dame Dawness remained firm. "There was a break before you answered. Must I remind you that withholding any information about these criminals would make you equally guilty? I'll allow you to read it again, as your eyes may have failed you in your age."

The monger, above his deboned fish, gritted his teeth and leaned for better inspection. His look was a puzzled one. "A thief with an unknown name. Pharloe Hull of the East Wynd sent you, an anvil, for such a petty crime? I believe you know more than you let on," said the fishmonger.

"The proper information has been written," she insisted, her tone clamping.

"Ralph," said the old man, clarifying his name.

"Fishmonger," Dame Dawness reaffirmed, her eyes narrowing. She hammered the flyer to his little market stall, each beat an aggressive one. "A reward stands for any individual willing to provide valuable information," she announced to all within earshot. "Your reward: a pound of gold petals."

Everyone went abuzz. Raihn, however, was quiet. His eyes were fixated upon a foreign girl depicted on the poster Dame Dawness had nailed. Perhaps he stood out too greatly, for she looked his way.

They made eye contact, his muscles taut from nerves.

"You there, state your name," the anvil ordered.

Abruptly, all eyes fell on him. *Does anyone recognize me?* he wondered before sputtering, "Lance Peddler."

"What have you to say, Peddler?"

"Nothing worth hearing," he laughed off.

"What is your contribution to Cobblestone?"

Stunned by the question, he realized he had contributed nothing. Regardless, even if he had, he could not speak it under this new persona.

"My petal is my tribute," Raihn answered, making himself a character. "I found myself going nowhere, so I went somewhere, a place where I might sell."

"Hence the name Peddler," she remarked, a bit of amusement rolling along her breath.

It was a quick exchange, and Raihn noticed the fishmonger's eyes flick at him briefly. They were acquaintances. That was It. *But did he remember?* Raihn asked himself, *He wouldn't snitch, would he?* The man was given the right to Wispy River through a contract with Raihn's grandfather. *Surely,* he wouldn't snitch.

"What do you know about this girl?" Dame Dawness continued, her palm resting on the pommel of her sheathed sword.

A mere game of intimidation, Raihn figured hopefully. "I have nothing of value to offer, as this is my first sight of her. My apologies," he said. A bead of sweat rolled down his face.

Dame Dawness's eyes tightened. The Black Anvil surveyed the crowd once more before leaving in silence, with her apprentice following. Raihn let out his gut as his lungs relaxed.

The travelers murmured more openly once the mercenary departed, but Raihn was reeled in by the face on the poster. So was another, whose robes became clenched under Raihn's heel.

"Oh! Excuse me, sir," Raihn apologized.

The robed man shook his head with a faint smile. "I come from caverns where there are no sirs. I'm just an old, curious man, my memories still flickering, my eyes fading, and my body growing lazy. My grandson, Halba, guides me to the Wall of Thorns. I hope to make my crossing."

"To pass the wall?" Raihn asked.

"To depart this world and enter the next," the man corrected. "Such is our way, made ever slimmer as we near the mountain."

"Grandfather," Halba interjected, as if the old man had said too much.

"Quiet, Halba," the man rasped. "Lest your fear bring us more concern than kindness."

"What do you mean, 'made slimmer'?" Raihn pressed.

"We solmners are hidden before our journeys begin, but the tradition itself is not," the man explained. "Unfortunately for you, only we are granted this religious path. We are foreign folk."

"You are a mystic!?" Raihn said.

"Keep your voice down!" the grandson urged. "And we prefer solmner."

"Sorry," Raihn apologized. "My father sort of prohibits any interest or knowledge of anything deemed unworldly," Raihn said regretfully. "But around here, that caution is warranted. I sometimes forget that myself."

40

"Like the king and his Authority. I can see that I have flapped my gums more than I should have," the old man croaked wearily.

"No, no," Raihn assured. "Thank you for sharing it with me."

"Not to worry, until your father finds out," the old man replied, straining a laugh. Then he looked at Raihn for a moment, his eyes looking dull. "I can see even with my partial sight that you have a lingering interest in this girl. Why is that?"

"I'm curious about why she would be wanted," said Raihn. "She looks innocent enough."

"And how is it she appears?"

"Dark hair, small nose, rounded lips—she's an Endolander. It says that her crime is theft, but even so, what kind of theft would warrant this great of attention? Why would her name be unlisted?"

The solmner seemed less buoyant after hearing this, as if he knew something Raihn didn't. His voice became forlorn and narrow. "How old is she?"

"Nineteen. Do you know her?" asked Raihn.

"Grandfather," the grandson intervened.

The old solmner lifted his hand to silence the boy. "She's free," the old man said, his dull eyes managing a twinkle.

It was unclear to Raihn what he meant by this, but his curiosity was interrupted by the familiar sound of cawing overhead. He glanced up to see it, the dark messenger. The raven still lingered, eclipsing Eldhos, its wide wings casting a gliding shadow. Chickens clucked in their cages, and other livestock stirred madly through the market. Raihn detached himself from this little bubble and saw an abundance of Hull soldiers questioning merchants. Raihn neared them so that he could listen, but babble buffeted the air. Something was up.

He sidled along the crowd, aiming to appear disinterested and to lie low. The old man ensued, as well as Halba.

It was odd to see the Hulls outside of their own wynd, but here they came like a landed fleet let loose from a slob cardinal. They stormed like one dark cloud and poured in through the streets, heavy like a downpour. They roared thunderously and pushed Cobblestoners to the dirt as they ripped them from their carts and homes, searching for the missing thief.

"Grandfather, we should leave," said Halba. "Grandfather!"

Fear welled up inside Raihn, too, but they remained like frozen fools, watching the berated townsfolk against Halba's protest.

The Hull soldiers locked it all down, rounding up Cobblestoners and sequestering them. Some resisted, though it was futile as they were battered into submission. Raihn was afraid, unable to move. *Benjin and Marnie and Tassy.* He feared for them, but some sense emerged with the appearance of the bailiff, who begged for understanding amidst the madness.

"This is not how we treat Cobblestone!" yelled the bailiff. "I disbelieve willful agreement by lords that this behavior had been granted."

Dame Dawness appeared before him, her metal mounting over the sight of villagers. "Another wynd blows in," she said. "Tell your cardinal. Relay tidings of my power, and might he be convinced to plea to Pharloe from my sudden wrath. For by the time a letter reaches your lesser cardinal's talons, I'll have the fugitives in mine. I will return to Cardinal Pharloe Hull with my contract fulfilled."

Bailiff Kelce rested his palm on his pommel. "Then what of the king? What might he say about all this: he who rules the Eight Wynds. The cardinals govern their small plots, but not without a say from him. You overstep your boundaries as an anvil, Dame Dawness. I am a far-reaching spear for the king in what is ultimately his town. There is a reason we are called the King's Authority. And I, with my constables, would not have you tarnish its reputation, for we are also its shield, its watch."

Dame Dawness took a stance, her plated forward leg taking the lead. "Once King Stamen, in his tower of gold, can see the value of our fugitives, he will understand," she replied. "Though if you persist in standing in my way, I am sure he will favor a harsh judgment, one I will command happily before having heard it."

Beside Dame Dawness stood two bullish Hull soldiers, ready to heed her command as her hand looked to hoist. One of them looked to be a knight with his heraldic tabard, and even he stood by her. *But why? She was a mercenary. Was she entrusted that much by Pharloe?* They eyed the bailiff, snorting and spitting like the fowl-folk they seemed to be.

Kelce forfeited his contest.

"Now then, find the fugitives. Flush them out," the dame ordered. "I desire proof of the town's honesty."

Raihn had spectated the travesty until it got even worse. Another knight of the East Wynd herded two heart-stopping villagers. Raihn gasped.

The solmner came beside him. "What do you see?"

"My friends. They have them!" Raihn replied. After standing aside, hearing them faintly argue in the distance, Raihn stumbled closer, paying caution no more mind as reason evaded him.

The old solmner came and gripped his shoulders. "Don't go any nearer," he warned.

The knight had wrangled Benjin and Marnie, then kicked them to the dirt, their faces made swollen.

"What have you done to them?" the anvil demanded, seemingly enraged by their mistreatment.

"Had to loosen some tight lips."

She launched her metal gauntlet into the knight's mouth, knocking a tooth.

"You should have brought them to me first," she scolded.

"Indeed." The knight spat a glob. "The constable confirmed these two to be Benjin and Marnie," he said, cradling his jaw. "They run the Mousehole with another by the name of Tassy, though she has yet to be recovered."

"And?"

"There was also a patron collaborator—drunk, but no less right about this pair. This leads me to believe his word on Raihn as well. It seems the tavern hostage had offered the guise, 'Lance Peddler.'"

"Lance?" she repeated as she and Pate shot Raihn daggers.

Raihn froze as they headed this way. "Damn you, Hardy," he cursed the drunk beneath his breath.

"Leave me, Halba. Your journey is over," the old solmner said.

"What? So will yours, you addled old man!" Halba cried.

"We are fated to perish. Since following the flow of the river, I accepted my fate. Whether I die here, I will not abandon another… Not again."

"Rotted blot!" Halba cursed, "And you know what? Black spurs too."

"Look, please do not stay on my behalf. I'm just a nobody," Raihn said, true of heart. "Unlike me, you have no obligation to stay."

Halba's grandfather remained silent, standing firm against Raihn's bold words. When Dame Dawness loomed over them, her mere presence vanquished Raihn's courage as she donned her helm. Pate, in company, bit her lip in anticipation, excitement flickering in her eyes as she hovered close. Her hip tilted in a coy, snarky bow.

"What is it you want?" the solmner asked her.

"Do not interfere, lest your tradition be quelled, mystic."

Raihn glanced past the dame and her "pigeon," catching sight of Benjin being escorted toward a growing group of detainees.

Suddenly, Benjin elbowed his escort, breaking free from the soldier's grasp. "It's a trap!" he shouted. His voice rang out in warning. "They mean to ensnare—!" An abrupt interruption cut his cry short. His blood forked out, staining the stone street from a blooming arrowhead.

Raihn froze, his eyes locked on Benjin. His mind raced, but all he could do was silently beg to whatever great power that might heed to save him, though he knew how fruitless that plea always was.

"Please, god," Raihn blubbered.

The anvil whipped her neck in aghast surprise, clutching his mouth as though he were about to swallow gold. He trembled in her gauntlet, his cheeks bulbed.

"The only god to exist is a proclaimed one in the tower of gold, and if he is not the grace you speak of, his Authority would then have you reminded. And be thankful I am no Authoritarian, lest thy mouth be hollowed out," she warned.

Her voice was that of power, but despite that, she was resisted. Not by Raihn, but surprisingly by the old solmner, who had swiftly drawn a short staff from his robe.

"Don't," the dame warned again, her eyes hawkish through her helmet. Her voice was subtle this time, as though it were a secret between them. "Quell that rebellious will to fight back," she said. It was a mellow tone, tinkering through her metal.

The solmner cracked her helm with his staff. Her hold of Raihn fled. And when she went to snatch him, the solmners both walled her off. She faintly shook her head. Against the egregious anarchism of these supposed lawmen and soldiers, Halba seemed suddenly fortified as well.

"I knew you had it in you, Halba," said the old man. "If only I wielded such bravery at your age, I would have no regrets. And so, I know you would not look back and regret this moment in which you are brave."

"Now would be a good time to run, Raihn," Halba cued.

Raihn paused at that moment, thinking to argue, but they were determined. Raihn could see it.

The first place Raihn thought, and nearest, was the empty alleys of the town. He sifted through there like a grain of wheat while the hulls pursued, their broad armor scraping plaster walls.

Raihn broke for the tree line as they spilled nearer. The son of Parcel scrambled from the valley, nimbly scaling the steep incline despite struggling through a blurred exhaustion. The gap between Raihn and his pursuers was closing when a shadow joined the fray—one grander than a mere raven's. Raihn saw it lurking through oak and elm. Alas, he was tired, light-headed, and woozy, seeing shapes. Then the air whistled, and the grass hissed, though seemingly not by wind.

Behind him, the men drew their blades before crying out and spitting their sorrows to the sky. Raihn ambled up the clustered bark of an elm, hearing the thuds of their fallen swords. His heart sank. It was real.

Terror pursued him as he climbed higher up the highest trunk, corking his breath into a jar. There he clung, sweaty and peering through sprawling lanes of oak. He heard no more yelping, screaming, or thudding. The wind seemed to blow again, this time akin to a bitter breath, for there was the wafting scent of something, though singed. He cursed himself as he despised his own beating heart, pumping endlessly and loudly. Then he cursed again, for the shadow of the tree looked feathered. The begrudging wings seemed to follow him wherever he went.

Raihn steadied, listening past the beat of his heart. The wind stilled, and from behind him, he heard a low croak. He froze, rendered useless like an opossum.

Finally, Raihn managed a look over his shoulder. The omen was there, leering, abyss-eyed. The crescent beak halved, and it squalled a rotten gurgle between razor-like bristles.

Like a flightless hatchling, Raihn dropped and fell far. He left behind familiarity as he headed to not grass, but a crashing blue. Yet, he was far from that too as he plunged between a jaded sky and an endless sea. The elms were gone and so was the valley. He feared for his life of which appeared thieved, wondering how it was all possible as he soared.

He plunged deep. The blue foamed over his black hair. Bones unbroken. Skin not stung. He was alive and not utterly shattered into sea debris, though it suffocated him. His lungs trailed bubbles to a far-away surface he wasn't sure he could reach. He paddled fiercely, refusing to drown.

The waving water calmed. He saw the sky through the surface and he reached for it, though it resisted him, his finger tickling the edge of his boundary. He flurried bubbles from drowning screams, scratching at what seemed to be ice.

Raihn begrudged the vile sea, smothered in salt, his tongue buttery. The sea ensnared him, and bubbles spurred from his thrashing. The water's surface was elusive, casting a dark forecast, but he saw through it the manor, and upon the doorstep, Dame Dawness. She marched there with Pate and four men. ...*Mom,* Raihn's mind lent out. She was still home, and worse, she answered the door.

The dame barged, knocking the aghast Angeline onto her back.

"Search the manor!" the dame barked. "It's here."

"What is!?" his mother cried.

"The key," replied the dame.

Raihn flopped, smacking the surface, his arm bewildered by the slow-rendering sea. He tapped it far too lightly, flopping still like a netted fish.

"The proclamation!" the dame added, but his mother was clueless. Dame Dawness made it clear. "'For those truncated, a stayed hand': the eldest carving upon what is impenetrable bark!"

Angeline's eyes widened. "No. No! I shan't speak of graven images!"

Raihn knew not of what they speak. And the void below, ever thirsty, swallowed his conscious as the black crowded his vision into a shallow lagoon.

CHAPTER SIX
Doubled over

There was a constant, unyielding flow as Raihn lay on the muddy bank of a river, his insides churning. He vomited, rinsed his gums, and vomited again. Then, he flopped aside and wondered why his cheek was sore.

"You're alive! Good. Your salted mouth is ruining what is left of my drink!" a man exclaimed from his rocky perch.

Raihn jumped up, wobbly on his feet as though he hadn't been on land for decades. "Who are you and…why does my face hurt?" he asked, caressing his cheek.

"That's the price unconscious men pay, lest I be a thief and take your silver petals instead."

Raihn dug into his waterlogged pockets, prompting the stranger to repeat himself, "I said lest!" Regardless, Raihn checked his satchel that was on land just as well. It was somehow utterly dry, to his relief.

"Alright, so I still have my things. Who are you? What's your name?"

"The man who saved your life. Is that not good enough? And I believe a thank you is due before my name."

"Never mind it, I haven't the time anyway," Raihn groaned, wringing his clothes.

"So be it. I am Lostar of Lakewane, a plateau among the sands of Endura."

Their face sounded boastful. "Is that supposed to mean something?" Raihn asked.

"Hmm…" Lostar pondered. "I suppose not," he said, pinching a flagon over his lips. He brought it down, rattling the remainder of it. "Hardly a sip," he muttered.

Raihn briefly noted the strange bandage on their ring finger that curved over their flagon. "I think that what you call a sip is what I'd call a mouthful, just like your name."

Lostar's eyes narrowed. "It is a deserving name, peasant. It follows my back from the hot salt flats and the rolling dunes and the oases of Endura. A name of two syllables is hardly a 'mouthful.'"

"Not when you slur it."

"Maybe so. And what may yours be?"

"I'm Raihn."

Lostar scoffed. Their tongue slow, he said, "Dull."

Raihn stepped up. "No! It's interesting. Very interesting."

"What's interesting about rain?"

"Well, it nourishes us and brings crops. And fortune!" Raihn pointed.

"Firstly—" Lostar whipped Raihn's finger away and raised his own. "Firstly, that's not interesting. Pleasant, sure. Interesting? No. Secondly," he went on with another finger, "it looks to me you've been unfortunate as of late, washed up like m'self. And here I save you, and you flood me with bitter banter, and so far, no good fortune. I'd be better off saving someone not so poor-looking," his throat squelched.

"Whatever, it's not so dissimilar from the name of my father. What does yours mean?" Raihn asked, but the Enduran was silent. "Fine. I was only being polite. I've got more pressing matters."

"Oh, the 'polite' peasant has somewhere to be? Got to drown somewhere else?" Lostar mocked.

"I wish."

"I should have left you in that river," the Enduran remarked.

Raihn, still trying to understand what had just occurred, wasn't sure what to make of his recent events, but it didn't help that this badgering fellow was clogging his ears with jibber jabber.

The Enduran hopped from the rock and pursued. "A town is supposed to be around here," he said, voice about as wobbly as his legs. "Where might that be?"

"It's straight up that way," Raihn answered, his finger pointed ahead.

"What do you know!" Lostar exclaimed. "Looks to be where you go. Mind if I tag along?"

Raihn glanced back, wincing upon catching a whiff of their breath. Recovering, he looked Lostar over curiously, noting their ornamental scimitar and slung bow bearing a four-legged fish crest. They sported a short and scraggly beard and long, oily hair. And beneath their crimson cloak, faintly glimmering leathery scales could be glimpsed. Their company may prove beneficial when venturing into what became a hostile place.

"I'll show you the way," Raihn told them. "If you want to come sightseeing and find drink, then where I head has the right place."

Lostar smiled, bits of bug limbs strewn over his teeth. "I have not eaten well for some time, but you have some insects to scavenge. Your worms here in Eldhona are juicy ones."

"Not an insect," Raihn answered tersely, holding his sickened stomach under his sodden cloak.

"Pardon?"

"No backbones," Raihn clarified, sauntering off. "They're invertebrates. I used to pull them up from the dirt and take them to the fish as a boy—to that river, in fact. Sometimes, I just played with them in the palm of my hand."

The Enduran followed, still tripping over his feet. "Why?"

"I don't know... That's just what we did."

"Were you ever picked on as a little one?"

"So, what if I was?" Raihn's voice ticked.

"Might the cycle go unending—big ones pick on the little ones, little ones pick on the smaller ones..."

Raihn glanced over again to read their face, but this time, first, he spotted a pail full of water in their hands.

"Water for the horse," Lostar acknowledged. "Your animals seem simple and thoughtless behind their eyes. Easily tamable."

"That so?" Raihn said, dry-breathed, turning back his head.

Raihn walked on, unsettled by the silence. He glanced back yet another time, checking on the Enduran; the fellow seemed delicate, like a crisp autumn leaf on the verge of crumbling, yet they weren't old like some greybeard—perhaps just a bit older than Raihn himself, which is to say they were still spry.

"...Where's your horse, anyway?"

"Just up a ways, not far," Lostar answered. "We've been heading that way by luck. I would say otherwise if not. The trees became dense, and so I tied 'im up. You'll see."

"I believe you, it's just a horse," Raihn paused, a hunch bulking, his eye peering around his shoulder, "...but from where did you buy it?"

"Do I appear endowed with riches?" Lostar asked, fingers squirming through holes in his pocket.

"I knew it!" Raihn spun around, taking a stance. "Of course he's tamable, for he was tamed already!" Raihn accused. "You're a damned brigand after all!"

Lostar sputtered, "What else was I supposed to do?"

"Maybe try not to break the law the moment you step into Eldhona. I've got enough trouble as it is," Raihn said dismissively. "You sure you're not planning to rob me naked?"

Lostar snickered. "I'd sooner gouge my eyes than see you without breeches."

Raihn smirked. "Fine, maybe you're not a brigand."

"No, just a tired wanderer... But if you insist, I prefer Highwayman. Sounds more stoic."

"You don't want to be called that... How about I call you vagrant?"

"Cold," Lostar stated. "Suppose you are out late. That why you're in a flap? Mother'll flog you," Lostar teased colorlessly.

Raihn froze; his mood dampened. "Don't speak of my mother."

Lostar sobered. "Fair enough. My mistake. Anything else worth of warn before we continue?"

Raihn sighed. "I suppose it's worth addressing. I don't know what it's like where you're from, but here, the king has a strict rule. He doesn't like foreign beliefs breezing through, as I've been reminded, unless they're profitable. So, I hope your tongue is well-mannered before them."

Lostar fell quiet, and Raihn wondered if he was being overbearing. Then he wondered if any of that would matter. Cobblestone has been turned on its head. "I'm sorry if that came off a little crass. It's not been my day, to say the least. You're right, I'll be flogged."

"Is it often that you apologize?"

Raihn reconsidered—the vagrant might now become overbearing.

"No fortress is ever submissive," Lostar continued. "A lord should hold committed servants, and the lord will face times to act decisively, unapologetic in his choices, lest he lose himself and all his people." He pulled a finger from his pocket, wagging it pointedly. "Be submissive or take action. Hesitate, and you might find yourself with holes in your pockets without a thread left to mend them." His hand sank into his pocket, his finger worming out of the bottom.

There seemed to be a matter on the Enduran's mind that still eluded Raihn, much like the point, and for what he understood was disliked. "Let's just wrangle the horse already."

They pushed through the dense thicket and emerged onto a dimly lit trail beneath a fading Eldhos. The surrounding trees appeared shockingly barren and twisted, devoid of their usual luster.

"I must have been out of it for a while," Raihn muttered, half-joking, a sense of unease creeping over him as he surveyed the surroundings. There was no way he had lain upon the bank for so long, but he couldn't shake the feeling that something was wrong. The trees should have been in full bloom at this time of year, not looking sickly and bare.

Glancing at the vagabond, Raihn considered honesty; he noticed the signs of hardship already carved into their fatigued face, and he ought explain his crassness and the potential danger ahead, but fear gripped tighter.

The path less narrow came. Lostar seemed confused, swinging his eyes up and down the path.

"Something amiss?" Raihn asked, noticing the Enduran's agitation.

"Do you see my horse?" the Enduran replied sharply.

"No, afraid not," Raihn answered.

"Then yes! Something is amiss!"

"Are you sure you could trust your fingers to tie a knot?" Raihn teased.

"I'm hindered, not helpless…"

After a moment of searching, Raihn called them over to a rope around the base of a tree. "Look. It was severed. Rope's frayed."

"A no-good thief," the Enduran hissed, inspecting it.

"A 'thief,'" Raihn echoed in amusement, dismissing the incident as he turned away. But Lostar insisted on further investigation. Raihn halted, swung his shoulders, and said, "Look, I don't have time to be sidetracked, Enduran."

"Are you not curious?" Lostar pressed.

"Of what?"

Lostar scoffed. "Helpless and hapless," he laughed. "You don't even see it. Nay, you trample the curiosity with your feet."

Raihn stood in place, puzzled.

"Blind too… I'll tell you. Tracks. There is but one set, the one I made from my ride. And if my horse were stolen, don't you think the culprit might leave a little trail? Or what of my horse's trace? They do not double back, and the thicket is too dense to traverse anywhere else. It's as though it flew away."

Raihn laughed, which seemed to offend Lostar. "Like the horse, Prosporos."

Now more intrigued than offended, Lostar scrunched his brows. "Eldhonans have flying horses?"

"It's just a story," Raihn said, but then he heard the abrupt flapping of wings above. His body chilled from a bloated-sounding caw overhead.

Their heads tilted up, and they saw the raven perched atop Lostar's mutilated steed in the woven branches and boughs. Blood dripped from cuts resembling bloody wings.

Lostar's breath quivered off his lips. "My poor horse!"

"Quiet!" Raihn shushed, sensing a foreboding presence, the same as when the raven had faced him before.

"I have been cursed," the Enduran stated, eyeing the bird. "I'll kill it the next time I see it, then might there be no more unsightly things!"

Lostar sped off, and Raihn had to scramble in hopes of not being left under the umbrella of death. The raven croaked a wry laugh through the dead trees, more terrifying than once considered a mere nuisance.

Neither muttered more than their breathy exhaustion after a mad sprint. Eventually, Lostar broke the silence. "This mountain in your land is guarded by godless men, but I fear they are the least of my concerns…"

"That's why you're here?" Raihn huffed. "You know it's forbidden, right? Unless you were an Endolander on their pilgrimage. You can't go near it," he continued, but Lostar was yet to indulge him in their business. Raihn groaned, frustrated, feeling as though he was babying a boy who got into Father's ale.

The village loomed closer, though beyond sight, as Eldhos sank below the horizon, leaving the white freckles of stars to dominate the sky. Raihn's prolonged absence from home cut at his patience. *Please be okay, Mom,* he thought. Memories of the morning's rushed bounty surfaced, and he longed to share a meal with her again, almost catching the faint scent of sausage.

50

The trees became sparser, and there was an orange tint in the sky. However, it was not from Eldhos, but the village, and there was a scent of burning fat and smoke. He started uphill in a panic, and atop the valley, he stood disarmed by the nightmarish blaze that devoured Parcel Path and Cobblestone. *The manor must be soot.*

Wind whipped the fire's blistering heat up the slope, crucks crumbled down the hill, and sparks twirled. Lostar came beside him and was gone the next moment, selflessly charging into the inferno.

Fear pulled Raihn down upon his hands, his limbs melded to earth like candles over a grave. He held himself in a contemplative yield, too weak to see the manor burn, spurning its view. But he forged a brave glimpse onto the hill. The home stood spared from the flames. It inspired him to leave the top of the valley's side and to delve into the fray as Lostar had, searching for survivors in need of aid.

Raihn descended with lungs full of smoke and his eyes running rivers from the might of the dark plume. Despite his tears, he could see the charred corpses of the villagers strewn about the valley. With mindful steps over the rubble, his eyes were gritty and unable to shed more tears. "Lostar!" he called out, his voice hoarse between coughs. A nearby cruck collapsed, sending up a cloud of debris that singed his skin. He shielded his face and cried out again, "Lostar!"

Lostar emerged from the dark cloud, each step sounding like crunching cicada shells. "We can't stay here!"

"Are there no survivors?" Raihn asked.

"Raihn!" Lostar's voice barked, more serious than ever, "Come on!"

Fleeing from the devastation, he found a sustained path before breaking into a fit of mumbles. "They abandoned us. The cardinal. The king. His Authority… The Hulls from the East Wynd go rabid…" Realization struck, his eyes widening despite the burning. "I need to go home." If there even was a home to go to. He glanced through the haze ahead, where the sky was not lit with doom and where the path would take him up the hill to the lightless beacon. "I must ensure my mother's safety," Raihn explained.

He navigated the peril until the manor crept into view. It was untouched by flame, and Raihn cheered before face-planting. The hill peeled in and out of view as he rolled, overcome with pain stemming from his temple.

"Are you okay?" Lostar asked.

Raihn pressed his hands to his head and groaned, suffering from a sudden migraine, his head torn open like an envelope.

"What's wrong?" Lostar asked again. "Where is your home?"

Raihn mustered a point up to the hill where the manor sat.

"Peasant my ass!" Lostar remarked.

It seemed fate was playing with the heir to Parcel, for the hilltop where the manor stood suddenly ignited as a cracking torchlight against the stars.

"Raihn!" Lostar encouraged. "Come on! If you want to make sure she's safe! Get up!"

Raihn ground his teeth, his head pounding like a hammered anvil. He struggled to know why this vagabond took interest, a passing thought as pain swelled within his right hand. "Something is wrong with me," he said, clutching his wrist.

"Don't let a little joint pain get you down now!"

It was a race uphill towards the ever-growing ball of fire that was Parcel Manor, the door before them a gateway into damnation. Raihn barred Lostar from entry, arm out. "I admire your willingness to help me, a stranger to you, but you mustn't put your life over mine."

Lostar's expression contended, but he ultimately nodded. "Be swift."

Raihn rammed the door before a burst of black smoke plumed out of the crash with a wave of heat, the vestibule like an oven. Fire climbed the walls, cooking the hanging leather jerkins and filling the air with the stench of charred meat.

"Mom! Dad!" he cried, hoping to hear a reply. He scoured throughout the manor, but wherever he went, the fire had beaten him there, licking at the ceiling. Only one place remained: the second floor.

Raihn covered his mouth and stepped meekly up the stairs, reminding himself not to touch the teetering banister.

He'd come upon the corridor with the study on the right and two chambers to his left. The first was already open, revealing nothing within but firewood. A few more steps and he squared the entry to River's old quarter, which was burning away, books smoking, paintings already ash.

Tears cut a trail down blackened cheeks just when he thought none were left. Wiping them away from his stung eyes, he spotted a bright singe upon the corner of his satchel—the journal within being the last remnant of his brother, and the satchel the last of his mother. He patted it out, looking to flee before it, and he was toasted beyond what could be repaired by hems. But as he turned, he was snagged by the sound of a tiny yet distinguishable scrape.

"Hello?" His head swiveled, the scratching too curious to abandon, himself too entrenched. He glanced under the hot bed, but nothing was there. Then he turned and searched the rank trunk. *Where is it coming from?* It was an unintelligible sound, yet it seemed intentional somehow, as though meant to be heard. It cried out for him, screeching long scores. Then he heard it again as he seemed to close in, almost center of the chamber.

He stopped.

It was coming from beneath his sole. A light scratching through the flooring. He pondered it, presuming it was maybe a strong-willed rat or the fire was cracking the wood. Whatever it was, Raihn abandoned the chamber, knowing nobody he knew would fit there besides the critter from earlier. And worse now, as he fled, he suffered pain in his hand once again.

Raihn popped out like a kernel through the front door, coughing like an old pipe smoker. He relished the softer air, which soothed his chimney-lungs. He glanced up at Lostar helplessly, clutching his right hand.

"Your hand—is it burned?" they asked, their voice tinted with concern.

"No," Raihn replied between puffs. "I'll be fine… But my family… I can only presume my mother is in the hands of that damned anvil contracted by the Hulls. My father would be next."

Lostar's face turned pensive, his brows furrowing.

Raihn sighed, the truth burning through him. "Suppose I have been vague, to say the least."

"You mentioned the Hulls before. What's happening?"

"They, as well as their anvil, tore up the town searching for fugitives, then turned on me… They take issue with, well, my father. I might just be their placeholder of ire until they find him. I managed to escape them, but then," his voice hitched as he considered the raven, "I blacked out and woke beside the river," he said, skirting that part. "You know the rest."

"Still feels like a lot is missing…"

"I know the feeling," Raihn huffed. "You can ask my father to fill you in when I find him…wherever he may be."

"We'll find him," Lostar reassured, "and your mother."

"We?" Raihn echoed, his tone incredulous. "I led you to this chaos with my lips…" his voice croaked as he searched for a term, "sewn by my own fear." Raihn let out a laugh from shock. "Lostar, are you not livid? I knew there was danger."

"Not with you."

"But what about the Hulls?" Raihn asked, fear taking hold again.

"I can hold my own," Lostar assured, brandishing his blade. "I already know of these callous Hulls from the East Wynd."

CHAPTER SEVEN
Brimstone

Not far from the manor, Raihn sat and gazed at the sky while the Stars twinkled overhead, pondering his next move, feeling lost in the vastness.

"Like lost ships of Barynn sailing. It always makes me wonder," Lostar said, standing beneath them.

"Wonder what?"

"For where they sail, and for why."

Raihn scoffed. "Still whimsical on that aftertaste of booze?"

Lostar wobbled as he attempted to correct his crooked stance. He fumbled with a pouch upon his lower back until retrieving a cylindrical shaft of which he brought to his eye. Presumably, it showed through magnification, the valley below, this divot that comes hither of scorched earth and the dead that litter it—an unkind sight that Raihn wished not to visit again nor look upon.

"See anyone?" Raihn asked, his eyes keeping to the sky.

"Not yet. Survivors cannot always be seen, but that does not mean they cannot be found. And if they are not found, then might they ran far away."

"I appreciate the effort, but if that's the case, I suppose there is nothing else for us here. Right?"

"Quiet," Lostar shushed, pocketing the spyglass and pointing cautiously to the forest behind them.

Following their hush, a rustle of grass pricked Raihn's heart and brought him to his feet. He became just as alert as Lostar, who snatched their bow and nocked an arrow with absurd speed, pinching the shaft between their fingers and anchoring it beside their cheek, arrow pointed at the nether.

Sensing something predatory, Raihn stepped back.

"Don't," Lostar warned. "Do not show yourself as prey."

Regardless of their speedy fingers, Raihn doubted them. "Can you fight in this kind of state, burdened by mead?" he asked.

"I'm about to find out."

"No, 'we' are about to find out," Raihn corrected, his guard up and his breath shallow.

"Good. You'll never find your kin by running from the first crick you hear."

Raihn breathed and squinted at the dark tree line where a figure took shape. Whatever, or whoever, it was, it instilled fear, yet he stepped nearer, heeding the Enduran's advice.

Lostar kept his eyes forward, ready to call out to the lurking stranger. "Identify yourselves!" he demanded. "Who are you, and what do you want?" There was no reply. The aura under the cover of the trees felt even more threatening. "Raihn, listen carefully. I have a dagger in my pouch—the other spyglass."

"Spyglass?" Raihn repeated. "You seem confused, drunkard, and I do not mean to sound picky, but—"

"Just grab the one with the snake crest!"

Raihn did as he was instructed and snatched the spyglass. "Okay?"

"Extend it and untwist the lens before removing the barrel shaft," Lostar explained.

Following those steps, Raihn discovered a hidden blade within the metal shell. "Genius," he said. "But it's not much."

"Be grateful you have something."

"What about your sword?"

"It does not leave my person, Raihn the Ungrateful," Lostar taunted. "Have you ever wielded a sword?"

"Well, no…"

"Then I cannot entrust it to you," Lostar snipped.

"How hard could it be?"

"The weapon extends us. They perform only as well as their master. I advise you not to insult them by the insinuation of their ease of mastery."

"That's some spurious wiseman nonsense!"

"For your sake, I would hope so. I am feeling tipsy after all," the Enduran teased.

"You might put that too lightly. 'Tipsy' my buttocks."

Interrupting them, a disembodied voice called out a demand, deep and rugged. "Surrender your weapons and abide by the will of the king," it said. "We do not want you, stranger, but the boy. Stand aside and go about your business."

"Aye! Go find someone else to argue with!" another, though softer, voice reiterated from the brush.

"Shut your trap ye damned fool, Pepin! They've not argued yet," said the rugged one. "But aye, foreigner!" they began again. "If it be reward ye require, then arrangements can be struck. If ye disassociate yourself from the fugitive and walk in haste, that is. Mayhap the heft of petals in your pocket would suffice? Then some mead and some food to last ye 'til the journey to another village," the voice went on.

This 'master of a blade,' as Raihn had understood, seemed awfully quiet. On edge, he awaited their answer.

"I need not silver, gold, or steel. The metal I carry is fine enough," Lostar replied at last.

Raihn exhaled in relief, though his thoughts remained unsettled. He couldn't decide whether Lostar's choice was admirable or a display of sharp survival instincts. After all, there was no guarantee the Authority wouldn't double-cross him, especially given Cobblestone's state. Perhaps Lostar truly was as genuine and principled as he appeared—or perhaps the contents of his flagon had clouded his judgment. Either way, Raihn was grateful for Lostar's steadfastness.

While the Enduran's actions were pondered, Raihn failed to notice the two burly arms that wrapped around them from behind. In a flash, Lostar was wrenched backward, lifted by a powerful force that hurled them downhill like a stone skipping water. Lostar and the assailant tumbled until stopping against the fiery backdrop of the village's roaring flames.

Raihn glimpsed them as he leaned over, now left alone with a man shrieking on his knees near the tree line. The stranger's curses pierced the air, drawing Raihn's attention. Amid the chaos, it seemed Lostar had managed to loose an arrow in time, its fletching still visible as it jutted from the Authoritarian's side.

"Shit!" the wounded soldier cried. "Ye bastard boy!"

"It wasn't from me!" Raihn cried out.

"Get 'em!" the Authoritarian blared, but to whom?

A horse-teethed fellow, lanky and oblong all about, crept out, looking rather timid.

"Get him, Pepin! Go on!" The wounded man rallied through his pine bristles.

The lanky one neared, his head between his shoulders, his thin lips pressed tight. He resembled a rat, having big ears and a dainty chin.

"What are ye waiting for?" the stricken one went on.

"Wait-wait-wait," Raihn waved, retreating from the advancing soldier.

Pepin drew his longsword.

"I'm not the one that loosed that arrow," Raihn continued. "I've done nothing wrong!"

"Don' matter. Ye coulda come quietly. Now I have to suffer this damned arrow!" the gruff one squealed. "Get 'em, Pep!"

Raihn's mind raced, evaluating the situation. *He's thin. There's less muscle than the other, but he appears confident. He wields a longsword with two hands. I'll just wear him out and dodge his strikes. His blade will do the rest.*

Pepin, close enough to lunge with a heavy swing, was easily evaded. Raihn felt the blade whizz past his ear before it dug into the ground. They fought it out from the dirt and swiped at the scrambling Raihn again, their momentum pulling them to the dirt. *Weak. Young. Impatient. Must be a re-*

cruit, Raihn figured. This could very well be their first encounter, and he could not have been any luckier.

Raihn could end his foe with swift stabs to the throat, but he wasn't sure if he would, delicate whispers careening into his ear, insisting mercy. The question became much heavier if he would, conflicted, for he's never slain even a chicken. But the light in the valley, refusing to die, took his gaze and shone a memory hitherto. He recalled the brutality as the village and the town were still burning. *The Authority did that.*

Raihn's arm loosened, his anguish fastening his blood lust, and his emotions lubricated his conscience. He pulled back his arm and knew he would not falter. Then, strangely, his hand mysteriously hurt again, making him flounder.

"Stop strikin' to kill!" the wounded Authoritarian coached. "Detain him, Pep, ye buck-toothed dolt! I told ye that sword was too great for ye!"

Raihn dodged another strike and moved toward a defenseless Pepin. He faltered a moment and thrust his dagger, though the blade could not penetrate their mail shirt. Raihn froze, cursing his meekness. His jaw clenched, and his eyes shuttered.

Pepin had the upper hand now, and he moved forward aggressively, bashing Raihn's back with the pommel of his sword.

Falling after a valiant effort, Raihn's body hit the ground like a sack of oats, where he continued to bemoan a nagging whisper that deterred what would have been a kill, for Raihn could have aimed for the throat. It was there, meaty and red from a recent shave.

Loathing himself and lying limp, Raihn was surrendered to Pepin's muddy boot on his tender spine. He wondered now about Lostar's battle and whether they would succumb to the same fate.

The gruff one changed places with Pepin, who ambled down the hill in search of their third man, clanging and ringing from down the way. Raihn awaited them, hoping that the vagabond was not just a horse thief but an outstanding warrior, considering their arms. Then again, might they have stolen those as well.

The two men clanged metal through the valley and up the hills. But eventually…it stopped. Raihn thought on, wondering if Lostar was alive until they emerged from the slope in chains, but alive no less. *What now?*

"Stronger than heavy steel. Lighter even! A fine rarity that I would celebrate beside a wench, but I'm afraid I'd have to stick my cock in ash!" the triumphant soldier cackled as he neared.

"But I helped you in that triumph," said Pepin.

"Shut it!"

The other one, still with the arrow protruding by his side, kept still beside Raihn. "Pepin, collect them weapons and toss 'em in the carriage, will ye."

"Why me?"

"Like I cannot be bothered to leave an arrow to rot and fester in some minced flesh, shit-head."

"But that Enduran, drunk as he seems, stood victorious. But there I was in the nick of time to clobber him good!" Pepin argued.

"Quit yer foolin' and get to collectin', damn you. I'd not entrust my damned side, let alone my leg, to your tree-hangin' hands. Colby here can mend me fine, and then I'll mend ye well if you insist on backtalkin' me! You no-good, horse-mouth, rat-lookin' son of a rancid pony—eyes buggered by flies with shit smeared on yer hindlegs."

"Hey there, pedal back now," Colby waved. "I mend that gnarled fuck-all belly o' yours?"

"Aye, that be right," answered the wounded man. "And ye better."

"Damn all. Better not squeal like a damned pig," said Colby before glancing at Raihn. "Right? Oink, oink!"

"I ain't no damned pig, Colby, fuck. And I ain't gotta take that slop you spew. Just mend me, dammit! I'm tired of this fucking shaft skewering me!"

"Oh, shut up about it and be nice." Colby grinned, but so did Pepin, seemingly enjoying the rawhide banter. "Fix that smile, piss-face. Not like you can be trusted to cauterize a wound like myself. That's why I gotta deal with the coming whinging. Now move your twiggy ass!"

"Fine, fine," Pepin waved his hand like a white flag. "But what's that there sword? It twinkles like a star, yeah."

"It's made of simic, don't ye understand?" Colby replied. "Mighty fine it is. And it be mine too, Pep. Ye got that big o' cutter, so it's only right. Besides, my fingers like it very much and I would hate to let it go, but I must. To stick it away for the time bein'."

"What about Dame Dawness?" Pepin wondered. "That dame-of-a-mercenary with that fine hind."

Colby, looking mighty fed-up, looked over again, scoffing. "I know of her, yeah. What about her, dammit?"

"Well, if she's here to make a big splash, I imagine that sword will cause quite a ripple. And she'd have us to thank."

"Foolish-brained toad," Colby cursed, vexed by the tall fellow. "Forget it. We aren't the bailiff. We are no more than simple men, scraping by. Far as I know, there is no writ and no bailiff. Even the watchmen, patrolmen, whatever the shit, failed their town. After all our poking in the dark, we see a fire, and here we have these two fellow culprits. It was the start of their short-lived rebellion I'd surmise, but what the fecal fuck do I care? I am a simple man that believes in equivocal exchange, aye. This blade serves just that. That honored mercenary wench can sort the rest with these two, as I'm sure they'll pay for their crimes. Might they be part of them fugitives even. Better for us if so."

"Doesn't seem equivocal to me," said Pepin.

"No, it doesn't," Raihn chimed in, grass prickling his inner ear. "Nor does it seem right to me that we're judged by you grunts that take us for tinder folk. You appear as though you dropped your pitchforks for swords and wiped your green thumbs for red hands just yesterday. You betray us, honest people, for the real criminals!"

Pepin stalled a moment, gawking at him with a crooked lip while the other balled a fist.

The wounded one growled. "You know not the grit under my nails, boy," said he. "No amount of peelin' of my eyes would take back the sights I saw as a farmhand to my pop's tindered acres. For the likes of you, spittin' up fire and lies, no bailiff or constable will do… You know, I shall take you to Dame Dawness myself, for a fine hind she has indeed that I'd dream of rippling…and she will take care of us both." Turning his attention to Pepin, he said, "Be off already, will ye!?"

"Fine."

"And fetch that one's satchel, too."

"Alright!"

"Oh, and Peppy, we don't bend our ears for rabble. Mind that."

CHAPTER EIGHT

The ant mill

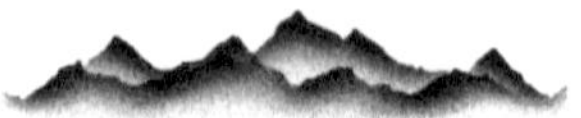

Pepin escorted the unlucky duo toward the grimy prison carriage while dragging a sack of armaments that made his body slump under its weight. Raihn glanced back at Lostar as Pepin fed them into the rusted, rotting carriage. The hinges groaned, and a haunting howl echoed from the wheels as they clambered inside, their heels thudding against the wooden boards. A distant, pained cry sliced through the wind as they were seated across from one another, sounding as though it came from the stricken soldier.

Pepin tossed the weapons overhead, securing them with knots before settling down across from them. "Bet he'll come back to us ripe mad," he said, presumably meaning the soldier. His buck teeth peeked out beneath his upper lip, a smug look spreading across his face as he surveyed them, chains rattling in his hands.

All were quiet until Colby and the one still nameless had rocked aboard. Colby seemed to take the horses while the other, angry and stripped of cloth, entered. His skin was a knotted mesh from the hot steel he seemed mended by.

"It hurt?" Pepin asked.

"'It hurt'? Yes, it bloody fuckin' hurt! And it still hurts. And the pain from giving you this wallop is well worth it," he added, swiping the back of his hand across Pepin's shoulder. "Now, scoot over. As if I'd be the one driving the wretched carriage with nagging nags dippin' and bobbin' with horse flies flyin' in my shoulder, dammit."

Raihn then heard the driver, presumably the greediest one of the bunch, whip the horses into a trot.

"It won't be long," said Pepin.

"For what?" Raihn asked.

"The checkpoint! We'll have you there soon enough, and just as soon I'll have some ale," Pepin smiled.

"Shut it! Quit fraternizing and keep an eye open. You were told to mind it, weren't ye? I need a damned good nap before we get there, but it won't happen with ye gabbin' with the prisoners." Colby shut his eyes and leaned to the side. Pepin, however, gazed up at the ceiling, likely thinking of the sword just overhead.

Pepin seemed the last of the two awake, and Raihn felt spry. "So, you meant to take only myself earlier, but you sounded intent on gathering us both, taking us for fire starters."

"Quiet you," said Pepin. "I ain't meanin' to talk to you."

"Then I'll just help myself and drone on while you listen," Raihn snapped. "It was those Hulls and that dame herself that trashed the village and Cobblestone. The Authority was bullied into submission, but as you know, they—you—are the greatest force over all the wynds in Eldhona, making sure all is in accordance. You don't have to take that, and I shouldn't be suffering it. So, this is all a misunderstanding."

Pepin pressed his lips tightly.

"Pepin…listen to me." Raihn leaned, squinting, thinking to himself they'd not known who he was to the dame. They seemed clueless about it all thus far. "You didn't seek me out…right? You just seen me, and you tried splitting me up with my armed friend here, right? Well, he did no torching. I've been beside him just as he'd been beside me the past, uh, I dunno, five hours? The Hulls are working with the dame," he insisted. "They'll be with her. Wherever you take me, if she is there, so will they be, and that means you'll be bullied even more than you are by these two you ride on with."

Pepin finally leaned in. "Okay, so what then? Why'd they burn it? I wanna know!"

Raihn shushed him, raising his finger. The other Authoritarian slept. "Don't want to wake him," he said softly. "Look, I'm not sure why, but no reason is good enough for me to accept."

Raihn waited a moment as they looked pensive. But instead of an answer, he'd taken a kick to the shin by Pepin. Shutting his eyes tight and pursing his lips, he minded the things he wished to say to the laughing pest.

Raihn clung to the side wall and cast his gaze beyond the feeble light of swinging lanterns. The stiff wind hissed past his ear, and the horses clopped, but loud snores from their careless guards persisted, and Raihn was flung every which way as the wheels buckled over pebbles. He struggled to understand how they could remain unbothered. Eventually, the cart flung him sideways before the Enduran's pressing eyes.

"Can I help you?"

Lostar leaned back, his eyes heavy. "What do you know of Endura?"

Raihn shrugged.

"How about its ruler? Oleandor, the present Elgar of Endura. Heard of him?"

"No," Raihn replied, sighing. "But I've got a feeling you'll enlighten me."

Lostar ignored the quip. "Endura's sands have always guarded more than meets the eye. Beneath the iron-streaked flats, we unearthed a metal unlike any other: simic. Stronger than silver, harder to forge, but so brilliant it could light a sail aflame with its reflection alone. Simic became our pride, forged into blades wielded only by Enduran royals. But such treasures breed hunger, and hunger has a way of unraveling traditions."

Raihn raised a brow. "What kind of hunger?"

"The kind that ships once sailed to satisfy," Lostar continued. "A fleet crossed the greatest lake of Adjurrah long ago—calm waters, fast winds, a sailor's dream. But the lake betrayed them. The surface cracked open, drinking the fleet into what became a dust bowl. All that remained was a single, winding river—the Nexus of Adjurrah. It was then, amid the chaos, that simic was discovered beneath the lake's bed."

Raihn leaned forward. "And those ships? Where were they from?"

"The East Wynd," Lostar continued. "The Hulls clutch their secrets of that voyage, and Endurans only speculate. There is only a shipyard now where lowly Endurans take shelter in vessels from an old world that we yet understand."

"The old world," Raihn chimed. "It was before the reign of Rosen Kings."

"The Endurans once sailed between islands," Lostar continued, restlessness in his tone. "Those islands are now mesas, buttes, and plateaus—the very foundations of Enduran cities. Endura itself is a marvel of strength and survival." He paused, his gaze steady. "Our strength lies in our traditions, passed down through generations. The gars—children of the Elgar—inherit not just his throne but his legacy. To succeed, they must first guard their father until his death, as the custom demands. Marriage is required before their ascension, and during that ceremony, they are entrusted with the generational Binder's Blade."

"Even so, it can be stolen, right?"

"It can be." Lostar's eyes narrowed. "The efforts to forge it are great, and to protect it, even greater. If the sword is stolen from a gar, then he is shamed and his title struck. And the thief is fed to the deepest cracks of Endura, or shelled away in a very hollow place...."

"Assuming they're caught," Raihn added.

"Assuming they are caught," the Enduran echoed, hinting the faintest grin, seemingly figuring what Raihn was getting at. But then his grin faded.

"Our sacred swords should never fall into a foreigner's hand, but times have changed. Hunger outweighed the traditions of my ancestors, and while trade feeds our people, it left many angry, including the Elgar's chief advisor—a man that tried persuading the Elgar, to no avail, mind you, to cease trade. 'Simic strengthens our enemies,' he mocked bitterly. "But the Elgar believed in a peaceful relationship... It was a hard choice for the lord of our land, but he never faltered from what he deemed right.

"When the Elgar fell ill, he abdicated, allowing his son, Trussgar, the Heir Apparent, to wed and he named Prince Regent to Ambroseah."

Lostar's voice grew darker. "But during the ceremony, betrayal struck. Chief Advisor Oleandor, in league with the Lowland Kraters, conspired against the family, so Trussgar claimed, though his vows to protect his parents came to nothing. He failed to act in time, and as a result, his parents' throats were crossed by daggers, much like their legacy. He lost everything—his mother, his father, his betrothed—everything," Lostar continued, his tone made ragged by this recount. "A tragedy you might understand, Raihn of Parcel," he added, his eyes saddle-bagged by sadness. "In Trussgar's failure, Oleandor could usurp the throne."

Raihn stammered, "Well, surely something could be done, right?"

"'Something could be done'?" Lostar repeated, bluntly mocking him, as though taken aback by such naivety. "It is not so simple. And now, thanks to Oleandor, simic is never to be traded again. This hunger for power has brought tension between countries and a growing lust for simic, though this is more of an empire, whether admitted or not..." he remarked offhandedly. "Anyway, now these fools have this sword of simic—the Binder's Blade."

"And one wishes to keep it as the other wants to take it to Dame Dawness," Raihn filled in.

"I can't let them take it anywhere," said Lostar, his voice chilled.

"Well, you might have to."

"Did you not hear what I just said? This sword, in particular, is the generational Binder's Blade. I have to return it to proper, deserving hands. Should I retell the story?"

"No!" Raihn shouted, realizing his excitement, his voice dwindling into a whisper, "No... But if your hands are unfit, how did you attain it in the first place?"

"The sword is...in a transitional phase," Lostar muttered. "If it wasn't in my hands, then worse fingers would curl around the grip." His head dipped low. "It binds our people together, but it has another name—Truthseeker," he said, his eyes jumping up at Raihn. "And while it currently binds nothing, I deem Truthseeker well-fit to prevail. Its master was Trussgar Drackis. And down in the depths of its surrounding despair, I had come upon this blade deserving of reclamation, Raihn of Parcel."

Raihn smirked from his dramatic display of theater. "Stop calling me that. Parcel is gone."

"Only when its last living resident is dead will Parcel Path's embers die out."

"More spurious nonsense. You sound an old-robed gabber... But I appreciate your positive...wisdom, even though my hands are what's bound... I mean, what does it matter? Dawness will have me by the neck."

Lostar's face became shadowed by disappointment. "Feeble words."

"Nothing matters when you're dumped in a lightless hole," Raihn mumbled. "What was it you said, hollowed out in a shell of a place?"

"It matters all the same, just not to those that give up...or those too cowardly to face the turmoil..." Lostar said.

Raihn exhaled his witted demeanor. "Thanks for the history lesson."

The carriage halted, the whole compartment creaking from the wood's unease. "We stopped," Raihn pointed out.

The carriage teetered for a moment as the driver seemed to step off. Silence ensued, the two napping Authoritarians unbothered.

Raihn listened, only making out rainfall for a few moments, when suddenly, the door broke from its hinges. The Authoritarians woke and scrambled to unsheathe their swords, but something yanked them out and flung them down into the muck. A hard stomp squashed in the dark.

Raihn struggled to parse the foe from the dark, their skin glimpsed by the swinging lantern. Whatever it was, it was more powerful than a horse, cloaked as parsed through the glow.

"At least they didn't suffer long," said a feminine voice. "Still brutal, though."

That wasn't the killer. *Couldn't be.* Their voice was much daintier than Raihn imagined.

The killer peered in, silver irises gleaming from under the brim of their cloak. Their skin was hard to see, but it looked as white as snow, and the same could be said for the strands of hair dangling past it.

"Should we be thanking you or begging for our lives?" Raihn asked, noting just how tall they were.

Their lips were soft, and Raihn, at last, noticed they accented a woman's strong jaw, but a sneer crossed her otherwise soft face, revealing two sharp canines that interposed wildness.

Another face peered around the corner. Also a woman, but much shorter. Her skin was olive-tinted and mostly masked by mud. Torn rags hung from her body, and her hair was cut short as if by a dull blade, uneven and frayed like cut rope. Her dissatisfied eyes darted around. "Nothing," she declared, disregarding them. She was *no killer,* just an accomplice to a disproportionately sized woman.

Raihn became offended. "What do you mean, 'nothing'?" he scoffed. "What about us?"

"What have you?" she asked.

"What have I?" Raihn repeated.

"Yes, what have you got on your person? What do you possess?" the girl clarified. "I would assume it was all taken by the Authority."

"Thieves," Lostar blurted.

"We are not thieves," the girl protested promptly.

"Scavengers," Lostar corrected.

"Wrong twice," she said.

"We are wealthy—made of money, you could say—and you'll be rewarded if you let us go," said Lostar.

"Or I could just steal it off you."

"What if my belongings are not with me?"

"I have no interest in detours," she said. "I'm already late as it is. And it's not like I can trust any ol' prisoner anyhow."

"We may be prisoners, but to whom?" Raihn mused. "The Authority? They are not so reliable in nobility. They will take anyone away, including minor offenders."

"That I understand…but of what interest were you to them?"

"Well, it's a big misunderstanding…"

"I'm listening, aren't I?" she sassed, her head pidgeoning forward. "I told you I don't have the time, so make it good."

"They grouped us with some other offenders when we did not correlate," said Raihn, simplifying the matter.

"Okay, but just because you say that does not make me believe you. I need trust, so how about you point me in the right direction? Where is Cobblestone?"

Raihn stammered until Lostar intervened. "He can take you there! I was looking for it myself when he helped me find it."

"I only need a direction. Point it, and we can be on our way," she claimed.

"You could try, but I doubt it would do you good with all the twists and turns in the road," Raihn contended, following Lostar's lead. "Surely you would only get more lost. You could unknowingly traverse into more Authoritarians, but I could easily lead you back there through a shortcut."

"So be it," she agreed, albeit reluctantly. "But try anything, and my friend, my big friend, Amarra, will do to you what she did to your captors."

Amarra grabbed a chart made up of the alphabet. Pointing to the letters for Raihn to read.

He read aloud, "You be dead," then chuckled nervously. "Yeah, I don't doubt it." She was like a horse on its hind legs but mightier.

"Better that you don't doubt it," the girl assured. "Come now, lead the way."

"Wait," Lostar said.

"What is it?" she half-whined.

"You got a little something," he suggested, gesturing to his face, insinuating she should wipe the mud off.

She rolled her eyes and left the carriage.

"I guess it's just her style," Raihn shrugged, a remark trailing. "If you like to look like a pauper."

The girl had returned with a key and unlocked them from the carriage, and one after the other, they exited. Raihn gazed momentarily at the giant scowling down at them. Then, he noticed the sack of weapons leaning against the carriage. She was collecting them, *but for what reason if they were not thieves?*

"Sorry, but consider your weapons the price of saving your skins," the *pauper* girl said.

Lostar looked itchy, likely thinking of protesting as Amarra continued to glower. "What for? For your big lady to turn us into jerkins?" he said. She was so big that he arched his back and head. Still, her eyes were pressing down upon him. "What is it? What?" he snapped. Amarra leaned down and reached for his hip, snagging his corked flagon. "Don't you drink it," he threatened.

"Why is the flagon so important?" The giantess's dainty companion asked.

"Why is it you speak for your giant?"

"I asked first," she replied. "And **she** isn't **my** anything besides friend."

And that giant friend raised the flagon, much to Lostar's distress. "It's the last mouthful of sweet mead from Endura," he explained. "So, don't!" Against his wishes, she unplugged the flagon. "Don't you do it," he warned, his finger pointed. Bottoms up it went before her mouth. "She's drinking it!" he stomped. "Scavengers!"

"We only take what we need along our travels, though neither of us has had a good drink in a while," she said.

"What's done is done," Raihn excused. "How about we introduce ourselves? I'm Raihn. My somewhat incapacitated, sobering companion is Lostar. What should I call you?"

"Well, I already introduced my friend Amarra, but as for why I speak for her, she's mute. I figured you might figure it from her chart, but alas, you're fools. And she crushes any foolish man that harms me—or tries to, by the way. As for my name, I'll let you wonder," she teased, her lips rising into a half-sneer beneath her nose.

Raihn tried crossing his arms, forgetting the chains that forbade him. His embarrassment led him to play it off. "Boy, I sure wish there was a key to get these off," he said, his tone playful.

"Nice try," she said.

"Alright, alright. Then, at the least, do me this one favor. I need something that the Authority took from me. It holds personal value and means nothing to you, my satchel. And before you ask, there's just a journal within, and a spyglass had they stuck it in. Anyway, it belonged to my brother."

"The spyglass?"

"No, the journal."

"S'pose that makes more sense. Fine… You are so materialistic," she quipped in a mock whine.

After the girl peered inside the satchel to test his honesty, she tossed it back. Then, to the surprise of both men, she started to detach the horses from the carriage.

"What are you doing?" Raihn asked.

"We can't just leave them."

"Well, certainly Amarra cannot ride a horse." Then he looked her up and down and then back at the girl. "She's enormous! Perhaps eight feet tall!"

66

"Don't be daft—she's eight feet and four inches. Also, we need an extra horse."

"Why would we need an extra horse?" Raihn asked.

"Are you going to gawp and question all night, or should we get going?" she snapped.

Moving in a single file with their horses in tow, Raihn and Lostar led the way through the dense forest, the others following closely behind. The interlocking branches overhead shielded them from a drizzle as they forged their path. The horses, held steady by their reins, occasionally shied at the rustle of reptiles, their nervous snorts breaking the quiet. Raihn, too, startled now and then—though his fears went beyond the skittering of lizards after dark. There was no civilization nearby that wasn't Authoritarian, and death seemed to permeate the air around him, the image of that slain horse shadowing his sense of reality.

A shiver crawled over his spine as he wondered that, just maybe, whatever tore Lostar's horse was the same thing that got those men who gave chase outside the village. It could come for these horses just as well.

Many times, Raihn tripped over what he could not see. Light was sparse. And though he was dirty, there was a bright side. The dirt and mud helped deter blood-thirsty mosquitoes haunting his ears like raving banshees. But the gradual transformation from forest to swamp was concerning. At this rate, they'd have to get used to smacking the back of their necks. The 'shortcut' seemed more of a nuisance than he'd thought.

Eventually, the tight overgrowth receded, and the two could now walk shoulder to shoulder and properly speak to one another.

"What do you propose will happen once they discover that Parcel and Cobblestone aren't exactly a village and town anymore?" Raihn asked Lostar.

"I don't know. We'll cross that bridge when we get to it."

"That's how people end up in tight spots."

"Sounds familiar…" Lostar remarked. "I don't know, Raihn. We act surprised, throw up our hands, and put on a show?" he said sarcastically.

"'Oh, Wow! I cannot believe my eyes! My village has burned down. What am I to do?'" Raihn exclaimed, feigning surprise.

"…Work on that," the vagabond suggested.

"You really want us to lie through our teeth?"

"What's wrong with that?"

"It makes me uncomfortable. I usually like to put everything on the table."

"Have you put everything on the table for me?"

Raihn didn't answer, too busy reflecting. "Well, not exactly. I figured you would think I'm crazy or that I was a criminal."

"You are a criminal. We just escaped our now-murdered jailors… So, tell me."

Raihn sighed, "Fine. I was running from the soldiers, and then something attacked them. I say 'something' because I honestly don't know what it was. But I sensed it. I went up a tree where a raven brought about my fall."

"A raven, you say?" Lostar perked.

"Yes. The same as the one that perched your horse. It was in the tree, staring deep into my eyes as it cawed. I fell. Struck a sea that seemed iced-over after I had submerged. Became trapped, forced to witness a vision of my mother being assaulted by Dame Dawness through the ice. Then you came along…"

"That's everything?" Lostar asked.

"Do you think I'm crazy?" Raihn asked, dodging his question.

Before Lostar could say anything else, the girl's questioning from the rear preceded him. "Are we almost there?" she called out in a tone that worried Raihn. Her impatience was growing.

"We're making good progress!" Raihn shouted back before admitting to Lostar under his breath. "I really hope I'm not lost. I'm pretty sure we're headed north, but still east of where I met you, assuming the carriage was to wrap the village…"

"'Assuming.' I thought you said we were making good progress?"

"I'm trying to keep her happy."

"Well, shouldn't you know where you're going by now? Does anything look familiar?"

"I've never been this far from Parcel. I just know we head in the right direction…I think. Listen, we're in a swamp, and by Parcel is the river. If we keep heading this way, we should pass it. We must be heading to Cobblestone…I think."

"…Reassuring enough."

Chirping rickets and croaking toads abounded. Barynn trickled through the overhang, barely lighting their path. And it was muggy, infested with things that bite.

"You know when people say it can always be worse?" asked Raihn, his boot brimming with murky stew. "They're full of it."

Lostar agreed. "This is all so…different," he muttered, nostalgia lacing his remorse. "So cluttered and wet and full of mosquitoes," he went on, swatting.

"You sound homesick," Raihn said. "Is Endura not a miserable place?"

"To some—those that lived beyond even the shadow of Lakewane, far from the river, in the Lowlands. 'Rodents' some might call them from up in the Highlands, 'clinging to the hulls of ships.'"

Raihn itched, and not from bug bites. "But you're from Lakewane, as you said before." Lostar ignored him, their boot squelching through muck.

"Lostar," he pressed, his voice hanging a moment. "How do you see them? Those that live beneath you."

"I don't believe there is one man, woman, or child that lives beneath me. It's impossible to be any lower than a vagrant like me."

The tired two pushed on through a temperament, which had transitioned into a bog with abundant vegetation slothing about. Deep roots anchored the trees, while thick moss and low-hanging tassels covered them. The party delved between them, passing small ponds of murky green water adorned with lily pads adrift and spinachy debris.

"The Authority sure took us out quite a way," said Raihn through his exhaustion. "Though they very well wouldn't want to cut into the bog when they have a path. This is our best route to not get caught."

"The further we go, the more I understand the Authority's decision to go around. The water here is—" Lostar stepped into a camouflaged pond, "abundant."

Raihn cackled at his misfortune.

"Do you find my misery funny?"

"I sympathize with your misery, but yes, it is funny."

"Then we'll keep it to ourselves and laugh when the ladies make the same mistake."

Soon thereafter, the sound of a loud plop was followed by a sharp cry. Raihn and Lostar derived some joy in an otherwise terrible night until an angry downpour sounded off a roaring applause against the broad leaves. Raihn darted towards a towering tree for shelter and paused midway, attempting to relay the coming shelter to the women.

"What? I can't hear you!" the nameless one shouted back, the deluge overwhelming.

"Forget it. Let's go; they'll follow," Raihn said to Lostar.

"Come to think of it, I hope the big one didn't get her feet wet. Her being angry is the last thing we want," Lostar considered, as he and Raihn tied their horses to a small tree that neighbored the giant one. They both removed their boots, draining out any hitchhiking water and tiny tadpoles before scratching their soggy heels against the rugged bark, unwinding as their captors drew nearer.

For a moment, it was quite enjoyable to see them so miserable, but as they came closer, Raihn couldn't help but feel regret and shame. The shorter girl was shivering through her teeth, soaked. Her raggedy attire clung to her like a big wet sock.

Amarra tied their horses and sat her down in the tree's nook, comforting them as their teeth chattered like a leper's clapper. And unlike they hoped, she was angry.

CHAPTER NINE
Unmasked

Raihn dreamt of three shadows taking shape, their dominant hands emerging as they reached beyond the darkness, now steeped in white light. Their fingers spread out. Bent like awful branches. One hand fell off its stumped wrist before him, and another continued its reach, while the third remained still—all of them white as salt.

Fear snaking through his ribs, Raihn jolted awake, his left cheek sore. "Again?" he moaned, rubbing it tenderly. "I'd appreciate you not hitting me every chance you get."

"Wasn't me," Lostar denied.

Raihn opened his eyes and saw Amarra hovering over him, her hood bulging from her large mane. And from her shadowed face under Barynn's glow, her silvers peered cold on his outstretched hand, strangely curious of it. Knees bent, claws dangling, she squatted, refusing to help him up. The ball of each knee parted her cloak into an open curtain. Thick thighs flowed down before curving, linking muscle and plumpness around her tight, full-ered calves. A loincloth hung between them, and animal furs wrapped around her chest. Her silver eyes starred brightly under the sky.

Raihn swept his look elsewhere, the other cheek now turning red. She rose, her knees sinking back into the folds of her cloak, eyes much harder than mere sparkling stars.

"I think she enjoyed that too much," Lostar laughed thickly. He'd stepped forward and offered his hand instead, his voice dwindling to a whisper, "I think you liked it as well."

Raihn accepted their aid, eyes narrowing on Lostar, hoping to dispel further remarks as he rose. He wasn't one to lust and think of such things before marriage—or at least, before finding the *right* lady—though his hormones were hard to ignore.

"You could have warned me about that pond," Amarra's companion whined.

"Ah, now I understand the hospitality," Raihn muttered, holding his stinging cheek again. "I suppose I deserved that." Then he paused, his heart skipping a beat. He saw her face clean of muck; the tumble into the pond must've washed away her disguise. He looked at her soft olive hue and recognized her from the wanted flier that Dame Dawness had shown in town.

"Sorry," he began, "I misjudged the depth of the pond. We mistakenly thought you'd merely get your foot wet."

"Then you may as well make it worth it and laugh," she retorted, but he did not. "Guess it was for nothing, then. I don't have time for you two."

"What's so important there, anyway?"

"Nothing you need worry about," she replied.

"I'm not worried," he lied, wondering *what if they think we burned down the village? What if more Authoritarians are there? She's wanted, but then again, so am I.* "Alright, if you're in a hurry, then I suppose I'll untie my horse."

"Don't worry about it. Just take the key and go," she said, holding his liberation from chains aloft for him to take.

Raihn sighed, letting the key hang. "Listen, there should be a river not far from here, and over that river is a bridge. It's not in the best shape, but it holds. Though it was not made for folks as…well, tall as your friend. I wouldn't recommend she take any horse with her. But if I double back and take a second horse across, so the bridge only takes on her weight and her weight alone, she should be clear."

Her lips pursed, hand wobbling in the air. "Why? Why help us? You're free now."

"I'd sure hate for another one of you falling in and getting wet on my account."

She watched him carefully, considering his offer. "Fine." Her arm fell, and she said, "I don't wish to tread a frail bridge more than once, so lead the way," and pocketed the key.

"What about my restraints? I meant to grab it. I just meant to make things clear first."

"I reconsidered," she said. "Your willingness to help me screams suspicious. And I don't like being put on edge."

Unfortunately, Raihn had only a catnap, awakened when the deluge was over. The night persisted, deepening a pit in his belly when he heard the river running near. He'd never been here at this hour, the darkness was only bright enough from Barynn to see through.

There it stretched, a relic of the past, barely holding on, with the river rushing beneath it—the bridge.

"No one uses it anymore," Raihn explained. "After the Authority came, alternative paths were made for better, safer routes."

"You seem to know it well enough," the girl remarked.

"My father used to bring me here to fish, but that was a long time ago," he said, taking a beat. "That was with the fishmonger… Anyway, I'll take my horse and double back, just as I said."

"Are you sure about this?" she asked. "It appears hardly held together but by tooth and twine."

"I know it looks scary, but considering who you've got with you, any other path is too risky."

"Don't speak another word about Amarra," she warned. "Especially to get your way."

Ignoring her notice, Raihn continued, feeling the tension rise as the women became provoked. "The lighter it gets, the better the Authority will see her," he asserted, prompting Amarra to step forward, a dim sharpness in her silvery eyes. "You're not hiding who you are," he added.

Though her cloak shadowed her face, Raihn could sense the lurking snarl. Her grip tightened on his collar, yanking him close, her towering stature making him feel insignificant. She lifted him effortlessly, his clothes taut as he was hoisted off the ground, yet fear hadn't touched him until he glimpsed the white claw emerging from her cloak as if from the dream.

Raihn breathed, battling her grip and the squeeze from his cloak and tunic. "You're not fooling anyone with that cloak," he said again, her grip tightening. He knew what she was, and she had to take this route for her own good. "This is the best and quickest route, I swear," he went on, beginning to choke. "Otherwise, you might stumble on another patrol."

"Stop," the girl ordered. "We should hurry. We'll do as he says." Her gaze flicked over to him. "But no funny business."

They all glanced at the bridge once more. The river below it was running quite fast, spitting up beside the rocks. She dropped him, and his body smacked the dirt.

"Does anyone know how to swim?" Lostar asked. They all remained quiet, their faces exuding dependence.

The dilapidated bridge was ricketier than he'd recalled last. And as it shook and swung, he regretted his workload, leading a horse, still meaning to go back and lead the other. "Please, bridge, do not fail me now," he uttered.

For most of the way, Raihn held his breath. It was a slow and steady process, but to his delight, he made it across. "Yes!" he cheered. "Only three more horses to go! Swell." His sarcasm couldn't be more palpable, though he couldn't complain much, knowing this was his plan. He tied up his horse and crossed the bridge again more easily than before. "Okay, Lostar. It wasn't so bad," he assured, patting them on the back.

"Yeah, right," Lostar scoffed. "So, you want me to go next?"

"Why not. Give me a breather."

Lostar took his horse by the reins, sighed, and crossed the creaking boards. He appeared to be sick and nervous, averting his eyes from the river before embracing his steed at the end of the bridge.

Raihn swiped away a bead of nervous sweat. He was just about to make another crossing, but the girl objected, pulling a fold of his cloak. "I think you should go last," she said. After swearing the bridge would be a fine route, he couldn't say no. "You said it was safe, right? I'll lead the pack-horse, then Amarra will cross, you going last with the final horse."

With a determined glint in her eye, the girl urged her horse onto the creaking bridge, her steed's hooves clopping against the wooden planks. Raihn held his breath as she darted across the wobbly bridge. She reached the other side in what felt like mere moments, safe and sound. Raihn exhaled, relief flooding through him. Still, the real test of durability in the bridge would come next as Amarra was to follow up.

A pit of doubt deepened in Raihn's stomach.

When Amarra took the first step, Raihn crossed his fingers and hoped for the best. The bridge swayed, creaked, and buckled, but she made it, too. He let out a breath.

"Alright, that's it. Pack it up because we are on our way," Raihn cheered in a feigned merry tune. He stepped forward confidently as he led the last horse. "You see, Lostar, no sweat!" he said at the midpoint.

But barely a second later, Raihn felt a lurch in his stomach as the horse dislodged a loose board with its hoof. He watched in horror as the steed's front leg dangled through the gap. The entire bridge teetered, and before he could react, it flipped upside down. The horse, tangled in the ropes, kicked wildly to stay above the water's surface. Its cries of panic pierced sharply into Raihn's ears. He clung to it tightly, his heart racing, fighting its frantic actions and the powerful current. He felt the wind off its kicks, inches away from his head.

Without hesitation, Amarra dived in, leaving her companion behind. Raihn's breath hitched—whether from the cold water or from the fact he saw her wading toward him, he wasn't sure. The water on Amarra was nearly chest high because of her height, bouncing along her collarbone. He imagined her ox-strong legs pushing her off the riverbed.

The speed of the current and the horse's thrashing made the situation even more chaotic. Raihn gripped his satchel tightly with one hand, holding it high above the water, while his other hand, dragged nearby from his restraints, clung to the horse's mane.

Amarra reached him, putting herself between him and the flailing horse, her back taking its blows. Raihn felt a strange sense of security in her grasp. A sharp contrast to the terror of moments before. Certainly better than facing another one of her powerful right hooks.

She took him to shore and set him down, where he shivered uncontrollably, his teeth chattering. He flopped back, his eyes under both women, the sky-raking branches from the near trees hanging just above. Both seemed frustrated.

"Maybe you should have warned me about that small pond," the girl mused, her tone light, as if drawing a connection between their earlier mishap and this ordeal.

"You're still on that?" Raihn groaned. "Well, then, how come he didn't fall in?" he asked half-seriously, gesturing to Lostar. His lips pulled into a faint grin, his chest still convulsing. But his breath was lost when Amarra dove back into the water. He gasped, shooting up, realizing she meant to save the horse.

The animal kicked and thrashed, rattling the bridge and nearly dragging the entire structure into the river. Amarra had no time to waste. She swam toward the panicking horse, grabbing its snagged leg with one hand while prying the bridge planks apart with the other, creating just enough of a gap to set it free. But the battle wasn't over—the horse, still wild with fear, fought against her aid.

Amarra's strength was enough to wrestle it into submission, her arms locking around its neck as she struggled to tug it ashore. Twice, she nearly lost her footing, the current threatening to sweep her away. Yet, by the skin of her teeth, she dragged herself and the horse to the riverbank.

The horse, still riled, bolted into the forest, its hooves clattering as it vanished among the trees.

Amarra bent over and gasped for breath, then took a knee. Her companion was quick to be at their side.

Regrouped, they tracked broken branches and the imprints of embedded hooves, following the lead of their determined guide: a nameless girl. "This way," she urged, her voice cutting through the eerie silence of the skeletal trees—a foreboding sign of wickedness, perhaps leeched by the shadow, as Raihn had mentioned to his father. The mountain hung high in the sky, out of sight from this dusk. Raihn, ever vigilant, sensed something amiss. The surrounding decay snarled sinisterly, and a sudden caw from the treetops shattered what tranquility they had. Raihn tensed, his senses heightened by another sound, one that was distant. "Wait," he cautioned.

"What is it?" the girl inquired.

"Can you hear it?" The noise grew louder—a heavy rhythm drawing closer.

"The horse?"

"Not a horse," Raihn detected, another tingle running up his hand, "something larger, more menacing."

The sound of its hooves was heavy and strong. Whatever it was, it riled up their remaining horses, who pulled away and snorted. And while kept at bay for a minute, they had to be let go lest they'd drag their riders through the mud.

"Damn!" Lostar exclaimed. He turned his attention to the giant woman. Her power bested her horse's, which happened to be the pack horse. She kept it in place with the greatest effort so it would not flee. The horse carrying Lostar's belongings was terrified, whining wicked neighs.

"Let it go! We have to leave!" Her friend pleaded.

74

"No!" Lostar barked. "That horse possesses worth greater than my own life! If that beast takes off, I will have no choice but to search for that horse all night!"

Mud seemed to tremble beneath their feet as they felt the continent, Adjurrah, quake. Branches popped in the distance from within the brush, each breaking into the wooded applause of cracks. And suddenly, out from it, the creature responsible for all the terror had burst through the clamor.

Into this dead zone, they saw it head straight for them, wasting no time as it killed the distance before jutting its tusks through their horse. The thing was on four hooves and rode with a coat of short, dark bristles. Amarra dove back as it had tossed back their pack horse with a flick of their meaty neck. Glaring at the party after demonstrating its strength, it was like the beast had a vendetta.

"That's a big boar," the girl uttered, less serious than the situation demanded. The others were quiet, frozen, for the boar was so close that they likely felt its warm snorts graze their skin.

"I could really use my sword," Lostar hinted through managed panic.

"Well, the beast is between it and us, so what can we do?" the girl asked.

Amarra reacted first, her snorts combating the boar's. She lunged toward this elephant-sized boar and gripped its tusks, fighting in a way similar to her earlier corralling of the horse. But this wild beast was greater than any horse, and she struggled against it.

Thankfully, as Amarra grappled with it, her companion could think; Raihn saw a spark in the girl's eyes just before she took her cue to sneak off to the battered horse that was flung away. She hovered over its broken body when Raihn approached and heard it whimper. It jutted its muzzle as the girl knelt before it, laying a soft hand between its eyes and then to their chest. Shushing the animal, she reached for the bag on the harness and emptied it. The weapons spilled into the mud.

She took the sheathed blade and tossed it to Raihn as he was closest. And just as he was about to pass it over to Lostar, the boar overcame Amarra and flung her into the Enduran.

Raihn acted swiftly, drawing the sword with a determination to slay the beastly thing. His gaze locked with the overgrown boar's as he took a deep breath, the scimitar shimmering like a star, poised to strike. However, to his surprise, the boar showed no signs of aggression, even dismissing him. He sighed, nearly crumbling, his bravery fading. But the boar reared its head at the girl, and he reignited.

Ignoring Lostar's warning cries, Raihn charged forward. He maneuvered around the boar with agility and speed, avoiding its deadly tusks. With a daring leap, he thrust the blade shallowly into the boar's neck, the strike nonfatal. The boar shook its head violently, throwing Raihn off like he was a mouse.

Helpless and weaponless, Raihn tumbled and crashed to the ground, the sword shallowly remaining in the beast, out of reach.

"It's a curved sword!" Lostar bellowed. "It's not meant to thrust!"

The boar again turned its attention to the vulnerable girl and her injured horse. Raihn felt a surge of urgency. "What do we do?" he asked, turning to Amarra for guidance.

Amarra turned to Lostar, her gaze pleading for him to act before it was too late. Lostar, caught between uncertainty and urgency, looked to Raihn. The unspoken despair in his eyes mirrored Raihn's own—both seemingly powerless against the looming threat. The giantess clicked her tongue and took matters into her own hands, charging at the boar. She grabbed hold of its tusks and engaged in another grappling match to protect her companion from harm. And like her, Lostar sprinted into action, leaving Raihn to wonder where he might fit in.

Raihn stood back, his gaze fixed on the unfolding spectacle. Initially questioning Lostar's motives, he soon realized the true mission at hand was retrieving their blade.

Determined, Lostar gripped the handle of the sword and pulled with all his might, but it remained firmly embedded in the boar's unforgiving muscle, and despite Amarra's valiant efforts to keep the beast at bay, the sword remained out of reach. Raihn could see the strain on her face, glistening with sweat, a bulging vein stressing her effort. As she fought to maintain her footing in the slippery mud, Raihn's eyes flickered to the collapsed horse and the kneeling girl, realizing the danger that loomed ever closer. "Move!" Raihn screamed at the top of his lungs, but her concern for the Giantess seemed to paralyze her, so Raihn swooped in and pulled her up to her feet, his heart racing. Amarra, the boar, and Lostar plowed toward them.

This battle of strength was tipping, and Amarra seemed to give way, her biceps pronounced with a rivering vein. Raihn froze, but the girl clutched him, pulling, and they both fell out of harm's way. Amarra glanced over, seemingly understanding their safety, and she lost more strength. She avoided stepping upon the horse that lay there, then was mashed against a nearby tree. Her back ground against the bark like cheese to a grater, her face surrendering to agony. She was doing her best not to be gauged by the oversized boar, but the tusks swung endlessly past its squeals.

"Get back!" Raihn warned after stealing one of Lostar's arrows. He leaped and swung down, piercing a pitch-black eye. He then fell back and watched the animal flail, nearly stomping him with its thrashing hooves. The giant woman had not yet let go of its tusks and took this opportunity to fight back. She kicked its leg, bowing it. And with another whine, the boar fell to its side, the sword pushed deep by the force of the world, Desekreus, drawing a horrid, dwindling, final whine from the felled beast.

After a time to breathe and collect themselves, they gathered around the beast. Raihn exchanged glances with the others, making out a glaring development. In the heat of battle, the giant's hood must have slipped. His gaze locked onto two pairs of horns atop her head—one set, no larger than an adult's thumb, rested on her forehead while the other spiraled out like hair buns made into ivory horns. Her ears, pointy and whimsical, resembled a sheep's, with delicate hairs. They befit her cloudy white hair and milky skin, with a collar of curls rolling around her long neck. Everything was seemingly sculpted from alabaster, as opposed to her northern kin, beyond the Eight Wynds, grey like razed coal.

Raihn broke his gaze away, still hung up on her imprinting beauty, though an angry caw hurled itself through his thoughts from above.

He shook in a start, eyes up. The raven bore its eyes down. "I don't think this encounter is by chance," Raihn stated through the gloom.

Lostar swiftly took up a rock and hucked it but missed, his hands fumbling from the chain. The raven laughed wryly, its voice sounding too human for comfort. It warped, sounding feminine, like a knife twisted under its feathers.

Raihn winced, remembering it from the window. It was no ordinary raven, as it followed him every step of the way, atrocities in its wake.

Amarra sneered and pushed Lostar aside. She clutched a mightier rock, the size of a large striking head from a flail, her palm encompassing half of it. And without waiting, the raven ceased its laugh, flapping off into the sky. Still, she tipped back her weight, left leg arching away. She heaved with all her might, and the rock soared, beating the limbs off trees. It narrowly missed the bird's wing. She bent past her knees again, her palm now scooping many pebbles. She twisted and then cannoned a grapeshot, many pellets scattering between the branches. The raven appeared struck, yet still escaped with its life.

"Not much for the wildlife, are we," Lostar kidded, stepping toward the boar carcass. He pried his hands beneath it and struggled to raise the animal to free his sword.

"Keep it up. I think you almost got it," Raihn said, level-toned.

Amarra shook her head and shoved Lostar out of the way once again, his feet unable to find footing as he fell. Raihn wondered if she just enjoyed bullying them. She squared up to the dead boar and cracked her fingers with a grin, ready to show off. Squatting down and hooking her arms below the animal, she lifted.

"What are you doing? You're going to worsen your back!" the girl cried. Amarra did as she pleased and disregarded the concern. She flipped the beast over and retrieved the sword, her silvers lit from its majesty. "That sword," their companion breathed, "I see. That's why it is so important to you," she gasped, taking notice of its rarity. "Remarkable."

"The sword must get back into the right hands," Lostar asserted.

"Fine," she said, snapping away from the glimmer. "Let him have it. If any more danger comes our way, it's better for you to have it than not.

Might as well take the keys," she added, tossing the rusty ring to Raihn. "You know we have nothing. You can see that by looking at my clothes. Or my face. Besides, my giant lady friend will peel you like a banana if you feel spry."

Raihn laughed at this, evidently offending her.

"What?" she asked, annoyed. "What is it?"

"Skinned like a potato is a bit more intimidating than peeled like a banana, but I get the idea."

"I am not a brute; my terminology is softer than your people's vegetables."

"I know. I can see it on your face. I know where you're from—the only place to speak of bananas."

The girl seemed to panic. "What do you mean?" she asked. "See what my expression?"

"That too, but no. I hate to break it to you, but you seem to have lost your dark complexion." She ran her fingers across her cheek, gasped, and reached for mud.

"Stop!" Raihn said. "You don't need it. You're both in this together. When Amarra is spotted, so are you. Like I said, her cloak isn't fooling anyone. I know where she comes from. Harboring an Outcast could have you sentenced for life, or worse."

"Not that it's your business," she sharply began, "I have an acquaintance to meet in Cobblestone. Amarra will have to sit it out, unfortunately."

Raihn sighed, unwilling to hide the truth any longer. "Look, I assure you there were wanted fliers with your face stuck on them," he said. "Yes, I know who you are, but I may be the only one."

"What? What do you mean? Say it straight!"

Raihn tensed up, his shoulders rolling. Honesty wore heavily upon him. "Everything is gone. The entire village. Cobblestone, too, along with anyone there."

For a minute, she stood silently, disarmed of her senses. When she recovered, she blurted out, "Why didn't you tell me before?"

"It was not Raihn's idea, but my own," said Lostar. "As shackled captives, I considered our best interest just as you did as a fugitive."

"Any kind of Authoritarian is not just your enemy, but ours as well," Raihn explained. "Don't you understand? That village was home to my people. The name Parcel is the name I bear. That was my home, but now it is mostly made ash by them—Hulls, the dame, whoever. It doesn't matter. And even though it is burnt, there is nowhere else for us to go."

She seemed to relent and understand him as her eyes softened. Then, beside her, the giantess collapsed, perhaps from pain. "Amarra!" the girl cried, flinging their cloak aside. The giantess's back was revealed, shredded. "We have to dress her wound," the girl said.

Within no time, Lostar had cut a portion of the massive cloak and bandaged the bleeding giant.

"If you need time, I can wait," Raihn said.

Amarra shook her head profusely and fought to rise. Raihn put out his best hand to aid her. She paused to regard it, her features soft at first, then tense. She ignored him and shoved her hands against the earth, but the trio lent her all their strength to erect her like a mighty statue.

The littler girl glanced at Raihn with unkind sharpness and then softer at Amarra. "Are you sure?" she asked. Amarra nodded. Then, speaking in a tone as brittle as charred timber, she flickered to Raihn. "Show me the ashes."

CHAPTER TEN
Embers of a fire

The quartet fled the forest on foot, sparing no time to search for their fled horses. The trees thinned at last and the coming ridge before them peeled, soon to reveal the village. First, the mountain peered over the ridge as a dark shape under parting clouds. The full glow of Barynn even touched on the near-equally distant Wall of Thorns. Suddenly, Raihn's mind cracked. He stopped. The pain pushed him down to his knees.

"What's wrong?" Lostar asked.

"My head! It feels like a rat chewed through the back of my skull and brain," Raihn replied. "It's chattering away."

A voice called to him from afar, as if beyond the wall, echoing as if from a grave. Then it boomeranged from the village, tugging the hairs along the back of his wrist. His head warmed, a pot whirling like stew for the rat to pilfer. And beneath his skin, his veins felt wiggling like worms as if grounders shook his flesh.

Chattering, first just a noise, became clearer. It was a crisp whisper, something beyond his grit, fine like a sharp wire grinding through his bones and ushering unintelligible things over his lobes—chattering still.

The girl turned to him. "It comes as a faint whisper riding along the wind. Sometimes, it's a tingle in your hand. Other times, it's like hot sand pouring through your ear," she said, somehow familiar, her voice drenched with a longing lamentation.

"How do you know this? Who are you?" Raihn asked the girl through his teeth. "Why is it that the Authority were so fixated on you?"

"Unfortunately, who I am no longer matters," she said dimly. "I had my suspicions before—when your sleep couldn't be disturbed and Amarra woke you. You dreamt of it, didn't you?"

"I'm not sure what I dreamt of, but something seemed to reach for me then, or rather gotten ahold of me, and I don't mean that smack by your friend."

His quip didn't amuse her. "You're not the first. But congrats. It's your responsibility now," her voice lolled.

"How can I get rid of it?"

"Is that all you want!?" she snapped, as if offended. "I am utterly lost as to why it chose you."

Raihn grimaced, holding his head for a moment. "What is **it** exactly that chose me?"

"The hand hewed from a tree turned pale—the Undyed Tree. It paled near Hullgain Castle, sprouting a Stayed Hand, made impervious to any blade—it called to me. I saw it," she said remorsefully, her voice tired yet harsh. "I snapped it free from the tree, reading its carved wood and feeling things I've never felt." She spoke of it, clasping one hand within the other, as if desiring its promises. "I lost it."

"What?" Stayed Hand. That's what the dame had called it before his mother. It was some sort of key. "Did you drop it somewhere?"

"Fool," she said, broken from reverie, her voice now low. "I've become unfit to hold the Stayed Hand and bear its grace, for I lost my own grace. Though through you, I know it is still out there," she said. "See, I have an ally in Cobblestone who smuggled it in after it was gone from me. And if it were impervious before…" she mumbled, hinting at indestructibility.

The pain lessened. Raihn breathed and continued, "You think it survived the fire… This unbreakable branch, shaped like a hand, pale as a dove, and all that. Well, why did you split up, anyway? If it is so important."

"No choice. Hulls were on our tail. From the eastern castle, Hullgain, we escaped Cardinal Pharloe Hull and lost our pursuers. Then we got lost in the process… Pharloe will want me back," she said, fear crashing over her visage.

"You or what you've taken?" Raihn asked, trying to discern her meaning. "I imagine such a trinket would grab his desire."

"Don't mistake me for a thief like Pharloe," she hissed. "If I were a thief, then the conduit would not have ended up in my possession, to say the least."

Conduit? "Relax, I'm not calling you anything, including your name, which was absent from that poster, by the way."

"My name is too important for some to hear, though I suppose you are not just anyone now. My name is Tepparna Fila Ranada. Not Teppa. Tepparna," she insisted.

"Sure… Look, even if this thing is calling me, how do you suppose I find it?" he asked, masking his hunch. "You don't plan on digging through rubble all night, do you?"

Tepparna looked to ponder it briefly. "What does it chatter to you?"

Raihn settled, listening, hearing a faint scratch as if upon wood. Bark from the tree, perhaps. *No.* He couldn't understand it, but it wasn't near him. It was scratching out for him, heard from afar, though near. "I'm not sure," he said, unsure to elaborate on his knowledge.

"'Not sure'? Too early to properly commune, I suppose…" she remarked, her phrase intriguing Raihn. She glimpsed him with a suspicious sneer, then wiped it away. "You said this was your home, right? The village. Would you know where the Mousehole is?"

Raihn had asked what this branch was for, though Tepparna hardened. "It'll come to you," she sneered.

Coming over the ridge, Raihn prepared her for what she was about to see—bleak remnants of what was once a thriving town at the end of his ashy village. Horror lay before them: charred bodies strewn about the grass and stone, and most of the buildings had been reduced to piles of soot. Though they could barely look upon it, they forced themselves to come closer.

After pressing on into the market, Tepparna's sudden change in demeanor became alarming. "I hate them," she snarled, meaning the Authority and the Hulls, or so Raihn assumed. She was even more agitated than before. "I hope they get what's coming to them."

"I want to get back at them, too," Raihn agreed as they entered the once bustling town of Cobblestone from the southeast. "This town is where my only friend gave his life for mine, where that dame sicked her men on me."

"An honorable man," said Lostar.

"You have no idea," Raihn chuckled. "But he wasn't the only one to help me. And the strange thing is, only my friend's body is gone," he said, taking notice in the market square.

"Perhaps he survived?"

"No, there's no way." Raihn didn't want to get his hopes up, but he couldn't help but wish that Benjin somehow got out, hard as it would be, to believe that amongst all the charred bodies.

Raihn looked westward, where the copper sign stretched, and spotted the corpses of his two saviors: Halba and the old man. Tepparna seemed to spy them just as well. She went to them and knelt before their robes. Neither were scorched, like some others, the bigger one of the two facing down.

"They aided me, too," Raihn said.

She revealed their face, rolling them over. Suddenly, she choked back tears and balled her fists.

"Do you know them?" Raihn asked gently.

"Why?" she wept, her sorrow palpable in the air.

"I don't know," Raihn stammered. "It just seemed—"

"No, why would they sacrifice their lives for you?"

Raihn struggled, his mouth agape. "Oh," he uttered, his eyes descending from her glare.

Lostar intervened. "Sometimes, people value the lives of others more than their own. Perhaps they knew there was more for Raihn to live for than themselves. It's an honorable death that many warriors strive for."

"He's no warrior. This man, and just him and not this boy, was a coward—a coward that betrayed his family, and me, abandoning me when I needed him. He remained while I..." she shook her head, throat rattling. "There was more for him to live for... He shouldn't have been here. I mean, he abandoned his sanctuary and begot a family, one he refused to fight for. And yet…he fights and dies for you?"

"I'm sorry," Raihn said. "I still ask myself why he, a man whose name is unknown to me, fought for my sake."

Tepparna seemed to take a breath and collect her thoughts. "Pohl was his name, and apparently content with dying while knowing where his daughter was," she said elusively. "Whatever he lived for, I hope it was worth it… Maybe he went back to his old ways."

Raihn cleared his throat. "You know, after an anvil had put up your wanted poster, he came up to me, guided by Halba—that unfortunate boy beside him—yet he asked me what your face on that poster looked like. I described you. That's when he seemed unburdened. It was like he knew you were better on the run than wherever you were before."

Suddenly, her dam cracked, and then she burst, her grief flooding out. "I guess you were right. We're all fugitives with nowhere to go."

"Not just yet," Raihn said. "You still want me to take you to the tavern?" She nodded, so he took her hand, pulled her up, and said, "It won't be long now. We're almost there."

Amarra looked to him kindlier then, as if noting his compassion, even though he knew himself to be a reluctant recluse.

Raihn gestured ahead. "This is it—The Mousehole."

"What's left of it," Lostar added, for it was a stripped-down structure, barely standing.

"Where you meant to regroup," Raihn added before pushing on alone.

"Are you sure that is a good idea?" Lostar asked.

"No," Tepparna answered on Raihn's behalf. "I'm sure he's aware of the buckling posts."

Raihn pushed the blackened door, which fell from its hinges and crumbled into a charred heap. Above, the second floor had partially collapsed and came down in toothy timber. The tavern was in a state of fatigue and disarray, held together by the flimsiest wooden scaffolding. He hoped the rest of the second floor would not cave in more than it had. At the very least, the bar was safe for now, but as he gazed above it, his heart plunged.

"I don't understand," Raihn said, aghast.

Lostar murmured outside, "Something's wrong."

Raihn stumbled out of the building and fell into the dirt. The others spilled in to investigate. Tepparna and Amarra followed Lostar, who gripped the door frame, causing it to chunk away into his blackened hand. All three locked up. Before them was a skewered man propped up over the bar with spears puppeteering his body, and gone were his lips and eyes and much else of his charred features. The biggest tell to discern him was their missing tooth.

Amarra fled out steadily.

"How can they be so cruel, these Eldhonans?" Tepparna asked, still locked. She broke from the sight, peering back over her shoulder, likely curious about Raihn's state.

He looked off, his thoughts muddled. Amarra, beside him, gently guided him back. She knelt, one knee touching the ground, her hand resting with surprising gentleness on his shoulder. With a slow, deliberate motion, she lifted his chin, coaxing him to meet her gaze—those silver eyes that had once been so stern were now softened by an emotion he hadn't seen before. It struck Raihn that this might be the side of her that Tepparna relied on. This shift in her demeanor seemed to come from a place of care, as though she had recognized something in him that needed protecting and had stepped into that role without hesitation.

Yet, even as Raihn recognized this newfound tenderness, he couldn't ignore the unfavorable glare from Tepparna—a look of envious disapproval, as if she was struggling to reconcile this softer side of Amarra with another. But it didn't last. Suddenly, a burst of grating caws rang out from a raven— the same as before—landing before them, antagonizing them. The bird's sudden presence frightened him, disrupting the moment. Amarra pulled away from him, annoyance clear. Jumping to her feet, she unleashed her rage on the raven with a swift stomp, all manner of tenderness fleeting. The bird evaded her foot, only to be trapped between her clenching fingers. It pecked at her hand furiously, tearing bits of her skin away, but this only enraged her further. She snarled and slowly squeezed the life from the raven. Its little heartbeat likely puttering through its little bones before, at last, it popped.

She had held her breath in her rage, then let it out. Her chest deflated. She looked to her companions, and they all looked back, though Tepparna's chest was rigid with fear, her lungs holding air in captivity.

Amarra looked down at the remains of the raven in her hand, its head dangling past her thumb. She let go. Its frail body thumped into the soot. Tepparna dissociated, her eyes cast down to her feet, and her breaths finally came out, though shallow.

Amidst the disquiet, Raihn partook in being a monster. He stomped the raven flat under his foot, feeling a faint crunch. He hoped to save Amarra from feeling across the fence, but it made Tepparna feel ill by the look of it. She headed back into the tavern, mumbling, "Why him?"

Raihn lifted his gaze to Amarra, wondering why she was so kind to him suddenly. Then again, might she only have a nurturing nature. Either way, it left a mark. Still, he felt cautious as to stirring any jealousy. Not that there should be any, *right?* The giant didn't care for him. She was only mothering, like with Tepparna.

Raihn ambled toward Tepparna, intending to check on her, but paused as the awful stench wafted at the door. Grimacing, he pinched it shut and stepped inside, avoiding the temptation to look at the horrors surrounding him. Tepparna was rummaging through the debris, her movements hurried and tense. The buzzing of flies filled Raihn's ears, and he imagined they plagued hers, too. The sickening scene made his stomach churn, and he pulled his hood tighter around his face to block out the stench.

"Tepparna," he called out, his voice muffled. She didn't respond, only sifted through the remains more frantically, tossing aside charred tables with hands blackened by soot. A groan escaped her lips as the task's weight took its toll. "What are you doing?" he asked her.

"Silence yourself," she snipped through a stifled breath.

"If you're still on this quest, then…I don't know. It's all gone. You can't beat them, and you said the hand is gone from you. Why do you fight it? Look at your hands, dark as coal. That's from the forces after our throats. There is a dame after this thing, after you."

She found a pewter tankard through the rubble and whipped it at him. It smacked his gut and tumbled, hardly rolling aside because it was warped. She noticed it, a glint in her eye and a tremble upon her lip, like she felt similarly broken. Or, maybe, that was Raihn's silly presumptions. Maybe he'd not yet understood social cues from being locked up every day. She fled the potent tavern, pushing him aside. Raihn followed, watching her gasp for air. She fell to her knees in a crying fit to regain her breath, and like what she did to Raihn, Amarra engulfed Tepparna within her great big cloak. She really was just a kind giant under that cold exterior.

The flames from the town seemed to persist as if softening the wax around her wick. Raihn was glad. He was nobody to care for, after all. He was just like Lostar, a vagrant. But at least Lostar had a purpose.

Lostar sifted through the ashy remnants of a scorched guild member's treasures outside the tavern. He dug through the miscellaneous items left behind until he found a cart that had been knocked off its wheels. Peering into the cart, he muttered, "These will do." Raihn watched as he took four shovels and headed just outside of town, where he laid them down and dug with one.

Raihn and the others gravitated toward Lostar and the tools. Soon, a plot was dug as close to the tavern as they could manage. Then they dug another and another, knowing it would be disrespectful to honor only one of Raihn's saviors.

CHAPTER ELEVEN
Rekindled

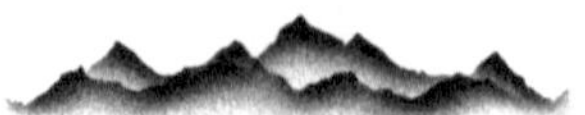

"I just don't know," Tepparna began, standing before the burial. "My contact. Is he even alive?"

"Wherever he is, it's likely where the King's Authority and the Hulls are not," Lostar mused.

"Unless he's been captured," she wondered aloud. "Or perhaps he's fled. I'm not sure there's any real reason he would stay and honor his word. Maybe I was a fool to trust him."

Raihn observed her, intrigued by her conundrum. He had been so preoccupied lately that he hadn't considered this possibility—her intent to meet more than one ally. He linked pieces together, but before he could speak, Tepparna's eyes widened. She dashed away, leaving him and the others to pursue.

Catching up, Raihn deciphered figures in the dark—men greeted happily by Tepparna. As the two groups converged, Raihn scoffed. "Of course."

"What?" Tepparna asked. "Do you know them?"

"Against my will… Just this morn, I was their hostage," he stated with a dry-witted edge.

"Now, hold on, let me explain," said the roundest member of the four with the orange chops. "Herb and I arrived in town before dawn. We kept watch as we awaited the full party when none other than Raihn himself appeared."

"And like a couple of creeps, you both followed me," Raihn said.

"**Buffoons** would be a better description," said the brown-haired one, frustrated. Around his neck, Raihn's eyes sharpened on the brooch of a hound.

"You were there," Raihn reminded. "I could feel your glare from the back of the tavern."

"I should have introduced myself sooner," he admitted. "But we wanted to keep a low profile. I didn't expect to find Authoritarians in that sleazy hole, so I shied away," he sighed. A grin spread across his face as he extended his hand. "Name's Magnus."

They shook, with Raihn noting the strength in Magnus's grip.

"Apologies for the poorly coordinated effort," Magnus continued. "My nerves were frayed, so I rushed, hoping to find the rest of my party. But upon that failure, I returned empty-handed, and the Authority swarmed outside. Sorry we'd not met on better terms."

"Indeed," Hodge agreed. "I am exceedingly sorry for putting you in such an uncomfortable position and even more so for what befell this lovely town and…your village."

"I—" Raihn began, but then he shifted his mournful tone, remembering who these men were. Neither their suave behavior nor their heartfelt condolences change the stress they induced. "You tied me up and held me captive. You hurt my friends. You…"

Amarra and Tepparna shared concerned glances.

"…It's fine," Raihn sighed, his energy deflating.

"How about we use the term 'restrained'?" Hodge suggested. "Perhaps 'borrowed'? If you are willing?"

"Fine. While I was—**restrained**—you were waiting for Tepparna and Magnus?"

"Well," Hodge stammered, "we would still be short, but yes."

Tepparna cleared her throat. "We'd have made it sooner if we weren't lost, though, apparently, by some odd luck, we found these two as captives."

"And you didn't even know we planned to meet!" Hodge laughed heartily. "Like destiny, if you believe in that sort of thing."

"But why me? How do you even know who I am?" Raihn pleaded.

"A good point," Tepparna chimed. "Consider me lost, Hodge, at least before the news I've yet to relay, considering his disposition."

"May as well say it plainly," Magnus intervened, grabbing Raihn's shoulders as if he were some familiar friend. "It was your father and I that organized our gathering." He seemed to be waiting for a response, but Raihn's eyes glazed over. Tepparna appeared just as shocked as he.

"Your father's and Tepparna's absence were the root of our panic," Hodge added.

"I promised to let him tell you himself," Magnus elaborated. "Not one for promises, I'm afraid."

Raihn blinked. "Why would he make any promise to fugitives? My father is a lord," Raihn attested. "No offense."

Magnus nodded. "So he is." Straightening up, he withdrew his hand from Raihn's shoulder. "Tell me, Parcel's son, are you familiar with the white branch, the Stayed Hand, as they call it?"

Raihn glanced at Tepparna. "Sort of," he replied, reluctantly nodding, unsure of becoming tangled with these fugitives.

Magnus flicked his eyes between him and Tepparna. "I have a history with your father. He owed me, and by accepting this branch, we were made even. See, I required a haven for the white branch—some place where the Authority wouldn't suspect, with someone I could trust. I planned to stay until my companions arrived. But when the time came, your father never showed… We were supposed to take that branch. Do you know what happened to your father?"

Before Raihn could answer, Xander butted in. "What if it was a trap? Those Authoritarians came awfully quick."

"My father would never!" Raihn retorted, detesting the hint of accusation. "Nor would he betray any supposed friend. There was a wicked dame after him until he vanished."

Magnus's eyes narrowed thoughtfully.

Xander grunted. "The girl lost the branch anyhow."

Tepparna opened her mouth to respond, but Hodge interjected passionately. "We can't just let go of such a discovery! If we don't unearth whatever lies beyond the white walls, then no one else will."

"Wait," Raihn halted. "That's what you mean to accomplish?" he said, drowned by a growing fervor. ...*To use a key.* His heart palpitated.

"Maybe that's a good thing, brother," Herb replied, his voice tempered with caution. "But count my hopes dashed by all this risk. I desire the same knowledge, but I understand the cost. Besides, the branch has forsaken her—it's forsaken us all."

Hodge sputtered. "We won't get far with our faces nailed on fliers in every city." The group fell silent, invigorating him more. "I've invested my life in this and can't so easily pluck out those weeds. I'll go, even if it kills me," he said finally, with a childlike determination.

Raihn stepped forward, intending to speak, but Herb raised a dismissive hand. "What about me, Hodge?"

"What about you, Herb?" Hodge snapped. His brother appeared wounded, but Hodge pressed on. "Why can't you just back me up on this?"

"I share your dream, but I'm not blinded by it… I'm a scholar, Hodge, not a gambler. And I won't let you roll a set of loaded dice against our favor. I don't want to see you dead over a dream."

"You don't have to let me do anything," Hodge argued. "Dreams are for those who sleep on their wonder, but I, a scholar, learn. I research."

Herb shook his head and sniggered. "A 'scholar'?" That word hung in the air as Herb seemed to reconsider it. "Are we scholars anymore?"

"Let's hold on," Magnus interjected. "We can't lose sight of what's important, and that's trust and loyalty to each other."

"And what quest is not treacherous?" Lostar spoke, his voice cutting through the tension.

Magnus, surprised by their inclusion, briefly acknowledged their presence. "Yes! What quest is without danger?" he repeated. "We have a group, each member with their own skills. We can do this, but only if we stick together. I need—no, we need—our scholars."

"I am not a scholar. I'm a contract killer," Xander reminded them, his voice cold.

"One who failed at that," Hodge commented, unable to resist.

"Don't make me change my mind," Xander threatened, his eyes narrowing.

"We're all here for one reason," Magnus reminded. "Some just have more urgency than others."

"I'm only here to repay my debt," Xander grumbled, crossing his arms.

"If that's the sole reason you came, then I expect it to be paid in full," Magnus replied sternly, his gaze locking onto the mercenary.

"How about you ensure all your 'friends' are square," he remarked, his tone brimming with accusation.

"Enough! Your paranoia is showing more than your scalp," Magnus snapped.

Tepparna reached a boiling point. "Shut up! I once held hands with our future. It has forsaken me for true, but not all of us. If you'd cease the squabble, you'd learn Raihn has the same symptoms as I did," she explained, her enthusiasm fizzling as though disheartened. "...It reaches for him. Raihn."

"Then hope is not lost after all," Hodge said smugly defiant as he side-eyed Xander.

"I would agree. Right, Xander?" Magnus pressed the merc.

Reluctantly, Xander answered through gritted teeth, "I suppose not." Looking at Raihn, he asked, "Where is it then, eh, boy?"

All eyes fell upon him.

Tepparna impatiently assisted. "You've felt it, right? That...tingle. Did it point you anywhere?"

Point me anywhere? He held up his right hand, and that 'tingle' returned, guiding him. He pointed, the tingle a light fuzz until the sensation slithered to the tip of his pointer, ringing west. "There," he guided, pointing outside Cobblestone. "Home. The manor... No," he aired. "This is crazy. You're all nuts. I did not sign myself to this contract."

"We know," Magnus agreed, "but the hand has. Will you indulge our madness?"

Raihn sighed, feeling his back against a wall. "What if the dame got it first? And, I mean," he stammered, "how can I trust that you're not all looking out for your hides?"

"Hides?" Magnus repeated. A scoff slipped out of his lips. His eyes appeared pensive, his mouth agape before a breath could escape it. "A man of great wealth risks losing everything in their hunt for more," he mused. "For those cornered, such as ourselves, don't dream of their fortune. We fight for it. Like...keen foxes."

"Well, foxes are opportunistic," Raihn remarked.

Magnus's persistence dusted away the comment. "Together, we can achieve what none of us could alone," he said. "We go not as beggars or highwaymen, but as foxes drawn from their holes, baring our fangs at our hunters," he said finally, his smirk made of self-approval.

Herb shrugged and gave props—a minor strut for Magnus's rally. "But his question stands, even if on paws."

Tepparna sighed. "Idiots," she called them before turning to Raihn. "Do you know where it might lie?"

"Maybe," he answered, hung up on the 'hunters' part. "I have a hunch that I'll be able to find it when I near it," he said, looking at his finger.

"You will," she assured.

A fox. *Yeah, right,* he thought, feeling cornered like a mouse.

"But if we follow this boy, keep in mind he comes from a manor," said Xander. It was a rather cheeky way of saying he was no fighter but a "soft-handed ninny."

Raihn wasn't oblivious to their remarks. However, minding the uncouth mouth, Raihn did appreciate Magnus's rally. Still, his gaze wavered away, and Tepparna seemed to regard it unkindly.

Returning to the northern tree line from where Magnus and the others had come, they returned to their tied horses.

"Okay, Raihn," Magnus began, "you should have something to defend yourself with. I believe a short broadsword should suffice," he said, removing a short blade from the horse's pack. Unsheathing it, he played with its weight and continued. "It's not too heavy, so your swings won't pull you off your feet. Give it a try."

Raihn took it, finding his footing and giving it a swing. Magnus swerved away. "It feels good," Raihn said. A smile came across his face as he handled the blade, albeit stiffly. The others also took a cautious step back.

"Well-swung and a good fit," Magnus cheered. "Familiarize yourself. Practice. Loosen up your wrists, but keep them firm. Think where it is you intend to strike. Plant your feet. Hold your ground... You'll be a master soon enough."

"You sure I'll need it?" Raihn asked. "I mean, it's not like I'm riding into battle or aught."

"Equal responsibility," Magnus asserted. "You must also bear your fangs, son of Rahim." His smirk inflated once again.

But that's exactly what Raihn feared, just as resilient as he was to be a lord. He was neither lord nor a fighter.

"There be one entrance to the mountain," said Xander, "squirrelly as it may be. Your best bet is we'll face steel. When that time comes, you best find us the Stayed Hand and scram," he said, his voice taking a turn. "I don't want no boy swingin' blindly." Xander looked at Magnus, lowering his voice. "He'll just cut us down."

Magnus pursed his lips and clenched two whitened knuckles, visibly frustrated by the grotty, loose-lipped offender. "Pay him no mind," he said to Raihn. "He's a mercenary. Killing is his trade. But you, Raihn, you have the promise to be a good man."

Raihn felt a tinge of admiration that was swiped as Tepparna smacked the saddlebags she'd been rooting through closed. Something was obviously, and doggishly, chewing at her bones, and her ear looked keen from its bend… Still, the comparison to little beasts pestered his head.

Magnus briefly regarded her and then looked back at Raihn with some kind of a glow of realization. "Maybe you should just snarl and keep the fangs to us," he shrugged. "After all, what good man can be called a killer, eh? Don't want you losing that grace of yours."

"You can't always find a way around a blade," Lostar disagreed. "No matter the swiftness of your feet, and no matter the shield, you must know that one of those blows will eventually land upon you. Staking one's companions to act as a shield is foolish, for that shield might split, and they might be gone from your protection. Fasten your bravery."

Magnus twisted around. "And who are you again?"

"Lostar," Raihn answered for them. "He comes from Endura. He's with me."

Magnus's frown flipped. "Well, any friend of Raihn's is a friend of mine."

Lostar did not budge a grin.

"Right, well," Magnus began, turning back to Raihn, "sheath it and strap it on. Consider it a token of goodwill. Use it if absolutely needed, but mind your good graces…" Magnus bent closer. "Don't make me regret it, hm?" he whispered, patting Raihn's back while holding eye contact with the Enduran.

"I won't," Raihn assured, feeling further roped in than he intended to be.

He returned the sword into the snug scabbard and fastened it across his waist. "I have a question," he said. "My father, was he going to the mountain as well? I mean, was he going to leave?"

"Asking the tough questions," Magnus grinned, seemingly by force. "He'd mentioned something very important lay there—something that he would rather come across himself—something that would have thrilled you. Do you know what that might be?"

"So that's a yes," Raihn gleaned, promptly yet evasively.

Magnus pursed his lips. "Yes. Perhaps you can ask him about it yourself, then. We'll find him," he assured, patting Raihn's back again. "He just…thought it would be best to tell you in a comforting place."

Lostar stepped forward with crossed arms, interrogating Magnus. "Raihn's father owed you this, what, a favor?"

"If you refer to the Stayed Hand, that's right," Magnus replied as he checked his horse. "Would have been best to trade under the table at the tavern, though. He was a bit more peculiar about being there."

"What do you mean?" Raihn inquired, his brows tight.

"I mean, it wasn't just for you. He was a cautious fellow; he wouldn't bring the branch to the mountain. Instead, he demanded to meet first and make sure all was square. Then, if it were a tight knot he could trust to hold, he'd take me to where he hid it. All the while we would instruct you to remain at the tavern. He deemed this to be the safest route."

"And look how that all turned out," Xander remarked, drawing a frosty glare from Magnus.

Lostar leaned to Raihn. "Watch out," he breathed. "He seems to be a man who holds you to your debt. Maybe return that sword when we're through with this."

"Don't be silly," Raihn said. "It's a gift. Like you said, a shield might split."

After checking the harness, Magnus abruptly exclaimed, "Alright! Shall we be off?"

"Not so hastily," said Hodge. "I can't take another step without something to eat."

"I'm feeling rather peckish myself," Herb agreed. "What have you in that satchel of yours, Raihn?"

"Just his brother's journal," Tepparna cut in. "Nothing we can eat but dry old goat skin. I was hoping you had some food."

Xander quipped, "Well, if you can round up some food, let me know."

"I have four sticks of dried pork," said Hodge.

"I have a fork with nothing to stick," Herb whined.

Xander scoffed. "What have you, Magnus?"

"Empty pockets."

"Right," Xander scoffed again. "I have salt, but nothing to be salted."

"And my dried pork has had enough of that," Hodge stated.

"I have something," Raihn said at last. "And it can use that salt of yours…" It was that great big beast south of them, still dead on its side.

"Okay, let's say there is such a beast. Who would collect it? Who will cook? Who will prep?" Hodge questioned.

"Oh, brother, these matters infest your predictable mind? Your belly's insatiable pursuit is stronger than your exuberance, yet you choose work to fret over?"

Raihn quickly intervened, recognizing Hodge's hurt, and emphasized the importance of planning. Lostar supported this sentiment. Hodge suggested sending the strongest to retrieve the hog, Lostar, Xander, and Amarra, while others prepared a fire, but Magnus challenged the idea: "I can't deem it wise to part the strongest from the—well, pardon me for saying this, but weakest."

"Then what do you recommend?"

"I, along with Amarra and Lostar, should do it. They know the way, and I know she can handle some weight. Xander can provide the rest of you with some protection."

"Great," the grizzled merc grumbled. Even the two ginger brothers seemed dejected.

"No gripes," said Magnus. "Remember, you all listen to me, and I listen to Tepparna. So," he started as he turned to her, "what say you?"

"It's adequate," she agreed, though reluctantly, hardly included. "I'll see you guys soon enough." Her eyes lingering on Amarra, she seemed to mourn their inevitable departure.

"Alright," Raihn began. "Who knows how to—"

"I know how to start a fire," Tepparna interrupted sharply, "but I'll need wood, some string, and tinder."

"Or Hodge's tinderbox," Herb said.

"…That works too," Tepparna said, looking disappointed.

"You best believe I wouldn't depart without it," Hodge grinned.

Xander prodded Tepparna. "I'm surprised you even know how to start a fire."

"It's been long since the Eldhonans suppressed my self-reliance, but my skills are still intact."

"Is that so? Ye know, I wonder… Did you fill Raihn in?"

"Raihn!" Hodge began abruptly, searching for something to say to him. It seemed there was something unsaid that Raihn should hear—or so he thought.

"Oh, quit!" Xander blurted. "Tepparna is an Endolander from far east, and here she is in Eldhona as a fugitive with an Outcast from north of here. Peculiar, innit?"

"Of course she's wanted," said Herb. "She took what they consider property of their domain. That is all."

"Quit pussyfootin'. You're both scholars. Surely you can put two and two together."

"Xander!" Herb barked. "That is quite enough."

Xander relented, but a faint grin on his mug suggested his enjoyment in stirring trouble.

Flickering, the heat gyrated like a sultry belly dancer along ten pupils. There was still tension between the brothers, and Raihn felt a thicker heat radiate from Tepparna.

Finally, through the awkward disquiet, Xander grunted. "I have to piss."

"As do I," Hodge said, jumping to his feet.

"Ye big baby, waitin' to not go it alone. Come then."

Herb slapped his thighs and rose. "May as well."

Raihn and Tepparna remained. His lip quivered before he broke free of his timid bind. "So, I'm pretty sure you're not okay, but I'll feign ignorance. Are you okay?"

"Aren't you unconventional?" she scoffed. "To answer your question, none of us are okay. But me specifically? No, Raihn, I'm not. But I'll feign ignorance just as well."

"Is it me?" he asked, leaning closer to the fire.

"Do you care, truly, to ask me this? Or do you inquire from the burden of guilt?" He was too stunned by her directness to answer. "Don't worry about it. I already dislike everyone else. I don't deliberately dislike you, but," she paused, searching for the correct verbiage. "It's just not fair. I'm trying to catch a break. I was more than willing to commit to the task, but here you are. You didn't ask for this, I know, but have some guts! You selfish Eldhonans," she insulted before cutting herself off. Perhaps too much verbiage.

"The branch has forsaken me. I am hopeless without it and discolored like it," she continued, forlorn. "I'm nobody once again. And with Magnus and his rallied allies, they heed his word. I'm just here without recognition."

"Is that really what you want?" Raihn asked.

"What I want is to matter again," she corrected, hugging her knees. "To be respected. And to be selfish just this once. Because I'm taken piece by piece as time wanes."

"Well, you matter to Amarra, right? Besides, why would you want Xander's respect, anyhow?"

Tepparna laughed, expression souring. "…My goals weren't dissimilar to yours, you know. I often seem in search of those that aren't beside me. But the wickedness about unspun my grace and my self-reliance burned my spool. My kindness seems to smoke eternally from the wick, and I go without reignition. You seem alight, though I feel you will not tend that light long. I see hints within you, beyond your kind shell. Might you succumb to a similar fate and burn us all. The thought challenges my trust in you, but may that just be my own guilt, my own prejudice, my burden."

Raihn couldn't help but reflect. Still intending to ask for clarification, Hodge returned with the others from relieving themselves.

"Much better!" they exclaimed. "And look at that ham!"

What ham?

"Well, I'll be," Herb gasped. "Raihn spoke true."

What are they talking about?

Raihn twisted around. The Outcast appeared with a leg hanging over her shoulder like a club. The gatherers returned.

"Enough dallying! Skin it and spit it!" Hodge cried. "Whether Hulls, Authoritarians, or even Anvils lie in wait, let them! I'm famished!"

'Twas fine meat, still unspoiled. Amarra was perhaps the loudest among the feast. Hodge seemed to enjoy her gust and regarded her as a feasting competitor. Herb sat and ate uninspired, contentedly dining with the fork he carried.

After reducing the leg to a fine bone club, the two competitors nestled against a nearby tree.

"Magnus, you suppose we let our food digest with a brief nap?" Hodge asked.

"Keep up the laziness, and he'll leave us, brother," said Herb.

Hodge continued. "It would be no good getting a cramp amid battle, right, Tepparna?"

"Fine with me," she said flatly.

Magnus looked to disagree. "Well, we should keep to the dark," he said, but then he glimpsed all their faces and reconsidered. "Herb, Hodge, Xander, you have blankets, right?"

"Herb and I have ours and carry one extra."

"Xander?"

"Just for myself."

"That makes four, between eight, or seven of us rather, and Tepparna should have one. We also need a lookout, but this will be a brief reprieve."

Hodge fluttered. "A game of grass, fire, water, then! Loser keeps watch and forgoes the blanket."

"No chance, you cheat!" his brother exclaimed just like before.

"Do not! My wrists ache and are made slow—Rheumatism!"

"Then someone take my blanket," Xander grumbled. "Nobody'll sleep safe with you on watch, petulant scholar. I have a cloak anyway."

"Good on you," Hodge said, elated, disregarding the insult.

"Whatever, just take my blanket and fight among yourselves."

"I'm not so tired," Magnus yawned. "I'll take watch instead."

Herb looked concerned and proposed there be two watchers in case one were to fall asleep. Xander looked to speak up again, but Herb put his fist out to Hodge. "By a game of grass, fire, water, it shall be decided between us."

Raihn pondered Herb's choice, considering he'd just called Hodge a cheat, but Hodge accepted, and they threw down hand signs, picking elements. Hodge won after a stutter and began to play the next round, but Herb bailed.

"It's alright," Herb said, looking troubled. "You won. Water extinguishes fire. You can keep your blanket, and I offer my own to whoever wants it."

CHAPTER TWELVE

The dream of a one-winged mourning dove

"Benjin?" Raihn said. "Benjin!"

"That's my name," the taverner responded, slamming down a pewter tankard.

"I thought I'd never see you again!"

"Then here, drink up," he encouraged, scooting the ale. "Maybe you'll see two of me and be twice as cheerful. Not too much, though. I don't want to be the one to clean the mess."

"Marnie too!?" Raihn exclaimed, for she was there as well, serving patrons.

"Should I wrangle up Tassy so that you can say her name as well? Repeatedly, perhaps," Benjin teased.

Raihn swiveled and saw many drinkers, blowhards, adulterers, and fraudsters here in the tavern, unburnt and livelier than ever. There were also some agreeable ladies and honest men from his village. Regardless of background and status, they all joined in this hole to laugh and sing hurdy-gurdy tunes, a croaky chorus under well-oiled fingers. Drinks spilled and swayed to the rhythm, and Marnie lived it beside them.

Amid all the ruckus and jolly joes, Raihn twiddled his thumbs and returned his gaze to his friend behind the bar, his smile dropping. He knew the truth and recalled he'd rolled over on the dirt for another nap. "Benjin…"

"Raihn?" Benjin mocked. "See how annoying that is?"

"Dammit, I'm just trying to level with you. That's not a simple thing when you are being, well, yourself! I need you to shut up and listen."

Benjin, taking a hint, leaned in.

"Is any of this real?" Raihn continued. "Be straight."

"Have I ever been anything else but that?" Benjin laughed. "Yeah, it's real," he confirmed. "Or so I'd hope."

"I bet you hope. It's elbow to elbow in here, Benjin. But maybe I should rephrase myself. Is this truly you? The last I saw you…"

"Would you like me to ask the girls to pinch you to ensure you aren't dreaming?"

"Look," Raihn sighed, persevering their jest, "while I can say it, thank you, Benjin. For everything. This was a good place for me when all seemed bleak."

Benjin spit-shined the counter and ignored Raihn. Frustrated, Raihn went on, demanding their attention. "Benjin, I'm spilling my guts here."

"So am I!" Benjin grinned.

"Come again?" asked Raihn, rather confused.

"What?"

"What?" Raihn echoed.

"Drink up. On the house. Can't let it go to waste, scamp."

Raihn looked at them queerly. They seemed off and dense, but Raihn obliged. "Here's to your popularity tonight," he said with a swig. A strange consistency coated his tongue. "Thick," he said, poking his eye over the tankard. Raihn sloshed the drink. "What is it?"

"House specialty," Benjin chortled, muscling his cloth over the counter.

"No head to it this time." There was a bitter aftertaste that curled his toes. The drink looked dark. He scrutinized it. Benjin droned. The music crawled. There was a voice in the crowd, a familiar one. Raihn glanced about and studied those who lurked and spotted Will. *Him too? Why?* "What's Will doing here, Benjin?" Raihn asked.

"To drink and fuck like the rest of us," Benjin answered. "For some of us, that's all we got. We drink to forget, and when we forget to drink, we take up our tankards as fast we can. So, wouldn't you like to forget…what you've done?"

"What are you talking about, Benjin?"

From the crowd, a voice blared. "Yer why I've been pickin' away in the mines." The tune stopped. All the patrons looked Raihn's way, their eyes bitter and sharp. "Yer why, and your father's why I've been bound here, and my father, and his father too. My blood be lesser than yours it seems, all clotted up, but yer blood is why mine dried up. The blood of a coward runnin' through ye. And only now, I see the flicker in yer eye. You lookin' to flee an' leave me—us. 'Ere. Come ball up them fists again."

This was no refuge and no sweet dream. Raihn had enough. "You're all dead! Him over there? Dead. Oh, and him? Yeah, dead. That guy? Well, I don't know him, but probably! And him too," he said. "But it wasn't my doing! I'd no idea this would happen!"

Will pushed patrons aside and fought toward Raihn with a furrowed brow.

"Shit," Raihn cursed. He excused himself, realizing he couldn't just wake up. He pinched. The pain was real. "Shit," he cursed again.

Raihn bumped into Mrs. Acker, her clothing green-stained.

The woman put her hands on him, reaching low, her gloves getting caught on his fabric. "We're just pullin' your weed, son."

Raihn pushed her down, her body bursting into ash. He froze, noticing all the fowl looks he was getting, his hand trembling.

Will was near. Raihn dashed, panicking, and shoved patrons. "Pardon me. Excuse me," he said, bumping and smacking into them as the air became staler and quieter.

Bursting through smoke clouds from pipe smokers, Raihn coughed and wheezed. It felt almost malicious to suffer through such a hostile disquiet; they sneered through the haze. Their eyes were suffocating and their snarls shiver-sending. He collided with them again and again. They spat indiscriminately into a spittoon of copper, and within the pool of black, Raihn saw drowning feathers flapping. It was a little bird that was struggling to escape their spit. He stepped back to avoid these churls, failed, and bumped into another. "Sorry!" he said to the smith, who clenched a hammer in their hand. "It's not real. Not real," Raihn reminded himself. *It's a bad dream, a very vivid, lucid, ever-realistic bad dream.*

"Let me show you how real I am!" Will threatened, lashing the patrons away in pursuit of Raihn, who was trying to squeeze his way out toward the door.

"Think you can run away?" growled one man in a surly voice.

"And leave our village in ash?" spat another.

"To think, the irresponsible heir of Rahim still hasn't the backbone to put mine at rest. Aye, a wallop I should give ye, indolent child."

"I bet 'e still wets the sheets," another jeered.

"His mother wipes his ass too, I'd wager."

"Why should he be the one to live?" a nursing mother hissed.

"I'm sorry!" Raihn cried out, but they cared not, grabbing at his garb and spewing insults.

"Sloth-of-a-son that brought fire!"

Raihn shoved them, watching in horror as their crumbling bodies scattered across the floor like burned tobacco.

"No, I didn't mean to!" he gasped, running frantically through the meaty maze with no door in sight. The only way was up—the stairs. He broke for them, shoving the men dogging his heels. Raihn passed the bar and saw something out of the corner of his eye. He regretted his pause from curiosity, for what he saw behind the bar was the house specialty: a minced brew of spilled blood from Benjin's cut belly.

Benjin poured another for him, raising it. "Drink up, Young Lord."

A dry heave seized Raihn and sent him tumbling into a woman coming down the stairs, Tassy. She twirled his hair between her fingers and pulled him in, burying his face into her pillowy chest. "Where's the hurry?" she asked. "Still holding out on me? I know you're spry in the britches, just itching to let go for the first time."

Her violation suffocated Raihn, his ears cupped within her bosom. He pried himself away from her ashy stench, looking directly into her jade-turned eyes. She leaned for a kiss, but he took her by the hair just as well and whipped her away. Still clenching her blonde strands ripped from her scalp, he stood aghast, watching her tumble. "I didn't mean to…"

The temperature seemed to rise, and the diamond-shaped bars along the window looked to glow red-hot by the booths. Raihn fled up the stairs and then looked back down them. The foot of the stairs seemed to hold the raging pool of flesh at bay as they all, including Will, formed a wall of malevolent gleams, Will and Tassy with eyes of jade.

Raihn found the corridor, where all the wood seemed to pale. The layout mirrored the eldhorium at the manor. With all the doors closed ahead of him, a footprint trail led to River's quarters just like he saw in the manor. Once at the door, he heard voices from the other side. Lending his ear, he identified Rahim's voice. *They're his footprints,* Raihn pieced together, but what of the other pair?

Reaching for the knob, he felt the heat around it and halted. Raihn desperately tried to break the door down, kicking it with all his strength. Its hinges repelled him time and time again. Though there was a keyhole, at the least, he may peer inside. He sank to it. As if he were someone else looking in, he saw himself sitting before the manor, speaking to his father.

"Can't really say I feel much grace sitting above a village of our laborers, though."

"They understand why we have this hill, and you know well enough, too," said Rahim. "We don't look down at them, we look over them. And without them, I wouldn't be here—we wouldn't be here."

"Is that why you will not grant the serfs freedom? Because we need them?"

Rahim leaned. "If you are so concerned for them, then be a man, Muna Raihn… Then you can inherit the land and liberate them yourself."

"Why? That's not what you would want."

"I want you to take what is rightfully yours! Because when I am dug into the soil, they will look up from the foot of the hill and wonder who will lead them. Those who toil offer me their grain and their eggs, as Amos intended. For us to prosper, dammit. His dream was to secure his kin a good life."

"To prosper in a tarnished plot? Withering lands under the shadow of a mountain?"

"Do you fear it?" his father asked.

"Of course," Raihn answered against the door. I'm afraid." He wept, trembling. His father's voice triggered his bottled emotions to flood. And then he heard not a memory. It broke him as it seemed directed at him through the door.

"Be brave."

CHAPTER THIRTEEN
Visions

Raihn woke to Amarra hovering over him, her hair backlit under Barynn's light. Concern bunched her cheeks to her eyes as she gripped his arm too harshly.

He masked the pain. "I must have been tossing in my sleep," he murmured, then whispered, "I'm okay." He assured her quietly, aware that the others still slumber. "Just another nightmare. Nothing more," he lied.

Her eyes drifted downward, and he became acutely aware of his induced stress, quickly whipping his cloak closed. But there, against his hip, lay his satchel, slightly open with his journal poking out. She reached for it, curiosity piqued.

"No!" Raihn exclaimed, fear surging as he snatched the journal from her grasp. Her eyes glossed over delicately, showing a hint of hurt. "It's okay. I'm sorry," he said, softening. "It's just… It's all I have left of my brother. He was curious. Like you."

Amarra retrieved her chart and spelled out her question, tilting her head. *What happened?* Raihn read. "He left home."

Raihn delved into the pages of the journal again, half awake, but then his eyes shot open from a sudden revelation: another page had been torn out— one he'd not yet read. "How could this be? I never let it out of my sight!"

A twig snapped in the trees. His back twisted into a knot, and he feared there were unwanted watchers, but it was just Magnus returning, who shushed Raihn before sneaking to Xander, kicking their muddy boot. Xander stirred and switched sides. Magnus scowled and kicked a second time. Harder.

"What?" Xander whined. Magnus raised a finger to his lips and pointed to the dark of the trees. Suddenly, the bushes twitched before a fading clang.

Terror befell Tepparna as she was jolted awake from the excitement, throwing aside her blanket. She shot up and rubbed her eyes. "What's going on?"

"We'll find Herb! You find the branch!" Magnus ordered, darting to the trees with Xander as though in chase.

Raihn glanced over to see Tepparna staring into the darkness, momentarily lost in thought. She then turned to look at him, Amarra by his side. She was dismayed. A lonely look came over her.

"Well, then!" Hodge burst out. "What are we waiting for?"

Raihn found Hodge's optimism somewhat strange, but he took comfort in the assurance that Herb was in good hands. He turned back to Tepparna, who seemed steeled. Now wasn't the time to address it, and thanks to his dream, he pieced together where the hand lay. "We must go to the manor."

She agreed, likely feeling the same. "We have four horses. Let's use them for speed. It's best to get there and back as quickly as possible to regroup."

"What about Amarra?" Raihn asked. "She's a bit big for a horse, and there are five of us."

"Right," Tepparna said. "I don't suppose you've seen an Outcast run freely before."

Raihn, along with Lostar, Hodge, Tepparna, and Amarra, crossed buckled crucks and dead cattle through the ramshackle town and the ashy village. A steep incline ahead led to the manor and its smoky hill of bare dirt. The manor wheezed as the wind blew through the gashes of crooked oak.

"Be glad of it," said Hodge. "A house made not of stick and straw."

"I'm not so sure. Even sturdy oak could break apart and bury me with ease from perhaps one good wind," said Raihn. "It should have been made of stone."

"Let it be me to enter," Tepparna said. "I'm the smallest."

"I agree, you're the smallest, but it is my home," Raihn asserted. "I also have a hunch I know where the branch is lying."

"That hunch could get you killed!"

"So be it," Raihn said. "This whole damned village and town would rest easy."

"Now don't go risking your life over some survivor's guilt," Hodge said, but Raihn pressed forward.

Through the charred threshold, Raihn stepped onto brittle wood. The building was soggy and dripping from the storm. Mushy gobs of gray puddled at his feet, and if that was the state of the first floor, he feared what the eldhorium held in store. "Here it goes," he said, a sensation guiding him there.

One foot before the other, Raihn minded his step as he reached the stairs, feeling that itching presence up there—his hunch thus far seeming right. *It's still here,* he thought. They slanted and buckled under his careful tread.

At the top, a long corridor lay before him, blackened and gashed. He pressed his hand to the sooty wall, mindful of its stability. The door to his brother's chamber was off its hinges, lying flat against the ruined floor. Just around the corner of the frame, he could see a reinforced haven, the most supported chamber in the manor, but the ceiling was waterlogged and dripping, perfectly awful.

Holding a deep breath, he shuffled along the brittle floor until he heard scratching, just like he heard it last time he treaded here, the same as he heard it at the edge of the trees. Some boards were still solid enough, and from beneath one, he heard the sound persist. He stepped forward, and the scratching felt like an itch beneath his foot as the board chilled his heel with a slight vibration.

It was no mouse, his finger tingling as it pointed down. Stepping back, he saw a thin gap in the floor and knelt to investigate. He pried it open and saw a ghastly sight—a small 'coffin' with a decrepit, severed hand bereft of pigment. And as he peered at the hand, it cricked its fingers, sprouting vines and shooting them over the back of his hand. There was no time to escape it. He fell back in terror. The boards slumped, and his gut shivered, foretelling the collapse.

There was a faint darkness as the stars faded and gave way to the dawn. Flickering light and waving shadows danced around him, and a feminine cry echoed down the dark space. Light beamed on a spiraling staircase of sandstone that led to the deep cavern he was in. Then, a chamber flickered alight to his side, and a tapestry embroidered with a pale tree gazed from it. He hardly looked at it when the above entrance was eclipsed. Darkness suffocated him, and the wind's faintest whispers hushed.

Clops of oncoming guests descended from there, one stranger's jade eyes the only visible feature. The cavern collapsed beneath roaring cackles, but something shimmered in the distance: a tree appeared, white like the one embroidered. Its branches swung out and hung down like long tassels. It was a weeping willow, pale as Amarra. But then it blackened, flaming like a torch, oiled and lit. Hope fled his heart, and he became terrified. Then, there was a break in the insanity as the fire died out, and he became smothered by rock.

Particles from the sanded stone were huffed, indenting his mind, striking fear and temptation; images pounded his anvil, sparking more and more fear, his chest overcome by this weight until there came an ease. Boulders lifted from the rubble, and Raihn felt sausage-like fingers pull upon him. He escaped the collapsed manor and the plight of the dream. He saw his companions standing before him, their hands sooty. Raihn sighed. A wild dream had overtaken him once again.

"Glad to see you're not dead," Lostar said with some levity, but his smile faded, replaced by concern. "Raihn, look at your hand."

Raihn's hand interlocked fingers with one that was severed. Thankfully, the hand did not bleed nor show bone, merely a branch. "I suppose that wasn't a part of that ghastly dream," Raihn groaned.

"Not a dream," Tepparna corrected.

"Yes, it is," Hodge disagreed.

Raihn stood and immediately fell, breaking their disorder. Amarra caught him. "My ankle," he squeaked.

Upon closer inspection, Hodge declared, "It's not broken," to their relief, "but it is sprained, and we have no horse to ease the pressure as they were spooked upon the collapse."

"It's okay," said Tepparna. "We'll get back either way."

Amarra hoisted the injured Raihn once more, then draped him over her back, still warm from blood, like a cape. It reminded him she had braved a wound earlier.

"I can walk," he lied, but she gripped his forearms and let out a titter.

"Splendid," Hodge rejoiced, happier had this hand made him. "Hope is not lost after all. We have our new host!"

"Yet you don't believe in visions or sorcery," Tepparna snickered.

"Wait," Raihn halted. "You knew about this and didn't warn me?" Raihn said. "I mean, I knew it was a branch, familiar like a hand, but... I was scared half to death as it latched on! I was nearly dead, resurrected by you folks because it startled me into the collapse!"

Hodge shrugged, seemingly about to comment on resurrection.

"Aht," Tepparna waved her finger. "Whatever it is, it will be with you by some sorcery... **Sorcery**," she repeated, her voice thick against Hodge, her pupils pointed.

"There is no such thing as sorcery," Hodge replied.

"How would you know? You said it yourself before. You know very little of it."

"Anything without understanding is magic in the sense of whimsical imagination, and it is my job to understand it... I just don't quite grasp it yet."

"What do you think, Lostar?" Raihn asked.

Lostar looked standoffish. Cold. "There once was something, but then there wasn't," he said, like a mystic. "I know nothing of it, and never will I—unless we find the answers ourselves, like Hodge said. And if any understood it before, they wouldn't anymore."

Hodge, despite not fully understanding by the look on his face, agreed, just happy to be there. "Let's move on! I can't wait to tell Herb!"

Raihn also struggled to make complete sense of it but shrugged it off all the same. "Yeah. Sure."

Briskly, Tepparna led them into the forest, with Hodge marching along, his stomps drumming. Lostar drew Truthseeker as they approached the trees. They pushed beyond their camp after finding it empty, heading deeper. Raihn's eyes struggled in the dark but eventually spotted a shape in the grass sprawled out: a body. It seemed the battle had erupted here, but the fallen wore neither armor nor leather, nor a surcoat, but dark overalls.

"There he is!" Hodge exclaimed. "What are you doing sleeping in a time like this, Herb? Wake up! Herb, come on! No time for a catnap," he said before kneeling and shoving him. Their body sloshed limply. "Get up. Raihn found it. We have it again. The hand! We can know what lies beyond the wall!" He yelled, begged, and pleaded, growing pink in the face. "Brother!"

Lostar stepped beside him and grabbed Herb by the shoulder before rolling him on his back. Hodge lost his breath as he looked at his brother's slashed throat. He trembled and clasped Herb, cradling them tenderly and tightly, perhaps to stop shaking.

After a moment, Hodge set Herb down and picked something loose from his brother's garb before dropping it into his pocket.

The same cruel fate may have claimed Magnus and Xander, so Raihn and the others scoured the area, searching for them, leaving a reluctant Hodge to mourn. Their eyes swept the surroundings, but there was no sign of their missing comrades. They regrouped in a clearing illuminated by Barynn's gentle glow, where Hodge arrived last, his face still flushed, but then something caught his attention. He knelt, his hand brushing the grass. The dew revealed faint wheel imprints that pressed the grass flat, leading away. "A wagon," Hodge stated. "It heads to the southern checkpoint just before the camp north at the Wall of Thorns."

"A camp?" Raihn questioned. "You'd think it'd be a more permanent fixture."

"You'd think right, but alas, the wall has… 'magic' in its vine." Hodge's eyes rolled. "The 'keyhole' seems to move away from them, or so I thought. It has yet to flee their lesser dwellings. But there's no reason to bring in more masons if the wall would only tease them further."

"Sounds magical to me… Wait. Are you certain it's still there?"

"If they'd taken up their bags and moved, I'd be concerned, but they have not," Hodge replied. "And there, they will likely take Xander and Magnus to their cells and hold them at the camp as hostages, but first, they'll check in at the checkpoint. From there, we can rescue them before it gets too cumbersome. They'll also have an armory, which will be most beneficial to us. We could use some weapons. I need something sharp," he said coldly. "You're well-accommodated, but Amarra has only hatchets."

"Tepparna should be armed as well," Lostar added.

"Should I?" she asked.

"If worse comes to worst and none of us is around to help you, you should be able to defend yourself," Lostar doubled down.

Hodge agreed. "As for you, Lostar, you're more than suited already. Just as much as we need weapons, we need sustenance. "We'll die of hunger if not by wound. Somewhere lays a store of food at the checkpoint, likely a cellar. If we are so lucky, I would find a sack of potatoes and maybe a bundle of carrots. Eldhos has yet to complete its cycle. We have the darkness to sneak about."

CHAPTER FOURTEEN
Bloody drunk

Well after midnight, the ragtag group hastened toward the checkpoint, their blazing hearts set on rescuing their companions. Raihn, being carried because of his inability to walk, pondered his role in the upcoming fray. Apart from wielding his modest sword, he felt as useful as a barber offering his services in a battlefield. Midway, Amarra froze with ears sprung.

"What is it?" Tepparna asked softly.

The Outcast remained alert, leering into the woods, stirring paranoia.

Raihn squinted over her shoulder, sensing something as well. The hairs upon his arms stiffened, and goosebumps erupted along his skin, possibly from trepidation about the deep dark.

She set him down, poking his forehead and pointing to where he sat, as if to say, "stay put," treating him like a wayward pup. She prowled off, her movements reminiscent of a lioness stalking through tall grass—or perhaps a bloodhound on the scent.

Pure darkness filled the mouth of the rock, exhaling a foul breath. Amarra ventured in past it and emerged moments later, dragging something Raihn struggled to make out at first glance, the smell worsening.

"A corpse!?" Tepparna exclaimed. "Who would have done this?"

"Or what? For all we know, it could be a wolf den," Hodge said grimly.

Amarra withdrew a second putrid shell, and Hodge began examining what might have caused their demise. Lostar stayed behind to safeguard Raihn, though Raihn couldn't help but worry when he noticed the tremor in Lostar's hands. He pondered it, his mind drifting over their recent chill demeanor.

Hodge returned with a perplexed expression.

"So, what did you discover?" Raihn asked.

"Two bodies of opposite sexes," Hodge began. "From what I could discern, the woman was…" He paused, choosing his words carefully. "Eaten. There wasn't much of her left. The man, however, had deep scratches on his body—his chest the focus."

"And what about their rings?" Raihn asked further.

Hodge's eyes narrowed.

"There was talk of missing villagers: a couple," Raihn continued. "The husband vanished, and the wife sought after him. It makes me wonder…"

"Then come get a gander at their gnarled fingers and tell me what they might tell you," Hodge instructed.

Raihn felt a surge of apprehension, but the expectant gazes of the others settled on him, urging him forward. Hodge and Amarra had already shown their bravery by venturing ahead. To ask someone else to retrieve the rings would strip him of any remaining dignity, especially with Tepparna's piercing glare fixed on him. He needed to prove himself and be as brave as at least a young harrier pup.

Raihn approached the corpses, pinching his nose against the overwhelming stench. The wooden palm knotted tight around his hand, as if from the dread. Kneeling on his good leg, he creaked, ignoring the squeeze as best he could.

He examined the fingers of the corpse, noting the maggots wriggling about their ring and through the mutilated flesh. He deciphered what he needed to before wondering what had happened here. Shielding his breath with the tail of his cloak, he leaned in closer, studying their features: sunken cheeks and torn ears. On the man's neck, he discovered two identical holes resembling bite marks that didn't look to be from any animal he knew. And though his nerves were already swimming, he thought to see their fingers spasm, though only from his peripherals. Blood iced still his veins. He gazed at their ring once more, awaiting its next jitter. His heart raced on edge. Nothing. He swiveled back to reexamine their face, thinking he might recognize them. His chest squeezed tight. Hands clenched. The corpse's head hovered, its fishy eyes trained on him.

Raihn yelped as he stumbled backward. The dead man was pulled up through a sluggish animation. Maggots spilled from their wounds and hollows. Raihn tried to call for help, but his voice was caught in his throat like a hook into a gill. He couldn't summon the strength to shout for Lostar, floundering a breath from fear.

The maggot-ridden man lurched toward Raihn. Motionless. Body torn and lifeless. They stood. It seemed conscious of Raihn, almost fixated. There was a greenish hue to their slick-made decomposition. Black snakes looked to slither beneath their frail, rotted rags of skin that slipped from eggy gashes. And as they reached out, Raihn clubbed the jagged ground with his elbows in retreat. His one heel peddled against the ground, but his other ankle panged. Meanwhile, the corpse, husk, whatever it was, seemed driven. And when it got too close, its fetid breath faintly bellowed between its resinous gums.

The corpse strung up a grin, pausing just inches away.

What. What is it?

Raihn crooked a brow in question, then glanced down after a strange grip overcame his thigh. Their hand. Then, an old air dusted from their chimneyed throat, their eyes glowing green. "You will be mine."

Raihn shuddered, cold as the breath from their sodden, sluggish lips.

The ghastly head suddenly flung from its shoulders, its ribbed chest hanging in a brief suspension, remembering to crumple to the side. Amarra knelt in place over the corpse, strategically avoiding the gore.

Raihn had to freeze and register what had just transpired. She had cleaved the corpse's skull with her rugged hatchet. It rolled just a foot away. Tarry trails oozed.

Amarra extended her hand. He took it, murmuring his thanks. As she helped him up, she patted him like a dusty carpet. Bugs flew from his clothes, and she nearly knocked the breath out of him with her vigorous slaps. Still, it was better than a smack across the face. But why did she care? Why'd she even think to dust him off?

"Where is Lostar?" he coughed, gasping for air. "Lostar!" he called again. "Where could he have gone?" Not so far, it seemed, as they'd come from around a tree.

"It was about that time all that drinking haunted me," Lostar said, drawing disgust. "What's going on?"

"Nothing," said Raihn dismissively. "You missed it. He's dead."

"Did he hurt you?" asked Lostar.

"No. Amarra came before he could do anything," he answered, still dismissive.

Lostar took a step back, his grimace portraying a slight offense.

"Did he attack you?" Tepparna asked, approaching with Hodge.

Raihn couldn't answer, and she took that for a "no."

"Then why did you kill him, Amarra?" she asked, turning her attention. "He could have been a survivor of some malicious animal attack."

"No way," Raihn denied... He was dead. There was no denying that."

"Then how can he be killed twice?" Tepparna asked.

Hodge seemed to ignore their bickering, searching for real answers. "There is skin beneath her nails," he said of the female victim. "Good chunks of it. And by the look of his shredded chest, I'd say it was obvious that he attacked her. Was he breathing?"

He did more than breathe; he spoke, but Raihn could hardly believe a man in that shape could be anything but dead. They seemed arisen, as if waking from the dead. And, too, Raihn wouldn't relay what it said. "No," he lied.

"Well, on the contrary, I believe he was, just very little. With the swampy skin, being mottled with those black forks beneath his skin, I'd say he's been ravaged by extreme hypoxia—a state of low oxygen, for his blood is dark. I believe he was lying here for some time, knocking on death's door... I'd just assume death was on a retreat..." Hodge rolled his shoulders into a shrug. "I wager the fool was gone from senses, stirred from being dragged out of that recess. If anything, he was put out of his misery, and justice has come for the lady in the cave."

"That's fine," said Raihn, disregarding the rather detached *word salad*. "But I can't imagine anyone from my village doing this. Not even the worst of them, especially to each other—them both being married and all."

"So, you've figured out who they are? How?" Hodge asked.

"I saw their rings of Parcel copper, engraved with a stalk of wheat. The Blacksmith made them, and my father officiated them."

A long night it had been, and longer would it be. The group was tired and hazy-eyed. Maybe that was why Lostar started stumbling.

The Outcast side-eyed her passenger, Raihn, to which he asked, "What is it?" She closed her eyes and mimicked a nap. "I can't. I mean, I can, but it wouldn't be fair. Not while you all walk on."

Amarra flicked his forehead and furrowed a brow of disapproval.

"Amarra... What if I have another nightmare?" Raihn asked.

Reaching into her sack and retrieving her board with a list of letters and common words, she spelled, 'Then when?'

"I guess you have a point," he sighed. "Fine, but if you sense that anything is wrong, please wake me. The faintest twitch or the softest sigh. Please," he pleaded, fearing what might creep into his slumber. She gave an enthusiastic thumbs up, beaming.

Tepparna peered over her shoulder, observing them.

"Wait!" Raihn woke in a start, eyes bulging. Sweat clambered down his brow. For a moment, he was dazed, appearing like a frightened hare, far from a dog, even a fox.

"Quiet, or you'll get us all caught!" Tepparna hissed, her anger as sharp as her glare.

Raihn shifted under her gaze, still shaking off the remnants of another nightmare. "Did we catch up to the wagon?"

"It's just up the trail, but the soldiers seem dead," Lostar replied, his voice unexpectedly loose. "It's strange."

"What do you think? Should we investigate?" Hodge asked.

Tepparna remained silent, and Hodge didn't offer further input. Amarra seemed ready to move, but before she acted, Lostar darted ahead, his steps unsteady, as though the flat ground was uneven. He passed two bodies lying in the dirt near the seemingly abandoned wagon. Soldiers. Likely the drivers. Lostar peered inside the wagon, gripping the hilt of Truthseeker.

Amarra grabbed Tepparna's hand, and they hurried after him. When they caught up, Raihn saw Lostar's sword pointed into the wagon, then at whom it was pointed: someone rummaging through a dead Authoritarian's pack.

"Who are you!?" Lostar demanded.

"Whoa, whoa, easy now!" The ratty man waved his hands, eyes wide. "The name's Pocket."

"Your real name," Lostar said, tone hardening.

"Mine name it is," he said with a flourish. "'Pocket' be what people call me."

Lostar jutted the tip of his sword toward the rat-like man's nose, menacingly close.

"Honestly, it is Ernest!" Pocket squeaked, his voice wriggling like a worm's.

Lostar scowled, his unsteady blade swaying slightly.

"I said it already. It's Ernest, honest!" Pocket repeated, sounding more desperate.

Lostar sneered. "What were you in the life before this one, a cardinal's fool?"

"A fool, yes, but not for any cardinal. What's it to thee?"

"A man is nothing without a name," Lostar stated.

"Pocket, I said twice, and twice again I said Ernest! That should say plenty about me. It says enough about you."

"It tells me you're a scrounger. But what I would like to hear from you is whether you found other prisoners aboard this wagon."

Upon that query, Raihn noticed open shackles lying about the space.

"Perhaps a drink will help loosen my chapped lips." Pocket smiled, spotting the flagon and smelling its potent reek on Lostar's breath by the tell of his wince.

Lostar pressed the tip of his blade into the scrounger's nose. Blood trickled out.

"Fine, I yield. I was picked up for scrounging is all, like you surmised. Then they picked up two others. They gave a good fight but were bested."

"Bested!?" Lostar shouted. "Explain."

"Look-look-look, they got shoved in here with me, alright? They ain't dead. I picked our locks, and they fared better the second fight and took off. Aye? I helped them, and I am willing to help you! Even after you poke me in the face with that glimmering blade. But they were a nice couple, those fellas."

"If that's true, then I suppose we should ease up, right, Lostar?" Tepparna asked.

Lostar lowered his blade, and the scrounger's eyes followed it. The sword wielder looked hesitant to trust wriggly snakes and didn't seem to like the sparkle in Ernest's eye. "Which way did they go?" he asked.

"Well, in the same direction you came. I was actually waiting for the lot of you to return," said the thief.

"And why is that?" Tepparna asked.

"As I said, I am no fool for a cardinal. I'm but a humble thief. If you have a bone to pick with the Authority, I'll pluck off the armor first. Upon the return of those I helped, you will find that it's all been agreed upon."

"You're a rat," Lostar lashed.

"Exactly. And a rat knows their way around rubbish. So, do we have a deal?" His hand reached out, but Lostar ignored it.

"Shake his hand," said Magnus, coming through the trees. "What's another ruffian in our company?"

"The end of our lives if he can't be trusted," Xander answered, following. Lostar agreed.

"Just because gods are barricaded from men with manmade palisades, does not mean we cannot have faith, Xander," Magnus retorted.

"Might it be why I falter. My belief needn't barricades, for I've none. But I'll go along with it," Xander said before directing his attention to Pocket. "But y'listen 'ere mouse. It ain't as easy to pull one over me like it is them," he warned with a pointed finger.

"Fear not for me. I know the way like my bladder knows piss and my kidney knows stones. I'll get you there, aye," said Pocket with a rotted grin.

During the regroup, Hodge appeared more anxious and dejected. Magnus and even Xander quieted as they seemed to recall they were down a man.

"Saddle up!" Xander exclaimed, breaking the silence.

"But there is only a wagon," said Pocket. "The horses sped free."

"That's not what he said," Magnus chimed. "What he said was to straighten your swords. Point them in the direction of these assholes that killed Herb, because we are going to shove them so far up their ass they'll go on limping with the crossguard against their taints. Isn't that right, Xander?"

"Ab-so-fucking-lutely, Magnus."

"Swell," said Hodge, shuddering. "And I have a plan."

After hearing out Hodge's plan, it was fortunate they had come across this thief. Hodge explained that they knew the checkpoint where the thief could be a swell ally.

Xander, unconvinced, spoke out. "Are you sure we should be trusting this 'ere rat, Magnus?"

"No," Magnus answered. "My trust runs thin anymore, but we need any advantage to get into this den."

"Then I hope you keep a tight leash on him. He already looks a dog's asshole, puckering his lips, whistlin' like a damned fool. He'll have us caught."

"And what about those weapons he looted off those corpses?" Raihn asked.

"We'll get our own, Raihn." Magnus steamed. "We just have to work together. And if we can't get along, then let's just shut up, aye?"

"Raihn, eh?" the thief echoed, catching his name and snubbing a wise Magnus. "What about his white nag?"

"What did I just say about the talking?" Magnus recapped with a swell in his tone.

"Her name is Amarra," Tepparna corrected, her fist clenched and ready to forgo her pacifism.

"Not a subject to be touched. Got it," said the rat.

Raihn held a feeling deep down in his gut that foretold this would be a pattern, that the rat would be a chatty one.

"Thief's proffered grief and stunted stumble heard a lopping offer for his hands come their mumble. Evince of name, and to Dame Dawness they grumbled. Reckoned now a free bird. It's all thanks to thine words," sang Pocket.

"Chain him, leave him. I don't care, just keep the cheeky cunt out of our hair," Xander mocked in a half-assed song.

"Quiet, both of you. I won't say it a second time," Magnus ordered.

"What would thou prefer, father or leader?" Pocket jested.

"I'm the initiator of this quest," Tepparna asserted. "And stop talking like that. It reminds me of my bloodless father. Furthermore, don't speak of yourself third-tongued."

"So, thee art flint. Mayhap Magnus be the flicker and spark?"

"Why must you echo the dialect of lords? You never steal a mirror to see your mangy self as lesser than them?"

"'Tis more fun to do as ye wish once knowing ye may, but hardly am I free to do more than wink lordship through my teeth… Don't you see? I can speak as I wish, no matter the hierarchy. And I can do as I wish so long as I look down the fork an' mind the rust of the prong."

Magnus sighed and asked, "Just how far along are we, Pocket?"

"Take a gander and see," said the thief, a shabby checkpoint coming over the next hill.

"It's just a pile of sticks," Raihn remarked.

"A dam built by beavers," Xander reiterated.

"It's not meant to be a castle," Pocket said. "The cardinal sleeps on the thought of any siege here, knowing all wynds protect it. No way a group of fanatics could take them down, let alone go unseen. Besides, they never know when to pack their bundles and move."

"Ain't nobody cutting down his tree, just his daisies," said Xander.

"You halfwit-fanatics mean to pick apart his dam and spring leaks," Pocket argued. "My eyes see it all."

"So, you side with the Authority?" Tepparna presumed. "Magnus, I'm not so sure about this."

"Endo backwash," the thief cursed. "Westward water."

Magnus snarled, snatching the thief's raggedy garb, pulling him close. "Any more remarks and it won't be your hands missing," he said. Dropping him, he continued, "And the river is the Annex of our people, which flows east, cardinal's fool."

"Fine." Pocket shrugged, dusting himself off. "I know where they're posted. I can get around them and lead you to the cellar, then our deal would have come to a swell conclusion. And by the way, I said 'backwash,' turd."

They snaked through the forest, their gazes sweeping the checkpoint keenly. The watchtower loomed tall at the far end of the road on their right. Nearby stood a stable, and beside it, an armory stood in formation. Across the road, opposite the armory, the barracks were perched. The cellar hatch was in the center of it all, exposed and vulnerable. It was adorned with a rusty handle and iron studs.

The Authority had commandeered crops from nearby farms, which were delivered to the checkpoint and rationed out by the cook. The root cellar served as a storage space, where barrels might be hidden, summer spuds nestled, and a vigilant cook might keep watch while guarding against hungry greenhorns—at least according to the thief.

"S'how y'know of this place anyhow?" Lostar slurred, staving the surrender of his tired eyes.

"I'm a thief. I get around," Pocket said sharply. "Now, look at the tower and see that it is lazy. Sleeping on duty, I presume. These men have gone unchallenged since the last harvest and been made tender like boiled eggs," he said.

Raihn's eyes narrowed, considering the validity. "What do you mean unchallenged? What happened last harvest?"

"Death. A bear, they said, from what I could hear."

But Raihn had never heard of a bear attack. "A bear? One bear?"

"Can't say I ever heard the term 'a pack of bear' before," Pocket snickered. "Or even a murder of bear—a school of bear—"

"Shut up about bears!" Magnus barked. "I want to hear about swords and carrots, not claws and death. And I want you to tell me more about these posts."

"A'right," Pocket sneered. "Two in the Armory, and one in front of the barracks," he said, leading them to the armory. Peering through the gaps of timber, he informed them the guards slept.

"Aye, real lucky," Xander remarked. "That one guard between the cellar and barracks and two more dozing here sure has us pissin' ourselves."

"Arrogance will have us dead," Pocket replied.

Hodge interrupted, "I must express some concerns. I don't deem it wise to carelessly lump ourselves down that cellar like fish in a barrel of oil or crowd ourselves in one shack."

Tepparna agreed. "Amarra and I shall wait here at the armory. She might be too big for the cellar."

"Along with Raihn and Lostar as well," Magnus added. "He can keep watch with a bow. First, you can rid us of that guard across the way," he said to the Enduran.

"If that is what you deem best," Pocket said doubtfully.

Raihn couldn't help but notice Tepparna's leadership get buried yet again, though he couldn't help but agree with Magnus, and neither could Lostar, who twitched, sniffled, and swung off his bow, taking action.

"Then it's settled," Magnus continued. "Hodge, Xander, Pocket, and I will go. The rest of you will stay here."

Lostar clumsily knocked an arrow, to which Raihn pondered his quaking anchor.

"Well?" asked Pocket, as the arrow wobbled in a long pull.

"Shut up!" Xander barked. "Let him find his aim. He can't miss this."

Lostar looked to be made nervous, but that in itself was strange. He was never nervous about meeting his mark—or so Raihn had thought, considering the last time. They breathed again. The arrow soared, punching the enemy's throat.

"That's for Herb, bastard." Xander quipped.

The sentiment did not quite resonate with Raihn, for it was just an old man armored by the king. Their plan was in motion nonetheless.

"The three of you should be enough to gather food a plenty," said the thief. "Meanwhile, the Enduran, the Outcast, and 'this one,' I guess, can collect the weaponry."

"What's that mean?" Raihn asked.

"You're an inconvenience—a backpack," Pocket explained, "and like one, you should carry food, not weap—" His voice choked when Amarra clenched his neck, lifting him so high that he couldn't find the ground with his flailing legs.

On the other end of her temper, Raihn fought a grin. But was her outburst for his sake or hers? He laid his hand gently on her arm, soothing her. She drew back her tunneled vision. The thief was let go, coughing and gasping. Raihn believed to have found the answer.

"Keep it down, you fool, lest you wake the guards," Xander callously reminded before praising Amarra. "Good arm."

Anguish replaced the fear on Pocket's face. He clasped his throat. "Can't believe I oblige an Outcast," he spat. "Follow me," he said to the others, his eyes lingering on her.

Pocket led one half of the group towards the cellar, nearing the felled guard. Raihn watched from the back corner of the armory. Magnus slithered, gawking contemplatively at the tower and the dead soldier. He seemed to have his guard up.

Raihn refocused. "We'd better hurry."

Tepparna agreed. "I'm sure they won't take long."

Lostar clasped the iron knob, but it resisted him—locked. Of course, it is. Looking at the small door, Raihn hopped down from the giantess's back and landed on his searing ankle. Surely, he could do something, but what? Couldn't break the knob or kick the door in even if he wanted to. Not without waking the guards or further injuring his foot. But just then, something small and dense beat against his scalp and tumbled to the dirt. A key. Confounded, he searched the sky, finding nothing. *Where did it come from?*

Lostar picked it up, fit it in the lock, and the door swung away. "What do you know," he said.

There were racks of assorted weapons—pikes, glaives, swords, bucklers, maces, and even ones that Lostar scoffed at, crossbows. There were also arm splints, padded tunics, stout visor sallet helmets, and kettle helms. Notably, there were also two young guards sitting at a table. The one on the right rested a hand over the splintered table with a knife stuck in it. "Who could go without chopping off a finger the longest?" Was clearly the start of this, but before either lost any blood, they drank themselves into a stupor.

Raihn entered with his companions to follow, Amarra ducking the doorframe. "They're young," Raihn pointed out before recalling he'd seen these two at The Mousehole.

Lostar unsheathed his sword.

"Wait, it's not right," Raihn said in a tense whisper. "They're just sleeping. It would be no better than what they did to Herb." The last man they'd murdered weighed on his mind enough.

"It must be done," Lostar stated.

"They won't stir if we remain quiet—" Raihn felt dismissed, Lostar ripping open the guard's throat with his blade. They woke in a start, gasping for only a moment.

"We shouldn't kill them," Tepparna agreed, though reluctantly.

The Enduran seemed to comply with their mercy-wishes, but then he'd looked her with a cold stare, his eye between dark strands, murky and glossy. "Kill the other one," he ordered. "You're here to either fight or die. This is the line you came to. They'd kill you or worse, had they the chance."

"Knock it off. If you want him dead, then just do it yourself," Raihn said.

"If I stand in the way of her training, she'll die," he slurred.

"What are you babbling about? What training?" asked Raihn. "We're not soldiers."

"Precisely. That boar would have her striped red in the forest if not for us. These two guards are no different than that boar. Amarra cannot watch her every move every second. Tepparna cannot rely on her protector."

"Then what about me? Do I need to train?" asked Raihn, whisper-yelling.

The Enduran reached for the dead man's tankard. He lifted the brim to his nostrils, cultivating a wheaty scent.

Raihn slapped the tankard out from their hand. The ale seeped into the dirt floor. "Don't you think you've had enough?"

"What are you accusing me of, huh?" asked Lostar.

"I don't know where you got it from, but don't take me for a fool who wouldn't notice how you've been acting. The way you stumble and slur. At some point tonight, you found what you were looking for, and it's jeopardizing this quest. You're worse than when we met," Raihn snapped.

"You think y'know what's best fer me, inheritor of Parcel?" Lostar slurred a mock, snatching Tepparna by the shoulder. "Don't you hate them after what they did to Parcel Village, the town? Remember Pohl."

"I can't," she said, resisting his provocation.

"You'll continue to lose control unless you fight, yet you refuse. Why?" asked Lostar, extending Truthseeker to her.

Tepparna trembled. "Because, Lostar, I cannot truly piece back what is broken. You're right… I hate them. I want them dead. I was once as sharp and shining as a sword fresh from the smithy. But now I'm shattered, abandoned, and adrift," she confessed, a tear tracing its path down her cheek. "Eldhonans are a brutal people, taking and destroying. I will never be whole because I've already fought back…taken lives. And that unearthed a certain joy from my tomb, filling me up again. That feeling is why I lost the Stayed Hand to begin with. I thought that if I pretended to change, I would win back its favor. I tried to hide my true self, hoping for approval from it. But I was wrong. I was a bloodstained sword in a sheath, gone of its grace by force."

"No," Raihn breathed from understanding her. His stomach deepened.

Her grip tightened around Truthseeker. "I won't deny who I am again." She lunged forward and plunged the blade deep into the sleeping guard, then paused, twisting it through his padding. She quivered, her shoulders shaking. Her elbows pulled back before she swung an arc, lopping their head. The young guard's head tumbled to her feet. The sword released.

Something seemed off, her head low. She stumbled back as if overcome by sickness, collapsing into Amarra's arms.

Raihn faltered. "What's the matter?" he asked, circling her. His eyes widened—there was a dagger lodged in her chest, the very one that was stuck in the table.

"You Eldhonans," she muttered. "You pluck unripe grapes from the vine. Death will find us all, and for them, I pray it be most ghastly."

Her pupil fell heavily upon Raihn, and he suffered her ghostly glaze, fighting his loss of understanding with guesses. The light within her eyes faded, even before her death. Amarra fought for her gaze, but it persisted to curse Raihn and all of his kind.

Amarra dropped to her knees, holding Tepparna, her heart likely sputtering as she'd looked gone of breath. There seemed a cork in her lungs, her face taut from her strained anguish. She took her ear to Tepparna's chest as if searching for life within, but it was gone. Raihn knew it to be true.

Gently, she lay Tepparna to the dirt while shooting a frenzied scowl at Lostar. Her willful gaze appeared harsh as a curse, presumably a stain for his memory. She erupted and lunged at him. Her fingernails dug into his skin, scratching as she'd slammed him against the wall. Weapons along the timber bobbed and Raihn swore he heard a crack in the wood.

Unfinished, she swiftly nabbed an arrow from his quiver and stuck him against the wall with it in his right palm. He looked in pain, but he seemed to accept this punishment without a fighting twitch. She snarled, her thirst for retribution seemingly unquenched. With a swift motion, she grabbed another and drove it through his other palm, pinning him to the wall more securely.

Raihn couldn't believe his eyes. He reached to pull her back, but she whipped around and shoved him to the floor. His sunken and disheartened eyes aligned with hers into a muted gaze.

Amarra faltered, letting go of Lostar. Her erratic breaths hitched, simmering. She glanced at Lostar, then back to Raihn. Her big, pointy ears drooped like a disheartened dog's. Quickly, she went to Tepparna's corpse, took her up into her arms, and fled out with her shoulders smacking the frame.

Raihn detested his subdued voice, his mind once racing for a word to spew—any word. Amarra was gone. It was a mess, as all had gone awry. "Fuck!" he cursed. "You idiot," he blurted, turning to Lostar. "Did I not tell you it was enough? Look at what you have done! You got her killed! You couldn't just leave her alone, could you?"

Lostar hung against the wall, his head low, chin to his chest. "Raihn, try to understand."

"It's time I look out for myself. You're a detriment to all those around you."

"I'm sorry," said Lostar.

"I would hope so, not that it does any good."

"She was untrained," Lostar excused. "She knew not where to strike."

"Then you shouldn't have coerced her into it," Raihn retorted.

"Guilt does not lie solely within me, Raihn. You're…maddened, angered…by her unresolved life. Am I wrong? You stole her urgency, Parcel. You did."

Raihn floundered in a frustrated stutter, knowing it to be true. "The difference is that I could not help that, you sour son of a bitch. I didn't ask for this hand," Raihn excused, waving it, "for my village to burn, to lose my family. I didn't think it'd become tethered to me. Don't you think I wish Tepparna kept the hand? I'd have rather followed her if it made her happier. She treated this thing like the key to her life, and I took it from her!" Raihn hobbled to Lostar and landed a firm right hook. Lostar's hair swatted his cheek. "…How long?"

"What?" Lostar groaned.

"How long have you been drinking? Where did you find it?" he asked. "You bog us down with your ailments. You could have missed with that arrow back there!"

Lostar merely gazed at the ground, where blood and ale pooled.

Raihn huffed and puffed, awaiting an answer. But the Enduran was far gone. Raihn turned his back, but then he heard the Enduran muster a meandering breath.

"It was there. Upright. Against the tree by the cave. I heard my name, as if it called me," his voice trailed. "I was so thirsty, and it had been so long," he whimpered. "Listen to me. I need your help."

"At least you admit it," said Raihn. "That's the first step, as they say. But the only way to help you is if I let you dry up in a dungeon—if you don't dry up here first."

Raihn, on the verge of departing, heard a disturbance outside. He turned and ducked against the wall, peering through the window facing the center of camp.

"What is it?" Lostar asked.

"It's the Authority," Raihn murmured reluctantly, his words more to himself than to Lostar. "They've converged on the cellar. The others are being loaded into a wagon… It's just me now."

"You can't—out there alone," Lostar slurred, dragging his tongue.

"Yeah?" Raihn said, his head snapping to them. "Try completing a sentence in the next couple hours, and then maybe you can aid me," he remarked sarcastically.

"You can't be serious," Lostar said. "Don't fool yourself. It's over. You'll be minced. You're no fighter. Like Tepparna. She would have to defend herself when the time came. Like my consort when she couldn't save herself."

Raihn double taked. "What?" he aired, somber-toned, his brow relaxing from its furrow. *Consort?* It clicked. "Trussgar?" He quickly smothered that empathetic kindling. "No. Don't hold onto that until it's necessary to be honest. Do not use some sob story to make me feel sorry for you and to let this all go. Besides, you're wrong. I don't believe she couldn't handle herself. She killed before and lost the hand from it. She tried to change course, but already had she steered wrong. All you did was break her moral path that led to salvation." Raihn eyed the pale hand and pondered. "You pushed her back into what she tried to escape… But then again, this hand seemed to know better of her fabrication."

"Then she was damned from herself, not the hand."

"So, now you're blaming her? She'd still be alive had you not… I'm going in damn circles."

"I merely want you to understand," Lostar reasoned. "I can't refute the blood on my hands. I never did. I desire solely to serve my name—my forsaken name."

Raihn shook his head, a withheld breath suddenly a gale from his nostrils. "Yeah, as you hinted—your grand secret, shed in a time most convenient." He comprehended Lostar's disposition, though he did not blame him any less. They embodied the retreat of a butterfly, clawing to break out of their cocoon once again. But Lostar continued to regress, a pitiful play.

"If I were an honorable man, I'd have died by my own blade, but I simply could not let that be our legacy," Lostar continued. "I had nothing left. Far from the throne atop of Lakewane, I became a vagrant in the sand, made lesser than those of the Rivy Chasms—lesser than the butte folk for their baron—lesser than the folk of the mesa, Ebbtide. I failed my people and my blood. I mourned my love and my life, though I was given time to spend on whatever I chose that was not part of the royal life.

"I thought upon the solmners that would come down the river. I sought out those not meant to be sought after—the mystic kind. Eventually, I reached their temple after much determination only to discover the rubble and ruin of it," he explained, fighting to be coherent. "Once again, I was left with nothing, for they were all dead. I was bewildered, and so I followed the river they trailed upon for their pilgrimage, where they would find Eldhona and then the Wall of Thorns, where they'd take their lives. I hoped to find some pilgrims along the way, but they're all dead."

Lostar's voice rattled before morphing into a smooth, somber drum. "Similarly, you seemed to have lost everything. And, too, you wander under the stars. I should rot on this wall, but I can't let you go alone with nothing but the distant stars to watch over you. I couldn't allow it. Forgiveness is not what I ask for, Raihn Parcel, though, with this journey, I might die after all with some dignity restored."

Raihn began to feel a tug at his perception of them. He shut his eyes, feeling himself give in, detesting it. "How do I know you're not just a thief?" Raihn's voice whipped, eyes opened. "Why should I trust you're not traipsing in disguise?"

"Remove my bandage," Lostar said.

"Bandage? What, your finger?"

Lostar nodded.

Raihn, curious enough to abide, hobbled up to him and pinched the loose fabric. He pulled and revealed their finger, which was ringed with a simic band.

"How low of a thief do you believe me to be to steal this ring of simic?"

"You'd be damned low…but a thief would have pocketed it."

"And a husband would wear it, a fool would flaunt it… I am sorry that I lied to you."

"Trussgar…"

"Do not attribute me a corpse's name."

Raihn huffed. "Then forsake that blood lust, or you'll be dead next. Make an oath to be spared eternally from the drink, not to me, but to yourself."

"I would rather die twice than succumb it again," Lostar assured.

"Good," said Raihn before reaching for the arrow stuck into Lostar.

"No, no," said the drunk. "Not yet! I want a count of three!"

CHAPTER FIFTEEN
Blood upon his hand

Deeper into the trees, glancing about like a frightened animal and maintaining a low profile, Raihn led the hastily bandaged Lostar, who carried with him some swords from the armory for their allies. Raihn brought a 'walking stick,' stabbing the ground with the blunt end as he waded through the forest like a dirtfarer.

Raihn couldn't believe he would try to face the king's boots with only a vagrant drunk at his side. He wasn't even sure why he was doing it. Herb's corpse flashed, Hodge still out there. Maybe he just couldn't allow the same fate to befall them. "Stay on your toes," he cautioned. "There's no doubt they will see the bodies in the armory and come searching for us."

"I'm not so sure," Lostar pondered.

Raihn shoved out a look of confusion.

Lostar elaborated. "They expected us, and now they have hostages. They have a plan, but do we?"

"My plan remains," Raihn asserted. "I have all the power so long as I don't mess this up."

"What plan?"

"You are duller than an old kitchen knife, Lostar, but we—no, you—can mend that," said Raihn without regret for his bluntness. "Without me, they can't get beyond the wall, so we'll use that as a bargaining chip if it comes to it, but my highest priority is to save the others first."

"That's not a bad plan," Lostar said, smiling lazily.

"Lostar…don't get too comfortable," Raihn said before taking a beat. "I'd be selfish to allow my judgment to keep you from helping the others, but still…"

"I suppose I am held within your court," Lostar replied with some snark.

Raihn grunted. "Don't make me out to be high-strung. I feel sick about what I just saw," he said, wincing from a tinge of pain in his ankle.

"Let me help you."

"I got it," Raihn insisted. "It's why I took the walking stick. I'm aware of my limits."

"A 'walking stick,' he says. It's a spear."

"Then it's a killing stick that helps me walk," Raihn rephrased.

"So is a cane, if used properly. Anyway. How about the crossbow slung off your shoulder? That only weighs you down," Lostar stated. "Sometimes less is more."

"And sometimes, more is more."

"What?"

"Look," Raihn's tongue clicked, "Its weight is opposite my aching ankle. I'm fine."

"You're being stubborn," Lostar argued.

"And so are you," Raihn batted back. "You're hurt, yet you carry a bundle of swords. Weight and pain is worth it to us both, clearly."

Lostar grunted his disapproval. "…You plan on using that Eldhonan contraption?"

"If you mean aim to kill with it, no. I have seen enough death," said Raihn. "I have no will to bring about more if I don't have to. Besides, I don't think this hand wants any bloodshed, either. Not after what Tepparna was saying, as vague as it was… Maybe a well-placed bolt would at least subdue them."

"So, what then? You're also making an oath to go without killing?" Lostar asked.

"And don't you pressure me for otherwise," Raihn said.

"Get down," Raihn whispered, throat clenched. The dark of the night relented, and the dawn reared its head. It was that transitional phase when the sky greyed, revealing, dully, an encampment ahead. Raihn and Lostar flopped down and scouted.

"Behold those tents." Raihn was awestruck by the stretching encampment at the other end of a dirt trail.

"And that wall pecking at the sky with thorns. None of your people's siege ladders could compare," Lostar added.

Raihn remarked upon it. The Wall of Thorns. It stood against them on their left with a dominating height. It was the only structure to stand up against the King's Authority, so great that even the grand encampment below it now seemed meager and fruitless. There was some kind of power—an aura radiating, posing many questions to Raihn that he had never thought of before.

The tangle of white thorns, the sight of all sights to behold, was woven like a basket, carrying who knows what within its grasp. But it was also a *colossal palisade,* shunning all without a key. Raihn glanced at his hand, the branch eerily similar to the weave of the considered palisade.

Lostar suddenly appeared discontented during his scouting. "Where is that thief, Pocket?" he asked.

Raihn trained his eyes, only now taking notice of their allies bound in a row at the base of the wall. Lostar was right to wonder. Pocket wasn't among them, just guards.

Raihn shrugged it off. "Doesn't matter. Come, we have to save them before that dame arrives," he said, rising, but Lostar pulled him back down by the fold of his cloak.

"There's not a chance that she's off somewhere else," Lostar told. "She's here waiting. Few soldiers are about. Some watching those guys, but that's it. The second we take one out, the whole camp will stir. We need a plan."

"I have one," Raihn reminded.

"Well…that's a broad plan!" Lostar blurted, his voice sounding numb from booze. "This is a delicate matter that deserves precision upon getting a proper look."

"Then you stay back with your bow," Raihn argued. "You can cover me. I'll be safe. They know they need me alive."

Lostar pinched his temple and groaned, scouting just a second more. "There are five guards. I can't let you go out there, especially on that foot. Use your crossbow here, not your sword out there. Safer that way."

"Fine," Raihn conceded, catching a curious glimpse of a paddock full of horses. It spurred imagination, his eyes made into contemplative slits. "If you insist on me staying, look to your right."

Lostar glanced there and back. "Horses?"

"You wanted a less broad plan, right?" asked Raihn. "We have to get the guards away. You follow?"

Lostar paused, pondering Raihn's concept until his face blossomed gleefully, seemingly understanding. "That's a plan I can follow," he said with a gleam in his dilated eye.

"And 'those guys,' they're friends," Raihn corrected.

"Sure, except for Xander, at least, right? He's kind of a dick," Lostar laughed.

"Definitely rough around the edges," Raihn agreed. "But it doesn't mean we have to leave him here. I'm sure he'll redeem himself when the time comes… But Lostar."

"Hmm?"

"…I don't see my parents."

"If they are here, you can bet Dame Dawness will bring them in."

"Bargaining chips," Raihn surmised, glimpsing his hand again, considering its value. His fear whirled like a sickly potion in a caldron. *What if they lop off my arm to reclaim this branch?*

"You have that bastardized bow with you. Don't let any get close."

Raihn snapped from his ill-minded swirl. "Huh?" Lostar seemed to read his mind, reading the sinking fear that Raihn was facing. "Yeah…" Raihn said in delay, patting the stock of the crossbow, hollowness in his tone.

Lostar elbowed him to signal their time to act. They began to stand just before hearing rustling right below the mound of which they had lain. They synchronously shoved each other back down, both of them stifling a groan spurred by their injuries.

A man from the encampment had come near. *We're spotted!* Raihn thought. His body tensed up, and his heartbeat drummed against the dirt. Through the brush, he watched the figure come closer to only seat themself on a stump. Raihn sighed in relief, *like an idiot.*

The man twisted and glared into the forest.

Raihn shut his eyes tight, sensing the curses flying through Lostar's head. *Just the wind,* Raihn suggested, as if telepathically planting the thought into them.

They straightened, but Raihn continued to hold his next breath hostage. It was eerily quiet. No birds. No bugs. Just the tickling hairs of grass against Raihn's nose. Time seemed to drag; he could hardly let out his breath.

"See something, Wallace?" a voice asked. Some other man was approaching.

"Nay. I just got the chills. Hate this place," said the soldier on the stump.

Raihn had cracked his eyes. The two soldiers flapped their gums. The one on the stump, Wallace, removed his mail and padding. Beads of sweat rolled down from his receding hairline and over his wrinkled brow.

"You goin' mad on me, eh? You know we ain't heard no damned owl at night. No birds. No fuckin' bees. Ain't nothing out here. No bewitching beauties. Nothing sweet like honey. Just that tar, mo-lass-ess shit. Them wheat farmers 'ere love that sugarcane shit. No. No honey 'ere. No, sir. Not in this neck of the woods. So, I wouldn't blame ye, but I sure wouldn't want you goin' mad dog. Lunatics 'round here aren't good for the lot of us trying to get by. Wouldn't want another incident on our hands."

"I'm not going mad, Ruth. I'm not. I'm just tired. Besides, if someone here went mad, I'd be just fine," said the balding fellow on the stump, gripping the pommel of his sheathed sword. "Moreover, them men were tore up. A bear, I reckon, like some others reckon too. Just this time last year about."

"Even if there was a bear out here, in the animal-forsaken trees, you think you could take it?"

"Aye, better than them fellows before me a year ago, I reckon," said Wallace.

"Poppycock. An insensitive dick you're being," Ruth laughed, his bottom lip hanging over his scraggly beard.

Raihn eavesdropped, minding what they spoke, finding the topic of a bear ripping through particularly intriguing, as Pocket had already remarked upon.

"Dead, aren't they? I'm not hurtin' no feelin's," said Wallace, unfastening his boot straps.

"S'pose not," said Ruth, resting his looping thumb through his baldric strap that crossed over his ripped, blue gambeson.

"They just spent a little too much time with too little food. Lucky us, our wait is 'most over. The men seem spirited to feast today. Maybe it'll all be over soon, and we can scoot on from this place."

122

"Then I s'pose you believe this gibberish, Wallace?"

Wallace, removing a pebble from his boot, grinned. "That bitch has been jabbin' my heel for too long."

"Wallace," Ruth called, leaning over him.

Wallace tilted his head up at them. "If it gets me out of here, it's best to have hope in it, I s'pose. Make me happy for a little while. Let's hope, too, they show."

They? Raihn echoed in thought. *Us,* he realized.

"Right," agreed Ruth. "Well, I'll leave you to that ripe boot. I'm going to see what's for feastin'," Ruth said, parting ways.

Wallace sunk his foot back into his boot and started removing the other boot. Surely, after this one, he would leave. But first came a spider with more legs than Raihn felt comfortable with on any insect. This plant-resembling spider descended from a single strand of webbing above his hand. The tiny arachnid landed, and he kept his mouth shut tight and held his breath when it crawled, dragging its camouflaged body across his skin.

Lostar glanced, expression pinched by concern, his sight trained until the soldier slipped on his other boot and took off. He then crushed the spider between two fingers and tossed its mangled bits aside.

Raihn was dumbfounded.

"You looked like you were trying to lay an egg," Lostar stated, stifling a laugh. "It was but only a spider!"

"It was a Peeping Tom!" Raihn was alarmed, voice strained thin.

"A what?"

"It's poisonous."

"Thanks for alerting me now!"

Raihn shook his head and toyed with the crossbow, ensuring he was familiar with it. "I'm just glad it's gone. I hate anything dangling by a thread."

"You sure you can handle it?" Lostar asked.

"It's simple enough. Point and pull," Raihn replied, but he felt his face flush upon working it.

"Those are harder to work than you might think."

"I've got it," Raihn dismissed.

Lostar crept toward the paddock on Raihn's right, shushing the uneasy horses. On Raihn's left, about thirty feet away, the weary Xander was kneeling. Raihn spotted the mercenary, whose eyes caught wind of their ploy, and swiftly, Xander rammed their head into the guard—perhaps the best use of their thick skull yet. All attention fell upon him, the reaches of the dirt path clear. The guard buckled, turned toward Xander, and struck him across the cheek for the others to witness. The captive was yet to surrender, spitting upon the guard before laughing.

"Snail dick hits softer than a pair of fat thighs!" Xander blared for all to hear.

The guard looked embarrassed in front of his cohorts, so his gauntlet was raised for another strike, but it was prevented.

"Rest easy that fiery heart o' yours." Ruth stepped in, wielding a half-eaten carrot in one hand and gripping the assaulting soldier's right hand in the other. "Wouldn't want 'em blacked out and missing their friends, would ye, Lemmy? What would the Dame say 'bout that?"

Lemmy, more petite than Ruth, yanked his arm away and sneered. Ruth chomped on his carrot and gleamed through orange chunks until there came a sharp and feminine cry.

"What brat out there cryin'?" asked Lemmy.

"Sew that mouth o' yours, boy," Ruth warned, pointing his carrot. "That might be the apprentice to Dame Dawness. I hear the Dame takes good care of a li'l girly, and I wouldn't be mincing words like that if she's even a hundred acres from here. And if that be her apprentice, the Dame must be in tow, not four acres."

Then there was another cry, one for alarm. "The horses are loose!" It was one of the men from the camp. "The horses are loose!" They sped up the dirt path towards Ruth and Lemmy. Huffing, their hands clasped their knees. "They escaped the paddock!"

Raihn glanced at the empty paddock and swept his eyes right back.

"Son of a bitch. Who locked the gate last? You, I'd bet, 'snail dick.'" Ruth accused Lemmy with a tease.

"Don't matter. Just help me gather 'em," Lemmy replied. "Must be what that girl was on about."

With the paddock vacant and the guards hectically scrambling to corral the horses, Lostar retreated into the treeline for cover and made his way to the fugitives.

"Why they spooked?" Lemmy asked. Unbeknownst to him, Lostar had pricked the tail ends of all the horses. It was a success—or at least the first half of his plan was.

All that remained was the untying. But when he approached his companions, he waved and tilted like the ground was a teetering boat in a mad sea. Falling behind the bound Xander and dropping off the bundle of blades, Lostar made it.

Raihn sighed, his palms of sweat gripping the crossbow. Then he spotted Pate. His heart sank. She was approaching from the field before she stopped dead center of the trail. Her expression was twisted by confusion. Lostar's face wasn't plastered on any wanted posters—perhaps that was why she hesitated. Fortunately for them, she was still a ways down the road.

Xander seemed to have seen her gawking and warned Lostar. "Hurry, they see you!"

Raihn was uncertain if Lostar groaned anything back as Xander was already hardly audible, but he began to cut at the merc's binds, spotted much quicker than he'd probably anticipated.

As the soldiers danced around trying to wrangle the horses, Pate alerted and rallied them.

"Quickly, untie me so that I may help fend them off!" Xander strained.

Lostar's voice grew. "This rope is thick and very coarse. Just keep your hands still. I'm trying to keep from cutting them!"

In truth, Lostar's metal was more than sharp enough to cut the binds like butter, so why not use it? *Likely seeing double. Twenty fingers he'd wished not to cut a single one of,* as Raihn thought, frustrated.

"They're getting close. Where's Raihn?" asked Xander, his stress rising.

"He's here," Lostar assured.

Raihn kept quiet, watching from the brush.

Xander asked of Amarra, but Lostar said naught. Then he cried out in alarm, "Snail Dick is returning!"

Raihn took aim to aid them, and lucky for them, he landed a bolt in Lemmy's foot, sending him hopping along the dirt. And after a blink, Xander was free. He'd plucked up a sword and, rather than deliver a cry before battle, whined, "Short broadswords!?"

Lostar snapped his bow in hand. "They're heavy!" he replied, pulling an arrow from his quiver.

Raihn caught sight of blood spurting from Lostar's hand, the injury worse than he'd realized. Then he paused, almost impressed by Lostar's determination. He could see the man stifle what must have been a sobering twinge of pain before he knocked the arrow and anchored it. A stampede of soldiers rushed toward them, Ruth and Wallace among them. Lostar had his target in sight.

He released the arrow, and Raihn watched as it flew. It struck a soldier's neck, though not the one Lostar had aimed for, surely. And considering their condition, Raihn thought it would be impossible to aim precisely. Still, with so many enemies closing in, it hardly mattered. Luck was on their side. The blood from the fallen soldier spurted out onto the man behind, blinding them for a precious moment.

Raihn's perfect opportunity arose when the soldier, wiping blood from his eyes, slowed down. He soared a bolt from the trees and struck their foot. The soldier fell, and there was just enough time for Lostar to take up his blade and finish him with a drunken flourish.

Lostar and Xander stood side by side before the oncoming Authoritarian soldiers reached them, but the Enduran was heavy on his feet. He'd done his best to keep up with the clanging strikes of metal, but his duel was long and arduous. Raihn grew more worried. Much time was being wasted, and he could feel it. Saving just Xander would not be enough. Lostar's condition was too weak. Their hands struggled to clasp their sword and blood dripped from the handle, yet he tore down his foes, including Ruth and Wallace.

Together, they wasted no more time and dashed for the other prisoners while they could, who then took up their blades upon a swift-made freedom.

After Raihn stood to return to them, many more men clad in armor spilled from the camp, a mix of Hulls and Authoritarians. He was terrified, but he had to do something. He flopped back upon his belly and pulled the whip-cord of his crossbow, much like tugging a keelboat ashore. It was very strenuous to do more than once—at least for him. It took all of his muscle to tug it, but finally, the cord landed in place. His biceps bunched in pain, but he powered through.

Raihn realigned the weapon and took up aim with the iron crosshair before pulling back the trigger and ejecting the bolt to topple the soldier to the ground. Another tripped over them. Then another.

Raihn smiled, feeling empowered and able. He kept to his oath, the index finger from the pale hand tapping him as if approving it. *Creepy.*

He struggled to ready another bolt before lending his focusing eye behind the sight. He wiped his sweat upon the grass and returned his index finger, resting it against the curved iron trigger. His breath slowed as he searched for his mark.

He pulled. None of the men had noticed him, as they merely fell from stricken legs. They were clueless husks charging blindly, their vision narrowed through their helmets.

Masking the support coming from under the trees, Lostar also let loose a flurry of arrows to topple the soldiers before them. Those soldiers then became trampled, and over them, more had swarmed with a disregard for the dead and wounded. They just kept coming, ready to overwhelm their enemy at hand.

Lostar and the others became surrounded. Outnumbered. Their efforts futile at best. The steel tide closed in as the fugitives formed an inner circle, pressed upon one another's backs. Their elbows clashed as they held no more room to wave a simple short broadsword. Their weapons fell from their hands. Surrender.

Raihn felt laden with fear. Surrender seemed the only way, and yet he resisted. Now was not the time to be rash, even if the sight of their surrender encouraged hasty action. He forced a breath. His hands gripped the crossbow tight, and his body had shaken as he thought on the matter. His finger could not be trusted, yet it could not be removed from the trigger.

Then, as if designed to tempt him more, Dame Dawness appeared from the camp with Pate by her side. He aimed as he thought about Benjin, Tassy, and Marnie. He became angry as he relished the revenge of the fallen. His village. Possibly his parents. The kind solmners. The hand squeezed, its bark biting him as if disliking his rage.

Dame Dawness was at his mercy. Was it the right move? Did it matter? He didn't care to know for a moment before adhering to the grip from the hand. He breathed again and calmed the itch. The grip of the pale hand loosened.

Like oil in water, the dame came before the prisoners, including the newly added Enduran. There was no pride upon her face, no vanity, just relief. "Finally," she said. "Where are the others? If they are here lurking, wave them over before I must retrieve them myself."

"Not all of us remain. Some lay dead not at the hands of your men but the mistakes of ours," said Lostar, perhaps stupidly, yet honestly.

Magnus squinted. "You mean Herb?"

Lostar kept his eyes on Dame Dawness, and she kept hers on him. Her posture corrected.

"And what of the others?"

"They're dead. The hand is gone. I aimed merely to rescue these men and to get out."

"…You mean to say that you outlived an Outcast?"

"She turned on us, sticking me to the wall with my arrows. But the wounds I left her with will take care of her," he lied.

The dame seemed to look him over, likely taking notice of his wounds. "Might some of that be true. But you're not one of them," she said, meaning the fugitives. "But if by chance you care for them, I'll clip their fingers. One by one," she assured. "Might the truth reveal itself then… We shall end this campaign."

"Their campaign is never-ending," said Hodge. "Pharloe's and the king's, both with their petty desires. The mountain is to be pillaged and stripped of any meaning," he said, even though he'd not believed the same as solmners. "The king loathes this unknown marking on his map—his 'Compass' as he calls the land. And his dog, Pharloe—"

"Pharloe has been put back on the chain," said the dame. "The king re-takes the helm, seeking the key that Pharloe had squandered."

"Now wait just a minute." A man pushed himself through the crowd of men. It was a knight of Pharloe by his look, wearing a tabard of red and yellow. "You were contracted by Pharloe, Frinjen Slayer. You're bound to that duty. You're here not to reclaim but to retake the hand and deliver it to Pharloe himself, as well as his Outcast and his—"

"A new edict has nullified the contract. The Outcast is dead, and I have received word from the king himself to open this thicket once and for all. Take what fugitives there are when I am through. But until then, stay out of my way." Her tone was as sharp as the barbs on the wall.

More bickering ensued, the man becoming frustrated. But he appeared to withhold his ire, for she was right to rebuke his contract. The king may make any alteration to an anvil's contract, so their services could indeed be allowed to remain in flux. And even though the pale branch was in their wynd, King Stamen rules all eight of them, and thus, it belonged to him.

The knight stomped at the details. "Where's the letter?"

Dame Dawness summoned Pate. She stepped forward and pulled out a rolled piece of parchment.

The knight of Pharloe snatched it from Pate's hand and read it over, mumbling the words under his breath before exclaiming, "Unfruitful for ages, and when it grows, it gets plucked by scroungers! The Stayed Hand is ours by right."

"The real key is a villager in our very midst, as I've been told. It means nothing without him," said the dame. Then she'd turned her gaze back to her prisoners. "Now, bring him forward and be free from peril," she said. "I swear no harm would come to him." She squatted before Lostar, resting her elbows on her knees. "I am not so callous as to derive pleasure through pain, but that is how dire this is. I plead, even to those lowly such as your-selves." She wrapped his hair around her metallic fingers and pulled him close. "Tell me the truth." A certain desperation touched her voice.

After a moment of trading gazes, she sifted the truth. "He is alive," she gleaned. Her eyes left him briefly, then returned. "Lostar is your name, but upon your hip is a sword of simic." She removed it from its scabbard and admired it. Lostar's eyes followed her as she stood and held it aloft. "Re-markable," she said, looking it up and down before returning it to him. She snapped to her feet, took a firm stance, then nodded to her men.

Raihn was to be caught, but before then, he could finish her here and now. Unbeknownst to her, she stood directly in his line of sight, but he waited and watched. His chest tightened. His finger itched. It wrapped around the trigger, ready to pull, but before he could, two spears nestled behind each of his ears. He froze. It was over. He'd be taken to the anvil now, where he would be forced to surrender and give up his purpose. Raihn had nothing else to cling to, and the idea of sitting behind bars was a dreadful one if his punishment would be so light.

But then, seemingly at his most desperate plea, his captors fell beside him, a hatchet in each of their skulls. He turned, a sense of disbelief washing over him. Amarra towered over him. He stretched a wide smile. Then it fad-ed. Her face was all cuts and bruises. Raihn meant to ask of them, but be-fore the words could escape his lips, she pressed her hand over his mouth. Her eyes flickered ahead. There was a rustle. It must be Hull or Authoritari-an men.

Amarra let go. He looked to see them cross the tree line. Too close for comfort. Amarra bent her knees as her eyes tracked them. Slowly, she pulled her bloodied hatchets from the skulls of the dead men. It sounded sticky, as if taken from a dense beehive that coated her hatchets in honey.

She stowed the hatchets upon her legs. And from her waist hung two eight-flanged maces. With them, she stormed forward, her feet kicking up dirt. Wielding these massive weapons, Amarra drew the enemies' attention, luring them away from Raihn, who was impressed with her choice of wea-ponry, realizing she must have returned to the armory. And even after what came of her best friend, she admirably returned—then again, where else was she to go? Maybe she was just bloodthirsty. But, Raihn wanted to believe she came back for them. There was, after all, a softness in her gaze when he looked at her. Maybe she even came back for him.

Amarra stood in the middle of the road as all watching eyes turned to her, even Dame Dawness's. The anvil's head whipped back to Lostar in disappointment.

"From my lips, I offered truth, and from yours, I was gifted more lies," Dame Dawness said, glancing at her men and back as her hand strangled the hilt of her sword. "Where is Raihn?" She drew her sword in contempt.

Time seemed to wane as Lostar must have seen the end of his life gleam upon the tip of her sword, but he appeared calm. *Why?* Raihn wondered. He looked to accept his fate, unwilling to betray him.

Meanwhile, Amarra was swarmed by men from all angles who focused on her. They offered their best war cries and surrendered their lives to her might. Bludgeoning many to a bloody pulp, she was seamlessly warding them off as she brutishly slugged around the dirt with her weapons, piling high a ring of corpses. One by one, a ferocious ocean of oncoming foot soldiers amassed at her feet as her cloak twirled. Her force caved in their chests and broke their ribs, but many were luckier. Those with that luck pushed themselves up again with a second wind. They were relentless, working in numbers, piling on, clinging to her back and legs, cutting her dense skin with biting daggers.

Amarra dropped her twin maces, exchanged them for her hatchets, and began chopping the soldiers down like they were shrubs. Kettle helms flung from their heads.

As difficult as it was to forsake Amarra, Raihn knew Lostar needed him most. He took a deep breath and aimed through the crowd, finding his target. Dame Dawness's sword was mid-swing. He pulled the trigger. The bolt soared through the trees and met its mark, but it snapped against the dense armor on Dame Dawness's back and ricocheted into a soldier, who grasped needlessly at his wounded hip.

Lostar appeared distraught, probably cursing Raihn for outing himself. The anvil glanced the surrounding area, her eyes quick to fish in the trees. She then grabbed the Enduran's hair and yanked him up to his feet. He'd been strung up in a presentation towards the forest's underbelly, as if hanging from a gibbet at the gallows. The tip of her sword slid into his belly, however shallow; Magnus and Xander gripped her crossguard, to Raihn's surprise. She recalled her blade, seemingly moved by their gallantry.

"So be it," said the dame. But the damage was already done.

Lostar fell free of her grasp, smacking the dirt patch. The others rushed to his side and pressed their hands firmly against his wound.

Raihn clutched his weapon, trembling in the bushes, feeling it was all a farce. To win meant to succeed, a hope and a dream now fading. But he could kill her. He could avenge his village—hardly a consolation after he'd failed them, but it was the best he could muster. In truth, this was for his comfort. Another bolt found itself snug against the whipcord. Aiming it, Raihn felt the branch loosen more.

All this struggle, he'd aimed not to kill but to maim, though now, his iron sight was set on her head. His finger tensed up, about to pull. The Stayed Hand continued to detest. Tepparna's plight echoed how she lost the hand as Raihn thirsted for blood himself.

Then, a dagger grazed his cheek, a hardly tolerable voice coming over his ear. "Don't."

Raihn clenched the handle of the crossbow, then threw it down. "I wondered where you were, thief."

"Just come easy."

"Bastard."

Amarra tossed soldiers like dolls from her back as Raihn left the foliage. Their eyes met, and she seemed to cave in defeat, the light in her eyes dying. It seemed it wasn't just a thirst for blood after all. She stepped towards him, many armed soldiers still weighing upon her. But then she seemed to realize who stood behind him. She swung her mighty legs in her quickly determined stride, as if she was adamant to tear the thief in half.

Pocket gripped Raihn in place with one hand firm on his shoulder, their dagger jutting dangerously close to his neck, close enough to tickle a hair with its tip. Eldhos continued to rise beyond the mountain, casting a planetary shadow well beyond the road's end. The charade seemed at an end, the light marking defeat.

"Amarra," Raihn began. Many bloody cuts and wounds laced her body. "It's over. Don't make them hurt you anymore."

Although reluctantly, she surrendered.

They stood beneath the menacing, wormy visage of the white wall. While white wood might feel more discolored, the wall, perhaps 'gate,' was more alive in person than previously imagined. Its thorns are plentiful, its roots deep, and its branches weaving. All of it around a strange imprint of a hand. But this was remarked upon momentarily, for Lostar's fleeting life clung before Raihn. They were hardly gasping for air.

The reluctant Outcast surrendered herself. She looked sorrowful—they all did, except Xander. He was fuming, a gravelly hum of frustration emanating from his throat. His eyes burned like little pieces of coal, glaring at the thief.

"If you had accepted the inevitable, you would have saved your friend," the dame said to Raihn. "Instead, your head was full of whimsy, beside a beast no less. I gather your misunderstanding of the world. Suffice to say, much worse will your understanding dawn, Young Lord Raihn."

"The world doesn't revolve around you or any man," Raihn whirred. "The king is but a decorated man of riches. Your fealty is made up of dead animal skin and ink. By that ink, you sell yourself no differently than a tavern's whore. And now, my friend, my companion, whom I value, is dying," Raihn said, his eyes remaining on Lostar. Raihn consoled him and pressed upon his wound. No matter what, the cherry-red blood just kept gushing between his copper-tinted fingers.

"All this suffering… A choice derived from a gambler, for what?" the Dame asked. "A peek at what's over the Wall of Thorns."

"Derived—spurned, from something, from somewhere," Raihn said. "I didn't choose to be the sole survivor of my village, which you invaded in search of my father, torturing my mother in your scheme. You talk about needless suffering, yet it began before I had any part in it."

"The manor yielded nothing for me," said the Dame. "And I'd not—" she leaned in, "lay a finger, nor touch a hair on your mother's head. You hear too many stories." The Dame straightened up. "Nay. I intended to use you as bait, hoping the fugitives and your father would come to me," she explained. "Funny," she remarked, noting how he fell into her grasp from opposite circumstances. "My party is not infallible and let loose their lips around too many ears. The death of your tavern friend was hasty and undeserved."

"Benjin was his name," said Raihn. "Did your men also string him up in the tavern as some macabre joke? Did they then burn my village under your watch as well, Black Anvil?"

"You are mistaken," said the dame. "Quick are you to trust these criminals."

"I haven't walked among them long," said Raihn, "but I know they would never."

"How are you so sure none of them lie?"

"I'd trust any criminal before a bluecoat."

"Only more disappointment," said the Dame. She beckoned Pate before placing a hand upon her shoulder. "You betray yourself. So naive and gullible. Blind hope in friends will stray you to places such as this, abandoning you at their convenience. Heed my words. You'll never see them again."

"What is your point?" Raihn asked. "Is it my wellbeing you look after now?"

"In my pouch is a crumpled letter," she said, reaching through the flap on her sword belt. "The moment the prisoners escaped I was contracted to bring them back by order of Pharloe. Later, I discovered where you were going and why, though not without help," she mused. "I received many letters lately, but one in particular was without so much as a seal. That's because a man on the run scribbled it," she continued, her eyes flickering to Magnus. "I encourage you to confess," she demanded of them, straightening the piece of supposedly damning evidence.

"I'm so sorry," Magnus's voice shook out. His head hung between his shoulders, his gnarled hair curls somewhat concealing shame in his eyes.

"Don't be sorry," snarled Xander. "Just tell me it's not true."

"This pitiful quest," Magnus began, "a child's whimsical dream. We could not realistically defy the King's Authority or an anvil. It would only end gravely, and you see how it played out now. I could have prevented this, perhaps gone free, but Dame Dawness did not keep her end of the deal."

"Another lie," Dame Dawness declared. "You did not live up to what was promised."

"And I told you I would do it alone," Magnus retorted. "Yet two Authoritarians sat near me in the tavern!"

"Two measly patrolmen were not foreseen," the Dame agreed. "But someone like yourself shouldn't be so easily spooked by them."

Between their bickering, Hodge cried out, "You betrayed us and said nothing all this time!"

"No!" Magnus barked. Starting with Dame Dawness, he pleaded, "He just did not arrive. I left to make the second-best bargain, and guys," his head turned, "I faltered once, and when I discovered she would go back on her word, I ran. I still saved you all. I came to your rescue, remember? The back window to the tavern! Either way, I swear, I was looking out for you," he persisted. "If they got Tepparna and the Outcast back—"

"You mean my father, right?" Raihn interrupted. "'**He** did not arrive'? After Xander questioned my father's trustworthiness, it was you who stabbed them—and my father—in the back? I mean, I had my suspicions of you the second you lurked in that tavern, but..." Raihn said, disgusted. "I hardly know you, but for some reason, I just...believed you were a real friend to my father."

"I'm so sorry," said Magnus. "I didn't mean for any of this to happen."

"Of course, you did," said Hodge. "That's how they found us so quickly... Herb could be alive had things been different."

"Magnus," Dame Dawness began, "I only sook the key and the fugitives. You do understand the irreparable damage you could have caused? You nearly tarnished the name of the Cardinal of the East Wynd. How can you say you did not mean for this to happen?"

Raihn roared in his throat, interrupting, "Little do I care about your petty quarrels, failure, betrayal, or decree," before Magnus could answer. "Even if you're not to blame for my village, I know you ransacked it. I also know you're the reason Lostar lays dying, and that's enough for me to know that whatever you do or say, you're no better than him, dame." Raihn motioned to Magnus. "You sentenced an already surrendered man to death."

The dame did not contest.

"Neither of you have honor," Raihn continued. "My friend is dying. So, give me a moment of god damn peace while I still have him. Have at least that much decency and respect."

Her expression surrendered to a quiet, mournful glower through her helm. She removed it out of respect, somewhat weakened by him, or so it appeared.

132

Raihn held on to the wandering warrior that lay cold, every breath of his shallower than the last. Raihn gripped him tighter and tighter, stealing himself, for soon, he must let go. Silence settled, and Raihn faced only the truth of what was to come. "You wanted this, didn't you? That's why you came all this way?"

Lostar rested in his arms, pale and weak. His remaining energy went straight through his lungs as his lips seemed to part.

Raihn listened carefully.

"Open the gate," Lostar said, tone sapped. "Let me see what so many lived and died for. I must know. Though I will die here, as I deserve no entry."

Raihn—a reluctant recluse, no better than a failed warrior—lay Lostar down. He rose, looking at the wooden hand that hung upon him. He was in no position to judge, judged by the hand himself, but he damned Lostar for their feeble breaths.

Dame Dawness distanced herself, and the others also offered space so that he may grant Lostar's wish. Raihn poured all his hope into fulfilling that wish and marched the cleared path. There seemed to be an aisle of grievance that he limped through, but soon, there were only the links of interlocking wood, white with hollowed points. The thorns spread open wide, showing a hand-shaped hole.

Raihn plunged his open right palm into the hole, filling it perfectly. He took one deep breath and shut his eyes tight, enduring the pain from all the thorns. The pale hand loosely holding his seemed to line up with the wall.

Anticipation for the culmination of this tremendous effort—an effort to find the secrets of this beastly heap of stone—was left unfulfilled, for nothing came of it. Deflated, Lostar's life drained away as Raihn could not fulfill his only wish. "Come on," Raihn whispered, but nothing seemed to happen. "Please work," he begged quietly, but nothing came of his want, and no better would come from his demand. "Open!" He swiveled his head and saw that Lostar was fading away. Panged knowing that their mission had reaped only suffering, Raihn persisted as their only hope. Regardless of how hard he breathed, the air seemed to choke him from the inside, as if out of spite. The mountain appeared displeased, but he'd suffered enough for its hunger, for it was gluttonous.

Raihn launched his palm into the hole again, and inside it, he was hooked by the thorn legion. His blood spilled over the splintery, alabaster-like twine in a bright color.

"O mountain, please. I'm begging you, o mountain, heed my call. We're lost, and this is our only light. We offered everything in our darkness, with little else to give, our lives forfeited. I've not come in wonder or excitement but in need. Do not forsake me now, because you would them as well, something I cannot bear. So abide by my words because that is all I have left to give." And the pale hand was felt no more around his fingers, let go.

CHAPTER SIXTEEN

Circlet's dread and a horn's howl

The dark of the mountain's shadow doubled as the sky filled with clouds. Fitting. Raihn closed his eyes. The darkness prevailed even greater. Time acknowledged truth. There were no marvels, no respite from life's grindstone. He slumped against the wall, thorns that he accepted ripping into him as a means of some reflection.

A dense fog crept through the tents and the trees, encroaching upon them, swallowing all in its path, as dense as his desolation. Raihn paid little heed at first glance, but its thickness was akin to a plume of smoke, the color of thick webbing. It rolled over them, above and under, blockading his vision. Hardly could he see his own feet, but still, he felt the same ground. He looked up, unable to behold even the sky. It was eerily quiet.

Those around him appeared confused. And when he lurched forward to find the hand, it was gone. He knelt, his hand brushing the surface of dirt, and then he crawled in search of it. Concern filled his heart as another realization struck. For when he circled back, there was no wall. And even worse, no Lostar. *But they have to be there,* he reasoned.

The thick, white tide engulfed them when Dame Dawness broke the silence with a mutter. "What is this?" She held out her hand, fog slithering through her fingers. She was the only one Raihn could see left, yet he was undetected. Her senses seemed to knock her eyes awake, and she became alert. "Nobody move!" she barked. "Don't let them escape!" She donned her helm and carefully ebbed away into the veil, searching for him and the others.

Raihn stood up, away from the thorns. He fought the dense obscurity, piercing it with wonder before looking back. *Is this the other side?* Suddenly, he was grabbed and pulled. The dame found him.

"What's happening?" she demanded to know.

A strong bellowing sound roared from up high and cut between them. Sharper than a cry from a newborn, mightier than an ox, and deeper than any thunder. Raihn clenched his teeth to stop them from quivering under the deafening assault of some mighty horn.

The dame scrunched her face, unable to hold him any longer. She let go and whipped away her helmet, then clamped her head between her palms.

The cacophonous blaring persisted, sending Raihn to his knees. The earth against them seemed to quake, spawning him upright like a worm beneath a grounder. When the intensely deep howl had finally lifted, Raihn, and surely the ears of all those whom befell its power, was left with a crying ring.

Raihn fell again to his knees, his ears feeling stuffed with cotton. A muffled boom came to the right of them, and he swore he heard something crumble.

Raihn took advantage of the dame's shock by slithering about until he found Amarra. She knelt, bloodied and dirtied, but had suffered no fatal wounds that he could see. He stood upright, his legs still feeling the vibrations. He wiped her face clear of blood to see no cuts beneath there, either. She was okay, which he was more than happy to see, though surprised.

Upon her knee, Amarra surprised him with a sudden lunge, happy to see he was okay. But the moment was spoiled as Raihn saw something appear over her shoulder.

There was a tree fading in through the ebbing fog, and from it was a hanged man. It was an awful sight, their neck looped with a thorny tassel. They clawed at it, eyes piercing down at Raihn as they cleared the density. And then others just like him were revealed, equally distressed, all of them naked.

Raihn, frightened, held Amarra and shied his eyes. Still, he felt their pleading gazes. But there was nothing he could do. They were too high for him to reach, and he felt unsafe in this mist. And if he were to spare any time for another man, it wouldn't be any of them.

"We must get out of here, but we can't leave Lostar behind."

Amarra's expression knotted.

"I know. I know," Raihn tempered. "But I can't just leave him. He has too much to make up for. And I know he isn't the only one." He spoke so close to Amarra's ear that she must've felt every erratic breath off his syllables.

She nodded, her ear flagging from his wind.

They scoured about for some sign of Lostar but only found hanged men, even women, who pointed in a direction opposite of where Raihn headed, to where the mountain presumably began to rise.

Several soldiers rushed past him, following the pointed fingers, hindering his search. Their armor and drawn blades blunted and scraped against him. And from where they had come, he heard howls of pain echo past into a point as narrow as the swords that nicked him. Bloodcurdling terror weaved its own wall ahead of Raihn, demanding he turn back.

The space around Raihn started clearing. He looked to the dirt below and still found nothing. The more ground he crossed, the steeper the shadow of terror loomed as the air settled into a disquiet.

Making it back to the white wall at last, Raihn was flustered. "He can't be any further than this. Did we somehow miss him? He should have been back here!"

Amarra looked to him ponderously, but then something stole her gaze. Raihn followed her attention, spying odd figures in the fog that soldiers engaged in a rise of clamor. Stringy silhouettes with thin tufts of hair. Unsightly wretches. Woe for their sounds of throaty bleats, terrible and inhuman. They were things "organically wrought from a desolate swim in the fog," as a passing soldier had articulated in a way that sounded a curse.

The fog became a perimeter to a hectic battlefield or, perhaps, an arena. More woe, Raihn detested the thought of presuming the role of warrior with his little blade, but his back was to the wall once more, thorns spurning him to action.

Raihn questioned whether this place should have ever been visited and whether this fate could turn out better than lying in a dungeon. Still, might there be some reprieve ahead.

He accepted the pointed way by the hanged men and crept through the fog with Amarra, wary of any danger in their path. They sidled around combatants with Amarra slaying any who dared attack them before snaking around again, finding more men dueling these creatures.

Shadows clashed about them with quick clatters, spilling blood on the ground where the fog broke. Men fell in their path, whom they quietly stepped over. Raihn looked back at their horrid faces, their mouths agape, eyes wide open. Raihn and Amarra's best defense was the fodder from the encampment, but that was a limited resource.

Things seemed to quiet after many clangs of metal met what was now a stone pathway. Raihn squeezed Amarra's hand tightly, then dashed along the path, stunned by the firmness of his ankle, realizing there was no pain. They might survive this with the slack they were given. As for the others, though, Raihn could only hope for the best.

Raihn's foot struck something in the grey and put him on a swift balancing act upon his toes. What he smacked rattled and clinked like armor from a dead Hull soldier. Then, he gained footing to only plow into one of the things that had appeared from the fog: a woman in rags. She was growling from the caverns of her stomach past thin chapped lips. She was bony and slender, fat and muscle absent, her hair equally frail. Her eyes were sunken deep into the bowels of her skull. The paleness of her skin hinted at a lack of light ever shining past the mountain and wall.

Raihn's tomb of fear now froze over as her expression mirrored that of a dog about to pounce, her lips peeling from rotted teeth. His eyes shut to block her out, for that was the least he could muster.

Nothing.

Upon peering back, Raihn saw Amarra's forearm reaching down from over his head. Their hand was clenching the hag's skull. It caved in, its left eye crawling out from its socket. Amarra threw her down like a wet rag, her behemoth foot coming down right after. There was a dull pop as crimson oozed between her toes, as if she stomped a cherry pie.

But the vile woman was not the only foe. Another seemingly materialized in the fog, for they could hear it only. Suddenly, Raihn's leg was clamped. Looking down and buckling his jaw, he saw it was but a child that lingered below their line of sight, ready to teethe.

Amarra snatched the little boy up, and it nipped at her fingers until it was catapulted away. She gripped Raihn's hand so tight it might go numb. And like the child, he was whipped across the terrain, trying to match her speed.

Stragglers from the Authority had evidently reached this point as well, but no further, their bodies scattered and lifeless as far as Raihn could see. The figures that emerged from the fog were cannibals, bent over corpses of blue fabrics, cupping pools of blood. It was a grotesque sight, *but so long as it kept them distracted...*

"They look…happy," Raihn murmured, low enough to maintain stealth.

"Run faster!" A voice urged from ahead beneath an orb of fire bobbing through the grey. "Just follow my light!" they called out again.

Raihn and Amarra exchanged a glance, then pushed even harder. In the chaos, Raihn faltered, his legs sputtering as Amarra's sweaty palm slipped from his grasp.

"Wait!" he cried, but she was already out of reach. In his desperate attempt to close the gap, he tripped over a dead soldier, stripped of both armor and flesh, their underbite jutting distortedly over a chewed lip.

The battle seemed over. There was nothing left to hear but the ominous silence. The bones of the fallen would surely be picked clean by now, and Raihn, still carrying ample meat, knew it spelled bad news for him.

His mind spun, dizzying him at the worst possible moment. He pushed himself up, sword drawn, eyes alert, fearing a cannibal would leap from the fog and tear into his throat. After a moment, he continued, hoping to reunite with Amarra. The fog provided cover—so long as he didn't unwittingly stumble toward one of the cannibals. Aside from the chattering of his teeth, all he could hear was the sickening slush of his feet as they pushed through liters of blood.

Raihn halted, spotting a man seated ahead on the path, dazed, as if unsure of where he was. He gazed into the sky, sharp, pronounced cheekbones jutting like cliffs above a disheveled beard. His legs sprawled in opposite directions. And what looked like a torn potato sack was draped over his bony hips. Raihn watched them keenly, sidestepping while pointing his sword. Distracted, he carelessly elbowed something else. A sudden jolt sent him off his feet.

He twisted to see a similarly ragged woman, alerted. She snapped her gummy maw with few teeth, and her hair hung like webbed curtains. Pronounced ribs rowed under her taut skin, which was likened to a dried lake's riverbed.

With all her might, she yanked Raihn down and pulled at his hair to expose his throat. As the foul woman pinned his wrists with her sharp knees, she knocked his sword from his grip, causing it to clatter. Her rancid breath singed the hairs in his nostrils, and he nearly lost what little food remained in his belly.

The bearded man, catching the scent of potential prey, slogged toward Raihn, making the situation even direr. Crawling on feeble legs, he inched closer, his milky eyes fixed.

"Help!" Raihn cried out, desperately trying to summon Amarra. "Please, Amarra, I need you!"

His back pressed against the rough stones. Pebbles dug into his skin as he realized he was about to be torn apart by this ghoulish pair. He had become reliant on Amarra's ability to appear just in the nick of time, but he seemed abandoned. In his desperation, his last maneuver was to butt the assailant with his head. That allowed him to wedge his foot between him and them before ferociously kicking the hag away. She fell back and cracked her skull upon stone. One foe left.

Raihn retrieved his sword, and without time to spare, he lopped the head of the oncoming man clean off, sending it rolling onto the ground beside him. He'd slain what seemed like twisted remnants of human flesh distorted into grotesque vestiges of their former selves. Humanity lingered in the glint from the rolled head, but it quickly faded. He huffed and he puffed as thunder blew through his veins.

Raihn fell, hugged his knees, and tried to gather himself in the return of silence, his thunder gone. But the hag awoke and leapt for his throat again. Raihn pointed his blade up and fell back. The woman was impaled, yet she clawed at him still. She slid closer and closer as the blade of his sword plunged further through her gaunt figure. However, before her body reached the hilt of his metal, her head finally fell limp. She was snuffed, the back of her head like a sodden bird's nest.

Raihn dropped her body aside and stood, battling a scream. Just a moment to recoup was all he'd wished for, but his shoulder was suddenly gripped. Raihn spun and waved his blade, his stony expression limbering. "Amarra!" he cried, nearly missing her. Thankfully, her arm stretched out further than his blade. "I'm so sorry. That was close," he apologized.

Amarra embraced him again, trembling, whether from this awful place, because she was alone, or for losing him, he wasn't sure. But he was glad of her return, cherishing the embrace even. He'd realized he didn't want her to vanish again.

Before they could truly regroup, that same voice called for them. "This way." It seemed to be annoyed.

They weren't far now, and the voice persisted from somewhere above. Looking up, Raihn saw the flame of a torch bobbing through the fog. Faintly, he glimpsed a staircase under its flicker. But before they could reach the steps, the anvil made it through the fray and cut them off.

"What did you bring upon us?" she bellowed from the other end of her leveled sword.

"If you want to live, then just follow us!" Raihn exclaimed.

Dame Dawness lowered her blade contemplatively. She looked to the stairs and then back. With a breath of despair, she let them off the hook. And when a scream from a young girl broke, she raced off in the same direction Raihn and Amarra had just fled.

Raihn's stomach churned at the young girl's scream. It was just like when the horses were freed from their paddock. *Pate?* Raihn found his body tuming towards the sound, but Amarra gripped his arm. Her head shook.

He and Amarra had their own battle to fight, so they squared their bodies abreast and moved onward up the rocky stairs.

Raihn climbed, the faint pitter-patter of footsteps behind him growing louder. He swiveled his head, fear tightening his chest. Cannibals were overrunning each other in a tide of flesh, giving chase. They drew closer, and his legs, already weary, screamed for rest. But he had to keep going, to gain more speed.

The gap between him and the cannibals was shrinking fast. One managed to scratch his swinging elbow, and then another pinched the flesh over his humerus. Panic surged; something had to change, but he could do nothing.

The foreboding caw of a raven echoed through the air. There was no time to question if it was as damning as the last as he spotted a lurking figure above. Raihn could only hope they were friendly, for there was nowhere else to turn with deadly drops beside them. Before he could call out, the figure raised a bow and loosed an arrow into the cannibal on Raihn's tail. Then they fled up the stairs.

"Lostar!" Raihn exclaimed. "Is that you?"

Raihn found the energy to climb up the stairs and become level on a bridge. Raihn's calves were burning as though set ablaze, but that was a far more acceptable pain to endure than what those creatures' pursuit would bring upon him. Thankfully, not far ahead was a black stone arch. But as he neared, he saw the bridge end abruptly past it. Only the fog persisted, but there was no place else to go.

Barreling through, they were soaring momentarily, his heart climbing to his throat. Thankfully, they plummeted into a vast body of water, their bodies slapping the surface as if it were solid ground. Raihn was knocked into a haze before coming to his senses beneath the surface.

He swam to the surface, gasping for air, seeing that Amarra's head was already above water. Together, they peddled ashore. Raihn expected the horde to free-fall behind them, but nothing came besides his expectation. He thanked the sky, arms weighed down by sopping cloth. His eyes returned to the water, his cloak snaked around him. "Maybe they were behind us, and I missed them," he said. "Maybe they cannot swim. Either way, I'm not com-

plaining. Let them drown. All that matters is that we made it," he exasperated.

The fog thinned, better revealing the lush landscape unlike anything outside the wall. "I suppose we're safe," he said, then glanced over. Amarra
was not beside him. Spinning around, he discovered her some distance
away, smelling roses. She sauntered back to him, his face feeling flushed.
She grabbed his hand and tugged him along like he was a gentle flower, her
hand a soft breeze.

After the terror they'd just escaped, this wondrous forest seemed too good
to be true, as if some realm old but very much alive, with moss scaling the
trees and vines lounging over their branches. Wild mushrooms grew in
herds, and butterflies fluttered over mounds of flowers. It was a much-
needed infectious pleasure, numbing him sedately. Raihn teetered upon his
heels to spot all the birds flying from branch to branch in the great big trees.
These magnificent woodland monoliths were like the greatest man-made
towers, reaching high into the azure, with sprawling boughs like winding
bridges for critters to cross.

Raihn murmured a curse. "By the bells," he said in amazement. Continuing to follow Amarra, his neglect of the path ahead led him to clash against
her. It would seem that while he was distracted by his wonderment, Amarra
stood in awe of a more foreboding sight that spread beyond the cliffside.

His attention twinned hers thereafter, his eyes taken by the same shivers
of rock and stone in a grey expanse ahead. Stone as far as the eye could see,
amid fog just as dense. And glimpsing through the rock's billowing wig,
though faintly, was the Wall of Thorns. It rose up and up, and then up some
more, racing away, clear of the fog's wisp. They were illogically high on
this mountain but insufficient to peer over the wall.

"Miryam's grave," he cursed softly, "we made it."

Amarra looked at him with an honest grin as they overlooked the rest of
the staggering mountain. Butterflies fluttered within his rib cage, his hand
inching toward hers. He clasped it carefully. Her smile faded. Her hand retreated to her chest, and his butterflies returned to their cocoons. "No. No,
I'm sorry," he pleaded. "I was but in the moment," he continued, but Amarra retreated by a few steps. "Amarra," he breathed. Her dismay left him
floundering.

In his distress, Raihn fled, following a winding path. Around a mound, he
came across a cave wedged amongst a rocky outcrop along the grassy hill.
Thinking this was surely where the others had gone, he entered. And closely
behind him, stress gripped his shoulders and breathed down his neck, cold
as a river's lick.

The dark innards of the cave wrapped him in uncertainty. He wondered if
he'd made another mistake by running. *Surely,* she'd thought of him even
less. He was no giant like her, let alone big for a man. The more he thought

about it, the more it was detrimental. He felt himself a fool to open himself up once again.

AMARRA was alone, unable to speak her mind, when everything seemed to splinter apart. She chased him, but he had already vanished into the cave's dark belly. A shiver ran up her spine, briefly stopping her chase. She was before the cave's maw, where light remained only at its doorstep. She was frightened, but her foot lurched forward and pulled her into the black. She spanned out her arms to find the walls for comfort, leaning left and right. Nothing. She reached up. Nothing there either. She glanced back at the entrance. Her heart wrenched to discover it gone.

Amarra pushed forward, searching for an end, battling a fear concerning not her safety, but Raihn's. Her ferocity was a constant shield, rarely lowered—but the thought of Raihn being just as lost in this darkness clung to her mind like a leech. Yet, that wasn't the only thing leeching. Something lurked here. She skimmed her surroundings, trying to sniff it out—some kind of stalker, not just the burden of her self-judgment. She twisted herself into a web of fear, many judgments flying in.

He was somewhere in here.

She rattled her head by the horns. Lowly, they are men, and, lowly, she's an Outcast. Inside them all, tender yolk. She steered razors down her scalp and plowed a fist to the dark, but the dark forbade pain. She turned over her knuckle, angered by its numbness. She beat her chest. Harder. She pulled back for her hatchet, her head in a whirl and her heart in a plunge. Memories had her in a daze, made by men and Outcasts alike. Her hand fled the reach of her weapon, bells nearly tolling in her ears.

She launched into a steady sprint, but the darkness offered no reward for her effort. Eventually, her pace slowed to a brisk walk, then to a wandering shuffle, as time, light, and all sense of direction remained elusive.

Then she sank and hugged her knees in a curl. She thought she was brave to fight on, but it seemed feigned. Accepted was defeat, and the dozen shed tears. Darkness enveloped her, prevailing over her. And though her efforts seemed fruitless, she found a morsel of comfort in the isolation, strangely heartened by reminiscence. She felt nothing beneath her, but out in the black, she could sense iron bars inches from the tips of her stretched fingers. She recalled the hope beyond them, within her memory, still fearing it. There was always another heart to pry that metal.

A faint noise arose before her—a gentle ring—and a glowing beam of hope lifted her chin. Before her stood a crownling flower; it peeked through the pitch black, sprouting from nothing and appearing to hover as it uncoiled from its root. It was so vibrant that Amarra couldn't help but admire it, feeling thankful for this delicate flower to keep her company. She'd only ever learned of it through Tepparna. Its perky, intoxicating fragrance was finally tangible and not just a blurb. She reached out and caressed its dainty stem, marveling at how small it was when more flowers sprouted, popping up and stringing a path before her. She stood up, beaming. Bursts of energy seeped into her bones as a newfound sense of direction blossomed. Wherever the crownlings led, she'd follow.

At the end of the growth, Amarra heard babbling before witnessing something emerge from the dark: a boy with grey skin, an Outcast like her. He lay on his back beside a river, a musky scent clinging to him. Suddenly, he jolted upright, eyes darting wildly alert, like a deer. His breaths turned ragged as he was visibly shaken, lost, and hopeless. Then, heavily, he sobbed.

Amarra stepped closer, intending to calm him, taking notice of his petite horns. Seemed a warm place for an Outcast. He was far from the north with tear-streaked cheeks. His face lifted, his gaze nearly meeting hers.

"It'll be okay!"

She whipped around.

A human boy broke past the foliage, echoing her unspoken reassurance.

"Don't cry," the newcomer urged.

Amarra realized, with a shiver, that the horned child wasn't looking at her, but straight through her. She was a kind of visitor, trapped between worlds, peering through the vines the way she felt something peer at her.

The new boy had a warm, Eldhos-kissed complexion, black hair, and eyes like acorns. Concerned, he called out, "Dad!" But no guardian—human or Outcast—was in sight. He knelt beside the crying child, studying him. "Wow…you have horns!" he said, reaching out thoughtlessly to touch them. The Outcast child flinched.

The boy withdrew his hand. "I'm sorry… Are you lost?"

A sharp crack shattered the moment, twigs snapping, branches splitting under substantial stomps. A man pushed through the thicket with a frustrated crook in his back and a fishing rod in one hand.

"Don't run off," he grumbled. "And mind your manners, Muna. If words won't teach you, my hand will."

He froze mid-step, his body tense. "Get back."

"Why?"

The father dropped the rod. "I said get back, Muna!" The man's hand shot to the bow slung over his shoulder, gripping it instantly. "Move out of the way."

"He's lost!" Muna yelped. "He's alone."

The father's gaze flicked around warily. "He's not alone. He can't be. Think, Muna Raihn. How did he cross the Line?"

Amarra stiffened at the realization. *Raihn.*

The father's voice hardened. "Use your head and quit acting stupid." He slung the bow, snatched Muna's arm, and then turned his attention to the Outcast boy. "Where are your elders?"

The child curled in on himself, head tucked behind his arms.

"I asked you a question," the man pressed. "Answer me."

"I don't know," the boy blubbered.

"Why are you here?"

"I don't know! I swear!"

The father exhaled sharply. "Dammit." He wiped sweat from his brow and paced.

"Can't we take him home?" Muna asked.

The father stilled. His brow arched way over Raihn and his "Stupid question."

Muna flinched at the words.

"No, Muna. He's not a pet. And I won't endanger Parcel Path for him." The father shook his head, jaw tight. "But we can't leave him either. If the fishmonger finds him—or worse, if he wanders into town—" He trailed off grimly.

"He's safer with us."

"You ever consider whether we're safer with him?"

"But you always said putting others before yourself is part of being a leader."

The father's jaw clenched. "…Of all times to remember my teachings."

Muna stood firm. "So, should I put his life ahead of mine?"

The father scoffed. "Don't pretend you have stout shoulders when they aren't even leaves yet to grow broad." He resumed pacing.

Muna's voice wavered. "Then what do you want to do, Pop?"

"That's what I'm trying to figure out!" The father's shout cracked louder than any branch he broke from stomping.

Muna was startled, his eyes burning. His lip trembled.

The little Outcast shuffled forward and draped himself over him.

The father exhaled. His hands found his hips in a way that relayed his surrender.

"…Shit."

Amarra relished the meager reverberations after the family turned to dust, but that reverie was short-lived. The well of black boxed her into a cluttered room filled with moping paintings and miscellaneous objects, much like this other Outcast, with their nose buried in a book at the wall.

Beneath a circular inset window, the Outcast sat with a book balanced in their lap. Amarra quickly recognized them—the grey child from the river, now appearing in their mid-teens. They seemed detached from reality, lingering in the chamber of their mind, their expression clouded by some implicit emotion.

Outside, a ball of laughter bounced through the air. Amarra leaned over the boy to catch it through the window. Below, Raihn and a girl lay beneath a tree, lost in their made-up whimsy.

Her gaze drifted downward again, tumbling as if down cellar steps this time. And there, in the dust and dark, lay something forgotten: a core cast aside from the lathed bowl. Like that core in the cellar—shaved away, discarded—he could remain undisturbed while those of a prettier shell retained purpose, brimming and finely finished in a highlighting light.

Her eyes fell on the book cover they held: Bees and Honey.

It snapped shut, and she recoiled.

The young Outcast tossed it aside, slumped their head against the wall, and listened, resembling a lop-eared bunny. Muffled voices arose from below—a restrained feminine voice and a much louder, huskier voice. They seemed to go back and forth beneath the floorboards, the man sounding more stressed than the woman. Amarra listened closely, going as far as pressing her big pointy ear to the gap in the floor, the timber tickling the soft little hairs of it.

"Raihn cannot bring her around here," the man muffled below. "Have you told him? Because look. There they are."

"They're young," the woman excused. "It's natural. We can't just forbid him from courtship, Rahim. I know how you'd react if your father had done what you're trying to do."

"We live under a constant risk," Rahim continued.

"Maybe it's time to let River go. He remains cooped up. It's not right."

"Taking him in has complicated everything," the man griped.

"Such is life," the woman retorted. "You knew what path that choice would take you. 'An easy life builds no character.' Remember that? You used to say that about that girl you once courted. Is that what this is about? Her now having a daughter, who's out with your son?"

"Don't be ridiculous, Angeline. I'm glad Bart ripped that rotted rag off my hands; I wouldn't hold that against their…spawn. That was the best thing he ever done for me because it led me to you. He's a snake for doing it, but…it worked out. And if he were ever to discover our secret with those loose lips of his…"

"You've done the right thing once, Rahim. I'm sure you'll do it again."

"No, Muna—Raihn did," Rahim corrected. "But even so…a good thing can stretch so far."

"Then maybe you can confer with Raihn, you know, make this a family matter. That means including River."

"Perhaps…a cabin," Rahim mused, exasperated. There was an audible silence just then. It was as if the two lit up and gave each other a look of *radiant discovery*, or so Amarra imagined.

"There's plenty of space out here, and surely, off the path, he can be secluded but not alone," Rahim continued. "We can visit him occasionally, and Raihn can be groomed for the position of Village Head with… Aggy," he added, his voice lowering in distaste.

144

"I know she's rough around the edges, but I think Raihn is fond of that," Angeline reasoned.

"He shouldn't be, yet he goes against all the grain in all the oak in the valley. She bears no fruit but grows like a thornbush. I hear Lady Charlotte Helmsworthy of Majella suffered a significant loss," he continued. "Now a lonely widow, I would place Young Lord Muna Raihn Parcel in her late husband's stead. The Majes, surely, would adopt him quickly. And a fine dowry she would offer. Or similarly…"

"Rahim…" Angeline interjected softly.

"Lady Brunnie of Mulberry Woodlot. A shame about those wasps, but after all, they are Bushwalkers. She'd come here with her feet all—"

"Rahim! Must she be a lady, a baroness, or anything more than what Muna Raihn loves? Was that all I was, purely?"

"Purely, you are the salt of my lake," he replied tenderly. "I look out for you, for anyone under my roof now… However, I cannot sit and abide, knowing how peculiar our life on this hill has become. The floors creak heavily over my head from an Outcast who cannot espouse any woman that Raihn can. Nor can he go as Raihn pleases. And worse, what would happen to Raihn if he were to take a hand under my roof unfamiliar with the creaking? River cannot remain here forever, Angeline. He needs his own home."

"Perhaps that discussion should come first, then Raihn's suitress. You've got the idea already; time to lay out the design."

River took an ink pot from his desk and pulled up another book. The back, binding, and cover were all of worn leather. It whined sorrowfully when split open. He dipped his quill and scratched the page until three knocks came at his door. He jumped up and slid into bed, taking the book under the covers.

"Are you okay?"

Raihn peeked through the doorway.

"Yeah, I'm fine," River replied.

"What's going on? Not feeling good?" Raihn asked, entering the room.

"Why do you ask?"

"You're in bed with the covers pulled over your head," said Raihn. "It's hot, stuffy, and past lunch."

"Well, what else am I to do?" asked River.

"The opposite of what I just said…and to eat—or did you eat?"

River didn't answer.

Raihn sat on the edge of the bed and tugged on the blanket, revealing River's horns. They quickly pulled it back. "You don't need to hide them, especially not from me," Raihn said earnestly.

"Then why am I forbidden to pass even the back door?"

"For your safety."

"That's part of it," said River. "But your safety is the other part. I'm a stowed burden. Even if I was to be stowed someplace else, I'll always be on his mind."

"Whose?" Raihn asked.

"Father's."

"Then what is the right choice? There must be one," asked Raihn.

"Sleep sounds fairly good right now," said River. "I think that's my first choice."

"River, Aggy's gone," Raihn said. "You can stop sulking. Let's do something." He pulled at the blanket. "I can make barley tea!"

River shifted, his horn tearing at his feathered pillow as he glared at Raihn with purple bags draping under his eyes. "I must sleep."

Raihn bent back. "Perhaps you're right. Look, tomorrow is Aggy's birthday. Her friends will celebrate with her, but I still wanted to surprise her with a flower. I'll be back after that, okay?"

"If she's your desire and you hers, then why is she celebrating with her friends?" River muffled beneath the blanket.

"It's just what works for her," Raihn excused. "Besides, tomorrow is special. It's the day we found you. Remember?"

"I remember," said River. "See you then?"

Their horns poked out of the blanket, and they nodded.

Raihn slowly stepped back to the door and glanced around the room, taking in all the paintings, almost wistfully, watching River as if he were no more. He closed the door, and the atmosphere petered like a hushed candle.

Darkness purged the chamber of all its dwelling things except River. He bunched the covers into his fists, hiding, but suddenly sat up.

"Raihn!?" Their voice bounded through the dark, the bed frame creaking. Then, there was a scratching sound beneath it. Like fingernails dragged along the wood.

Silence loomed, heavy and unnerving, until scorched hands emerged from the bed's underbelly. They coiled over the sides, latching onto River and forcing him flat against the mattress. The bed rose, sprouting countless legs beneath it, just as many as the hands pinning him down. The flaking limbs tilted the bed, and in the darkness before him loomed a pair of silvery eyes.

"Who are you?" River choked through a grip.

Amarra raced to the bed and attempted to pry the hands away, but they were unrelenting. Though River didn't notice her, he and Amarra watched in dreaded suspense as the silver eyes blinked away, a voice taking their place.

"Interesting."

The voice was fragrantly creamy yet wicked, intrusively buzzing over her auricle like a bumblebee. She heard the unsolicited voice bend her ear as though she had lost control of her mind. "My heart aches, and it yearns. I loathe, and I wish. My passion lies beneath a mountain of anguish."

Get out. Leave!

But the voice persisted, louder and more unpleasant as it cusped her ear. "I am dead-alive, and you will be too," it said seductively. "I am within you always."

On the final word, Amarra felt the voice's molten breath drift over her neck. Instinctively, she glanced behind her. A pointer's length from her nose, she came face-to-face with his ethereal kind, for she sensed it in the dark, worse than a stalker in the vines.

"Second born and forlorn. Much like our kin, we all suffer under the same skin." The disembodied voice rasped, its buttered throat drying as the words tangled with fervor. "Yet the more they sprout, the further they descend from their roots, their minds consumed by rage. White spires will blacken, and the wings of fat birds will be shorn as they heed my call from clouds most dark. Feathers will flutter down from the flightless bird. I cometh."

Amarra writhed from the pluming voice, netted by weaving arms. Just like River was.

A visage spewed in a creeping push through the tarry darkness that ebbed from dainty cheeks. He neared with fair features touched by an artist, skin soft and firm as crafted alabaster like hers. He hummed a lowly tune as he came, grabbing the back of her skull with deft fingers.

Their heads clashed softly until they joined like molded clay.

"They were so close with you," he whispered.

Amarra shut her eyes but felt nothing come of this melding, like when her fist punched the black space. And then the bed fell and its arms receded. For a brief moment, she heard a delicate song played off some kind of string as though it were a memory that had come to her. Something within her wriggled along her veins, forcing her eyes to her hatchet out of a primal fear. Echoing within her, an aura dark, she thought to drain it out. She looked to the edge of her hatchet, afraid of how far she might go, knowing the cave had starved her of pleasurable pain.

"Do it," the voice whispered.

She sprung for the weapon, then yielded. Sudden stabs pricked, thoughts of ticks rummaging beneath her skin.

"Do it!"

Amarra gripped her bloodletter, raising it to her chest with her eyes shuttered. She'd blindly swung down, swift so that it may be quick. Just as swift, resistance came, but not from herself.

Halted, she felt no sting. Her hatchet suspended before her, unpermitted by some other force. She opened her eyes. Nobody was there. She flung the axe and it fell flat without a skid, without a sound.

Amarra fell forward like a mote with broken chains, not yet released from the snake's venom. Against the black void, she lay flat with a cheek pressed on spotless glass. And from around her shoulder, she saw pale ankles stepping her way.

Amarra's skin no longer itched from the intruder. Even so, she could not move. Her muscles were burned out like blown wicks. Her skin began to flake and drift, and so too would her mind. It seemed the end was nigh, but then a bright light gleamed over a boulder. A beacon. She could hear a running river and held steadfast. Normalcy at last, as she could smell the scent of river birch. It seemed to burn sweetly into her nostrils, her cheek on pillowy flowers.

Strength began to return, and Amarra found the will to push herself up at last to confront the coming thing. However, no one was there, unlike she thought. Instead, she saw a door misplaced by some trick of her mind. She glanced around and saw naught else.

She went to it and entered. She was led to the same chamber as before, where Raihn sat, reading a familiar journal. She moved toward him and peered over his head to see just what he was reading.

"I'm sorry. Forgive me. I should have been there," Raihn wept over it. "If only you knew. In the mess of things, I forgot, and I'm a fool for it. Any risk to have you back would be worth taking. Even if worse came to worst, I'd rather suffer with you than without you. Though if shearing us brings you peace, I hope you found it and that you suffer no more."

Amarra smiled at Raihn's vulnerability, finding solace in familiarity through his loneliness. Raihn took the journal and fled what was now a dusty sanctum, swept into black.

She spotted Raihn in the shadow. He smirked, with a bulb of fluffed crimson upon an emerald stem: a rose he contentedly caressed. He approached, and her heart fluttered in a panic. Her chest tightened from uncertainty. A whirl spun in her head. Every time she saw him, she saw a reflection of kindness but also pain. Deceit. Not that the former was his fault or a sign he'd shown. She had to decide how she'd react this time; her chest ever snugger, but he pushed through her like an electric current. It dawned on her that she was just a visitor once again. Gravity overtook Amarra's heart as she became unexpectedly heavy, relieved, and somewhat jealous. Raihn stepped towards a red-headed girl standing in the distant dark, the same as the one under that tree: *Aggy.* With every step, a scene developed around him: bramble, a fence, a path, grass. But the girl had yet to spot him, occupied by merry companions no matter the scene's livery.

Raihn hid and lurked around a hut's corner after noticing her company of three. Amarra skulked just over him.

"That's quite the dress. It kind of suits you," one of the two boys grinned condescendingly over the white frilled garb of blue that the redhead dawned.

"Yeah, if you lived on the hill, where you would look down upon us," a girl with dark hair added.

Aggy, whose red curls engulfed her freckled face, seemed embarrassed. Her dashing green eyes, vibrant like the rose's stem, avoided them. "It's not bad," she said. "It came from the market town. He left it on my doorstep with a note saying he couldn't wait. So, go easy."

"It's just not you, is all. I'm used to seeing you in 'spenders and a coat of mud," said the boy. "You'll probably miss the splinters, too."

"Being on top won't change who I am," the red-haired girl blushed.

"So, you're just wearing it to play nice," the boy figured. "I ain't blamin' ye."

"Easy, Will," said the dark-haired girl. "You're soundin' jealous of good ol' Aggy."

"Never! No offense," Will said. "I says it true when I tell you I am attracted to mud and dirt. Work. Fightin'."

"Well, I'd say what she was doin' is work enough," the dark-haired girl remarked. "I can respect that."

"You're not lyin'. Raihn probably thinks he's the top, but his head is in the clouds."

Aggy chuckled, but she seemed nervous. She swiped back a curl and seemed to flick and itch off her dainty ear.

"What?" a second boy asked. "You haven't snuck off to a bush and frolicked a little?"

"We're taking it slow," said Aggy. "It has to be special…for him." Her eyes rolled.

"As if I can regard him less," the second boy said, his grin smearing across his cheek.

"Don't pressure her," Will snapped. "If he wants to wait, so be it. That only means she goes unspoiled. A fresh egg yet to be eaten."

"Gross," Aggy winced.

"Look, he may be chocolate, rich and tasty, but it ain't good for ye," Will drawled. "Is the position worth it?"

"Will," the other boy began. "You mean to say you wouldn't hitch onto an ugly horse even if he were ahead in the race?"

"Shut up, Bubs," Will said, his fist waving. "Aggy, what of it, huh? You going through with it? Tomorrow, you gonna lock it down and spend ye grace er what?"

"Yes, Will. Don't think I'll be persuaded."

"No, I don't have no alms full o' silk and gold for that, I s'pose," Will remarked.

Bubs scoffed and scratched his elbow, saying, "What about Bart? He feelin' like me or Will do, Aggy?"

"Pa encourages it as redemption, and he's miserable anyway I'm sliced. Pa wanted a pie but got a cake instead. Though, still he calls me cherry rather tenderly, 'cause I'm so sweet." Her face briefly went pensive before she continued. "'You shake that boy down yet, cherry?' he says. 'Well, why not?' he says more." Her head cocked to the side. "So what do I say? He's a sissy. Makes Pa smile I guess, but for a second only. Then he gets bitter an' talks about 'that no good swine, Rahim,'" she mocked with a deep voice and a chug from her arm.

"Figures," Bub said. "Pops is old and crusty. Tell him to flake off."

"Lock it up, Bubs," said Will. "Papa won't be matterin' much to ol' Aggy when she gets the best seat in Parcel Manor with the likes of them. No matter what 'e thinks. But neither will we matter."

"That's not true! I'm telling you, I am who I am. I have no frills," Aggy argued.

"Other than the ones on your dress, Aggy Arbordale Doncane," Bubs remarked.

"Cram it," Aggy snapped. "I'm going to bend by a bush with Raihn—him being quirky about my feet in that manor an' all. This village'll fall into my hands, and not the other way around. Because I owe no sores to those tyrants."

She pranced her tongue like a snarky playwright in a pageant wagon, painted like a droll number in a broadsheet of whores from the rich North Wynd's undesired district—a place Amarra was familiar with. The same as she was familiar with the way men paraded women in a theatrical light, owed painted faces brighter than the broadside of their barns there. She seemed to drape herself over the arms of these men's banisters, a piece of cloth steeped in some linseed oil, cheap, flammable, with a glossy finish ready to burn if all else fails.

"Then be sure to keep Rahim impressed as well then," Bubs said.

"Not easy to do as daughter to a copper-mining serf that embarrassed the lord back in their heyday. However, I've heard tell of mistresses taken not for power. That Raihn is so thick-headed. I'm confident in my wiles to make me one such mistress." She smirked and popped a hip, followed by a wink.

She was aware. Selling her femininity: a droll number, but it meant power. Her wink to her mud buddies clued them in on her self-awareness.

"So, forgive my dress and let me shake my leg a while more."

Will sighed. "It's a lonely village, and Raihn'll run it up or down, doing as he wishes."

"Either way," Bubs continued, "until Rahim's rule is over, I doubt Bart will get any favors or slack. They think so little of us. They have nobody tending the manor house besides themselves. I never see no serf come down that hill. Strange folk they are."

The plot enraged Amarra. Stomping towards the no-good scamps, she reached for their throats one at a time, mimicking a harsh thrashing as their bodies aired about her clench. Then she attempted to dust away their image, but they persisted.

Then, she heard a rustle from where she came. She and Aggy both glanced over, but only Amarra investigated.

Raihn was missing, and in his place, a smashed rose.

None of the boys took notice, but Aggy was the one to remain alert on her toes. "Guys. I think I've had enough talk about the subject," she said. "You told me you were taking me to celebrate, not lament. Let's get some tankards and put on our drinking smiles!"

"Right, I s'pose it your day after all. S'pose we may not get too many more, so let's say we trek over to the Mousehole."

"Deal. I'll meet you there, 'kay?"

"Why not come now, Aggy?"

"Because I says so."

"Right o' right. C'mon Bubs, Ags is gonna change first, I'll bet. Wantin' proper attire for the hole," said Will.

Aggy had watched them leave before almost leaping off to the side. She discovered the rose, her body spelled by petrification.

Amarra grinned out of spite, sensing a plunge from Aggy's chest, who plucked the rose and held it close, gaze drifting longingly into the distance. Amarra noticed him, too: Raihn. He was shuffling away with his hands buried in his pockets, head low. The redhead darted after him, and Amarra followed closely, contempt swirling within her. The redhead quickly caught up to him, pleading, but he refused to listen.

"Leave me," Raihn muttered, sounding truly like a lord. But when she pressed again, he spun around, nostrils flaring, his anger coming in huffs. His status took over. "I don't want to hear any more you have to say. Today was to be spent with your friends, so go spend it. They're more important anyway, right? Minds full of alms with silk and gold. And well, this is a valley of common copper after all. That's all they'll be, and gold is all they will wish to be. Take your dress off and join them in the mines."

Raihn stormed off, and Aggy hung her head, curls dangling past her face that she'd not flicked.

Amarra was so busy being poisoned with a mix of empathy and contempt that she hadn't realized how happy she was to know more about Raihn. When she simmered, she had discovered a sense of intrusion. She was pushed into Raihn's life journal that had been, for the most part, shut. She then considered her intrigue, wanting to see more regardless. Raihn was a struggling lord of copper and men, but an oddity.

The darkness bent and twisted into something new, showing her his stomping trek uphill to a grand building. He was met by those Amarra presumed to be his parents. Rahim asked nothing, but Angeline inquired much from her rocker.

Raihn grasped at the knob, ready to flee her, but Angeline hopped up and held his wrist in place.

"Talk to me," she said, most motherly.

"It's over," Raihn admitted. "She had a single desire, and I'm not it. What she desires is no different than any other suitress's."

"I knew it!" Rahim jumped, slapping the arm of his chair.

Angeline insisted he quiet down, though futilely.

"Barthalmass Doncane undoubtedly plotted this," Rahim continued. "With that river as his stake still."

"It's not about Bart," Angeline maintained.

Rahim exhaled and collected himself. "How'd this come about?" he asked, leveling his tone.

Raihn sighed, ambled past them, sat himself upon Rahim's rocker, and explained, "I overheard her with Will."

"Well, at least now you know to stay away from her," said Rahim. "It was dangerous anyhow. I've said this many times over. If anyone listened to me, this would never have happened!"

"Calm down." Angeline fanned her hand. "I'm sure your 'I told you so' doesn't help any."

"I'm getting my axe," Rahim huffed. "Imagine what the rest of them will think after hearing about how they toyed with us."

"You mean toyed with Raihn? And what, are you going to kill him?" asked Angeline.

"No," Rahim replied. "But that sounds like a good idea!"

"Come with me to the back. I'll make some tea," Angeline told Raihn.

Amarra pieced together the events, which were woven out of order, and felt the distress in the family as they were crumbling apart. Poor River had no clue…

…He would be forgotten up in his sanctum.

After that day, Eldhos would rise again, and Raihn would be changed. Like River, he lingered in his walls and the village would wonder why. Stories spun on a spindle, lies winding it thick. And, too, the globe seemed to spin endlessly. Night to day and day to night, Amarra waited out this hasty pace.

And then the night remained, darkest of them all. Eldhos was gone, and the manor and the village had been swallowed utterly. She was left alone in a place that seemed forgetful. She bore close to her heart a wick lit by a wish to return…to reconcile with such a fragile egg and to remind it of warmth, as Amarra meant to lower her shield once again.

The end of the cave revealed itself.

152

CHAPTER SEVENTEEN

Her name was Adfirna, and tenderly, Ogormin

RAIHN searched aimlessly through the dark, ample space. The seemingly never-ending slate raised goosebumps from a falling chill.

Cries boomed, cracking into a kind of gate; streaks of light ran like a web over the air, annulling his isolation. The pang of the corvid roar wrung his bravery, but as he trickled through the crack, he seemed shrunken not just by fear but by the size of this new realm. Before Raihn loomed a bleak forest of massive, unparalleled black trees caked in hoarfrost, regal and crowned with tines, some cut, lying like logs the size of rivers. Might a mountainous giant with an axe's haft as thick as an oak's bough and its head as large as a wagon wheel, had felled these snowy, black tines from the main beams of old that Raihn had heard tell of. But his imagination outpaced the tavern folks' rumors, dreaming of what else there might be, and if these were not trees, but literal growths from something beneath the dirt and snow.

Raihn peered deeper into the forest. More tines and beams, not felled but tall and wildly crooked, standing spirely. Beyond them, a white veil blanketed the source of terror. But the cries seemed to grow near as he entered the forest, knees wobbly. The trees bent over him, their tines jutting away. Eventually, he came upon a severed tine with a draped deer skin over yak hide covering the arching entrance. *Here,* he thought, hearing the wailing pierce his eardrums.

Shivering in the cold, the log appeared inviting and warm. In an attempt to gain entry, he discovered the intangibility of the yak hide. His hand passed through what he considered a hallucination, had he known what a hallucination was other than something the Bushwalkers would drone about while lying bareback in the grass.

"What kind of magic…" his voice quit, the howling persisting beyond the boundary of animal skin. Raihn retook his hand, and like planes visibly parallel, he peered through the otherworldly hide. Within the tree was a channel where shaggy furs were hung about and strewn across the floor, some of them wet. Tools dangled: saws, hatchets, tongs, and mallets. Stitching needles, an awl, and a leather slicker were in a basket. But most notably within the channel were two Outcasts of opposite sex.

The female braved a dire labor; her dam burst, her heels glistening, the furs cold. The to-be father exchanged the yak furs for dry ones before occupying her side.

Clasping his hand and pushing, the child came with a shallow wind. The father took the newborn and severed the umbilical cord with his fangs, bundled the child in what looked like wolf fur, and swaddled it.

Still extremely tense and tired, the mother only thought of the child. "May I see him?" she asked, oddly speaking common-tongued.

"She," the father corrected, his tone dreary, his language just as understood by Raihn.

The mother was clearly disheartened by the news. Wishing for a boy, she appeared more worried as the baby continued to lie silently. "Why is she so quiet? Hand her to me," she said firmly. But the father was reluctant. With her arms reaching out, the mother now demanded it. "Give her to me."

The child was passed, and the mother's once beaming eyes dimmed. "Is he coming?" she asked.

"All of Norrekdorr in Nomankra must have heard," said the father gravely.

Raihn feared who else might lurk in these neighboring black bark trees and huddled beside this family, expectantly eyeing the yak hide over the entrance. Who could these giants possibly fear, and what was wrong? Raihn looked back at them, struggling to see the wrapped child.

"What will you do? Tell me it's something," the mother said, her voice trembling, the syllables not matching her lips. The father's demeanor seemed less than hopeful. And before his answer was pried, the yak hide swung aside.

Another had entered the room—the one they seemed to fret over. A male Outcast, lurching past the yak fur. Like his long ears, his stately horns were adorned with metal rings. He wore yak fur over a leather tunic, and his hair was braided with dangling beads. His piercing eyes were lined with soot, just over rigid cheekbones. Stillness befell the dwelling. He snorted, eyes piercing past his stout nose at the mother, the child clutched at her bosom. The baby was fully wrapped. The new arrival snorted a white cloud of discontent once more.

"Show me."

"Yes, Onurra Tarinorr," said the father. But the mother resisted.

"Show me the child!" Tarinorr demanded.

The mother took one last look at her baby and unwrapped it. The chief-looking one, Tarinorr, became quiet like the child before him, looking upon her small tuft of wispy, white hair over her white as snow scalp.

From what Raihn could see, she appeared nothing like her kin, so he breathed her name as he knew it: "Amarra..."

"Shame has blown through the tines upon this night," Tarinorr said.

"Onurra..." the father whimpered.

Again, he said it, *Onurra. What does that mean? Is it their first name, or does it merely precede it?*

"Nay, Ogrrek, Lyra lives, her blood subdued," Tarinorr began, calling the father 'Ogrrek' and the mother, 'Lyra.'

"The child is bald and merciful," he continued. "The grand burr beneath the soil has gifted a teindorr naught," he stated. "The mother still draw breath, disappointing what lay below the teins and beams. I expected not a bloodless crown of magnolia betwixt her thighs." Tarinorr's hand extended in wait for their apology, a confession of their mistake.

The mother's nostrils flared, her hands firm on her offspring.

Tarinorr, their *might-be-chief,* retook his hand and fled after a final snort.

The father neglected the gaze of his fraught love and sunk his eyes to the ground. Balling his white-knuckled fists in anger, he stood up proudly and flew out. Raihn followed.

Not keeping pace with them, Raihn finally came to a clearing where the father was surrounded by what looked to be his tribe: a race under wood and stone, adept wielders of axes. Carvers, whittlers, and those capable of lathing with the smallest branches they could manage.

Standing dead center, the father faced Tarinorr, who slumped upon a throne carved into the lopped trunk of a black horn tree. The massive tree arched in a slight bend, its dark limbs stretching overhead like frozen talons. Beside the chief stood two more giants, both brimming with dissatisfaction. On the left, a thinner Outcast with a fair face watched silently. To the right, the meanest-looking one leaned against a long, blood-red staff, her eyes peering beneath sags of warty skin, her gaze as horrid as her posture.

Gazes narrowed as the wintry newborn and its mother advanced. The father grimaced, looking to dissuade her approach.

"I will walk," she said, her legs quaking. "And I will carry her."

The male relented, briefly snorting. His hunter eyes narrowly peered beneath his brow to the Outcast court, his head crooked at them momentarily before he self-corrected.

Tarinorr proceeded, his gaze unyielding as he cued his slender Outcast with a soft wave.

"We are not unforgiving, Lyra Hokskarn," the speaker declared, his throat contemptuous. "Renounce your parentage. Sacrifice the dull and nameless child as it stands against the image of our forbearer. Or be exiled.

"Will you offer your mistake unto our Onurra and take your solemn grievance, or—"

"Nay," she interrupted. "My child has a banner to wave."

"She has named her offspring," Onurra Tarinorr gathered. His expression remained unmoved as if he had predicted their defiance. He idly scratched the coarse, dark hairs on his chin.

The thin Outcast sneered and requested their child's name.

"Adnafir," the mother answered.

Raihn's breath caught. *Adnafir.* Hearing Amarra's true name mesmerized him. It was far more beautiful than the one he knew.

Tarinorr's stern expression was unyielding even after he spoke. "I was thinking closely to a little wolf—those puny southward things akin to our ogorm," he remarked. But then it broke. A rare grin spread across his face, revealing a surprising, almost eerie glee. "Call her Ogormin," he laughed, the sound harsh and commanding, his heartiness tapering off abruptly.

Tarinorr shook his head, knocking his jest. "Adnafir," he continued through a deep hum, his voice tender bone marrow. "I admire your tenacity as a clan; however, with your child named, your backs are already turned against the north."

The father, visibly shaken, thanked Tarinorr and knelt, his weight dropping harshly as though the strength fled his knees. "Ogormin…" he echoed, his head bowing low. "Our ogorm howled their last howl yesternight. It is his fur that keeps Adnafir warm. Fitting."

Tarinorr's eyes seemed to soften, but then he looked reminded of his stature, eyes igniting as he issued his final command. "Turn south with her, seek the fir trees. Leave your belongings to fire. No cursed thing may remain, especially those sodden furs. If this frail child survives exile, then strong enough might she be to live." And finally, he said, "The child we seek shan't come nameless, for they must embody Sikrubur before us, claiming that name. Plainly, I've witnessed the failure of your seed."

The Hokskarn clan, defeated, parted from the tribe. They had nothing with them, and only the father was able-bodied. As soon as they left the others' view, Lyra, weakened by her labor, succumbed to the arms of her mate.

While they may have accepted this exile, Raihn had to follow them longer than he wished, his feet plunging into their stamped pits. He'd already come to sum up this mess, considering it a ritual. Despite that, he followed, awaiting an end, until *Amarra* had grown a little older, maybe six years in an hour, no longer carried. She was upon a much smaller log, as she and her family were closer to who they called 'tiny folk.' They suffered smaller things like these frosted firs in which they could not live within, like their teindorr dwellings. She neighbored a fire, wrapped in her father's arms, as they waited for a skinned deer to cook. But time seemed to slow again.

Raihn watched them, seeing Amarra as a happy child despite exile and a broken throat. Her parents seldom spoke, their words limited to tasks. Ogrrek remained close to his family, standing among the little trees by their thatched dwelling.

On a somber night, Raihn caught some shut eye while the Hokskarn Clan sat, nursing another fire. But there was a rousing, and he seemed late for alarm. The clan already watch the forest from the front of their meager home.

156

His eyes studious among the darkness, Ogrrek became swift, abruptly smothering the fire pit. And when Raihn questioned their distress, he felt it, the slight rumble of earth. He'd removed his shoes and put his foot to the cold soil. He'd not recalled such a hasty shake in the ground before, but the clan seemed to understand its wild vibration.

Ogrrek whisked *Amarra*. "Come, Ogormin," he said tenderly, sticking to the nickname.

Lyra followed as they fled their new home, and Raihn tried to keep up with her, but their speed could not be matched by an ordinary man such as him.

The rumbling doubled. Something was catching up, and whatever it was, Raihn knew it would consume him first. He began to hear the drum of hooves and packs of supplies clanging like washed tin dishes. Shovels and canteens, swords and spears, axes and lanterns. It all clanked.

Whooping and hollering riders rode past and waved their weapons. All but one of them appeared to be rowdy. And this one man watched from behind the mane of his steed, riding cautiously.

Raihn's stomach sank. He knew what was coming. Heart pounding, breath ragged, he sprinted after the riders as they vanished into the night.

He chased the endless dark, snow stretching infinitely before him. Then, a trail of blood threaded to an inevitable end as the ground peeled away beneath his aura of light, revealing the fallen. Dead men lay scattered, spears jutting from the snow like fractured bones. Panicked neighs echoed, then silence. A heartbeat later, abandoned horses thundered past him.

Pushing deeper into the late frost, Raihn stumbled upon a man still standing. The leader of the charge, as he recalled, now clutching a bloodied blade over Amarra. She knelt beside her slain parents, silent sobs racking her small throat.

Raihn froze, his heart leaden, watching as the little Outcast was about to be struck down last.

Despite knowing his presence was intangible, he lunged forward. "No!" he cried, falling through the foe. Sprawled on the ground, he turned just in time to see a cloaked figure emerge from the darkness, steel flashing—a blade carved across the attacker's face before burying itself deep in his belly.

The rider staggered, clutching the blade stuck in him. "Alvin, you bastard," he gasped before collapsing beside Raihn.

The one named Alvin removed their hood, revealing themselves as the trailing rider, the best-tempered among the party. "Stay bleeding in the snow, whimpering and fighting with your last breaths," he said. "Or remove the blade and die swiftly. I strongly recommend the latter—no, wait, there is a choice appendage: forgiveness. It might be wise before your end."

"Forgiveness? From who, if not the king?" asked the outrider.

"Whoever you wish, just so long as it is not from me," said Alvin, nervously chuckling, his big spectacles bouncing upon his rosy cheeks. His words cut sharply, like the grit of his foe's appearance, but he was quite the opposite, well-kept.

"May the Ivory's Knight smite you," the outrider cursed him. "Only the king may forgive me, for he sits above all, traitor!" the wicked Outrider howled. He unsheathed the dagger from his flesh, eyes freezing over.

Alvin sighed and turned to Amarra. "I am so utterly sorry," he earnestly apologized. "As you may have heard from his vile tongue, my name is Alvin. And those men should not have been out here, but then again, neither should you. But I digress," he mumbled as he twiddled his fingers. He then carefully retrieved a handkerchief and slowly approached her.

Amarra just cowered there, clutching her parents' lifeless figures.

"I know you are frightened," Alvin continued, "and I don't blame you. Cry out if you must, but I will not hurt you." He neared, gently wiping a drop of blood from her face. "It is a dangerous place to be, and surely more will come when these outriders do not return, though I would suppose more will come again and again regardless. Quite frankly, you are not safe. And while yes, I know, south of here is no safer for you—but with me, you might have a chance where I may keep an eye most watchful. Would you mind coming back with me to my study? I promise to not leave your side."

But Amarra was unmoved.

Alvin slapped a palm to his head. "Of course, how silly of me. You would understand only Atnaarr." Alvin cleared his throat. "Unchak sarra gono," he said, "I mean no harm." He continued, gentle rolls coming from his tongue. "Sakra unrek. Sakra unrek," he repeated, his finger poking his chest, throat bobbing.

Still, the girl clutched her mother and father. The young Outcast froze a twist in her expression: a quiet cry. However, no sound escaped her lips, raw emotion in her contorted face and trembling body. Tears streamed down her cheeks, her narrow eyes pushing them out.

Alvin took ever more pity on her by the look on him. He came beside her and wrapped her in his cloak. The girl's body shook the way a scared pup would, and her anguish was palpable, but in Alvin's embrace, she finally began to settle, her sobs subsiding into a still, heart-wrenching silence.

Raihn observed, his sight becoming congested by a snowy gust. He braced for the blinding chill that seemed to sweep him elsewhere.

Black brittle stone in the heap of night. A glow at the end of a hall before many cold bars of iron. Occasional taps of rat feet skittered across the floor. Raihn witnessed the storm fade and was parted with this. Amarra was still before him, but this wind had brought her to this dark place where she sat behind iron bars, still young and still weeping.

Looking at her, he saw her horns, petite and sprouting. She banged them against the bars, ringing her sorrow. Again and again, she bashed the bars until her skull inevitably bled.

"Amarra!" Raihn cried. But they clanged, a reverberating clong filling the dark maze of iron.

She stopped as if she had heard him and seemingly acknowledged his gaze with her eyes affixed to his. He hoped, as he could only hope, to be seen, but from her eyes was a hollow gaze—two murky, forlorn ponds. She fell back into the darkness, chains around her wrists and feet rattling.

"I'm so sorry." Raihn wept remorseful tears, finding himself a runaway fool fleeing from foolish things after seeing Amarra lied to. Abandoned. Put in a cage. Tepparna was her stripped-away candlelight.

Raihn became shrouded in remorse. Amid his own self-judgment, a latch reverberated a shiver as timber gurgled. A door had opened, and a light cut in. The beam parted the black air, illuminating the walls of stone and high-lighting the bars of iron, pushing rats into the bookending dark. Raihn expected a jailer, but he saw another girl, young and with a soft face. She held aloft a little lantern, stepping through the block with her dainty feet prattling along the stone.

And she, with olive skin, ignored Raihn as he expected, then faced the same cell within the block. She held the lantern before Amarra and looked upon her. She was bundled in a massive cloak.

"You're chained!" the girl exclaimed, a frown stretching her lips. "Pale as well! What are you?" Her words went unanswered, swallowed by the dungeon. "Hello? Stop ignoring me!"

Amarra glared at her, covering her mouth to signal her muteness.

"You can't speak? Or won't. Hold up a finger if you can't," the girl continued. One finger crept from Amarra's cloak.

She understands, Raihn realized. *Did Alvin educate her?*

"I finally found someone to talk to, and she can't even talk back," the girl whined. "Okay. Shake your head or nod to answer. Understand?"

Amarra nodded.

"Good! Can you read?" she asked, to which Amarra rocked her hand as if to say "so-so."

"Really? Well, I can't read too well, but I'm learning. The strange men said I should be 'ladylike.'"

The girl slumped to the bars, seemingly deep in thought. "Wait!" She straightened, and her eyes bulged happily. "We can learn together! Would you like that?" she asked, to which Amarra nodded again. "Yay! I can also bring what I've been taught and teach you." The girl applauded. "Well, at least you can understand me… Oh! How old are you? You can use your fingers."

The jailed orphan did, and the once presumed jailer counted them.

"Seven? I'm six. My name is Tepparna, but my mom calls me Teppa. We're sort of new here. I have to relearn everything. Like, how to refer to 'His Grace.'" her eyes rolled as she curtsied. "It was far scarier at first, but I'm glad to be off that bumpy wagon and to have a floor to sleep on. No more slivers…"

For a moment, Tepparna looked glum, but then she brightened. "Now, I just need to know your name. But since that might take a while, why don't I give you one?"

Raihn sat back, blowing a steep exhale. All he could see was that visceral outcome in the armory, a fact harder to swallow seeing her so young. It was so real and grounding, dashing any preconception that they were untouchable adventurers. And more, seeing how far they went back emphasized the pain of Amarra's loss.

Before he could dwell on it for too long, there was a flicker. Tepparna vanished in a blink, and the same clanking as before signaled Tepparna's approach yet again. With her was the same lantern, the only light besides the tiny hole in the wall upon the closing of the door.

Tepparna approached the cell, looking at the age Raihn knew her to be. She wore better clothes than before, cleanly prim and proper, but at a cost. There were sores upon her knees and bruises wrapping her wrists.

Tepparna knelt more gracefully this time. Her hair was long and braided, and she wore a lavish emerald dress. Over her hands were silken gloves not long enough to hide evidence of her captivity. She shone her lantern over Amarra and joyously grinned, her cheeks eclipsing her eyes, but the Outcast's dull expression shared little of this happiness.

"Mother is in His Grace—I mean…" Tepparna shook her head to seemingly fight her teaching, "that fat toad, Hull's chamber with all the other chambermaids. That should offer us some time," said Tepparna, jingling a ring of keys. A deviant smirk crept along her lips.

Amarra's eyes remained narrow. She fell back and shook her head in profuse protest at what was being proposed.

"What, why?" asked Tepparna, her smirk gone. "This is our chance to escape! The light of Eldhos will recede shortly."

Amarra picked up a chart of letters and began to spell.

"Too dangerous. You cannot die for my sake," Tepparna read aloud. "No, Amarra, it is not for your sake but ours. You're not the only one trapped here, you know. I'm going, but not without you. If you stay, then you're keeping me prisoner just as much as they are. I tire of these walls, servant to this glutton. The both of us deserve freedom, my mother, too. So please, let us both escape and be free."

"The three of us, you mean," said another from the dark of a neighboring cell.

"I know what I said," Tepparna snapped.

"I'm like you. I've done nothing wrong," they went on. "What I did was right, and now look where it got me. So can't you do right by me?" He leaned into the light, hands clutching the bars.

"Magnus," Raihn gasped.

"I can help," Magnus continued.

"You're a tracker, as you said before, correct?" Tepparna inquired.

"Among other talented professions," Magnus answered not so humbly.

"Tracking will do just fine as is. Look. I know my way around here, but out there? That's different entirely. Neither me nor Amarra are natives to that world."

"Undeniably. It would be mutually beneficial if we help one another. But as I said, I am a tracker. Are you looking for more than freedom?"

"I search for what is forbidden to seek. I wish to go where no one else has, beyond the Wall of Thorns," Tepparna said, a spark in her eye.

"That's impossible!" Magnus scoffed.

"So they say, but today I tell you otherwise."

"Why?" asked Magnus. "Those dreams you blabber about have you ill-convinced?"

"Look, whether I find and attain the key or not isn't really important," she said. "If I scratch your back, you scratch mine."

"My back has been awfully itchy lately. This isn't my fanciest living space after all," Magnus sighed. "Fine, you have a deal." He reached between the bars to shake hands.

"Not quite." She looked to Amarra for affirmation. The Outcast appeared reluctant, yet she nodded in agreement.

The lantern's light puttered into a musky plume, darkness prevailing the dungeon.

Then a light cleaved the gloom. The door creaked an invitation.

Amarra's out there, accompanied only by broken promises.

CHAPTER EIGHTEEN
Cedric's foil

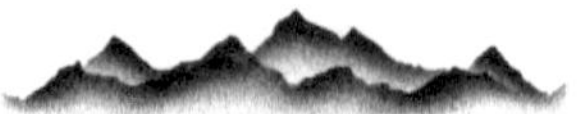

An arresting light flashed, propelling Raihn into a new realm through the door—a vast space cradled by lush foliage. Bright freedom buzzed within him as he became entangled in a lazy vine. There was no pain, only the tickle of his tumble onto a sultry seasonal bed, earthy and sweet, teeming with flowers from every corner of the world.

Raihn reveled in the sway of the blossoms, breathing deeply their intoxicating scents. The flowers bloomed as if it were late spring, early warmth touching the earth, and the fret and sorrow seemed to shed down his spine like dead leaves in fall. A smile spread across his face as the untidy things festering within him burned away to their core, leaving hardly a breath of smoke.

He laughed, though he wasn't sure why. Perhaps it was the grassy spears tickling his ankles or the delicate brushes against his ear. Or maybe it's the airy sensation in his head, the world subtly twirling around him. Raihn looked to the sky with relaxed eyes as he lay in comfort, as if shrubbed by Bushwalkers. Then, a shooting star, in the mid of the day, caught his gaze: Amarra's hand beckoning him to stand and walk with her.

"Amarra!" Raihn exclaimed joyously, his memory flickering. "I'm sorry. I shouldn't have been in such a hurry," he murmured, his voice slowing to a crawl.

She whisked him to his feet, the clouds returning as he tried to recall how he had come to lay down upon the grass. The coziness of the moment lingered as his questions did, but she enveloped him in her arms and broke his concentration. His feet left the ground as she pulled him close under her chin, and he smiled once more, feeling her warm breath against his nape and her sheepish neck brushing his face. When she set him down, she ruffled his hair.

They stood upon a grassy knoll, encircled by an array of flowers, as a chorus of voices buzzed around them, each one asking, "What?" Yet no other man or woman was in sight. They were surrounded by whatbugs, whose buzzing sounded like a chirpy "what?"—the source of the common joke about repeating oneself after hearing a whatbug.

"This place is wondrous," Raihn said, repeating himself to the inquiring whatbugs. Yet, he hardly bothered to wonder where the other fugitives were, as his sense of wonder overtook any concern. He plucked a yellow flower, indulging in its scent. "Crownlings—well—Cedric's foil, as a bed of them is called…" Raihn paused, the tale flashing through his mind. They'd turn red just before wilting, when their sweet scent turned bitter. Strange, for they hadn't done so before Cedric's death, as if they mourned for the martyr.

Butterflies fluttered, bumblebees zigzagged, and harvest mice nestled in the tulips. The dark world seemed to dissolve, giving way to a warm one, untouched by man. This new environment awakened Raihn's dormant senses, stirring his taste buds with the fresh finds around him.

Beyond the bush lay an even greater splendor. "A cabin!" Raihn exclaimed. "Old and overtaken by growth…large, too. I wonder if anyone still lives here." The answer was not far from the entrance. Raihn spied it—a mound with soft earth and a blank headstone. "A fresh grave, but the cabin appears hollow, and hollow it's been for some time."

The cabin was quiet and oddly luxurious, with two floors—strangely— and grew even more imposing as they approached. Raihn paused, taking in the scene like a fine, aged wine—not that he had ever tasted such a thing, even as a lord.

"Big," he said, flapping his arms. "We probably shouldn't go in. It could be dangerous if…" He trailed off as Amarra, without hesitation, entered the cabin, not even needing to stoop through the massive doorway. "Amarra," Raihn called out, exasperated. "Guess I'll just come on in unwelcomed."

Like a guest in a home never visited, Raihn stood awkwardly, glancing at the many things. "Hey, look! A fireplace with a bundle of pokers." He paused, caught up in his thoughts again, remembering a clack and a crick from logs on a cold night. He nearly forgot that night, which brought guilt. Then again, a lot was going on.

He ducked into the chimney and spotted a nest of sootbirds—a type of Caprimulgiformes—chirping for their mother.

"A nameless bird watcher named the birds here, often called the Selfless Woodsman." He continued, more to himself than to Amarra, who was off stomping through the cabin, "He never cared to make his name known, as notoriety did not ring in the halls of his head. He lived in a cabin, watching, inking birds around it. One day, he came home to his newly built cabin and slept cold, for black birds were nesting in the chimney, feeding their hatchlings. And for the sake of the birds, he bundled up and braced for the night."

Raihn retreated from the chimney and went on. "A different man, who refused to name himself in honor of the woodsman, found the journal with all these notes and shared the findings. I can't help but think of that story from when I was little."

Raihn realized he was talking to himself and said, "Amarra?" but she was too occupied.

Raihn reached up, stretching on his toes, but his fingertips couldn't brush the ceiling even then. The space seemed perfectly suited for Outcasts. And the one inside dashed around excitedly, exploring the cabin with a rare joy, finally able to stand upright in a dwelling without stooping. Raihn joined in, his curiosity piqued. He discovered little whittled characters near a pile of junk in the corner.

"Funny," he murmured, kneeling to examine them more closely. "One's fat, the other thin. One has a sword and bow, another a dagger. And this one here, it's tall."

The figures were peculiar, yet oddly familiar. Before Raihn could ponder them, darkness suddenly enveloped him, briefly reminding him of the cave. Startled, he ducked and stepped away, only to realize it was Amarra playfully covering his eyes with her one hand. If she could speak, she might have teased, "Guess who?"

Her spirited behavior caught Raihn off guard—he wasn't used to seeing this lighthearted and mischievous side, and she didn't seem to linger on any awkwardness from before. He supposed that was a good thing, making no other comments.

But as the moment passed, a hint of unease settled over him, his curiosity deepening as his carefree attitude waned. He glanced back at where the figures had been, but now there was only a pile of junk and random odds and ends. The figures were gone.

Amarra continued to poke around the room, occasionally glancing at Raihn with a playful side-eye. She sidled up to a tall cabinet, her broadness blocking his view. Raihn, unable to resist his curiosity, sneaked around her to take a look.

"Fishing rods and traps," he noted, recognizing the clutter in the cabinet. The sight triggered a memory of fishing with his father, a simpler time.

The Outcast had shut the cabinet and wandered off, leaving Raihn to explore alone. Without her presence, a growing sense of disorientation crept over him. He glanced back, hoping to glimpse her. "Amarra? Amarra," he called out, but she was nowhere in sight. His gaze shifted to the other end of the cabin where a staircase crawled away. "Amarra?" Raihn called again as he approached the steps.

Upon reaching the top, he found himself in a room larger than expected, filled with more furniture than seemed necessary. In the center was a massive bed, large enough for two Outcasts. But only one lay upon it, sprawled out with a leg dangling from beneath a bear hide and off the side. The midday's heat explained why her cloak lay discarded on the floor, and too, her loincloth and pelt—but still—*she's naked*. Raihn's heart skipped a beat.

He stammered, considering to either leave or announce his presence. "There you are. You wasted no time," he chuckled.

Amarra lay flat on her belly, her broad back exposed, revealing old scars that sparked a flicker of concern in his mind as memories surfaced. *That beastly animal,* he remembered.

He hesitated, thoughts momentarily tangled. "Amarra, we can't stay here," he urged as he clambered onto the bed, his bashfulness fleeting. "Amarra." She breathed heavily, almost snoring. "Asleep already?"

Raihn paused. Weariness washed over him when he touched the bed—a crude structure of reeds, grass, and furs. He continued to hover, trying to reason with himself that they shouldn't sleep, though his reasoning waned into triumph as exhaustion overcame him. He unfastened his sword belt, set it beside the bed, removed his cloak, and then ambled back.

Curling up at the foot of the bed like a house cat, he positioned himself facing the door, maintaining his distance.

Black. A tar pit bubbled, its dome expanding—perfectly round even as it thinned before bursting. Raihn broke into a sweat, emerging from the subterranean pitch as light returned with the next day's early morning. His mind felt scattered, thoughts splattering, regrouping, and then bursting again. The cycle continued—his consciousness constantly on the edge, jumping, splatting—a pocket of air rising in his head until it burst. He felt woozy, fighting against a tilt. His heart raced, pounding like hooves against the ground. Yet, he wasn't scared, and there was no nightmare; instead, he found himself comforted amid his plight, excitement stirring as Amarra's clammy body held him close, their hands interlocked. She must have rolled over in her sleep… He pondered this, smothered by the fullness of her silky alms. His mind wandered further, wondering if he had moved closer during their slumber, or if she was aware of their closeness.

Raihn slipped away and nabbed his cloak before escaping downstairs, his body still gripped by the vulnerability of the early morning. An inner voice nagged at him, pleading for his grace. Guilt flushed his cheeks. He moved lightly on his feet, heading for the back door. But as he passed the fireplace, a boar rug caught his eye. He paused. It seemed out of place, yet oddly fitting. He vaguely remembered the boar but not the act of taking its hide. *Amarra must have slain the beast, and we must have shared its splendor… We did.*

A fleeting memory of her glistening lips sparked in his mind. Her beastly nature, disregarding norms, was erotic. She must have saved the hide. Why not? It made for a good trophy rug.

Raihn sat upon a large boulder, and the river eased down as long tree tassels glid over it. In a strange way, he felt like the tassels, floating in place as the current passed him by. He was complacent, yet there lurked a certain restlessness below the water, which he could not see, for it was a shallow veil.

Time seemed to wane as the river flowed beneath his feet, the water carrying little dark ripples away. The wind blew, soft and gentle, whispering to the trees, which waved in greeting. Peace settled over him, making Raihn neglectful of his duties—whatever they were. He delayed finding work, becoming lost in the harmony, his rashed thoughts fading their itch.

He could hear Amarra's rustling approach but didn't expect her to grasp his hand. Still, his gaze remained fixed on a strange, familiar fog rolling over the water, filling him with unease as if something within it was watching, the same feeling in the vines but somehow harsher.

Amarra proceeded to tug his hand onto her inner thigh, igniting a longed-for warmth between his loins, his gaze stolen. It felt dense yet soft. She drew it higher, and he felt no loincloth.

The fog crept closer, brushing against the tassels like his fingertips brushed a sheepish tuft.

Raihn scrunched his thighs together under his cloak, taking back his hand, for she was suddenly hasty. He floundered, turning his eyes short of her face.

"There's…an axe…I should prep some wood for tonight," Raihn said, his voice tinged with nervousness. "It must've gotten cold for you last rest… Stave the cold… Cook up something tender." He recalled the fishing gear he'd seen the day before.

That's right. There is work to be done.

"…I'll be right back."

Raihn found the gear and shut the cabinet, but there was more clutter than before—a familiar trunk and a satchel. He couldn't recall placing them there, let alone what they contained. Still, perhaps a quick rummage through old things might jog his memory, driven by curiosity in this cabin that had felt like home for so long. Besides, he was in no rush to face Amarra—he must have embarrassed her, or so he thought.

The trunk whined open, its hinges creaking with a wistful familiarity, even in their grating yawn. Inside, nestled among the contents, were many books. Raihn soon found himself immersed in one of them: a book of tales. He began with the story of Cedric the Golden Martyr.

Cedric met his end at the hands of the Reds. As he fell into the crownling bed, the flowers turned crimson, mirroring the banner of his foes. These flowers, which he had tenderly cared for in his mother's absence, now seemed to care for him, leaving a remembrance of a scent.

According to Cedric's father, his son's tenderness for soft things led him to overlook sharp certainties, sealing his fate. This tragedy emboldened his siblings to harden themselves, vowing never to trust the Reds again. With the support of their king, they banished the Reds to the Lesser Wynd. In a cold inflection, their father remarked, "To stoop low to the flower bed was to lay upon one of death."

166

As Raihn set the book down, his eyes fell on another: Bees and Honey. Memories, though faint, flickered like flint on steel.

Determined to refund his memory, Raihn reached for his satchel, feeling an inexplicable connection as if it whispered from its stitches, stitches fanning away the fog.

Then darkness. Large hands curtained over his face.

"Amarra?" he called out.

The hands pulled away, revealing her firm abdomen before his eyes. His gaze climbed past her naked alabaster until it met a mischievous grin.

His body stiffened between surprise and surrender as he followed her lead toward the stairs. Her body flowed with gentle bends and curves, like a lulling river meandering through a valley, yet her belly was firm and defined like a washboard nestled beside smooth waters.

Raihn trailed, but unease grew within him, for not only did he feel incompatible, but his thoughts were still shrouded by a veil. Along the staircase, he noticed a shaky stool and a tankard. A name echoed in his mind: Benjin, tugging at a loose thread of memory. Clarity suddenly pierced through his vulnerability, and he whispered, "Tassy," recalling his past rejection of her advances on his grace.

"I can't," he said, his voice faltering. "Not yet. There's something about this place that I don't remember. Maybe...I don't know. You have to first remember what it is you've forgotten. Then you ask yourself, 'How could I have let these important things go?'" His voice softened as he tried to discern his thoughts, straining a smile to mask his unease. "I mean, they feel important."

Then, as though a candle was lifted between his ears, a memory warmed in a flickering light. The stairs that Amarra led him to reminded him of the ones that led to the eldhorium. And as he squinted through the haze of memory, he noticed portraits lining the walls.

"My brother," Raihn gasped, realizing the importance of his satchel. Something inside it held the key to understanding. Breaking free from her enchantment, Raihn rushed back down to retrieve it.

Amarra followed quickly, her feet beating a hasty rhythm on the stairs, and planted her lips on his. They were seductively gummy, but Raihn recoiled, backing away from her lurching advance.

There was an audible break of suction from the part in their kiss.

"What's gotten into you?" he asked, appalled.

She snatched his hand, and Raihn, shocked, tried to pull away, but her grasp was unrelenting this time. Her hand, dwarfing his, closed, knuckles spined. The bones in his hand grated one another.

"Amarra, please understand. There's something wrong with this place," he pleaded, but her grip only tightened. His heart sank, heralding a deep suspicion. "Amarra, let go," he demanded.

Her grip tightened.

"Amarra, you're hurting me," he trembled. "Enough… Amarra!" Raihn struggled harder, pulling away, but she was as sturdy as a cruck.

Her eyes daggered through his bubble of pretense that she was only playing, slicing through the fading morn, time seemingly reversing, her visage one of death, devoid of remorse. Her eyes turned to stone, the darkest edge of the mountain through them.

Desperation took over. He lurched forward and snapped his jaw over her hand, but she whipped him down in retaliation. His head cracked against the edge of the stairs, a groan slipping out, her claws rolling under his neck hairs.

Turned over and dragged away, his heels thumped up the stairs. And as he came to his senses, his fingers scrabbled at them.

He was pulled through the door and thrown onto the bed, his cloak flapping open. His heart pounded as he sat up, parsing her figure at the door in the dim light. She crept, her movement a shadow in the dark until he felt her breath run down his throat again. She—*an eerie imitation of Amarra*—loomed over him. Her eyes lit into bright jades, just like Tassy's in the nightmare. They were all he could see above him, floating in what could otherwise be mistaken for empty space.

Suddenly, it struck him—*this was just that, a nightmare.* He bellowed, crying to be woken. She bent closer, eyes narrowly upon him, her granite horns caging him in.

Raihn whispered a stammer, "She wouldn't," but the figure's haughty expression remained unchanged, as if a mask. She strapped him beneath her weight. "Amarra," his voice rattled.

She clamped around him, her spearing legs bent at the knees that dug under his armpits. Her touch was familiar yet twisted, and he struggled to break free, his breath hitching as she leaned closer.

Raihn turned a cheek as he reached for his sword, but she grabbed his hand and plied his fingers into crossroads. Then she reached for his breeches, her claws slinking down his belly, sending a shiver through his hips. Her eyes remained focused, her face as still as black water.

Raihn shut his eyes to spare himself from her jades when a distant commotion broke the tension: a tangle of screams and crashing trees. Raihn opened his eyes, seeing the assailant's skin now greyed and her hair dark as tar, but her glinting eyes remained. The cabin seemed dissolved, revealing the same woods he had fled earlier—he was awake.

She pressed her quad horns down, corralling his attention, a fingerbreadth between their noses. Raihn snapped his jaw at her with the intent to tear her lip off, but she was quicker, swiping his cheek with her horn. She sneered and then pinched his bottom lip between her fangs as some sort of revenge. First, just a nibble, then they sank. Some kind of warm liquid sieged his lip and ransacked his inferior labial vein, and warmth bushed out through his face.

She reached again for his breeches, yanking them halfway, but the ground shook. Trees clattered under the sky and then crashed down around them. Another Outcast had arrived from a hard tumble, their arms and legs bent in ways they're not meant to be bent. But the one on top of Raihn, with jades past her tarred strands, her head craning off a long raven-feathered neck, was undeterred.

Before she could finish her cruel intentions, a blur of movement tore her away from Raihn, perhaps the thing that flung the other Outcast through the trees. He saw a small, frail-looking girl battling them, rolling and tumbling with surprising strength. She called for him, insisting he seek the light of the cave, their voice vacillating under their foe's might.

Weary and mutilated, Raihn pulled up his breeches and ran, though his legs felt full of lead and his energy was nearly spent. His head, flushed with heat, slumped to the side as his strength ebbed.

His ankle rolled, pebbles flinging from his fall.

And though his mind was foggy, he still questioned—*why?*

When the dust settled, he heard one of them return—the victor, their grey-as-ash ankles stepping into view. The corpse of the girl who interfered lay as a backdrop to them, beaten to a pulp.

The cold fog enveloped his body, and he lamented its curse; it was a harrowing moment before his bones settled, leaving him petrified with nothing but the echoes of what once was. His tomb of flesh despaired, burdened by the gravedigger.

He had wilted, stained in crimson as she raked his crownling chest, chanting, "Chahken dau, go-unrek. Dunaul, un-narek."

CHAPTER NINETEEN
Close to the chest

"All these years built up only to be knocked down by the crutches. What's the point of moving forward if we have to crawl?" grumbled an old, rusty voice to someone unseen and inaudible. "But how?" he asked the receiver of his groans before seemingly being filled in. "If you want me to be blind, then so be it. Suppose you want me mute too."

There was a long beat suggesting they were being scolded.

"Consider it minded."

Raihn lay, a twitch in his ear, as he picked up this buzzing dispute, just barely, from the rusted voice. And with his body a staff upon the ground, his neck stiff, he could only wonder where they were, what they looked like, and so on. But he was immobile, seeing only a blurry cloud in the sky. It sprinkled his cheek with temperate drops. *Odd,* he thought, regarding the inconsistent shower.

But none of all that mattered. Not the bickering fuzz, or the rain, for he pondered his body to be mistaken for a corpse. *Would they send me by flames?* The image of a pyre tucked him into prickly thoughts of firewood. Uncertainty played his mind into twangs and scratches, his spine fiddle-necked. However, he thought, *I'm alive,* looking up at the cloud—thinking and looking being all he could muster from himself. He lay trapped within cursed muscles, entombed in a claustrophobic shell. He seemed to be spellbound by sleep paralysis. *How did I even end up here?*

A thick and muffled voice reached Raihn's ears as though he'd been submerged. He deciphered the words with concentrated effort, "So, how do we…fix this?" The voice was softer, less bitter than the other, but elusive beyond clear perception.

Raihn managed a breath forward, relieved that his grain was acknowledged.

"What's best is that everyone stays calm for now, including the others, when we regroup. I have one duty, and that's more than enough for me, so keep that in mind before you start asking more questions," replied the rusty voice—the same one grumbling earlier.

"Then I demand you tell me your duty."

The rust twanged a scoff. "Even if your highest lords sifted through that wall, they'd be disarmed of demands. But if you must know, it's to keep an eye on the lot of you. And, suffice to say, I'm not impressed by what I see."

"Nor do we need you to be. As you said, you have one job, right? So, setting all else aside—will he live?"

"He will."

"Is there no more that you can add?"

"He will live," the rust burst out, gravelly and impatient.

"For how long?"

"Until his heart stops beatin'! Happy now?"

Raihn's heart hadn't stopped yet, but it did skip a beat.

Another drop from the cloud. Raihn's vision began to clear, revealing not rain but tears. And neither was there a cloud, but a wildly frizzy mane. *Amarra,* he realized.

"Anything but!" boomed the other in response to the mention of death. "How could you say that before him?" The voice exploded in Raihn's ear like a cork popping from a bottle.

Lostar.

"You pushed for the truth, and I gave it to you harder than you could stand," said the stranger.

"Surely what was done can be undone," the Enduran retorted.

Is this how it feels? To be burdened with empty breaths.

They raged on, voices turning from ripples to waves, foamy and turbulent.

Lostar…

"Do you take me for a mender of flesh, greater than any herb-slinging wisewoman you know, with only the bones and muscle that make up my hand?" the rusted stranger said.

Please.

"Do you think li'l ol' me tends to this garden, feeding venomous snakes along the way?" they continued.

Amarra.

"How do I know you didn't do just that?" Lostar accused.

I can't…

Amarra put her hand over Raihn's arm. Kindred hearts rallied through their eyes, both muted. She caressed his shoulder, her white *claws* creeping in and out of his peripherals… The bickering from the others had subsided, and silence took hold for a moment.

"Look, there is one way," the stranger said reluctantly. "But it is no easy feat. It is the point of your being here, so I may as well tell you. It'll be entertaining, I s'pose. To place my hopes in you would be challenging; alas, I will allow hope to you, but not you alone. Come, the others wait. I need not waste my breath twice."

"You hear that, Raihn?" the one bickerer, Lostar, asked, coming into view as he knelt. "There is hope, Raihn."

Alcohol was carried on their breath.

Raihn lay cradled in the Outcast's arms, carried along a ledge path lined with lanterns. His heart pounded. Crimson vines coiled around the staked lights, their murmurs easing through the heavy air. Everything felt increasingly strange, especially the stout stranger with the bulbous nose and coarse fingers.

Not exactly a carpenter, despite the bucket of nails he carried, but he was all they had—a grumpy old imp. His unkempt appearance suggested he hadn't bathed in years, and he reeked of rotten eggs. With bushy brows and crooked teeth, he was an unpleasant sight. Yet, Raihn's head lolled to the side, his vision fixed on him, unable to look away.

Thankfully, they turned a curve along the mountainside where the others awaited. Some cheering staked his bitterness.

"Raihn!" Hodge cried.

"You'll be happy to know he isn't dead," said the warty imp. "His arrival was made a late wind after your breezes."

"He's paralyzed," Hodge surmised. "Was it poison?"

"A toxin," the short fellow corrected.

"Snake?" Hodge inquired.

"Serpent," the imp refined, grit in his breath. "Snare might be a better fit, as I liken her to that."

"Her?" Hodge repeated.

But the imp clapped his hands together and pressed on. "So," he began, "I will relay a portion of my knowledge unto all of you," his eyes sweeping over them.

"Why not all of it? And who are you?" Hodge asked.

"Aye," Xander agreed, "you told us to stay put and fucked off. And here we are, and there Raihn is."

"Don't get your teeth crooked sucking on the tit all the damned day, like Henry. Patience, boy. I am Ghor. Some have called me Crum as a perverse joke, thanks to my stature. Well, I am not one for gags or perverse things. I am short and quick to the point, lest I feel invigorated… No lollygagging, I say, nor gum smacking."

"I'm tired of your babbling, two-fourths. Tell it to me straight, as you say you do," Xander demanded.

The little outburst from Xander seemed to amuse the imp, as his sly grin deepened across his face. He had certainly identified the temperamental one in the group.

"Listen well, sour of mouth and gum-smackers," he said, his eyes flickering through the party. "What burdens your minds most is undoubtedly the condition of your friend. You must endure the hardships. If you can't bear such a task, you may abandon this quest."

Swiftly, the stranger produced eight white wooden whistles that dangled from his grip. "With one shrill breath, you could be back within the comforts of home, though you'd be abandoning your friend. So the question is, are you homesick?"

"Well, he and I aren't exactly friends," Xander muttered, earning disapproving glares from the others. "Just a clarification…"

Ghor continued, "Then reach Weeping Giant's Head—the summit where the warmth of an eternal flame will revive his independence and stave off a plague, so long as you tend it. Lest the sickness spread, eventually making you starve like those bags of bones down there."

"But just how high is this mountain?" Magnus asked. "The peak pierces the clouds, rising higher than the wall. No man has ever conquered such a beast."

"Not yet," Ghor clarified.

"It isn't just clouds—it's fog. Fog everywhere!" Xander exclaimed.

"Shrouds are the least of your worries," Ghor mused. "Worse is the climb itself. And unfortunately for me, I'll have to endure it alongside you."

Xander appeared skeptical. "Is that it?"

Ghor tucked his fingers into fists. "Have you ever climbed a mountain, Xander?"

"I've done my share of climbing. We'll be fine."

"Don't forget, Hodge lost our climbing gear," Magnus reminded him.

"Fuck!"

Magnus sighed, crossing his arms over his chest. "Look, you mentioned a plague."

Xander echoed the concern. "Aye, the fuck is that?"

"'Tis an old mountain, and it breathes an air of discontent, struggling to keep these walls whole, barring the realms from its flesh-eaters." No matter how much this imp spoke, he seemed elusive in nature, joyous in his knowledge over them.

"Whether you want to take on this challenge is up to you," he continued. "You can still live your life to the fullest. But if you leave now, you'll carry the weight of what you abandoned for the rest of your days: your friend, your companion—whatever, and more." Ghor stepped forward, lifting the seven whistles higher. They knocked together like wind chimes, signaling a wind of transformation.

His gaze locked onto Xander. "So, what's it going to be?"

"I…" Xander muttered, the words catching in his throat. He snatched a whistle and held it aloft in his palm, likely feeling the weight of the others' eyes on him. "Oh, relax! I'm not going home!"

"Oh? Saving it for later, then?" Hodge asked nervously, inching closer. "Why is the whistle around your neck?"

"For safekeeping," Xander replied. "It's not like I want to throw my escape away. If things go sideways, I'll have a backup plan."

"Fair enough," Hodge conceded.

"The rest of you can take a whistle as well," Ghor said, his voice calm but insistent. "Like Xander, you can wear it if you choose. There's no shame in it."

"Your name is Ghor," Lostar said, cutting past the subject at hand, "but that tells me nothing about you."

"Agreed," Xander rang in with a new tune. "You show up with Raihn, limp as a wet rag, and offer us these sorcerous trinkets. It's a bit much to swallow."

Ghor chewed his teeth. "I keep these grounds, and these grounds keep me," he said. "'Tis all you need know."

"Some keeper of the grounds," Xander remarked, looming over Ghor. "Those husks of flesh—they nearly ate mine! Couldn't you have kept them at bay? We could have died before even starting this vague rescue mission—one that's necessary only because of this mountain!"

"Blame the serpent for that," Ghor said glibly. "They were turned loose." But Ghor seemed as glib as they come, sparking more frustration with ease betraying gravity.

Xander growled. "But I still wonder—are **they** going to find us again?"

Ghor shook his head. "Keep to the light," he urged. "Follow the rowed lanterns."

"What if Raihn uses the whistle? Would he be sent home?" Lostar asked.

"Now you're getting greedy," Ghor smirked. "If you lent it to his lips, and his breath was full of intent, I suppose he would. But don't think you can escape and find some antidote beyond these walls. It grows in only one place." Ghor glanced upward to the highest reaches of the mountain. "I've told you all what to do."

"Then you have my answer," Lostar said firmly. He took a whistle and flung it off the cliff.

Amarra followed suit.

"I'm not sure if you're brave, naive, or foolish," Ghor snickered.

"No doubts are about me," Lostar replied, and Amarra nodded in agreement.

A wicked smile crossed Ghor's weary face, crow's feet pinching over his cheeks. "So be it. I've answered your questions; now, relieve me of these last trinkets."

He glanced around at those who took the remaining whistles. Each of them toyed with the idea of using it, their faces betraying their thoughts.

"You know what, Xander's right. Nothing wrong with holding onto it," Hodge chuckled nervously.

Xander rolled his eyes.

"That goes for me as well," Magnus added.

"That still leaves one whistle unaccounted for," Lostar noted.

Ghor pursed his lips and then smacked them. "You can come out now. There's no hiding behind those rocks," he said, his voice carrying a knowing tone.

Pocket emerged timidly from behind the stone rubble.

"Go on, take it and go, traitor," Magnus spat.

Pocket winced at the word but snatched the whistle, glaring coldly at Magnus.

"You're one to talk," Lostar spoke up. "You betrayed your companions, and I saw the glint in your eye when you first heard there was a way out. You go wherever the wind blows."

"He's right," Xander agreed, his eyes turning on the tracker.

Magnus shot a cold glare at Xander, then turned a glower on Lostar. "What's it to you, Lostar of Endura? I have no ties to this party. Tepparna is gone," he snapped. "Her death, still murky to me, happened under your watch."

"She shouldn't have been on this quest," Lostar shot back. "Who was she to you?"

Magnus scoffed. "She was nobody to everyone but me...and Amarra. She was our key to freedom, just as much as this place was hers."

Xander curled his lip while Hodge buried his hands deep into his pockets, their closed-off gestures conveying their mistrust.

"I did what I had to!" Magnus snapped, wrenching in frustration.

Magnus stormed off, rounding the curve, leaving Raihn to anticipate the sharp cry of his departure. But moments later, he returned with an exhausted look—and, surprisingly, without a whistle that Raihn could see.

Did he throw it?

"You don't get it," Magnus murmured, his voice heavy. "I had no choice. The dame stood between me and Gayle, my wife, and I tried to strike a deal—a fool's bargain, vagabond. Gayle and I planned to have a family, but the cardinal took her as one of his maids..."

Lostar's expression softened.

Magnus wasn't finished, his eyes turning upon Hodge. "And it's all because Xander and I spared **him**."

Ghor allowed a beat, then took a breath. "I suppose you all know what this means," he said, but all looked confused. "No one is going home! The adventure begins—or continues," he explained.

His brow scrunched. "Hold on," he said, pressing his ear against the rock as if listening to it. "Ah, yes!" he exclaimed, peeling away. He dug into his sack and pulled out a chest. "You know, I'm tired of lugging this thing around. It's rather hefty—so how about you do me a favor?"

"Hold on," Xander waved. "What's this now, crazy old imp?"

"It's a chest, can't you see?" said Ghor, shaking it.

It was a wooden, white chest, and over it was a dainty white hand clutching it shut.

"I see, dammit, but what sits in it?"

"Well, isn't that the intriguing part? You have to carry it all the way up to Weeping Giant's Head without knowing too. How about that?" the groundskeeper teased.

"You mean to say you never peeked? Never got curious to lift the skirt and see what was underneath?"

"Of course, I was curious. Still am," Ghor admitted. "But even if I wanted to, it won't open for me. It's not meant to, not yet. Those little fingers keep it sealed tight until the right moment—when it's properly courted. Lose this hand, and you lose the journey."

"People have died to get here, and you treat us like pawns in a game!" Xander snapped, frustration bubbling over. "Every answer slips away like a leaf in the wind! I can't shake the feeling you're holding back the truth."

"I'm just a groundskeeper—maybe a shepherd, too," Ghor considered. "You move your feet, reach the peak, and sing a merry song... Reasonable enough?"

"No," Lostar replied. "But we'll ask no more of you."

"Good!" Ghor clapped his hands. "Just follow the path. Stay within its glow, for there's no coming back if you stray. Those lanterns along it will repel unwanted guests—like those cannibals, if they were here, which they are not."

"Another one of your strange rules," Lostar muttered.

"It is not a rule, nor is it strange. From me, it is merely advice. Whether you adhere, well, that's on you," Ghor said, wagging his finger devilishly. He then held the chest firmly in both hands, his arms shaking feebly.

"Just as Raihn was entrusted with one hand, so shall he be with another," Ghor continued. "What awaits this rabble slumbers still, its flame barely a flicker. It lies in wait for this party of a crooked-tongued man, a killer, a drunk, an Outcast, and a buffoon. I wonder if ye have any compassion and how ye might fare under its light." He spoke to them all, but his glibness gave into an irksome contempt for Amarra, his eyes and tone a nasty cookery catered at her.

Ghor squinted, scrutinizing the rest after. "I believe Raihn shall keep it, yes. Quiet as he is, he's yet to prove me wrong in trusting him. And while he lies dormant, this chest will find a place in his satchel, where he would not be so burdened as I am," he said almost coyly, gently laying the chest within it. "He may seal this plague."

Moments later, the groundskeeper groaned, appearing beckoned. He pressed his ear against the rock again as if listening for some hidden signal in the unyielding stone.

Finally, he muttered, "Fine," as though conceding to it. "Now, a final warning," he added, turning to them. "Nothing too alarming, just that if you don't reach the peak in time, you'll also hear a shrill cry—a sound that signals the end of your journey, for the walls will rot from its plague, and all that."

"Come again?" Magnus stepped forward. "You seem to fumble the last part yet again."

"It's a race," Ghor clarified. "Its beginning marked by the blow of a horn, its end cradled in a cry."

"How long do we have before this 'cry'?" Xander asked.

"I don't know," Ghor answered dispassionately. "That's why you should scurry quick. To reach the peak an' put a cork in. Things seem to develop, and I try to keep up. It wasn't meant to be this way, but here we are."

"What about our children?" Magnus asked. "Are they in danger from this plague?"

"By the sound of it, you have nothing to worry about," Ghor snorted.

Magnus raised his fist, hovering it over Ghor as if contemplating the strike. Ultimately, he must have deemed it unwise, for he backed down.

The groundskeeper smirked, unbothered. "Type of behavior I'd expect from the nasty she-beast among you," he remarked, nodding at Amarra, "not the everyday man."

Amarra, likely offended, became the first to step away. Lostar followed.

"But who am I to be the judge?" Ghor supposed.

CHAPTER TWENTY
Barking dogs

XANDER watched as Amarra and Lostar navigated the rocks ahead, their once-narrow ledge trail widening into a plateau. Yet, the lanterns kept them close along the path. The mountain, described as "broad," had been likened to a "cow lick on the back end of a scalp," conjuring the image of a sweeping mountain that narrowed into a lofty peak at its rear. But no matter how it was cut, Xander felt its long, broad draw in his ankles.

Raihn's head dangled off The Outcast's arm, his eyes distantly cold upon Xander, driving an even colder shiver up his spine. They looked helpless and miserable, but also creepy and hard to ignore. *Thankfully,* the she-beast adjusted Raihn's head, supporting it with her bicep, and inadvertently spared the mercenary, Xander, from the boy's peering eyes.

Now, with his peace, Xander looked to his hand, counting his fingers and the stipulations, goals, and so on:

1. Race to the peak to save Raihn.
2. Race to the peak to stave a plague, *apparently.*
3. Race to the peak to see what lurks within that chest.
4. If all that fails, blow the whistle and *fuck off* so he can *at least die in a better place.*
5.

Xander paused at his pinky during his finger counting, wondering if he'd missed anything.

Along the path, countless trees spired as temples praising the sky, their barren branches forking, unbothered by stagnant air. It was quiet. There were no bugs buzzing or birdsong, just dead air and eerie lanterns aglow. Upon each side of the rugged path, two rows of these lanterns emit a foreboding crimson upon the rock, haze alight. Did the groundskeeper light them? Does he maintain them day and night? They resembled no lantern Xander had seen before.

"What are these?" he questioned.

"You never seen a lantern before?" Ghor replied.

"You know to what I refer," Xander growled. "Their red-like glow soaks the ground like the stain of blood. From their centers crawls a red vine that snakes around the black cane. It isn't right."

"The lanterns are your guides, but if you turn your back on them, they will turn their back on you. Respect that much and stay the course."

Xander grumbled, remembering the stipulation.

5.   Stay with the lanterns.

Xander marched up a sloping trail with the troop. Fog swam through valleys, crept within chasms, and rode up ridges, veiling all that surrounded them in the distance. The time spent here thus far was meager but enough to strip the mercenary of patience. It was a whole lot of nothing, and Raihn's pigment was fleeting before him—*or might he just be greyed out by fog,* Xander wondered.

Amarra tried to force a smile, but with each worried glance at Raihn, her lips sank further, eventually turning into a pout as she watched his condition worsen. Xander grew increasingly anxious as he watched the nurturing giantess ahead, his frustration mounting as they encountered more of the same terrain while Raihn continued to sink in her arms. It felt pointless. The only things that changed were the shapes and sizes of the rocks.

Eventually, a bend appeared along the path, and Xander found himself grateful. It wasn't a climb or a long flat stretch. Still, weariness nipped at him. He wondered how much longer this could take. He asked Hodge, who knew the most among them, but the answer was far from comforting.

"A few months, you say!?" Xander exclaimed, unable to believe the estimate.

Xander picked at his scabs along the way to occupy himself. He dug out wax from his piggish ears, dug dirt from under his nails—bit those nails… His walk turned to a meandering saunter. Ghor laughed all the while.

The mephitic air choked Xander as the fog became thicker than ever, but he couldn't take a bite of it even as dense as it was. His stomach grumbled and twitched. His fingers clasped what fat he had and gnarled his skin to make his belly suffer for always being hungry.

There was no food.

Maybe a speck of salt from Hodge, but what good would that do when he was cotton-mouthed already and without a morsel? What really could be the final straw for him at any moment would be the ringing in his ear. As though a granular musician snuck beside his drum in the night, played a bad bagpipe, and blew a discordant, never-ending shrill.

There was smoldering tension among the fog concerning Raihn and food. Perhaps a day crept by as they meandered up the mountain through a white river. And through the fog came stone lit red. The miasma forbade the tell of time for a while, but they had guesses. Now, though, the fog thinned, light prevailing it. "Stone and more stone," Xander grumbled from its reveal, which included the sky-touching wall that ringed them. "All the trees have abandoned us, save for the valleys we cannot venture. We see nothing more than miserable rocks. I just want to get high enough to see beyond the wall and get a look at home."

"Home sick already?" Ghor asked a second time, loving that phrase by the look of his gnarly grin.

"It is the mountain that I grow sick of. It's mountains upon mountains! It's like we're at the bottom of the ocean, and the water is rock! I'm suffocating. No wind, no animals, it's depressing! I, withdrawn from noise, save this bell in my ear, burdened by the confounded ringing, cannot stand this solitude. I just want some freedom from this enclosure," Xander said, fumbling with the whistle.

"You're not planning on leaving, are you?" Magnus asked, concerned.

"I…just need some rest," said Xander, winded.

"And I need food," Hodge groaned between heavy breaths. "I'm utterly famished."

Xander concurred.

"That isn't going to change," said Ghor.

"Pardon?" Hodge stopped.

"No food is to be found here."

"No food? Not even squirrels? No berries, no fruit, nor mushrooms?"

"Only meat here is yourselves," said Ghor. "Can always become like those flesh-eaters down below." The groundskeeper grinned slyly. "You do have a mountain goat with you," he snuffled, still scornful of Amarra.

"Disgusting." Hodge recoiled. "What are we to do? We can't make it on an empty stomach!"

"Relax, you'll live," said Ghor. "You will be hard-worn, but you can make it. Is it likely? No, but there is a possibility."

"How do you reckon? We'll be starving," Xander barked. "And not much longer…we'll be dead. Pray, how can we climb? Up this mountain. How? All that way without provisions? All this walkin'…we won't make it."

"You'll live," said Ghor. "And don't you think I'm hungry? Under my garments is skin and bone." Ghor peeled his cloth and revealed ribs lined beneath his tired skin. "But you…just think of it as a motivator," his voice stumbled, less shallow. "The sooner you reach the spiraling peak, the sooner you can rest easy with food and drink in hand."

"It isn't right is what it is," Xander mumbled, his head slumping.

"There's always home," Ghor taunted. "It is just a whistle-blow away."

Doubt permeated their silence as the group exchanged glances, little rocks rolling under their hobnails.

"So you keep saying," Xander griped.

Ghor took a breath. "You are all aware, I assume, of the eight realms—wynds, you call them, the ones I've heard tell of, with your houses of pearls and thorns that yield to a rose. This realm under your boots is not governed by any of those eight liege subjects you call cardinals. This realm bends no knee to a rose and never glances up as it only looks down."

Everyone appeared weary of the stubby stranger and his roundabout ways, and even Xander had ceased to engage with him.

They fled through two shoulders of rock and followed this crack in the stony realm for some while, until Lostar and Amarra moved ahead to a tight passage, disappearing over a brief climb before rounding a curve to the openness again. Xander followed, paused, and sighed, relieved of claustrophobia.

His aching feet planted firmly on the winding path's edge as they entered a break in the murk. The fog parted oddly, revealing the vastness of the rocky hive below. Valleys dipped and jumped endlessly; through them, the fog stretched out in wisps of gray, gradually solidifying into white, like strings of cotton sweeping along the curves and breaking apart in others.

Xander squinted, barely making out the white bramble wall in the distance. Its true measure—be it leagues or acres—eluded him. It loomed far ahead, the fog thickening at its base as it slithered past chasms.

Then he turned his thinking back, noting they hadn't begun at the mountain's base. The journey hadn't been long enough to cover such a vast distance to be at this elevation. It pricked him the longer he considered it.

"Whether this makes me lesser, I do not know," Magnus murmured, stepping up to the uneven ledge trail over the valley. "But I cannot help but see man's destruction as more beautiful than this gray rock."

"Stay here long enough, and you'll appreciate certain evils," Ghor remarked, as elusive as ever.

Xander scoffed and then creaked. "Ridiculous. I can't so much as gawp at home, forbidden by that wall."

"Look at it this way," Hodge began, "maybe this will make you appreciate what we once took for granted. Like blind men seeing for the first time, if such a marvel could happen."

"I'm not blind," said Xander. "It's a steaming bowl of shit porridge— maybe with some corn in it. Furthermore, a marvel that surely would be, but you can put a lid on your glass-half-full muck and let me close my god damned eyes—and yes, here I may say that, god—damn—it," he repeated slowly. "There are no marvels. Darkness will help me imagine things brighter than this. And if you yap more, I hope the ringing in my ear drowns you out, as I'd rather hear that than any say on marvels."

Past a curve, in a nook deep on the ledge trail, the group stumbled into the night and found themselves suitable claims for rest. The terrain was unaccommodating already, but at Xander's side, the thief wedged himself between a coarse indentation in the mountain, much to his displeasure.

"So, the thief aims to lie by my side?" Xander laughed thickly. "I don't think so. Find a new claim."

"Cut him some slack," said Lostar.

"You mind yourself, Enduran. I haven't got a quarrel with you, so don't bring me any cause to have one. Though this one here," said Xander, pointing a thumb at Pocket. "He's a thief. who betrayed us once and is likely to do it again, I'd bet...

"Move," he ordered again, sneering and propping himself near Pocket's face.

"Then cut the rest of some slack," Lostar reiterated sleepily, waving Pocket over.

The thief freed himself from the crevice and ambled toward the Enduran, minding the cliff.

"Don't get too cozy," Lostar said. "I may not be as harsh as that man over there, but that does not mean I am willing to turn a blind eye."

Pocket lay still for a moment, his cloak draped over him. Then, startling the others, he abruptly rose and hopped toward the ledge near the lanterns. There was about three feet between him and the edge, with the mountain face looming just five feet behind his back.

"What do you think you're doing?" Hodge asked.

Pocket's hand beat against his chest, ripping the whistle free from his neck. He'd catapulted the whistle into the grey depths, forfeiting a prize above all other frivolous treasures.

Pocket shuffled away from them and lay alone by the crimson lanterns.

Xander scoffed. "It would seem I don't want to be around him, and he doesn't want to be around you. So where does that place you?" A sly smile followed.

"Wherever you deem. Makes no difference to me."

LOSTAR lay chilled, yearning for his homeland, the thought of it a rock in his boot. His cloak offered meager comfort, for the stone was cold, unlike home. While he suffered the discomforts of sleeping abroad, Raihn appeared cozy with Amarra. Lostar was glad of her care, though a twinge of jealousy arose within him. Thoughts of indulging in a flagon of sweet cactus mead or perhaps sampling the famous ale from Raihn's wynd crossed his mind; however, Lostar desired his then-to-be consort most. Much to his favor, a swift drift into a warm, sandy dream swept him to his betrothed atop Endura, where he would reign as Trussgar.

And much to his loathing, he'd been stolen away by Xander's and Pocket's violent tussle. He'd awoken, the dark mountain surrounding him again. The thief and the mercenary were locked in a turbulent struggle for the whistle looped around Xander's neck.

Lostar, embittered, remained and watched. As did Amarra.

Evidently, the group was not unified, but it wasn't Lostar's obligation to rectify that, and apparently, it wasn't Ghor's either. The ones to protest were

182

Hodge and Magnus. But that didn't work, so they tried to pry the battlers apart. But both Xander and the thief refused to yield.

"Back off," Xander barked. "I've had enough of this rat! You either help me teach him a lesson or leave me to it!"

"But why now? When we finally get to rest!" Hodge cried.

"He couldn't follow through with his decision," Xander explained. "His grubby hands were all over my whistle when I woke."

"He's lying," Pocket groaned through a jab. "He was trying to abandon us!"

"What does it matter to you?" Xander asked.

Pocket finally pushed them off. "Because why should someone like you get to leave?"

"Like me!?" Xander stepped forward, shoving Pocket to the ground. "Because I shouldn't be here!"

"So, you don't deny it," Magnus sneered.

Xander snapped his eyes over to them. "You sold us out, Magnus. I'm not with this thief, and I just can't say I'm with you either. So, I know where I should go… Where the wind blows."

"What of our kinship?"

Xander looked to Magnus pensively, his mouth agape, hindered by some sort of restraint. He sighed. "I had wondered it the same."

"Fine, all you do is bitch and moan anyway," Magnus's voice climbed. "Who needs it?"

Xander's restraint seemed to dissipate with a scoff. "Look around you! You think they're going to trust you? I don't even trust you. I may be ill-tempered, but unlike you, 'friend,' I am no traitor. And neither am I a fool."

Then he gestured at Raihn. "To wait for him to die, for Amarra and Lostar to fall apart without him… This is a lost cause, and I would be damned to let a traitor ride his high horse and tell me what to do!"

"Shut up," Pocket shouted, scrambling to his feet. "Shut up!" He shoved Xander through the lanterns with one hard push, the mercenary catching his balance at the ledge.

"This was all a waste of time," said Xander. "I'd not expect cats and dogs to survive together, regardless of a dog's debt to 'em."

"Just get on," Magnus harped, waving him off.

Xander stood there, seemingly coming to grips with the situation on the other side of the lanterns. Little red flickers catching in his eyes. He looked to have calmed down a bit before finally reaching for his whistle, but he only found his tunic to claw at. His bulging eyes shared his surprise.

"Looking for this?" asked Pocket with a smirk.

Glancing up, Xander spotted the whistle dangling from the thief's deft hand. "You bastard!" he roared, a vein bulging from his forehead. Xander attempted to march through the lanterns to retrieve the whistle, but the blazing barrier held him at bay. His feet plowed the dirt, forbidden to pass the light. "Damn it," he cried. "I cannot get through!"

"And I have your whistle," Pocket taunted.

"Give it to me," Xander demanded.

"I have a better idea," said Pocket with a flicker of his own in his eye. His arm arched back, ready to pitch.

"Don't! Please don't!" Xander wailed in desperation. "How will I get home? If you are to throw my life into the bowels of this mountain, you may as well just kill me!"

Pocket's stern expression softened, and his arm fell aside. "Just fuckin' with ye," he said with a pitying tone. "Here, take it." He tossed the whistle to Xander. "I wasn't really going to throw it."

"Right," grumbled Xander, seemingly in disbelief. "Fucking mongrel."

The mercenary puckered his lips and blew into the whistle. Lostar couldn't help but feel lightheaded in its wake, his vision failing. All went black.

XANDER saw the group collapse at the whistle's blow, leaving only him and Ghor standing.

"What's this all about?!"

Ghor stretched a maniacal grin under his nose, indulging in some kind of spite as Xander felt the ground rumble. It pulled apart, and his feet sank between rocks that ground at them like chomping teeth. His ankles broke, and his body collapsed, his hands scrabbling at the ground. Xander howled as the rocks caved down, pulling him within. His legs shredding into bits, he'd felt the wrath of a smith's grindstone.

"Lying sack of shit, bugger! Your whore mother should have swallowed you, you no good stumpy, repugnant, recluse, haunter in the mountain! You little trog' toad! Aventail would fall to your quill of a pecker and your pair of boils for a nut sack!"

Xander relented and spared his remaining breath in hopes of waking the others, screaming and hollering until earth plowed his mouth and broke his jaw, shattering his teeth into shards of broken glass.

CHAPTER TWENTY-ONE
Catching rain

AMARRA blinked awake sometime in the day, and the battle between Pocket and Xander flashed. But only one of them woke alongside her, the other gone.

"What happened?" Magnus asked first.

"Your friend went home," Ghor answered with a crooked lip.

"He's not my friend," Magnus corrected, his sorrowful gaze contradictory.

"The sound of a petulant child is a cursed one," Ghor remarked. "Either way, I care not. I just want to know if you lot are coming. I think you got decent enough rest."

"Always in a hurry," Magnus sighed. "Anyway, suppose we know what happens on the other end of the whistle—a good nap."

Most were not so attached to Xander, but regret seemed to touch Magnus's eyes. He kept glancing as though to assure himself the merc were gone.

Amarra found her footing, and the others, with her, marched around the steep mountainside without a gripe. Pocket led the way, Magnus and Hodge following next, while Amarra and Lostar trailed. After perhaps two leagues, Hodge relished a glimpse of green beneath the wisp of fog yonder from the lanterns on the ledge. The sharp stone mounds shepherded the grasslands upward.

"Come, Hodge," Pocket said, ushering him away.

"I only hope we can cross it down the way," said Hodge, looking out to the vegetated valley. "…Or up the way, I should say…"

"In that sense, then, might we have a glimmering light ahead of us—"

"This is nothing short of an excursion," Magnus interrupted. "Are we merely reduced to backpackers?"

Smirking, Ghor said, "You sound disappointed. Enjoy the walk while you can. I assure you, ascension is not so mere."

Magnus groaned, paused, and questioned if Ghor ever reached the summit.

"If I have, I wouldn't be here to suffer alongside you."

"And I'd rather frolic with the Bushwalkers, munch on mushrooms, and get shrubbed," Magnus replied.

Hodge hummed dreamily. "Delectable thought morsels."

Amarra walked the night, darkness obscuring the white wall from sight. Around a bend, a challenge peeled out and dared her and the unit to confront it head-on: a wall of rock; it stood tall, casting a daunting shadow, even after the evening, over Amarra's courage.

Hodge exhaled wearily, eyeing the steep incline of stone before them. "It goes straight up."

Magnus scoffed and feigned positivity, all while delivering a backhanded remark. "We can climb it, regardless of you losing our hooks, and regardless of the night, for despite not having gear, many mountains have been conquered before this one, and in much more dire conditions."

"Conditions more dire than his?" Lostar gestured to Raihn.

Magnus's gaze followed their motion, his expression conflicted as though he'd forgotten. "Right… Ghor?" he questioned, desperation creeping into his tone.

"If you can manage to bring him along," Ghor replied coolly. "Do it."

Lostar turned to Amarra, a soundless question in his eyes, as if to say, "Can it be done?"

She nodded, jailing a breath as she examined the imposing cliff face.

Hodge exclaimed in the same moment his pointer whipped towards dense foliage beyond, "Look!"

Amarra's gaze followed, and Lostar dug out his spyglass. But his haste betrayed him as the cylinder slipped from his grasp, clinking against the rock. Hands trembling with urgency, he plucked it up and aligned it with his best eye.

"Anything?" Magnus pressed impatiently.

"Fog is too dense," Lostar replied.

Then, Magnus turned to the scholar. "What did you see, Hodge? If you saw something, tell us. I don't see anything, either."

Hodge stuttered. "I'd swore I saw something move out there."

"They're trees in fog. A leaf may take shape of a bird." Magnus's voice climbed. "You could have seen anything, which could be nothing. Who knows! Just keep hold of that excitement when I'm on the rock."

Lostar sighed, shrinking the rod into folds. "Nothing."

Ghor groaned. "All this stalling, and you might have the Outcast carry a dead body up the side of the mountain," he said, to no favor. "But what's it matter, the end seems nigh as he is rather glum looking. Might you cut him loose and try your hand at carrying his satchel instead. It would be lighter than his lifeless body smackin' you from its plunge—if the rabid snow bunny drops him from above."

Everyone traded glances, but Amarra tightened her gaze.

Ghor snickered, "Debate among yourselves." Then slithered up with ease.

"Well, he sure is a quick one," Pocket stated. "Who is next?"

"We should wait for morning," Hodge suggested.

Lostar reminded them that time was the enemy. Even though it cut at their heels and blunted their elbows in its draw, it would never lose a grip on Raihn lest they persevere.

Hodge fiddled his fingers in a swift forfeit while Amarra beheld Raihn's paling tint. Ghor's past assurances seemed unsustainable. Breath shivered from her throat.

Ghor's remarks—advisory, however you cut it—seemed to influence Magnus. Or maybe Magnus was simply looking out for himself, as had been displayed before. He adamantly took the lead without a rope (a tail of it left in Hodge's pouch proving insufficient) and seemed disgruntled at even the thought of Hodge going ahead of him. So they followed, with Pocket a nervous third.

Amarra came next, as Magnus insisted, with Lostar acting as a brave spotter (who stressed frustration in having no belayer), choosing the lowest position to keep a watchful eye on Raihn, whom Amarra carried. His limp figure complicated her reaches for crimps, fingers pinching stone into her palms. He wasn't heavy, but his awkward, unresponsive body made the climb all the more difficult. His wrists were bound around her neck with a parcel of Hodge's rope, his weight shifting, pulling at her windpipe from many directions. If not for the fur on her neck, she'd be left with a burn. But his safety weighed heaviest on her, his belly pressing and swaying against her back.

The climb was going well, even without a rope worming through the rings of anchors, looping around a pulley, until a cold tingle befell her nose. It sent a shiver down her spine, stalling her. Her gaze straightened as a bloody streak peculiarly stared back from the rock wall. It was dry—too dry to be from the others.

"Why did you stop?" Lostar's voice echoed from below.

Amarra froze at the warning sign, her mind racing with the possibility of more hardships. Her ears perked up at a small, crackling sound emanating from above, and her heart skipped a beat. Raindrops fell gently at first, then more urgently, as if the sky itself was preparing for a deluge. A bolt of lightning shattered the veil of fog with a horrendous flicker, the streak flashing a warning.

The sprinkling could escalate into a downpour at any moment, but Hodge was struggling in place just above, and the lanterns on the wall offered only so much clearance. She peered down to check on Lostar, who clung to the rock face securely as if he were a renowned cragsman. Not one of his fingers wobbled in place, clutching as firmly as the stone they clung to.

Then something caught her eye again—the forest. It seemed shifty. She focused upon it, straining her eyes to make out any details in the reaches.

Taking Amarra out of her reverie, some sort of work of metal soared down past her, missing both her and Lostar. It clunked against a rocky point and bounced off, rattling. Hodge resumed his climb then, and the lightning halted, but not before it highlighted rusted bits of iron lodged into the mountain before Amarra's eyes: little spikes with rings, no rope tied to them. And without any more clanging on the stone, she pondered whether someone else had left them behind. Or, maybe, Hodge or Magnus carried cheap tools.

She shook her head. *No,* recalling Hodge lost their gear along their journey.

She ignored the rings for Lostar's sake, knowing she might be too heavy for them, given their rusted condition. She pushed ahead, hoping the harshness would pass, but the group faced another hurdle before long. A shivering shower of pearls fell, bombarding them and making the rocks slicker by the second—there came the deluge.

"Go! Go! Go," Lostar shouted through the dampening volley, but upon his third cry, there was a tumultuous clap of thunder as a streak of lightning ripped through the sky, his voice drowned out by the din.

Amarra gave him space, taking long strides up the slippery rock, accumulating weight as the water soaked into her wool cloak. She slipped, slicing her palm. Another streak of blood was donated to the rock heap. Her hood swelled behind her, tugging at her neck all the more. Her sizable hand slithered across the wet stone as though discerning a lover in the dark.

She groped and searched for leverage, but all the crevices, though suitable for the smaller members of her party, were not large enough for her to fit even a finger into. Instead, Amarra had to grab hold of larger formations and heave herself up quicker. But this came at the cost of her safety. Also, because Magnus, Hodge, and Pocket preceded her, there was a cap on the speed at which Amarra could ascend the rock wall, which only upset her more.

Her state of climbing was dreaded, pitons embedded in her head as much as the crag, tempting her along every groove she clasped. Unfortunately for Lostar, she couldn't alert him of the gear.

Then she questioned herself as to why he was taken into consideration. Maybe she should pull them, snap them by their rings after what he did… But she didn't. *If Raihn ever—when he wakes, he'd detest me, never to reach out again for certain.*

The lanterns, rooted like the pitons, glistened upon the sharp stone as the downpour clinked against their glass. Occasionally, they revealed valuable ledges, bringing a sharper focus unto her mind, but upon one fateful swing, a raven appeared just beyond the light. Its eyes bottling the red glow. From it, a sudden caw echoed through her head, rattling her brain. She faltered, and her grip loosened. The rope around Raihn's wrists slipped loose.

She clenched a ring of iron in one hand and, at the last second, reached down and snagged his wrist with the other. His foot swung and swiped Lostar across the face, the ring flexing out of the rock, a bucket's worth of water pouring out over Lostar from her hood. They lost their footing and slid further down, grating their hands along the way.

Amarra lost sight of the Enduran and slung Raihn over her shoulder, the ring breaking in half, the pinot flinging out from its wedge. She took a moment to breathe, gusts of air coming in waves. She saw no more of the raven, nor did she see the others above. She only heard lower rumbles in the sky as drops tapped along her forehead.

She pressed on.

The end had to be nigh, and Amarra knew she must find it soon. Her hands were cramped, and her mental and physical states stretched beyond their limits. She wasn't as familiar with mountains as others of her kind. She glanced up at the men above and the dark abyss below, wondering how she fit between the two and if the men's hearts could endure. Beyond the edge of her vision, she questioned again whether the end was imminent. Her fingers felt brittle. She smeared her blood across the stonework, navigating its crinkles, asking once again: *Is the end near?* The thought struck a rhythm of fear on her heart's chords, but it eased. She spotted a root protruding from the mineral wall. It was just an arm's stretch away, the perfect tool. Was it safer than the pitons? She wasn't certain, but she grabbed hold.

Her fingers, like weak bramble, pulled. It held, so she let herself go in a heart-sinking beat. She heaved herself up high, finding a haven at last. The rock gave inward, creating a ledge. She hauled half her mass over it, triceps straining for a mantle, taunted by the nearness of salvation.

Safe in a concave shelter in the mountain, her fellow strays sat, seemingly forsaking her. She glared at them in silence, hoping they would see her. Her remaining strength was dim. Another whip of lightning illuminated them, highlighting their selfishness clearly. But the harrowing wind was more dreaded than the thunder and lightning. She braced for it, her long ears blown back.

Amarra's weakness came as a humbling surprise. Her eyes were tired like the dwellers within the mountain's refuge. Wearily, they closed.

Faintly through the rampant storm, she heard the coming of one man. She looked up and saw the thief hoisting Raihn from her back, and she was thankful. Wonderful mercy had it been. Raihn was heaved aside to safety.

Amarra kicked her stomach over the ledge and pushed hard. Pocket pulled her up like she was a bag of wet sand before they both collapsed, her hood sloshing over her, spilling once more. He said nothing and retreated to shelter.

She thought to go and slap Magnus and Hodge, but they weren't worth it. Her next thought proved more important. Diligence brought her near the ledge, hoping to see their last companion: Lostar. As angry as she'd been with him, she realized she did not wish to see his demise here. And while she had yet to forgive him, she felt his actions were guided by some other force that carried along his pungent breaths. And so, she kept looking for him, watching the lanterns' glows upon the rock.

Raihn appeared at the end of his rope, barely holding on to his last threads. He was at the forefront of Amarra's mind, and she saw the weather pelting him with shivering beads. Shielding him with her cloak, she brushed his skin, pondering what he was thinking. And pondering more, she questioned whether it was right to make him suffer and whether this was all a fool's errand. But she had nobody else in the world. If he were to die... Darkness engulfed her mind. She trembled, knowing this was still only the beginning. She gripped his hand, recalling how he reached out to her once. But it was damp and cold now, a reverberation in her heart. But another hand fell to her shoulder, summoning her gaze—Lostar. He made it, and Amarra shocked herself when she embraced him. He was small to her, the size of a young boy to an adult. To make up the difference, she knelt, feeling a bit smaller then, his kindness as generous as the differences between them.

After all, he couldn't perish just yet, not when blood was on his hands yet to be cleansed. Tepparna is owed that much. Lostar is owed that much.

After their moment of solidarity, Amarra brought Raihn to the crevice, shielding him and herself from the raging weather. As they recouped, Hodge began glancing around nervously.

"Where is Ghor?" he asked, his voice concerned.

"Who knows," Magnus sighed.

"I'm over here, waiting for you slugs," Ghor's voice called out from the shadows.

Hodge looked in Ghor's direction and groaned, prompting Magnus to ask, "Why're you whimpering?"

"Take a look," Hodge cried, pointing.

"Damn, it's not over. Though I don't know what else I was expecting," Magnus muttered, his eyes widening.

Amarra glanced. The mountain curved into an ever-narrower ledge, barely wide enough for Magnus's boots and even worse for her big feet.

"I guess I paid it no mind. I only sought shelter," Magnus said. "How are we meant to cross that?"

"Suck in your guts and hope for the best," Ghor said with a grin, dashing to the ledge and hugging the rock as he sidled away.

Magnus rose, smirking in disbelief. "Just that easy, I guess," he said, clapping his hands on his hips and turning to the others. "I guess that's it. We follow him."

At this point, Amarra and the others were distracted and neglected him. Hodge tilted his head back to catch sparse raindrops in his mouth while she

190

clasped her hands together and bucketed her mouth to the sky. Pocket already half-filled his rotten shoe with rainwater.

Magnus partook in the corner of Amarra's sight, tilting his head, craning out his tongue just before the rain ceased. "Of course," he grumbled.

While the others kept their precious water to themselves, Pocket reluctantly held out his shoe. "No, thanks," Magnus said with disgust.

Amarra sidestepped along the slick ledge with the others, her eyes focused and her movements unhurried. The rock's sheen revealed its slippery dangers.

"At least the rain has come to an end," Hodge said, trying to find some bright side; but cursed were his words—almost immediately, they were smitten with another downpour. "I know these are stressful times. Let's be rational and consider the ill-timed coincidence," Hodge added, his voice strained with forced optimism.

The ledge was slender but, at times, tamer than their last route. It was a glint of hope, dashed by disaster, a crack in the rock giving way under Amarra. She tumbled down, smacking the mountain as she shielded Raihn within her arms. She kept falling…and falling…down into the depths and towards the forested valley at the wayside.

"Amarra!" Lostar shouted, his voice nearly lost in the storm.

CHAPTER TWENTY-TWO

A clamoring darkness

Amarra spun uncontrollably until she smacked down into a patch of mud, her body coiled around Raihn. The mud was cold on her wounds, clasping her bludgeoned body the same as she clasped her cargo. Her body was briefly frozen by the sting of pain, neck staffed, eyes up at the ashen tufts she speared through.

As if struck by a mace, she tasted iron. Her tongue prodded out a loose tooth, then spat it and a gob of blood. And her gums bled a winery, longing for the popped cork. By the end of this adventure, she would be lucky to have any teeth left.

Attempting to stand, she fell back to the ground, her body's weight doubled. The fog above barred the others from her sight, isolating her.

She knew the others would remain up there, and might she hear the faint blow of a songbird as some victor among them claimed the last whistle. The one around Hodge's neck. But what hope would they have without Raihn and the little chest? For all she knew, they could be locked in a battle royale above, each one fighting for survival.

Amarra couldn't ponder long as shadows gathered over her. Panic surged as she scrambled to her feet, only for pain to knock her back down, gums barking for the runaway canine. The pull from Desekreus was relentless, demanding, and impossible to resist. The thin silhouettes inched closer, reaching for Raihn, whom Amarra clung to with all her strength. Despite her efforts, the skeletal figures pried him away with their filth-ridden fingers. Fear gripped her as she remembered the talk of a 'plague' within these walls.

Next, they came for her, their arms reaching out as if she were royalty, as if her touch would bring them fortune. To them, she must have seemed like a clean silk rag, something pure to be soiled by their disease.

Amarra shut her eyes, bracing for their touch, only to feel forgiven by gravity. To feel—feathery. They lifted her to her feet without leaving another scratch. She opened her eyes, seeing ordinary folk adorned only with woven twigs. Some were garmentless, but their expressions were clothed in kindness.

There was a shift in the air, a troublesome wind that stole the breaths of the remaining group that clung to the rock wall.

POCKET cried out, his face pale, "They fell! We're doomed!"

Ghor despaired and fled, leading them to the cave ahead, where they could rest and lament safely.

Hodge gawked at the cave walls, his lamentations non-existent. "Caves strike a similar chord as the rings of a stump. But unlike a stump, there are other possible means of taking shape than merely being hacked into."

Pocket rolled his eyes, wringing out his clothes. "Really? This be your focus right now?"

Hodge pressed on, disregarding him. "The mountain speaks of ancient forces. Of how these hollows have deepened," he said, running his fingers over its curves.

"Talk about deep ends." Pocket sighed, exasperated. "Hodge, we've got mightier concerns."

"Rainwater," Hodge clarified. "It seeped through the rock for ages and carved these caves. The earth's warmth makes puddy the stone, aiding the water's labor… Just listening to the drone of rain out there proves this work of art, typically recorded by grand minds. Marin Mott, one of my inspirations, was a great discoverer from the Wynd of the Blue Pearls."

Pocket snapped his fingers in front of Hodge's face to ground him to reality, but they'd seemed in a daze. "Hodge. Focus. We gotta figure this mess."

Hodge's eyes flickered with a kind of desperate clarity. "Steam and vapors, too. I'd love some steam. Is anyone up for some cave adventuring? Might we see what lies within Mt. Miryam. What a splendid chance for discovery that only I could make. Herb would…he'd be so thrilled."

"And he'd be quite literally a better fit for it," Pocket remarked offhandedly. Then he snagged Hodge's suspender, tugging, forcing the scholar to look at him. "Snap out of it. We must get out of here, not be lectured on geology."

"Leave the fool," Magnus said. "He can't face the truth that all is lost."

Hodge snapped out of his ignorance, looking at Pocket with earnest eyes. His gaze dropped, then lifted again, and he patted Pocket on the back before seating himself on the stone, as if finally submitting to the truth. But the thief felt like the real fool, standing there in a panic. He was sinking, desperately clinging to the smartest of them, dragging them into his despair…

The mountain would freeze and thaw, cracking like they, time breaking them down.

Lostar had dropped to the hard stone ground, soaked and shivering, but eventually scurried to the cave wall, keeping a wary eye on its maw. But Pocket couldn't bring himself to look out, waiting for someone he knew was surely dead. He sat dourly, gripping his sopping knees to his chest in frustration—a frustration that Hodge seemed to notice. The quiet cave was heavy with the weight of their emotions, but the strongest aura radiated from Lostar, who appeared the angriest.

"What's with you?" Magnus questioned.

"They're down there," Lostar began, "and we're in here. I wonder why I must be the one to survive."

"It's chance," Magnus said. "Don't put too much stake into it. Questioning things without answers can make you go mad. And I deem this mountain maddening enough already."

"Exactly," Pocket agreed. "We're just flat-out fortuneless."

Ghor hobbled halfway to the open mouth of the cave before peering over his bony shoulder. "You deem and question all you may. I shall return."

"What is out there that isn't in here?" asked Magnus.

"Privacy," Ghor said, lumbering into the dark. Even he sounded glum.

The rain picked up again, sadly for Ghor, fine for them in the cave.

"What I really want is a fire. So how about it?" Magnus said to Hodge, who was across from him.

The scholar had finally settled, their leather haversack dangling off their shoulder.

Magnus continued. "We're all wet, our hems spurting. As I speak for us all, we're needlessly cold when you've got that tinderbox."

"A fire?" Hodge repeated nervously, his head bouncing at attention like an alert squirrel.

"Yes, you know, heat, flames, warmth," Magnus reminded. "The very thing we need after getting soaked out in the cold of night. Pull it from your bag and get it going."

"Yeah, my teeth would thank you," Pocket clacked.

Hodge's face appeared subdued by anxiety as he twiddled his fat thumbs. There was something to be told, surely, and they all wanted to hear it.

With a pucker, Hodge averted his eyes. Apprehensively, he muttered, "I don't have it."

"No fire!" Pocket blurted.

"I'm sorry," mumbled Hodge through his thick hair. "The climb was steep, and it weighed me down. I dumped it. I didn't have a choice."

Magnus's subdued expression concerned Pocket and likely Hodge even more.

"To willingly toss aside such a valuable asset… That's just lunacy," said Pocket.

"Do not scold him," Magnus said plainly, leaning back against the curvature of the cave. "I know Hodge, and he isn't lacking sense, just backbone. It gets lost in the fat, where he buries all concern until they outweigh his might."

Magnus went on, far too relaxed. "Hodge, it is in my best interest to have a source of heat on bitter nights like this. I brought you along thinking you were a scholar. It's no wonder you gave up your studies. You're a fool to succumb to your every whim. Just look at you."

"What does that entail, exactly?" Hodge challenged. "I did right to leave that cursed castle."

Hodge leaned back, hands clamped over his tucked ankles. His lip curled as if tucking tobacco. Low and under his hair, with a smidgen of bravery, he uttered, "I forgive you."

"Excuse me?" Magnus leaned in, a throbbing twitch in his eye, voice scaling. "Me? You toad, I'm not the one who left a heat source behind!"

Hodge flared his nostrils and turned his head. "Curse this miserable weather confining us in this incommodious cave made cold and bitter! If my load was offered, I'd have suffered the same grumbling. That I'm 'weak.' This mountain, still towering, will sour you all more, and more will I disappoint you. Habituated, I understand that. But it does not mean I'll be your distressed pell for whacking."

As Magnus looked to speak, Hodge continued his flurry, dashing their chance. "Yes, I was weak to shrivel under the thought of your judgment, that I'm not strong enough, that I chose to throw it instead. I regret that—I regret not being strong enough for those who needed me," he said before a pause. "But if you think reminding me of it will help us, then try and try again until you find yourself with one less ally. I will not sit idly by to be belittled," Hodge huffed. "Now, it pleases me none to say this, but it pleases me less to hear you drag on with insults. How about we worry less for ourselves and more for those who got separated. Even if they are…"

Hodge seemed to simmer down, more anxious for Raihn and Amarra than fighting mad with Magnus. "I still think of them over my well-being, for at least I have a shelter… Lostar was right. They lay out there, and you…you gripe about warmth."

"Was it that 'Rheumatism' that buckled your strength, or your toadish—" Magnus sighed, waving Hodge away, forfeiting his rebuttal.

It was too late. Hodge fell back, his anger looking replaced by just plain hurt.

Pocket looked upon the salivating mouth of the cave from where he lay on the stone. The rain prattled, smacking the stone outside. "I could listen to it for hours," he sighed. "The rain, I mean, not you two," he clarified. "If you keep quiet, I might fuckin' focus on counting sheep."

As flustered as Hodge was made minutes ago, he'd knocked a fresh look at Pocket. "How do you make your lay look so comfortable?"

"It's Habitual," Pocket replied cheekily.

Hodge floundered. "But why? I mean—what made you a vagrant?"

"I know what you mean, but it's a rather personal question, friend," Pocket said, turning to the wall, clutching his hole-ridden cloak."

"Is the title of 'friend' not personal enough?"

"Sometimes words are just words, and when they might mean something, that's when you've said too much."

Hodge scoffed.

Pocket sensed them to be hooked from the thought. That's when he realized it was too quiet. He drew his dulled dagger from his splitting scabbard and carved the cave's cheek to kill time and scratch out the quiet. Moments later, he heard shuffling behind him, stealing him from his brief pastime after a mark. Lostar was stumbling away.

"And where are you going?" Pocket asked them.

"I cannot rest easy knowing my friends are out there," Lostar answered.

"So, what, you're gonna go searchin' for 'em?"

"Do not mind me," Lostar insisted.

"I'm trying," the thief assured, turning back to the wall. His eyes widened, then narrowed. His carving was gone.

AMARRA, amid the mud and clamor, a stranger had howled to her a dire warning: "You must leave now! The beast comes for you, stray lamb. There is no going back. You must hide, for there is no outrunning it. Go!"

She dashed into the murky fog of night, where Barynn illuminated through a low cloud. She navigated carefully, hoping to avoid the trees. Luckily, the rain masked her stomping feet, and the lit fog concealed her fleeting self. Her feet squished and slapped against the muddy terrain, *giving away* her position.

Amarra slunk against the base of a tree where the light was faintest, wondering of the beast. Could it sniff her out? Were its ears honed in on her through the rain?

Panic set in. She felt cornered, relying on hope. Not knowing from where the beast could come. She pulled Raihn closer and listened carefully. It was pitch black and silent, a time best suited for her keen ears. Forcing her teeth to stop chattering, she clenched her jaw tight, staving a thirst for warmth.

Time waned, and it became both more difficult and more vital to keep her eyes open. Amarra was weary and battered, with bruises surfacing and cuts festering. She'd survived much and could not endure more without at least a wink of sleep, the rest induced from that whistle dissipating. She slumped over but caught herself, then slumped and jerked again.

Jolting her head up, she caught her hand as it reflexively moved to slap her awake. She couldn't make a sound, so she bashed her skull into the tree instead, making a dull thud that had to suffice. Another bruise.

The rain ceased again, more abruptly than ever. A sharp snap cracked fear into her heart, and her eyes broadened. She thought of darting off, but the stranger's voice echoed in her mind: *There is no outrunning it.*

196

After a few tense moments, all was quiet again. Perhaps the beast was sly. Might they be instigating Amarra to flee so that they could find her.

Time was slow going and drawn out. She'd festered there, like her cuts, clutching Raihn. Anxiety-induced, she sat, her head still bobbing sleepily, possibly concussed.

"Amarra?" called a feminine voice. "I've missed you so," it said. A long silence followed. The voice was young, yearning, and familiar. Amarra glanced at Raihn, wondering if he recognized the voice of Tepparna. And then she wondered if he'd sensed her curious itch to meet her. It was hard—very hard not to, but she'd kept heeding that stranger's warning of a beast. It had to be evolving with wild tricks.

"Are you there? Amarra! Please! I don't know where I am. I just remember that pain within me, and I don't know where to go. Help me!" The voice faded, as if moving away.

Amarra shifted as if to stand but decided against it. She pondered how the beast knew Tepparna's wound, assuming that was what they referred to. Emotions overwhelming, Amarra knocked her head against the tree again. Pain slaked her.

A long, eerie silence debarked Amarra's nerves until they were made raw.

Tepparna's voice cut sharply through the fog, sounding braver. "Amarra," she called. "I saw you here…Amarra." Her tone chilled.

The silence resumed, leaving a haunting unease over the Outcast for only a moment.

"Help!" Tepparna's desperate squeals from the forest curdled Amarra's blood as they sounded horrid. Her voice wrenched as if forks raked down her body, splitting her skin into roads.

Unable to sit idly, Amarra placed Raihn down, pressing his shoulder affirmatively. She darted deeper into the forest, seeing no strangers, blood, or trails. Determined, she searched the mysterious realm and found a dainty footprint glistening with dew. She followed it, discovering more footprints leading further away until, finally, she saw Tepparna, who startled her with a sudden appearance.

"You were here the whole time," Tepparna said, heartbroken. "Just ignoring me, as if I didn't exist, as if I didn't matter…because you've got someone else now—more important than me—someone I should have left detained, but I freed you both. And look how you repaid me, harboring him even when he is to die, denying me all the while."

Tepparna's words recounted the basic events but lacked depth, like her state of mind. Amarra stepped forward to console them, but they stepped back. She tried again. Tepparna retreated once more. On Amarra's third attempt, the spry Endolander shocked her by lunging with an attack, stabbing her belly and then even her back, for they were quick in their scrambling.

Amarra winced as shallow wounds and even teeth marks marred her calf. Her once-trusted companion seemed to have gone rabid. Amarra donkey-kicked the girl without hesitation, despair catching up with her in a sudden gasp. She had never struck Tepparna before, but what faced her now wasn't the same little Endolander.

A soft thump reached her ears, and she assumed the girl, who could not possibly be the real Tepparna, had struck a tree. That might give Amarra a moment to collect herself. Blood gushed from the gaping wound near her navel, warm against her skin, while her calf, too, drooled. She hobbled away, each step searing through her nerves.

Feeling emptier than ever, she'd resign herself to die alongside Raihn, believing it was all that remained for them in this desolate, lantern-forsaken forest. She just had to get back to him first. But as she searched, turning tree after tree, she struggled to find him, questioning which one she had left him by. The more she searched, the more panic set in as she found nothing. She fretted she had taken the bait and left him as a prize for the jealous Endo-doppelganger. He was simply gone.

A wave of dizziness overtook her, and she crumbled to her knees. Slumping against the nearest tree, she bashed her skull against it, punishing herself in her anguish. She struck it hard enough to shed the bark.

How quickly there came a glimmer then; she froze. Two glowing jade eyes watched from the darkness. The beast, at last, was on the cusp of revealing itself in her weakest hour, having surely taken Raihn within its jaws. The sight gave Amarra enough strength to stand and reach for her hatchets. Then her ears perked up. Something rustled behind her. She spun around the tree, rising to her feet.

It was Tepparna. She closed in, lodging their foot into Amarra's wound for leverage and propelling themselves over her shoulder to clamber onto her back. They reached around and thrust a dagger into her chest with a reverse grip. Fortunately, it lodged in her rib and missed her heart. Tepparna then dove to the front, grasping for the firmly stuck dagger. But before they could pull it free, Amarra slammed them against the tree, causing them to stagger away.

Amarra turned for the jade lights, but they faded into the dark, Barynn-lit fog, replaced by a man approaching: Raihn. Somehow, he marched purposefully, his limbs limber. Amarra beheld his impassive face as he closed the gap, his hand gripping the handle of his sword. It hissed out from the scabbard, drawn to a stubby length.

Fighting against her instincts, she refused to allow any more distance between them. Her thoughts touched the distance of many years, his once unopposed kindness to her familiar to a decade's past. The blade pushed deep. Gripped by her hand, it was pulled closer, its sting a payment filling her void.

Her chest fluttered, eyes boarded up. *That's it.* A tender pain, reminding her of follies, that she was a mark to be scratched out, already pale as a corpse. She held him tight for a moment, palm on the back of his head, savoring the sting as if it were a long-awaited hug from her father. At least, that's how it felt, a tender pain, comforting in a way that her desire bent it to be, as it resonated throughout her body, like a blade ringing on stone. It was her voice.

CHAPTER TWENTY-THREE
Deeper cuts

MAGNUS side-eyed Hodge when they sighed exasperatedly. "What is it?" he asked them, the lanterns flickering on him and the recess.

"Can a downtrodden man not relieve some pressure?"

"Sure he can. But is that all it is?"

"Do you really wish to know?" Hodge asked.

"Honestly, I could use a distraction," Magnus admitted.

"Well, I'm just thinking ahead. That's all. What lies above," Hodge clarified, looking up. "Snow to fill our boots and freeze our toes into icy pebbles. We'll waddle just to keep them from shattering."

"Great, now there are two things I want off my mind." The other being their missing crampons.

"You asked," Hodge retorted with a shrug.

Magnus finally locked eyes with him just as a swift wind blew in. A small figure appeared at the cave entrance, capturing both their attention.

"What is this?" Hodge cried out. "A girl? And in her arms, Raihn and Amarra! How? She looks so young and frail!"

Lostar dashed into the cave. "Mind her not and look upon Amarra!"

She lay in the girl's arms, impaled, a short broadsword lodged within her chest.

Shame washed over Hodge's face. "You're right," he said, his voice remorseful. "My sincere apologies."

The girl neared, the lantern's light rolling over her. Amarra's body was too large for the girl to support properly, her head dangling, hair hanging. Raihn lay atop her by the sunken steel. Magnus leaned, recognizing the sword.

"You fool!" Ghor cried, darting into the cave next. "Have you no brain at all, Rayah?"

Magnus felt a wave of unease, every flicker of the lanterns casting a gloomy light in what truly was bad weather.

"Hey, what's he gabbing about?" Pocket asked. "She restored the party. Well, what she could," he added, seemingly out of nervousness, not heartlessness.

"True," Magnus agreed. "You once wanted him out, then when he fell, you lost your composure and found solace out there, Ghor. Even when it started to shower again. And now that he's back, you're angry. So what is it you want, little man?"

"I want to cross the snow," Ghor answered. "There are rules!"

"Are you sure it isn't mere 'advice'?" Magnus countered.

"'Twas the chest that my concerns fell along, not so much for Raihn," Ghor muttered.

"Oh, hush, Ghor," Rayah insisted, sidestepping the others as she pressed deeper. "Since when do you care about anything other than yourself? It's a wonder you're a guide. You couldn't even keep the grounds at the sound of the horn's blow."

Ghor's brows raced together. "How are you still alive, girl? Is it because you could not keep Raihn safe…back when he was pillaged from the intervening jade serpent?"

The air grew dense, a fog of fear settling in. Rayah's eyes were heavily domineering in her glare, like a malevolent mother, even though she looked so young. Magnus could see time glaring back through her gaze, stretching him thin. Reflections of himself bent over her pupils, magnified tenfold.

"We all get a second chance," she said firmly.

"No, we don't. Not yet. No. No sense at all," Ghor muttered more. "…Can he not fail?"

"He needs a fair chance." Rayah's voice strengthened as she gently lay Amarra and Raihn down in the back of the cave, her expression softening.

"Things are not fair. Never have been," Ghor grumbled, following.

"I invite that change," Rayah went on. "Is that wrong? Is it fair that things are not just? Only because you wallow for yourself?"

Ghor snarled. "It's mighty peculiar," he said. His eyes floated about the cave as if he looked beyond it. "This mountain seems to favorably tip scales for some… Mighty peculiar indeed."

"Your words are spoiled. Ilk of a rotten brain. Soon, you'll be just like the ones below, addled minds alike…"

HODGE oozed with concern while the two bickered. Rayah seemed to have a needle and thread of sorts to patch this mess up, and he was eager to see his companions mended.

He cleared his throat, drawing their attention. "Perhaps we can cast aside any quarrels and focus on the task at hand?"

"You're right. My sincerest apologies," the girl said. She sat beside her a weighty sack, uncinched it, and from the top, she pulled a small stone.

Hodge's efforts to maintain silence were withdrawn as a scoff escaped his lips, a fragment of his doubtful thoughts slipping out. *What would she do with a polished rock?*

Rayah dislodged the sword from Amarra's chest and set it beside her. Hodge's fidgeting stopped, realizing that the sword belonged to Raihn. But the girl kept going. She placed a red stone against Amarra's chest and spoke words unknown across Adjurrah—an incantation.

Before his eyes, the Outcast's wounds miraculously closed. Hodge sat slack-jawed, his head spinning—though that could have been due to his hunger.

Rayah turned to Raihn when Hodge meddled. "Don't suppose you have leeches in your sack. He's got venom slithering through his veins."

"Worry not your head, Hodge, and rest easy," Rayah replied. "I will relight him."

"And he will seem normal," Ghor added, earning a sharp glance from Rayah.

But it was too late. Hodge and the others were curious.

"What do you mean, 'seem'?" Lostar asked.

"Quiet," she snapped. "Unless you do not want him to return, give me just a moment. I'll bring him back, and you will see he is just fine."

Ghor brooded while the others anxiously watched Rayah perform. She examined Raihn's lip and discovered two marks but couldn't draw out the venom. Instead, she claimed she would reawaken his muscles, continuing her murmuring while holding the rocks.

Once finished with her strange work, Rayah, small and delicate, rocked back and forth, her presence disproportionately commanding. Though she seemed a tad bit more youthful than Raihn, her eloquent speech and authoritative demeanor made her age hard to guess.

"Yes, Hodge?" Rayah asked, as if his gawping at her was sensed.

He fumbled. "Just a thought-provoking turn of events. I can't help but be curious about who you are."

"Yes," Magnus agreed. "You haven't introduced yourself, though I caught your name. Will you be staying with us then?"

"I'd like to know that as well," Ghor added sharply. "Are your services still needed?"

"Well, I certainly hope not," she replied, unfazed by Ghor's gruffness. "But hope doesn't change much, does it? You've already heard my answer, Ghor. Did you think I misspoke?"

"Quit being coy and speak plainly!" Ghor demanded.

"I said my purpose here is unfulfilled," Rayah clarified. "He deserves a fair chance, which won't happen without me." She glanced at Raihn, as he'd yet to find his strength. There seemed a definite thought in her, some hatching decision. "Besides, they'll need me in your absence."

"What absence?" Ghor growled.

"Your guidance is no longer required," Rayah continued, her gaze returning. "I hesitated to act, but after hearing from you again, I realize there's no need to wait any longer."

"Excuse me?" Ghor snarled, his temper flaring.

"For the good of this party, I bid you farewell."

"Preposterous!" Ghor spat. "I keep these grounds, and they keep me!"

"And yet they are poorly kept," Rayah retorted, stone aloft in her hand.

"I've been here ever since—"

"And you will continue to be here ever since," Rayah interrupted, her voice steady. "Just not with us. Stay with the grounds, with those at the base of the mountain—the ones who hang in eternal hunger, their minds waning with passaging time."

Ghor appeared menacing and vile as hatred seeped from his eyes. "So, I've waited decades beyond to be treated as a stump just as I ever was," he said. "This is unjust… Why should I change when—"

"Say no more and be off while you still can," Rayah broke.

"Is that a threat?" Ghor's voice lowered menacingly.

"A warning," Rayah replied gently, almost pitying him. Her head tilted then, like a mother's. "Understand?"

"Aye," Ghor muttered.

RAIHN'S body surged awake, his sovereignty restored. But while he was a fresh blade snugged into a scabbard, he wasn't exactly fresh coming out. He glanced at the others through a haze, finding Amarra's body. His blade dulled ever more.

Since the incident with his assaulter, he'd yet to speak to her—or anyone for that matter. He had, however, witnessed her resilience. She took many blunts for him, her body his shield. But now that he'd regained control, she lay flat upon the stone because of it, her cloak drenched in blood from a wound he had inflicted. The cheering from Hodge and even the tepid claps from Pocket bounded through the cave, still deafened by Raihn's plight.

"She'll be okay," Lostar said.

Raihn knew she'd live; he'd heard everything, but that knowledge did little to ease his sorrow.

Pocket leaned in eagerly. "This lady, Rayah, stitched her up good. Well, not really—she kind of said some things. Her wounds mostly just—" he mimicked a closing gate with his hands, "healed up, except for some scarring. Weird, right?" Pocket blurted out. "She seems to speak twice as much as I can. Don't know what she was saying over her, but it sounded like goodwill," he babbled on. "Already an improvement from Ghor. Oh, that's right, he's gone now. More good news, right?

"Anyway, what was it like not being able to move? Was it like, 'I'm a swaddled baby,' or, 'Help, I'm having sleep paralysis and I can't scream, somebody please help me'?"

Pocket's rambling must've struck Magnus's nerves repeatedly as if he were a nail hammered crookedly into timber. He grew hot and ill-tempered, crossing his arms and squeezing his brows together. Finally, Magnus, bent out of shape, planted his hand over Pocket's mouth, ending the chatter but at the cost of one thief's dignity.

Magnus let go, and Pocket blurted again, "Right, well, she appears fine and proper now."

Raihn continued to sit, subdued by Amarra's frozen figure.

A hush fell over the cave, seemingly constricting Pocket, who aimed to break it with his banter. "He's still broken, Rayah."

"Aren't we all?" she mused.

"Y'know what I mean. He's unlike himself."

"Are you so far removed from human understanding?"

"I…don't understand," said Pocket, dumbfounded.

"Apparently so," Magnus snidely remarked.

"She didn't tell you," Raihn clued in.

"What?" Pocket asked, dropping his carefree demeanor.

"You're a terrible thief," Magnus interjected again. "Don't you see? That sword belongs to his hollow scabbard. You should be one to notice these things. He's rightfully glum."

Raihn was so exhausted that he had no care to sigh or to speak any level higher than anything monotone. "It was like I was in a wagon without the reins as a horse tugged me along," he explained. "I could feel my body as usual, but sinking forward. It wouldn't obey me… I didn't want to do it," his voice rose. "I looked right in her eyes, and I…" His knuckles whitened as he gripped his cloak into folds.

"It wasn't your fault," Rayah assured, touching his shoulder.

He shook off her palm, shrinking from her. Taking a beat, his eyes dropping to the stone, he questioned himself. "It is. I will always be a danger to Amarra. I am but a poison to all the good wells around me."

"Raihn, it was **her**," Rayah reasoned. "The vile Out—woman, Uklarta, did this to you, to both of you. You were," she hesitated, "her pawn because you were outside the lanterns."

Raihn babbled quietly, hidden within his cloak. "My weakness stayed me. I, like a moth, flutter to fire, burning my wings, only to be scooped up time and time again for tending. And when came your kindness, I lay with open ears… I remember what was said around me." Raihn's eyes lifted as if brought to a glint. "That venom… What did she do to me?"

Reluctantly, Rayah replied, "She—Uklarta—made you an extension of her mind, Raihn."

"The serpent?" Hodge inquired.

"Yes," she answered, her gaze returning to Raihn. "You were beneath her will. Uklarta poisoned your mind, flooded you with bad blood. But the lights will keep you afloat so long as you steer between them and do not stray again, at least, until you reach the summit and tend the Eternal Flame to stave a plague that she means to spread."

204

"What exactly is this Eternal Flame?" Raihn asked.

"A fire, now dim, hoping for a spark. You've seen the dwellers here. Cold are they. There must be an end to their plight. But no easy task will it be, given this mountain," Rayah explained. "It cracks, weak from the seasons."

Raihn caught Magnus's keen eye on the sword. They observed it, perhaps wondering if it might be swung again. "What are your thoughts?"

Magnus appeared dumbstruck by the straightforwardness and chewed his lip.

Hodge intervened with a hasty defense. "He's himself, isn't he? Raihn's in the path among the lantern light. Let's find comfort in that and not dwell on dark imaginings."

Magnus, still quiet, nodded as if to avoid a mob.

"You should worry, concern, what have you," Raihn acknowledged, "because trust in myself is thin. I wish not to harm any of you," he said, his eyes flickering to Amarra, "and certainly not her… She's been through enough."

"We all have been through enough," said Pocket. "We all have…dents in our metal. Slivered swords. Buckling at the knees," he said, long-windedly before a deep inhale. "We would have blown that whistle—all of us would have if not for our willingness, through pressure from those around us, to prove our mettle. We're fools for it, but I'm glad of it because we might skirt the end yet."

Pocket was admirable then, but Rayah aimed to make an additional supplement. "And if Amarra wakes the same as you, you'd be her last bastion. Don't fear yourself in despair and do more harm than you intend. You're no danger to us, but…Uklarta is a danger through you. Remember that."

"Uklarta," Raihn mumbled, his voice growing. "The jade-eyed serpent."

Raihn retook his sword and snugged it into his scabbard.

The Outcast's eyes cracked open as her silvers peered back at them.

"Look!" Hodge pointed.

Raihn felt queasy, the memory of Uklarta parading under Amarra's skin still vivid. Her head tilted, her eyes curious, perhaps of his restless expression. He feigned a grin before she took his hand, weaving her fingers with his. She, too, forced a smile; he could tell.

Raihn began to fester with an unkind spiraling from a bewitching wretch still groping his thoughts, making him feel dirty. His breath shook, as did his hand.

Their fingers untangled.

Faintly, Raihn heard unpleasant whispers, some unintelligible and some more refined and loud. He softly squeezed his sword by the grip.

Tighter.

The whispers antagonized him. "Kill the jade witch," they creaked in repetition.

Raihn's arm was gripped. He flinched, his fog wrung out; Amarra took him from a trance, his hand distancing the sword. He'd told himself the vile snare-of-a-woman was gone, but the vast mountain was dark. Even within the mountain's design, he felt no safer.

Then his and Amarra's eyes met. He thought her attention would soothe him, but his rigidity hadn't abated. Even though her eyes were not of jade, her face was a reminder…

It appeared that none could hear the deplorable whispers. Raihn hugged his knees to his chest, and from behind them, he glared back at Rayah, who stared. *What is it?* Raihn wondered. *Can she hear them?*

He tried his best to ignore her, his thoughts consumed by the useless fruit he'd been robbed of—a raging ocean bottled, his vessel tossed upon choppy waters. Concealing his distress, he lifted his forearm to veil the tear slipping down his right cheek. His elbow rested on his knee, palm pressed to his head, fingers raking through his hair, nails scraping against his scalp.

He thought to elaborate more to Amarra about the blood within him, but then he questioned whether she had enough concern on her plate—an excuse to avoid acknowledging what happened. And so, he knocked back the thought like it was an ale from his ol' taverner friend and elected to show gratitude instead.

Rayah suddenly made a demand. "Follow me," she said, promptly leaving.

Raihn tailed her and exited the cave. After all her glaring, there was something on her mind.

The cave seemed shifted to Raihn upon his and Rayah's return. Pocket was nearer to the cave's mouth than before, strangely quiet. He and the others seemed to feign disinterest in Raihn's personal matter, looking everywhere else they could, paying mind to mundane amusements.

"Hear anything good?" Rayah inquired.

"Huh? Who? Me?" Pocket scoffed, occupied with a flipping petal. "No."

"But you tried," Rayah accused.

"Of course I did," he swiftly conceded, a faint grin tugging at his lips.

"Well, that's to be expected, but it wasn't you to whom I was first referring." Her gaze alluded to another: Magnus.

He kept his head down, nail picking seemingly his focus. "Strange to have secrets kept among us, is it not?"

"It was a private conversation," Rayah explained, "but if Raihn wishes to share it, that is up to him." She looked up at him with big, unassuming eyes, voice unguarded.

The thief chortled. "Well, Raihn, she sure put you on the spot."

"Yeah…she did," Raihn mused, looking at Amarra helplessly.

"And if you refuse to elaborate, then it becomes a secret," Pocket went on. "And there's little use for secrets within a guild."

Raihn shifted, scalp itchy. The eyes of his companions brought ivy upon him. "We spoke for a bit, and while I may not share everything, I suppose you ought to know who is after us—or—me." He stammered. Just thinking her name sped his heart. "Her name is Uklarta." His eyes filled like pouty clouds, distant, his thumbs spooling.

"We know," Pocket interjected.

"Yeah, well, she—the serpent I heard Ghor speak of to you—is a pillager, a ravager…a brigand beside every road I wander. Even now, there's a hint of her in every syllable I make, my bottom lip stinging. My tongue licks the wound like an animal would lick theirs."

Pocket squinted. "A thief, you say? I didn't know you had anything of value," he snorted ignorantly.

Raihn shifted his burdened gaze to him, fighting a pout. "Even with the ashes of the manor flying through the wind, I was not without something precious." He slunk to the rocky curvature, sighing. "It was easier when I couldn't talk," he managed to say. His phony, nerve-struck grin wiggled into a frown. He'd struggled to maintain this casual demeanor, his eyes glassy and turning red.

His fingers found the hem of his cloak, fiddling with it. "Her fangs sank while I was deep in what Rayah called the Depth, a majestic place I did not want to leave. It was just me and…" his eyes dug deeper into his fidgeting, keeping sight of **her** from his view, "Amarra."

Her gaze rose to him. He could sense it. "I don't quite understand why, but it was like a dream intertwined with reality," he continued. "I was half asleep, and this mountain—as well as Uklarta—can conjure things. For Uklarta, you must slumber, but the mountain, I fear, beholds more power than that." He'd opened his mouth to say more, but he stopped himself.

"And?" Pocket pried, seemingly on the edge.

The cave fell silent. They seemed to know there was more to tell. Raihn glanced, a tight knot contorting his chest as Lostar was side-eying him. His heart chugged a river of blood, entwined with another stream. It raced through him, bleeding through his pores, clear and salty. He dropped his hem, clutching his ribs, his heart batting them. He meant to storm out to the cliffside, but Lostar gripped him.

"That's enough," Lostar said in a low bristle from the back of his throat. "You don't have to explain it to us, but you don't have to run either."

"Are we safe?" Hodge fretted.

Raihn sighed, exhausted from the badgering. "Just stick to the light," he told them, knowing the answer. "Please."

"Together," Rayah added.

"If it be unity you want, Rayah, I would expect you to keep us in the know," said Magnus. "Or rather, Raihn, if it be up to you, I will ask you directly what happened down there that is so hard to say?"

Lostar gripped his sword's handle, staring daggers at Magnus as if he already knew.

Raihn gently laid his hand upon Lostar's knuckles, sheathing their temper. They nodded, and Raihn turned his attention to Hodge, speaking the truth the only way he could without running sick to the wayside, "Chahken dau, go-unrek. Dunaul, un-narek."

Raihn's gaze persisting, Hodge slowly melted their uncertainty to a droopy dread. This confirmed Raihn's suspicion that the scholar knew the giants' tongue.

"What the fuck is that?" Pocket asked.

Hodge took a beat, looking to Raihn for confirmation. Raihn nodded. "He speaks Atnaarr," Hodge relayed. Then he translated. "'Tonight, you are mine. Next, I am his.'"

The shared expression among the group was mostly that of confusion, but the truth seemed to find them swiftly, their gazes like vices on Magnus's conscience. He staggered back against the cave wall as if unable to withstand the intensity of their judgment.

Amid the shared tension, Raihn felt a crushing weight, his breaths stifled with suppressed whimpers for what he had admitted. Desperate to escape, he bolted for the exit, tottering along the way. The cave wall hooked him with a jutting point, his palm slit. "Just need to get my sea legs," he stammered, forcing a grin. He stumbled toward the exit, lightheaded and barely keeping his balance.

Rounding the corner, he collapsed against the wall, holding out his bleeding hand and wondering how much of the blood was his own. The dark against the mountainside seemed even more black, pushing him against it.

When Amarra appeared, he couldn't meet her eyes, overwhelmed by a shame he couldn't control—a shame for his helplessness and the loss of his composure. "I lost my grace," he confessed.

Her finger gently pressed beneath his chin until he found himself staring up into her silvery eyes. His heart fluttered, and sweat broke out on his brow. She embraced him but quickly released him, likely sensing his trembling against her naval.

Raihn grimaced from his thorny reaction, knowing it was her for true— Amarra, not the beast who'd ensnared him.

As she pulled away, Raihn grasped her hand, their eyes locking again. His other hand brushed her skin, then traced the scar he had left. "I'm sorry," he whispered, relearning he'd hurt her just like *she* hurt him. But she was resilient. He admired that.

Her hand bandaged over his throbbing ribs. His heart thumped against her palm, quick as a pony's gallop. His arms found their way around her waist, braving memory. Reminding himself. Reminding…

Amarra tugged at his cloth before proceeding, but Raihn's blade whispered, stealing his eyes as it peered from the sheath. *Chahken dau, go-unrek. Dunaul, un-narek.* He pushed it down, silencing it under his scabbard.

CHAPTER TWENTY-FOUR
To tell the truth

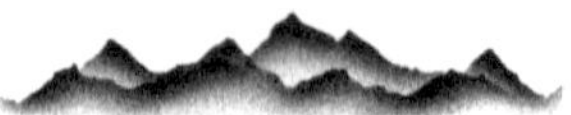

The party tiptoed into a new expanse, where the fog rolled down humps, billowing through fingers of rock. The terrain eased, and the haze retreated. Raihn cursed it, for he had found solace in its embrace. Sharp pillars prodded from ahead, mocking him. They *heard* his utterance to his party and *mocked* his fare, like hunchbacked crones pointing crooked fingers. Had the fog kept dense, he'd not be hassled by them. *Curse it all.*

The formations relented, and Raihn dared to lift his gaze once more, beholding the strange crescent-like trail in the mountain. It looped an ascension, its curves serpently and on guard.

Lostar continued sulking in solemnity until inspiration struck from the spiral. "Shit."

"Please don't grace my presence with such harsh chords," Rayah smiled.

"Don't carve into the mountain either," Pocket warned. "You might make it angry."

Hodge let out an exhausted sigh.

Pocket seemed offended. "Feeling burdened, are we?"

"Just fatigued from the trek. The climb ahead looks daunting," Hodge explained.

Pocket scoffed, "I've never felt burdened, and never will, as long as I'm a free man. But our pockets are lined differently, it seems. With your wide-eyed reaction, one would think you've never faced a challenge, thanks to the cardinal's wealth you're used to."

Hodge bristled at the comment, and Raihn observed the tension between them. Pocket continued, needling Hodge about his scholarly past and the luxury he once enjoyed.

Hodge, clearly uncomfortable, had no desire to banter with the thief, who remained the outcast of their group. Pocket, possibly sensing the lack of camaraderie, muttered to himself as he raced ahead to ascend that *unending* spiral of stairs.

Raihn, Amarra, and Lostar followed behind Pocket. Trailing them were Hodge and Magnus, one or the other always grumbling and struggling. The climb up the side was arduous for everyone, quickly fraying tempers. Occasional bickering broke out, understandable but no more tolerable.

Climbing resembled navigating puddles, as Raihn determined to avoid any splash. He kept to himself, dwelling on memories that swirled within his own cavern. Unspoken. Unresolved.

Eventually, they settled on the decrepit spiral staircase to catch their breath. A heavy silence permeated, like the wisps of fog, each exchanging glances laden with unspoken questions. Their expressions ranged from weary to skeptical as they were hinting judgments on the no-doubt arduous journey ahead.

Raihn's attention found Pocket at the furthest edge, daring to glance over the rocky brim from curiosity. Their hand slipped on the ledge, and Raihn's heart lurched quicker than he.

The thief nearly tumbled into the abyss, saved only by Lostar's firm grip on the nape of their clothing.

"Stay put," Lostar ordered sternly.

Pocket sank back, queasiness trifling his expression.

Raihn couldn't help but steal the briefest of glances wayside. The fog, a sheer silk over the spiral, wisps over a journey's start, inducing vertigo. He recoiled, everyone a blur, Lostar's disapproval waving through his vision. Then there was Magnus with a burden chiseling his features, his mind elsewhere.

Raihn was the first to rise, the others struggling to their feet. Lostar swayed, fringing too close to the cliff's edge, prompting Pocket to pull him back.

"That was a close call," Pocket remarked.

Lostar yanked his arm free. He snapped before a mutter, "I'm fine," followed by a belch, then a bend over the side, vomiting.

Raihn considered steadying Lostar by grabbing his cloak, but refrained, not wanting to embarrass the Enduran further. He watched carefully, ensuring Lostar was stable before starting up the staircase.

Up the way, Raihn had to glance; Lostar was still following behind, but the sight eased his concern. The weight of his satchel began to drag on his shoulder, feeling heavier than before. Raihn shifted the pack to his other shoulder to alleviate the discomfort and pressed on.

Amarra nudged him, gesturing towards the satchel. He shook his head, understanding her offer, but she had already done enough. He felt a sense of responsibility for it, entrusted with not only his brother's journal but the chest from Ghor. The contents remained at his hip, bobbing against him as they continued their climb until finally reaching the final step—or was it? It seemed to depend on them.

The stairs raced into the fog, but he managed to break off into a nook with a soft trail. The stairs continued on, and the lights now split into two lanes, begging Raihn to pick between two lit paths.

Lostar arrived, clinging to the center of the spiral staircase, like the bile clung to his chin hairs. Raihn considered he might be sick of heights, but he comes from high plateaus. He couldn't be.

The thief emerged next, and Magnus pushed out afterward, Hodge squeezing near Lostar last.

"There are two paths, but surely one is correct," Hodge observed, glancing between the two. One continues up, and the other is more level.

"Eenie, meenie," Pocket began counting.

"My fate won't be decided by chance," Magnus interjected. "I'll let my joints decide, and they insist on the flat ground."

"That's the trick," Hodge mused.

"What trick?" Magnus snapped.

"Why would there be two paths? It suggests a choice. We're meant to deliberate. Consider, should we take the safest route?"

"I have considered, and the safest sounds best to me," Magnus retorted.

"So have I," Hodge countered. "I find it odd to be tempted by what seems obvious."

"There is no test of temptation here, just a trek, as always. What's the matter with you? You don't believe in such eccentricities. It's all this walking that has you jumbled. We had multiple routes back home. These lanterns are for safety, and either way must be safe."

"But why two now?" Hodge questioned. "Someone laid out these lanterns. We're meant to choose."

"I don't know," Magnus admitted. "…The stairs might be quicker."

"'Might'?" Raihn interjected. "Then we should take the stairs, and quickly."

"So, you're leading now?" Magnus challenged.

"I just want to be considered," Raihn said, his tone building. A new breath diminished the swell of frustration. "You can do as you please. If it pleases you to follow the path, then do so."

"What about the chest?" Pocket interrupted. "Lose it, and we forfeit the journey, as Ghor warned. Have you all forgotten?"

"Then we should stick together," Hodge insisted, "like Rayah said."

A tense air settled as Magnus stared Raihn down, the same chiseled expression on his mug.

The others continued to spectate.

Raihn considered asserting that carrying the chest gave him the final say, but he knew further division was unwise. "How about we ask Rayah?" He paused, suddenly aware she was absent. "Where is she?"

"So much for any guide or aid—whatever she is," Magnus said. "She's gone."

"A vote it is then," Pocket chimed in.

"You know my preference," Magnus stated.

"Mine as well," Raihn countered, glancing at the others in anticipation.

212

Amarra initiated the voting process and stepped closer to Raihn, with Hodge following. Pocket and Lostar remained, and the odds were stacked against Magnus.

Pocket sided with Magnus. "Sorry, but I always look for the most comforting place. I'd rather traverse this path quickly than climb the stairs slowly. Nothing against you guys, I'm just—"

Magnus patted their back hard enough to draw a choke.

"...Right."

Three to two. If Lostar sided with Magnus, it would be a draw, but Raihn was confident in his friend to keep beside him.

Lostar teetered a glance to each candidate, then the trail, eyes almost yearning for it.

"I vote for the trail," Lostar ushered out. "But not for your sake, Magnus."

"Appears to be a draw," the tracker said. "Both of our choices are null—until one side wins, that is."

"Wins what?" Raihn asked, his voice bitterly tinged.

"Truth, and only truth. No dares. The first to refuse their truth fails."

"Fine," Raihn agreed, "but how do I know you'll honor it?"

Magnus scoffed. "Lying once...maybe twice, shouldn't brand me a liar. I know you've lied just as well, haven't you? Keeping secrets of your own, not just the ones born on this mountain."

Raihn's eyes narrowed, his mind made. "Who goes first?"

"Pocket?" Magnus prompted.

"Finally," said Pocket. "Eenie, meenie..."

"No, no, no. It could be rigged if he's got a side to root for. That won't do," said Hodge, being fair. "Perhaps, if I may, I suggest a gentlemen's game of grass, fire, water," said Hodge.

Magnus snickered in acceptance.

"A game of luck without outside help," Raihn stated. "Best two out of three." His right fist balled over his left palm. "Ready?"

"Only if you are," Magnus batted.

Raihn stood firm, his hand itching to make shapes. "Count it down, Hodge."

"Wait!" Pocket exclaimed. "I have dice," he suggested, digging them out from his pocket before presenting them on his palm. They looked to be made from shaved bone.

Magnus slapped their hand, and the dice flew down the mountain. "Stay out of it, Pocket. We've already decided. Besides, them dice'r likely loaded. Count it, Hodge."

The thief rushed to raise a sinched bag that looked weighted by marbles. He insisted on playing a different game yet again, but Magnus, more angrily, took the bag and flung it further than the dice.

"Fuck!" the thief cursed. "Have you no regard for personal property?"

Magnus played his hand early, giving the thief a vulgar finger. "Hodge," he barked, "count it down, god dammit!"

Hodge recoiled and began. "Three…two…one!"

Raihn raised his hand and pointed his fingers upward, all touching and not spread apart, symbolizing fire, while Magnus lain his flat, mimicking a grass bed.

"Perhaps it was ignorant of me to assume you'd use water subconsciously due to your name," said Magnus.

Raihn rounded his fist and took a deep breath. "I'm not a child," he said. His heart began to beat faster, and his palms began to sweat.

But water did cross my mind, he thought.

He felt sure of his next move, but still, his body proved a mess as Hodge began the countdown.

"Three."

Magnus appeared confident.

"Two."

They wore a smirk as if celebrating their imminent victory.

"One."

Magnus's fingers lay flat as he played grass a second time. "Got you," he smirked, winning this round.

Raihn's heart thumped louder. If Magnus won, he got the first question, which may be deadly. From the sureness in their eyes, Raihn wondered if this was about the path at all. But he acted as calmly as he could. Maybe the best odds were to avoid overthinking.

He coiled his hand into a fist once more and beat his palm with a determined thump. He was quick, his hand not revealing the next symbol until the very last moment. Braced for the worst and hoped for the best. This was it.

"Grass, fire, water," he muttered, fingers forming fire again. But Magnus laid down water, extinguishing Raihn's fire with an air of triumph. They grinned.

"I win," Magnus declared, voice sopping with satisfaction. "Now, for my question."

Raihn steeled himself, ready for whatever Magnus might ask. The stakes felt higher than ever, and he knew the question could delve into anything.

"I ask of you to tell us the truth of what happened. No talk of 'snakes' and beating around the bush. This Uklarta woman raped you, am I right? But for what gain if not pleasure?"

Raihn glowered at him, tongue-tied.

"That's rough, Magnus," Pocket murmured.

"Answer," Magnus pressed. "You fear hurting Amarra again, losing trust in yourself, overcome again and again by this ensnaring witch. How could a man, without trust in himself or his companions, lead? And you said Amarra was there as well, right? Do you hold it against her for not saving you?"

"I think that's two, maybe three questions," Pocket said. "Four, perhaps?"

"Shut it," Magnus cracked.

It was more important to explain to Amarra than to let loose his wrath. Raihn tried, as best as he could, to quell the bulging veins in his forehead. He spun and looked at her, their eyes wide. "It's not true," he sputtered, "not really... My veins, spoiled by her, might be freed if we conquer this mountain... But still, there will be others just as terrible—my people, like the outriders. Amarra, I know what they did. And I know more could come for us, or rather, you. I'm afraid. And...and, damn you Magnus, you son of a bitch," he said, turning to them briefly.

Raihn's chin was anchored down until Amarra took her hand beneath it, again pulling his attention. He was weak to it, anger dissipating. Her nostrils flared as if signaling thoughtfulness. A gloss sheened over her eyes, telling more.

He began to muster more truth. "You weren't there, Amarra. Uklarta—" he froze, apprehensive, "she manipulated the place meant to tempt me to remain with you. I don't know, like it was some trial or obstacle. But Uklarta slithered into it like a fog, molesting all that was good, darkening the images of those around me... I can't get her out of my head..." his voice stopped short, but his inner voice continued, ...*when I look at you.* His guilt mounted again, its creeping fingers clamping his throat.

She remained still, her eyes undeterred and no longer decipherable. A long-standing pause brought writhing squirms to Raihn's soiled nerves.

"What about the reason for her pillaging you?" Magnus pushed.

Raihn sneered. "That's another question, right, Pocket?"

The thief nodded.

"I answered one."

"Maybe two," Pocket piped up.

"Thanks...Pocket. But the game continues. I have the next ask."

At first, Raihn was going to ask Magnus if they'd snuck a peek through his journal by some off chance, but whispers crept into his head, prompting him to ask a most dreadful question—one he couldn't possibly know without their nudging. His lips parted.

"—I forfeit. You win," Magnus said, hands up.

Raihn gasped, dumbfounded first, infuriated next. This wasn't a move he'd even considered, to be robbed like this. It was unjust. Even the scholar's eyebrows furrowed as he and the others watched Magnus shed his dignity—or what remained of it.

Magnus said naught else, already ascending the stone spiral.

"It's the man without dignity that cannot be trusted," Raihn said. He looked down upon his sword and felt himself become heavy, the blood in his veins thickening.

Raihn passed Lostar, refraining from acknowledging him, and chased the endless flight of stairs again. Uncertainty festered, and he questioned the whispers over his ear, wondering if they were correct about Magnus, if they were a *slaughterer.*

An inconceivable metric of madness polluted their climb, unable to be measured in acres or leagues. It felt like a punishment for Raihn, who wondered if his belief in the right choice had been foolish. He sensed the others' loud thoughts pressed upon his back.

"Stop worrying," said Lostar, as though he had read Raihn's mind.

"It's hard not to second-guess myself when others do," Raihn replied smarmily.

"That comes with being a leader," Lostar argued.

"I'm not a leader."

"Are you not the reason we follow these stairs?"

Raihn pondered. "Why do you care? You wanted to take the cushy trail."

"It doesn't mean I don't respect your decisions. To ask your friends to follow you blindly would be foolish. Differing solutions or opinions are not betrayal. Feeling such indicates a lack of a mature grasp on the responsibilities of leading."

Lostar appeared present-minded, sober, and soft-spoken—a surprise to Raihn, but a welcomed one. Might Raihn be taking it too personally after all, but *even so...*

A silent slog ensued. Raihn despaired, curious as to where they headed. Might there be a dry pair of socks that would not beg an itch to his wet feet at the end of it all. And better, might there be a hearth too.

His mind was yanked from its gloom. His posture perked, and his shoulders squared. He saw the end of the ascent, eyes wide. "We made it!"

Smiles bloomed all around him like a field of marigolds. The group scrambled up the stairs like they'd reached the end of a rainbow, though there was no cauldron of gold but a dark, lonely cave nestled between shoulders of stone. Still, their smiles did not waver. Any place was better than where they had been. Hodge kissed the ground beneath them, twenty feet from the cave. Much praise was hailed when on their knees.

A feeling of accomplishment enveloped Raihn as the lanterns continued along the path into the cave. It was a relief to him, to them all, it seemed. Lostar patted him on the back and settled off to the side.

"A flat surface will work wonders now," Hodge laughed with a heavy breath. "I declare a moment, or a minute, perhaps an hour of rest... or—"

"Just relax," said Pocket. "We'll get up when our legs are done screamin'."

The exuberant voices faded, replaced by a chill in the air. They wrapped themselves in their cloaks, enjoying their well-earned rest, finding a strange coziness and comfortable silence around them. Their effort had led them here, scattered across the stone. Raihn, however, had not forgotten about

216

Magnus. He glanced over, pondering whether it was spite down there or something else.

Breaking Raihn from his reverie, a sound, like a whistle from the rock's yawning mouth, shot into his ear and down his spine. Goosebumps rallied along his arm as his attention turned to the black hole between the jagged-shouldered rocks. His hand gripped the smooth handle of his sword as his eyes stared deeply. The cave hissed, and then he heard a cry of terror, followed by one of pain, then a plea for aid, calling his name many times. "Raihn!"

It was a soft, feminine voice he'd thought of often since the flames overtook the village. *Mom?* He glimpsed the others. They were unmoved.

His attention was lassoed again, her voice gnarling, imaginations howling at his mind. Might she be upon the rack, stretched by the wrists and ankles. Or might rats be gnawing at her chest, trapped under a bucket. There was no knowing what had her, but Uklarta came to mind, the lasso shrinking around Raihn's neck, hastily pulling him in, tightening like a noose. He kicked up dirt in a scurry.

"Raihn?" Hodge said, confused.

CHAPTER TWENTY-FIVE
The dark house

Another cave, hollowed within the hallowed mountain, dark and devoid of life. Suspicion of trickery grew. Despite the risk of deception lurking among the rocks, the quest to find his mother felt imperative, though daunting to pursue alone. He glanced back, hoping to see the others, but the cave's mouth was sealed tight, the familiar darkness a grim companion.

The mountain seemed to tighten its grip, a sensation that puzzled Raihn, especially after being rescued by its young steward on her second attempt. This place was ill-suited for someone of her ilk, or so he'd think; she was strong but, unfortunately for him, missing. Maybe he was the one ill-suited for the harsh mountain.

Raihn exhaled, deciding to take the plunge into the deep. He waded through the dark chill, silently praying that the ensnaring witch wasn't there to stir mischief and that this was simply the mountain's miasma at work, for the cave had fallen silent.

"Mother!" His voice became lost in the dark, and he looked for her as it shrunk repeatedly through an echo. Despite the potential heartbreak or loss of sanity, he anticipated seeing them, even if they may only appear as ghostly visions. Even an illusion in this hole, devoid of granite, was welcomed…

Raihn realized he was a fool, lured by a glint in the obscurity that only shined his weakness. Lost in this in-between, he felt trapped, wondering if he'd veered off the trail. The mountain seemed to forsake him this time, truly. But he persisted, rummaging, sprinting through the dark marathon until he smacked into a wall, face-first. His nose smashed, he fell back, checking for blood. Surprisingly, his nostrils were clear.

He got back up and felt the surface he had rammed into. It had indents like wood planks, but they were sanded beneath a fine lacquer, unlike any peasant home. The only walls this luxurious—that he knew of—were the manor walls.

"Okay, you got me—but that was dirty," Raihn joked, trying to fill the pit in his stomach with a feigned laugh. He didn't even know who 'you' was— just some kind of…entity of magic.

Hugging the wall, he continued to search for a door, his thoughts racing. His fingers traced the smooth wood, looking for a seam, a handle, anything.

"It's like I'm the character of a cautionary tale that every child neglects to learn from. Then again, this is more like a tale where some creep jumps from the shadows, and everyone forgets the point."

He stopped, peering into the surrounding darkness.

"If there is a point to this," he muttered, "maybe I'm getting some form of mountain madness, if such a thing exists. After all, nobody else seemed to hear the screams but me…"

He fingered the wall, talking only to himself to fortify his nerves, until he found a deformity protruding from it. Curiously, his index slid down a bump that waned into a concave shape, then over something soft and cushy. Like a man reading braille, he felt the unforeseen page. It was undeniably a feminine face, with a nose and soft lips turning it cursive. With this sudden realization, his hand shot away in fear, brushing abrasive strings too coarse to be hairs from a scalp.

Heart hammering against his ribs, his breath paced.

"Hello?" he said at last, to no reply. "Hello?"

Nothing.

Raihn considered that, perhaps, his overactive imagination was toying with him, for when in the dark, anything could feel strange.

He reached again, slowly wagging his arm through the black. They were gone, so he coiled his hand against his chest and froze. Rationality kept him still. If he were to move, he might stumble into the thing. But then again, it knew where he was. He couldn't debate it forever, but his decision was rendered moot when he sensed their presence. He, honing in, could feel their gaze, determining who—or what—was standing right behind him. Maybe it was the very thing conjuring these visions.

Raihn gathered his courage, his thoughts battling. He took a step. *Betrayed*, the *damned* floor beneath him creaked with every movement. *Am I near the cellar? How did I even get inside?* He crept forward, feet tentative, trying to evade the stranger. He shuffled onward. Again, he collided with her—a woman's body. Her frigid breath brushed against his neck, his heart hopping like a startled toad.

He stumbled in his frantic retreat from the woman and crashed to the floor. The edge of his journal jabbed into his chest, sending boomeranging pain through his gut. As he rose, the chest tumbled out of his satchel.

Raihn, both frustrated and in pain, clenched his fist, knowing now was not the time for this. He swept the floor, hoping for a quick retrieval, but the chest eluded him. *Where had it gone?* Desperately, Raihn reached out, searching in vain. He crawled forward, his fingertips brushing the floor, but found nothing. Persisting, he continued to feel around until, at last, he touched something—a string.

Curiosity overcame him as he followed the string down with his thumb and index finger. Gradually, his eyes adjusted to the faint light, revealing it led to a sharp hook and pinched flesh. Raihn withdrew in horror as the figure, wired and unnatural, seemed to glide forward, its toes dragging, for he heard them skid. Tears of pure fear welled in his eyes. There was no escape from this puppet.

Raihn abandoned his attempts to flee, his voice trembling as he pleaded, "Please, don't hurt me! I've done nothing," sheltering his head beneath his arms.

Then, a flicker pierced Raihn's eyelids and drew his gaze. The puppet of flesh was gone, and he spotted an orange glow on a rocking chair, the same one his mother often knitted in. This was indeed the manor—or a twisted imitation of it, and on the chair sat a candelabra with one lit candlestick. Clearly, it was intended for him, within what looked to be the Lady's Chamber. Raihn cursed its horror-drenched aura.

He found the courage to approach the chair diligently. And when the candelabra was nigh within his grasp, the creaky seat reclined, and the candelabra fled his touch. He bit his bottom lip and dove again for the tri-pronged piece of metal. This time, it remained.

Just as his fingers wrapped around the cold cylinder, three knocks were at the front. Raihn jumped, and the candelabra fell from his grasp. He scrambled to the floor to retrieve it and spare the manor from a second torching.

The candlelight ahead of him, he daringly tiptoed toward the noise. The door was there—unlike before—and the knob glistened in the light, mocking him as he tried to turn it. Then, something scurried below and through the gap. It, an envelope addressed to him, bumped his foot. His breath hitched.

Reaching for it, he found the envelope immovable, just like the knob. He'd seen it easily slide through, yet it seemed affixed to the floor. Muttering a curse, he let go and studied his name upon it. The 'h' was missing. Might it be from an illiterate peasant?

A click echoed from behind, and Raihn swung out his candelabra. The light flickered upon the walls, revealing a shifted space: the vestibule. Coats and things hung about on fancy hooks, catching the glow along their loose threads.

Raihn supposed the letter beneath the front door would make sense, but he certainly wasn't there moments ago. If that be the truth now, the clicking sound must have come from the private meal room, where he'd last eaten at home. He reconsidered the sound, realizing it resembled the clink of silverware. The image of a knife sliced his bravery in half. Despite that, he investigated, nudging himself forth and peering around corners. The back door was open, the concern of knives fading, for it was only the lock. And through the door was the cave, a way out, it seemed, but the chest was still missing, and that envelope still nagged him. Everything refused him, except the candelabra and an exit that seemed all too easy.

Then, a heavy clunk above loosened dust in a cascade, and there was a shriek across the upper floor as if a weighty object skidded along it. That had to be his stolen chest.

Raihn brushed out the dander and thought if he were to go up there, it best be with more light. He attempted to use the one lit candle to light the others, but when he pulled the flame away, the other two wicks remained unlit. There was a *strange* stipulation to this, hardly worth questioning at this point. The envelope, the door… He was a doll in a little horror house, abiding no decree of his own making, other than his might to shun the back door, *unbelievably* heading to the stairs for the above floor.

Another wick ignited of its own volition just then.

"Sure," Raihn whispered, trying to cope. *Why not. I must be doing something right.*

Raihn stood at the base of the ever-fading stairs as they stretched into darkness, his legs trembling. He forged courage and took his first step, with his candelabra aloft. The steps groaned beneath him as he ascended. The light danced along the walls in a flicker, where his family's portraits hung. They deepened a pit in Raihn's stomach; River never painted himself with the family.

The second floor was cooler, thicker with dust. Two rooms peered narrowly from the left wall—the first, his father's forbidden chamber, and the second, his brother's. This was the first time his father's chamber was cracked open, the door never ajar from its frame. And unfortunately, it was where Raihn believed he heard the thud. It was time to disobey his father once again. His shoulder brushed the door open, and faint objects peeked back through the dark. Closer, his candlelight orbed over a desk that sat to the left of the chamber, a stately bed to the right, but, with his puny fire, Raihn could only see the foot of it. In the center of the room, there was a wall-to-wall red carpet.

Raihn slunk, dispelling imagined legends, yet each step felt like treason. So far, no chest, so he knelt with his candelabra and crawled across the carpet. His palm burned from the friction, but he pressed on. His eyes fell upon the large bed with a lush blanket draped to the floor. Curiosity piqued, he flung the bedding aside and peered below the bed, where his candlelight did not reach. Head against the bedframe, he earned a blind reach, the tips of his fingers brushing what felt like the chest. Wiggling it closer, he recalled doing so under his brother's bed. There was a rat at that time, but now, he considered that anything could scream out of the underbelly in a mad dash. He scooped it into his palm and began to pull, a sense of ease creeping only to be ruined.

A tight squeeze clamped around his wrist.

Raihn's imagination was validated—not that he wanted it to be—as he yelped and yanked his hand back. Whatever held onto him was dragged into the orange flickers. After a moment, he accepted what it was: a female corpse, hooked with strings. Setting down the candelabra, he tried to pry her free, but she clung tight. Her grotesque body and red hair sent a tug of war through his stomach. The dry skin felt chilled and flaky, as if she had just come in from the snow. While her features weren't evident, her dress pulled his bile into his throat, his realization a sickening one.

"Aggy!?"

The strings pulled away from her, reaching the ever-black ceiling, becoming taut. Her head lolled over, revealing a sullen eye beneath her red strands.

"I'm sorry for what happened to you, but please, let go of me," he pleaded. "I know I evaded you, retired to the manor, but I heard the truth."

Aggy began to move, strings tugging at her arm, hand, and pointer, until she directed him to the desk nearby.

Raihn, now released from her arrest, stumbled there, his legs like gelatin. He pulled out a drawer. Inside it, he found an envelope with a broken seal. His face scrunched as he scrutinized it. The writing was just as scratchy as the one beneath the door, the 'h' missing from his name. He put the chest down on the desk and pinched the envelope, removing the letter from it.

Dear Raihn.

I havent heard from you in quite some wile. I know what you heard and in turn I also know what you must think. Thoe it aint right to leave me in the dark to loath my own misgivings. I think Ive the right to speak my halves. I shoulda said it sooner but I was too afraid. But perhaps it is the way you have discarded me that makes my own truth much easier to be said now. It is something that I ached to say before but the outcome scared me. my father more so.

Raihn I will make it plain. I began seeing you threw the insistence of my father. To make him happy I tried to make you happy. Thoe in the end I fell for you. a rotten turn but maybe it evened out justly.

Wile I kept my act up in front of Will, what we shared was not staged like my shows. And even if I dont hear back I only want to breathe the truth. Please just dont hate me. That is all I really want.

If you decide to talk about this come see me by the river before Eldhos sets.

Sincerely,
Agata

The weight of these inked words—though roughly penned—set Raihn off balance. He fell against the desk, nearly whimpering. "I'm sorry," he muttered. "I didn't know." He was apologetic, but his candles were held up like a shield, the light dressing her skin with a carroty tint.

Aggy's head tilted. Her hair parted at the other eye, a dark purple ring revealed to be puffing around it, like a bruise. Hooks pinched her pale skin into a suspension, evoking the image of a kitten's nape in its mother's mouth.

"Of course, you'd no idea," Aggy's throat rumbled. "Ye neglected my half. I could say nothing, explain nothing. You were a coward, hiding beneath your mother's dress or hugging your father's calf while I cowered under mine. Your self-pity cost me everything while I gained a wallop upon a wallop. You, too immature to lead, lost us what could have been."

"I know…"

"And you'd do it again," she mused.

Raihn shied his gaze from the flickers in her eyes. "You're right. If I had received that letter. If it had not been hidden from me. Maybe things would be different. I should have braved the truth," he admitted. "Or sought it. Instead, I slunk in my manor, overcome by my wallowing. I am sorry, Aggy. It's not how I envisioned our courtship. I thought we were just petals in the winds of our fathers' breaths, but I could have spoken for myself and you, had I elected to… I fled the remains of my village with the ashes of the serfs in my socks. I scratch at my ankles, for every speck of ash is a serf clinging to my skin…"

Raihn took a breath, reflecting on the smithy, the wisewoman, and all the others. "It went quiet, that metal, once crying at my window by the morn of each day. Without it, I'd say this manor feels quite hollow and cold. I can't help but feel this is an echo gone shivering for my atonement. I know I could have saved you and kept you from the mines… I've considered a story of the pig and how I betrayed it with a feast upon its kin. Maybe it had a right to come after us. Moreover, I've betrayed my oath, lopping the head of a cannibal, a hungry echo trying to take me into its plight. I am the fire that takes and takes. Never satisfied. It makes me afraid."

Raihn breathed a beat, his burning wicks coming under consideration below his gaze. The smell of tallow wafted below the bulb of his nose. "You could have worn the rags or the dress. You could have kept playing puppet shows for the kids—maybe our own, had we any. But the deafness came before the fire, taking me before the village. Because I'm a fool always. And I am sorry for that, Aggy."

Aggy hovered, her arm creeping up, her hand coming near. "Then stop bein' such a fool all the time," she said, her thumb over his lip.

Aggy's strings singed, leaving little plumes of smoke. Some remained, igniting with great flames as they crawled down to her. Raihn drew his sword and swung. She, cut free, fell, and was then strewn across the floor.

The stench of death filled the air. Raihn stifled a breath as Aggy's body began to writhe upon the floor like a fish out of water.

"Aggy?"

Her body ceased all motion, and a horrible flame engulfed her corpse as if she were doused in oil.

"What do I do?" Raihn shrieked, looking to his candelabra. All three candles were lit. "It's over, right? Stop this madness!"

He took the chest and dropped it into the satchel, ready to leave this scarring mess behind. He turned his back to Aggy, the candelabra still clutched, when came a different glow on the edges of his sight. Raihn glanced over his shoulder and saw that the room had caught fire, flames rapidly climbing the walls around Aggy.

The candles had to mean something, for if not, then even powers beyond him were futile. Was this pain just another play, like the one in Cobblestone, before all went to flame?

The blaze accompanied her corpse. Without any string, she sprung up on limp ankles, heels snapped to their sides. Afflicted by torment, her visage gripped him, her hair singeing away, her skin blackening upon its shedding, exposing an unadulterated white beneath and an eye of silver. She seemed to grow, with nubby horns blooming from her head as if a cocooned beast was now rearing its head from her body. The wall behind her blew away, and through that gash, Raihn could see naught but darkness with swirling fire and debris—a powerful vortex that pulled in all the furniture, and eventually, Raihn himself.

The candelabra was sucked away as he held onto the satchel only, struggling against the pull that was too great. The maelstrom consumed everything in its wake, dragging him towards the abyss. He clawed at the ground, his fingers scraping against the floorboards.

Finally, he'd found a crook in the floor to latch onto, but the darkness quickly enveloped his environment, and the last thing he saw was the beast emerging fully from Aggy's remains, its eyes gleaming malevolence. He stared into them, his eyes aflame as though he gaped into Eldhos.

A voice called out to him from the door and spared his vision. From there, he saw a hand reaching out to him, dirty, with crud beneath its nails.

"Aggy!" Raihn exclaimed. Her hair was lush, though whipping over her head. Her skin, through the flagging hair, was as pale and freckled as ever.

"C'mon," Aggy beckoned. "Take my hand!"

Raihn grabbed hold, and she pulled him down the steps, the intensity of the fire ever fiercer. The thing above seemed enraged by Aggy's intervention, and it consumed the stairs down which Raihn fled into bits of charcoal. With Aggy's help, he found the last step. He covered his mouth with one hand and pressed through the orange waves until coming upon the private meal room.

The backdoor was still open, just inches away, when he lunged for the knob. His fingers narrowly missed it, the vortex still pulling him back. He paused, leaning forward with all his weight, his lungs burning. Suddenly, he felt her hands on his back as they pushed him forward.

He managed to grip the knob of the open door. Looking back, the vortex chewed near, taking his tears with a great suction. Aggy was clinging desperately to the table, her hair pulled back by the grip of the vigorous whirlwind.

"Go!" she ordered.

"I can't," said Raihn.

"You have to," she said. "There aren't more chances than ones already labored, other than the ones we wished we labored since."

Raihn strung out his one hand for her to grab, the other still holding the knob. He gasped, the vortex behind her stealing his breath.

She hopped towards him, taking his hand and pulling herself to the door, grasping the left side of its frame with red-hot fingers. With her right hand, Aggy pushed Raihn through the doorway, the fiery vortex swallowing her.

The door shut.

Raihn jumped to his feet, his heart sunken. He gripped the knob, but it scalded his hand. He relented briefly, then howled.

The door had been beaten on, on and on, for several minutes before finally he retired, exasperated. He fell to the cave's hard ground before punishing his knuckles upon it with another pounding.

There aren't more chances than ones already labored—

Raihn sat, held in by his own arms, trying to regain his composure from the torment he had just endured. His wounds reopened afresh, bleeding questions to a pool of loathing. He was plagued by it, thinking…thinking…

O Agata…

CHAPTER TWENTY-SIX
Silver to silver

AMARRA snagged Lostar by the neck of his cloak and tugged him along, whether he wanted to go or not. She wouldn't allow harm to befall Raihn another time, nor would she go it alone.

Unfortunately for her, a blinding light broke inside the cave. And for the briefest moment, her hand left Lostar to shield her eyes. Her vision adjusted, taking in a surrounding, lush wilderness with a wealth of stumps, no mountain or wall in sight. It seemed almost too good to be true, but before she could fully grasp the change, the sound of loud, chunky clops drew her attention to Raihn, who was felling trees. It was only he with her, Lostar absent. The cave was toying with her once again.

"I see that our newly fashioned beds aren't so bad," he said, tossing the butt of the axe over his shoulder upon approach. "Not as cushy as…well, never mind all that," Raihn laughed, realizing his rambling. "Glad to see you well-rested."

Amarra was taken aback, for unlike her previous experiences in the cave, she felt acknowledged. She lowered herself, her cheeks pulling into a wide grin. They embraced.

"I'm glad you're awake," Raihn continued, releasing her. "I'll need some help."

Amarra grabbed his shoulder firmly and glanced about. She seemed to have just come from a half-completed cabin. No sense was it—not to her anyway.

"Something wrong?" he asked, his eyes narrowing.

Amarra exhaled, cursing herself for not simply basking for more than a moment. She presented her chart, spelling out, 'Remind me how we got off the mountain.'

Raihn's expression took a flat note. Still, he managed a chuckle through it. "I suppose you forgot. It's kind of fuzzy to me too, I must admit."

He fidgeted contemplatively, making her nervous.

"Well, we reached the peak, and…" His face scrunched, his brows furrowing inward. "Look, I held up my end of the deal," he said defensively. "We stopped Uklarta and secured a future. We're not obligated to anything else but our solitude, and here we are—alone. Can you believe it? Solitude," he said, spreading his arms wide to encompass the land beyond.

Amarra pondered Raihn's words. He sounded conflicted, guilty, and vague. She gripped his shoulder even tighter.

"Amarra, please," Raihn implored. "Don't make me remember."

She allowed him his peace and let go of him, somewhat disenchanted. Still, she wondered if this was a page ripped from the end of a book—a fairy tale she would get to live, and that was why only he knew the truth. She had yet to uncover the secrets resting atop the mountain, but that time would come, and so she refrained from further inquiry, but not contemplation.

A soft hum in the distance interrupted her thoughts, growing louder, the beat of drums pounding. A shiver slithered up her spine, a thought bursting into her head: *Someone comes.*

Raihn, seemingly hearing it as well, gasped. "Come on, you know what to do. Just like we practiced."

Amarra was confused. *Practiced?* Raihn dashed past her and pulled the door to the cabin. It whipped open, banging the outer wall. She followed.

Inside, there was a hatch on the floor which he threw open, revealing a partially dug ditch. He squatted beside it, his axe still with him.

"The cabin my father started isn't finished, and I was inspired by the cellar back home, though this one is for more than ale and barley—" he'd shaken his head, dashing his rambling yet again. "No time for chit-chat, Amarra," he said, gesturing to the hole with the head of the axe. "Well?"

She resisted. He even attempted to push her in, but she heard the wild cries of those approaching, nostrils flaring as she smelled them. In a swift move, she shoved Raihn into the hole and slammed the hatch shut. He bellowed from below, and she firmly planted her heel on the hatch to prevent his escape.

"You're in man's land, Amarra! They'll kill you, or worse…!"

She kicked the hatch, silencing him, then stood at the door as the impending arrival was heralded by much tramping.

Soon enough, before her loomed a rising tide of grey flesh, Outcasts like her, spilling in with overwhelming numbers—an army of a tribe—a leich. Amarra couldn't fathom what this would mean for the land they had stormed. Each step they took broke the First King's Word, an oath that no Outcast would ever cross Crossguard. As far as she knew, she was the only one who had ever crossed, and that was only because of Alvin. Due to the First King's Word, her presence across the trenches and the battlement could never be known, for it could spark a riot led by the masses.

The Outcast army leered, their dark eyes gleaming under horns. They cleared a path for their Onurra, who emerged from his warriors and disciples. She saw only a boy in appearance, but she could read the Onurra's true age in his silver globes, who stood about Raihn's height, adorned with petite horns, with the fur of a scarlet bear draped over his charred body. Half of his face was marred by burns, looming closer as he strode near, like a white snake.

The Onurra addressed Amarra with a rascally grace, "O pale-skinned maiden with a shuttered cry," he began, ages resonant in his voice, "how fare thee in the wild, I would ask, but thou'rt forsaken by thy tongue, silent amidst mine own followers."

As he approached, his piercing gaze stretched Amarra's composure, drawing her into its two silver-ringed abysses, echoing Rayah's gaze. She remained steadfast, refusing to betray any hint of guilt. She wondered of his common tongue, for never had she heard it from an Outcast before.

With a playful snort, the Onurra—*the tribe leader,* momentarily acknowledged Amarra's stowed treasure, his eyes flicking to the cellar behind her. Her eyes curiously followed, suddenly understanding he had not spoke just to her. And when she returned her attention, the boy, with a dramatic flourish, produced a decapitated head from beneath his fur, its ghastly visage frozen with a grimace.

The boy clicked his tongue, adopting a more commanding tone. "Randy Rose, descendant of the weak, accompanied by a sizable retinue. He begged, offering information, such as the whereabouts of a 'pale Outcast' who consorted with a man. Thou'rt not so well-hidden," he remarked coyly, toying with the head's lips, glancing the cellar.

"I am older than I appear, the wind in mine pipes blowing dust. Mayhap my chords seem old-strung, yet I have listened for many a year. The winds shift, and I listen well. Mine ear ever attuned to the rocks, the earth where feet tread and stones are set. Now more than ever, I hear the impending rain, the trickle of water over hewn stones…whispers of those plotting a raid," he said dully.

The boy spun the head, eyeing its grotesque shape. He seemed to speak with a new breath, shifting demeanor. "These deceitful brigands boasted of your demise and of defiling what they found repugnant. Whooping and clamoring to retrieve the head of an Afurja—an 'Outcast' beyond the trench," he said, his eyes jumping back to her. "They fancied their names inscribed. How ironic," he mused, his brow furrowing, his voice becoming unkind. "I approached them, and for a moment they mistook me for a mere child and laughed—my skin a brand of frailty perceived by yet another court—yet I pried loose this one's decayed teeth." With a deft hand, he pulled open the mouth, revealing naught but gums. "Thus, he spilled all, gurgling truth. I dragged him back to his camp, for he could not flee the retribution owed. He pleaded to know the fate of Bedfort.

"Beyond the ivory Line of Bedfort, in the northern reaches of Nomankra, Norrekdorr, I hailed," he continued. "I found mine head sprouting between two thighs, crowned after a long darkness. I was rebirthed, and I rejoiced to see gathered kindred." His voice droned before raising its intensity, his lips bending. "'I, Sikradau, have set them free,' I told Randy upon his plea, the

228

palisade wall of ivory tusk and bone was breached, and we crossed the trench, battling even the stoutest defenders: the anvils, for I was born and destined from Norrekdorr, where old Norrek's ambitions were nurtured by his kin—his son, Tarinorr, their Onurra that exiled me."

The boy flung the head to the yard, where it rolled over crownlings. He calmed, seemingly recalling the Onurra before Tarinorr, his voice breezing. "Being an 'Outcast,' as they call us, exiled from such a tender age, thou likely hast no understanding of Norrek's tenacity," he said, his eyes glinting up at her. "He, born full of curiosity, oft asked his parents why he must never venture south, and no reply sufficed.

"Ere long, he questioned his Onurra, doubting him, and other Afurja heard his voice. And when he came of age, he challenged the Onurra before their leich upon the great stump of a felled tree with a thousand rings. In this challenge, Norrek bested him, conquering the stump and claiming the leich," he said, referring to what Eldhonans called a tribe.

"He then sieged sacred *blood pits* with mating rituals, seeking the one they called Sikrubur," *Darkroot,* Amarra deciphered, "to bleed out the mother… Barbaric and misguided. They bred failure after failure. And that tradition trickled down even to Tarinorr, the Onurra we shared. And I, like thee, was *exiled* by him. For I was bald, my skin pale and marred since birth, touched by a distant flame.

"In my anger, within the Frinj, where I was exiled to, I slew outrider sportsmen. I returned to Norrekdorr with weapons collected, killing all in my path with them," the boy said, impassioned.

Amarra backed away, to which the boy pressed forth, entering the hardly assembled cabin.

"I then sat upon the many-ringed stump, awaiting Onurra Tarinorr. And with my little horns, silver eyes, and pale body, I overcame him." His fist clenched. "The leich addressed me, Onurra Mupnarek." *Leader of the ex- iled.* "And I spoke broad of throat and swelled of lung, decreeing myself as *The Darkroot.* I stand a legend before you, a pyre for the ages—Onurra Mupnarek, Sikradau."

Amarra dug into her dusty Atnaarr recollection when he paused, letting the weight of his words settle. She parsed his tongue with her own thought- out translations, stowing her grim feelings behind a firm visage.

Then, with a steely gaze, he continued in an almost sing-song tone, "I ask of you to join beside me as a tine to my burr. We shall break the Compass from within, and no wind shall blow any more oaths of division. Gone would oppression be by righteous shields, my lambkin. No longer shall we be shadows prodded by the spears of man who dug trenches between our skins. I shall smite them, not guide them. And I shall start with the one thou harbor, for man and *Outcast* are forbidden after all."

Amarra knew little of what he spoke. She knew not the traditions of Nomankra beyond her exile. She knew nothing of the pits of blood nor the line of Onurra, but she disliked the inklings she was given, realizing she wore a look of disdain.

"What say thee, exiled lambkin? Wilt thou turn him over and march with thy kinfolk?" He reached out his hand, disregarding her demeanor, beseeching.

Likely, the boy, Sikradau, expected rejection, but still, he scoffed from her neglect. A fang peered between his lips. His eyes abandoned her rigid gaze at last, darting to her fist.

"There is no great stump," he breathed, "but we shall make do with this field…" Sikradau watched her, dipping down his head, his horns pointing at her, his silver eyes peering upward just below them. "If thou turn over mine meager body, then I assure thee mine leich will abide thee henceforth…" the rascally grin crept back. "Che-rekra rarta nau kolu oskta, na du dunuk oskta rarta."

Amarra clenched her jaw upon understanding him—it was the first day of challenge out of the two per week, thus insinuating she may be challenged endlessly by his warriors until the end of it, if she were to win. She surveyed the legion, spying their discontent already. And within the crowd, she saw things even stranger than herself and Sikradau—beings that looked warped, one of them spiderly.

"They now accept the askew variations of our kinship into the leich thanks to m—"

The boy choked on the sudden force that filled his mouth. Her skin taut around a jagged white-knuckle peak, Amarra rammed his jaw with a mountaintop blow. There was no need for an arena, a field, or anything of the sort. She only wished to quell his infatuation, distrusting all he said.

Blood trickled from his crumpled nose, but he remained, his heels firmly planted, predator eyes regarding her.

Amarra swung again, and to her ample surprise, she found her wrists clenched by his dainty hands. The boy held his ground and twisted with ease, her imprisoned arms spinning like wind-up toys. They gnarled, contorting Amarra's face. She fought a grin, pulling him back beside the hatch. She kicked at it, her grin spreading.

The hatch croaked open before Sikradau suddenly fell to his knees, his eyes alight with misfortune. His mistake was believing an exiled Outcast would abide by her kind's tradition, but Raihn had sprung from the hatch and swung his axe. The Onurra's ankle was lopped, they'd tumbled over, elbow cracked on the surface.

Raihn swung again, but down so to cleave their skull.

Sikradau caught the belly of the axe with his palm. "I've said it. I am a boy, still mightier than grown men."

Amarra, towering over him, kicked up her right leg, prompting Sikradau to grimace. He clamped his other hand around the belly of the axe handle, his fingers curling under the shoulder likely in hopes of controlling the axe head. But Amarra shot down her foot upon the butt of the tool, and like one of Raihn's trees, Sikradau was felled, the axe wedged across the bridge of his nose, crunching as if bark was split.

Raihn clambered out of the hole and embraced her as the jeering Outcasts roared in the yard. "I got to live a bit longer in a world where I could love again," said Raihn. "And that is far better than slumming in a world without that touch, even if it means a flood, so to speak, to the valleys, for alas, love can be selfless, but also can it be selfish…"

Amarra, towering as a mausoleum over Raihn's stout figure, held him as if clutching an urn, her gaze fixed on Sikradau, whose narrow, silver eyes remained locked on her.

The daylight wavered, casting shadows that flickered before settling into complete blackness. The Outcasts fell silent. In the stillness, all she saw was Raihn and Sikradau's corpse. The pale lips spread into a thin grin, whispering, "Un-ukra du amurna, na un-ukra Raihnrek sikranu."

Eldhos blinked awake, its light filling the void. The unfinished cabin and even the Outcasts were back. And the visage from the corpse resumed rigidity.

As the leich stampeded, the cellar began to glow an odd hue, and Raihn promptly stomped on Amarra's toes with his heel, causing her to dance on one foot. Then, with all the strength he could seemingly muster, he shoved her into the cellar, the hatch's lock squawking shut above her.

The army's footsteps thundered overhead, spears and swords piercing the oak flooring.

Amarra shrank into the shadows, and like it, her mind went blank. She was overwhelmed, deciding to hush the inner voices the best she could. But amid her attempt at peace was the shouting remembrance of Sikradau, crystallizing—*I see this conjuring, and, too, I see Raihn's negligence.* Sikradau had seemed almost gleeful about Raihn's *supposed* recklessness. That unsettling satisfaction, combined with Raihn's evasiveness, left Amarra deeply troubled.

CHAPTER TWENTY-SEVEN
To endure

LOSTAR'S skin cindered, his clothing hot to the touch. His hand turned up as his shield against Eldhos, breaking an induced blindness. A captivated audience beyond the left and right of his arm faded in, as did a familiar old friend beside him.

"Khaleel!?" Lostar exclaimed, his eyes falling to the man's hip, where a ceremonial simic scimitar hung. "How?" Lostar blurted with a west-attuned tongue.

Khaleel grimaced. "Spit the devised venom-speak of Eldhona," he said, speaking natively. "That old sage, Antahn, must be proud of his understudy, but please cork it until making nice with its speakers." Their expression softened, voice melting. "Keep your eyes forward, Truss. I should be the last plat of Lakewane on your mind right now," he hinted, smirking from under his larvalwig—a type of headscarf. But Khaleel's headscarf was strung from the powers of their oasis farms, full of mulberry trees and silkworms that would eventually cocoon the noble heads of the "plat" people.

Lostar's mind snagged. *Plat.* That was what they called the residents of the Lakewane Plateau, somewhat derogatory if by a Lowlander, endearing by his good old friend, Khaleel, who he could not believe was before him, or his magnificent courtyard atop the plateau.

...Home.

As he shifted his eyes and pinched his tongue, a *mirage* appeared before him... "Ambroseah..." Lostar whispered in awe.

She was beautiful, her hair flowing beneath a sheer white veil, like her silken dress fluttered in the wind. The dress wrapped around her body, cascading like a loose sash from her neck to her ankles, with her waist cinched by a golden brace. A glinting necklace held down the folds with jewels, accentuated her delicate collarbone.

"Truss?" her head tilted.

'*Truss,*' his name that was appended with gar to title him as protector to his father, who, too, was there, watching from above, across the courtyard of nobles. He seemed given another chance to maintain that name, faulting him into a daze, memory hindering his composure.

"Don't fray me with a hint of cold feet," Khaleel smirked again, even slicker. "Get in there before I make you walk the sand barefoot!"

They butted 'Trussgar' in the back with the hilt of their sword, but already Truss's heels burned, akin to the returning honey in his comb made ever sweet and spicy. He stumbled forward, heatstroke drawing near. Those around him bowed in a distortion of heat. His tongue, a raisin, he pushed on, knowing it would become saturated, for what was to come may turn spit to blood. This was his wedding ceremony, the same one he had relayed to Raihn. And on the altar, he was gut-punched, choking on the sand in the wind. His vows became discarded, fear taking over. He must be a gar again.

"You must retreat. They're coming," 'Trussgar' urged, reminded of his native tongue. "They're coming!" he repeated, voice mounting. He gripped Ambroseah's shoulders, spotting his ring of simic already wrapping his finger. His heart quickened.

The once-silent crowd began to murmur and turn their heads in disquiet. Even Khaleel sunk his head into his palm, muttering. Ambroseah looked at Khaleel in a panic and demanded the ceremonial blade, her two fingers gesturing for Khaleel to fetch it. Her eyes darted back to 'Trussgar.'

"Are you drunken?" she asked. "The plats—I mean—these people are watching. Your father, the Elgar, is watching. Coup your mind."

Without consoling her or reassuring Khaleel, he blurted his dire news. "Oleandor and his rebels will uproot my rite with his betrayal."

"What—Rebels?" Ambroseah asked, her brow scrunched into little rolling sandbanks.

Having dwelled upon this day for so many years, 'Trussgar' knew himself ready to face it a second time, but he couldn't verbalize another warning, refused when he tried.

Khaleel pressed on with a sheathed sword presented upon a lush purple pillow with a golden fringe and four tassels—one for the groom, bride, mother, and father. And through the nesting sword, they shall be secured.

Announcing to their audience, Khaleel said, "To the new man and Heir Apparent to the Elgar, to become Prince Regent, a sword of simic unrivaled by steel, glinting always, the Binder's Blade!"

He then kneeled, continuing with a reverent chin tucked against his collar bones. "Take it, allow Ambroseah's blood to be sewn along the fibers of your family and to weave its future. Join together, Trussgar," Khaleel said, holding the rite aloft. His voice quieted, "Your father is time-spent. Allow him this peace so he may abdicate soon and make you Elgar."

Trussgar hushed, tempering. Knowing he required the ceremonial scimitar, he accepted his rite from the lavish pillow with little to no grace, his arm still riled from excitement.

Ambroseah hastened the union, glaring over to the Keeper.

"I, the Keeper, pronounce and declare Trussgar of the Enduran Capital, Lakewane of the Highlands, and Ambroseah of the Rivy Chasms of the Lowlands, as husband and wife. From this day forward, Trussgar, you shall bear the title of Prince Regent, and Ambroseah, the noble title of Lady. May you serve your people with honor and wisdom until your last days. May the mother-to-be bless you with many heirs to uphold your legacy and strengthen the bond between Highlands and Lowlands."

Trussgar's betrothed completed their union through lip lock, her veil already whipped away by her own hand as she became his consort. Their audience, unsure as to cheer or not, murmured.

The new lady gave Khaleel a hard nudge, prompting a slow clap from him and thus spiriting a mounting applause from the audience. Trussgar, still worried, strapped the simic blade to his hip and rested his palm on the hilt, his eyes alert.

"Can you relax? What has gotten into you?" Khaleel asked. "All is well, is it not? Might you strengthen the bonds between Highlanders and Lowlanders. Quite a step for you to embark."

"Khaleel, my friend—my best friend. We are not safe. There is soon to be a turnover, a ruse. My father—" 'Trussgar' choked, measuring his tone, "—will die, and not from illness or age, but assassination."

Khaleel appeared fed up, his eyes momentarily shuttered. "Truss, if the heat has gone to your head, seek shelter," he beseeched. There is no shame in it."

"No. Khaleel, I tell you this not from heatstroke," said Trussgar.' "I lived it already. I swear it by the Eldhario Highlands—Ebbtide, Sereno, even this one—I swear… I shall perform the duties bestowed upon me as Prince Regent. Khaleel, whether you believe me, I am not just your friend. Not anymore."

"But you are not yet the Elgar," Ambroseah reasoned, waving off the nosing Keeper. "You govern under his command as his voice," she resumed.

"But I am a lord no less, taking action to defend my people and the Elgar until he abdicates." Trussgar then pressed his gaze upon Khaleel, affirming his power, "Escort Ambroseah to her chamber, then watch the door. Not even an ant may pass you."

"Trussgar…"

"Obey me. I… I am Trussgar, protector to the Elgar—who is a protector of the realm, the very one that endures hardship. Now go," he said, his voice sizzling. "This sword is of binding, and now I am bound to it, as is the rite to protect."

Khaleel, eyes wide, appeared rattled, then stable. Nodding, he placed an affirmative hand on Trussgar's shoulder. "She will be safe."

All the celebrating people of the plateau quieted, spectating, casting judgment. It was quite the spectacle, and Trussgar's warning had not yet warranted any merit, and the wedding was already in disarray.

Despite the lack of proof with Trussgar's warnings, Khaleel guided Ambroseah through the aisle and then the courtyard as Trussgar tailed them, eyes peeled for any strange movements in the crowd, any eye looking shifty in the slightest, any man unrecognized. But that was not so easy. Sure, he recognized the Pavilion—the counsel of elective noblemen, and, too, he saw the concern upon Antahn near them, but his gaze looked for those non-familiar. And with his hand firm upon his sword, he was ready to strike down any who dared step out of line.

The crowd was divided, some jovial, jesting about Trussgar's rush for consummation, while others scowled at the shameful display. "A mockery of tradition," one whispered. Yet 'Lostar,' now reclaiming his name as Trussgar, persevered and sped upwards through the Pillar of the Els—a grand staircase leading to the Elgar's throne overlooking the courtyard.

Upon reaching the Elgar, who the distasteful Oleandor accompanied, Trussgar was met with expressions of disgust.

"What is the meaning of all this?" barked Chief Advisor Oleandor, his fists balled tight, veins like roots.

"Calm down, Ollie. I am the one to ask of him," the Elgar hushed with a bite. "My son, tell me what ails you."

Trussgar faltered, overwhelmed by seeing his father again and so vividly. But there was another beside his father, Trussgar's brother. Their eyes went unblinking through a scarf, narrow from a broad smile under their silk, and they could hardly contain their purest excitement for their brother, hands waving.

"Harfaz!" Trussgar exclaimed, his heart swelling. Harfaz's eyes narrowed even more, his simple gaze relieving Trussgar of pain. But he couldn't falter, stepping forward, his own smile breaking through. "It's good to see you, brother, Faz," he said tenderly. But that was all the time he could offer them.

The Elgar's stern gaze gentled from the sight. "Trussgar, tell me what troubles you," he repeated, his tone laxer.

Trussgar tore his gaze away from Harfaz, refocusing on his father, his tone turning stern. "Your Elegance, there is much to explain."

Despite his meager, aged appearance—beaten by time yet clothed in silken riches—his father's presence remained commanding. He leaned upon the arm of his chiseled throne, his eyes sharp despite their narrowing. Beneath him, all was rock, carved into lordly appendages. The plateau was his. The stairs, his. The throne... All of it, rock, imbued with order by man's design. Betters at the top, lesser men below, and even lesser still beneath them. That was their system and the hierarchy in which supplies were split, uppers more imperative for delivery. He was truly a lord above men, and some men took much less than a liking to that.

All that his people despised lay within a chamber brimming with 'fool's hide' and 'oddments.' And it was the chamber of their Elgar, who'd sit snugly in his 'sandcastle' dressed in banners allied to him, not the other way around. But Trussgar stood before a man he'd admired, who'd been dusted in their tenure, modern morality brandished from their throat.

"Ambroseah, get inside and lock the door. Don't come out until I say," Trussgar demanded.

She hesitated and worriedly glanced at Oleandor, who returned a similar look.

Trussgar huffed, irked by any assurances to his wife that came from the scoundrel. He then glanced at Khaleel, who affirmed his word with a nod, escorting her through the nearby doors, the heavy stone lock audibly grinding into place.

Oleandor Cirro, the Elgar, and his consort, Eleken Kane, all glared at Trussgar, awaiting his plea. It seemed he found council. With regret, he informed them, "We're under siege."

His father leaned in. "Presently?"

"I see only chaos from your foolery," Oleandor remarked.

"Silence," the Elgar ordered, waving a feeble hand.

"They draw near!" Trussgar insisted.

"Who?"

"The rebels—Kraters, Your Elegance," Trussgar clarified. "They wish to end our trade relations regarding simic."

"Trussgar!" Oleandor boomed. "You blanket this union so quickly to blister our ears with caution for Lowlanders—"

"Kraters, not Rïvians," Trussgar interjected. It was important to him to clarify this, for the Rivians were directly below them in close proximity, still considered to be a higher class of people than the Kraters.

"—without a droplet of blood?" Oleandor persisted, tapping his heel on the paled sandstone. "There is peace here, yet you roll in calling for a storm without a single cloud on the horizon, nor a speck of sand along the gust of wind," his voice rustled, then leveled. "Take Ambroseah. Greet the nobles with a grin. Assure them they have a worthy successor. We are not a fear-mongering people, and we will never cease our relations if that is what you expect to gain." Oleandor smirked, nearly sneering. There was little bite at the end, his traitorous glee hardly contained.

Trussgar felt his face redden hotter than Eldhos already made it, enraged by deceit. "Lies," he howled. "Pretender! Oleandor leads this treasonous act to end our trade! He will divide us from Eldhona!" he cried, frantic in his plea. "Your Elegance. I beg you to heed my words, for I've only ever had the best intentions. Does that not have worth? Am I not Prince Regent?"

The Elgar's eyes escaped his son momentarily and peered around him pensively, likely spying a concerned audience. "That you are, but I am the Elgar, son. Regarding what you speak, I believe your intentions are in line, but your mind..." His mouth gaped, hollow, his voice crawling from its deep burrow, "I stand with my Chief Adviser."

"Father—"

"And the stench of fermentation lingers from his breath," Oleandor added.

"Under suspicion of you being ill-fit to rule, I must have you restrained," Trussgar's father declared.

Oleandor leaned in, suggesting, "The Hollow would sober him up, Your Elegance. Under lock and key, we can entertain our guests without concern for further disruption."

The Elgar leaned on the other arm of his throne, scratching his chin. He seemingly pondered Oleandor's suggestion, doubt and concern permeating his pupils. The Pillar of the Els seemed to hold its breath as he weighed the decision. In that crucial moment, Khaleel returned, offering a semblance of relief.

"Ah! Khaleel, my good, loyal spine," the Elgar called. He paused, the words lingering in the air as if he were still debating the course of action. "…Escort my son to the Hollow," he commanded at last, his order a reluctant one. "But first, strip him of his rite. Keep it discreet. Let no one see my son detained. I will handle the busybody nobles."

Khaleel appeared torn, his eyes hopping between the Elgar and Trussgar.

The Elgar's tone brooked no argument, yet it was clear he did not relish the decision. And as he fell into a coughing fit, a trident vein forked from his wrinkled brow, making Khaleel look even more reluctant to stow Trussgar away.

Trussgar was stripped of his blade, but they might as well have torn the cloth from his back and left him bare; the coming pit sunk his belly into its depths before he'd even set foot within it.

Once there, he clutched a prickled name: Lostar, for 'Trussgar' was *doomed to fail.* He was escorted to the spiraling dungeon that is hollowed sandstone. Questioned was the point of this mirage of a memory, where Khaleel had assumed the role of a soldier—a spine of the Elgar's Glochidium—rather than the role of a friend.

Lostar stepped through the gate, the keys already jangling around the lock. He rattled off many thoughts: fight back, accept it, or plea for understanding. But Khaleel, the spine, had the backbone to be a prick at the right time, his duty usurping his friendship and taxing the choices. What a fool. Khaleel sheltered the sword in his sash near his groin. He was unassuming, never seeing Lostar pushed into a corner.

Lostar's breaths in the cage had been uncontrolled, as he knew the turn of the lock would calcify the same outcome. All thought was cast aside, rationality a failed route. A void blew between his ears, his demise already within it, but he was a gar, after all. He whirled around and snatched the blade before striking Khaleel's skull with the ornate pommel, his arm wagging through the iron bars. He dropped the sword, clenching Khaleel's garb as he guided their fall, and let himself out. He couldn't waste this second chance, not when the reclamation of his title was so close and the end of the Drackis bloodline was within reach.

Lostar was cornered and made wild, grasping beyond destiny, refusing to be inept in a plunge as deep as the sorry hole in the hallowed dungeon. Something had to give.

"I'm sorry, Raihn. Another oath must be broken."

Lostar was panting doggishly, locking a gaze with Khaleel when they finally arrived, a big mark on their head. But Oleandor's torso was already crossed with a streak of seeping burgundy, his upper half slumping off, organs spooling out. Khaleel was too late.

Lostar's imprisonment would surely extend to a lifetime, and the Pavilion of Nobles would soon elect a new bloodline—but thanks to Lostar, it would not be Oleandor; he'd served his people by pruning the diseased vine. He understood that, by his actions, the rebels would have no leader left to serve, thus preventing the attack and more death. But the crowd erupted in an uproar, leaving the Elgar breathless. Lostar sheathed the blade and set it down, finding a sense of balance amid the ridicule.

"Khaleel, restrain him!" the Elgar barked through a gasp. "Truss is not a gar!" He rose, his knees wobbling. "He could not endure or adapt, and from this moment on, he is not of my ilk!" He turned to his audience, his voice rising with renewed strength. "To the Hollow with him, behind the iron. Let this rotted pear blacken further in the dark, where none shall see its mold. Let him feast on the lizards and choke on the arid puffs of the bellows beyond the cracks." The Elgar summoned his might, his gaze sweeping over his people. "I say unto you, the Pavilion and those of the Rivy Chasms, let it be known—this is not my son!"

The Elgar stood tall while Eleken cradled her head in her palm, shielding herself from the turmoil. "This is not my heir!" he continued. "This is not your future! Endura is a democracy, and we are not savages! My people, we endure. We sprout legs, feet, and noses from the lake to the sand. And from my grandest father's gills, my line has delivered me the power over my Glochidium—loyal glochid men, my loyal spines, and…" His voice caught, his eyes reddening as tears welled. He looked to Truss once more. "…a disappointment," he aired, his speech faltering. "I have no gars!"

Lostar found himself once again dragged to his sandstone enclosure, taken to the Hollow, a place where criminals and enemies of the Els languished in near darkness. The air was hazy, hot, and stuffy. The stairs ran round and round, down and away into an even darker depth, cells blocked out of the wall along the way.

When he awoke, he was smothered by fluttering particles of sand illuminated by a sliver of light seeping through a gash in the wall. His entire body ached, particularly his sore rear, from being kicked into the cell of the death spiral—a place likened to an ant hill—the Hollow. It seemed a cavity he'd never leave.

238

Springing up, he gripped the dusty iron bars, his eyes locking onto Khaleel, their expression harsher than the metal between them.

"Eldhos burns away the impurities of the Eldhario Highlands through endurance," Khaleel said. "And those failed by its shine must be put away. You—a worm that crawls from the rotted pear—may dry up here, where I shall see you last. Or, you may crawl again from your hole and tumble down the cliffside to be picked over in the Rivy Chasm."

"You speak ill of my mother, linking her to a rotted fruit?" Lostar retorted, his voice trembling with anger. "I am no worm, my hand firmer; I secured our people and my father through strength."

Khaleel turned his head away as if ashamed of the thoughts that had crept into his mind. "You are more broken than your—" he paused, his anguish momentarily sheathed, then suddenly sparking again. He struck Lostar on the head with the pommel of his sword right through the bars. Lostar tumbled within the small space of carved rock, his fall causing his shackles to ring, his ears singing with a single-tuned whistle. Seemed to be payback.

"I am a good, loyal spine, but I speak of what I know and what I see. And before me, I see a cicada shell with nothing inside it. What better of you there was is gone. And all that is good is parted into your broken brother, made a failure. If he weren't sick, he'd inherit the Glochidium," Khaleel sneered, clenching his jaw. "But because of his state, he could not be a gar, thus opportuneless." He relaxed, swiping back his black hair, his eyes dashed. "You, however, had a perfect path, cut like a river, and all you had to do was float downstream. You had a beautiful lady and a friend beside you…"

Lostar sat upright, crossing his legs, eyes downcast and unable to meet Khaleel's gaze. But this might be the last time he would ever see them, so he lifted his chin and forced eye contact. Their words had been coarse like the sand, but their gaze was softened by a hint of friendship, sternness betrayed by it.

"Thank you for looking after him all these years," Lostar said softly. "Please, ensure his safety upon the next Elgar's rise."

Khaleel hung his head and blew a hard sigh. "Antahn and I will be good to him, you know this. Unlike you, we are not kin to him, but we bond just as well. But Harfaz will ask of you, lost from understanding. Thanks to you, I have to relay your misguidance, though in a simpler way."

Lostar nodded, accepting that fact. "Antahn will be disappointed."

Khaleel's silence hinted agreement.

Lostar lay against the rock with his only belongings—a waterskin and a bucket that reeked in the horrendous heat. A warm and putrid stench stained his nose with something foul. He kept his distance from it but could not stay far enough away as the cell was tight. He took up the waterskin that was sucked thin and empty already, and hurled it at the wall in frustration. Next to him was the gash, big enough for him to crawl through, a steep fall—a plummet, outside, into the chasm, where poorer folk meandered: Lowlanders.

The dungeon was a solitary place, with few prisoners holding out their empty waterskins from their cells, the backs of their hands dry and cracked like the stone. Lostar questioned whether they still drew breath or if they, too, were cicada husks. He also wondered what was going on above, whether the Elgar sought counsel or if the counsel sought him.

Then he heard a faint buzz coming from outside the gash in the wall, growing into a howl as it neared. Truss stepped closer, bending his ear to listen. The howl was racing down from above until he saw a man blink past the hole briefly. The howl continued its descent as he peered out to witness the man's tragic fall. But even after the man hit the ground far below, the screaming persisted, multiplying as more figures cascaded down the stone side like tumbling sacks of spurting mulberries. These were not prisoners flinging themselves from the upper rows to escape their sentence—they were his companions, soldiers who had once lined the courtyard, the Elgar's Glochids.

A screech rang through the hollow, unmistakably the door he'd come from grinding open, and someone fastly approached, keys clinking as their feet tapped down the stairs. And when they reached his cell, they madly fumbled through them, their body caked in blood.

"Khaleel!" Lostar blurted. "What's going on?"

"You mean to make me say it?" Khaleel replied, eyes focused upon the keys. "You were right, but do not bask in it."

"…How is Ambroseah? Is she safe?"

Before Khaleel could answer, an arrow pierced through his padded linen garb and past his ribs. He touched it, his index finger coming away with a spot of blood, eyes wide open. His other hand dropped the ring of keys as a second arrow drove through his body and stopped just before Lostar. Khaleel stumbled until tumbling down the stairs.

Lostar lunged forward, watching them vanish from sight. His eyes then caught the keys lying just outside his cell, tantalizingly close, but possibly out of reach. He clawed through the narrow gap between the bars, straining to grasp them hard against the warm iron as he groaned desperately. A fingernail finally latched onto the ring of keys and towed them, but just as hope flashed, a sharp blade came down and severed the reach.

"I liked that finger too," said the assaulter, a woman.

Lostar grated his teeth, clutching his maimed hand as Ambroseah came before him, a composite bow slung around her shoulder, veil gone from her face. Her fingers still wrapped the grip of the Binder's Blade, its metal curved, crescent-like, and blood slipped down the ornate fuller a bloody river, drooling past the starry crossguard.

Lostar sat there, gutted, his stomach sunken like the desert ships.

240

"I see the shallow ponds in your eyes," said his consort, "dull as ever. Unlike the metal you moan about and the silk you plats farm," she groaned, knees bending out, sinking her into a close position.

"All those times you caught me training, insisting I'd never need fight—a Highland privilege," she remarked, her gaze falling away. "I was a fighter since birth, first toying with horned lizards, even to when I was eight. As elusive they were, blending in, as if cloaked. I'd find joy in their hunt, watching them sluggishly skitter along with their little round bodies, their stubby snouts leading the way. When they didn't get away from me, they'd puff or spurt little blood streams from their eyes as a defensive response…

"Mother always scolded me for it, telling me I was too young to look messy like that, especially in front of boys. I didn't know what she meant then…but I got older… The first time I'd squirt blood, I felt like the lizard, made defensive from a predator…"

Her head fell, eyes between her spread legs first, then her feet, and then her toes. "They feel full of blinking stars," she said, standing up. "Better to distribute that energy through the whole body than in one place; otherwise, it will numb my feet," she said, mindfully turning her head to the depths of the spiral.

Lostar shook his head, dashing her rambling.

"I know. It's a lot, but I've not spoken my truths in many a year," she went on, her eyes returning.

But he persisted in striking no conversation.

"Truss, I did not come from the Rivy Chasms. I am a Kraterian. I lived in the Lowlands, dingier than the likes of the chasms, without even your stoic shade."

He listened more tentatively, his expression grimmer as her lie unfolded.

"The days become hotter," she continued, "and we are becoming defenseless. Your father was sealing our doomed fate to think that honest terms would hold even after our precious metal was mined out," she excused, her voice rising. "Endura becomes more barren. We deserve more as a people than to be arms laborers," she said. "By the age of eight…I was pulling simic ore like my father, Truss." She beheld the mirroring blade. Her thumb caressed the curve of the guard, then the ricasso.

She fortified in his silence, starting up again. "Khaleel was a well-intentioned man, strong as the spine of this sword, sharp as if from a cactus, protecting the greater self." Her fondness for the blade ceased as she tossed it into the bowels of the cavity. "But good intentions don't always make good men; a good man wouldn't turn a blind eye to forested beasts that bring about our first blood."

Lostar's eyes flickered to her as he grasped who she referred to—the Eldhonans.

"When we have nothing left to give, we will no longer be a resource to them," she said, meaning no more supplies would come. "We would become ever more defenseless, staving the very blades we forge." She quieted. "We merely wear weaponry as a symbol—for what, hierarchy?" she shrugged, her hand feebly clasping the iron bar before her, eyes more polished than it. "Is it not tormenting enough to look upwards at your towering mesas, buttes, and plateaus? I worked my way just to meet you, soliciting myself, bribing—what did it matter anyway, soiled like I was. Gone from grace, as those Eldhonans say," her lips bent.

"It was not by chance that we aligned, Truss. Nothing earned is by chance," she continued, now impassioned. "That's why you killed Oleandor. It's that festering duty—that resolve in you. That's why I was taking up stars," she said, an old term drafted by the Enduran people that embodied the stance of anchoring arrows.

Lostar remained silent, his eye piercing through his sand-weathered hair.

"Still, nothing to say?"

"What do you want me to say?" he replied.

"That you understand the ones who struggle," she snipped. "The ones out there in the hulls of ships, braving the grit of wind to feast on prickly lizards, scorpions, cacti, pears, and beans," she continued, her voice exasperated. But then some other thought seemed to cross her mind, her breathing becoming intense as a lead-up. "Why did the wester-folk come here—that fleet with ill intent, loaded with brigandine, bows, barrels of ale, and swords? I believe they came to enslave us—or slay us."

Ambroseah now gripped the bars with both hands, her once-shining mind dulled into a patina. "We, once islanders, minds minded, were to be sieged by the wester-folk of Eldhona. But thanks to the cracking grounds from Desekreus, their copper hulls sunk to sand, lending homes."

Lostar shook his head, for that was all speculation. He scooted away, and the back of his head thumped against the rock.

"Truss," she prodded. "Truss. Entertain me with your thoughts."

Her mind was *sandblasted. Nothing matters.* There were two heads to the snake, and Lostar pitted Adjurrah, the continent, into a worse state.

Her eyes widened, glazed, unpleasant. Her breaths froze, and the air paused, grains of sand still mid-drift.

Lostar choked, gagging on sand in his throat as if they were little biting spiders. She observed, her eyes gleaming with a flash of silver in them. He rolled over, clasping his throat, his nub gushing. But she just had to get closer so that she could enjoy as much of his agony as she could. And might it be the lack of air, but he'd even sworn to see her skin whiten.

"My father," Lostar coughed, beginning to speak to her at last.

She took a breath, her color filling in.

Air seemed to find him again, and after a gasp, he continued through a rasp. "He traded simic to ensure their lives. There is no need for death."

"Tell that to the Eldhonans who make deadly weapons," she resumed with a blink. "For what do they prepare? They say it's an attack from the Out-

242

casts—a prophecy from the First King. That's why the cardinals aligned with him. But it is also said there was more turmoil than that—a war torn the land before the alliance. Ironic, is it not? Bloodshed to prevent greater bloodshed."

Lostar's eyes hopped back at her, a tired darkness ringing them. "What if they are right about the Outcasts? If you mean to overtake Eldhona, they could seize you when you're weakest."

"I will not overtake all of Eldhona, but I would welcome the Outcasts into the rest."

Lostar shook his head. "…Insanity."

"Ensuring the firmness of our borders is a duty that a good lord would uphold. We shall take the East Wynd to ensure safety and good farms. At least, that is something we can negotiate through our war. Then I will pledge our simic for the day of the Outcast's reckoning. Then, those green thumbs will rue all their gardening…

"Truss…" she continued. "I have seen Eldhonans with swords of our own make as they come in the night and take our women on the border, hacking down their sons. Even our own skirt about under your father's purview, taking girls from Endoland and trading them to Eldhonans… But we endure, right? I suppose that's what being an Enduran means…"

Lostar became wise to this tangle, spurned from redemption. A laugh broke from him. Then he pondered his hand. It pained him. His smile faded. "Be careful. Another dragon is always on the lookout for treasure."

Ambroseah cocked her head, as if finding his allegory amusing. Another flicker of silver skipped across her eyes. A rush of whispers scraped from her lips, nigh audible. All he could make out was "Raihn" and something about him being some kind of "absolver." Her fingers spidered as if fighting for life under poison.

But that was a fleeting haste. Her lips were calm, eyes dark again. She continued as if she'd never sputtered her gibberish. "I shall ride out and rally our people for a purpose you cannot grasp. I will forge armor unbreakable. Neither blades nor arrows will pierce it." Her eyes pressed through the bars, promising her curses, leather-throated. "Our will lives on, and they will see the shine of Eldhos two-fold as we march for our spoils."

Lostar scoffed, fighting a shudder, and cautioned himself not to confront the irregularity again. "Seems a bit much for Oleandor. I am sure you both laughed behind my back amidst your plot to overthrow my father."

"Oleandor and I?" she clarified. "Feigned laughs, sure," she said, fingers choking iron. "You had done me this favor of killing him. Foolishly, he believed in the simic, as if it were…a deity. He would babble on about tradition, to which I suffered quietly. He was an eccentric man who thought to end trade and make our people self-reliant. The fool, confusing dreams with actuality," she said. "The Eldhonans would surely come for our simic whether we liked it or not... I planned to gut him myself to ensure that wouldn't happen, opening up our leading strike."

Not that she'd have much success, Lostar knew. Disregarding that, he continued to converse. As he must, considering part of this mirage to be true to Ambroseah, the other a strain between it and the mountain—a leech that seemed to interfere, or perhaps that witch, somehow, even through the lanterns.

"Even after all your treachery, I made no mistake in not heeding my father's concern over espousing a Lowlander," Lostar said. "After all of my pleas. He accepted it to show him that our wedding could bring solidarity through our land. Deep as the chasms, the fault between us was your betrayal—one worse than Oleandor's."

Ambroseah pulled away. "My mission was at the forefront of our people's needs, not mine..."

Lostar's breath hitched. "So, you do care for me, just not enough."

Ambroseah's tenacity dithered, her darkness thinning. "Truss, I..." Her voice cracked, revealing a hidden tenderness as valuable as the ore in their ground. She breathed, moved, and shifted from her spite, though Lostar hunched out her motives to remain true. "I can't falter now. Our people need a leader who can endure and fight for them. I can't afford to be weak, not now. If you go free, I know you will only stop me."

Tears welled up in his eyes as he saw the conflict in her, as if the silver was her own void, blanking her mind when come a tight corner. The game was over, and he spoke not to appease the mountain—or whatever induced this nightmare—but to put his heart at rest.

"No, I don't know if I could. I'm not much for this life," he replied. "That's why it is best that the past stays in the past. Because I will remain a failure, as I am meant to fail."

The gash in the wall hushed him with a warm blow, and he looked upon its light. "I've yet to achieve what I've strived for my whole life. Unfortunate for us, I cannot serve you."

She reached through the bars, her fingers lightly brushing his cheek. She guided him back to her, his head cradled upon the metal. Her finger twirled his hair, her breath like the warm wind.

"No, Lostar, that is very fortunate." She withdrew her hand, her expression feigning its firmness. "Even a seed can be more resilient than its rotted past, growing fuller than ever."

Lostar pushed himself, understanding what he must do, regardless of where it would take him. There was no reservation other than the one before him at the hole, where Eldhos shined an end.

CHAPTER TWENTY-EIGHT

From the dark

RAIHN and Amarra reunited, quick to tremble in each other's arms. Raihn had narrowly escaped the fiery vortex that consumed the manor, haunted by an old flame, and the way Amarra held him so tightly suggested she had faced something equally dire.

"Damn, guess I'm third!" Pocket exclaimed, snapping his fingers. "Never first to grab the gold, and if no silver is left, I'll take the bronze," he went on, exiting the cave.

Raihn heard but paid little mind.

"…Tough crowd. I'll just pat myself on the back. It's okay. Good job, Pocket," the thief self-congratulated, hands restlessly fidgeting. "Got you good, didn't it, yeah?" he chuckled. "It wasn't so bad…" A forced grin scraped from cheek to cheek as he looked back at the cave for a while too long.

"How long?" Raihn muttered.

Pocket flinched as if prodded, his head whipping back, grin fading. "Pardon? Come again?"

"For how long were you in there, Pocket? You must have grown a few inches because your head is in the clouds," said Raihn in jest.

Pocket reinforced, wiping what was becoming a frown. "Someone's got to be," he joked. "Though I don't have to grow to touch the clouds. I'll reach the top with you folks and pass through them."

The thief hunkered next to Raihn and Amarra, his grin fading again, hands bracing his ankles into place. "This mountain," he began, as if considering how to describe it, "it's—y'know?"

Raihn shook his head. "What?"

They didn't answer.

Raihn looked them over studiously, noting how stirred they were, rattling in their shoes. Whatever they went through in that godless cave must have been punishing, so Raihn put his arm over them as a means to share some comfort. They appeared grateful.

AMARRA twisted in the ebb and flow of time, its channel dark to a sounding line. Recovery was slow, but eventually, the trio found a semblance of rest along the waves of rock and fog.

Her nerves eased, her heart palping in a steady rhythm. Raihn's body quieted beside her. Now was a good time. She retrieved her chart and spelled from dire concern, her memory of his demise the ignition. She swore it had to be a vision, like she—like they all must have been—made into seers of sorts.

Raihn focused on her chart. "Whatever happens, be selfless. A life of solitude is not meant for us," he read aloud, one brow lifting in question. His mouth hung agape as if searching for a reply, irking her.
She nudged him.
"Yeah," he stammered, "I'll do my best."
Amarra huffed, unconvinced. Her nostrils flared, her eyes narrowing skeptically.

"I swear," he assured through his equally agitating yet endearing smirk.

Amarra playfully shoved him, perhaps a bit too hard, then nodded. She pulled him in again, her fingers caught in his hair, her chin lent upon his scalp, pondering if she should write more or whether she was meant to. But in the end, she will be there for him, assuring he doesn't become a fool without a compass, selfish and reckless, building a cabin. Surely that's not what this would all amount to. Peace just isn't meant for someone like her, and maybe she was a fool to fall for him, selfish in her own ways to consider against it, thinking to tuck some place into a forest like his brother was planned to be.

RAIHN heard the pitter-patter of footsteps emanating from the cave's mouth, becoming heavier in a meandering shuffle. "Hodge!" he exclaimed. Hodge was as glum as could be upon his exit. Raihn's excitement dwindled.

"You revisited a time of your life that you wished to change, didn't you?" Pocket said curiously, his tone playfully snarky.

Hodge's gaze kept astray. "Hm. Suppose we share a common space in this circumstance for once." His voice was dry, frayed.

"Unfortunately," Pocket agreed. "Not that my choices differed much. I don't see the point in dredging up these memories other than to rub inevitabilities in my face."

Raihn stepped in. "I think it's to move forward and learn from it, to make better choices when they present themselves next." He glanced at Amarra. "I think that was the point being made," he said.

She smiled.

"Well-spoken," Hodge nodded.

"That's a nice sentiment," Pocket remarked, "but it seems a bowl of shit when I faced death all the same in that hole back there."

All the smiles dropped, and Pocket leaned in, his eyes reflecting a distant pain. "I was back home with my family. Now, that may sound nice, but I'm glad to be back here," he chuckled, his smirk brief. A shadow crossed his face, and he continued, "Where I lived, it never felt like home. Those who raised me weren't my parents. No mother would ever stand by and watch the father of her children do what he did."

He paused as if to stifle a tremble in his throat.

"Go on," Raihn encouraged.

"I was soft-spoken, and Father said I'd grow up to be a nobody because of it. Despite that, he treated me favorably compared to my sister. I relished that favor because I couldn't tolerate the thought of being treated worse. And that made me just as bad as he was, for I did nothing to help her. I thought I did, convinced myself in fear that I'd helped, but I was just afraid.

"I only gave advice knowing she'd ignore it. That way, I could say I tried. I was a terrible brother, and for that, I believed I was cursed. To be ignored forever, a rat in the mud, scrounging and thieving. I nearly got you all killed because of it. Beyond the poisonous relationships I keep, I foil truer ones because of my well of debt."

Pocket looked at Raihn in a puppy-dog kind of way. "I deserved no better, and I would be selfish still to think otherwise unless I change. To really be recognized for something other than being a coward."

Then, a moment passed, long enough for the thief to notice Hodge's continued stare. Pocket shifted his eyes and body. Finally, he caved. "Yes?"

"Your sister," Hodge said, "could you tell me more about her? What memory did that cave take you back to, assuming that's what it did?"

"Well." Pocket distanced. "I was taken back into the throes of my father's reign, where I was tending the chicken coop with Mother. Just outside the window, I could hear him—Pa—scolding my sister inside. Not that this was unusual in my house of sticks, but…

"She may be my sister, but she always had more balls," the thief broke, chuckling. "So big and long, you'd think she'd throw them over her shoulder rather than those sopping towels she'd washed… Yeah, she said what she thought and did what she willed to do. She was far more rebellious than I ever thought I could be. An' to tell the truth, I was always jealous of that, not that she'd know." His head shook.

"That day, she and Father fought like they never had before. The walls couldn't muffle them enough, nor could the unsettled chickens' commotion quiet them. She was like the tides beating a cliff too tall, makin' pointless splashing. I think that's what bothered her the most: there being no effect. So, her words became sharper." His gaze lowered.

"In exchange for her brief freedom to express herself out of the pent-up anger, he would... he'd... hit her," Pocket continued, angered. "His right, callused hand, flat like a pan," he said, mimicking the gesture, "crossing her like steel. It was as if he had this notion of a perfect world where he could bend it to how he'd seen fit. And to him, it wasn't yet right. His vision of us wasn't what he predicted, making him a real-weathered rock. Quite unfair for us little pebbles, I'd say."

He tensed, fists balling on his knees. "Their relationship was extremely unhealthy, and whenever she was disciplined, it was put on display so that I would only become even more obedient out of fear. And what he'd do, y'know..." Pocket reached out, his hand clenching the air, "he'd grab her by the throat and give her a good thrashing. Her little hands feebly pawing at his arm of fur."

Pocket lowered his hand and became somber beyond his sigh. "She was supposed to be outside helping Ma, not me. Nothing wrong with a boy gathering eggs or apples, but Pa thought the work wasn't fit for me, like the stable work. He thought my sis should do it instead because 'she was too frail for anything else.'

"She wanted to work hard, but all he wanted was milk, sewing, scrubbing, picking, and a shoulder massage that seemed too personal by the end of the day...

"You've heard of butter fingers, surely, but not udder fingers, I'm certain. Some cockamamie, off-putting joke of his. He used to sit and watch her milk the cows for a good while and told her she needed soft palms for his shoulders. But she wanted to churn butter, which isn't easy work. That's why it was her favorite whenever she'd get to, handling the farm like a man, not washing his clothes at the river. Yeah, whenever she mucked about, she smelled worse than I did," he laughed. "And she'd chase me with her buttery fingers...

"She'd seek out the tools to prove to our father she could do it, but that wasn't the point, sadly. She would heave hay whenever Pa wasn't around, working to gain some muscle. And Pa began to notice her string-bean-like arms thickening into cobs of corn. But he claimed it was just fat, taunting her and refusing to acknowledge her strength. But she was strong, going as far as wrestling great fish out of the waters, dress hiked up, the local fishing folk hollerin' at her to stop spooking the creatures."

Pocket smiled through the pain, seemingly remembering his good sister. "Her feet were caked in mud like no other. Yeah, my sister was against the grain, eh. Though I told her to just listen, that it could be easier. That just wasn't her," he sighed again. "I hated the hard work, sweatin' through my breeches. I couldn't lift my arms, and yet my sister didn't call me a pussy— not until she asked me a fifth time to leave with her that is. To run. I figured she would stay just as she had the last four damn times after asking, but she proved me wrong. I just didn't think she'd go that far… I should've left long ago. I was tying her down with my, uh, reluctance."

"Why? What do you mean? How far?" asked Hodge.

"Well, she was still very young, but she was very strong… Her corn cob arms… I woke up feeling refreshed but strangely distraught. I must have slept hours extra, as Eldhos was already beaming down. I didn't know why I wasn't whipped awake earlier, and then I noticed the silence." Pocket scoffed at it. "Strange. No yelling… Outside my door, I found them… Pa, I got, but Ma?" Pocket scratched his prickly stubble. His hand blossomed, fingers spread, a look of confusion crossed his face. "My sister had lost it, yet she spared me… And why, she just sat there, at the table, as if everything was fine, but she knew what she did. Yeah, sittin' there, waiting for me to see what she done. I mean," Pocket stuttered, "she may as well say, 'bad dog,' and rub my nose in their blood. Damn well I was standing in it, my toes swimming in it." His eyes stared off, shimmering, as if looking at his memory.

He scoffed again. "She said to me, 'You did this,'" Pocket pointed ahead. "She was no longer the regretful child, Burenna." There was a long pause as Pocket tried to force the truth out, his knee bouncing.

"Then what happened?" Hodge asked, laying a hand on the thief's back.

"She said there was a place for someone like her, so I asked if I could come with her as I had no place else to go, but she said it was too late, and it was not a place for me.

"Then she burned the cottage down without turning back. Wattle and daub. Smelled like hot dung…I got by, though."

Hodge leaned in, "What about her? You think you'll see her again?"

"On the road, I heard rumors of such a buster of bollocks and knew it was her. She's always been out there, causing mischief, like myself." His gaze fell on the boulder sea.

Raihn leaned in. "You ever find her?"

Pocket nodded. "Finally. I tried to make amends, but I'm not sure if that's possible anymore. I don't think I could do anything to get her to forgive me. Even when I did return to that memory in the cave. I left with her, but Pa was hot on our heels, racing towards death… So, sure, I can learn to be better, but that seems to be my point of anchor, where I have to understand it. Regardless, she had blood on her hands. Little I can do but accept it."

Hodge patted their back. "Then maybe all you should do is forgive yourself and try to move on," but his eyes shifted, belying his assurance. "Maybe we all should. Then we'd not put ourselves in places as loathsome as this one."

Raihn pondered the sentiment and whether Amarra's experience was similar until Magnus finally strode out. His hands dug into his pockets, and his eyes glared down at Hodge. He seemed disturbed and livid, frightening Raihn, Hodge likely more so. Thankfully, they crossed, gaining distance.

Time still passed through a wane and Lostar was yet to emerge from the cave, his absence concerning Raihn. *Did he fail? Could he fail for that matter?* Raihn pondered, for it seemed a challenge pitted against him in there. His head was crowded by unwelcome thoughts, making him anxious, so he stood up. "I'm going after him," he declared.

"Are you out of your fish fightin' mind!?" Pocket burst.

"I'd lose my mind if I wait for him any longer, and I know he would do the same for me," Raihn claimed.

Amarra rose too, and so did Pocket and Hodge, but Raihn waved them back. "No. No sense in us all facing those terrors again. I'll go alone," he said. They abided, albeit reluctantly. Magnus, however, had only lurked, his eyes peering from over his cloaked shoulder.

Raihn fearfully approached the cave's mouth, hoping that the Enduran would shuffle out. "Lostar, are you in there?" he cried, but there was no answer. All that came was a ring of simic, tumbling along the stone and then rolling to his feet. "Lostar's ring," he said aloud, plucking it.

Raihn entered the cave and felt around—nothing. He went wall to wall, back and forth, feeling only the shivering walls that lap over one another with jagged edges, enclosing him within the dark vestiges of his nightmare. Then he carefully raked his feet over the ruffled rock until he struck something firm, kicking it curiously.

"I am here," Lostar assured, grunting, sounding mid-shuffle. His hand landed on Raihn's shoulder. "And that was my shin," he grumbled.

"Lostar!" Raihn cried, celebrating their return.

"How many?" Lostar rustled. "The others. Are they back?"

"All who entered, thankfully. Still no Rayah. But Lostar—"

"Good," the Enduran said, patting Raihn's shoulder, and leaving.

But Raihn wasn't finished speaking.

...Your ring...

Raihn followed them to the edge of the cave before the others flashed smiles, though Magnus merely glanced as Lostar crept out.

Raihn took a few steps ahead and spun around to see them in a better light; Lostar was washed-looking, seemingly toying with their once ringed finger, pondering it almost. Raihn offered them the ring, but they continued to deny interest. Whatever happened in there seemed to be between him and his once-beloved. Raihn pondered the ring a moment, then dropped it to the stone.

"So, we still waiting for Rayah?" Magnus asked in a grumble. "Should we go?"

"That would be dearly impolite," remarked a splashing voice from up high.

"...Rayah?" Raihn said, twisting around to see her atop the cave, beaming. "Good timing. Where were you?" he asked.

"Away!" she giggled, her hands knit together in her lap.

"Awfully coy and gleeful, aren't we?" said Pocket. "I think that is what we need most dearly, my dear. Glad you are back."

"Nothing awful about it," she replied, hopping beside Lostar, her knees still pristine after the drop. "But we really should get going."

Raihn glanced at Lostar once more and then beyond. The cave mirrored an unshrinking black hole at Lostar's back, restlessness in their eyes…

Following a day's—*or perhaps a night's*—rest nestled along the rigid cliffside, Raihn woke with a pained back. He wished for furs to soften rocky blows and ointment to soothe the ones he'd already accrued. He, with the others, continued along the path, deftly clambering and scaling, finding new heights, fingers shedding skin and knees scathed like battle-worn shields. His cloak billowed in the wind, catching on the jagged rock, daring him to slip. But he fought on, clambering up the narrow spine of stone, eroded to a fine point. Bits of rock arrowed outward, challenging him, leaving cuts.

Above, the daunting peak loomed as Raihn pulled himself over the stone, looking over the bed of fog. Shrouded by clouds, the peak gleamed through a sinewy break. At times, it had seemed almost mobile, as if it mimicked their every step. But now, there were unmistakable signs of progress. It appeared closer than before they entered the cave, as if the cave had somehow propelled them further along the trail, aiding their journey. Raihn felt a strange comfort in the peak's looming presence that promised a bastion of safety.

Exhaling, he hoped for another leap closer. Rayah's warnings gripped him, and he clung just as tightly, stealing another glance and momentarily delaying the others. He could see the wall tangled with knotted vines and thorns, dense fog clawing up against it from the mountain's broad valleys. He presumed it to be the western side—perhaps the north—he wasn't sure.

And he recalled their first look upon it within the ring of bramble, where all had seemed safe. His tongue brushed against the lingering scar on his inner lip—a reminder of his encounter with Uklarta. He shivered, perhaps from the memory or the chilling height, but observing the wall's progress soothed him. The white rampart of branches rose above the bouldering sea of fog, making him awestruck. A little higher, and he might see distant green through the white, forking branches—if not for the clouds lurking overhead.

Raihn lent himself to the ridge, his mood weighed down like a saddlebag of tools he wished to have for this climb—*a grappling hook and whatever else a mountaineer needs.* But good boots: *a nice pair of hobnailed steel toes* would suffice so his toes don't lick the mountain every step, wedged into nooks and cracks. Even better, a dark-clawed set of alpine iron soles. But with a grappling hook, he wouldn't have to fear the fall ahead of him so much, nor would he stall as much as he was.

Just one more look.

His eyes rose to the clouds ahead, where the mountain seemed to narrow and broaden through their approach. Then he braved the sight below, where he must descend back into the foggy torrent. His cheeks rounded from his final exhale.

His foot crept over daringly, and down he went, a (thinner) cloud of fog swallowing him again. "Wedging" down the crack, as Hodge called it, Raihn filled the spaces with a twist of his foot and fists until he descended unto his wished-for trail at the bottom. The fog thickened at his landing feet and rushed past as if something shunted it forward. It felt alive, ebbing back from where it came; the fog pulled and slithered ahead before sinking and wisping under a bridge made of red vines, like beetroots steeped in bull's blood. That bridge stretched like a pathway into a world of mountainous valleys, a realm grander than anything Raihn had ever known. His stomach seemed to bite itself like a dog, his leg already a mere bone. His raw-made hand clasped his meager belly, a sheath of dry skin. He was tired of walking, and still, there was a way to go...

As he drew closer, he recalled the memory of that bridge that had collapsed before, where their horse had fought against the river current. He gulped. The sea foam fog swirled below the tangled bridge. At the least, this one was wide enough for two to walk, shoulder to shoulder. And the others, save for Lostar, grouped near him at the edge of the red root's bond, trading glances as if wondering who'd first set foot upon the woven pathway.

Raihn told them to go no further, seeing as Lostar trailed behind.

"Trust me, I'm in no hurry," Pocket remarked, cautious of the terrain.

The Enduran, wrapped in his cloak, slogged over the path with all manner of direction and balance cast aside. Might he be downtrodden, like a drunkard trudging through the street from the Mousehole with nothing but the wind at his front, or might he be starved into a daze.

Raihn slowed as a sharp wind howled past, nearly pushing his kite-body over. He looked back, nodding to the others as if to say, "Go on."

Lostar halted before him, his eyes concealed beneath his hood. "You don't have to worry," he said. "I come at my leisure."

The wind hissed through their cloaks. Raihn stiffened, mirroring the rigidity of Lostar's tone as he discerned their forceful front.

Maybe it was just the cold. Maybe Lostar was sick from the heights. Maybe Raihn wasn't detecting the shaky undertone of drink in Lostar's lungs. Regardless, it didn't help Lostar's case, clutching their cloak through tremors. Then again, maybe it was fear, for where and why would ale, wine, or mead be up on these rocks?

"I won't ask anything of you, and if you wish to walk alone, I will respect that wish. But my feet will not travel far," Raihn said.

Lostar's eyes seemed hollow, perhaps mined out by unknown fabrications. Raihn, not wanting to intrude or pry, stepped away, respecting his word.

"Wait," said Lostar. "…You may stay."

The others had already picked up their feet and begun crossing the bridge, overcoming their fears. Pocket was the first to dare lay foot upon the crimson tangles, Hodge following closely. They moved along, their hands gliding through the fog as they steadied themselves even while having enough space beyond the perceived narrowness. They each made it to the end soon enough, and so did the others. And then Raihn, just before Lostar, crossed as well.

. But Hodge did not continue forward, as if snagged by the deeply rooted vines. He squeezed on back to it, knelt, then studied. "Who wove this bridge?" he asked, though his questions vibed more closely to interrogation. Not to Raihn or the others, as they'd no clue, but to the mountain itself. "It is not a natural thing, and without it, we would be stranded. What are you?"

The scholar's hand shot away as if barbed.

Rayah's eyes narrowed. "It does not matter," she said from within the cluster, her tone untrustworthy. "All that matters is that it gets us across." That part, at least, was true.

Raihn was already interested in Hodge's wonder and was further intrigued after Rayah's attempted dissuasion. He touched down beside Hodge, his palm planing across the bridge. Then he stopped, a pulse against his skin. His hand shot away soon after, no different than the way Hodge's had.

"Surprisingly profound," Hodge began, before the cables of red.

Raihn quickly discerned that the remark was not made simply because of the red lengths, nor their warmth, but the additional strand, white like the hairs on a village elder's chin. And after Hodge had had poked at it, Raihn had to just as well. "Profound indeed," he murmured back. It was no different from the wall's pale thatch, peering between the colorful webs. Another peculiar tidbit was that it was cold, or rather, lacking the unnatural warmth of its red siblings.

The steward spoke, so Hodge and Raihn glanced over their shoulders.

"I know," she said preemptively, her eyes frozen, "it runs cold. But it holds dearly to guide, with some fair roots. Much more lurk beneath them, old and still tethered, committed to the herd's design."

Magnus evidently became impatient, he stood with a look of disinterest and crossed arms.

"Alright, let's get a move—" Hodge began, but a chill ran through his words, cutting them short. His hand shot out, snagging something from the bridge's clasp.

What was that about? Raihn squinted. Funny enough, their snag mimicked an action that a prospector might make. But from that comparison, Raihn began to wonder what kind of valuable trinket—or whatever it was, snug as a bug in the folds—could be. Hodge's thick clench hid its value, his eyes fixed ahead. *Guilty enough,* Raihn thought, but he chose not to pry. Instead, he and Hodge rose, ready to rejoin the group. But Magnus walled himself between parties. His arms knit tighter under his damning judgment.

Hodge paused.

Magnus pressed closer.

The scholar turned away, shielding his gold—or, maybe—his pet mouse from the group's taken-in stray.

"It's nothing," Hodge assured, tuning his voice to be nonchalant. "Just a fancy mineral. I think I'll take it home and start a collection."

"Show it to me," Magnus said. His tone was soft but demanding, and without a doubt.

Hodge's palm bloomed, revealing only a plain pebble with a jagged point. "See? It resembles a mountain."

"I do see," Magnus replied, tension persisting beyond his calm composure. "That's a nice souvenir you got. I'm sorry, Hodge."

"It's quite all right. Let's just put it behind us, shall we?"

Hodge started a determined trot, but Raihn had noticed a sly action from Magnus, which planted him in place. Nobody else moved either, maybe because they took notice just as well or because of Raihn and Magnus's locked stances.

Raihn caught Pocket with a glance and nodded as if to say, *Did you see that?* They nodded back in acknowledgment.

Hodge halted, finally taking notice of his lonely road. He turned back to face them when Magnus revealed his pickpocketed prize. Not the pebble but a whistle. It dangled from his hand.

"You don't have to be a thief to be deft," Magnus smiled.

Hodge stomped back, bravery bubbling between his cheeks. "Give it back!"

"You mean, you want two whistles?" Magnus asked.

"No, I want one," Hodge replied.

Magnus's face contorted. "What happened to yours?"

"I threw it away."

"Did you? I didn't see you throw it," Magnus said. Everyone abandoned theirs, but not you. I remember well that you kept it safe around your neck, tucked against your chest."

"I threw it away when no one was paying any mind," Hodge insisted. "I felt guilty just holding onto it when no one else had one."

Magnus snarled. "Lies. You'd have thrown a self-congratulatory party, so we'd all pat you on the back. All you ever wanted was to be stuck here, even when Herb thought against it!"

Hodge recoiled, huffed and puffed, and argued back. "The rain was thick, and I clung to that rock for dear life!" His breaths steadied, the truth finding its way through his anger. "I took it out and thought about blowing it before my fingers could fail me, but…I would know that Herb died for nothing if I blew it. I say the truth, confound it. I let it go so I could go on without temptation, but somehow, it's like it came back, peeking through the roots of that bridge… All to taunt me."

"Sounds a burden," Magnus stated. "Why do you insist on keeping it?"

Hodge stammered. "Because…"

"You were a scholar, loafing with scribes, and yet you say, 'because,'?" Magnus mocked.

"'Feebleness' comes to mind," Hodge sputtered.

Pocket glanced at them all as if brewing a scheme. His feet pushed off the ground, he took only one-and-a-half steps to secure the whistle. His other foot touched down, and he tossed the whistle to Hodge.

Resentment rumbled in Magnus's throat, then cleared from a sigh.

"I did not hide it for myself," Hodge continued. "Magnus, if you return home, that would be just another regret to feather your cap."

Magnus stiffened, Hodge's concern bouncing off him. "Hand it over. Now," he demanded, his hand finding the handle of his sword. The steel peered between the crossguard and scabbard as if daring Hodge to protest further.

Hodge shrank back, shielding the whistle against his chest, but Raihn pushed his palm against his pommel. Magnus, noticing it, raised their other hand to stay him.

"Don't concern yourself, Raihn."

Hodge pondered, his gaze narrowing on Magnus's steel. In that moment, Raihn could see the scholar's decision emerge without a word spoken. Perhaps, if Magnus would stoop to threats, it would be better for him to abandon the journey altogether. Raihn found himself almost giddy at the thought of their departure, his hand slipping off his pommel, as both he and, apparently, Hodge saw the light of the matter.

"Fine. Go ahead and take it," Hodge nearly sang.

Magnus wasted no time. He snatched the whistle, wound his arm, and hurled it into the fog with a whipping motion. His scoff interrupted the faint sound of it disappearing into the air as he turned to lead the way forward.

He left them with this supposed truth: "Now none of us can abandon Raihn, or the journey to contain the ailments of this mountain."

With that, he walked off, and so did the others, albeit reluctantly. Raihn, however, huffed. And without want for favors—if he could accept that's what it was, a favor—was pecked from the gesture. He went as far as to bounce his hand back to his sword, choking the hilt of it. The leather grip groaned under his pressure as his eyes trained on the back of Magnus's head, just as theirs had at the tavern, where he ratted them all out.

Magnus might have been well-intentioned, but his approach was meanderingly indirect. It was almost as if he was using bait and tackle on purpose to toy with them, promising good character along the way.

Raihn only glanced at the ledges above, where lanterns speared out, wondering to whom the whistle had last belonged before he caught up with the others.

The party continued along the path, crimson orbing in rows to guide them. Raihn wondered whether time kept on dwindling or if it was just as affixed as the lights. The fog thickened and thinned sporadically, shielding them from the sky as they dipped up and down slopes. Lanterns dimmed and brightened with the fog's ebb and flow until they plunged deep into a chasm where everything seemed dense and warped. The winding path, lined with rocks and cliffs, narrowing and widening, became steeper and more callous as they descended, all progress feeling lost.

It felt like a forsaken chasm, locked deep with only a hint of light, stone walls closing in. In his mindlessness, Raihn continued to watch the stone rise above them until he smacked right into Magnus's back.

"Sorry," he said, seeing only the back of their tattered cloak. But then he saw what lay ahead of them. Like the others, Raihn stood still and gawked. "A gate…" It was made of stone, unlike any barbican gate or portcullis. The lanterns lined right up to it, deep in the chasm, and though the gate merely blocked the guided path, there was no wall around it.

"Well, ain't that some shit," the thief said. "If only—"

"Yeah, yeah. If only…" Magnus echoed a mock, pushing the thief aside. He stepped up to the gate and heaved his right shoulder into it. Nothing came of it, and so he relented. Leaning against the immovable object, Magnus was exasperated. "Well, I did all I could."

Amarra stepped forward, swiping Pocket and Magnus aside, leaving them teetering on the path's edge. Her apparent pride in her strength bolstered her confidence, and she popped her knuckles, ready to gloat as her grin suggested. Placing both hands flat against the gate's surface, she dug her feet in and pushed mightily, her taut muscles straining. But the gate refused to budge. She glanced over her shoulder with a reluctant plea in her eyes.

Raihn, as well as Pocket and Lostar, joined in, but the sturdy might of the unrelenting gate resisted them just as well.

Magnus had yet to push, and Raihn wrangled him in with a sudden glare. Magnus dusted himself off and pressed his shoulder firmly against the giant stone tablets. Almost all had pushed now, but even so, it withstood their persistence.

Raihn groaned, turning his back to the doors, exhausted. He looked over to Hodge and Rayah. They grinned, still lifting no finger.

Pocket asked her, "What's so funny? And you, Hodge? You mind helping, not gagging on saffron, my lord?"

Saffron being lordly spice, Raihn snickered in amusement.

"Contrary to your belief, I don't believe I could have helped, Pocket. This isn't like a door to your hovel." Hodge's grin faltered through a visible wince, acknowledging his foolish slip of the tongue, yet he persevered. "Gates aren't meant to be pushed down; they're meant to ward off unwanted guests," Hodge explained. "It's not sloppy, is it? No. This is precise. The lanterns led right to a gate—this gate. We require a grant of access, not a bulk of muscle."

"Rayah, what is the meaning of this?" Raihn asked. "Who can open the gate for us?"

"Erratu," a raucous voice thundered from above.

Raihn shrunk down, eyes darting upward. And so did the others', from the beastly boom. The monolithic gate ran up into the fog, where two littler lights were robed at the top. Like a dark cloud of knotted fur, the thing was webbed in wisps of fog, its mane a cloak of fur interspersed with patches of exposed, scarred skin. It perched there, its teeth old and dull, its nose slanted as if blunted by a boulder. And over its mighty skull stretched two horns, flaring like a worn crown with many cuttings. The creature pawed the gate like a mangy cat. Yet, within its round eyes was a contradiction—a gentleness contradicting its crooked fangs and manginess.

After working up some courage, Raihn dared ask it, "Who are you?"

"Erratu: Afurja, akin to her, bean," the creature answered, indicating Amarra with its big, gleaming, goat-eyes.

"What does that mean?" asked Raihn, exchanging glances with her before they both returned their gaze to it.

"'Bean'?" Hodge repeated. "I could go for some pork and beans."

Raihn pinched his nose bridge, not to relieve stress but to emphasize his frustration. "No—I mean yes, me too—but 'Afurja'?"

Hodge nodded molasses-like, his head dipping back. "Right," he mouthed. "That's Atnaarr for 'Outcast.'"

Afurja...

"Planted in the same garden are we, and rotten are we," the beast went on.

"Planted? For what?" asked Raihn.

"Curious is the bean," the beast said, leaning closer from his perch.

"I am," Raihn said. "Though maybe I get ahead of myself. I am Raihn. What might I call you? Erratu, was it?"

"Erratu, yes. Aberration, not 'ohurmarr.' Not 'ogorm.' Erratu," said the creature hastily.

Hodge laughed. "Of course you're no monster, nor are you a beast. You're…you!"

Pocket side-eyed Hodge, clearly disagreeing, but Raihn kept his focus on the 'Aberration,' stomached his fear, and continued to chat. "And you're okay with that name?"

Erratu pondered this question a moment and returned its bright gaze rather woefully. "Erratu is me, an 'ogorm' without fangs," Erratu's voice trailed. "Does bean understand?" it asked, but Raihn pondered. "Unsure?" asked Erratu. "Small bean stuck and lost?"

"Stuck, yes. Lost? Nay," Raihn answered bravely. It was close to a mutter, but his voice gained traction. "The lights guide our way, but if you would be so courteous as to allow us passage, we would be stuck no longer."

Erratu scratched its gnarled chin hairs, its other burly hand clinging onto the top of the gate the same as its curled toes. "But still, bean search. Bean seeks beyond the light. Erratu knows. Be careful, little bean."

"That's all well and good," Magnus intervened, stepping forward, arms signaturely crossed. "But what has any of this got to do with the gate? Are you going to let us pass? We are to reach Weeping Giant's Head. Heard of it? The top of this mountain."

"Maybe allow passage," Erratu considered, nodding, then giving a snort and a grimy grin. "Maybe. Beans come in different sizes, differently intentioned. Erratu allows passage…for a price."

"Our pockets are empty," Magnus explained, inverting his pockets by the inner folds.

"No," the mangey beast boomed. "A more valuable sacrifice is required." It roared ferociously and pounded the gate. "Sacrifice!" Its maw gaped wide, breath heaving out a rancid smell.

"Sacrifice!?" Magnus recoiled. "For what reason should we do that?"

"Passage," Erratu stated.

Magnus protested, waiting for the others to join him, but they simply stared. "Well?" Magnus asked.

Hodge's jaw clenched, nerves taking over. "Why?" he asked the half-furled creature. "I gather that there is more to this mountain than once presumed. I can admit that. But where does betrayal fit?"

"You have come far," said Rayah, "already a great sacrifice has been made, but you must make another. What many of you faced was nothing short of insight between you all, leading up to this. One of you will be cast out, whether by vote or force; it is up to you all to decide. Perhaps the most burdening one," she said slyly, her conniving voice swiftly succulent. "So, choose wisely. You can vote however you like. Whether you wish to drop the weight of the weakest, the ailed one, the deft one, the liar…" Her pupils danced along their grimacing faces.

"You know," Hodge began, "you're a whole other entity when serious."

"Too serious for my blood," Magnus agreed. "What is this, Rayah? I mean…really? I thought we were a troop. We're here to save all that lives, up from the clouds down to the roots, everything between them, that death not take over from some plague."

Her gaze cracked briefly, shying from them. "Make your choice and deliberate," she said, doubling down almost dutifully.

"To nominate excess baggage is barbaric… But I suppose if the boat is full of water…" Hodge mused.

Magnus's head goosed back in protest. "What are you saying? You suggest she's right? You never believed in this type of shit before!"

"We all know who must go. I've known it for some time now."

"No way. Simply unright!" Magnus replied.

"The world is unright," Rayah retorted. "It is full of aberrations," she elaborated, looking kindly to Erratu, then antagonistically at Magnus. "Though some can prove their innocence. Has any of you proved it yet?"

"So, you're with the beast completely, and you think this is acceptable?"

"It is necessary to fulfill the journey. For the dog to scratch off its flea," Rayah replied calmly.

The silent nominations began quietly. Lostar watched Magnus from under his hood, and Magnus looked at Pocket.

"Why are you eye-fucking me?" Pocket flinched. "Maybe you should look at yourself. You still have a bit of betrayal stuck in your teeth."

"I was strong enough to free us of that whistle's temptation, remember?"

"There it is," Raihn groaned, his frustration justified. "You did no favors."

"That's right," Pocket agreed. "I wasn't gonna blow and go."

Even in his passion, Magnus spared a brief moment for a double-take. "I'm just considering the most logical choice," he replied, his eyes feral. "Who has the most business to finish and has the least. Unlike you, I have someone to go back to. Someone that needs me."

Pocket appeared stung, becoming more complacent, or perhaps more like a whipped dog. The thief backed down, mumbling, "That's not true."

"She's gone," Raihn reminded rather abruptly, referring to Magnus's spouse. "Don't waste his life so you can continue your quest to reclaim what is lost! The Hulls are ruthless, and they will never give her back."

"Yeah? Can you live by those same words?" asked Magnus. "I am not the only one to put lives at risk for another—"

"What?" Raihn asked, caught off guard. *What did he mean by that? Does he know?*

Magnus had stopped, their lips compressed, words tugged at bay. But he seemed to pick back from another thought, "—and you suggest I go?"

"…I'm just saying let's not point fingers," Raihn assured.

"Then how will we move on? Someone has to go. I'm just being rational. My Gayle was taken by the cardinal, and I was jailed because of…" Magnus flashed with a new light, his eyes falling upon Hodge like a heavy landslide.

Pocket intervened, stepping between them. "Allow myself to be the sacrifice. I'm just a rat, right?"

Hodge shook his head. "To let you serve up yourself would be unfair."

"Unfair to whom?" asked Pocket.

"Me," Hodge huffed, fiddling nervously with one of his two suspenders. "I want to go."

"You don't have to," said Pocket. "I mean—you insist on snuffing yourself out?"

"The same as you," Hodge retorted.

"Why? Don't tell me it's simply because of Magnus's pestering little eyes."

"It is the most rational course of action," Hodge replied.

Lostar began to step forward, clearly about to offer themself, but Raihn was quick to stretch out his arm. "Quit trying to die on me, will you?"

Magnus appeared relieved at all their willingness to be sacrificed—a reaction that drew Raihn's ire out even more.

"I've done nothing but hold you all back," Hodge continued. "The values I had are lost, along with my better half. If I were to be sacrificed, maybe I could find them again…"

"Hodge," Raihn breathed, tempted to insert Magnus as a sacrifice.

"No. I fumbled the tinderbox. I lost us our gear. And most damning, I was meant to be dead already. It's only thanks to Magnus that I am here," he clarified, turning to the tracker. "Thus, my debt to him. If he'd not spared me, Gayle would still be beside him and not locked away. I shouldn't be here." Then, he spoke to Magnus directly. "And that weighs on your mind."

Returning his attention, Hodge continued his plea. "If I stay, I'll just keep dragging you down, and we all know it. I'm only willing to say it because you're all too kind. Well, most of you."

Raihn awaited Magnus to refute these claims, but they kept firm, their silence speaking volumes. "Well? Aren't you going to say something?" Raihn asked.

Apparently not. Magnus stepped away, and Hodge's decision hastened. Raihn begged Hodge not to do it.

"I have to," Hodge insisted, his voice steady but his gaze not. "It's the only way I can make things right. I want this," he assured him. "I want this so that I can make at least one contribution. I'm just the portly and carroty one of the group. The joke."

There was no arguing. Hodge's mind was made up. But the worst of it was the despair in the recesses of their pupils, forcing them into submission. Amarra placed her hand on Raihn's shoulder. He relented, defeat blowing out between his chapped lips. "Then I can't let you go thinking you're a joke when you're braver than the man you apparently owe yourself to."

HODGE found it difficult to bend his knees before the lurching beast, assuming it would slay him or eat him. His lips pursed tight, and he closed his eyes even tighter as a moment of silence filled the air. The anticipation was killing him.

Then the wait was over. There was a clawing descent along the gritty stone as the beast sounded to come from its perch, followed by a non-oiled hog-whine spurred from something archaically mechanical. Hodge heard the others gasp behind him, so he unfastened his eyes. The gate was open, and no hair on the selfless scholar's chops was grazed.

"Why?" Hodge breathed.

"You sound almost disappointed," Rayah said enthusiastically.

"I just want to know…"

Rayah smiled, deliberately ignoring his exhausted question. "I had to put on my most grave little girl act."

"I'm…" Hodge stammered.

Rayah leaned in, her voice a whisper in his ear. "What you said, most noble Hodge, was admirable and selfless, but we both know the winds guiding your sail were turbulent ones. Take an oar instead. Keep paddling."

Hodge looked at her, his surprise evident. He felt exposed/ vulnerable for a moment, but the rising commotion around them quickly pulled him back to the present.

Rayah straightened and addressed the group more loudly, "Hodge and Pocket, opposite sides of the coin. It wasn't the best, but it sure was a spectacle!"

"I beg to differ," said Raihn, clutching his chest.

"Still, ye've got some things to resolve, so it's lucky for ye to still live," Rayah said, her tone flamboyant. Then she winked at Lostar, "Don't squander that chance and spoil what many do not get."

Raihn pondered this momentarily, but Rayah's attention had already shifted. "And you," she said, turning to Pocket.

"Don't say it," Pocket cut in. "Whatever it is, don't. I don't need affirmations."

Rayah's smile creased under her cheeks, and she let him be. "Well, I can sense you're all itching to go, so I will say this next and first. Hodge had asked where betrayal fit. Well, it doesn't." Her voice turned cold, her gaze fixed on one person.

Magnus, bristling with resentment, stormed through the gate. Alone.

"Pieces gone and images incomplete, the return of them will make the one whole, and an unsightly betrayer is always there," Rayah stated. "Always."

Hodge found his footing as he dusted himself. Not that dusting did much good after all this hiking, but he wouldn't be happy unless he tried. Still, he looked down in disappointment as he remained quite filthy.

He sighed and slipped through the gate in search of their next obstacle, all the while burning a hole in the back of Magnus's skull with his appended gaze.

POCKET was the last to pass through the archway. He noticed Rayah side-eyeing him and made eye contact. "Shit," he cursed, averting his gaze. It was too late.

She skipped to him, a playful grin on her face. "You backed down easily," she teased.

"Maybe I'm not that eager for death. Might not be all it's cracked up to be. Besides, what kind of sendoff would I get down here?"

"Well, I praise the true reason you stayed," Rayah said. "A pity it would be to bequeath us your demise so soon."

"Oh yeah? Why did I stay?"

"Because of what you found," she replied.

"Rayah," Pocket sighed, looking at her, feeling the tired saddles under his eyes droop.

"You found something precious, worth living for, and worth dying for," Rayah continued. "A gem that could not be stolen but earned. And yet, you were going to give me the sacrifice, not of your flesh, but of what you finally mined. It's a thing more valuable than the trinkets you trade in any barter town."

"Well, you must indeed be older than you look. There aren't many barter towns left. But when you put it like that, yes. I suppose I'm not so bad, huh?"

She was right. He wasn't so lonely, and he also felt a growing camaraderie that changed his tune. He even wanted to hear more.

CHAPTER TWENTY-NINE
Wars in the muskeg

RAIHN sensed an ominous waft lingering over him that could not go unheeded. His eyes sharpened because of it. His head on a swivel because of it. Meanwhile, Magnus seemed to become more detached from the group—the newest outcast, a man who always led and provided now ostracized.

Pocket broke the silence: "Is anyone else concerned in the slightest that it's following us?"

"Relax," Rayah said. "And '**it**' has a name," she added, as if offended. "You may go by a nickname, but he does not."

"Okay, I can respect that," Pocket replied. "But why is he, uh, you know—tagging along like I've got a piece of meat hanging out of my back pocket?"

"Might he like your ham, but the rest of your body would be more filling than that. Isn't that right, Erratu?"

"Erratu hungry," said the misshapen Outcast through a hungry breath.

Pocket quickened his pace.

Gone from the deep fissure, with its gate pointed through the chasm, came crisp gales and a deep depression in a broadened "plateau," as Hodge surmised. A dark trench was slithering through a snow-dander field, dug like a moat, with paper birch trees along it.

Magnus knelt, his fingers rummaging through the soil, plucking clumps and pinching them. He retained his findings, quiet and studious with fingers blackened.

Hodge, too, found it worth a look.

"What do the experts think?" Pocket asked.

Hodge considered the dark ground, stepping into the trench, sewing a soggy smell from pushing his weight on it. He stood at its center, his knuckles turned on his hips. He spun slowly, surveying the area. "Huh," he aired.

Pocket, confused, gestured with his hand, showing his dissatisfaction. "And?"

"Odd place," Hodge replied simply.

"'Odd place,' he says. 'Odd place.' Yeah, I suppose it is," Pocket told the audience. "Don't suppose you'd, uh, elaborate, perchance?"

Hodge exhaled, his hand now rocking like a boat in choppy waters. "Eh," he said, his lips pursing out. "It's peculiar. But after you've encountered this big," he paused, his finger pointing beyond them, "not 'monster-nor-beast' fellow, I suppose you lose some of that wonder to this mashed-potato-like mountain."

Raihn scrunched his face, struggling to understand.

Hodge expounded, "I say, peas weren't meant to be in there, but golly if it isn't easier to swallow that way." A wistful elaboration. "Look, I'm rather whacked, gentlefolk. But yes, soil is prevalent on my mind," he remarked sarcastically.

His feet danced in place, teasing the ground, sewing more of a stench. "Cakey," he deliberated. "Too much sugar," he added, hinting some density.

"Are you done?" Magnus questioned. They nodded, so he glanced back at the others, his pupils narrowing on the strange mountain dweller that trailed them: Erratu. "Then let's get moving, preferably away from…that."

"Okay, okay, I will say this," Hodge snagged, evidently irking Magnus. His hand whipped off his hip, finger pointed up as if a caricature. "It's truly odd to find such soil at this altitude," he said, facing the trench. "My hob-nailed heels should scratch the rock beneath me, not skid this boggy bath. There should be a hook upon my fingers, grit upon my touch, not something so…mushy. This feels like a place belonging to a peaty moor," he said. "And consider, we all see it, out of those dreadfully hallucinogenic caves. It's real." He paraded yet another twist, eyes appearing to mirror the lantern's flame. His intrigue let out. "But you know what that means?"

"What's that, Hodge?" Raihn indulged, allowing a rare moment of curiosity to slip into his voice as he watched Hodge delight them with his bits of knowledge.

The scholar's face lit up with a small, triumphant smile. "We don't have to rest our backs on gravel," he replied, tapping the soft earth beneath them with the tip of his boot.

Magnus maintained a closed-off distance, his arms in his signature fold, broad shoulders casting a shadow over the patch of ground Hodge had been examining. His frown deepened as if disapproving the optimism.

Hodge caught the dour look and furrowed his brow. "What's wrong, Magnus? Surely this is better than those jagged rocks we've been contending with for days."

Magnus's eyes shut, briefly pestered, then cracked into slits as if he were fighting slumber, eyes puffy and purple, little more than a groan here and there from him since the gate. He glanced at the shadowed soil, his lips pulling into a taut string of yarn. "Muskeg, not a moor," he answered simply.

Hodge seemed deflated while Pocket found air. "Fertile as an ill-starred wench from the Wynd of the Black Deer," said the thief, prodding the soil with his pointer. "Accursed lands, good for burnin' with all its peat."

Raihn caught a whiff of something earthy ahead—damp and faintly honeyed. It was oddly pleasant, a welcome change from the usual scentless, stagnant air.

Magnus, however, was clearly unenthused; his expression soured, head hanging low. "It's tender-footed, and it will grab at your feet. Yes, like sponge cake…"

That, coming from a tracker, even a bastard one, Raihn understood trouble lay ahead.

"The lanterns guide ye passage," Rayah stated. "No way around it."

Magnus's sleepiness turned ill, his eyes sinking into the trench, his concerns still withheld more than was liked by Raihn. The man-made channel winding through the fog was ominous, its sides like crescents under the looming lanterns, their posts sprouting through moss.

"But fortunate for ye," Rayah continued, "it is not dug so deep into the direst muskeg…"

The even-more-whited paper birch trees loomed faintly, accompanied by some black spruce that were native to the muskeg's edge. The trees guarded tufts of shrubs lurking under them, spying the adventurers' crossing. But, shallowly in the recess, Lostar stumbled into the inner walls, dark vegetation slapping his stained cloak. His shoulder took the brunt of it, while his hands nested under his pits—perhaps from the cold, his shivers hard to ignore.

"Are you okay?" Raihn fretted.

"I'm fine," Lostar answered firmly.

"You shake and you walk as if on stilts."

"I'm cold," Lostar snipped.

Pocket, taking precariously wide strides, tilted his head toward them and remarked, "It's as soft as my ol' father's belly, an' the walls drool like his jowls. Point is," he snickered, "it's not just him struggling. The mud's givin' me cankles."

Raihn ignored Pocket's intrusion of jest, sighed, and retired from his concern, for he could truly do nothing with the curt replies from the Enduran. Eventually, he nestled along the inner crevice and suggested rest.

The wailing winds blew overhead, and it seemed fitting for the mountain to give pardon with this hollowed depression. The ground was cushioned, though the cold was biting. Dark, cold debris clung to them, and a dark, shallow water slapped their soles, running their hems, trousers, and britches cool. It felt like a comfort trade, all that the terrain would barter.

Magnus was right to be reluctant, but the terrain hardly seemed worthy of a deep grudge. Raihn's legs tuckered out, so he called for a break. He and Amarra squashed beside each other as the others snugged against the wall. His foot braced against the muck above the stagnant string of water, his back pressing the other side of the trench wall. All that mattered was that his tailbone remained dry.

Magnus's concern continued to lodge within Raihn's head, his mind hooked like a thread on a nail. Pocket's blurb about the Wynd of the Black Deer seemed to trouble Magnus the most.

"Hey, Pocket," Raihn began, "I've heard mention of the Black Deer. You seem familiar with that, wynd. What curse do they speak of?"

"What they're named after—the Black Deer," Pocket said. "If you ever see a black doe, spare it, lest their mate lay curses upon you from their imbued antlers," he went on, miming antlers beside his head.

"So, does that entail they killed a black doe? What came of it?"

"If I knew, I'd have told ya, but I don't," Pocket replied. "I just know that if you ever see, whether by sight or dream, of an animal, rare in some particular way—disfigured or discolored—you get it—they might be a Wyrd."

Raihn scrunched his brow. "Meaning?"

"Harbingers, foretellers, omens, heralds—"

"Okay, I get it," Raihn interrupted. "Wait," his mind snagged, "discolored, you say?"

"How many black deer do you recall seeing?" Pocket remarked. "See, that's the rare part right there!"

Raihn sidestepped the blabbing, cutting through. "Like Prosporos, the gold, winged horse?"

"Sure!"

Raihn's mind adrift, his tailbone slid down this pig-trough-of-a-trench, purring out squelches from the slop. He kicked himself back up, brows knotted, his boot rigid but caked in soft mush.

"Silvers, too," Pocket added. "Gold for yearning, silver for malleability, red for loss—"

Raihn gestured to speed them up, still ruffled from the mess.

"Each can be paired with an animal—typically," Pocket said, pausing to ponder. "Mostly animals. And might they then be disfigured too, becoming quite cryptic…"

"What about giant wild boars that try to kill you?"

Pocket stammered, unsure. "Never heard of 'em trying to kill head-on before."

Raihn grunted, picking at the memory like a scab. When Pocket inquired whether there was something on his mind, Raihn assured it was nothing. His questions were met. He nestled his hands beneath his cheek, and Amarra swung over him as if he were her pillow.

The chilled winds abated.

Stirred awake with a racing heart, Raihn freed himself from under Amarra in a sudden rush. She peeled off of him, her eyes glossed with hurt. Guilt flushed his cheeks, or so it felt. "Just a nightmare," he said. "I'm sorry." Yet

266

she appeared unmoved. He sat there, contemplative, glancing a couple times, his mouth unsure when he'd speak up. He just couldn't help what nightmares he'd have, as they befell him even within the lantern light.

Her hold of him must have incited his nightmare. And with the way he pushed himself out, he knew it was best to explain himself, not that he was any good at it.

"Not that I wanted—her determination—Uklarta's, but if I hadn't come to know you, it wouldn't have been so…no, that's not what I mean to say," he'd interrupted himself, anxiety-ridden. She grabbed his shoulder, easing the burden with a brushing thumb. "…I just wish we could get away, some-place secluded. Unfortunately, however, the memory would haunt me there. Then again, I don't know if I'll ever shake it…" his voice faded out, then returned sharply. "I have to see the head of the mountain, Amarra. Maybe then I'll come down from this sickness."

Amarra nudged him as if to knock loose that kind of thought, her strength nearly pushing him down. He laughed it off, but she was serious, her expression the only rock in the vicinity.

Raihn strengthened his voice again, quelling his nervous grin. His chin fell, and he spoke indirectly, "Lucky me, though, this wasn't like those ines-capable dreams laced by her presence or that of the mountain's will. It was purely a nightmare of my own deep conjuring. It's easy to tell, actually, compared to those bad dreams. I thank the lanterns for that…my regular nightmares."

He took a breath and studied his worn hands, recordings of his struggles. "I foresee that secluded cabin, unbothered by miasma. That's your free-dom." His hands balled into determined fists, his eyes gliding as he turned his head to read her emotions. A tear slipped down her cheek, and her eyes gleamed from beneath her hood. Her grip tightened before pulling away, but her hood caught his grasp. He gently pulled it down, revealing silvery eyes, distressed, with a red tint.

His next questions faltered as her gaze stretched far beyond him. A swell of concern clenched his heart, his body ransacked by anxiety. She snorted, seemingly annoyed by his prying. He surrendered, wondering if it was something he had said—or if she still ached from his escape—for there was a memory within her gaze. Whether it lingered from moments ago or from long before, he was uncertain. But it was there, sharp with pain. *Something from the cave,* he considered.

A blue-hued darkness spread through the muskeg, snowflakes fluttering into the lanterns' glow. *Hardly a mountain.* This place was outlandish at every turn, the lanterns arching over them with a dim protection all the way. The trench was damp in most areas and always prone to collapse, and yet, it still felt like a bed compared to the frigid ridges, rocky slopes, and flat crags they had daredevilled.

Sometime later, after an indeterminate stretch of more rest, Raihn awoke abruptly again, as if his body had buoyed itself into consciousness. His eyes cracked open to an unusual sight: a rock weighing down two pieces of parchment. *Peculiar,* he thought, seeing it rest just outside the light.

No longer tangled in Amarra's arms, he eased his crooked back from the dark, damp soil and quietly slipped away while the others remained at rest.

Climbing to the top ridge, Raihn reached past the light, plucked the piece from under the rock, and ducked down against the inner wall of dirt. Holding the parchment tightly, he smoothed out its wrinkles.

Journal Entry 20
Era of King Stamen, Year 26 under his reign.

After heading out and laying upon the hot boulder, I slept. Easily, I was at peace with the relaxing flow of water and the comforting light. Even if it was unwise, I had to remedy my sleeplessness. I'm glad I did. A maiden, horned as I, with rich skin gilded and accompanied by luscious tresses, reached out her graceful favor. She beamed like Eldhos in my dark slumber, cradling my sanity within her gentle palm.

I must accept her hand of old grace, her fingers like crownlings soft to the touch that beckon me, lest my infatuation with the mountain degrade my mind.

And on my anniversary, just as I came to them, I now depart. Though it is with a pit in my stomach, even if softened by this new infatuation.

I take my leave, no longer a hindrance, guided to what is forbidden. I just wish I could inform them of my travels, but unfortunate is this stipulation; by her one rule, they cannot come, and they cannot know, for it is forbidden.

If I could be greedy and steal just an ounce more of peace from this gold, I would write goodbye, even if they cannot read this.

But there was still more on the other side.

Journal Entry 21
Era of King Stamen, Year 26 under his reign

I have finally arrived. Just outside the camp at the Wall of Thorns. I sit at a comfortable distance, where the gilded maid, who visited me in my sleep, instructed me to wait here for her. So, I write, hidden, listening to the guards carry on with their nasty banter.

It's strange seeing men. I don't know them, and they don't know me. If they did, the entire village might be uprooted in search of more of my kind. In fact, I am surprised it hasn't been already from my mistake… Still, I can't

A stern focus settled over Raihn as he read, his mind fixated on this 'mistake.' He pondered whether it was something first penned on the missing page—the one mysteriously torn out during his first night with the party, and his thoughts spiraled deeper, the world around him fading. Then, without warning, a hand gripped his shoulder. Raihn's heart leaped into his throat, and he nearly jumped out of his boots.

Raihn glanced over, noticing Amarra's white claws. "Sorry, I was really lost in thought," he apologized, quickly folding the page. "Did you happen to read this?"

Amarra nodded.

"That's…alright. It's been a long-kept secret, but…" He hesitated, debating with himself. "I have a journal—my brother's journal, as you already know. He's been gone for," he pondered, "about a year. Silly me. Can't even keep up with the days. Anyway, he showed me his book in a dream," he chuckled nervously. "But it's actually not funny," he added, clueless, somber. "I guess it's all just silly."

"But.

"It was…difficult—both finding him and losing him. I don't want to go through that again."

Amarra broke a grin, taking him in close.

"You know, I was already wondering if he'd come here, that I could find him again. I looked at the path and wondered if I was walking in his footsteps. Thanks to this page, I know he was here. Except, in that event, wouldn't the 'Eternal Flame' already be tended…or something like that? Our journey up would be moot. Yet, it isn't."

Raihn paused, stressed, running his fingers through his hair. "I think my brain's molding over," he continued. "Everything's fuzzy now, but I'm trying to keep fresh and sort this all.

"In his recording, he wrote of screams. Like there was an attack. At first, I thought it might've been a bear, as others taled. Except my father searched near the gate around that same time of year, just after River went missing. And he said he was turned away. By who? Corpses? Why not just tell me the truth? Did he think River could have…"

He took a breath, clenching the page as Amarra continued to pull him in. "This is also proof that it was something else. And whatever it is, I have a hunch it's what killed that couple in the cave and strewn Lostar's horse up in the tree—you weren't there for that," he annotated. "But now I'm stuck with the idea that my father died under the assumption River was a killer. As well as other concerns. Such as the whistle. What if River blew it to go home but was found by the King's Authority? And when he came to me in my dreams, would that mean he's…"

Amarra plugged his mouth with her warm palm and then let go. It was brief and tender, but he felt her nails scrape away…

He began again, his tone calmer, breaths controlled. "These questions just make everything fuzzier, like my brain's turning to mold, aging like bread, hard as all the rock this side of the Wall of Thorns.

"Because…he's an Outcast—an Afurja." He twisted and looked deeply into her eyes, baring truth, bravery stemming from her touch. "That's what worries me most. We could never vouch for or claim him if he was caught. That's why we couldn't even gather a search party when he disappeared. That's why our manor was barren of anyone not kin—he was a secret, meant to be stowed away. In a cabin. Out in Father's woods."

Amarra appeared grateful for his honesty, but a shadow of doubt took shape in her eyes when he'd, again, mentioned the cabin. And that was cause for concern.

She grabbed her chart and spelled: 'Whatever comes at the peak, think not of us. Hearken to my plea, not to the promise of a cabin.'

Raihn nodded, noting she wrote out of her own concern, yet again. She seemed to look ahead while he looked back, but he considered there might be a balance in that.

Then he glanced about to assure himself nobody eavesdropped, and all those around did not stir. Rather *odd,* considering the discomforts of the trench. His suspicion was enough to retire his prattling. They returned to their rest, with Raihn asleep in Amarra's muscled lock.

When he awoke, Amarra and the others were gone. He found only himself submerged beneath a muddied brim, decorated with moss—an undrained hole in the muskeg. Fear gripped him as he realized he was chest-deep in the murky water. "No… I'm in the lanterns!" he cried out, but all he stood in was a mere pool of burgundy wine. "Is this a vision from the mountain then?" he asked aloud, his voice teeming with terror.

In the wine-colored pond, a mangled face surfaced, following bubbles and squelches. It appeared to be Erratu, and around him, more bodies canoed like they were leaves in fall, all misshapen with wild horns and vastly differing sizes. One of them was painted red, but he could see her face, her unmistakable quad horns—Amarra.

Suddenly, standing tall, others surrounded the crater in the bloody muskeg, their eyes down like cast stones. Judgment and dread weighed heavily on Raihn, his acorn eyes wide with fear. Towering Outcasts loomed over him, each varying in shape and size, some grotesquely irregular—possibly aberrations like Erratu. One of them was long and slender, with low-hanging hands and crane-fly legs. Hair draped down like dusty curtains, concealing their eyes beneath thick bangs. A fringed shawl swathed their slenderness.

Beside them stood a bulkier figure, more beastly in appearance. The hound of the group, with a large snout sniffing out from beneath their cloak. Thick stalks of grey hair bushed around their wet muzzle. They leaned on a cane, their humpbacked, crooked.

At the center of the group stood the largest Outcast. His horns stretched like the limbs of a paper birch, and over his broad shoulders hung the scarlet hide of a bear. A dreadful foreboding permeated the air, his presence as dense as deep peat. His silver eyes polished the memory of the manor-swirling vortex.

Raihn attempted to clamber out of the pond, but he became tangled after kicking his legs into what he could only assume to be submerged corpses. He became locked by ropes of hair and bramble in the rising pool of bobbing skulls, simmering into what felt like a tomato-ish tarn to him.

He fought harder and harder to get out, the rim crumbling from his touch. It was a quicksand kind of soil. Amarra's dyed mane swam across his face during the struggle and the waves he made. He loathed it all.

A yellow leaf fell from the sky and nestled upon the red pond before capsizing. After that, white ravens rained down to the pool and cawed helplessly as the blood stained their reverent feathers. Their wings slapped and splashed as they flailed helplessly. Little droplets had fallen upon his tongue and lip, the taste rotten and far worse than the stench tying his nose hairs into knots. Raihn nearly spit up from it, but he choked it down and continued his desperate bid for freedom.

Raihn ended his struggle, realizing it only worsened his situation. The ravens dipped lower, their talons tranquil. Amarra's sodden hair followed, anchored by her plunging corpse. He looked up again, seeing only the hauntingly pale lapis remnants of the sky—the beastly creature with the cane and the *crane fly* gone. Yet, Raihn remained stuck.

Panic began to creep in as he swiveled his head frantically, searching for something, anything. But nothing was coming next. That panic swelled like the blood pool. And worse, Amarra's arm erupted, then dunked him into the depths of the putrid tarn.

Kicking and swinging against his rotting restraints until he was finally shaken free, Raihn peddled through the thickness until there was a gurgle through the soil. Everything became still and black, yet he was aware, as if at the end of a lucid dream. His body quit, his peddling over. At the very least, he found himself out of the tarn, breathing. The stiffness returned like the moment he miraculously found himself away from Uklarta.

"Nothing has changed," a voice whined, clearly Pocket's, who exclaimed in false surprise. "The grey. The cold. What's with this place? I don't even know how long I slept!"

"And now an aching back," Hodge grumbled.

"That's nothing new to me," Pocket remarked.

"It was enough time," said Rayah, chiefly. "We must hasten our feet. Every extra second we do not need is a selfish indulgence. We mustn't give Uklarta any more time."

"Can you guys see the crust on my eyes?" One asked, unmistakably Pocket. "I feel like my face is covered in crust. Like. A nice meat pie. Fuck all, I want a meat pie."

After all this echoing back and forth, they seemed to finally quiet when Raihn felt himself shaken to be roused from slumber. Their hands were mighty, presumed to be Amarra's. He was familiar with them being half the size of a buckler.

"The fuck is up with him?" Pocket asked, his voice chirpily nearer.

There was a pause. "Rayah!" Hodge called out from over Raihn, his voice booming. "We're within the lanterns. That dream walker can't pierce him through it as we're led to believe, so what's this? He will not wake from her shaking!"

"Leave him," the steward demanded, her tone dry. "He'll wake."

Nearly on cue, he broke free, sweating and panting. His upper body shot upright, narrowly missing Amarra's chin. He caught his breath and rubbed his temple, feeling her firm grip lingering on his shoulders. All eyes were on him, save for Rayah's and Erratu's.

"I'm fine," he assured, annoyed. All the yammering and concern only worsened his headache. Lostar, however, was the quietest among them, looking sleepless. Raihn noticed him gazing up at the pale, shrouded sky.

"You get any sleep?" Raihn asked, but Lostar didn't reply. There seemed to be a toll taken on him, and it was getting worse.

Raihn glanced at Amarra. She still caressed his shoulder tenderly, perhaps aware of her tight grip from before. She looked to only worry for him. "I'm okay," he lied firmly.

They filed through the trench, one by one, marching like soldiers in the despair of war on a path to oblivion. The scenery was so dull that even a swerve here or there roused their excitement. But inevitably, the path would straighten back to its monotony.

Raihn considered the *nightmare—or vision, whatever it might have been—*and speculated its intent, coming up with not even a spark. What was there to interpret? Raihn tugged on the strap of his satchel as he pondered, mostly wishing to retreat into the vision of his cabin, and he thought of Amarra more than anything. The weight of the satchel grew heavier.

Amarra nudged Raihn firmly. He glanced up at her, his neck aching. She was gesturing for him to hand her the bag. First, he hesitated, then he pulled the strap off. He was relieved already and about to pass it on, but then Lostar stumbled over to them in a hurry, feet splashing.

"May I?" they asked, their hand already stretched out in trembles.

Raihn looked at Amarra. She nodded, easing his people-pleasing mind that couldn't decide on its own.

Lostar's eyes swam in envy.

"Take it," Raihn said, leveled.

The hefty satchel descended into Lostar's outstretched hands, and their body teetered as though it accepted iron.

Magnus scoffed, shoving Pocket aside in his pursuit of it. "Allow me," he snorted.

"I've got it," Lostar grunted.

"Sure," Magnus chortled. He thieved the satchel in a swift cradle, hips dipped back, face made of twists. He fell. It would have crushed his fingers, but luckily, the ground was soft and wet. "Well, don't just stand there, take it!" he barked.

Amarra leapt forward and clutched the strap, pulling at it, but its traps frayed from strain.

"The seams!" Raihn cried.

Amarra fumbled for a moment and cradled the heft of the satchel with her big palm and pressed it to her chest. The strap dangled with ease, still intact. Raihn sighed in relief.

"So, what? It's just a bag," Magnus remarked, standing up.

"Everything has its worth," Pocket said.

"My mother made this for me," Raihn fought.

Magnus relented. "My mistake," his soft and genuine voice rumbled. He caressed his dog-shaped brooch, which clasped his cloak at the collar, his eyes still upon the satchel.

Hodge spoke up, his hand busy with something in his pocket. "We've all got silly little things we've become fond of."

Magnus surrendered his fiddling fingers, seemingly aware, and his tone was more annoyed. "I get it."

"So then, what is its deal?" asked Pocket. "How can it be so heavy and light all at the same time?"

Rayah let out a cold breath: "It's as heavy as thy inner self, and physically, you would be burdened by its manifestation… That's how you may be granted access to the Eternal Flame, light of heart."

"Why detail us now, girl?"

Her little, peppery eyes shot up at him. "Self-conscious pilgrims would be unsavory, not that you can hide your true intentions…" she remarked. "You refer to the chest, but it is not the chest that weighs you down. And seeing ye that struggled, I would reflect. Thou'rt deep in the beetroot now."

Her tone seeped from a commanding heart, but seeing her heart waver from a piddling flame to one of a giant's was odd. Her demeanor ever shifting, old and young, revolving.

"You know," Pocket began, "those Endolanders were onto something, taking their own corpses to the wall, choosing death. But what's it all for? What are we meant to be worthy of?"

Like some amongst them, her visage was careworn, her glint ferried off some distant place. Dim was her socket-lanterns, regarding Pocket somewhat coldly. "Consider thyself tender peat for the flame," Rayah murmured, her voice soft yet melancholic. "It wavers from yore-time, burning endlessly. O flame, wavering, wavering—Dimming." She spoke from a mind adrift a foggy pond, her voice lower, now a whisper.

"Of course, steward," said Pocket with a smirk. "And might there be a dragon to slay along the way?" His brow wormed smarmily.

"There are many," Rayah replied, a gleam before a wink, the edges of her broad smile tucking into her cheeks; her childish nature shined through again.

Pocket blinked, his smirk fading. "Wait, really?"

"Relax, it's farcical," said Hodge. "It's all a ruse."

"Pardon?"

"She's being facetious—cracking wise," said Hodge. He squinted, perhaps waiting to be corrected, but Rayah only petted Erratu, side-eyeing Hodge with her light seemingly returned to harbor.

"Go on then, 'scholar,' why don't you give it a go?" Pocket teased, gesturing to the satchel.

Hodge crossed his arms. "It's just a chest. Her words are more weighted than it. I won't partake in mind-games." And then he fled off through the trench.

MAGNUS groaned. "Let him go," he said, clasping his aching hands together in hopes the pain would subside.

"Are your hands okay?" Pocket asked.

Magnus resented the hospitality. "They're fine," he groaned.

His friendships had grown thin, and as the thief had noted, "he seemed adamant to break them all by this point."

Burdened by his troubles, Magnus trailed the group loosely, his boots slushing through the mud. The pain in his hands wasn't unbearable, thanks to the soft soil, but it lingered just enough to keep him aware. As time passed, the soreness dulled, and he found himself following Erratu, the hairy, ogre-like Outcast who had clambered over him to join Rayah at the front.

Moseying through the furlongs, Magnus scrutinized the beastly figure ahead, its fur matted like that of a stray dog, its horns arched like a longbow. The creature glided effortlessly through the gutter, its broadness leaving no room to spare in the narrow path. Thin strands of its hair trailed along the walls like wriggling worms, while its heels flung muck back at Magnus with each heavy stomp. Any hope of finding humor in the situation seemed about as distant as the bottom of the ocean.

A prudish man once insisted he be prim, but then a stranger—a woman—encased him in mud, insisting it was the way of a tracker to become one with Adjurrah. It seemed that Magnus molded himself into her ways back then, still following her trail even now. He reminisced, but an old face reared its conniving voice through the recesses of his memory. "Remove that filth and scrub behind your ears," it demanded.

Father. Their dirty child was never to look a street rat lest he scurry dirty streets, treated as one, spurning lady folk of finer clothing that mean to spill their coin purses for hard wax.

Beneath his crusty garments, Magnus pondered, and deep down, Gayle's memory urged him to bury his doubts beneath a chunk of mud. His dragged cloak slithered behind him, becoming grime-ridden. Eventually, it became taut, snagging on something. Magnus glanced back, but there was nothing visible to be caught on. Nothing. Yet, it felt as though cleats or crampons pinned down his cloak. Still, there was only the fog. He ignored the inconvenience and pressed on after the weight lifted, chills tapering down his spine.

His companions fade into the fog ahead, and with a quickened pace, he began to close the distance between them. But just seconds into his effort, his cloak caught again. The sudden jolt punched his throat as the brooch cut into his skin, sending him crashing into the cold muck, gasping for breath. The cloak tightened around his neck, stifling any attempt to cry out. And then it grew even tighter as he was dragged toward the source of the pull on his back. Desperate, Magnus twisted around, trying to see what had snagged him.

There, half-buried in the muck, was the culprit—a decaying hand with forked fingers hooked into his cloak.

Magnus struggled to free himself, and a desperate tug-of-war ensued. He yanked at the cloak, wrestling with the rotten appendage, but all he succeeded in doing was raising the decaying arm further out from the deep recess. Magnus pulled harder, his efforts growing frantic, until finally, a figure emerged—a being with eyes gleaming like lit candles.

Magnus faltered at the sight, his heart pounding. He scrambled to his feet from his achieved leeway, his breath hitching as he stared at the apparition. "Gayle?" he whispered, hardly believing his eyes. The figure was femme and furry, draped in animal hide, and skeletally thin. Her hair knotted and floated in the still, black water with an oily sheen.

She yanked hard on the cloak, her strength catching Magnus off guard and sending him to his knees. He struggled to regain footing, but her relentless pull dragged him deeper into the muck. Then, as swiftly as she had appeared, she sank back into the trench, pulling him down with her.

Magnus pressed his hands to the ground, mud seeping between his fingers as he nearly submerged. The black water encroached on his face. At that moment, Magnus realized there was no winning, only a compromise. His brooch lowered to the muck, and he went through with it before long.

He fumbled to unclasp his cloak, his fingers fiddling in his folly, slick and grimy. The cloak constricted around his neck like a deadly snake. Magnus felt his face flush. He battled, struggling desperately to breathe, and by some grace, he prevailed, unclasping the broach from his taught cloth.

Peeled away from the black water, he coughed in a fit to breathe again. The assailant, though, had not relinquished his cloak. She clutched it with her rotting fingers as her head sank back into the waste. Magnus watched his long brown dressing slither into the ground, red in the face as he huffed and puffed.

He dove and gripped the tail of his cloak, pulling greatly. The mud regurgitated it with reddish brown chunks that reeked of dead cows and a dank alley's tallow. Flies and maggots were glued to the stained drapery. Magnus winced, his throat wringing up bile. He swallowed, held his breath, and pulled his ruined cloth closer. But the brooch was missing. And so Magnus tossed the cloak aside and dove back in. He clawed at the mud, each hand raking furiously with a fruitless effort.

Magnus stood and left his cloak to the trench. A bitter, battering wind wound through the air and chilled his mud-caked body. Cold and filthy, he discovered he couldn't stand it, his father's voice echoing, demanding he bathe. The mud beneath his fingernails, the splats of brown gunk in his facial hair and eyelashes—he yearned for a dip in a lake.

Magnus cursed his father's old tidy teachings that clung to his mind like one of Erratu's wiggling hairs. Ringing like the tongue of a bell, left to right in his head, his father's curses reverberated. "You son of a bitch," Magnus swore, burdened by their voice.

The tracker took a breath and then resumed. He fought hard for that brooch, wondering if Gayle had taken back what he no longer *deserved*. Then he considered himself caught in the tricks of this mountain. "She's not dead," he laughed. "And she's not forever gone from me. No matter what anyone or thing may suggest."

Magnus channeled his inner Xander and raised a spiteful finger at the mountain. "I'll pull my britches down, up on that summit, and deliver my own peat."

His mouth suddenly dried like a raisin in the sand hills of Endura. Thirsty, his gaze darted to the mud, tempted, his tongue as rough as a dog's. *Maybe just a lick,* he considered. But still, he feared that the *revenant—or replica—* swam down in the soil still.

Just mind games, he thought. What was the harm other than the trace of old boot flavoring the trench? *Well, dysentery,* he weighed. And if he wanted to count the risks, he'd likely find at least five other illnesses inciting some kind of diarrhea. But the mud was wet and seductive, like a fair maiden new to a brothel—or might she be a bitter old hand.

Magnus tried again to trick himself into this fancy. In truth, it did not look good, not like ale, once boiled, nor as swell as a well, but he was parched.

Magnus tested the ground beneath him, kicking at the muck, his boot splashing in the murky water. The light rippled in it. *It's all just a game. A trick of the mind.* He was safe. He told himself so. After all, they had only grabbed his cloak, stolen his brooch—mere scare tactics meant to be deciphered. Magnus scoffed, trying to shake off the unease.

On his knees, his chapped lips parted in a desperate second. He scraped his taste buds along the bitter trail of wet earth, finding some relief, thankful the others weren't around to witness this pitiful act. He really should return to them, he knew, but first, *just one more.*

His lips rounded, he drank in some still water, his tongue still dry as baked wheat in the North Wynd. He stuck out his tongue for a soak again, quick and fleeting. Magnus lowered his head, letting his tongue graze the wet slush, but instead of relief, he felt a sharp pain. Two icy fingers clamped around his tongue, yanking him down forcefully abrupt.

Magnus groaned, confusion and fear flooding his mind. *Why* did it hurt? *Why* weren't the lanterns protecting him? *This couldn't be real. Why would...* His thoughts spiraled as he struggled to comprehend. Perhaps this mimic was shielded from the light by his own shadow, or maybe it lurked so deep in the ground that the light could not reach it. But whatever the reason, Magnus was now trapped in its grip with the lanterns just out of reach.

Magnus, a mere fingerbreadth away from the mush, yielded only a moan for aid, and when he did, the fingers clamped tighter to spite him. His mind scrambled to cook up an escape plan. The thought of cutting his tongue free flashed—not that he meant to do it, *but...*

He could not part with his tongue like he could with the brooch. *No,* he thought definitively. And surely, that was not meant to be an answer.
Surely.

He had a blade, but it took time to garner the will to grasp it, as he'd done so with a simple plan devised. Reaching for his weapon, he fumbled with the hilt, feeling a sharp pinch as the enemy dug *her* nails into his tongue. Finally, Magnus found a firm grasp on his grip and unsheathed his steel. Now, all he must do is raise it single-handedly while pushing himself up with the other hand. He struggled to bring it up between his body and the trench floor, cursing the lies of the lanterns beside him along the way.

The pretender inched her way closer as Magnus pulled his strained tongue, and just in time, he shoved his other hand against the ground, craning his neck. It felt like his tongue was about to tear from his throat, but he gained enough room to swing.

It was done. A severed thumb before him, his tongue intact. But to his horror, the attacker angrily crawled from the muck. Magnus staggered back against the wall, realizing this was not a mimic of Gayle but a man he knew for a fact to be dead. He studied them a moment, their fingers somehow all in a row.

The figure, a young buck dressed humbly, his face unshaven and hair wild, lurched toward Magnus with a crooked gait. Magnus, his heart pounding, sheathed his blade, signaling that he meant no further harm. But the man drew closer, snarling.

"Thee a whoreson to a proud fool," they said, black water spilling through their teeth.

Magnus braced a moment, knowing there would be a clash. His brows knit-down from hearing their *condemning* voice, his body livened by an electrical jolt.

Magnus darted forward, tackling the figure to the ground. The man's knotted hair swayed and then whipped as Magnus pinned him down, teeth grit. And with a swift rise, he stomped hard, intent on sending them back down to *where they were meant to be.*

"I do not want to see you anymore!" Magnus shouted, his voice echoing off the surrounding crescent walls. "Just go back! Go back! Return!" With a forceful shove, he mashed the muckman back into the murky grave, like a potato being crushed into an oily gravy. It was brutal, but Magnus refused to believe that this was real. He couldn't believe it, and his voice was strained ever-so, wearing in and out, damning any truth of it.

"The light keeps any at bay that aren't meant to be here!" he insisted, but despite his words, the remnant, once thought to be Gayle, remained—a severed thumb lying in the mess. It was too thick to be hers, yet it wasn't his attacker's. Magnus dreaded looking at it, yet he couldn't tear his eyes away, tormenting himself with the grotesque sight as it began to writhe and bleed a milky substance.

"This place is strange," Magnus muttered to himself, feeling bizarre, all oddities pressing down on him. "Fuck this," he growled, his patience fraying as he turned to leave the eerie remnants behind.

Magnus returned his gaze to the reaches of the trench and saw that none of the others were within a visible range. Likely far and away they were, he felt, deepening a pit in his belly.

He took up his cloak of grime and flapped it in the wind, shaking free any excess bits. Choking back his urge to vomit, he threw the cloak around his neck and immediately felt the additional weight of carrying it, the wind too frigid to forego it.

Magnus breathed shallowly and stamped on the severed appendage, grinding it beneath the black water before resuming his path.

The fog closed in around him, thick and unyielding, but it wasn't long before he saw it—a corpse, sprawled in the trench ahead. He paused, disbelief mincing his features. "Fuckin' really?" he muttered under his breath. "I've not heard a thousand bells, only the sound of a horn, and yet here death lay."

The body lay flat, blocking the way forward, leaving Magnus with no choice but to step over it. He advanced cautiously, his eyes planted on them. The man before him was dressed in finery: an embroidered golden vest over white silk, the fasteners gleaming faintly in the dim light. His trousers were loose and airy, tucked into long stockings, and his feet were shod in clogs that pointed awkwardly to the side.

But it wasn't the clothes that captivated Magnus; it was the man's face— young, though not too young, with a chiseled chin and dark brown hair pulled back into a neat tail. The features were almost serene, as if frozen in time, untouched by the decay that should have marred them. Magnus stared, unease prickling at the back of his neck, wondering what cruel trick of fate had left this seemingly untouched figure in his path.

The man's heart did not thump, and he smelled like burning tallow. Magnus halted before him, whiffing it, his eyes mired and his mind dull. He stared at the body and was overwhelmed by it, his emotions amok. Where the corpse's thumb was supposed to be, it was but a stump.

Why this place insisted on tormenting him, Magnus did not know, but Rage whirled in his chest, pestering him even when he meant to abandon everything that spiraled around this very body.

Hand on his sword, Magnus placed one foot forward between the body's sprawled legs and then took a wider stride over the corpse, anticipating its stirring—possibly a lunging attack. Magnus felt as tense as a coiled spring, his limbs screwed tight. But as he finally leapt over the body, nothing happened. Magnus let go of his grip and looked back just to make sure the corpse remained still.

The body was bleeding from a deep cut across its stomach, a wide gash spilling thick white milk. Their eyes sprang open, gazing back.

Magnus spat and turned tail.

A baby's cry pierced the veils and staggered him.

He strode.

The cry of the babe waning, waning, gone.

AMARRA was far too wrapped up in thought to notice Magnus was missing, nor would she care even if she had. Her history consumed her, turning all thought upon an outrider: Alvin. Her head was swimming through the trench, memories coming back from armor strewn about, blades stuck into the walls. Signaling the others, her long ears pricked up and fluttered.

"What is it?" Raihn asked.

The others stopped and looked at Amarra for an answer.

She stood there like a frightened deer gawking off into the distance, listening. She heard strange hums and hearkened back to her last dream walk, whence came a silver-eyed boy. It was there that the hums preceded the Afurja Leich. She felt the tangibility in the soil as the hums grew into a pounding, her ankles abuzz. Ducking down, she pulled Raihn along with her.

The others followed suit.

"What's going on?" Pocket asked.

Amarra hopped back up, holding Raihn like a doll, still thinking of Alvin. Her eyes peered over the peak of the trench, skating down the flat muskeg where the fog thinned just enough to reveal a litter of outrider corpses.

She curled closer to her rumbling ankles, Raihn buried against her chest. Fear overcame her, her memories cutting deeper down this parapet.

It wasn't the Leich coming to slay Raihn, but a band of horses carrying men, as her ears deciphered. The men came to slay the exiles and steal their ivory for their palisade.

Hodge glimpsed her, deciphering her peril. Then they loosened, as if from a detection. "I believe I know where we are," said Hodge, dreadfully. "Magnus was indeed right. It isn't a moor. This is the entrapping trench just north of the Ivory Wall—part of a march that certainly should not be upon this mountain. A very unwelcoming border for both sides of the wall, a collision of cultures that begrudge each other. This little depth spans from west to east, accompanied by the ivory adorned stake wall—as in, a wall with sawed horns from exiled Outcast."

She heard, eyes slit open enough to see him. But she was numbed, feeling littler. Visions of horses cascading flashed, and blood filled the snow around her as she saw that field still up north. The voices around her droned into echoes.

The fog parted just enough to prove Hodge's observation correct. The palisade seemed to step forth, biting Amarra with its rows of staked teeth.

Raihn gawped, then inquired, "What grudge?"

"I'm not so sure. A lost lyric in the songs sung of our long endeavors, it seems. As a scholar, I was quite interested in the Afurja, for everything cast out, there must be a root cause. But I tell you, there weren't scribes then…

"Raihn," he started again, his voice low and grim, "this trench was made to impede and ensnare any Outcast that charges southward to that wall. What would come next is a hail of arrows. So decreed the First King: 'No Outcast shall tread our land.' And the marcher lord makes sure to uphold

280

that word. Their bloodline depends on it, ensuring greater privileges than the other wynds."

Amarra shut them out, her palms to her ears, her teeth grit.

RAIHN tugged at her, but she pulled away, her falcate eyes wincing through tears. He looked at her, more worried now, pulling at her hands. She glanced around once more before yanking him back down by the collar. "Amarra, what's wrong?" he asked between breaths as she hovered protectively over him. The others, too consumed by their fears, took little notice of Raihn's plight.

Amarra smothered him, her frantic clutches reopening his wounds. Scratches marred his skin as he winced and groaned. "Amarra, stop," he whispered, stifling his panic.

It seemed eerily quiet over the parapet of soil, where Pocket peered out. "Well, I see nothing," he remarked. "And I hear nothing either."

Meanwhile, Amarra wrestled with Raihn, unintentionally choking him as she pressed him tightly against her chest. His feet kicked as he struggled for breath.

Finally, the thief noticed, his brows furrowing in concern. "Amarra? Hey, I think that's enough. There's nothing to fear, alright?" But she didn't seem to hear him.

Raihn fought desperately against Amarra's frantic grip, clawing at the muscled noose around his neck. "Amarra!" he wheezed. Claustrophobia set in as she pressed him into the mud, guarding him fiercely, as if bracing for an imminent attack. "Please," Raihn begged, his voice suffocating into a whisper.

Lostar watched briefly, his attention grabbed when Pocket's was. He dashed forward, shoved Pocket aside, and attempted to pry Amarra's trunk-like arms away. Pocket stumbled and then joined in, but she wouldn't budge.

AMARRA finally felt their struggle and perceived it as a threat. She turned, snarling at them. They let up, and she seized Raihn's short broad-sword, pointing it at Pocket and Lostar. They fell back, Pocket's hands raised in surrender.

She saw men of a long-thought-over memory of a place, cold and foggy, from the cold footing over soft snow. Amarra saw their dirty old gambesons and thieving hands reaching for her horns. They, with their ivory-cutting saws, come from the moor of Bedfort, south of the muskeg peatlands, meaning to kill her and steal what was close and dear. Their hands bobbed about, her eyes following them. She bared teeth like a wintry wolf from the northern reaches of the muskeg where the firs populated the ridge of Nomankra, the Frinj.

LOSTAR watched as Magnus burst out from behind Erratu, panting like a dog that's been jumping through hoops. And that *dog* seemed confused, hands resting on their knees as they tried to catch their breath. Lostar cared little for them but glanced at Rayah, puzzled by her lack of concern. She stood, arms crossed, as if sealing herself from their troubles.

Lostar disregarded them and unsheathed Truthseeker. In a split second, he contemplated batting away Amarra's stubby stinger, though he wasn't sure where the matter might go from there, so he rallied his courage and first spoke his warning. "I would not regret slicing his blade if it meant easing his breath."

The trench wobbled beneath him, his head floating. He felt unfit for the task but the best suited for it. "You must release him," Lostar continued. "I ask you, lay him down before I harm what actually matters to him."

Hodge bravely stepped between them, gently pushing aside Truthseeker with his palm.

"Hold steady, and not too hasty," he said. "I wouldn't relish a fight between you two." He then addressed Amarra directly, kneeling before her pointed blade. "Amarra, put down the sword. We are your friends and mean no harm to you or Raihn. But you must loosen your hold on him—he can't breathe. Can't you see? Let him go, I beg you, as your friend and his. There is no danger. We're just trailing this old mountain, remember? This be only a flicker of memory."

Her snarls relented, her fierce gaze yielding to the gentleness of his words. Slowly, her eyes became friendlier, as if recognizing reality. She looked at Hodge, her guard lowering.

"I know of you, pale 'Outcast,' as we Eldhonans call you. But you, Amarra, are a legend to some nobles—an Outcast once harbored by another scholar. They say his party was slaughtered by ogorm, beasts that also killed your parents," Hodge said softly, his tone a cautious one. "I don't know the truth of it," he added with a small grin, "but that's what good ol' Alvin attested when he took you into his study."

Magnus cut in, still half-panting, "Then the Ivory's Knight came," he said, drawing their glares toward him, for that seemed a bitter addition.

RAIHN thanked his friends—or tried to—his throat was sore. Amarra had let go, clearly embarrassed by her behavior, though Raihn wasn't unfa-

282

miliar with it. He beheld Amarra in a pensive study. From what Hodge said, he gathered they weren't far from where her parents were slaughtered, but only he knew they were not slaughtered by ogorm.

Raihn breathed in carefulness. "It's okay," he said, harboring no resentment. But it wasn't okay; he was shaking, and he couldn't dare tell them how terrified he was. It wasn't her fault. Both struggled to overcome their history, old and new. But she wouldn't even look at him, as if in shame.

All stole a brief reprieve from the excitement, and Pocket seized the moment to ask Hodge for clarification. "So, this the infamous Line of Bedfort, Crossguard?"

"It is, and the first stand against the Outcasts, should they ever invade," Hodge replied. "With the Wall of Ivory at our backs. This is where the hunters—those outriders—ride out to find the exiled Outcasts, to slay them as sport, and to garner favor among their compatriots and, worse, the favor of the Ivory Knight."

"But why?" Raihn asked. "The White Ravens allow this?"

"The land of man extends further than the trench, and they eagerly watch for those who walk upon it," Hodge said, his gaze distant and glassy. "The true border begins where the trees grow denser—the fir trees. See, we're still on the muskeg. The Outcasts know this, and that's why they exile their own to walk that edge… It's the Frinj. Our slaughtering goes without tampering any peace, so long as it remains within the borderland."

That makes Amarra Frinjen, Raihn thought. "Maybe that's enough," he groaned, sensing the sorrowful aura in her. "I let my curiosity get the better of me, but thank you for answering." He gently touched her knee, lending his soft energy despite struggling with what had just occurred. Uklarta rang in his head, a fresher wound. But he knew it wasn't Amarra's fault. And he kept reminding himself of that.

"Raihn," Hodge addressed. "If we escape this dire mountain, be mindful of what else lurks outside these walls of thorn and these lanterns. If you are found with—"

"I got it, Hodge. Thanks."

CHAPTER THIRTY
Six melting candles

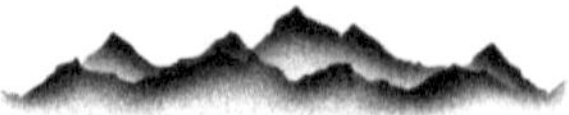

Magnus marched through the trench, pinching the neck of his cloak with its hem dragging behind. With the air calmed, he wondered aloud why no one had said a word about his disappearance, reappearance, or smell.

"Your face isn't that bad," Pocket cracked.

"What?" Magnus stammered. "Can you not see my soaked cloak?"

"Yes," Pocket answered. "It helps mask the smell. I use the same technique: mud smearing."

"No, the blood! Why've you not harped on it yet?"

"What are you on about?" asked Pocket. "You look like you fell face-first into some mud pies. What blood?"

Magnus, bewildered, glanced down at his clothing. There was not a single drop of blood on it, just mud, and he seemed to notice that fact at last.

"Damned mountain," he muttered. "It plays me like a fiddle."

Pocket waved Magnus off and looked ahead.

His eyes popped open wide, and he, annoyingly, slapped Raihn's shoulder out of excitement. "Trees!" the thief exclaimed. "Grass! The end of the trench!"

His excitement seemed to spread, and the party seemed revived with a quicker pace toward the distant end of the trench.

Still a ways off, Raihn could make out the first signs of freedom through the thinning fog—a grassy hill crowned by a cluster of trees.

"Finally, some green again. But I don't understand it," Hodge muttered. "Montanes grow at half altitudes, but we're well beyond half, I'd say."

"Did you not just elaborate we're an ass-hair's length from the north palisade?" Pocket said. "You can't question the altitude of trees at that point; there's no sense in it."

Hodge dashed ahead without a rebuttal. It appeared he took a shine to something: a rock with a small piece of parchment tucked beneath it. "What might this be?"

Raihn bolted after him upon realizing what it was. "Don't!" he called out, his voice full of urgency. "That's mine."

Hodge froze, his hand hovering over the crumpled page. He turned to Raihn, eyebrow raised. "How?"

Raihn softened his tone, deciding to be honest. "It's torn from my brother's journal, the one I always keep with me. I need to know what it says."

Hodge hesitated, looking at the page in his hand before slowly handing it over. "How are you so sure?"

"Because… I found another one earlier while you were all sleeping. I know there are more."

"What does it say?" Magnus asked, creeping closer before Raihn could even start reading.

"Not sure that's our business, Mag," Pocket interjected through the tension.

Magnus glared at the thief, their old rivalry threatening to reignite, but Amarra stepped between them, her presence diffusing the situation. With the brewing conflict at bay, Raihn took a breath, eyes falling on the page in his hands. He hesitated, unsure if he should read aloud.

He sighed, "Maybe it's time everyone knew," and looked to Amarra for reassurance. She nodded gently, giving him the encouragement he needed.

With a deep breath, Raihn read aloud: "As of now, I'm past the gate and inside the mountain. Much has happened since my last entry, as it's been a while since I dared open this book. I haven't even allowed myself to look away from my surroundings.

"All I want is rest, but I sit beneath rock, hiding in the fog. My writing is sparse because I've spilled much ink in my fleeing. And with what remains, I must confess. My heart's desire misled me, and now I feel its weight. A woman from my dreams turned into a nightmare. She is false, for I saw her as she truly was…" Raihn's voice faltered. His eyes lingered on the next line, the words catching in his throat. "She's an Outcast, like me."

The group fell into a heavy silence. Pocket and Hodge exchanged wide-eyed glances. Magnus remained unaffected, and Lostar, as always, stood off to the side, hood drawn.

Raihn swallowed and continued reading. "When she led me to the gate, I found it littered with corpses. She brought the screams of those I inadvertently damned, so their blood wouldn't stain my hands.

"She promised safety for me and the Authority, but I stand here alive, unlike them, with my throat unslashed. I saw her true self and ran with the key she claimed would save me: some strange hand. I followed the stairs, crossed a bridge, and now find myself in a maze, not a mountain. But at the end, I met two figures: a small, ornery man and a petite girl who seemed friendly. Yet, I sensed the little man's distrust. They gave me a chest, swearing it was valuable. A daintier hand rested over it, and it felt heavier than I expected."

Raihn was so absorbed that he nearly forgot he was reading aloud. His nose was practically touching the page as he continued.

"The girl warned me of a looming danger—Uklarta, her sister, and possibly a third. They're coming for me, one spared from the 'eternal dungeon.' My eyes must remain alert. The girl has fled, and I hope she's safe, but I'm not defenseless. I have a whistle imbued with magic. It could solve every-thing, but I seem to have lost it in my panic.

"Now, I am trapped in a place I was driven to, a most-damning rock."

Pocket let out a thoughtful hum. "Now, I'm no expert, but it sounds like there were three o' these women-folk after him, right?"

"There was a third," Rayah answered quietly. "Her name was Larnaskra, but she's no longer with us."

"So, he bested them?" Raihn asked, doubt clouding his voice.

Rayah took a moment *too long* to respond. "Yes. River found a way."

"Without your help?" his voice rose.

"Raihn, I did what I could, just…not at his side," Rayah replied, her voice soft yet defensive.

"What does that mean?" Raihn demanded. "If he bested her, where is he!?"

Rayah didn't answer, leaving Raihn to stew.

He huffed and marched off, his mind tangled in a mess of unanswered questions. He surveyed the ground, determined to find another page. When he finally spotted one, his heart leaped. Kneeling quickly to retrieve it, Ra-yah appeared, her face expressing concern. Raihn snatched it up before she could say a word.

"I know they're close," he read through a feverish mutter. "I can feel them now. It's like something woke up. The mountain trembled, pebbles rolling down like tears, then…silence. I know it's a trap. They're waiting for me."

Raihn glanced up at the trees, the montane ahead looming ominously. He tucked the page into his pocket and, without another word, dashed into the dense thatch. The others kept pace. Erratu pounded the dirt excitedly, and Raihn shared the same enthusiasm, for the cumbersome trench was falling behind them, as was the foul air about it.

"How about we rest?" Hodge asked, his breath labored as he struggled to keep stride.

"Not yet," Raihn replied.

"Not all of us are spring chickens."

Raihn shrugged. "Then, by all means, catch up when you can spring. The path will lead you back to me."

Hodge, undeterred, called after him, "Raihn, I get it. You're on the verge of something big. But discoveries can wait. I'm not asking for a break just for myself—look at Lostar. If you took a second to really see, you'd notice why there's concern."

Raihn spun around, frustration simmering. He was about to dismiss Hodge's words when he finally noticed the rest of the group sheathing be-hind. Lostar, in particular, was struggling—barely keeping his footing. And then, without warning, he collapsed face-first into the dirt.

Pocket rushed over, crouching beside him. "Are you alright?" Lostar didn't respond, so Pocket offered a hand.

Lostar pushed him away. "Get off me," he growled, his voice muffled by the dirt. He swatted at the air. "Damn flies," he muttered, though there weren't any flies at all. There hadn't been any bugs.

Raihn walked back to the group, uncertainty weighing on him as he looked from one weary face to the next. He wasn't sure what they should do, but he finally understood that pressing on without rest might be a bad call.

Magnus didn't seem bothered, but Raihn knew better than to assume that meant he was indifferent. Magnus was always observing. He had to think there was more to Lostar's collapse than exhaustion, even if he wasn't saying it out loud. Magnus stamped on the ground and hoisted Lostar back to his feet.

"I got it," Lostar muttered, too proud.

"If you had it, you wouldn't be on the ground, would you?" Magnus shot back, his tone sharp but not cruel.

Lostar swayed on base, like a toddler learning to walk. Raihn's gut tightened.

Hodge's voice cut through the tense silence. "He needs rest. This isn't something he can just walk off."

"No!" Lostar fought back. "We have to keep moving."

Raihn glanced. *Why was Lostar pushing himself this hard?*

"Why do you always refuse to take care of yourself?" Hodge asked, his frustration plain.

Lostar stated swiftly, "We need that page."

Everyone's eyes turned to Raihn, and he could feel the pressure of their stares as they awaited his call.

"I'm sorry," he muttered. "We should rest."

It was dark, but it continued to deepen. The forest nearly vanished into an abyss, its sprawling branches looming ominously over the weary travelers. Raihn could see nothing beyond the reach of the lanterns that uneased him back to his childhood—lying in bed, feeling that eerie sense of some unseen foe watching him from outside his bed curtain. But where it had once been pure imagination now felt probable, the valleys dungeoness to those paupers he once saw, perhaps folk whom swam off current. Next thing Raihn knew, his mind played tricks, Xander's face in the dark. *Nay, he was home. Lucky bastard.* But it wasn't luck. *Not really.* Xander was selfish, but the others remained, and maybe that was something Raihn should be more thankful of.

A wave of queasiness swept over. He sat down on the path, gazing ahead with his guard up, his thoughts tangled in the uncertainty of what lay ahead. And while he wrestled his unease, the others slumbered peacefully, their breaths steady as they lay sprawled out in their own lanes.

Hodge's voice broke, nearly causing Raihn to jump out of his skin. "It's not his fault, you know."

Raihn clutched his chest, trying to steady his racing heart. "What?" he stammered, catching their gaze from across. "I thought you were asleep. What is it, Hodge?"

"Lostar," Hodge made clear, his tone calm, cheek and lips bubbling out from his pillow-made hand. "You must be thinking about him—why he's been acting so strange. If I'm not mistaken, he's a drinker."

"Yeah."

"Now, forgive me for prying, but I could see it on your face before. You looked, dare I say, unsympathetic?" asked Hodge.

"No, that is not true," Raihn denied. "I mean, I didn't mean to look that way."

"Meaning to look that way and feeling that way, or exuding that feeling, are different things," Hodge mused.

Raihn considered choosing his words more carefully. "It's just, I think it is more complicated than that," he stammered. "He just needs to…heal. But he seems to sneak drinks out of the blue. And it can be, I don't know, scary. I don't like to see him that way."

"What is so frightening about it?"

"He can be unpredictable, for one," Raihn answered.

"Ah, yes, the lack of foresight can be something to fear. If I had that foresight, then might Herb still walk among us…"

"Well, it is his own beast to slay, I suppose," said Raihn, still on the matter of Lostar. "I will leave it at that. I tried to help."

After a brief silence, Hodge added, "Care for those who cannot care for themselves, lest we not be taken care of when we also need it most and be left by our sons and daughters and friends."

"But how can I help him when he refuses to help himself?"

"Remove your boots and walk with his feet," replied Hodge. "Barefooted, you might feel the struggle, whatever that may be. I will not pretend to know his past, but I would likely guess it was not an easy one to survive. He carries with him simic, and yet…well, here he is," said Hodge. "His fight is not over. This is a battle that cannot be won quicker than it has been endured."

"Perhaps you should have been a poet," Raihn laughed.

"And why is that?"

"Poems sound nice," Raihn said simply. "But I never know what they're getting at. You're also a—what's a good, scholarly term? An astute fellow."

Hodge grinned, nodded, and turned over. "Goodnight, Raihn."

"Sleep well, Hodge."

After allowing Hodge to fall away in slumber, Raihn pushed himself up to search for another page of River's journal. Not that he wasn't concerned about Lostar; it was merely that Raihn's instincts told him that finding the journal entries was of the utmost importance. Whether true or not likely debatable to the others had they been aware.

After glancing to ensure the others were sleeping, Raihn took up his satchel and surveyed the area. After scrounging as best he could in the limited light, there was a loud snap. *A twig, perhaps?* Whatever it was, it hadn't come from his group. The realization hit him like a stone in the gut. No one in the party had moved, and there hadn't been a sign of animals since they'd set off.

His heart quickened.

It's nothing, he tried to reassure himself. *The lanterns will keep us safe.* He clung to that small comfort, though it felt thin, almost fragile. Still, it was enough to push him forward, his curiosity pulling him toward the source of the sound, the backside of the lanterns.

As he moved cautiously through the light, something caught his eye. Just at the edge of the lantern's glow, a figure. Raihn froze, his breath catching in his throat. The shape was slumped against a tree, unmoving. Might it be one of those helpful strangers from a ways back and down. His feet moved before his mind could catch up, drawing him closer. His upper body leaned into the light as he strained to make sense of what he was seeing. *Horns?* His stomach dropped. *An Outcast.*

"River?" Raihn's voice came out as a near-breathless whisper. He stepped closer. His eyes adjusted to the gloom, the flicker of lantern light casting just enough of a glow to see.

River sat with his back against the tree, unmoving. His hand clutched a wadded piece of parchment, and a slit ran across his wrist, blood trailing down his arm. A sharp rock, still stained with blood, was in his other hand.

The sight hit Raihn like a battering ram, forcing him to his knees. He stared at the body in disbelief, his mind sluggish to process what lay before him. River was gone and had been for some time.

Raihn felt cold, nearly too dazed to mourn, as he'd never accepted their death before this moment. They were merely lost, but this was a hard confirmation. He contained his anguish, sparing the arousal of his companions, still demanding answers. *Surely,* Rayah knew of River's demise. *Why did she say that River had bested his foes when he clearly had not?* Raihn found some hope in those words only to have it dashed so cruelly. Perhaps he'd find the truth in the balled-up journal entry waiting in River's stiff palm.

He raised himself to his knees and leaned forward further, reaching for the crumpled, dotted red page. He stretched through the glow again for a second, and in that second, he was ensnared again in Uklarta's trap. She, whose belly was noticeably plump and firm, sprung from behind the tree in the nether of light, seizing Raihn's right hand in a death grip. She'd weaved a wicked grin, proud of her web.

Raihn's adrenaline surged, and he lunged forward, his instincts taking over. His knees anchored him in the light. And with his left hand, he grabbed River's rock and slashed at Uklarta's wrist.

For a fleeting moment, a glimmer of excitement stretched across her face.

Raihn swung the stone again, but she caught his wrist, her fingers clamping down like a bear trap. Her glee was just as toothy as she bent his palm back, forcing the rock from his grasp. Under her power, Raihn felt as malleable as steel in a furnace, her eyes glowing like jade coals in the dark, her breath a plume of sulfuric heat.

"Ohurmarr," Raihn breathed through a quiver. *Monster.*

He felt helpless, objectified as her plaything. At any moment, she could whisk him from the lantern light, but she seemed to derive pleasure from his fear, her other hand disappearing between her thighs. Her eyes, intrusive, distressing, gleamed. They holstered any bravery he had, taking him captive.

Slowly, like a weighed anchor, his knees were drawn toward the outer perimeter as if she were tugging him ashore before her free hand drifted back, snailing over his fingers.

Raihn grimaced and collapsed onto his belly, his feet dragging behind him now, not just his plowing knees. His fingers were forced into a spread, where she began tonguing the webbing between them. He couldn't look anymore, his sight subdued, like his voice. He felt her serpent muscle glaze his skin, then wrap his finger, her teeth lightly itching the base of it.

Raihn's throat tightened, choking words that struggled to escape—a voice caught like a furled sail in the wind. Just as his feet began to slip from the path, a firm grip seized his ankles.

"I've got ye!" Lostar shouted.

"Lostar!" Raihn cried out. "Please don't let go!"

The Enduran held on tight while Raihn hovered just beyond the light. She'd not let up, and Raihn wondered if she merely gamed with them. Whether or not it was hubris that kept Uklarta from pulling Raihn away from the Enduran, Lostar's intervention allowed the others time to arrive and grab hold of Raihn's ankles, too.

Raihn felt he was being stretched upon a rack, his ankles and wrists tugging in opposite directions. Uklarta seemed to relish the struggle, her eyes glinting with some dark amusement…until Amarra emerged from the shadows. Her grip on Raihn's shoulders became firm as she met Uklarta's gaze with a fierce glare, daring them to continue. *Please don't,* Raihn thought.

For a moment, Uklarta's smug expression wavered as Raihn's body shifted ever so slightly towards Amarra. The pale Outcast was strong. Stronger, perhaps, than Uklarta had expected.

"Guys! Do something before my arms are torn off," Raihn yelled, beginning to feel like a soft cotton ball.

In her dismay, Uklarta's claws dug into Raihn's knuckles. He stifled yelps to starve the woman of her pleasures, but his suffering would only worsen if his friends continued to pull.

Lostar pulled away and drew his bow. But upon pinching an arrow, he fumbled it to the ground.

"You fool!" Magnus blasted, as apparently he was there as well.

But, Raihn struggled to see them all past his shoulders. Erratu, though, remained at bay, Rayah there calming him. Raihn called for him, begging.

"No, Erratu," Rayah denied him. "I've interfered enough."

"But he hasn't!" Raihn reasoned. "Please!"

Erratu pounded the ground, tangled between them, his indecision briefly flickering until coming to a distressing head. Erratu had decided, already across the lanterns after a leap. His snarl loomed over Uklarta, bearing down upon her like a toothy gargoyle before he seized her arms. His mighty clamps forced the witch to relinquish her grip; her fingers raked out from pain. A roar from his belly followed his behemoth fist into her chest, which sent her tumbling like a dry weed into the abyss. After a satisfied huff, he waddled to the path.

Raihn was safe in the light again, now pulled over a pile of his allies like a net over fish, blood dripping from bloodied gills in his knuckles.

"You couldn't just wait?" Rayah finally snapped, stomping to him, her hand upon her hip.

Raihn shrugged, knowing he was wrong, but buckled, "Oh, so it's 'you' now, not thee?"

"Couldn't just allow Lostar to rest?" She continued.

Raihn, untangling himself from the pile, rose and clamped his hands within his pits for pressure. *She's right,* but her frustration fed his own. "How come you can never give me the full truth? Always tiptoeing around every subject. You're no better than Ghor! That's my brother over there! Dammit. I knew there was more to read. And this is the only way I might ever hear from him again," he said, raising the wadded entry.

"Well then, go ahead. See what it says," Magnus prodded through a whine, dusting himself off; his voice was tinged with annoyance and a strange curiosity.

Raihn unraveled the wad and smoothed it out. He looked to it a moment, his expression turning grim. "No, that can't be right."

"What's wrong?" Hodge asked.

Raihn flipped over the page and saw only a blank sheet.

Magnus sighed, his shoulders relaxing. "Raihn, what may or may not be written does not matter. You knew who he was," he said calmly, as if relieved.

Raihn shrugged off Magnus's sage words and balled up the page, holding it tight. "She lured him here," he said, picking the threads in his skull.

"Right, Rayah? Just like I was lured. She was that golden maiden…in his dreams."

"What are you saying?" Hodge asked.

"She's a dream walker… My brother wrote of a woman inside the journal as if she were his bastion. She brought him to the gate. It was her. She cleared the way for him and stole him from home. She killed those men, not a bear."

"He bested her," Rayah said. "Don't let her win lest his sacrifice be in vain. You, too, can beat her."

"Don't subjugate his memory to your own goal," Raihn shook out. "I'm not giving up for his sake, not yours." A thought took hold of him, guiding his inquiry. "But tell me," he continued, his tone tapering, "how did he get outside the path? How did she reach him? He wrote, detailing where he might roam in the last entry as if there were no lanterns."

Rayah's gilded expression melted. "The right precautions were not yet taken," she said, gesturing to the lanterns. "Even those like us learn."

"You knew of her before, and yet you left him alone, completely unprotected?"

"I had to fight them alone," her voice rattled. "Don't you think I get scared? I loathe the breakage of my bones, snapping time and time again, but I keep fighting. They left me shattered until Ghor, of all people, had to sled me up the mountain. I have died twice. Once for him, and once for you…"

That seemed a prickly plight of hers, Raihn noted.

Her tone flicked back to the matter at hand. "They brought River here for their gains. It's their first objective in this campaign. River could only stop them by removing himself from their path, but now, with you, it doesn't matter. If you have even a fraction of your brother's commitment, you'd not throw yourself—" her voice cut as she seemed to reevaluate what she was about to say.

"River didn't want to leave home," she began again, "but he knew he had a purpose. He didn't want to die, but he knew what had to be done. Instead of mourning his death, celebrate his success and learn from it. Be inspired and don't let them win…for his sake."

Raihn trembled in place. Rage bubbled beneath his skin, and it boiled over as he threw the wad at Rayah's face, leaving her stunned. He, overcome with frustration, lost any inkling of right and wrong. "I don't know how long you've been here," he said, "but if you've ever had any humanity in you, you've forgotten it. Whatever he did. If it saved all of the world-or-whatever, great. But it doesn't mean it hurts any less. If I wasn't made livid, then might there be something amiss; I am human."

Rayah relented, seemingly reflecting on her humanity, and heeded Raihn's passion.

"She burned my village," Raihn continued. "I mean, it must have been her," he breathed. "But first, she molested my dreams under his face, and then she… And later, lain these pages here under rocks for me to find." His right hand clenched the grip of his sword. "I'll put an end to her games."

"You understand what that entails. I know you do," Rayah said. "The reason you were ensnared. You saw her belly. I told you before…"

"Pardon?" Hodge said. Then he stiffed and shut his mouth, conscious that it was likely a private matter.

"It's okay, Hodge. I apologize for my frustration," Raihn said. "Rayah alluded to…Uklarta's pillaging—the very thing Magnus was so adamant to know about—what she relayed outside the cave is that Uklarta holds my seed," he admitted, glancing at Magnus, aware of their curiosity.

"Raihn," Rayah persisted. "Look at me."

Raihn ground his teeth. "I hear you," he replied, his eyes burrowed down.

"She manipulates you because you are human. She wants your anger to fester… Is that satchel, that chest, not heavy? Don't you listen?"

"Does he not deserve a break from a moral high ground?" asked Pocket.

"He feeds seeded animosity, and he will end this trek swiftly," Rayah argued. "She will win."

"A lesser man makes excuses, I know," Raihn said. "My father assured me of that, but I can't bow down to your made-up rules just as well."

"Your desires lead you astray. You just cannot see it because it is **him** inside of you," Rayah insisted.

Raihn assumed she meant his father and became red in the face, or so he felt. And within his ears, angry whispers clasped him. The satchel became heavier, just as she mused it might be, making him all the angrier. "You are not my sculptor; I am not your stone!" Raihn barked defiantly. "Nor my father's. I will steal out my bastard seed."

"…Right. Of course," Rayah's eyes dimmed, "I suppose you are human after all. And what you do is up to you, not me. I shan't interfere. If it is the rage you succumb to, then I will have an answer and remain here indefinitely…"

Her meaning was lost on him, but it mattered not. He spun his back from the others' pitying eyes. And the satchel was so heavy, he dropped it to the dirt, spurring a gasp from the steward.

Wondering who else may take it up, Amarra was the quickest to answer.

Some time had passed as they lined the path, brooding. The air was stiff with tension, a lingering effect from the intense temp from earlier. Raihn considered inquiring about Larnaskra, but his pride held him back after his outburst.

He began to dwell on it, wondering if he was wrong and how Amarra, now carrying the satchel, felt about the situation. Just as he glanced over at her, a strange glow permeated the forest, casting a red-like hue. Beyond the path, a great light flickered, and six figures, aflame, staggered. They howled, stumbling towards the lanterns before collapsing, rolling in desperate attempts to extinguish their great, horrible flames.

Raihn tensed. "Is this her doing? Or is this the work of the mountain?"

Rayah gawped at the inferno, seemingly as shocked as the others. "It's her."

"You think my wish for a vengeful murder is still in poor taste? It's already too late, Rayah," he huffed. "I had no choice before. I killed one of those cannibals. Why pretend I'm any better than…a killer."

"Now is an inappropriate time to prove your point," Rayah replied.

Raihn knew it was true. "You're right," he sighed. "We should do something."

"No," said Rayah. "She knows we can't, which is why she did it."

"Well, can't you pull them in?" asked Raihn. "Extinguish the flames? Look at them!"

She panted, her eyes alight from her glance. "I do as thou commands—the wavering flame, made sick from its lengthy post." Her tone shifted into a steady gait, her eyes firm, revealing this duo-like persona.

"By who!?" asked Raihn. "Who would tell you to let them suffer?"

"It matters not," said Rayah. "Better is it they perish once more."

"How could—what? 'Once more'?" Raihn stammered.

"It's another one of Uklarta's traps," Lostar mumbled, swaying. "Don't f-fall for it yet again."

"Haven't you noticed?" Hodge mused. "By my count, there are six of them, and six of us."

"Now thee understands—a theatrical display by Uklarta," Rayah said.

Lostar dropped his bow into his hand, hastened an arrow's fletching beside his cheek, then loosed it; a miss.

"Don't sulk now! Try again," Magnus belted.

Lostar took a moment, anchoring another arrow as well as his breath. Then, with a swift release, the arrow soared and delivered his mercy. One by one, the Enduran's arrows quickly found the remaining five targets, graciously sparing them from further agony. But then a seventh figure came, stumpy, screaming and hollering—though not ablaze. "Don't!" they screamed, flailing. Out of the forest stumbled the frantic figure, his ragged voice piercing the tense air. Ghor. "Let me in," he cried.

"He had his chance," Magnus muttered.

Unlike Erratu and the girl, Ghor was barred from entry, spurned by whatever protection shielded them.

Raihn's pulse quickened. He could feel the panic rising as he looked between Ghor and the others. "Rayah, we can't just leave him out there," he pleaded.

Rayah's expression remained stubborn. "The banished must remain so," she said.

Raihn's frustration boiled over. "But you can bring him back, can't you…?"

She ignored him, her gaze cast to the fire.

"You may as well damn him to an execution," Raihn carried on. "A village is governed by its lord, fine, but doesn't that mean the people should still look out for each other?"

"That is a dangerous way to think," she warned.

"And yet, I just want to save a life," Raihn shot back, his frustration turning sharp.

Rayah's eyes hid behind the fire's reflection as she spoke with a calm authority. "People need leaders because many cannot lead themselves. Responsibilities must be upheld by those willing to carry them out. But the selfish, they are too weak for it…"

"I only get to live once," Raihn argued. "I'd rather not spend that life under an iron fist, but you seem fine with it. Back in my stead, you'd be tightening your grip over feudal lords in some kind of creeping autocracy."

Rayah's patience snapped. "Then make the best of it! Make it better for others, even!" She pressed a hand to her forehead and sighed. "But you…will never understand."

"What about you? You got a second chance," he pointed out. "I saw you in shambles while I was numb."

Rayah faltered, her gaze softening. For a moment, she had no response. The silence stretched between them as she lent considerable eyes to Ghor, whose pitiful gaze reached up at them.

Her expression cracked, and a heavy sigh escaped her chest. "Grab hold," she said, wary but willing, extending her hand toward Ghor.

Ghor's meaty hook clasped her with a desperate grip, but before either could react, an unseen force yanked him back into the forest, Rayah along with him. Erratu's guttural howl vibrated through the earth as he pursued, dirt flying in his wake.

Hodge froze in place, his face pale as he watched them vanish. "She's gone," he said, a little firmer than a sorrowful hum.

"But she came back once. Perhaps she can again," Raihn inserted.

"I doubt it," Magnus snipped. "We don't know if there's such a thing as third chances. She failed the second she was to permit Ghor back on the path. It's her fault…and yours."

"He is not to blame but unfortunate circumstance," Hodge declared. "His heart was in the right place, and you can't fault him for that."

"Look, Ghor isn't great," Raihn began, "but if she got a second chance, then perhaps he deserved one as well. Maybe he learned," he reiterated.

"Keyword being 'maybe,' and 'maybe' is a risk," said Magnus.

"Words from a man who gave up," Lostar slurred, staggering closer.

"Says the lone drunkard, far from home, looking for someone else to protect," Magnus retorted through his teeth. "I had you made as soon as I seen that blade. One only a thief or a failure would carry."

"Rayah has been missing for seconds and already we bicker," Raihn said. And before he could scoff, a rustle drew his attention towards the fiery fog.

And just after Magnus groaned how Ghor wasn't even saved, they stumbled out with minor wounds, entering the path without strain.

"What of Rayah?" Magnus inquired hastily.

"She's gone," Ghor replied.

"Then how did you make it?"

"Bait sometimes finds itself off the hook. Rayah was the real prize."

"And you just left her?" Raihn asked, disgusted.

"What was I supposed to do?" asked Ghor. "It's better for one of us to get out of there than neither of us. I didn't realize what was happening until I escaped."

"Do you still believe saving this worm was the right choice, Raihn?" Magnus sneered.

"It was the right thing to do," Lostar said, his hand swatting the air as if fending off flies, "but the wrong outcome."

Disregarding that, Ghor wished to know what induced Lostar's limp-wrist.

"He appears to be swatting away his breath," Magnus quipped.

"That's enough," Raihn said, then demanded they get on.

"Someone's had enough of this place," Ghor remarked.

With each passing remark, Raihn regretted his decision more.

CHAPTER THIRTY-ONE
A cloud of flies

LOSTAR plowed through the earth as though it were a seafloor, his barnacled heels dragging, fists tied into salty knots—sweat sating him, dragging him into deep suffering. The others, though plodding, blurred speedily through the forest. But that did not matter. Seclusion was sating. Loneliness bottled in his chest, dry and harsh, nothing like the warmth of his favorite mead, but painfully reminiscent of home.

"The worst, isn't it?" a taunt floated behind him.

Without a glance, Lostar recognized them. Ambroseah. "Why're you here?" he muttered.

"I'm here because we both made mistakes," Ambroseah said, her tone smooth, teasing. "My back already clawed, they've still yet cut into yours."

"You nag in my ear like the flies."

She chuckled, her shadowy presence flickering in his peripheral vision. "The night is nigh. After brooding through the day, you'll brood through the night when the dark is most heavy."

"Be gone from me, fly."

"So you may sulk in peace?" she pressed. "You cannot see the path ahead with eyes cast upon your feet. Raihn is right there, treading almost as heavy."

Lostar shook his head, bitterness curling his lip. "No need for a vagrant such as I to saddle an already burdened mule. Lest he buckle, both of us only suffering together."

"Is it better to suffer alone?"

"He has her," Lostar vaguely gestured ahead. "Amarra, and she's better protected him. And thanks to me, Tepparna's gone from her. I'll not ruin another pair by wedging myself in as a third horse in this race. Not when that girl is dead because of the sand in my boots. I killed her—egging her on as I did, thinking of you."

Ambroseah's face twisted into something colder at the corner of his sight.

"True," she said, her voice losing its mocking edge. "But some paths remain unbroken, no matter how fiercely you chisel at them. Hers was a clandestine one."

"Be gone, fly. I will reach the end of my path, slow as it may be. Then I'll be free of you."

"A slow stride. Yes, because there are flies worse than I in your ear," she replied. "Accept it. The truth. You'd not fit the throne with the likes of me, but the lesser evil, in my miraged stead."

Lostar's teeth ground together from her probing words. Yet, deep down, he wanted to keep denying her, if only to keep her there, needling at his guilt. But the air quieted. He glanced around, uncertain. There's nothing but the trees.

"I know," **RAIHN** replied to Hodge. "But it feels like we're so close, and Uklarta is getting desperate. I feel like we can make it."

"If you say so," Hodge sighed defeatedly.

Magnus agreed with Raihn, albeit harshly, "You ask for too much rest and lack discipline. I say let's get this over with."

"Give him a break, eh?" Raihn said.

Hodge placed a hand on Raihn's shoulder, nodding as if to thank him. Then, turning to Magnus, he said, "I know what you saw in that cave, and I know what your regret is. But the fact of the matter is, you made the right choice already. Stop paining me by regretting it."

Magnus stamped up the hillside like a pissed-off pony and remained at the top, *at least kind enough* to await Raihn and the others.

It was finally conquered after some tiresome effort—effort that left Hodge nearly collapsing onto his knees over the ridge. "Okay, now I'm resting," he panted.

"We'll unwind here as best we can," Raihn declared. "Thank you for pushing on, Hodge."

Then he took a moment, his gaze brushing past flanking trees. And the light peppering between them. Something amiss took the horizon—they were short a man.

"Where's Lostar?" Raihn fretted.

"Huh?" Pocket said, glancing around with a start. "He was with us a minute ago."

LOSTAR was halted by another shadow: a man dressed in thin robes, encrusted with the sands of Endura, that draped over his hands and feet.

"Oleandor," Lostar greeted bitterly.

"You understand I do not seek war as your consort did," Oleandor replied calmly.

"You both agreed upon the same treason," Lostar spat.

"And yet, if she had her way, the Eldhonans would have our metal down their throats, and you would be left to rot in your cell. Her death and your

298

cowardice allowed my reign, leaving you murderous. You, a vagrant, lost in a strange realm."

Lostar's anger flared, bitterness rising from the lecturing of a traitor.

"I crushed the disquieted rebels and rallied the soldiers of Lakewane," Oleandor continued. "I made a promise: to guard them—as a Gar was meant to guard the Elgar."

Lostar pointed Truthseeker at Oleandor's throat, but they prattled on.

"Even now, you can't shake the sand from your boots. You sulk—a lowly vagrant, without his ring, forsaking his vows."

Lostar, enraged, whipped back the blade and lunged—but stumbled and collapsed at Oleandor's feet. He felt a stream as cold as a river trickling down his hair as he lay there.

"Might this satiate your thirst for a haze?" Oleandor mocked.

Lostar glanced up, seeing a tipped flagon in Oleandor's hand. He tasted the stinging nectar, spat it out, and rose to his feet. He wobbled on his hindfoot, then forefoot. Whipping his hair back, he raised his sword.

Oleandor held out the flagon. "Forgo your weakness, vagrant," he said, unyielding.

Lostar swung yonder the flagon, splitting the horizon. The dirt shook beneath Lostar's heels, and voices seemed to beckon beside each of his ears.

Oleandor did not fall away—instead, he sprouted oil-black plumage. Lostar's anger evaporated, replaced by fear from the greatest fly—a raven. The lanterns rattled, much like his hands, as the winged beast reached for Truthseeker with its beak. They clamped onto it, and Lostar struggled, battling for the sword until he pulled it free. He swung. The nightmarish Corvus was shorn. Black feathers fluttered over a red spurt as a murder of crows gathered into a screaming burden.

In his haze, Lostar could almost understand them.

"Stawp! Stawp!"

The large raven stumbled, its talons wavering, wings flapping like black flags.

It felt wrong, but *why?* The large raven cawed with a strange guile, sounding almost joyous. Its quills looped as the bird vanished. And to the ground, a quill settled into the earth's bosom—a lonely feather:

"Pocket?" Lostar stammered in disbelief. Was it truly him? *Did he...?* How cruel—this mountain. The realization stung worse than any vision—worse than the nose-hair-scorching scent of an Eldhonan tannery. Lostar stood over Pocket, noticing the shadowy wing of his sword lingering over them. Lostar gasped, fingers unfurling. His sword was relinquished of his grip, touching down momentarily until plucked.

There was no recourse. The sable birds closed in: Raihn, Hodge, Magnus—all of them. But it was Raihn who shoved Lostar, leveling Truthseeker at his chest. "Stay back," he warned.

"Come now, it's not that bad." Pocket chuckled through what looked like a sudden tinge of pain. "The more you fret over me, the more you'll worry me."

Hodge rushed an inspection. "Luckily, it isn't deep," he reported.

"I must admit, I am light on my feet," the thief added.

"Not light enough," Hodge countered. "A cut is a cut."

"So, what do I need? Some salt, pepper, lemon?" asked Pocket.

"Perhaps if you were a fresh fish," Hodge jested. "Nay, I haven't anything…other than my will, but where there is a will, there is a way. Amarra, if you would be so kind as to find your cloak ever smaller, I would be most grateful. I need a dressing."

After dressing the wound, Hodge sputtered, "Now, it would be wise to keep off your legs. We wouldn't want to tax the body."

Pocket dismissed his advice: "I can walk."

Hodge became insistent. "Just because you can, doesn't mean you should."

"It be my chest that's wounded, aye? Not my legs," Pocket retorted.

Raihn, still with the sword pointed, honed authority. "I don't want you to move or agitate the wound. Amarra will carry you, I'm certain." He exchanged a glance with her. She nodded.

Pocket shook his head. "I've had cuts before, and I never threw myself over a chirurgeon's table nor sought out a throng of well-doers, and certainly no barber—not that they'd like to have me with my stolen petals or my things for trade. It's but a mere scratch. I've suffered worse encounters with calculi stones, cutting up things more fragile than my belly. And I walked then."

"Ignorant fool," Magnus blew. "How do you still roam?"

"By the grace of my luck an' the skill of my craft." Pocket's voice trailed off as he strained to speak. "Lucky I was once that a traveler came upon me when I was off alone, sick. She treated me kindly, seeming to take pity upon this poor thief—a wisewoman, I guess. But I trust no word of the wise. Keep your valerian, I say."

Hodge gazed yonder. "By my guess, essence of valerian may linger in the miasma of this ambiguous mountain, or other hallucinogenic essences, and I wonder if it makes us dull butter knives." Hodge glanced in wonder at Ghor, who remained silent. His attention glided back to the thief. "I was once a scholar, but I, like you, am just a rogue," he said. "So, I speak more in our kinship. Take my aid, you damned, ignorant stray, Pocket."

Pocket seemed to set aside his pride as he relented. "Okay! If…the nice gal doesn't mind."

Amarra snorted with a grin, then effortlessly plucked Pocket off his feet and cradled him in her arms. With the satchel and the thief in tow, Amarra seemed like a walking wagon.

Now that Pocket was taken care of, Raihn returned to the Enduran at the tip of the pointed sword. "Where is it?"

Lostar regained focus after being absorbed in all their lovable chatter. "Where is what?" he replied.

"Dammit all, you're drunk! The drink you had—where?"

"Absolutely sozzled, brother," the thief added.

Raihn glimpsed Pocket, unamused, and then returned a glare. "You were slashing at the air, like your tongue, and stumbling! Pocket came to disarm you in fear of what might come of your state—and for fear of you harming yourself!"

Hodge's finger interrupted with a caution wave. "Allow me to propose another ailment on the same spectrum," he said.

Raihn huffed. "What might that be?"

"You see, if a fellow drank heavily to the point his body became accustomed to it—and I mean heavily, making ale seem like well water—then suddenly being restricted from that habit could have almost the same effect as if he were still inebriated." Glancing at the look of confusion on the others' gawking faces, Hodge added more simply, "I'm saying withdrawal."

"There is such a thing?" Raihn asked.

"How are you certain it's not the mountain?" Pocket inquired.

"I'm not," Hodge answered truthfully. "It could be both. I've only read about it." Pocket snickered, but Hodge continued. "From what I've read, I can understand that there are symptoms on display here: the dripping sweat from his brow and the way he shakes. Worst of all, though, are the hallucinations. I believe that's why he was slashing at thin air, you see. Though again, perhaps it's this unrelenting fog, or—"

"The fog," Magnus interjected. "I seen its conjuring before. I don't fault him, believe it or not."

"Don't tell me it's all in my head," Lostar snapped.

Hodge took a breath, maintaining his composure. "It has a name. They call it delirium. His body is struggling to endure withdrawal…"

"Well, whatever it is, he is a danger to us all and should be relinquished of his arms so that I may sleep better with at least one eye shut," said Magnus.

"I thought you didn't fault him?" Raihn asked.

"I don't, but it doesn't make me feel any safer."

"Well, his sword is already gone from him," Raihn pointed out.

"And still, I feel no safer," Magnus said.

Hodge patted himself down in search of something. His eyes lit up as he made a suggestion.

Lostar, a marshaled vagrant, shorn of highborn status, had his palms clammed together by Hodge's last tag of rope. Directed by shepherds, his thighs wagged like old tale-bearers, crone-made knees buckling with little will, until rest was decreed just a howl before nightfall.

Ghor sneered a twisty-lipped muse, "Enjoy it."

There was grit between Ghor's teeth that rubbed Lostar's ears raw. They snickered in a way that suggested darker shadows were encroaching.

Amarra docked Pocket into a comfortable nook, then went to Raihn not far.

RAIHN later stirred from a lonely dream. Everyone slept but Lostar, glowing from their nearest lantern, whispering to what appeared to be a large oak barrel. Planted on a boulder, his hands were unbound, bouncing off his knees rapidly.

Raihn peered over Amarra's shoulder as he and she braced against the cold. Without a blanket, Lostar hid most of themself ahead, within their cloak, just their hands in the biting wind. It seemed to get colder the higher they went, the squalling wind coming and going only to berate the party.

Lostar curtained their cloak's folds together, its fabric taut over their lurching posture. They whispered. Too faint for Raihn to discern. The flickering lantern light battled their shadow, and they, bedeviled, rocked as if despair pulled out a desperate prayer.

Raihn's gaze fell on a strange cactus branding on the barrel's spigot. Though the nozzle shone Eldhonan copper, this was no Eldhonan drink, making it all the more peculiar—and stranger still, Raihn witnessed its trick over another. For all he knew, there had never been a shared vision. But, clearly, not all the tricks of the mountain's crags had been revealed—if its tricks were even finite—it a dungeon eternally, it felt.

Raihn sounded off his approach with a meager cough so as not to put Lostar in a start. His weight carried itself down to the rock, finding it softer than he expected, with a fine surface to it. The space between him and Lostar aired his intended comfort and respect. But his gaze opposed the barrel with ire, his tone yet to contrast that regard. *What a deviant trick by the mountain,* he thought. They were tasked with conquering the mountain, but it fought them to an edge.

For a time, they kept to themselves within each other's company. Raihn hoped it said enough on his behalf, anxious of what else to speak. Lostar wasn't drinking nor sick from the sky-scraping height, just suffering through the determination to keep straight.

"So, it was your seed she was after," Lostar began. It seemed on his mind, only just now bringing it up. "Speak on it if you'd like, or let me know if I harp."

Raihn sighed. "I don't know… I mean, first time…seeding," he gestured uncomfortably, "and a first-time father… It's a lot. Seeing her belly like that. Knowing a part of me is in there… And I know what I said before, about uprooting it. But there is a better way. I guess. I don't know. Reaching the summit resolves it somehow. That's what Rayah said, but she didn't tell me how. I just know it must be before Uklarta gives birth to it. It's the only way to undo part of what she's done to me."

"So much for 'I don't know.'" Lostar mocked: a hard wall to overcome when Raihn bared all.

"Yeah," Raihn grinned forcefully, "but I suppose I owed you something after how I fell back on my pointed finger. I'm sorry. Honesty was the best I could do."

Lostar became docile, face aglow.

Raihn hummed. "What about you? You want to talk about this?" he asked, gesturing to the barrel.

Lostar shook his head. "I don't think so," he grinned, mimicking Raihn. But the smile faded, that meager joy fleeting.

Hairs trailed their head's motion, wobbling back. Consideration played from his quiet, on the cusp of breaking. "You don't owe me anything, you know. I've done nothing but get you carriaged off, serving nobody but my own goal to redeem myself. Amarra's got her wing over you just broad enough, as she's the better protector—I'm just a washed-up fish who needs to accept the truth."

"Maybe that's the true reason we're here," Raihn suggested.

"Or might I have killed a black doe in a past life..."

Raihn leaned closer, clouding his inner thunder. "If you can't keep the title of gar by acting as a shield, then let me protect you as one—so I can save one goddamned person under my own piddly feathers. I can't stand to see you before this barrel of gilded tar. It's more potent than any ale I've known; its scent is pungent across any hill. Don't give in to it—even if it makes me selfish. Lift both our curses. Prove yourself—to this mountain, if not you or I."

Lostar stewed between his greasy strands in a companionable silence, then stood and slapped the spigot harshly. The mead rushed out, and when the last drop dripped, Lostar reached beneath the barrel's belly and heaved until Raihn was summoned.

Together, they sent the empty barrel tumbling downhill until it vanished from sight, one of its copper hoops wheeling astray.

"...Go on. Take it back," Lostar said.

"I'm sorry. I was out of line."

"No," Lostar rejected. "The chest."

"Oh...I don't know..."

"Are you afraid of its heft?"

Raihn nodded.

"Take the damn chest, or I'll ply your fingers around it..." Lostar threatened.

He certainly has a different stroke about him now. His tactic, too.

"If the little imp entrusted it to you first, then surely it's true, for the worst of man recognizes the most apt. You just have to see it in yourself, though you won't even give it a glance."

Lostar's hands fell on his shoulders, hard as an uncle's promise. Raihn nodded—not that he believed much more in himself. His self-esteem was meager and his resolve reluctant. But, glancing at the chest poking out of the satchel, he considered the truth of it.

Raihn swung an arm, his hand assuring his honesty upon Lostar's shoulder. "I'm sorry I ever—"

"No more," Lostar interrupted. "And by the way, I…woke with the binds untied—honestly. I don't wish to make the others…uncomfortable."

Raihn's eyes narrowed upon their wrists, seeing the lingering marks from the chaffing. "Are you—"

"I'm certain," Lostar assured. "There'd be no hard feelings about it."

Raihn couldn't help but feel a wave of ease, certain the chest's burden would give.

CHAPTER THIRTY-TWO

Sand and vinegar

Eldhos broadened its gaze into a searing light, blinding and disorienting Raihn as he awoke. A complete turnaround from the chills he'd been buffeted by. He shot up in a heated pant, the others already in defeated squats.

"What in Adjurrah is this now?" Magnus grumbled, beads of sweat already bulbing on his brow.

"A hallucination of my home," Lostar muttered.

The dunes of Endura rolled beyond their shadows, and *little shards of broken glass* whiffled under their collars.

Distress welled up in Lostar's throat. "…I can't be here." Anxiety twisted his tone into a coyote's yowl. Then his fists met the sand in a flurry, the particles packed tight. "No!"

"I don't know about this one," Pocket remarked, eyeing Lostar warily.

"Me neither," Magnus replied. "I think he's lost his marbles."

"You mean like my marbles that you sent down the fuckin' mountain?" Pocket asked.

"Yeah, just like those," Magnus answered.

Raihn echoed the resentment for this place, eyes wide. "I can't be here either."

"Now, don't you get all worked up," Magnus pointed.

"Look around you," Raihn insisted.

The others skimmed their surroundings through a clueless gloss.

"There are no lanterns in sight!" Raihn blurted out. "And don't forget, my veins are infested with Uklarta's blood," he added.

Magnus's eyes cleared. "Ghor… What in tattered saddles are we to do… Ghor?" He turned around, finally noticing their absence. "Great!" he shouted in frustration, arms to sky. His voice bounded over the sandbanks, the whir of the dry wind emphasizing the vast leg to come.

"Let's not lose our cool," Pocket interjected, pun clearly intended. "We've overcome everything else so far. I'm sure it ain't as bad as it appears," he groaned, gritting his teeth.

"Are you okay?" Raihn asked.

"I'm fine," Pocket replied, though his tone belied his discomfort. "But damn, it's hot."

"Oh yeah, 'not as bad as it appears'?" Hodge mocked, fanning himself.

"Firstly, I don't sound like that. Secondly," Pocket glanced around, "where the fuck do we go?"

"Exactly," Raihn said.

"Listen," Hodge began, shading his eyes with his hand. "Hallucinations usually affect only one person, and this doesn't feel like a vision."

"Okay?" Pocket's face warped. "And?"

Hodge browsed the horizon. "There!" he pointed. "A man, lumbering over a distant mound. A mirage, perhaps?"

"A what? Mirage?"

"Some call it magic, but educated folks know it's an illusion caused by refracting light," Hodge explained. "Kind of a mirror in the wind—an inkblot to perceive."

"Either way, I don't trust him! Swaying and walking all mysterious-like!" Pocket said.

"Alright, alright. Let's all just calm down, eh? Getting to be too much excitement," Magnus groaned.

Raihn nodded in agreement. "I can't stand all the noise while the heat is so unbearable."

The group shaded their eyes, contemplating their move. Raihn, still eyeing the distant shape, gestured toward them. "Well, he's obviously got somewhere to be. Look at him go in his leisure."

"More of a stagger," Pocket muttered.

"However he walks, he's moving, and that's our only lead to follow," Raihn determined. "I mean, if we all see it…"

"Assuming it's a person and not a hallucination," Hodge cautioned, but he nodded in reluctant agreement. "But I suppose you're right."

"Everything will be fine," Raihn assured. "It seems an intentional spell."

Hodge rolled his eyes.

"Or whatever you make of it," Raihn continued. He glanced at Lostar, hoping for confirmation. That it would be okay, but they quieted more than he liked, lost in their own turmoil. "It will be fine…"

Raihn peddled beside Lostar, as they'd thumped through the sand with the wind billowing their heavy-looking cloak.

"Are you okay?" Raihn asked, thinking, "He seemed better at night, heaving that barrel. The only other heaving he may do would be dry like the desert."

"I'm fine," the exhausted Enduran replied, feet thumping less and less until dragging.

Hodge pulled Raihn aside and bent his ear a moment. "Don't hold it against him," he said. "He's going through a lot right now. Under these conditions, it won't be pretty."

"Thank you for the clarification," said Raihn. "But I know. Enough, at least, to understand he's not himself. I won't forsake him."

"Stop mumbling about me," the Enduran grumbled. "Damn! It is fierier out this way than I 'member."

"You've grown accustomed to Eldhona," Magnus asserted.

Lostar denied it feebly. Then he crumbled, smacking the blistering sand, mumbling curses.

"Lostar…" Raihn began, reaching out.

But he was refused.

"I'm fine!"

They weren't. And it was clear. But what can you do to help when that help is unwanted. The sight was just as unwell to see, Lostar sweating out something from deep in their pores, forlorn.

Hours passed, and Lostar staggered about with his cloak swinging side to side in tandem with the distant stranger. His lips were dry and cracked as deep and wide as the flats they encountered, its cracks painted like streaks of lightning towards the horizon where the distant figure met the sky. Raihn, however, kept a downward focus so as to not wedge his foot into the hollows. His skin bumped like the sand banks, agitated. Little grains nestled into his lashes and brows like dander.

Pocket braved the arid expanse on foot, his lips of molting lizard skin too dry to thread out a whistle. "O, I'd rather have mushy mud-caked toes than sandblasted soles!" Pocket sang instead, his voice carrying at least some merriment. "O place abandoned, sand acres vast, this weather can kiss my ass!"

"Please, shut your trap," Magnus requested through fatigue.

Pocket, ever the joker, grinned. "Now, Magnus, do you want those to be your last words to me?"

"Yes," Magnus replied humorlessly.

Pocket chuckled, "You know, sometimes it's hard to believe you like me."

"I wish I was dying," Magnus groaned, tilting his head back to gaze at the unrelenting sky. "I felt like it yesternight, that still water doing me in."

The thief's playful banter continued, "Too bad, I'll probably beat you to death—as in, first one to croak. Y'know I'd not harm ye. Not like I am now anyway."

Magnus could only muster a weary sigh.

The bleakness of the journey weighed heavily, but Pocket's antics, however irritating, provided a strange sort of distraction. Except for one thing Magnus had said.

"Pardon?" Hodge wheezed. "What do you mean, 'still water'? Tell me you didn't…"

Even against the grain, Raihn couldn't battle so much as a smirk. Pocket wasn't looking well, but Raihn was glad of the distraction for their sake, as they derived a fiendish glee from Magnus's exasperation.

Eventually, when their wound seemed too much to bear, Pocket was swathed in Amarra's bulky boughs—much to Raihn's appreciation. Still, he couldn't help but feel guilty that she was always stuck with the burden.

And eventually yet again, further along, Pocket couldn't quit squabbling even though sand rode straight down his gullet. He hacked in between jets and backbites, antics unending no matter his retching.

Raihn turned his head at them with a plucky tone. "You know, you shouldn't talk like that. You'll be just fine."

"Liars have their tongues cut out, ye know," Pocket coughed.

Raihn's lips ducked.

Magnus groaned. "And you know how thieving goes, yet you could still grab yer own cock, lucky for you. And need I remind you, you, too, are a liar?"

Raihn's lips pulled in from their purse.

Raihn crossed leagues of desert, away from the deep gashes, and up and down dunes again until the sand flattened out. Pocket wondered aloud how much further before they would see a color that wasn't "the same damned blue" above or "the same damned beige" below. Just two colors stretching vast, unbothered by any plants. Raihn wondered about it as well.

Eventually, they had come upon some grand burrows where they'd bicker whether to rest or stride onward so that the distant figure may not escape them.

Ultimately, they pressed forth without respite, and Raihn cursed the long-draw of time, thinking of Uklarta's rounding belly.

Plants rode into sight, rising over banks with tacked arms half greeting them with lifeless waves—cacti. Raihn and the others, desperate for drink, scrambled to them, but all the plants had been severed and robbed of any goodness that would be passed unto them.

They pressed.

Still thirsty, their tongues cracked like the flats they'd traversed. The space between the group and the figure persisted, and Raihn lamented it, his mind toyed with. He said naught of it as the complaint would make more tart the mood if he'd even be coherent enough. The elements discombobulated him, and he felt withered under the blaring light like some uprooted weed.

"Nonsense!" cried Pocket after they had all crawled over yet another hill. "We should pick up speed!" The thief groaned in pain once more.

"Stop wiggling about," Raihn commanded, glancing. "You're only going to make it worse for her and yourself."

Amarra nodded, her grip tight on them.

"And our speed is moot," Hodge added practically. "So, we may as well not exhaust ourselves into old grapes."

"Fine," Pocket conceded, though his eye maintained a mischievous glint. "But if I happen to see a statelier gal as a mirage, let me go. You can't keep me from drinking her richness in."

"Might the heat and light take your lips to the needle of a cactus." Hodge grinned.

But that was enough about Pocket. Raihn couldn't exhaust himself on them entirely, knowing how Lostar had been slogging. And just as Raihn glimpsed them out of wonder, their tumble was cued. All eyes turned to the heaving Enduran as he vomited sand-staining bile.

Pocket's head turned a notch. "With your tongue moistened, I don't suppose you could stick up a licked finger and lead us someplace wet, could ye?" He turned to Magnus. "Right, that's a thing? I mean, isn't that what you do? You're a tracker, right?"

Neither answered, and Magnus became drawn to something in the sand.

"Yeah, I'll just go fuck a cactus then," Pocket muttered.

"Will you shut the fuck up for a moment and look," Magnus groaned, his voice tense. "There are tracks here. We're not following a mirage."

"Of course," said Pocket, his tone suddenly more serious. "I don't suppose you thought the wind knocked down those cactuses."

"It's cacti, plural," Hodge corrected, ever the scholar.

Pocket waved dismissively. "Cacti, cactu, I don't care-iti. But instead of staring at the ground, might you wanna look ahead. Our strange wanderer has come to a stop."

Raihn gasped. "If we go now, we might catch up."

No oases were in sight—not even a hint of the half-buried vessels with copper hulls that might have offered some hope amidst this insanity. As they trekked on, Hodge, ever the studious man, prattled in his boredom about the life of Endura: how the cold nights would bring out rabbits and coyotes, or how rainbowed rolls and blood stones adorned fragmented lands, and v-shaped valleys had been scoured smooth by flash floods. But here, in this unforgiving stretch, none of that seemed possible. No rabbits to hunt, no rain to quench their thirst, no shelter from the elements, nor even the ghostly shadow of the long-forgotten vessels. Just sand, combed into neat, mocking rows.

Raihn glanced at Lostar midway through the gasp-laden teachings, their expression just as plain as the homegrown insipidness.

As they drew closer to what they presumed was their destination, there was an eerie, monotone note—a brassy kind of song. It was oddly beautiful, lifting the sting of heat, their plodding mellowing into feathery steps. Raihn wondered if it was anything like the horn from when they first entered the mountain's gate or if it was something native to Lostar's homeland. He glanced back again to question them, but they appeared entranced by the trumpeting, the function in their arms and shoulders forgotten. They were utterly locked up.

"Lostar?"

Their face was scoured blank, a vast scape of sand wasting infinitely beyond them—a shadow from a once near-boundless lake. Their legs yielded under the beauty of the song—or so Raihn interpreted until their lips bowed down. They might shed a tear if their eyes weren't so red from the sandy wind.

But why? Raihn pondered. Were they close to his plateau?

Raihn was locked onto them, but they refused to meet his squint. A moment longer, they continued without a word, their cloak flagging.

The song sharpened, becoming loud and clear. The figure they had been tailing disappeared into the sinewy heat, leaving in his place a massive grotto, once an island, that stood before them like a massive tooth—a bored cavity at its center underbelly. Its lapping edges grew thicker, like waves of tonsils in a mine singer. At the other end of the grotto, Raihn made out the exit. "It's an uncorked bunghole," as Pocket described, "given melodic licks." It was. The wind filtered into brass waves, its tone crying higher and lower as they came.

Shade gorged them into a faulting stupor, tempting pause. Raihn was the only one determined enough to forgo it and catch the figure before they lost it for good. Lostar took no part in the debate, and Pocket was managed. The direness was possibly dawning on him. The others gave in with him and Pocket in tow; there was still a long enough stretch in the grotto for the harboring shade to be savored.

Once they climbed out of the hollow, they were greeted by a distant rock craning toward the sky. It protruded from the river-dried crib of sand like a toppled pillar, expansive like a moor, leaning precariously until it reached the plateau's surface.

Raihn led the way, ascended the rocky tongue, and discovered two large sand mounds at the other end with a narrow gap between them. The vast desert sprawled low beneath Raihn, shivering his spine. His stride gained, the mounds flanking the path looming closer, casting long shadows from their size. As he neared their pinch, he noticed the mounds were riddled with "cheeky" holes, as Pocket annotated again.

Everyone investigated. At the left mound's backside, there was an entrance. They saw two dead men within and blood-soaked sand—the mounds appeared to be sand blinds.

"Looks like that fellow we followed was perhaps less friendly than we might have hoped," Hodge remarked.

"I never assumed he was friendly," Magnus replied gruffly. "Never trust a stranger until you know their intentions." His eyes narrowed as he charted the area. "I suppose the other blind is just the same…"

310

"Unless that stranger is there, cutting others down," Pocket said, anticipating it, voice wriggly.

With that, Magnus drew his sword and cautiously crossed the gap, leading the group in a single file.

The second hollow was identical to the first—filled with the bodies of the dead, with no one present to answer for them.

Past the mounds, the tracks led down a slope, guiding the party toward a secluded city of stone nestled within the heart of the rock, cloaked by it. Intriguing as it was, their curiosity was quickly overshadowed by the pungent stench that filled the air from other corpses that stewed under the relentless heat.

"Rancid," Hodge exclaimed, covering his nose.

"Watch your tongue," Lostar snapped, as if suddenly finding breath in company.

Hodge shrank back, muttering an apology.

The bodies were of men dressed in ornate clothing, lining their own kind of path to be followed. Magnus, ever cautious, issued another warning: "Be ready for anything."

"How much more ready can I get?" Pocket groaned from Amarra's arms.

"Besides you, you imbecile," Magnus cracked.

Through the pale rock, Raihn took wide strides over corpses in search of their foe. That's when he caught sight of a cloaked figure creeping through the maze of buildings. "There!" he shouted.

But by the time the others got to glance, there was only the tail of their cloak wagging around the corner.

Magnus scurried without hesitation, Raihn close behind.

Turning the corner, Raihn saw the back of the figure standing before a large dip in the sand that funneled somewhere else with a slab of stone as its first step within. The cloaked man removed their hood, their hair down in waves, with a glance over their shoulder.

"Lostar!?" Raihn cried out, double-taking between the pair.

The figure continued descending into the spiral, disappearing into a black void.

Magnus stepped toward the Lostar within their company, his lips tight. His hand shot out and clenched a fold of their cloak. "Is this why you can't stomach being here? I didn't know we had a ruiner of peace among us."

Lostar choked, words withheld as if fear shackled his throat.

"Answer me," Magnus demanded, but Lostar was distant. Magnus's patience snapped. "He's as crooked as the old nails in that tavern," he said, letting go of Lostar and watching him collapse among the dead bodies.

"Magnus," Raihn called. "Go easy. None of us seen him do it. He's not guilty until proven to be."

"My gut speaks truth enough for me, and my memory serves just as well. I recall his eagerness to fight 'til death, as he meant to impart onto you even." Magnus leaned in, then turned to the hole. "Maybe we'll get some answers down below."

"Magnus," Raihn began again, "this isn't Lostar's doing. He wouldn't..."

"How long have you known him? Huh?"

"About as long as I've known you," Raihn replied.

"Then not long enough to trust him," Magnus muttered, stomping off. "Are you lot coming or not?"

Raihn's concern deepened as Lostar looked far gone, unsure of what had them so rattled. Only pushing forward seemed the best route to shine an answer, as Lostar would speak nothing of truth in this moment.

"I'm coming," Raihn finally answered, steeling himself to follow Magnus into the unknown. "Don't go anywhere, alright? Everything will be okay," he told Lostar, as if trying to convince himself more than anyone else. He couldn't lose faith in them again, always betrayed by his thin rulings.

He entered the swirl, finding a spiral of dimmed stairs flowing into the deep shadow. They took him to a cooler grave in this hollow space, shared by many dead men with scattered blades as their everling flowers. As his eyes acclimated to the darkness, Raihn stepped off the bottom step and scoured the area.

"I know this place," he said. "I've seen it once before."

"How could that be?" asked Hodge.

"It was a vision, back when I hurt my ankle. In the debris, I saw it crumble. And I can prove it," Raihn said, his voice rising. "There's a chamber to the right of us, but I didn't get to see too much of it. There was a collapse, and then...her eyes. Uklarta. She was here." He stiffened, eyeing the dark. The others shuffled about, glancing. "You'd see her bright eyes predator in this pitch," he detailed.

Raihn looked for the chamber, but it was darker than before. He struggled, but almost on cue, the torches ignited beside the entry. More corpses lay there, robed like the two solmners that came through Cobblestone. He stepped over them, came to the arch, and entered. Another corpse lay within the room—only the one. The bodies all appeared fresh, many of them youthful. Except for this one, who looked ravaged by time: old and gaunt before decay could set in, with robes tied around their husk.

Hodge raced in beside Raihn and quickly skimmed the area. He seemed to spot something interesting and tugged on Raihn's arm, guiding his attention to a sand-embedded tapestry. The fabric was dull and gritty, but it bore the faint image of a tree, hanging up and above the body.

"What is it?" Raihn asked, his gaze fixed on it. "The Undyed Tree?"

"Nay, I mean yes, but this is a weeping willow," Hodge corrected.

"So, what, there are more of these white trees?" Magnus questioned, mid-approach.

312

"You mean besides the littler one with the hand-branch? Maybe," Hodge replied, kneeling to inspect the body next. With a handkerchief, he carefully turned over the dead man's hand, examining it. "Bruises," he noted. "They wrap around his hand like clasped fingers. And though his body is pale, it is not from death." Hodge double-checked, fingers upon their throat. "Nay. Warm. This death is recent, and it looks like this man had been hiding down here for a long time before meeting his end."

Magnus's eyes narrowed. "And this means?"

"I believe—no, I wonder… I wonder if the reason the branch was missing until its more recent discovery is because of this man," Hodge speculated. "Perhaps he kept it and refused to take on the journey, unlike Tepparna. Maybe only after coming to the mountain and…failing…the hand would regrow. For another to take. I mean, look at his bruises. They mirror the same places where Raihn and Tepparna's hands were clasped. This fellow hid with the hand here for all his life. For as I recall, there was a long period in which the tree was short of the uncanny branch."

"But why not take it to the mountain?" Magnus asked. "If these lemmings journeyed just to die…"

"That's just a myth," Hodge said, glancing back over his shoulder, "about the lemmings…"

"Stay focused," Raihn urged. "Look. Maybe he knew something we didn't."

Everyone seemed to stew on that thought a moment before Magnus said something about it. "I bet that Lostar knows a thing or two."

Raihn silently agreed, but Lostar was in a severe state to prod.

"Yeah? Good luck asking," Pocket laughed.

"I don't need luck. He withholds some kind of secret," Magnus said, his fist clenching his sword belt, thumb through the belt loop.

"And I don't believe he's the only one," Raihn remarked. "Who's to say what we all hide from one another. Does it change our current affiliation?"

Magnus's thumb squeezed the leather loop tighter.

"How about we just focus on what's in front of us," Hodge suggested.

Magnus hummed deep in his throat. "What's more to gather? Besides your best guess?"

"I don't guess, I estimate."

Raihn was nervous, disliking the aura in Magnus's sudden quest for truth and their trail of negative connotations regarding his friend.

"You don't have to guess."

Raihn flinched and spun around, seeing Lostar lean against the archway. They pointed to another tapestry that hung above the entry, facing the corpse. Raihn glanced up at it. The tapestry depicted the very same tree, but it was burning.

"Well, glad you decided to join us, Enduran." Magnus's clenched jaw relaxed, and his arms crossed. "How about you elaborate?"

Lostar, through a slobbery haze, confessed. "These solmners are a private study of belief. And I've come desecrating their temple with my heavy feet before. In my efforts, I mistook their temple to be in Endoland, but the truth is, the Endolanders came here, converting the eastward Lowlanders of Endura. Even as a Highlander, I had no idea of this well-kept secret."

"I don't understand," Hodge admitted.

"This tapestry," Lostar continued, "is a reminder of why he sits in this room day after day—a fear-striking image of the tree that burns. At least, that's as far as I can guess."

Raihn twiddled his thumbs, deep in thought. "When the manor crumbled, I was taken out of sorts momentarily. I saw a torch-lit willow, burning. I was scared, honestly. Now it's come back."

Hodge put a finger to his lips, his eyes fine. "From what I can best speculate—it is asinine, I know—but consider it a moment, and you might indulge in some madness as well," he said.

"Out with it," Magnus blurted.

"Presuming this solmner indeed remained here with the branch, and with what Tepparna said about her visions worsening in time, then I am sure this fellow had dastardly visions himself."

"Well, whatever else he saw must have been terrible," said Raihn.

"Exactly my point. He was afraid, just as you say you were, young Raihn. Furthermore, if he'd held onto this hand-like branch for that long, I wonder what more he might've seen. Might that tapestry be a reminder to him of why he lay here. But that is only my best 'guess.'"

"Fine," Magnus grumbled. "Solid of sound, I would say, for your estimate. But Enduran, why did **you** come here?"

"I was but a lemming," Lostar smirked, face melting into sweat. "I fled the Highlands. Then I thought to seek out these solmners. No easy feet. They journeyed across the river to the west, so I followed their trail and went east.

"They covered their tracks by some tool upon their sashes, so I waited on the bank and watched for where they had come from until more of them met the river. I discovered they'd carve around certain markers—big rocks and the like—that grotto. I eventually found myself at the mercy of their pointed staffs. 'Too close to home,' they alerted. They were rightfully mistrusting of me, taking me to their stone hold. I was too close to merely be turned away."

"Then what?" Magnus prodded. "They're all dead but sound alive and well in your tale."

"They were," Lostar clipped, winded yet coherent. "That did not last. I should not have come, for I was followed. It was a feathery shadow—a vulture, I thought. Then I heard this caw... I looked up, and what I saw was a raven. It flew over me when I was captured..." His voice wavered, and beads of sweat trickled down his sagging face. He clung to the arch for sup-

314

port, heavy-looking and disoriented. "It seems a haunter stuck to my back as compensation for my failures.

"The Raven brought down rocks from a cave-in. By the time I dug myself out, with hardly a breath in my lungs, I saw the toll it had taken on what was Overstone.

"Then the shadow followed me west, where I mistook a pilgrim in our herd for a peasant lain awash along the bank," he added, his gaze lingering on Raihn.

Raihn hesitated, searching for the right words. "And if none of that had happened, we might never have met. If this solmner hadn't known fear, likely seeing the flame I saw, and if you had never faltered…we might not be here, especially me, not on my own, and certainly not without courage. There's something greater at work. Something that's led us to this place. It means…something." He turned to Hodge. "Isn't that right?"

"It's a whole lot of something," Pocket jested.

Hodge lowered his head in thought before meeting Raihn's gaze. He nodded. "Indeed," he said, but he didn't seem sure and only meant to assist. There was no science to it, but it was absolutely spellbinding. Might that be why. Something he could not refute.

"Then let us be rid of our shadows and succeed where—" his voice cut briefly. "Where others failed."

Raihn gripped Lostar by the arm. "I feel your purpose, 'lemming.' Just as it swells within for myself." It was cheesy, but he was proud no less, being coy. "There will be answers at the end of this road."

Lostar couldn't give the same grip without both hands awkwardly coupled together, thanks to their bind.

CHAPTER THIRTY-THREE
Dark reflections

HODGE broke in a start, suddenly free from the scorching sand and blistering heat. He gawked around, frantic-eyed on the forest's slope. His heart raced like a rabbit from greyhounds—hare coursing while the other hares still slept.

"I say! Glad that's over!" Hodge rejoiced, selfishly hoping the others might stir. But they did not. Unease crept in, yet he waited patiently, hoping they would wake soon without further prodding.

An hour dragged into a dim morning. Nothing changed. Hodge's concern festered and turned maggoty like rotted meat pie until his patience fled. He shook his companions, shouting, "Wake up! Wake up!"

"Oh, give it a rest," said another, who was not within the lanterns.

"What!?" Hodge, startled, spun in search of the source of the voice.

In the dark, they sipped a cup of tea, their pinky raised delicately. "First time I've seen you play in the dirt," they said.

On all fours, Hodge stared deeply into the man's eyes where candlelight flickered. The man watched him from over the lip of their ornate teacup.

"Herb," Hodge uttered in disbelief.

His brother sat cross-legged, sporting a handkerchief from his collar, dabbing his lip with the tail of it. Then he nibbled on a biscuit, feasting from an array of finely plated foods along a long, candle-lit table.

"Where'd you snag all that?"

Herb recoiled. "Is that your first question? Is this bounty more exciting than my guest appearance? Come now, Hodge. Take a seat, then. I am famished, mind you, so don't mind my appetite."

"I wish I could, Herb," said Hodge wistfully. "I really do."

"You deny this ensemble?" Herb asked, tempting him. "Biscuits and honey, apple pie, tea, meats and cheeses…ham!? Not even a spot of butter over bread? A shame to let it all go to waste… What a shame indeed."

Hodge longed for a seat at the table where he could gulp, chow, and chat even, but he mustn't. He watched Herb peck and dabble like a desperate puppy instead on the other side of the lanterns.

"…I can't," Hodge repeated.

"Why not?" asked Herb.

"I know what you're doing."

"What?" Herb's face scrunched up. "Is it the lanterns? Don't you remember? They're here to keep others from getting in. I cannot come to you, Hodge; you have to come to me. I went through the effort of finding you already."

"Okay, so what about this lavish picnic?" Hodge asked. "Huh? Where'd you come upon all this, the pantry in the rock?" Hodge remarked sarcastically.

"There's a lot more out here. More than what you'd find on that lonely trail. There are lords, jesters, bards even! All out here, more amusing than that thief and better at song-making. Yes, they are. Eating, playing, laughing. And rich in food, just like this table is—like I am! But I made a little wager with a lord at his banquet first. I told him, lying as I was," Herb prattled on, cutting a sausage rather daintily. "I said to him I was wealthy. And so, I bet him that wealth for his table. You know what we played? We played the same ol' game you and I did. But the thing is, I didn't cheat—"

"Herb…"

The brother relented. "By the way, I seem to have lost my button. Criminal of me to dine improperly."

Hodge lit up and rummaged in his pocket, his fingers finding it. He'd taken it along with him, harboring it all this time. While toying with it, he contemplated giving it back.

"Yeah, I told you, didn't I?" Hodge asked, taking it out and holding it aloft. "It required some new thread."

"Hodge! You have it. Wonderful!" Herb cheered. "May I have it back?" Their open palm reached.

Hodge statued, a clear displeasure to them. Then he softened. "Herb. I did cheat," he confessed, plopping near the light.

"I know, Hodge," Herb said, their arm falling.

"I got you killed. Because I wanted to be cozy. It was selfish," Hodge wept.

"It was," Herb agreed bluntly.

"I'm sorry."

"I know," Herb repeated.

"Can you forgive me?"

"Hodge…"

"What?"

"There was a bit of a blanket shortage, remember? I'm older than you. That's just what we older brothers do. But first, I played your little game…"

Hodge reflected quietly.

"Anyway, brother, you were right about that button," Herb continued. "Been going mad, I have."

Hodge stood up and took a step forward. "How about one more game? If I win, I'll remain here on the path, parting you with your button. And if I lose…"

"You'll join me," Herb presumed. "Are you certain?"

Hodge nodded. "I think my rheumatism was healed when I stepped a foot beyond that wall," he smirked.

RAIHN awoke, the sky pale in the early morn. He rose, the rest of the party waking too. Lostar, Amarra, Magnus, even Ghor was there, waking. It seems the groundskeeper had not shared the same vision. But as for Hodge, he was first awake, waiting.

"About time," said the scholar.

Raihn ambled over his thoughts and noticed how collected Lostar seemed. Even Hodge had pep in his step. It appeared some sand was removed from both their boots, muck and grime from the muskeg departing their toes' webbing. However, he had a dropping feeling that it wasn't over—sinking after a short journey up since their rest. The muck nipped at his ankles with a freezing bite, and those ankles plopped deep. His muscles became weary from the extra effort in long strides that left goopy craters. And to make things worse, snow started coming down, albeit lightly.

Hodge struggled. "Like a jaunt through pudding."

Magnus, however, was the loudest complainer. "Ghor, how long will this last?" he groaned.

"What? I thought you preferred this to stone," Ghor sniggered.

"Ghor," Raihn snapped.

"I don't have all the answers," Ghor cracked. "You take me for a masochist?"

"It's just…from blistering sands to this? I ache for the middle ground, and maybe a moment of contentedness," Raihn said before a smiting hail ensued, breath nearly visible. "My feet will freeze cold and break free in these pits."

Pocket dramatized his restless groan, fighting to free himself from Amarra's arms. "Okay, that's enough time for healing."

"What are you doing?" asked Raihn.

"Shut up and let me suffer too," said Pocket. "I'm into it."

Raihn saw his reflection and related to that feeling of helplessness. "About time," he cracked. It caught the thief off guard briefly, but then they caught onto Raihn's sly grin and matched it.

"Raihn!" Lostar called out through the fierce hail and the icy clamor. Every element seemed to conspire to claim their lives, Lostar struggling with hands still bound. "Help!"

Raihn sprang into action, seeing Lostar's foot deeply wedged into a muddy socket and desperately needing a hoist from the swelling mire. Locking

318

his arm beneath Lostar's, he heaved with all his might. The Enduran rose to his feet, but that's not all; Raihn wrestled with the knot binding their wrists. Distress mounted as the bitter cold pecked his fingers into numbness.

Lostar looked straight at him. "Take your time. It is alright," he said, his voice barely audible over the howling wind.

Their steady energy somehow helped him focus. The bind was loosening.

Magnus, however, caught wind with his own flurry through the storm. "What are you doing?"

Raihn continued to fumble with the binds, growing increasingly frustrated. Finally, he gave up. "I can't."

Lostar smirked, raising the rope to his mouth. He bit and gnawed until it eased off.

"Well, I'll be…"

They shivered through volleys of hail toward a stone path nearing the dim morning, darkened even more by moody clouds. Their feet, caked in mud, slapped against the cobblestones that led toward refuge: one massive structure of dark stonework, a castle. It loomed just ahead, beyond broken pillars. The forest was spoiled, its trees bare, broken, and lodged in mud. But through the fog, just beyond the castle, Raihn glimpsed the summit lingering in the distance. His stomach dropped excitedly—they were nearly there, and he hadn't realized how far they'd come.

Early in his venture, Raihn had misplaced his foot into a puddle, but he could now take quite a step into a moat, mindless as he was being. Lucky for him, there was no such channel.

He stumbled over the jagged rocks and steered himself forward with renewed focus. The entry raced close, his eyes tied to the iron portcullis gate as it grew with red vines snaking through the grill. Its sharp teeth loomed above, sandwiched between barbican towers. Overhead, in layers of arches reminiscent of the grotto's tonsils, three murder holes gaped like the orifice of the gate itself. And through those voids, deadly rain could descend—rocks, scalding water, molten lead, or hot oil—meant to strike down or smelt out the skeletons of anyone daring enough to approach.

As Raihn's eyes drifted down from these menacing apertures, they settled on the massive double doors of the barbican. The doors, though grand, were marred by time and perhaps beaten by a siege, with studded boards splintered and grinning like broken teeth, *a grim welcome.*

"I've seen more ornate shitholes than this," Pocket commented. "You think some greybeard squats in there?"

"I'd bet only mice and rats, but this mountain seems cured of 'em," Magnus remarked sharply. "All but one…"

Pocket narrowed his eyes, seemingly letting the jab slide, refocusing on the door. With a swift kick against it, he bounced back into Amarra's arms, wincing.

"Will you settle down?" Hodge said through exasperation. "You're just making worse your wound."

Pocket crossed his arms. "No greybeard to pay homage to us louses, I s'pose, nor would they to a band of rogues." Then, his hands shaped around his mouth, he called out with an amplified voice. "Hello!" His voice echoed through the holes of the gate, each repetition deepening Magnus's sneer. "Don't worry. Nobody's home, Mag, ol' friend. This place has been ransacked, sealed back up, and left to rot. Or the victor croaked since. Probably a skeleton up in the keep, I'd reckon."

Amarra impatiently fanned the group away, eyed the broken door, and then shifted her thoughtful attention to the mangled portcullis gate above.

Taking a deep breath, she back-stepped, her right shoulder becoming the vanguard for the siege. She slammed into the barbican doors, forcing them apart with a thunderous crack. They snapped away from each other and crashed against the inner stone walls.

Raihn watched, thoroughly impressed. The path before them was laid bare.

The group rallied within, save for Magnus, who pulled Raihn aside, their hand gripping his shoulder. "What're you doing?"

Raihn was confused.

"Your Enduran friend. You let him go free."

"He's fine," Raihn stated. "I think it's over."

"Oh, you think? You 'think' it is over?"

Raihn lost his patience, swiping their hand off from his shoulder. "He's fine."

"He better be."

Raihn scoffed and entered.

He felt like an intruder in this strange place, even if it was abandoned. He and Hodge made brief exchanges as to who could have ruled here and who might have built it. Hodge wondered if there was once a civilization on this mountain, until stating, "Well, I suppose there had to be."

Raihn considered sharing his and Amarra's discovery of that strange crowd down the mountainside. That was, at least, until Pocket cut in.

"O castellan! O castellan!"

Magnus looked tense, his shoulders hunched high. Thunder rumbled, and light flashed through the cracks above. Beside him, Hodge looked queasy.

"Are you guys alright?" Raihn asked.

"Familiar territory," Hodge shivered.

Magnus reluctantly nodded at Hodge, sharing the sentiment.

"Daisies. The lot of ya," said Ghor.

"Oh, there he is," Magnus waved. "Haven't seen you for some while. Though my eyes likely flew over you."

"Laugh all ye may. You step only within the gatehouse. And might I add, all these torches on the walls take place of them lanterns. And they line many halls and many chambers. Feel free to roam. I'll be laughing at every wrong turn."

"A sugary tongue for him," Magnus remarked, "but a gleeful little troll he is."

"Stop flappin' your gums and flog the floors with your feet," Ghor sparked.

Pocket was wincing and holding themselves, so after Raihn took notice of a rocker at the wall, he guided them to it. They reclined back, kicking off their boots and then wet socks. Hodge recoiled from the sight, but after seeing how comfortable the thief was, the scholar couldn't help himself but do the same. Hodge's socks, once white of cotton, were now browned soggily. Magnus shrugged, going barefoot and scratching his heels against the stone, just under the arrow slits.

They all raised their socks over the torches and picked the grime between their toes. Raihn followed suit, but knew the longer they took, the more that witch would bloat.

"Come on, Ghor. Partake in some hygiene," Pocket urged.

But the little man only sneered, his eyes dark and unkind. "I would never stain these walls with my scent," Ghor said, backing away into the darkness.

Raihn pondered the groundskeeper before glancing around the gatehouse. He saw a woven trunk by the rocker and a simple wardrobe a few feet from Pocket. These were still functional commodities, but they were kept in a very strange place.

The weather continued sourly, dripping through the crevices and pouring through the gaps as the hail turned to a shower. Lightning flickered.

Pocket grumbled. "The rain can eat my—well—wait a second," he paused. "I don't think I want to say that," Pocket mumbled as he wrung out his trousers. "Why you gotta be named after such a common thing?" he asked Raihn. "No offense."

"None taken," said Raihn. "Apparently, if I ever cried as a child, the rain would come, and I'd stop—sometimes I mean—other times, I'd just cry and cry. But Mother and Father hoped I'd be like the rain and soothe others. I kind of disliked that concept at the time, so they called me Muna by request. Then I met my brother by the river, which, you know, we named him River. So, then I guess I reclaimed 'Raihn' as my name. It made us feel more familiar with each other…"

They'd sat awhile, the droning weather filling the break in their chatter.

"Well," Hodge began, "I, for one, am feeling clean enough to get dirty again. My intrigue over these lain rocks has me itching. Time for a stroll, and if any want to stroll with me, do so, because if I may be honest, it would be disheartening to go it alone in the dark."

"Alright," Magnus groaned as he pushed himself up from the musty floor. "Let's take a gander at the halls of early authority. Or a husk of it. Might we find, dare I say, the corpse of a lord?"

"Authority is a manmade concept, backed only by armies and fealty," Hodge said. "And I see no army here, therefore, no lord."

"Or Ghor could just enlighten us," said Magnus, his tone sharp.

Ghor shook his head in the dark, despair clouding his eyes. "'Tis a lonely place," he said. "Full o' memories—little things of the past…"

Raihn spoke up, his curiosity invigorated. "What was going on with Ra-yah? She's…strange. Her head twists on her shoulders, a new face every turn."

"She's been stuck here for a long time," Ghor answered, "just as I have… Countless centuries make us all a bit odd."

Ghor's voice trailed off, their words sparking even more curiosity in Raihn. "How did you become the groundskeeper?" he pressed.

"No more," Ghor snapped, suddenly defensive. "I've said too much… Go! Do what you want and leave me alone."

"What about you?"

"I'll be waiting at the end," Ghor replied, turning his back, chilling breaths echoing in the dark. "I wish not to be here any longer than I must." Then, he slid through the darkness toward the next gate.

"But aren't you our guide?" Raihn's voice echoed after him.

"We'll be fine," said Pocket. "Mosey about. I'm content in sitting this one out."

"Yeah, well, you got a fine seat. You're practically melting in it."

"Like a candle," Pocket smiled.

"I don't think he'll be going anywhere," Lostar added.

"Okay, well, Hodge…Hodge?" Raihn looked around. "Hello? Hodge? Oh, boy," he said, feeling a wave of panic. Magnus was also missing. "I don't think I like this. We should all stay together and get out. I think I agree with Ghor. He left through the next gate. Maybe through there we can keep on going towards the keep. Might that be the end? I mean, where should we go? Moreover, did Hodge and Magnus go that way or through a corridor?"

"It matters not," Lostar waved cooly. "If they only mean to look about, they shall return. The lanterns seem to go every way, and, as I understand them, there aren't that many places to go in gatehouses but up and to the courtyard."

"Right," said Raihn. "That's the problem," he muttered, looking at many corridors. All of them lit besides the one nearest Pocket. "I just don't know if we should waste time. We should hurry…"

"And we know Pocket isn't going anywhere," said Lostar, glossing over Raihn's concern.

"Right," Raihn said again.

"But he looks unwell," Lostar went on.

"Well, don't say that out loud," Raihn muttered.

"Easy. Already he is fast asleep," Lostar pointed out, nodding to the snoring Pocket.

Raihn raked his fingers through his curly hair, stressed as can be.

"The rain breaks on our skin, half-frozen," Lostar added. "Best we wait for the elements to die down."

"Right. Right," said Raihn, beginning to pace.

Raihn, still anxious and now opposed to pacing, leaned upon the wall run through by many cracks. A couple times, he'd moved already, thanks to the floors above, all torn up as they are. He suffered some tumbling hail and drips here and there before asking, "When do you think it will end?"

"If any of us has a guess, it would not be me," Lostar answered. "Are you feeling anxious?"

"It feels like we're being stalled—or perhaps **we** are stalling. Should this weather stop us?"

"I don't think **you** need to ask **me** that." Lostar mocked, their mood much fairer than usual.

"I don't want to dismiss your input," Raihn said. "I'd hate to be the one who says we should charge out into a storm."

"What I say matters little," Lostar replied. "I've seen you at the forefront, making decisions."

Raihn scoffed. "I was mostly carried through it all."

"Even so… You are why we gained passage to this mountain."

"I just followed along, grabbed onto the vine. I couldn't have done it alone…"

"I know… None of us could. Remember that."

"You know, I should really thank you properly." Raihn stepped closer. "I feel like I've only given you grief. I mean, I was carried through so much of the journey—literally," he added.

Lostar flashed a grin, saying all that need be told from it.

Raihn nodded, a nervous smirk playing on his lips. "I should probably return this to you," he said casually, unstrapping the ensemble of black buckles and handing Truthseeker back to its *rightful* owner. "Here."

Lostar took the hilt delicately, then fastened the belt around his hips. A glint flew through his eyes.

"There's one more thing," Raihn continued. "Why didn't you untie yourself earlier? You just, you know." He snapped his fingers, evoking the simplicity.

"You tied them, so you had to be the one to remove them," Lostar replied.

Admiration swelled in Raihn, earning Lostar a hard pat on the back. "Magnus and Hodge have been gone for nearly an hour. That's time wasted. We should go check on them."

Raihn turned to Pocket. They slumbered, head rolled back. "Bah, he'll be fine."

In the old ruin, Raihn, Lostar, and Amarra ventured through curtains of thick spider webs, sidestepping streams of water and falling shards that leaked through the cracks in the castle's rudimentary walls. The question of spiders being present murmured through Raihn's lips with contempt.

It was an ominously quiet heap. The age of the weathered rock allowed passage for rain to flow over black *granite*. But Muna Raihn came upon even sleeker black slabs and gazed into the shine, seeing his reflection stare back. The surface was polished into a mirror, and his body was made dark through its reflection. He crossed it, and then more, as the slabs stood on crude stands made of stone easels.

The torches guided, their light soft over grit. Howls blew through the hall and whispered through the cracks, wavering the torchlight. Something felt amiss. Raihn's steady gait felt crooked as he passed more and more slabs of black, again and again seeing himself duplicate in the stone. He noticed himself glaring, his reflection's brow even more crooked. He observed, then considered it sentient. Examining each slab, he felt his twin's presence, questioning his sanity: *Am I going mad or just glaring at myself?* Maybe it was all in his head, but he couldn't deny the sensation running through his body—crawly, restless vibes, like spiders hatched under his skin. The only kind of damned insect on this mountain it would seem.

Raihn straightened his gaze, trying to catch himself in the mirror, gazing without a head turn. A huff escaped him. "Whoever lived here sure had a fascination with themselves, didn't they?"

Lostar seemed far too uneasy to reply.

Eventually, the slabs of black rock grew sparse, replaced by something strikingly similar to the clutter in River's chamber.

"Paintings," Raihn breathed. Many aged, their surfaces mottled as if layered with milk fat. One hung askew, split open, and knocked off its nail. The others were either intact, hung in place, or carelessly strewn about. Yet one detail connected them all: a recurring woman.

She appeared in every painting. In one, she sat in a rocking chair, weaving a basket. In another, she ate. In others, she folded clothes, dressed a child, or dressed herself. One canvas even showed her bathed in Eldhos's polka-dotted light, her arms spread over her fanned-out hair as she lazed upon grass, eyes closed. But for each mundane depiction, there was a creeping sense of perversion, all confined to what Raihn assumed was her home. That was what made it so strange, so disturbingly voyeuristic. Her nude back, glimpsed through a cabin window, made Raihn feel as filthy as the hides stretched over the frames.

And though not naked, the one painting caught his attention: the torn canvas where she played an instrument, though Raihn could barely discern which kind.

It was all excessive, but the slash across the painting seemed a town crier of obsession. The grime that coated her face and body around the gash blurred her contentment. Her figure was still noticeably pulled tight into a glassy curve, as though fashioned for distant admiration. The greasy milk fat residue thickened over her peace, talentless gobs that exist thanks only to time and decay.

"Do you feel it?" Raihn asked aloud and indirectly. Some kind of disturbing aura.

"I can feel it," Lostar replied.

A dense vibration hummed around the corridor's corner. Goosebumps rose on Raihn's skin as a sharp note stung his heart and sent his hairs on end. He realized it was the melody of a violin, emanating from deep within the recesses of the dank brick channel—the very instrument he imagined was in the torn canvas.

The hum was gentle, almost mesmerizing, drawing them forward. The three followed the distant notes into the dark corridor where the light steadily faded.

Is it from her? Raihn wondered. *But why would she be in one of these gatehouse corridors? And why is it so long and labyrinthian, for that matter?*

They turned the corner at the edge of the light and faced a stretch of darkness. Raihn grabbed a torch from the wall, noticing that a red vine spindled from it down into the ground, becoming taut when lifted.

Lostar sliced through the fleshy cable with his scimitar. It flopped down, rose-colored oil spilling out. Raihn winced and backed his foot away.

They huddled closely, not to lose the torch's light, so they could return to the *path*. Raihn gripped Amarra's hand as the reverberating music rose upon their approach, bouncing off the walls and filling the corridor with—what still sounded to Raihn—an elegant timber. An overtone as sharp and beautiful as a violin may screech and croon. However, Amarra's expression denied all of that starlight. Her lips knotted tight, and her long ears flicked steady. She gripped back.

Perhaps it was an awful sound. Getting closer, Raihn's hairs remained on end, and shivers xylophoned up his spine. He began to understand her screwed expression. Croons bent into cries and racketed into his ears, ricocheting until landing and cutting at his eardrum.

It continued to degrade as they pulled themselves closer, the sight of a dull glow emanating at the end of the space, a mysterious radiance from beneath some ragged tapestry, as if a star veiled from a cloud. It was where the screeching howls resonated. Raihn's free hand crept to it. Then he shot the cloth away and the melody slit into a sudden silence. Before him stood his reflection, cast upon the blackest slab of glass he had ever seen; he stared into the darkened surface, watching as his image slowly faded. He leaned closer, and for a fleeting moment, he thought he saw a painting beneath the glass—something beneath the reflection.

The polished block shone the image like a reflection in a quiet lake: a woman in a rocker with a violin nestled under her chin. Beside her was a trunk woven from sticks. The woman looked to be in a cabin, her eyes of woe to the door, her head a bow of golden twine.

Seeing her made deep a pit in Raihn's stomach, the moving picture reminiscent of when he watched his mother become interrogated from below the surface of a sea. But his stomach dropped lower as three sharp knocks beat at the door within the reflection. The woman's eyes hollowed over her frozen hand.

Three more knocks.

The woman quickly set her violin inside a trunk and nervously adjusted the collar of her dress. She pulled a weathered bonnet over her hair and dragged her feet toward the shabby door. She tugged down her wool dress and cracked the door no more than three inches. A pair of bright silvery eyes peeped through the narrow gap.

"Sikradau?" the woman said.

Amarra became rigid.

"Elda, formal as ever. I couldn't help but hear that darling tune rolling down the hill and into my halls," Sikradau said.

"Really? I didn't know it had such a reach." Elda grinned nervously.

Sikradau stared. "Mind if I come in?" he asked with a rich, buttery voice.

"Abbas will be home soon," Elda assured. "He's out gathering wood with Rayah."

"I hope he doesn't plan on using that small basket for wood. It seems better suited for berries or perhaps fish. I could not help but notice he held a rod against his shoulder when he left just moments ago, and we both know how long it takes for a fish to bite. I can only assume you'll be bored and lonesome until then. I was rather feeling that way myself, see. And seems how Abbas has lost his will for adventure…" his voice trailed and his eyes relaxed a moment before flickering back. "Well, it's a shame, leaving you home alone with no one to hear your delicate music."

"Well, that's not true. Like you said, you could hear it downhill," said Elda.

"Right! Right, so I could. But won't you be so kind as to let me admire it up hither?" he said, flashing a quick smile. "The clarity is so much better without these flimsy walls in my way," he went on, his long fingers groping down the trim of the doorway.

"Sure," Elda said reluctantly. "Take a seat."

"Thank you, and please, call me Sira." The door swung in a slow turn. "It might remove stress from your tongue," the guest creaked.

He lurched under the door, straightening his spiny back as only meager folds of cloth ran from around his shoulder down to his thighs, cinched at the waist by rope. *Their* skin wasn't grey but white like pearls, akin to Amarra's—a connection Raihn couldn't help make. Even their hair resembled gathered cotton, grazing the ceiling as they towered with a body sharper than most Outcasts—slenderer, nimbler. High cheekbones and thin lips marked their face, and upon their head, two small horns perched. Raihn resisted the urge to glance over at Amarra for comparison.

Sikradau sidled up to Elda's rocker, sitting by the *familiarly* woven trunk. He lifted the lid and hastily retrieved her violin. Handing it to her, he asked, "Please, will you play it for me?"

Elda gazed at the instrument, then at their petite nubs for horns.

"But before you do, feel free to remove that intrusive bonnet," he added. "It's a warm night—let your pretty head breathe, lambkin."

Elda hesitated but obeyed, dropping the hat aside and avoiding Sikradau's silvery slits.

"There, Elda," Sikradau cooed. "Now, if you wouldn't mind, I am quite eager."

Elda's eyes remained fixed on her instrument as she ignored the invasive gaze. She played, and the pale Outcast ran fingers over the bottom of her dress. Between their fingers, the hem of her cloth ruffled a moan. She tensed, playing her song of lament.

"That's enough," Raihn forced out, realizing he'd held his breath until now. He quickly covered the slab with the drapery and inhaled so deeply his chest hurt. All quieted, and Raihn heard nothing from under the fabric but his and the others' erratic breaths. He turned his gaze to Amarra, but she continued to gaze at the sheathed mirror-stone. The fire from his torch illuminated her, and darkness whipped around the light, exaggerating her features. Her hand fell away, her eyes a bright silver from the torchlight.

Raihn's gaze returned to the jagged tapestry. A tremor began in his chest, twanging with each breath. It gripped his throat as he sputtered, "We need to go." Urgency mounted, his voice rising with it, as he recalled those silver eyes peering out from Aggy's skull. "We must go, now!" He spun around, colliding with Lostar.

"Hold," Lostar commanded, gripping Raihn's shoulders. "Don't lose yourself to this darkness. Keep your head clear and tell me what's troubling you."

"Isn't it obvious?" Raihn bellowed.

Lostar didn't reply.

"Sorry… If you looked him in the eyes, you'd understand," Raihn stammered. "I've seen him before. His presence… it feels like a vice around your heart, just like those jade eyes did to me. But he's different, something beyond anything you've encountered. I've lain awake, haunted by all their eyes," Raihn said.

"Raihn," Lostar began, his tone unhurried, "are we in danger?"

"Yes," Raihn answered, shaking. "Haven't you noticed? The very things littering the gatehouse—the guardroom where Pocket sleeps—the chair, the trunk… They were taken here. And who else would care to bring them?"

"And we've left the torches, Lostar. Look." He held up his torch, the flame sputtering low.

"Calm yourself," Lostar steadied. "Stow your fear and lead us. We are here with you."

Raihn nodded, then looked up into Amarra's silvers. Fear seemed to take hold of her the most. Raihn snatched her hand with astute firmness. "Come with me," he urged.

So they raced together through polished darkness, fighting to return to the light and the second gate.

POCKET rested in the old, creaking rocker near the woven trunk and the wardrobe back in the gatehouse's guardroom, among all the doors between the gates. He stirred, half awake, soothed by a barrage of rainfall. It sounded as though his awakening was being applauded. "Thank you, thank you," the thief said, blinking. He shifted and nestled his hands under his chin, closing his eyes once more. The guardroom waded away with all the sprinkling.

The rain droned, but through the droning, he'd parsed a creeping breath. Gentle wind blew down his collar, then sidled through his ear. At first, Pocket considered his mind playing tricks, but it seemed unmistakable that he heard his name, "Ernest," through the whir.

He jolted up and squinted around the space.

Dripping and pouring, creeping and trickling and pooling—all the things that rain does—but none of it was Muna Raihn himself, humming or pitter-pattering.

"Raihn?" the thief still called out. "Hello?"

Some torches in the corner by the wardrobe were snuffed. He waited, craning his neck, straining his eyes. He saw two luminescent orbs of silver peering at him from beneath the wardrobe. "What the f—" Pocket jumped like a startled cat, clutching his bandaged wound. "Hello?"

A whisper crawled out from there. "They're leaving you."

"Says who?" asked Pocket.

"They're going. You're hurt, stubborn, and holding them back."

"You're daft to mistake me for a gullible dullard, you…rat beneath the brim." Pocket feigned a grin, stifling fear.

"You are but a wagon without wheels," the whisper taunted. "And the horses tediously drag you up. You hold them down, raking earth as they speak none of it before you—a 'knave,' they say to your back, and a knave you are at the forefront of their ire."

328

"No, she—that Outcast woman, Amarra—carried Raihn just as well she'd carried me, slinging me like a rucksack. Had I not been slung, I'd not be considered a friend."

"Sheep on the pasture, driven by the shepherd and his stick, acting well with domesticated manners… Your sheepherder is gone, and the mammals roam freely with their tendency resuming."

"You know, I think I'm just gonna ignore you," said Pocket, falling back into the chair.

"Gone for already a day," the dark whispered. "They have been gone a day. Would you ignore that?"

Pocket rocked back and forth with eyes shut. His breathing quickened, anxiety cracking his will. The thief sprang up with a spurt of energy, gripped the chair and hucked it across the guardroom of the gatehouse before snapping his hand to his wound. It broke into many pieces, but that was not all the damage the thief meant to bring. He kicked the wardrobe, still holding himself.

Then his eyes caught the gleam of a handle peeking out from under it, through his rage. He grasped the handle and lifted a cracked hand mirror, his chest rapid. In its reflection, he saw himself echoed thrice, his gaze returning from the glass. This mirror was curious indeed, and more curious did Pocket become when his mirrored eyes morphed into acorn-colored irises, surrounded by copper-toned skin.

"Pocket?" Raihn said from the glass.

"Uh," Pocket sputtered, glancing over his shoulder. There was no one there to be reflected, so his eyes returned to the broken glass. "Yeah?"

"We kind of need your help," the mirror twinkled.

"Well, maybe you shouldn't have gone without me," Pocket said.

"Clearly, but I realized it too late. All that matters is that I realized it, though, right?" Raihn asked, threefold with blinking triplets.

"Aye. Just cease that gabbing through the gleam, and swiftly I'll come. Figure me in somewhere, I s'pose."

Raihn perked and excitedly said, "Just head down the corridor and listen for my knocking. We got locked in a room; we were coming back for you and heard your voice coming from in here. Turned out it came from a mirror, of all things. Then the door locked behind us."

Pocket scoffed. "Just count your sheep next time… I'm on my way."

"Of all the corridors, take the one beside your chair. Listen for our banging."

"Beside the chair?" Where the chair *was,* in any case. Pocket peered into the corridor. It was dark. "I'm not going in there," he said. "It's pitch black!"

"Then take a torch with you. Cut it free and take it!"

Pocket scoffed, leaning close to one torch, inspecting the red vine.

"And…don't mind its spillage…"

Pocket entered the corridor and followed a string of spaces with a leaky torch in hand. Eventually, a racket bumped through the passage, dense thuds foretelling the room's nearness. Afraid and alone, he clutched the small hand mirror. Raising it at eye level, he shuddered, "No more acorns."

The knocks boomed in proximity. "I'm coming," Pocket grumbled, crossing misshapen and ill-fitted doors with distressed metal ring pulls.

Finally, one ring rattled against one door as a knock continued to pound from the other side. Pocket noticed a locking bolt, but why on the outside? *Odd*, he thought, *especially in a gatehouse.* There was also a wooden latch, but luckily, neither bolt nor latch required a key.

"Hello?" Pocket called.

"Pocket! Is that you?" Raihn's voice cried from the cracked mirror.

Pocket raised the mirror again. "Yes, it's me. Is that you?"

"Who else?"

"I don't know—shut up," Pocket snapped. "And will you stop banging against the damn door? Damn!"

"No, it reeks in here, and it's cramped," Raihn retorted. "Get me out already!"

"Gimme a minute…damn!"

Pocket put away the mirror and unlatched all the fasteners. The door swung open, revealing nothing but a dark void.

"Someone really wanted to keep you here," he muttered. "I hope you can get back into the light, but you really shouldn't have gone in to begin with."

"Who?" Raihn asked.

"What do you mean 'who'? Y—" Pocket froze as a tap landed on his shoulder. He spun around, stammering at the acorn eyes staring back at him from the dark—**not** from his mirror.

"…You." His voice wavered. "Raihn. What are you doing here? You're supposed to be in there!" He pointed at the room.

Raihn, Lostar, and Amarra exchanged confused glances under their own torch. Pocket, heart hammering, lifted the hand mirror—only to be met with a skin-peeling glare. Perverse pupils gleamed in the glass with irises of silver.

The mirror slipped from his fingers, shattering into a dozen slivers just as a primal roar split the air. A figure lunged from the dark chamber, landing on Pocket's back.

The Enduran clasped the hilt of Truthseeker, feet planted, ready to strike—but Pocket reeled and thrashed, smashing the wretch against stone and door as his torch dropped, sizzling out upon impact.

"Cut the ape!" Pocket demanded, but a womanly voice tolled goodwill in his head. He'd no idea who she was or why she'd suggest suffering the thing, but she assured him it would be okay so long as he calmed. But Pocket continued thrashing and hollering. "Cut 'im!" he repeated, stepping toward the light of Raihn's torch. The foe screeched and sizzled (not that it was touched by flame), to which Pocket smelled the singed hairs on their arm. The wild thing raved and chewed through his trapezius in a panic.

RAIHN stood back, watching the disordered corridor. Lostar raised his scimitar over his right shoulder, looking for an opening as the thief wailed.

Pocket gritted, "Just, maybe don't kill him!"

Lostar hesitated to slay the rat-like fiend with outward teeth and egg white eyes.

The wretch was as lean as a tannery's hide, its mired flesh pungent and stretched translucently thin over a cage of ribs—something far worse than any churl born in the deepest quagmire of the Compass. It retched over Pocket's shoulder, gagging as it struggled to quaff down blood and flesh, strands slaked with sweat plastered to its brow. Its feet, long and ratty, clamped Pocket's waist, their nails like rake tines.

"Help me already," Pocket's tongue galloped.

"Make up your mind!"

"I did!" Pocket bickered. "I said don't kill it, but that does not mean leave it be on my shoulders like some mere monkey!"

"I'm trying! It is a feisty thing," Lostar assured, grappling.

"It's like a grey rat…with horns and lanky arms!" Raihn described.

The description prompted the thief to beg for a parasite cleansing.

Amarra pushed Raihn and Lostar aside. With a heave, she separated the two, the writhing creature kicking and screaming like a child. "No! No! Please," the depraved lunatic pleaded.

Amarra spiked the cagey thing to the stone, laying them out flat in a daze. She raised her foot to squash them, but Pocket insisted otherwise. Reluctantly, she gripped the thing's ankles and tossed them back to the dark chamber, sneering at Pocket in frustration.

Raihn quickly sealed the door, the locks jittering out clacks. Pocket slumped against the opposite wall, riddled with more wounds. The door continued to rattle, muffling a guttural howl.

"What was that?" Lostar cried.

"I don't know," Pocket groaned. "But I hope it didn't have rabies. Damn, I'm going to look like a patchwork quilt by the time we get out of here."

"You'll be fine," Raihn reassured him. "We'll just…wrap it up like always."

Amarra, ever ready, held the torn ends of her cloak, hesitating before tearing off another strip for a bandage.

"At this rate, Amarra won't have any cloak left by the time we reach the top of this cursed mountain," Pocket quipped, trying to lighten the mood.

Lostar, thinking quickly, suggested, "We could take some of Magnus's hem."

"Yeah, I'm sure he'll be thrilled to oblige," Pocket replied sarcastically. "Wherever that blowhard is."

"He wouldn't have a choice," Raihn said. "But he's not here and you need to be bandaged now."

Lostar stepped forward, unfastening his cloak and bending it over his knee. He stretched out his scimitar before it to make himself a butcher of his sparkly wear. "Take mine. It's strong and defensible—reinforced well."

"Are you sure?" Pocket asked. "That's a mighty particular cloak. Any good brigand knows its worth. We know not to cut it, not even in our imaginations. It's lined with the scales of their glimmerin' lizard steeds, shimmering in a thousand colors when directly under Eldhos."

"You seem to know quite a bit about my things, street rat."

"I've bartered with many on the road to Cobblestone," Pocket replied, gritting through the pain. "Royals and scoundrels alike, some of them Enduran, some of them loose-lipped. Them Daints—the Free Bird folk—would take kindly to that array."

Lostar nodded, understanding. "Our cloaks are brave brands, making me a thief like you; bravery should be buried with its wearer; it is my coffin, but I have not yet earned my keep." He cut a clean strip from his cloak with his sword and began dressing Pocket's wound, looping in under his armpit with a knot made there. "Take this to any den of thieves and show them what you came across."

Pocket was visibly moved, his eyes welling up, but he quickly swept his emotions when came a knock on the door beside him. The creature continued to claw and scratch. "You have my thanks, Enduran," he said, his voice steadier.

Raihn glanced at his sputtering torch, the flame barely clinging to life. "We don't have much time. My torch is fading just like the last one," he warned. But before they could despair, the dark corridor ahead suddenly lit up with torches along the walls—ones they hadn't noticed before.

Raihn and the others retraced their steps down the hall, their voices echoing as they called for Hodge and Magnus. Raihn's voice seemed to bounce off the walls, reverberating in every direction, but so did Pocket's meddling cries.

"Okay, just one of us can call out for them. Otherwise, it's just a wash of noise!" Raihn advised just before a startle. Hodge appeared out of thin air.

Raihn exclaimed their name, but his smile faded as he took in the scholar's appearance. "Hodge?" he repeated, noticing the dirt streaked across their face, with clean trails down his cheeks.

"Leaving?" Hodge asked.

"Yes," Raihn replied quickly. "Are you alright?"

"Of course," Hodge answered.

Raihn wasn't convinced. "What happened? Where's Magnus?"

"We got separated," Hodge stammered, avoiding Raihn's gaze. "I must have lost him while I was searching the castle."

"Find anything?" Raihn pressed.

"Just…things that inhabit castles," Hodge replied. "Like stones, dresses, animal bones, black mirrors…creepy things like that."

"Mirrors, you say… What did you see?"

"Oh, you know, just a big oaf," Hodge said with forced nonchalance.

Raihn squinted.

"Yeah, great bushy hair on his cheeks," Hodge added, his voice strained under pressure.

"Just yourself?"

"Well, generally that's how mirrors work," Hodge snipped, a tear perched on his bottom lashes.

Raihn let the matter drop. "I guess so. Just come with us. If we're lucky, we'll see Magnus on the way to the guardroom."

Hodge nodded, his demeanor still uneasy.

"Magnus!" Raihn's voice barreled. "Magnus!" He shouted the tracker's name repeatedly, which helped him stay calm as he and the others navigated through this maze of horrors. "Magnus!" His voice multiplied away, racing itself. "I wonder where he went," Raihn said to the others.

"He couldn't have gotten too far," said Hodge, "but this is a gatehouse like no other, full of oddities."

"Right, we could have passed him already," suggested Lostar in agreement.

Raihn grunted, suddenly stopping as Amarra's outstretched arm blocked his path. He and Hodge glanced up at her, puzzled by her sudden caution. Raihn tried to make sense of her actions. And then, with a firm grip, she twisted their heads as if they were a couple of knobs.

"Oh," Raihn muttered, head swiveled to the point of interest. Another corridor, as revealed by the direction of her pointer and the spin of his head. Down the hallway, he could just make out the silhouette of a man on his knees, seemingly conversing with someone unseen. Raihn presumed it was Magnus, but who was he speaking to?

"We should be cautious," Raihn whispered, his voice tinged with unease. He and the others crept closer, moving slowly toward them. "Magnus?" Raihn called. "Ma—"

"Can I not get one second alone!?" Magnus broke, his voice harsh.

Raihn froze under their grizzly eyes. It was unmistakably Magnus, but something was unsettling about his abrupt anger. Raihn's eyes skimmed the dimly lit room, and then he saw it—a black mirror standing tall over them.

Raihn could see the tracker's image staring back in its reflective surface. *Is he talking to himself?*

They all backed away.

"What's that all about?" Hodge asked.

"Don't know. Doesn't matter," said Raihn, glimpsing the hail that racketed through the castle's wounds. "It has yet to clear outside. We'll call for him when it does."

Promptly, the hail ceased.

"Oi, Magnus!" Pocket belted down the corridor. "Hurry your buttocks up! The hailing and raining—and all that shit, is over!"

Raihn's face twisted as he lamented Pocket's prodding. He squinted past his tense recoil, seeing Magnus first touch the slab and then approach.

Raihn could see those same streaks that Hodge had on their cheeks. "I'm sorry," he said.

But Magnus blunted them all with his shoulder as he walked through, no matter the apology. He glared at Hodge and then Pocket before proceeding to follow the torches. In his croaky voice, he said, "Let us go then."

This castle was big, but the group roamed only the gatehouse and its many corridors. It was dark and damp, and the fires of the torches bent and changed many sizes, forecasting the direction of the wind and, therefore, guiding them to the gate. Raihn, and surely the others, were tired. He wished upon the flames to free them from this mistaken haven that should be ripped stone by stone.

Going to where Raihn presumed the gate to be, there was just a large gash in the castle wall that framed the wilds just beyond. Thankfully, it offered a way to bypass the rest of the castle, with lanterns continuing outward. At the end of the corridor, Raihn spotted Ghor leaning against the jutting stones.

"Take a wrong turn? I've been here waiting," Ghor taunted.

"You knew about this place," Raihn accused angrily, stamping towards him.

"That be a pretty vague statement," Ghor replied, furling a smirk.

"Then let me be clear," Pocket interjected. "A fuckin' lunatic bit me in there, and you, who I would fuckin' assume knew he was there!"

Ghor's expression turned serious. "…Did you let him out?"

"It's more like he let himself out," Pocket snapped. "And no, we didn't— or rather, Amarra didn't. Thanks, by the way," he added, nodding up at her.

"Wait," Raihn said, suddenly distracted by something beyond the hole in the wall. "Look up there!" He pointed, his finger trembling with the realization. "A cabin."

CHAPTER THIRTY-FOUR
Truthseeker

The cabin huddled among a herd of trees. Firs and pines, once presumably stumped, now seemingly full-sprouted, for no bases remain. Hodge couldn't help but remark on it, something Magnus resented, his familiarity with the wild undermining Hodge's credibility in the field once again.

"Firs don't grow back," Magnus snipped. "Neither would pines. Not here, anyway."

Yet atop the incline, Raihn saw no other kind of tree, whether around him or above. Even from a distance, the cabin seemed to be assembled from fir and pine, all logged together, corners saddle-notched. Pocket claimed the trees crowning the cabin had indeed regrown, just as he knew the mountain held that power, something Hodge, rather uncharacteristically, did not comment on, his wonder suppressed. Their chin, in fact, sagged in a sad tilt. But Pocket prattled on, Magnus spouting more.

Willows were a kind of tree to resprout, despite being felled. "Call it a resurrection, if you were an Alabastard up north," Magnus said, then mentioned the White Ravens are a fanatical bunch. "They love their alabaster trinkets… Seems that there is some merit to their allowanced prayer. I sense the power at the center of the white wall."

A freezing jitter tapped up Raihn's spine. Magnus's breath haunted him with wild considerations, the hand once gripping him hewn from a white-barked critter.

Light snowfall marked their ascent, camouflaged within Amarra's hair. The breath of winter curled from her lips in ghostly wisps. Their new shelter was near, and beyond it, the spiraling peak of Weeping Giant's Head loomed.

The wooden house, perched on the side of a cliff, applauded their arrival with flapping shutters. Unlike the derelict ruins, it looked like a home for comfort. But Raihn wasn't dull. He saw the conjuring from the slab, and now he questioned the cabin up the mountain and what remnants it may harbor.

The fog seemed gone, clouds in their place slithering the center of the slope, sharp winds breaking them into separate tufts that framed the cabin as if it fortuned their destiny. Raihn could see the trees vaguely greying out from the erasure. Cool tufts misted on his chest. The lanterns shone bloodily and lit the snowy canvas, grass thriving at the base of their poles in a warm-looking radius. They led up in what was a somber place with limber trees, branches like dancers nigh frozen mid-twirl. Their skeletal trunks and forked fingers shivered in the sharpest breeze, their blueish-green needles rustling like whispering sycophants, and the mountainside rose comparably to a grand hall, and the trees, its flatterers, enchanted those who beheld their ball—clamoring for Raihn's attention despite the chill. He strode, lost in the bushy jitters, thinking of Rayah. She was said to be the daughter to this Elda, and that led him to wonder how long ago the accursed incident befell the cabin. That Sikradau, his eyes like shrapnel, feathery and fiendish through even his graciousness, pushy and long-fingered in his reaches—tainted the sight of the coming shelter, no matter its resilience in the cold. No matter the resprouts. The chill pushed, the mid-twirls iced.

"I hope she's okay," Raihn said, not clarifying who.

"As do I," the Enduran agreed, seemingly on the same thought.

Raihn looked up to Amarra to mole out her feelings, but her eyes were cold like the wind, made into little frozen ponds with a thin hoarfrost about them. She kept moving forward, as if in a procession, and so he grabbed hold of her iced hand as he chiseled a smile. Usually, this elicited some form of feedback, but she remained unchanged. He wasn't sure what to say, or whether he should speak at all, trying to make his finger nimble on the embedded hook she seemed to be snagged by. *Is it Sikradau?* He wondered. *She'd been different since the castle.*

Raihn turned his attention to Pocket. "So, how're you feeling?"

"Cold as a cock in a corpse. Unsure if I'm extra cold or just normal cold. Who knows, I could die any minute!" Pocket laughed, but no one else seemed to share the humor of it. "Wonder who he was anyway," said the thief, presumably referencing the wily dweller.

"Does not matter," said Lostar.

"No, maybe not, but it sure would be nice to know," said Magnus. "I…apologize I wasn't there to help."

Raihn was surprised to hear the tracker's apology, and by the sound of his voice, raw and brittle, he could tell he meant it.

Then Magnus said, "You're welcome to take my cloak. Freezing out here."

"No, thank you, but I don't need it," Pocket declined.

"Pocket, I'm—" Magnus began.

"No, I said," the thief barked hoarsely. "I don't want it."

Magnus relented.

"More than nippy out here," Hodge agreed, stomping up through the white bulk. "But there is a cabin on the way. Maybe a toasty fire, dry logs, some blankets…" he paused. "I wouldn't mind an extra cloak until then."

Magnus seemed to stir in his jaunt, his bristly hairs quivering like the limber needles. "You've enough meat on your bones."

The wind flicked the quieted Hodge. Only his crisp stomps along the wintry bed aired his grievance.

Magnus, even though kinder to Pocket, still evidently harbored some disliking of Hodge. Raihn considered speaking up, but like Hodge, he couldn't conjure anything, his mind blank like the deepening snow, his voice frozen in its hall.

Finally, Raihn huddled at the snow-buried cabin door, shivering with his hands tucked under his chicken-winged arms. Cold, his elbows flapped. The faded trees waved churlishly, indiscernible whispers rushing past him. His hood flung, his ears ravaged. With a creak and a croak, the cabin opposed the sycophant's solicitation with all its groans.

"Well, what are we waiting for, to get buried alive?" Pocket joked, for along their way, a blizzard began a riot. "You'd be first, Ghor," he added, turning his gaze.

"As much as I do take offense to that, he's right. It's up to my ankles," Ghor agreed.

But against their vigor, Raihn stood between them and the door, frozen over by hesitating fear. Magnus trudged forward, pushing in the shoddy door. It swung out rigidly, and they peered within like curious deer, hoof to hoof. Raihn watched the main room peek around the peeling door. The fireplace was hollow, the woven mats before the door askew, cupboards were ajar, and a tattered dress lay like a bearskin on the floor.

"It's been ransacked," Magnus breathed.

"Yeah," Raihn croaked, hesitant to enter. But a rope handle peeked to his left—part of a door nearly adjacent to the entrance. He wondered what mess might lurk behind it.

"A shabby place," said Hodge, entering first, blunting Magnus with his shoulder. The others spilled in, half frozen. "There's nothing. For what there is, it is broken."

"There's a torn dress," Pocket suggested. "Might you keep warm with that fine cloth."

"Let it lie," Raihn insisted, coming in without humor.

Hodge opened each crooked cupboard in the corner of the room, revealing their hollowness. All that he found from them was a little bowl. "Not all is lost. We can make do," he gleamed.

The scholar took up the bowl and stepped outside, returning with it full of snow. "If we can start a fire, then I might have a drink."

"With what logs, genius? What fucking tinderbox, eh?" Magnus snapped.

The wooden bowl nearly trembled out of Hodge's unsteady hand, his baby-tomato nose twitching. He'd pitched the bowl at the wall, where it bounced with a clack, tumbling into Magnus's ankle. After it settled, the air was choked into silence; Magnus and Hodge stared one another down. Raihn shifted his eyes between them, concerned.

"Y'know, ye got a twig lodged up that puckered shitter of yours," Pocket said to Magnus. "Ever since that cave, and worse now from that castle."

"Longer than that," Raihn remarked.

Magnus raked back his hair, revealing his purple eye bags under a softening gaze. The shutters raged then, clapping the outer sides of the cabin. Raihn hopped from the loudest of their smacks, and Magnus glanced at him, maybe catching wind of the unease. "…I'll go secure those shutters," he said, leaving.

Hodge massaged his temple just after Magnus had fled. "I imagine this place was abandoned. They took everything they needed and ran," he sighed, changing the topic.

"Never mind that," Raihn said. "Let's just clear the floor so that we can get on with our rest and warm up. I think we all need it."

"If we're lucky, they left us a broom," Hodge muttered. "Aha," he exclaimed a moment later, his voice ticking, "found the bugger." He ambled over the debris and took up his rough wooden staff with a head of fine twigs.

Hodge seemed well despite the recent tension, and Raihn began to figure that the scholar was the most adept at disguising his grievances.

The voices from the group had been dispelled in Raihn's unfocused blur. The breakage of clay that Hodge swept aside piled into a nagging sight. And pulled between there and the unaccounted-for room, Raihn was bookended by discomfort. Thoughts persist, pimpling his brain with a nasty curiosity. He had to investigate.

Quietly, Raihn slipped inside the room, where seven simple beds lined the walls, little more than bags of feathers. They were small, almost child-sized, and six were stripped bare—no blankets or pillows. However, one bed still had both, and it was stained from a deep, old red. The sight filled Raihn with dread, yet he couldn't turn away.

He shut the door behind him and searched the room, his eyes sweeping over every detail. Nothing lay out in the open, but after lifting the makeshift beds, he uncovered a few trinkets: a wooden toy horse and a hairbrush. The brush caught his attention. Well-crafted and smooth to the touch, with quills from a porcupine bristling from its handle. Strands of black hair were still clumped in the bristles. Raihn frowned. *Porcupines, up here?* The anomaly puzzled him until his gaze fell upon something else more peculiar.

On the wall, a line had been cut, running vertically with notches beside it, accompanied by numbers. It was a growth chart, at a glance, that recorded children's heights over the years.

'26, 8 years. Rayah.'

Raihn neared the scratches, his eyes narrowing pensively. *Twenty-six? What, years old? Eight years of what? What era?* The Wall of Thorns had stood for as long as anyone could remember. Then, Raihn recalled the age

338

that Ghor hinted at—their time-worn selves stretching into a mad kilter. He misunderstood the order after checking the rest. She was eight at year twenty-six.

Seven children's names were marked on the wall, six recorded as four years old in the same year—a long-forgotten time, it seemed. Rayah's name was at the top, ancient yet marked at a tender age.

Raihn faltered, lost in thought, but continued his investigation. He noticed that the one name, 'Hornbrow,' had been scratched out in every entry. Beside it, another name was etched: 'Larnaskra.' His breath caught, the name echoing in his head. *Larnaskra.* He had heard it before, mentioned by Rayah. If only he *hadn't thrown a fit,* he might have learned more about her. But here was her name, etched on the wall, just like Rayah's. What struck him was that Larnaskra, though recorded as half Rayah's age, was taller. *Of course she was—she sounded related to Uklarta. And Uklarta had a sister, so who was Larnaskra to them? And what was she doing living here with Rayah?* He wondered, as that was all he could do.

Raihn stared at the markings, his mind racing, frustration swelling in his chest. So many secrets lured over all their donkeywork. He breathed out, his chest deflating. He stared, realizing that many others were human, and some were not—clearly based on their names and heights. It seemed this place had been a home to both Outcasts and humans.

At a height similar to Amarra's, Larnaskra's name was etched again, but this time, the year was replaced with question marks, as if she had lost track of time.

Raihn continued to trace the names on the wall, his eyes lingering on each one: Kurl and Knoght were both etched higher than the others, except for Larnaskra's latest etch. He paused, finally considering the others. His gaze climbed down the vertical scratch, finding Adlah and Jeor, their names inscribed at more modest heights. But the final name at the bottom made his heart stop—'Ghor.'

Raihn saw enough and thought to return, swinging open the door. Amarra hung against the frame in wait, and much to his surprise, her silvers upon him. "Oh, hey. Sorry, I took a little excursion. Safe to say you don't want to go in there. It's in even worse shape."

She eyed him queerly before backing up to give him room to exit.

Ghor, with legs crisscrossed in a lean, arms folded, his eyes pressed from across the room. "You didn't find anything in there?" he asked with a roguish grin.

"This place is wasting away, and that room took the brunt of it," Raihn replied, glaring at Ghor and shelving his questions for later, perhaps when Amarra was asleep, considering how the castle had seemed to unsettle her. He figured he'd hash it out with her whenever he could steal a moment.

Hodge finished sweeping, saying, "I may be fit for a servant. No more broken bits on the floor." But in truth, the floor had been fine enough minutes earlier. He was just meticulous.

Raihn granted them a casual smile, being extra kind to Hodge as a gesture of goodwill, making up for Magnus's transgressions. "I'd still rather be poked by shattered wood and clay than lie out there," he said. "But now, this is a quaint burrow. Thank you, Hodge."

Raihn curled beside Amarra and Lostar, suspending his slumber to be the last awake. That proved a crucial challenge, but he wished to steal Ghor away at night and wring out some answers.

Raihn turned aside on the hard, uneven floor, but he sensed Magnus across from him, their back to the wall as they sat. He glanced over his shoulder. There was something on their mind that Raihn could tell through their pensive eyes and twiddling thumbs.

"You know, I may not have always been a tracker, but even as a kid, I liked being on the move. I was raised a chandler like my father."

Raihn flopped to his other side, listening, stifling a sigh. He hardly cared to listen to their babble, and hardly did they deserve an audience, but he was just curious enough to face them.

"Every day he'd sell his candles in his little red tent in a dark alley," Magnus went on. "I always smelled at least the one of them burning after he'd light the wick at cockcrow. They weren't great but better than the other rancid smells that wafted in that alley. I despised it, perhaps more than him.

"When I left, it was simply to make my own candles. Ones he'd laugh at when I'd make mention of them. I took what he taught me and made it my own out of spite." His expression hardened. "No orders. No demands. I even took some of his regulars," and it softened upon his next breath.

"I made candles that would stop the ladies mid-trot upon their heels… Made my father red in the face. I put flower petals in the wax and other gimmicky things of the sort. They loved it, and I did as well. Smelled dandy, right? Some were even subtle and kind of earthy, with a hint of sweetness. Like a grassy acre full of flowers. It was nice actually, opposing the rank city—the ass crack of Pharloe." A shine meteored past his pupils, gleaming a trail of sorrowful recollection.

"One day, my father began his business. He lit a candle at the front of his tent and sat in his chair with his cat, Wik. It was a black cat, if you couldn't guess it, with a bell around his neck. Bastard always hissed at me and bit my ankles, dashing away before I'd teach him not to, his bell ringing off. My father laughed every time…

"When a thief ripped through the alleys, my father, as stubborn as he was, tried to stop him. I wouldn't have given a damn, but he did. He always gave a damn. I could not figure why," Magnus choked.

"The man—the thief, with a pecker of a knife—cut his belly wide because of the damn that was given. And some of my father's enemies bitterly laughed and said it looked like a smile. They snickered because it was the first time they'd seen it from him.

"Through all the commotion, I shoved them aside and seen it myself. By that time, though, his guts were spilling everywhere, and the smile was gone. It smelled like the alley was littered in tallow, burning under my nostrils."

"They ever find 'im?" Pocket asked.

"No," Magnus answered. "No. And I did not want them to. It was a matter I took into my own hands because—well, I don't really know," he murmured, shifting. "Maybe matters between us felt unresolved. Maybe I thought he'd get better or that I'd keep working against him until he'd respect me. Maybe that was why I had to find his killer, so that my father could look up at me a bit, albeit from the bowels of his grave, though, that was more difficult than I had expected.

"I asked around, 'Who seen the butcher?' And, 'what did he look like,' and so on. But alas, that garnered nothing and still I couldn't find him, told only they looked twiggy. So, I decided to find myself a tracker.

"I went to the Sawed Paws of Elgen's hill above Ogden's deep. A man named Oleg offered a name to me—a 'suitable' tracker for the job—Gayle. She not only aided me but taught me what to spy. With a quick temper, I was easily intimidated, but I listened. She was impressed with my fast-learned skill," he went on, a grin finally pulling at his lip.

"Together, we found the man's hut in a forest outside of the city. I saw him through the crooked door of his mud home…" he said more, melancholy taking the wheel in his breath. "She allowed me to…take care of him…and so I did without hesitation, but had I not been so bloodthirsty, might I have seen his child in the crib before they bawled. My heart sank, and I just—I looked over and saw them with a bottle of milk, the milk the killer stole from the cow of my Father's buddy… Fresh milk is always set aside for Wik. Father just cared for that cat too greatly, and died for him, trying to get that damned milk back."

Pocket, sitting beside Hodge, itched curiously. "What of the mother?" he asked.

"Wasn't one," Magnus replied. "Not that I could find. If only I had allowed him a word, I suppose I'd have spared him and maybe asked where she was myself."

"And what of the babe?" asked Pocket. "It alright?"

Magnus looked to the space between his feet on the floor. "I thought I could take care of it, but I couldn't. I was so grief-stricken that the babe only reminded me of it all. I couldn't even be decent enough to care for it, but it was for the better. Gayle took me back to her people, where a man and woman accepted the child. I left before even a name was decided—and more than I deserved—Gayle accompanied me during my departure."

Pocket seemed to take a moment to think of all this information, then huffed through their nose. "There is more to us street rats than you presume, but I'm sorry for what it amounted to."

"He was fighting for the child he loved," Magnus added. "I can't blame him—a father better than my own."

"So, why do you spill your beans now, 'Sawed Paw'?"

"Because I was reminded that Gayle did not deserve a single thing that came her way thereafter, and a greedy man such as myself has yet to give up on her." Magnus laid back his head, which thumped to the wood, his eyes wavering through gloss like wicks themselves. "And Pocket," Magnus began, possibly to say something important.

"Yes?"

He removed his lucky rabbit's foot from around his neck and offered it one final kiss before tossing it to the thief. "Take it," Magnus said. "Might you find some luck in your ever-longest run ahead of you. Might you not marry the soil, or might you bloom from it in a field away from here."

Pocket held out the rabbit's foot in one hand, caressing its fur with his thumb whilst his other hand grasped his wound. "Yeah…might I not be a rat then, eh?"

The cabin fell quiet, the shutters shielding them from the wind in their guarding. And faintly, the closure plate in the chimney rattled periodically whenever the wind snaked through the chimney top, sounding even colder than their chattering teeth.

Raihn glanced at Pocket, who looked as pale as the fog below. "I believe we should get our rest. The next wake could be our last upon this mountain. Then, we'll be home," he said.

Raihn turned back over, cradling his head over his hands, ready to feign sleep.

"I had known a woman once," Hodge began.

Raihn grimaced, expecting another story. *Damn.*

"Congratulations," Magnus interjected, his tone dry.

Raihn, half-asleep, rolled over again, this time to face Hodge. "Who was she?" he asked, obliging the scholar.

"Linotah," Hodge replied.

"Can't say I've heard that name before," Raihn said.

"Laylish," Hodge clarified. "She's from Layland."

"Oh. Can't say I've heard of them either. Sounds pretty though," Raihn added, giving a lazy thumbs up.

Hodge continued, his voice taking on a nostalgic tone. "Few have. She sailed from across what was deemed endless waters. Chap-lipped and salty-haired, she sailed alone, her boat coming pale and hot from the East. Buffet-

342

ed by carving waves, her vessel docked in Endoland just through their archipelago. She was with an Endo guide thereafter who led her to Endura, and then a fellow from there to here similarly."

Hodge paused, his expression shifting. "Rumors started of a lady far from the east… King Stamen summoned Linotah, and so was I. But only…I was meant to…interrogate her." He looked down, focused on his fidgeting thumbs, his chin pressed over its double. "I was told of her presence in the castle—told that a knight had brought her in—sequestered, more like, but she seemed calm, not in duress, and rather gleeful of the banquet of gilded halls she'd mistaken for a charming hostelry," he continued. "She took no notice of her capture, but I knew, seeing the guards bookend the door to her chamber, she may never leave."

Hodge's demeanor dimmed. "I saw her for the first time from the doorway. She glided from her bed with the daintiest of feet, her hand careening over mine as she greeted me. She spoke gently, oblivious to her captivity, yearning to set sail on her old pale boat again to discover the world." He paused. "I didn't force any answers from her, and I brought her good food aplenty to replenish the meat on her little bones. I told her that her boat was gone and that arrangements were being made for another—a lie. In return, she shared invaluable teachings, praising her distant home…"

Raihn, now fully awake, pushed himself up. "Why'd she come alone from this apparent paradise?"

"She didn't mean to lose her crew, but the waters seemed darkened and angered. She alone survived the voyage, all skin and bone from pecking at reserves and spearing fish."

"And you were fond of her," Pocket observed.

"I was," Hodge admitted, his gaze distant. "But I wasn't the only one. Before word of her had reached the king, others were drawn to her exoticness. I suppose that was one time I could thank the Authority for stepping in, but the king is no better than those lecherous folk. He's a lustful degenerate himself, collecting exotic women for his pleasures and as chambermaids… like Pharloe."

Magnus shifted, crossing his arms.

"Yeah, yeah, a thieving king. More discrimination for my brethren," Pocket chimed. "What happened to her then?"

"She eventually recovered, and the nobles and their men took a liking to her, their eyes feasting on what was meant for the king. For never had a person come from Layland before, far from us, the waters severe.

"I continued to chronicle her life and her people in my journal, but the more I learned, the more I wished to forget," Hodge explained. "I understood her real importance to the king then. She was—before sailing here— outside his rule and knowledgeable of her heritage. You see, her ancestors were chased out from here long ago." His eyes flickered to Raihn. "Her bloodline failed to quell the unionization back then, and those kin sought their own independence.

"But most of you don't understand why I sit with you as a miscreant—why Magnus and Xander were summoned to track and murder me. Why I babble now, it's because, through that girl, I learned the truth."

Raihn, intrigued, bent closer. "What truth?"

"I've told you, the unionization—the Cardinal War," Hodge reiterated. "Everyone heard of it, but it was so long ago. What do we actually know?" he mused. "The houses that resisted the unionization of what would become The King's Compass—his land of Eight Wynds… Six houses lent their loyalty to the First King—the unifying prophet who drove the two resisting houses eastward and filled their hollowed castles with elected families," Hodge explained as though a schoolmaster. "They went so far into the east that they found land further out than a place later dubbed Endoland. But before completing their crossing, some cabinmates dropped down into the coves there, afraid of what might lie beyond and thus populating it.

"And in their pursuit, the First King's fleet sunk to the forming cracks in what became the dried lake before ever reaching them. They sunk into what would be known as Endura."

Lostar tensed, his fingers clasped, eyes hawkish. "You know of the first reign," he said, bending forward. "And what do you know of those felled ships?"

Hodge paused, seemingly considering his words. "Nothing," he said sharply, leaning back. "They didn't survive, from what I know."

"So, they weren't sailing to plunder Endura?" Lostar inquired further.

"No," Hodge answered firmly, as if to hush that interest.

"But what exactly was it she knew that fastened her stay?" Raihn asked. "I mean, by the king, here, in Eldhona. Why'd he hold her?"

Hodge's gaze snapped to him, eyes narrowing as if weighing how much to reveal. "Those sunken ships were filled with slaves," he confessed, "taken from what would become the Northeast Wynd, your wynd—a realm that dared to resist. The captured men were forced to labor, rowing the fleets, chasing their so-called 'traitorous' brethren who refused to join the unification…

"But as I said, that effort failed. The First King declared the fleeing vessels had been seized and crowned himself a savior, proclaiming there was no eastward land to escape to, that we were stranded here with the Outcasts in the north, and that we must brace for their invasion."

Amarra suddenly gazed upon him as though she knew something.

"I made a false report," Hodge continued, his breath lingering, "that a disease had festered between her legs so that she not be taken to the lord's chamber, and too, I spoke on her 'addled-made mind' from her journey. From that lie, it was ordained that I abandon her and let her be burned so that her curse wouldn't spread; instead, I escorted her out to her freedom and headed south."

Magnus scoffed, balling his fist. His teeth ground like coffee beans.

Raihn glimpsed, concerned, but continued to speak with Hodge. "What about your brother? Where was he?"

"He was there, but knowing how fond I was of her, he allowed me to tend to her alone in my study—back in the days when I would be unrecognizable to you," Hodge laughed, his grin fainting, hand on his belly. "Later, I dragged him into the mess I created," Hodge admitted. "Herb and I hid with her after that, working labor-intensive jobs to afford a vessel for the three of us. But she was rather upset when she discovered I'd lied about us getting her a vessel the other time."

"And then I foolishly let you go," Magnus interjected, gripping his cloak tightly. "You begged and fuckin' pleaded."

"Magnus!" Raihn barked.

"'Tis true," Hodge said, guilt along with his cold-embered breath. "I was getting onto that part."

"They gave her all their coin and wrestled me and Xander," Magnus persisted. "All so she'd get away." Then he peddled back so to elaborate. "Coming from the Northeast Wynd, Xander and I took on what we thought would be an easy job. Not from the local guild as usual, but some 'rich-looking stranger,' as I took him for at the time. So, I took his offer, making a name for myself, gathering my good friend Xander and all... Gayle stayed back, letting me track on my own for the first time, and... Well, we found the bounty: two redheaded dolts. We bound them up and thought to gag them with all their whining, but through their begging, I chickened out! Y'know why?" Magnus asked, leaning in, his jaw clenched. "You want to fucking know?" he repeated, pounding his chest to every syllable. "I thought about the man and his child and their milk—the thief I'd murdered and the grief that had stricken me. So I let them go. I figured, 'Hey, these fools'll head south, find the girl, and shove off with the Blue Pearl navy men in Brineberg.' I was just a tracker, after all. I'd say we killed them and take the fat sack of petals... But we were all fools." He leaned back against the wall, his energy spent.

Magnus's expression twisted angrily. "Killing Linotah would've been better, for she was on her own, running down the way with all them petals after we caught Hodge and Herb. But brigands got her, figuring out she, too, had a bounty. But first, they robbed her of her petals, blacking out her fucking eye with flotsam fists, for they were once brackish fishermen deprived of catches. And through their baying to the Authoritarians, they'd badgered a pardon out for their past transgressions, accepting that reward while ratting us out.

"Mind you, we'd no choice but to run and leave her behind for the Authority. I returned home, the king still on my ass, because apparently, those two fire-heads were so goddamned important." Magnus huffed and puffed. "Who knew, right? 'Two thoughtless geniuses, ' the stranger had told me. And then, because of all this do-gooding, I'd took a spiral as a supposed traitor. That blackguard, descendant-of-a-crook, king took that poor girl, and who knows what he…

Magnus rolled his fingers from his fist, popping them. "And that 'stranger,' as I told you about, he was the fuckin' son to that piggly Pharloe. How was I to know?" his hands waved, his eyes broadening. "I never seen him. But, apparently, he was so piss-stained in his braies, he was adamant to retrieve me, telling his king that he'd 'take care of me.'

"Well, one fateful morning, my spouse was tending the garden while I decided to get some shut-eye. I was stolen awake, ears tarnished from her screaming my name. The fool I was, I burst outside without so much as a dinner knife in hand, but maybe that was for the best. She didn't need see me dead," he said, stealing a quick breath. There was a terrible ire in his eyes, seemingly bending him into a shape Raihn had not seen him in before.

His voice trickled somberly past his whiskers as he went on. "The first thing I saw was her hair tangled in another man's fist. Then I heard the frantic moo of Spud's upset cattle. And then I saw Spud himself, lying in the dirt, drenched in his own blood," Magnus said, his hands gesturing at his clothes. "He was just an old man offering us lodging, who could do little against them.

"I blacked out before I even understood what was happening, then rattled awake in a wagon, my scalp bleeding. I was so out of sorts that I couldn't even think to wonder where Gayle was." His loss was reflected through his jittering eyes, fingers clasping his cloak. "But soon, I discovered that I was being paraded through the village as a 'hideaway rapist'—another one of their lies." His fingers clawed his cloak into furls, his voice ticking again, rage bubbling. "The scornful looks didn't matter to me when it all came back, nor the heaps of feces, mud, and rocks those people flung at me. That was nothing. I only wanted to see my wife—my Little Paw," Magnus trembled.

His voice began to wind down upon her name's utterance as if it were a spell over him. "All I had were my bound hands and my muffled screams. A rabid crowd lobbed heaps of dirt and worse as the wagon jostled me about.

"Other criminals and thieves lined up in front and behind me, and I truly blended in with that sorry lot. Then it began to rain, and under the fall of rain, we shivered until we passed through stone walls, led in our binds. We walked in a chain, baskets for our heads awaiting us at the end.

"Heads rolled. I thought I'd be next, but was guided away, still walking. Walking. Eventually, I walked right into a dungeon.

"After many days of eating slop there, taking a beating day in and out, I asked the cook yet again where she was. He taunted me. The 'cardinal's wench,' he said. The cardinal's wench…" his voice billowed.

Hodge squirmed, quivering, more likely from fear of Magnus's wrath than the cold. "I think that's enough chatter," he said, his voice frozen.

Lostar, with his hand on the hilt of his sword, watched Magnus closely. All was quiet—Raihn paying close attention to their hand.

The chimney plate shivered through the disquiet, and for a brief moment, Magnus looked to remark on the eeriness he'd stirred up but ultimately turned his back to them, lying, facing the wall.

Raihn was desirous to slip away but resisted the urge, keeping his mind active as he feigned slumber. His hood was draped over his head, his arms crossed. He shut his eyes periodically, jerking them open whenever he caught himself drifting too close to unintended sleep.

Amarra faced away from him, her touch distant. She seemed lost in thought, much like Raihn himself. He wondered what she was thinking. Then his thoughts turned to Rayah. Surely, she would have something to say about all this had she not been dragged away. *Hopefully, she's alright,* he thought, feeling burdened by her absence.

The moment eventually arrived for Raihn to act. When all the others seemed asleep, he rose slowly, carefully tiptoeing over them. He left behind his satchel, approached the dwarfish man nestled in the corner, and placed his left hand over their mouth, shaking them awake with his right. Once Ghor was roused, Raihn pulled them up and shoved him towards the room.

"What do you want?" Ghor snapped, muffled by Raihn's hand.

Raihn ignored him until he entered the room and shut the door. "What happened here?" he asked in a harsh whisper.

Ghor did not answer but asked a question of his own. "So, what, you waited for 'em all to sleep? To keep all the answers to yourself?"

"It's not that simple," Raihn said, miffed. He grabbed Ghor by the arm and marched him over to the height chart on the wall. "Look," he said, pointing to the recordings. "Here. From what I can tell, the one named Hornbrow is now called Larnaskra, and of course, here's Rayah," he said, pointing to her inscription. "She was eight at nearly, what I figure, the beginning of our time… I mean, year twenty-six?"

"The beginning of your time was when silver-eyed Outcast filth crept into this cabin," Ghor replied cryptically.

Raihn paused, trying to parse the meaning. His eyes lit bright and were made wide from understanding the next second. "We're his offspring…"

"You're a concoction," Ghor reiterated through a sneer. "But so am I."

Raihn slumped against the wall. "My head hurts," he muttered.

"Be careful, Raihn," Ghor warned, his tone grave. "This is where madness takes root, where the twine knots and unravels and some frayed strands are snipped." He continued, "You know of Rayah, the eldest. But after her came children less pure, born from that thief in the night…

"Abbas cared little for these children, favoring his true blood, Rayah, above them all. And there were many kids—too many for our mother to survive." His expression sagged. "Eager to be born, some came with horns already sprouting, cutting her from within as they fought their way out—'beasts,' as their father saw them, creatures he could not bear to care for. He discarded the rest, for even the bald were tainted by the blood of that silver-eyed Sikradau."

"So, where did he go? Is he still out there?" Raihn asked.

"Father? He abandoned us," Ghor replied, "and guardianship became a burden that Rayah took up."

"But she's so youthful," said Raihn, "and that was so long ago, before the eras of kings, I gather."

"And what am I?" Ghor asked, his feathery brow arched.

Raihn froze, noting how much older Ghor appeared, confusion clouding his mind.

"It's fine, lad," Ghor said with a weary smile. "I know. It's a mess of twists and turns that led us here, in and out of this mountain. I was no fairer in my younger years, and neither of the lasses would have suffered much with a body like this, bent so shortly. I've come to accept it…but not the holes in my chest," he added, granite-throated. "Father was right about them being beasts." His gaze strayed off.

Raihn squinted, following Ghor's gaze to the bed. "Are you saying that blood is yours?"

Ghor nodded. "My life was cut short by none other than the Afurja spawn himself, Knoght. The rivalry between us led to a couple of his horns in my stomach. After that, the others were frightened—or so Rayah told me later, after my…return. They went one way, and the Afurja, dubbed Outcasts, went another.

"Knoght committed the first crime against humanity—the second crime from an Afurja—and was cast into Sikradau's forsaken castle by his own kind, where he remains until the end of time as atonement." Ghor's eye flickered up at Raihn, letting the realization sink in. "When his kin fled north, away from the fairer ones, Larnaskra was one of them, who was yet to be so bitter… Some of them take a little while to come around before they thrust their horns into your belly," Ghor sneered again.

Raihn didn't like the inclination. "Those horns might as well have been daggers, for man turns on itself daily," he reasoned.

Ghor spat his blame with hatred. "No thanks to Sikradau and his blood trickling through generations."

"That blood you speak of runs in my veins as well, no matter how little," Raihn continued, "just like the blood of…"

"Abbas," Ghor reminded.

"Right—that runs in the veins of the Outcast. And whether this father was so great or not, he dumped a heavy burden on Rayah's shoulders," Raihn

348

said, his gaze hard on Ghor. "But you, Ghor, you can't hold a grudge against all of the Outcasts. Amarra isn't like that. If it stirs hatred within you, then you must hate me as well, because I hear him in my head," Raihn said, tapping his temple. "I know it's him—Sikradau. Ever since the markings behind my lip, I've been hearing his voice, telling me to do things or to feel a certain way. I can't stand it, but I can't help feeling that it's in everyone, just a little quieter. They're all brushed by it… It's in you just as well."

Ghor seemed greatly unsettled, his eyes shying away.

"What is it?" Raihn asked.

Ghor's eyes snapped back onto Raihn. He stuttered, "You aren't the first to say that. To speak of his voice within their head. Just like the cursed boy."

"Which one is he on this wall?" Raihn asked, concern welling up.

"Forget it, mister high and mighty. Write about your love for the bad blood in that book of yours. But while you do, you will still know what I say is true, of where it stems. You saw Sikradau's skin, white like it is." He grumbled some intelligible mutters. "Amarra's kind are ignorant of their history. They understand there was an old and powerful Outcast, leaving them ponds of his geysering blood, but they never saw…**him,** only felt 'im. They're a clueless folk, unknowing of their shameful flee, unknowing of themselves cast out as atonement. Because of this, they stir," Ghor's eyes glanced, "up north."

Raihn disliked that thought, as well as any negative connotations. "Stew all you like and be miserable," he said, "but Amarra has nothing more in common than, well, what you can visibly see. She's kind, soft, and…gentle—more so than anyone I've known. I'd rather die than betray her kindness to someone like me. I won't abandon her like Abbas abandoned you."

Ghor laughed heartily. "I've never said I looked up to Abbas—except physically—and I do share the resentment with him as a bastard above their lot of bastard children."

"…A bastard you are, Ghor—a bitter groundskeeper."

Raihn spun around to make his leave, but faced a blockage in the door. "Amarra?" he gasped. She slumped in the exit, her posture as bowed as a cane, so she could fit. A tear fell by the wayside, parting her with a glistening trail. She appeared relieved, the castle's frost melting away.

She entered, closed the door, and knelt. Her chin nestled over his shoulder, her horn grazing his ear as it did. Her cattle ear fluttered happily in his hair. Whatever darkness there was upon her now seemed lifted, but concern persisted in her tears. She pulled away, brushing his chin.

She took out her spelling chart.

"I don't ever want you to die for me. I can't bear another man's death on my behalf," Raihn read. A frozen block melted from the coldest chamber of his heart as if dispelled. His hand ran up the back of her neck. He saw Amarra and no one else, damning any disrepair between them. He pressed his lips to hers—both pairs somewhat cold.

Raihn heard a commotion opposite the wall, as if all the others had become restless. "Time to go back," he said to Amarra.

Ghor sniggered. "Finally."

Raihn ignored him, opened the door, and stepped out, his foot making a shallow splash. He faltered, his vision and understanding catching up to him—Hodge lay in a bloodied mess, drenched, Pocket similarly bloodied beside them. The Enduran appeared to be resting without harm, but Magnus was nowhere to be found. Raihn gripped the doorframe until he flung himself down to Lostar, shaking him awake.

Startled, Lostar murmured, his eyes closed. "What, what is it?"

Raihn shook harder, then pointed to where Hodge lay.

"What— Where's Magnus?" Lostar pressed.

"He's gone, and I had only just returned," Raihn replied, already moving to Hodge's body. The scholar's arm lay out, cupping his own blood. Raihn pinched their wrist and then their throat. No heartbeat. "Son of a bitch," he cursed. "Hodge…"

"Hope you'd be just as sad to see me go, too," a voice rasped nearby.

Raihn quickly glanced over to the belly-up Pocket. In an instant, Raihn rushed over. "I mistook you for a corpse!" he exclaimed. The sight of their fresh wound brought a grimace. "What happened?"

"Magnus," Pocket strained to say.

Raihn rapt Pocket's hand high in a tight bind of fingers, feeling the warmth that hadn't yet faded, their breaths shallow. His hand, and theirs, fell gently upon Pocket's chest.

"Why?" Raihn asked.

"I don't know," Pocket whispered, his words brittle. "I tried to stop 'im. I swear." Their eyes flicked to Hodge's corpse and back. "Magnus. He—" Pocket struggled, swallowing. "He's in a real dirge. I saw it. 'E looked at me like I was somebody else, apologized more earnestly than ever. But that's 'cause I'm dyin', ey." His breath hitched. "The tear on my cheek ain't mine."

"It's okay, Pocket."

"But you'd best scurry quick," Pocket nearly whispered, his voice barely a crawl. "He tried to take the chest, but it was too heavy for him by the look of it. I believe he knew he'd little time. But I'd not allow him swiftness."

Pocket managed a faint grin a breath later. "That Enduran… He sure is a heavy sleeper."

Despite the pain in his heart, Raihn couldn't help but crack a smile in return. "Lostar had a lot to sleep off, I suppose."

Pocket retrieved something from a little drawstring bag upon his hip and shoved it into Raihn's satchel.

Raihn peered inside and recoiled, quick to fish it out next. But with what strength remained in Pocket's body, they gripped his forearm.

"It won't do a body else 'ere any good, I wager," said the thief.

Raihn lungfulled a breath as he glimpsed the others to discern whether they noticed the gift, then exhaled. "Pocket," he steadied, palm to pommel. "Magnus can run all he wants. The lanterns will lead me right to him."

"He is not yours to kill. Now, step aside," commanded a stout voice.

Startled, Raihn spun over, the tip of his scabbard skirting the floor. Dame Dawness strode forward, her armor iced, feet thudding heavily near. To avoid being trampled, Raihn obeyed and scrambled aside. "What are you doing here?" he managed to ask.

"Leave me," she commanded.

Lostar looked instinctively ready to fight, but Pocket waved him off with a bloodied hand.

The dying thief managed a murmur to not only greet her but to announce her bond to him. "My sister, Burenna Dawness Hatfield," he smirked, side-eyeing Raihn cheekily. "You've come all this way…"

"Renna, if you insist on my curse-name, and Dawness if you insist on a last. Hatfield," she scoffed. "How quaint for a farmhand."

Raihn stiffened, questions withheld. "Let's give them some space," he said to the others, plucking the strap of his satchel.

Pocket hooted, his gut looking to wrench tight. His eyes glazed over as he beheld Raihn, flickering between him and the others. "Thank you. All of you."

Raihn stopped at the back door, unsure of what he was thanked; the thief had been treated roughly all this way, but Raihn flashed them a smile. "You're welcome," he said, then paused in the center of the frame, deciding if that was the best he could say.

He half-glanced over his shoulder. "Thank you as well." Then Raihn stepped out and shut the door, the outside chill harsher than ever.

In the elements, alongside Amarra and Lostar, Raihn kept tightly knit with the others to fight the cold. The wind was shielded by the cabin, its backside their haven, the window beside their ears.

The back door to the cabin flung, batting lazy clumps of snow off with its vibration. The dame stepped out. Her helmet and pauldrons were removed, sleek chains on her shoulders draped from her black gambeson, speckled in snow. She eyed the window, her narrow eyes very much perceptive of what could have been overheard.

"Why?" she asked, her voice steady but vague as she slammed the door behind her. More snow glided and jumped, much like Raihn's nerves.

He hesitated, unsure of how to interpret her ask. "Pocket suffered much trickery from the mountain, but Magnus duped him most in the end."

"Is that all there is to say?" the dame pressed. "Why did he betray him? What could Magnus stand to gain here?"

"Ask him yourself. He can't be far," Raihn said, his tone clipped.

"Does my presence so embitter you that you deny me an answer?" she challenged.

Raihn bristled but knew she was right. "I don't know. Pocket tried to save Hodge from Magnus's resentment," he answered, snipping details.

"You never should have trusted Magnus," she said coldly.

"Just like Pocket trusted you?" Raihn shot back.

She huffed. "Magnus will turn his back on you, made out to be gold when he's but a gilded fool. That's who he is. And your father fell victim to his whims."

Raihn's heart skipped a beat. "What?"

"Though his case was different," she droned. "Your father only helped Magnus for one reason—because Magnus threatened to destroy his family. That tracker has been a liar from the start. I should have taken him when I could instead of relying on his aid. Nothing worked the way I foresaw it. All of you, even I, are complicit tools in his shed, used, then hung all the same. 'Twas my mistake in coupling our efforts."

Raihn chewed over the bits of information, bracing himself against the wind and the voices that rode along it. They scratched at his eyes and scraped the inside of his ears. His mind latched onto the blowing of the dame's wind, retaliation bulking in his belly.

The cold in the hoary air made Raihn feel thinner, like the air in his lungs stretched thin by elevation. He thought through it, seeing through the mist that clung around him, realizing that Magnus always looked out for themself. They spoke what they needed when it suited them, wept for their sorrows, and clothed themselves in pity.

CHAPTER THIRTY-FIVE
Gutter plant

The dame strode ahead, her posture trained and a commanding presence that asserted confidence, pulling all who remained behind.

Raihn and Lostar slouched along the snow-laden land, the tip of the mountain drawing, but Raihn's gaze remained affixed to the determined legs ahead; there was a grudge in the dame's feet that stomped through the snow, and Raihn likened their weight to his grievances.

Snowflakes flocked in Lostar's hair, following wherever he went. Despite the cold, his breaths remained steady, though his nose ran wet. Trust in Dame Dawness couldn't possibly come easily from him. Raihn knew that much. They had only glimpsed each other before setting off, probably recalling their last meeting. And beside them, Amarra snorted and hocked phlegm, the anvil also prevalent on her mind, no doubt. Raihn could feel her tension, but he was too focused on his own discomfort to dwell on it. He clung to himself, shivering as the cold iced his lungs, his jaw frozen in a clench. She corralled him and Lostar into her cloak, and their feet danced to maintain balance before she mothered warmth unto them.

Ghor, though, trailed, quieter than usual, his bitterness apparent as he struggled to keep pace. It was *odd,* Raihn thought, how Ghor had fallen so eerily silent, his wide strides barely making headway through the snow. It was a first, maybe from a lack of an invitation.

A looming tower prevailed the snow's haze, drawing more and more, revealed to be the absolute peak: Weeping Giant's Head. Flakes of snow kicked up along the wind, and fir tree branches buckled, laden. Closer they came, ambling up the slope that seemed to turn hard, becoming rocky once more. Might all the visions of a bygone era, and their memory, be left to linger about the carpet of endless clouds. Might this end of their journey be what stunted Ghor's trap.

"Just through the forest, then it's over," said Ghor at last.

"And who is it that tells me this?" asked Dame Dawness.

"Someone that's been here far too long," Ghor answered wearily. "I keep the grounds here. Raihn had come before you, and he knows, unlike you, the way home is up there, at the tippy top."

She hummed interest, taking his word well.

Raihn—a perpetual thinker—worried, his thoughts like a bubbling cauldron. A tumult of questions swirled within him, but the most insistent of all was the simplest: *Why?*

His musings were halted as he heard a dreadful sound in the distance. It approached steadily, undeterred by the lanterns, its rhythm unbroken. It rumbled, drawing nearer as if an oncoming avalanche. Everyone froze. Adjurrah seemed to tremble as if the very ground beneath them was splitting apart. Snow jumped from their branches as the mountain appeared to awaken with anger and wrath.

"What shakes the trees?" asked Raihn.

The groundskeeper rolled their shoulders up to their ears, looking cold and worrisome. "Erratu."

Dame Dawness drew her sword, gripping it with both hands. "What manner of creature is this Erratu—a mountain giant?" she inquired.

"Well, yes, but he's quite harmless," Raihn reassured. "He wouldn't harm a fly. Just eager to return, like a lost dog finding its way home."

The anvil stood firm and vigilant, attuned to the ground beneath her, apparently requiring more than Raihn's reassurances to feel safe.

Amid pounding tremors, Raihn sensed an ominous warning. He fled from the large cloak that shrouded him, spinning around just in time to see the forest behind them erupt into a cacophony of snaps and cracks—an unhallowed discord of destruction. The trees bowed and splintered in Erratu's wake, shouldered. Snow flew in all directions by the force of Erratu's mighty knuckles as he pushed through the curtain of wood and bristles. He barreled, threatening to uproot what little remained of the wintry woods atop this mountain of dirt and stone.

"Are you certain of his harmlessness, Raihn?" Dame Dawness called out, her voice carrying over the disorder.

"Not so much," Raihn muttered, looking to Erratu as they came from way off the path. "Ghor, what's wrong with him?"

There was no reply, but perhaps the groundskeeper was frozen in shock, so Raihn called his name again, "Ghor?" Still no answer, only the growing thunder of broken branches and the distant howl of the wind. Raihn's gaze snapped back, and he saw Ghor fleeing up the mountain, leaving small pits in the snow. "Bastard," Raihn cursed under his breath. "He's really good at that."

Amarra tugged at Raihn's collar, urging him forward as the others already began their retreat.

The dame sheathed her sword. "Come!" she ordered, stealing Ghor's lead. "I have seen what a normal Outcast can do, and we shan't test this one's might!"

Raihn started up the mountain quickly and passed the stubby groundskeeper before long. The deep snow clung to his ankles, but the actual terror loomed behind him. Erratu was closing in, their howls growing louder. The wind pushed against Raihn as if determined to drive him back.

"Something is amiss," said Lostar.

"You think!?" Raihn cried.

Erratu come rotten, rabies foaming through their teeth.

"It has to be Uklarta! She's twisted his mind," Raihn shouted over the wind.

"Who?" Dame Dawness wished to know.

"A witch," Raihn summed. But his wits tightened. "I'd wager she's worked her blood-magic on that giant… Back when she took the mountain's steward from us, she drew him out…"

"'Mountain's steward'?" the dame mumbled back.

The tower loomed larger now, appearing like a watchtower atop the mountain. Below it, a final stretch of odd vegetation came into view, a hope amidst the chaos.

"Trees ahead!" Dame Dawness rallied. "They look to thicken and cluster once more."

"You think they'll stop him?" Raihn asked.

"Seeing how he's ripped through the stray ones? No," Dame Dawness answered. "But they might at least slow him down before we reach the next clearing. We must make our sprint there."

"What of the lanterns?" Lostar asked, glancing back. "He's yet to reach them."

"Judging by his sure stride and Ghor's fearful retreat, I'd say those lanterns won't hold him," Raihn said grimly. "He's under **her** influence, but it's still him; he's not been banished from the path yet in the same manner Ghor was. Remember? He returned. Either way, I'd rather not sit back and find out."

Erratu crashed onto the path, blasting through the lanterns as if to prove his point. The snow churned red as if wine spilled from their *vines*.

Lostar roared his correction, "He's on the path!"

"Then run! Break for the tree line and push through!" the dame commanded. She moved quickly, despite the weight of her remaining gear. "Push!"

They breached the tree line, finding a brief sanctuary where the trees were dense and old. Raihn pushed deeper into the forest, hoping the thick woods would fortify their escape. But the sound of destruction behind them didn't cease—Erratu's relentless pursuit was unstoppable. The sound of trees splintering by claw earned Raihn's glance. Before he could fully process the scene, Amarra slapped the back of his head, jolting him out of his stupor.

"He's nigh unstoppable," Raihn muttered, panic threading through his voice. "What do we do?"

Dame Dawness drew her sword with a sharp finality gleaming through the wintry steel. She pointed it to the clearing beyond this cluster of wood as the great Outcast plowed closer. "Ready yourselves as we must become armed in our taken stance!" she commanded.

Raihn's heart raced up to his throat as he reached the clearing, wondering if he'd truly die here just before the tower. He stood upon unleveled rock, his feet crooked in the best stance he could muster. He reached down for his short sword, its heft reciprocally comforting and terrifying as it was summoned from its lengthy post. He, too, noticed Lostar reach down for Truthseeker but saw the sudden dread on their face when they realized the sword was gone.

"Magnus," Lostar cursed under his journeyed whiskers. He spun, planted his foot, and reached for his trusted bow instead. Despite the unease of loosing an arrow on something that was once harmless, Raihn could see that Lostar knew there was no other choice by the look of their struggle.

The beast was upon them, its hot breath coming through snorts. Lostar knocked an arrow just as Amarra lurched forward, her face a furious scratch along their totem, hatchets raised like its eagle's wings. Together, they stood their ground.

Raihn adjusted his grip on his short sword, angling it toward the enemy's face. The distressing fear was still there, but he pushed it down, joining the others in a unified war cry. A fleeting bravery. Instinctively, he shut his eyes as Erratu leapt, bracing for the inevitable clash that would crush them all. He expected the weight of the titan to bear down upon them, but there was a sudden pause, followed by a loud boom.

Raihn, his head low between his shoulders, peeked through the veil of fear. To his astonishment, he saw their savior—Rayah—standing firm, her delicate-looking self engaged in a fierce tussle with the wild Outcast.

"Rayah!" Raihn cried out in disbelief. She had returned just in time, using her seemingly fragile arms to pin the rampaging titan down.

"Run! Get out of here!" she commanded. "I've seen Uklarta, and the end draws near. All of this will be for naught if you keep dallying! Do me this favor—reach the peak before she crowns a new lord of man!"

It tore at Raihn's heart to leave Rayah behind once more; the hardest choices in life are often the right ones, something he had always struggled to grasp.

They scrambled up the mountain. The broad slope they initially traversed narrowed into a ridge that forced them to make a turn, carefully following the sturdy path that continued to climb toward the tower, the highest point on the mountain. Below them, the clouds wrapped around the rock heap, shrouding all they had conquered so far in mist.

They halted when the lanterns that had guided them looked to be dead, their veins severed, leaking dark, bloody *oil* down the sides of the ridges.

356

"Veins," Raihn breathed, feeling a cold dread settle in his stomach. Veins. He knew they must be. Their leakage not oil or wine. Their spillage reeked of copper and iron.

"It was our shield against any deviant forces," Lostar added, his voice spurting through breaths.

The dame maintained a lead, stepping forth. "It didn't stop that rabid beast back there, so what does it matter now?"

Raihn gripped her hand, halting her. "Wait."

She turned to him, her eyes hard as stone.

He let go and continued, "The lanterns kept us safe until now, warding off Uklarta—that witch I spoke of. We wouldn't have made it this far otherwise."

Her brows dug down, thoughts tightening her glare. "Could she have cut them?"

"No. Magnus has forsaken us," Lostar explained. "He means for us to die. The lantern's source of ignition has been cut for some stretch…surely by my stolen blade."

"For why? What is so provocative up there?"

"I'm unsure of his motivations," Raihn stated.

Ghor interjected, "You had no place else to go, correct? The lot of ye, just a bunch of rogues, clinging. To hope for something—anything—that has meaning. That tracker must have caught a whiff of something delectable."

Raihn pondered it. "I'm betting he plans on whittling us down. Normally, we can't abandon the light and return without permission, though I have an idea," Raihn said, squatting. He cupped the blood in his hands, splashing what wasn't soaked into the snow over his face and body. "If it's what lit those guiding lights…" he mused through a shiver.

The others reluctantly followed his lead.

"Now, we just have to cross safely and make sure he doesn't get whatever he's after," Raihn said crisply, the blood as chill as an iced lake. "I don't care what that might be," he clacked.

"No, **you** have to cross safely," Lostar corrected him.

"'Tis true," Ghor agreed. "You're the one with the chest, after all."

"Hold!" Dame Dawness exclaimed. "If this thing, Uklarta, stops Raihn, what does she stand to gain? What did that spritely girl say?"

The air stiffened, and all eyes turned to the groundskeeper. He huffed, then spoke with his usual bluntness. "She's got a nasty loaf baking in the oven, stealing the batter from Raihn 'ere."

The dame looked visibly annoyed with the impish man, so her gaze shifted to Raihn. "If you'd oblige me with the sharp of the blade, I'd like to see the point."

Raihn, caught off guard, stammered through a flashing recollection of events. "He's right… Without Uklarta's arrangements, I wouldn't be here… If she hadn't lured my brother here…" he sighed the rest of that thought away. "A fool am I, pulling each thread she lay… She led me here, and she stole me in a small clearing… She—"

Dame Dawness initially struggled to parse his meaning. Her eyes pulled wide a moment before her hand tendered his shoulder. "That's quite enough. Thank you," she said, her tone steady. She was a sharp one. "What's up in that spire?" she asked Ghor next.

Ghor rumbled. "Why do you ask so many questions, anvil?"

"I'd like to know what I might die for," she replied.

"Regardless of what lies ahead, our focus must be on the path before us while we still have the time," Raihn asserted. "Unlike you, Dame Dawness, I refuse to lead this party to the edge of the world and emerge alone." His throat tightened, chords tuned a bit too tight. The dame seemed wounded at first, then offended, her hand leaving him before he could rectify his crudeness.

"Big talk of small gossip from one who knows not of what they speak," the dame retorted. "I had wished to venture out alone into the land of exiles—the Frinj, but my…partner. My friends. They insisted on accompanying me. Fools of the Foundry," Dame Dawness groaned. "'Twas a mission to harvest the gutter plant."

"The gutter plant?" Raihn inquired.

"Yes. It only grew beyond the muskeg of Crossguard," the Dame explained. "A bitter, earthy plant that was rumored to cure memory loss. It wasn't a guarantee, but for a father with few options, it was everything. For you see, Pharloe's brother, Phalen, was the unfortunate father with a daughter illed to forget his face."

Raihn nodded, piecing together the fragments of her story. "And that is why you ventured to the edges of Crossguard," he surmised.

"But not for a cardinal," Dame Dawness clarified. "There was word that those idiot men on the Line sent a bastard child to go fetch it—a wayward pup. 'No loss,' they thought—just an orphan that'd go deep enough and not stir the leich. But I would be damned to sit down and await my first contract while some girl walks alone into the cold, crossing the exiled Outcast, nearing that leich."

She paused, her gaze distant as she seemed to delve into her old chapters. "So, without anyone knowing, I left. Others caught on and came with me to ensure I was okay, but I only managed to bring back that girl with the plant thanks to my best, now fallen, ally.

"Phalen was overjoyed to receive the plant but saddened by the cost. The lengths those childless men had gone for it roused an upset among the lord and his company." She looked off again. "I gained favor in his hall but not on that…mercenary farm," she begrudged, her eyes returning. "I acted, putting my life in danger without any gain for Lead Belly. My sacrifice would send no gold to their bank, nor would the deaths of my comrades. I was pardoned from severe discipline, but wasn't let off so easily. Even entering knighthood angered them, it being a mere touch of gratitude. I'm forever a mercenary…

"To make up for lost anvils, I promised to forge a new one, something not done before by an anvil. But I wouldn't subject her to their facility or send her off to be a pauper or to find home at the orphanage again. That anvil-to-be was that sent-off girl."

"I'm so sorry," Raihn uttered. "I—"

"People I cared for died for that girl. Her life meant something. Take some inspiration… If you can save all the children out there, then save them," Dame Dawness said, surveying Raihn. "We can form a barrier around you and guide you across as we fend off this Uklarta."

"No, listen to me," Raihn begged. "I have her blood within me, just like Erratu. I could still turn on you the moment I step beyond the light. I should go alone first and—" Just as the word fell from his lips, Amarra snatched Raihn up, restraining his hands. "I might not be safe! I don't know for certain if this blood will spare me. What are you doing?"

"The only thing we can," answered Lostar.

It appeared they were all on the same page, for Dame Dawness nodded to Lostar, who nodded to Amarra, who nodded to the anvil. Lostar's grin was an ill sign.

They dashed him along the unlit path, crunching the blood-soaked snow. So far, so good as Amarra held onto Raihn, but 'so far' wasn't long. He'd felt a rushing heat beneath his skin, as if hot wheat slogged through his veins, a precursor to his thrashing in her arms.

Their strategy was working, but Raihn fought, the blood he soaked himself heating until burning. That blood seemed to subdue him for a time, but it wasn't enough. The lanterns' lifeblood became colder, dead from its host—the mountain, it seemed.

He felt fevered, losing all control. Suddenly latched onto Amarra's throat, her thick flesh resisted his teeth. Raw and tough was the flesh, but Raihn needn't chew. He bit and spat out a chunk of skin and craned his neck for more as though he was the wretch in the old room.

Amarra held him away the best she could, but he found her arm. Amarra winced and stumbled over the snow as she nearly succumbed to his bite.

"Raihn, no!" Lostar cried.

Raihn felt reduced to nothing more than a rabid animal, just as Erratu had been. But through his gnashing, his teeth clamped a salty rag. The dame's gauntlet scraped away from his teeth. Thankfully for her, that armor was something she'd not abandoned.

"Keep that in his mouth," Dame Dawness began to say, but before she could finish, there was a swift and blunt assault over her belly. She gasped for air, chunks of chain broken from her mail flying into the snow.

LOSTAR faltered at the sight of a swift blur, the dame battered from it. "What was it?" he wondered aloud, struggling to make sense of the sudden attack.

The dame caught her breath, full of curses, scorning him and the others for faltering because of her. Whatever hit her narrowly missed her ribs. It had to have been Uklarta. Lostar's mind raced as they crossed the mountain ridge, the rocky sides flaring like horns in rows. Was Uklarta scaling the mountain, flinging herself across the ridge?

The blur crossed them again, Lostar with clawed streaks across his chest. The party halted as he grabbed his trusty bow again, his hands steadier than ever. He knew he could make his mark if he timed it right. As long as Amarra held Raihn firmly and shielded them with her massive body, it would be difficult for anyone—even Uklarta—to reach them. Though if Lostar and the dame were to be weeded away, she wouldn't make it.

Lostar trained his eyes on the path ahead, defying the dame's concern. But before he released his pinch, a force wrenched the bow from his hands, nearly snapping it in two. Pain shot through him as claw marks raked across his chest again, as if a giant raven had swooped down in a flash and slashed him with its cross-stitching talons. The echo of feather and bone was followed by the mocking audience full of laughter. They croaked discordantly on the rocks, a murder of crows.

Amarra snatched Lostar in a bid to escape, the laughs haunting them all the way.

DAME DAWNESS suffered the sharpness of her metal plates as they bent deeply near her bones. The damage taken was almost too much to bear but not enough to stop her entirely. She sped along the lanternless gap, her sword heavier than ever. She covered Amarra's right, every step excruciating, as the Enduran steadfastly guarded Amarra's left with what pace he may also maintain.

Amarra's blood bridged starkly over her pale skin, seeping into her hair like blood on cotton, and Raihn continued to howl through the rag under her press, but the tower loomed larger, its lanterns glowing again just at the end.

Raihn's growls grew more savage, his struggle becoming harder to witness. Whether he was fighting Amarra's grip or Uklarta's control was hard to tell, but then, with a violent jerk, he spat out the rag and unleashed a deafening scream.

Raihn succumbed to his rabid state, his skin tinting red, something the dame glossed over. She couldn't help but be struck by the care that an Outcast had shown for him, a man, echoing memories of a past romance. In that moment, time seemed to slow down. She could almost hear the distant hoot

of an owl from her late-night excursions or the mournful song of a dove—
memories from her days of forging. But the flicker of Uklarta in her periphery snapped her back to the present.

She realized with a start that she had lost ground, falling behind. The pain
was taxing, and now was no time to reminisce. She quickly gauged the distance between them, noting how the witch's movements were calculated,
the intervals between her leaps precisely timed about a second apart.

Uklarta danced around them, teasing, but there was something in her
eyes—a glint, a tell—that signaled she was about to make a deadly move as
if she couldn't withhold excitement.

Steeling herself, Dame Dawness sprinted in a last-ditch effort, her eyes
locked onto the foe's next leap. She dashed beside Amarra, positioning herself as a shield once again.

The witch's strike came hard and fast, tearing through the remainder of
Dame Dawness's plate and mail. The force of the blow sent her rolling into
the red-splattered snow.

AMARRA and Lostar had only each other now, as she noticed Ghor had
fallen far behind. But Lostar, too, was struggling, his breath labored, his
steps faltering as he fought to keep up.

"Amarra," began the Enduran, calm and honest, "speed is your best
chance, and I know you have that mighty speed, yet you still falter. The
dame was right. There is no fighting it. You must go without pause—
without me. Don't yield for my sake."

Amarra glimpsed the sorrow in his gaze, his repentance. In a way, this
was his apology to her, to make amends. She glanced at the regret that was
not for here and now but for the time before.

"I know you will keep pace, so I will remove myself from your side." And
so he walked back into the wintry haze. "Run, damn you!" he cried. "Run!"

It was his war cry, fading wistfully until overcome by gusts and crows.

Amarra pressed on, her heart made heavy. Like a white horse fleeing the
battlefield, the Outcast ran, carrying her wounded soldier to safety. With
each surge forward, Lostar flashed in memory. He was back there, and she
couldn't stand to leave him.

Raihn thrashed, increasingly violent in Amarra's arms as if he were protesting all the sacrifices. Or perhaps it was merely Amarra's guilt that made
it seem so—guilt for delivering him into loneliness along with his safety.
But if any of them were to survive, it had to be Raihn. He must escape,
reach the mountain's peak, so that all the suffering would not be in vain and
that at least one of them might return ere tomorrow's dawn. She clutched
Raihn to her chest, gathered herself, and fixed her eyes forward as she focused on the next set of lanterns just within reach. She pulled his face close,

reveling in his bite, its pain a prelude to what Alvin faced before her. A pain insatiable, as though she must be feasted, her own kind of twisted repentance depending on it.

RAIHN found himself airborne, the world spinning as he crashed into the rocky snow. Dazed and breathless, he looked up to see Amarra standing at the edge of the light, just beyond him. She had made it, too, but something was wrong.

Her chest bore the grim bloom of a thorny rose—a bloodied hand that had pierced through her from behind. It withdrew, leaving a hollow where her heart had been.

Amarra's gaze met Raihn's, holding for a moment. A faint, bittersweet smile curled on her lips, a last gift from her enduring lifeforce. The light in her eyes dimmed, and she crumpled to the snow, her hand outstretched towards him.

Raihn, though steady on his knees, felt the world blur around him. It spun fast, pulling him down to his hands. He wanted to believe she was merely mid-sleep, but the cruel truth sat before him in the bloated form of Uklarta, her hand drenched in Amarra's blood, resting atop her swollen belly.

The witch flicked her blood-stained fingertips, her voice made slow in his language. "One's success often conflicts with another's ambitions," she purred, her tone layered and almost mocking.

Raihn's heart pounded with anger and grief, but he struggled to block out her words, trying to focus on anything but her gloating, Amarra's hand at the forefront.

"But there were things I couldn't grasp, like that branch," Uklarta continued, ignoring Raihn's attempts to dismiss her. "Yet, I could manipulate the splintered pieces around it."

Finally, his curiosity got the best of him. "Like who?" he asked, brooding. "Was Tepparna one of them?"

Uklarta locked eyes with Raihn, a predatory gleam in her gaze. "Tepparna needed just a nudge—a thought—before her desperation did the rest," she said, her voice deeper than most men's. "She beheld a spark. But in the end, more important pieces had to take charge. Sadly," she added, glancing down at her swollen belly, "I whispered to the brigands of Eldhona, men with dark appetites, so that she would unravel, becoming unfit. She tried to mask her rage with arrogance, clinging to the pretense of innocence, but she was never more than a pawn, leading the hand ever closer to you," she said, her eyes flicking up at him, her lips straight. She then leaned closer, her jades bright, tone intense, almost prophetic. "The world lies beneath towers and marble statues," she said, her breath of rusty nails. "All grovel at their feet, kissing their misconstrued image."

"Spillage of rot and mold," Raihn spat, his tongue oiled by anger. He gripped his sword's handle and swung his steel, stifling his urge to slay her, his swipe slow. Lostar and Rayah flickered within his head. "There's a fuller on each side of my blade." His eyes narrowed down his poised metal. "But at the tip, where they nearly meet, there's a fine line—your end, should you come closer."

Her jades faded into the whirlwind, though her voice still cut through. "I spared her," was all she said last. Simple and sharp.

Raihn recognized some truth; his bites were great and riddled through Amarra. Of course, if that's what the witch meant. Putting that aside, he stared deeply into Amarra's eyes so that no distractions take away her gravity in death. She looked protective of him still, her eyes relighting her briefed concern—*What is it?* He wondered.

He grabbed her malleable hand, which moved without her volition. The warmth was still faint, but her fingers, once released, flicked back into position. He couldn't believe there had been no response to his clasp. No gentle squeeze. Her stillness struck hard, as if her hand had never belonged to the vivacious person he'd known. There was no understanding within her gaze, no acknowledgement of his anguish, yet he wished there was. He wanted her to know how much it pained him to lose everything again, yet he couldn't. He felt a stem in his head break in two, unable to be mended, gravity, broken, pushing away his senses. Even his feet felt off the ground.

Raihn turned his back on lament, it now a husk to him, a benumbed moth drawn to a candlelight's petering, for the end was nigh, lonesome, and faintly understood. It glowed a word, not a promise, that the plague would end and that the unhallowed child be snuffed. The sheer magnitude of the mountain stretched as a dark road into a cloudless end, rapt up on high in doubts. He craned his neck for a discernible end, but even that certainty was a pitter. From the base, roots dug deep into the earth, shouldering slabs of stone in an upward spiral, leading—presumably to Weeping Giant's Head, the summit.

His ascent began, flesh pinched between his teeth. Red vines draped along the path like curtains. They pulsed unnaturally a steady rhythm that persisted no matter his achieved height.

The child would crown soon, Uklarta's labors coming to fruition, yet Raihn's efforts were immense, and the ascension was anything but easy. An echo sounded from beneath his feet. He paused, looking back with ears attuned. It was Uklarta's resonance: what the world might look like without towers supposedly safeguarding it—a thought bubble of feudalism dismantled.

Had the crown released, would the Eight Wynds revert power to state councilmen? What if what Uklarta mused was the end of all lords—alluding to barbarism, taking that of which you yearn. Or maybe the poor would no longer suffer empty bellies, left to sit on stumps, chasing squirrels' stashes, so to speak, while the king sat upon his marble throne, feasting before a stuffed pig. Might all the state taxes go to men, not a man. A king galloping bonanzas—carriaged from here and there on hunts and shows and jousts…weighing bounties for men of religious tongues, freedom of speech yoked by a highest rank.

Then he thought of the muskeg and the trench and the Ivory Wall. It all crept back, as well as the First King's word… There had to be some kind of unification; did that foresight have any merit? And thanks to his vision of a bloodbath, Outcasts reining over him and white Ravens, that oath from the king seemed nigh true.

The White Ravens safeguard the north, fortified by the king's decree, with resources more abundant to them than to other wynds. Even the eastern Endurans are of little concern, or so Raihn could gather through his journey. The Afurja were the main apprehension, and the witch, being Afurja, seeded rascally concerns into Raihn's forethought.

He shook his head, sweeping out the image of his village razed by men under a pledged allegiance. The villagers were men and women born in bondage, villeins, toiling for Raihn's father for a reason Raihn had not even known. He sighed. At least they weren't paupers, completely destitute. But they weren't free folk either. And worse than them were those down the mountainside valleys. Naked. Destitute. They, lordless there, without merit to their existence, not even as villeins to plow for a stead, twiddle.

Raihn's numbness dissipated.

Raihn proceeded with the maddest of sprints, fearing the wane of time. If he couldn't save his people before, he'd prevent a "plague" unto others. The crimson veins beat almost in tandem with his speeding heart. He clutched his chest, unable to keep running, slowed and cold.

He felt hollow-bellied, as if the wind blew right through him, whistling through his ribs like the tonsils of the Enduran grotto. The tower's peak taunted his wondering mind, so he peered over the edge of the staircase and consoled his curiosity, though the peak above remained indiscernible. Frustration pricked him, yet something nearby felt soothing and warm—the vines. They reeled him into their balminess, and he kneeled, feeling an almost irresistible urge to stay by them forever, to lie down, to let the warmth envelop him. Then, a sudden tug at his shoulder.

Raihn glanced back in a frightened jerk. "Ghor? Where have you been?"

"A fellow, small as I, needed a head start," Ghor replied with a sly grin. "Though it seems I was right to turn back. Come along, boy. We haven't much further to go."

Raihn frowned. *A head start?* He didn't recall Ghor ever getting ahead of him.

Raihn pressed his freezing hands beneath his armpits, stumbling clumsily up. His breath came in ragged bursts. Just as he rounded another bend, his heart lurched.

"Magnus!" Raihn screamed rawly. They were huddled against the pulsing vines.

Magnus steered from them in a slow creep, Raihn watchful. They approached a door at the end of the spiral, reminiscent of the wall where it had all begun. The door was a tangled mess of bramble, adorned with a solid wooden figure of a woman at its center, white like alabaster, carved into a wooden maid. She had only one hand, palm in bloom, as if meant to carry something. Her other wrist hovered above, a severed stump.

Magnus glimpsed Raihn with a sad smirk amongst his lumbering. He paused, half-cocked between the door and him. "I never saw myself as a gambler, yet I've placed many bets and lost more times than I care to admit. But just this once, I'm willing to wager that you seek my head. Though I suspect the chest wouldn't approve," the tracker remarked, his attention turning to the white bramble. He spun around, finally facing Raihn and Ghor. "It's just you left, eh?"

"Isn't that what you wanted?" Raihn asked. "You gutted the others."

"The end is inevitable," Magnus replied.

"Death, you mean," Raihn clarified. "Yours of which I would not be burdened from."

"…We are led to believe there is order in these faults, living in cracks. But her voice, over the mountain, echoes clear, and I'm climbing, clearheaded."

"And you trust 'her'?" Raihn pressed. "Uklarta?"

Magnus scoffed. "Not Uklarta. Gayle."

"Just say it clearly and spare me my guesses!"

"I saw her!" Magnus lurched. "She wants this. I want this. We will unite once again, at last, after all this hallow-walking."

"How?" Raihn asked, his voice strained. "How could she be on this mountain when she's been trapped with the cardinal?"

Magnus clasped his cloak with steady fingers, his voice turning cold like the wind. "Because she's dead," he replied. "Killed by the cardinal himself, made an example to the other maids."

"How do you know?" Raihn pressed.

"She told me—in the black," Magnus said firmly, throwing open his cloak to reveal Truthseeker. The unclasped cloth fell into folds.

"So that's what you saw in that abyss of tainted mortar… You don't understand the corruption amid all that stone. Don't lay your hope along its shadows."

Magnus gripped the sword.

"Stand down," Raihn said, clutching the handle of his own. Ghor lurked behind his leg, silent and tense.

"Do you not want your beloved Outcast back?" Magnus asked.

"Excuse me?"

"Death is an ugly consequence we do not deserve. It is only softened by wishful creeds, but I know the truth; I heed merit. She told me, Raihn. And Gayle has never steered me wrong. So, shouldn't I listen? For what reason should we perish?"

"What's he talking about, Ghor?" Raihn asked.

Ghor sighed deeply. "I wasn't meant to speak the full truth, and I'm still not meant to speak it. What I told you was true enough—there is a plague, and Magnus's wife is indeed afflicted. But she can be cured. If you get past this door—and Magnus."

"Still, you bend the truth with a breath of quicklime," Magnus sneered. "I'll cut you next, runt of the litter." He drew Truthseeker, and the blade glinted as it rose. "I know your secrets, little toad."

Magnus's gaze swam to Raihn. "Sacrifices must be made by the strong-willed so the rest of us can live for something," he said.

Raihn took an instinctive step back, his feet nearly numb. He almost tripped over Ghor, briefly flailing.

Magnus loomed closer, a maddened state of conviction in his throat. "There will be a rebirth, Raihn. My stains will be lifted." His cloak fell as he sprang at Raihn with wild swings, but Truthseeker's deadly arcs were evaded, and its strikes were a sloppy reflection of the skill its true master once possessed.

Had they been sober enough to show it.

Ghor quickly hopped aside as Raihn, light on his toes, narrowly dodged the blade slicing past him. His lungs pricked with frost, his mind still reeling, Raihn was unfocused. Yet instinctively, he evaded each blow, just as he had outside his village with those Authoritarians. But this time was different. Magnus meant to kill him, not toss him into a wagon.

"Please stop, Magnus. There must be some compromise, some space between the extremes."

Under Magnus's flurry, Raihn barely blocked Truthseeker's strikes. The clash of metal rang out and Raihn felt the impact reverberate through his arms. The might pushed him down upon his back, sword whipped out from his hand, clattering upon the stairs. The back of his skull slammed against the stone where he lay, trying to shake off the daze.

"They'll be fine. They're not really gone," Magnus assured. "Just 'plagued,' Right Ghor? Blighted by this accursed rock heap, clawing to be free from their jailors. There is but one power that will free them, itself jailed."

Raihn kicked Magnus in the abdomen. They buckled, and he hopped to his feet.

"No force of good would ever begrudge truth if it were not full of woe," Magnus groaned, stumbling back. "She has heard from what is passed down by the old tongues something wicked."

"You're cracked," Raihn said. "Beyond mad."

Magnus's eyes gleamed with a certain desperation. "Why must they be barred from what lies beyond that wall—those outside these lanterns, roaming hungry?" he asked, his tone almost pleading. "Why must my charity be refused? To live this curse alone… I could bring them all back. I can save them. I can reunite families and start my own. I can reinvent the world simply by standing aside, but you won't let me."

Raihn huffed, his breath fogging in the cold air as he considered Magnus's plea. 'They.' *They who?* Raihn recollected those strangers who came to him and Amarra back when they tumbled down the cliff.

"No…you just mean to scrub your stains of blood," Raihn retorted. "To undo all your past transgressions. But even if you can break these supposed chains upon them, you will always be a cold-hearted…slaughterer."

"Pick my brain like a buzzard, like this cursed place has, if that will make you understand," Magnus shot back. Then he pulled a whistle and a crumpled piece of parchment from his pocket and tossed them at Raihn.

He caught them, his initial confusion quickly giving way to anger. The dismissal, the betrayal—it all stung.

"You were sleeping, so I helped myself," Magnus smirked.

It dawned on Raihn that Magnus never threw their whistle, and he merely considered that they did. The realization ignited a rage deep in his chest. The satchel on his shoulder suddenly felt heavier, the straps straining as he pulled out the faux spyglass. Its metal sheath was engraved with the snake crest from Endura. It had still been inside it all this time.

…Lostar.

"No matter how many times a snake sheds its skin, it's still a snake," Raihn muttered, his voice growing louder. "You rummaged through my belongings; you're no friend to anyone, only looking out for yourself."

The weight of the satchel bore down, the straps ripping away. The journal spilled out, and so too did his anger, Magnus's smug grin fanning the flames. Raihn's oath not to kill was thinning, betrayed once already by the cannibal. He put away the wad and gripped the disguised blade, but before he could strike, a steel-tipped arrow pierced the tracker between their ribs. Magnus clawed at the shaft protruding from their chest, gasping for breath.

Raihn's eyes widened. *Could it be?* "Lostar?"

Gurgling through fleeting breaths, Magnus locked a gaze, his voice strained. "There will come a time when you will understand the importance of dirty work, just as I have." Blood fountained past his fingers, and Truthseeker slipped from his grasp, then clanged against the stone. He staggered towards the edge of the staircase as if for the warmth of the veins and slipped. Deep into the depths below, he plunged.

Uklarta's voice rang out in a broad reverberation like a brass bell in a valley, signaling an imminent end, her labor come, Sikradau soon to crown. But Raihn didn't hasten, for Lostar—bloodied and barely alive—returned to him from a few steps down, their bow let go.

"I am a sorry killer, after all," Lostar managed. "Don't you go and be an oath breaker like me."

Raihn wobbled a grin across his face. "Enough of that," he said. "You're severely injured."

Lostar tensed. "But I've secured myself the title of gar," he said, as if to say it was okay.

"Your lip is busted," Raihn replied, shaking his head in disbelief. "I can't believe you're here, **'Trussgar.'"**

"Neither can I," Trussgar admitted, his breath labored. "I thought those stairs would never end," he added, straining a laugh. "But this is a quest that I must see come to an end…by you."

"And I you, so rise," Raihn urged. "Stand beside me as we bring this to an end, just as we began. I've been selfish, surrounding you with poor manners, so let me be selfish again. I ask you to rise through the pain and to walk."

Trussgar dashed Raihn's hopes with a fleeting glance. "I am spent." His voice was barely a whisper.

Raihn's hope dwindled, but then he remembered the whistle Magnus tossed. He held it aloft, offering it to Trussgar, but Ghor snatched it away and tossed it over the edge of the stairs.

"Why!?" Raihn screamed.

"That would only make things worse," Ghor explained, his tone harsh but sincere. "Trust me this once. You wouldn't want it. Now, make it snappy."

Raihn heeded him, stowing his frustration. He could at least offer the sword if he couldn't offer anything else. He snatched it up and presented it. "Here, this belongs to you."

Trussgar refused. "My service is satiated, unlike the blade's."

Raihn's stomach knotted, his tongue tied. He lingered for a moment longer, searching for something to say, something to keep Trussgar with him.

"You should go," Trussgar urged, strength clearly waning.

"If I go, I know I won't see you return a third time," Raihn wept.

"There is nothing else for me to return to. Now, Raihn of Parcel, leave me, but keep the memory of what glory I have."

"You wanted this all along," Raihn said, his voice dithering. "I will go…"

Raihn hardly rounded the curve before taking out the crumpled page from Magnus. It felt almost as heavy as the satchel was.

"What are you doing?" Ghor groaned.

"Quiet."

The familiar scrawl of his brother's handwriting filled the page, and as the words sank in, more tears welled in his eyes. It was another entry from River's journal—of course it was. Magnus had always been looking out for himself, and upon reading the entry, Raihn cursed him under his breath, understanding Magnus always had a dagger up his sleeve just over his handshakes.

"What is it?" Ghor inquired, likely taking notice of Raihn's distress.

"Not long after meeting Magnus, I took rest. When I awoke, I noticed the journal was askew. I discovered an entry was missing… Just goes to show the crookedness in all manner of things," Raihn muttered.

"Uh-huh, yeah," Ghor dismissed, "but what's it say?"

Raihn hesitated. "Never mind it," he said, folding the page and tucking it away. "We should go."

Ghor frowned but didn't press further.

Raihn's hand trembled as he reached for the chest, his heart pounding. Each beat rang through him, and the chest felt equally heavy, almost as if it resisted his touch. His fingers hooked beneath it, but the weight fought against him, his back arching under the strain.

"No," he breathed in dismay. "Not now. Please," he pleaded, so close to the end.

"Heavy is the heart," Ghor mused. "Might you now share that page?"

Raihn stifled the rising panic, his forehead hot despite the cold. "Here," he said, handing it over.

Ghor read the letter. "Hmm," his voice rattled. "That Magnus was a sly one to hand it over, knowing he'd put a tac in your boot."

"Oh yeah? Real good, Ghor. Nice. I'm glad, even now, that Magnus can spite me," Raihn remarked, snatching the page back.

"It's not spite, Raihn. Quite the contrary, I'd propose. It's desperation— just in case he bit the dust—and bite the dust he did. That chest was heavy already when you saw the page, but now after reading it…"

I don't quite understand," Raihn said.

"…He wants to remain plagued with his woman."

Raihn sat beside Trussgar, who leaned against the tower's center, their breaths shallow. "I'm sorry, Truss. I guess neither of us gets our wish; I'm stuck here with you, whether you want me to be or not."

Trussgar's head lolled toward him. "What did it say?"

Raihn glanced down at the page before tearing it into pieces, the fragments caught by a sudden gale. He sighed. "River wrote about the moment he was discovered by a brown-haired man, one with a brooch of a dog, while sneaking outside the manor. He alluded to it in another entry, though I didn't fully grasp it until now." Raihn's voice wavered, then flared again. "Magnus worked as a strongman, collecting debts when it was time to pay—just like the dame mentioned.

"I don't know what Magnus was doing out in the trees, but it must've been before he was jailed…"

Trussgar sat in silence, his eyes downcast. He groaned, shifting uncomfortably before struggling to stand. His legs trembled, breaths coming raggedly as he pulled himself upright.

"What are you doing?" Raihn asked as Trussgar limped toward the chest. With surprising ease, they scooped it up and carried it toward the tangled image of the woman. The chest, which had once seemed so heavy, now appeared light and feathery in Trussgar's hands.

Trussgar offered it to the pale woman, his body a mess of quivers. The connection reestablished, the maiden somehow livened, made whole with her missing hand returned. Her body unraveled as the tangled vines around her fell away. With a gentle slither, she disappeared, leaving only the chest unlocked from her fleeting grip.

Ghor grinned almost perversely. "Aye, much like the gate… Keep going, boy. You're almost there."

"Just a damn second," Raihn snapped before rushing to Trussgar. "You did it!" he exclaimed, but Trussgar stood, stiffly silent. "Truss?"

Raihn stepped in front of them and witnessed their hollowed visage. After Trussgar teetered, their weight collapsed into his arms. He held them for a few stuttering breaths, then gently laid them down. The painful realization crept in that Trussgar's flame had burned out. They had been right to request privacy in death, for the weight of this dread was almost too much to bear.

Raihn retrieved Truthseeker and clasped Trussgar's hands around its hilt.

"Goodbye, dear friend."

CHAPTER THIRTY-SIX

The Eye of the Reaper

This was the end. Raihn considered the ease of a warmer horizon—a place to lay his head comfortably, where he might see a white cloud again and think of Amarra's hair. It wasn't the chill surrounding him that made him waver, but his nerves. This was it. Before him was a short corridor that spiraled away, lined by torches. Ghor staggered and rushed past him, grabbing a torch wrapped in a red vine. "He's here!" Ghor cried that way, his gaze coming back with a strange twinkle, "the absolver." His lips curled into a warty grin, and an old dusty laugh gusted from him.

Raihn paused, hesitating at Ghor's excitement.

"Hurry! No time to be shy," Ghor urged as Uklarta's howls echoed through the air. He gripped Raihn's hand and tugged him up and around the curve.

In a circular chamber, a massive white pillar stood at its center, adorned with a crown of woodland arms, each with delicate twigs and a veil of white tassels that draped mournfully from its branches. This was the tree depicted in the tapestry from the temple, the Weeping Willow. Its presence filled the chamber with a sense of antique wisdom and solemnity, yet it was so wondrous that it was also frightening and otherworldly; the journey of the solmners became clearer, despite their reluctance to deliver the hand.

There was no Eternal Flame that Raihn could see, just a well of water and a strange figure by it. They were faced away, looking through the gaps of bramble from under their dark cloak.

"Who are you?" Raihn asked meekly before a rush of frustration. "I want a straight answer. I mean, I deserve it after all this…what, trial and tribulation? You strangers reel me in like some carp along a shore of thorns. And I'm quite bled out from it all. I've got nothing left in me!"

"Magnificent is the tree, its willfulness evident in the delicate sprigs of its superior half," the figure said.

"Don't ignore—wait, turn around," Raihn demanded. "Turn around!" His fingers curled from the unmistakable voice. "Let me see you."

They turned, cloak thrown open, and removed their hood.

Raihn trembled. "River… No. You're dead. I saw you up against that tree… How?"

"…And thou hath come along with splinters aplenty," River said, nearing, then kneeling. "Reeled by many hooks upon strings, all leading hither. Now, with only thyself at the behest of the watchtower, flopping like a carp."

"Splinters?" Raihn asked, intrigued by his brother's cryptic words.

"We're all pieces," River explained, gesturing around them as if encompassing the entire world. "Scattered around Desekreus from the breakage of the willow before you."

"You mean from that crime Sikradau committed…"

River nodded.

"I was just following the string of weeds," Raihn said humbly. "I did little, all the work labored by my companions…"

"Nay, brother," River said, laying a hand upon Raihn's shoulder, his kneeling keeping their gazes level. "Thou'rt no carp, capering to the stream of fate," he said, mind changed. "Thou'rt a warrior, carving thine own path through the trials that have befallen thee. The cords that bind thee are of thine own weaving, spun from strength and the courage that dwelleth within thy heart. Thee swam against the current and found land as a man."

Raihn looked up, his eyes meeting River's. At that moment, he saw not just his brother but something more. But he was also dismayed, for this was not the brother he remembered; River spoke with an otherworldly air, like a king—or a vassal to one.

"I apologize," River said. "I am rather old-conceived, like Ghor and even Rayah. Sometimes, we servants forget who we even—"

Raihn wrapped himself tight around River. "I have made so many mistakes… I don't even know where to begin. I've missed you, brother. I read your journal—I know I shouldn't have, but—" Raihn hesitated, then let go.

"Ease yourself, brother," River interrupted. "You were right in some regard. Uklarta strung you along to read that which is nothing more than adolescent thoughts and mortal memory, bound by stagnating ink. That journal will never bring you joy with its old lamentations… Relinquish your burden."

Raihn's breath caught at the thought, but then he considered River's truth and dug for the journal. He grasped the leather-bound book, his stress tightening around it.

"Then, do you forgive me?" Raihn asked.

"No need to ask twice," River said.

Raihn looked confused, but River gestured to the great willow before them and explained, "I can become one with it and sense the lost splinters still wandering the planes outside, just like Abbas. But also like the stirring Sikradau, who lies trapped by Abbas's roots, slowly seeping out, growing bit by bit: a mound of termites. We can glimpse imperfect impressions of the past and future, like when you were in the eldhorium. I heard you then, through the hand of Abbas.

"But it was Uklarta in my dreams, right? Could you have come just as well?"

"If I were granted," River answered. "I couldn't intervene, but Uklarta is held to… a lesser standard. Now, you stand before thy bark of white, made pale by defilement, running colder than yore."

"I've seen him," said Raihn rather sharply.

"And much else have you seen as a late witness, made significant, for your arrival outweighs the scale of time—something the one before me could not grasp as her impatience begot rotten fruit," River said. "She—the Eye before myself—began to admire Sikradau. And by the history etched into the wall of that cabin, you have also seen her name. It is a memory engraved by the firstborn of that lot, the girl who watched over us all, like I watch now—Larnaskra."

Ghor scoffed. "You speak softly, as though they were good times to be had."

"And no better a time was it for those around you," River said.

"Surrounding me," Ghor corrected.

"You pushed them," River accused. "Nevertheless, Abbas allows your view beneath the might of his branches."

"His branches?" Raihn chimed in.

River's head gently snapped back. "…The tree is as sentient as you and I. He was flesh and bone once, righteous and happy—wrathful… You saw that as well. In the castle. The slab. Abbas—" River took a breath, looking overwhelmed by all his knowledge.

"It's alright," Raihn assured. "I'm listening." Though another cry from Uklarta echoed through the air.

"Abbas returned to the mess of his home, his love distressed. He turned away, knowing she'd never be safe out of his sight…paying visit to Sikradau's castle…"

"Aye, she was forsaken right after that fact," Ghor snidely remarked. "As though not stomached, for she bore what would be a strange litter also abandoned."

"He hath done that which was needful!" River's voice resounded, echoing through the chamber as he rose up, a spire. "T'was their sacrifice!"

"You say that as if she had a choice!" Ghor retorted.

"He'd not chosen their molestation," River went on. "Father withdrew from his stalemate with Sikradau and took her up in his arms. He ascended his erected mountain, knowing Sikradau would pursue, desiring to witness her final breath!

"There remained but one recourse to shield his offspring from Sikradau's presence," River continued. "Upon the summit of this mountain, they were joined, forever entwined. Abbas, Sikradau, and Elda. Yet, through her empathy and kindness, she flourished, offering solace. This journey was her divine gift to us so that one day neither may tread upon the soil but become one with it, intertwined with them. She pleaded to Abbas for it, to forgive, and now his progeny may also join them, for Raihn has proven their worth of accord. Thus…" River calmed, looking at Raihn, his chest deflating, "peace shall be wrought."

"River…" Raihn took a step back, parsing their meaning with all of them in his sight, his mind now tangled with bramble and thorn. "You mean to say this is eternity? For the rest of my life? To what, be dirt? Is that what this truly amounts to? So, this tree is a god, and I proved to be its dirt…" Raihn panicked, becoming hysterical, chasing his breath.

"You begin to sound like Ghor," River said cautiously. "You would feel nothing but the things you sense now, brother, but calmed and vast. And all the dwellers here may also rest."

"Is that the so-called 'plague'? What about my friends? What about family?" Raihn asked.

"That's the question, isn't it?" remarked Ghor. "You are not the only one opposed to this singularity."

"Is it Uklarta you speak of?" River asked Ghor. "For if not, then I would speak no more condemning words," River warned.

"Then what? What will you do?" Ghor asked, waving his torch. "Nothing. There is no repercussion. My murderer sits now in a room in that castle, and I toil here, praying for relief, that I can be dirt? Is that what it takes to find peace?"

"The folly of a man living and the stain of Sikradau's resentments," River said. "To live forever is to be condemned!" His voice rose. "Abbas and his might take their pain and sorrow, and he would quiet the minds of his lost children upon the return of Elda's courted hand."

"How can he be the judge of my future when Sikradau and he are melded into one?" Ghor questioned.

"Silence," River barked. "Thou art flawed men, and thou art shackled by thine own bias!"

Ghor sneered. "You grovel and plea that you are forgiven from your ill kin—Afurja—Outcasts. Mock me if it is willed, but you are bred the same, with the horns of a beast, Kurl!" Ghor's fat fingers and unkempt nails seemed to dig into River, pulling the wrath from their spew of anger.

"Never utter my misgiven name," River ordered. "You shall be dealt with in due time, but for now, we have our absolver."

Ghor fell silent, clutching his torch. He looked angered at being deemed of lesser importance, and his whole being trembled as he fought to contain it.

"…You're Kurl?" Raihn uttered.

River paused, taking a moment to focus on his brother. "An old name, shed as Larnaskra shed hers, after the first spill of blood. We fled and lived apart from the others in a harsh land. And upon her eventual death, Larnaskra was the first Eye suffering trials of time before I. She became restless, deeming to herself that no man was worthy, and heard the calling of Sikradau's voice for he, too, was restless as a stone in the stream."

Ghor neared. "She bore her children out of the same crime of which Sikradau also committed, and now Uklarta continues the vile act." His gaze met Raihn's. "You being her victim upon her tired wait for a worthy absolver."

River nodded, seemingly finding common ground. "I thank you, Raihn, for ending the cycle, as I could not from Abbas's one pardon. Though it was not for nothing, as I believe I was thrust into your little lap with a purpose."

Raihn felt nauseous, his head spinning, wrapping his mind around that idea of River being reborn before him, destined to absolve *god's* kin.

River knelt again beside him and said, "Deafen Uklarta's moans. Be still. Take heed. The suffering of his children will not end so easily. Sikradau's lineage, with his blood in their veins, marches on. Take heed," River said again, touching Raihn's shoulders. "I thank you for what has been endured, but I ask more of you if you so wish to oblige; the White Ravens require aid as they are in the North just below Crossguard of Bedfort. And only you can deliver a warning straight from this summit… But first, look upon the white chest and see gifts."

Raihn faltered, remembering the chest in his grasp. Now that the locking hand was gone, he fumbled and opened it, then peered inside.

"Fear not, brother," River continued. "It is the very thing for which you were entrusted. And by your hand, it is secure."

Raihn saw a dried ball of flesh, hard like a great seed akin to a beet but duller. He winced, forcing himself to gaze upon it in what he considered more of a coffin than a chest. "I've carried this all along?" he asked, whiffing its stench.

"The compassionate seed of Elda," said River. "Her heart, the long-lost love of Abbas, guarded from Sikradau. She hibernates, but still, her mind, attached to the roots, reached out, for her body was taken, not her being. The Lord Arbiter awaited her retrieval through your efforts so that he may forgive you.

"Elda's vacant plot was a sacrifice to all, but necessary, so that she may be safe. However, the time has come to bring balance and compassion to ignite once more and warm the eternal tree. Abbas would feel her again before they dissolve to the dirt of our plains, and the dead upon the mountain will not toil henceforth."

Beside the heart sat a wooden vial, stuffed with a cork. Raihn pondered it, to which his brother said, "Take it." And so he did. "Now, take up your blade," River instructed further. "Wound the tree. Accept its offering."

"River—" Raihn began, all his friends' images whirling within his head. They were here, somewhere on this mountain, but they would be gone utterly if he were to end his quest.

"A steadier hand thou would have from ears not sullied so hastily. Do not mind it and behold its splendor," River coached.

Raihn obeyed and brought forth his dagger-hiding spyglass. He swung, and the white bark wept red tears from a crimson incision. Raihn was further led to fill the vial to the brim.

"Pocket it and carry this sacred favor," River said.

"Sacred?" Raihn echoed. "I certainly will not carry it lightly, but why?"

"His vein, struck, was pure and concentrated with his essence as Sikradau is buried deep within his roots. It is greater than a mere herb or flower. It will repel any sickness."

"I could be unshackled from Uklarta's blood?"

"If you so desire it," River said. "With it, I offer you a choice: seclude yourself and be clean, with your journey at an end with a coming comfort of cotton ilk, or continue your righteous campaign with another quest and make an offering of charity to a sick lord in the realms of man, blind to his coming shadow… But earned is your rest if you so choose it, with your reward in hand."

"Just tell it to me straight. Is this the truth? You mean to offer a selfish choice and a selfless one? Am I meant to feel guilty for wanting this battle to end?"

"Your emotions are yours alone to harbor, whatever they may be."

Raihn briefly froze. "What's the reward?"

River laughed. "My air alludes your understanding. Your reward would be what you want most, as whatever you desire is surely worth such a great deed. But, of course, that is if you wish to end your pilgrimage."

Uklarta's howl tolled again.

"Better be quick," Ghor urged, his fingers spidering around his torch.

River clasped Raihn's trembling hands. "But first, take the seed and reunite them."

Raihn was released, his hands cold under the warm seed. He plunged it into the wound. The tree's wiry insides engulfed his arm until he pulled out, the gash stitching itself shut.

River continued, "Now go to the well, where it is most black. We shall rejoin when your time is over."

"Time unborrowed" is what Raihn heard, feeling temporary.

"The grimace upon your face is exactly how I felt when I found out," Ghor remarked. "But here I am with a will of my own. I have finally come before its deep roots and hanging tassels. I believe I, too, have come to my own choice." He then dipped his torch against the tree, blackening its pale bark that was just beginning to take hue. The tree groaned, whipping the torch from his hand with one of its tassels. The fire's blasphemy gleamed around him, striking fear into Raihn and drawing River's ire.

"You fool!" River scolded. "Raihn, you must go! The mountain must be buried and the flame snuffed before the willow becomes too weak! Our old-

376

est kin must sink away into peace, where Abbas may battle Sikradau no more."

"Brother, I—" Raihn began.

"Go, I said," River ordered. "Go where I cannot. Go to where there will be time in a most thoughtful place!"

"But I'll never see you again," Raihn fretted. "I never want to die—I don't want your flame to pitter out."

River froze, gazing warmly. "I will always be here," he said. "But if you stall, you risk bending Sikradau's bars of captivity."

Raihn nodded, and with River's hand on his back, he was guided to the well. He glanced back again, seeing a plea on their face that suggested some fear in them, doubt. It was the kind of look Amarra nigh whimpered before.

A breath inhaled, he delved into a blinding place where all was dark and lonely. He pictured a pale body, quad-horned and sweet, yet fiery and brave. He longed for her, his better half no different than what the tree had yearned for. He pondered why he must be tempted to have it rather than it be coupled with duty—a power admitted. Frustration swelled, his connection to Amarra strong.

He sank deeper, feeling himself shift in a sightless void, his thoughts chartering. *Hadn't I done enough? Was all this right? Should I even be the one to question it when Trussgar was truly worthy?*

There was a pit in his belly deeper than this well. Raihn plunged to Desekreus. The wind combed his hair, and the water washed between his toes as if he were the sand. It was calm, but then came heat around him like midsummer. It grew hotter and hotter, now boiling like a cauldron. His bark was peeling from the heat. But then came a new current, holding steady upon his oars. It cooled him.

Without a shore, before a valley with a large shadow looming over him, Raihn surfaced. His eyes opened, his gaze under, and to, a white cloud. It was a warm place, and he smiled at calm weather.

She smiled back.

Afterword

As a little cheat, I'm including this passage that was cut when Raihn left the cabin, as I felt it was a bit jarring and greedy on my part otherwise. It also felt like there was a lot of mourning in the end that was coming off as a roadblock. And at that moment, I liked sticking with Raihn's pov. If he didn't know what was exchanged in the cabin, then I felt the reader shouldn't either, even if it was "seen through the roots."

DAME DAWNESS removed her helmet, revealing what felt a rosy face. She sniffled from the cold and set the helmet beside Pocket. She unfastened her gauntlet, gently taking her brother's hand as if she could hold him back from death. The Black Anvil could see the end approaching in the thief's eyes—she could hear it in his fading breath.

Shallow puffs of air escaped his chapped lips. "Sister."

"Shut up," Dame Dawness replied, though tenderly. "Don't strain yourself." She held fast, her grip firm, refusing to shed a tear or to quiver her lip. As she looked at her brother, she noticed the foot of a rabbit hanging from his neck. "What is this?" she asked, grasping it with her other hand.

"A parting gift, I'd suppose," Pocket replied.

"Did I say to answer?" she scolded, her voice still soft.

Pocket strained a laugh. "I should have gone with you. I'm sorry," he said, his body shaking.

"I told you not to strain, brother Ernest. It's over now."

"'Ernest'?" the thief questioned, a faint smile tugging. "My sister, so formal these days." The infamous Pocket smiled, still shaking. "Might I then be more than Pocket, and more than Ernest, when you call me brother, if I would earn it. But truth be told—these Rogues anew—are not such bad folks. And a few days more, I'd give them their due, calling Raihn brother, myself, warmly-hued… And in fewer still…we'd have conquered this bloody mountain…"

"Shut it, you fool of a poet," Dame Dawness scolded, battling a grin. "I believe poetry is more than rhymes. And even then, you've got some practicing to do."

With a glint in his eye, Ernest attempted another grin of his own. "Sister," he began, abandoning the rhymes, "help them, please. Take Raihn to the peak."

About the Author

Jonah grew up loving kid-friendly horror books and spent countless hours 64-bit karting before transitioning to first-person shooters, system-linked with family and friends across rooms.

When not writing, Jonah can still be found immersed in video games or re-watching classic horror films—perhaps under a full moon. Or, you might find him mall-ratting, hoping the doors never close, with the bookstore and shops serving as a home away from home in the wild, wild Midwest.